ARCHER & ARMSTRONG

ROMANCE AND
ROAD TRIPS

RAFER ROBERTS | MIKE NORTON | DAVID LAFUENTE | ALLEN PASSALAQUA

CONTENTS

Collection Cover Art: Kano

Editor: Danny Khazem
Editor-in-Chief: Warren Simons

VALIANT.

Peter Cuneo
Chairman

Dinesh Shamdasani
CEO & Chief Creative Officer

Gavin Cuneo
Chief Operating Officer & CFO

Fred Pierce
Publisher

Warren Simons
Editor-in-Chief

Walter Black
VP Operations

Hunter Gorinson
VP Marketing & Communications

Atom! Freeman
Director of Sales

Matthew Klein
Andy Liegl
John Petrie
Sales Managers

Josh Johns
Director of Digital Media and Development

Travis Escarfullery
Jeff Walker
Production & Design Managers

Kyle Andrukiewicz
Editor and Creative Executive

Robert Meyers
Managing Editor

Peter Stern
Publishing & Operations Manager

Andrew Steinbeiser
Marketing & Communications Manager

Danny Khazem
Associate Editor

Lauren Hitzhusen
Assistant Editor

Ivan Cohen
Collection Editor

Steve Blackwell
Collection Designer

Rian Hughes/Device
Trade Dress & Book Design

Russell Brown
President, Consumer Products,
Promotions and Ad Sales

Caritza Berlioz
Licensing Coodinator

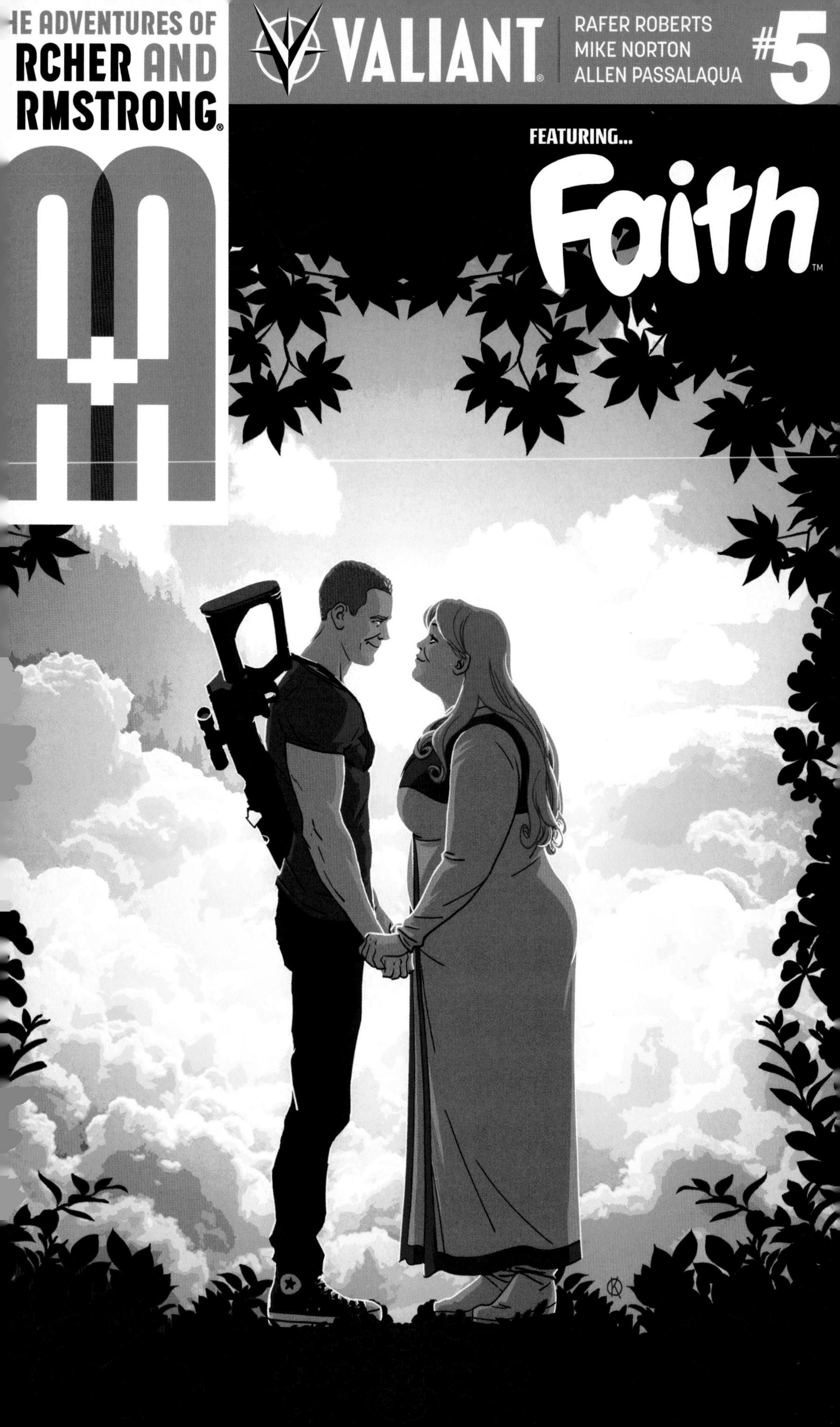
HE ADVENTURES OF
RCHER AND
RMSTRONG
VALIANT
RAFER ROBERTS
MIKE NORTON
ALLEN PASSALAQUA
#5
FEATURING...
Faith

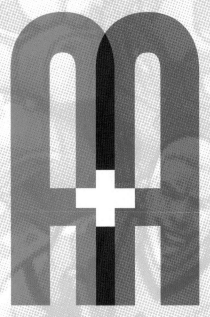

ARCHER & ARMSTRONG...

MEET ARMSTRONG. Since the ancient city of Ur, this immortal adventurer has spent the last 6,000 years drinking and carousing his way through history alongside some of the greatest merrymakers the world has ever known.

MEET ARCHER. A sheltered teenage martial arts master and expert marksman that was raised for a single purpose: to kill the devil incarnate. Little did he know that this undying evil was actually Armstrong (he's actually a pretty good guy...once you get to know him). Since hitting the road together, the two have become great friends and even better partners.

ENTER FAITH. Faith Herbert was raised by her loving grandmother and found comfort in comic books, science fiction movies, and other fantastic tales of superheroes. In her teens, she would discover her fantasies were reality when it was revealed she was a psiot – a human being born with the potential for incredible abilities. When the powers were activated, she discovered she had the ability to fly and create a telekinetic companion field that allows her to move objects with her mind. Faith then joined a group of fellow psiots called the Renegades to stand against the forces of evil. She's since left her Renegade family behind to take on the world's challenges on her own.

Let the romance begin!

ARMSTRONG. 6,000-YEAR-OLD HEDONISTIC IMMORTAL.

ARCHER. TEENAGER. EXPERT MARTIAL ARTIST AND MARKSMAN.

FAITH. PSIOT. CAN FLY. HAS COMPANION FIELD.

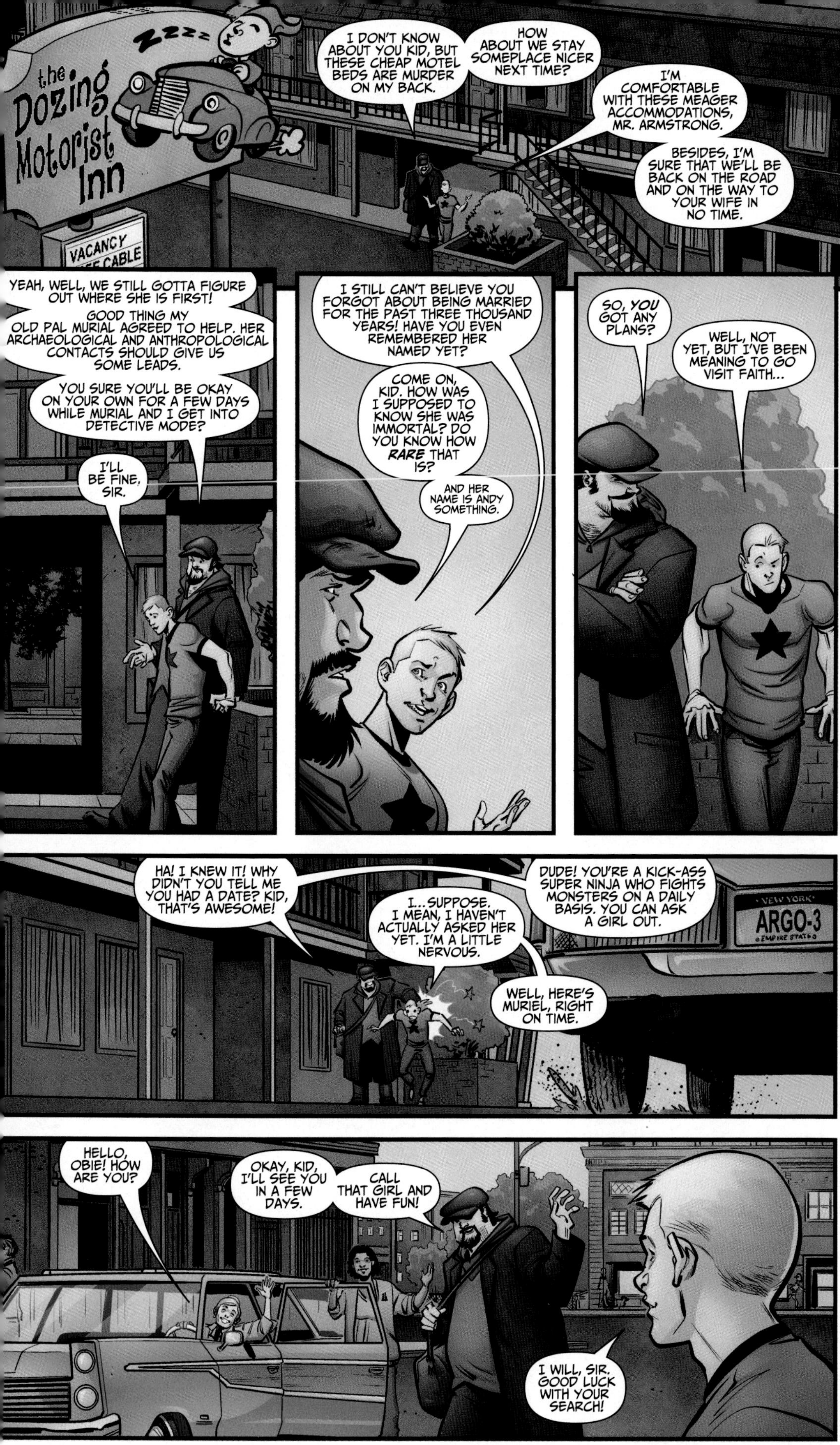
the Dozing Motorist Inn
ZZZZ
VACANCY
FREE CABLE
I DON'T KNOW ABOUT YOU KID, BUT THESE CHEAP MOTEL BEDS ARE MURDER ON MY BACK.
HOW ABOUT WE STAY SOMEPLACE NICER NEXT TIME?
I'M COMFORTABLE WITH THESE MEAGER ACCOMMODATIONS, MR. ARMSTRONG.
BESIDES, I'M SURE THAT WE'LL BE BACK ON THE ROAD AND ON THE WAY TO YOUR WIFE IN NO TIME.
YEAH, WELL, WE STILL GOTTA FIGURE OUT WHERE SHE IS FIRST!
GOOD THING MY OLD PAL MURIAL AGREED TO HELP. HER ARCHAEOLOGICAL AND ANTHROPOLOGICAL CONTACTS SHOULD GIVE US SOME LEADS.
YOU SURE YOU'LL BE OKAY ON YOUR OWN FOR A FEW DAYS WHILE MURIAL AND I GET INTO DETECTIVE MODE?
I'LL BE FINE, SIR.
I STILL CAN'T BELIEVE YOU FORGOT ABOUT BEING MARRIED FOR THE PAST THREE THOUSAND YEARS! HAVE YOU EVEN REMEMBERED HER NAMED YET?
COME ON, KID. HOW WAS I SUPPOSED TO KNOW SHE WAS IMMORTAL? DO YOU KNOW HOW RARE THAT IS?
AND HER NAME IS ANDY SOMETHING.
SO, YOU GOT ANY PLANS?
WELL, NOT YET, BUT I'VE BEEN MEANING TO GO VISIT FAITH...
HA! I KNEW IT! WHY DIDN'T YOU TELL ME YOU HAD A DATE? KID, THAT'S AWESOME!
I...SUPPOSE. I MEAN, I HAVEN'T ACTUALLY ASKED HER YET. I'M A LITTLE NERVOUS.
DUDE! YOU'RE A KICK-ASS SUPER NINJA WHO FIGHTS MONSTERS ON A DAILY BASIS. YOU CAN ASK A GIRL OUT.
NEW YORK
ARGO-3
EMPIRE STATE
WELL, HERE'S MURIEL, RIGHT ON TIME.
HELLO, OBIE! HOW ARE YOU?
OKAY, KID, I'LL SEE YOU IN A FEW DAYS.
CALL THAT GIRL AND HAVE FUN!
I WILL, SIR. GOOD LUCK WITH YOUR SEARCH!

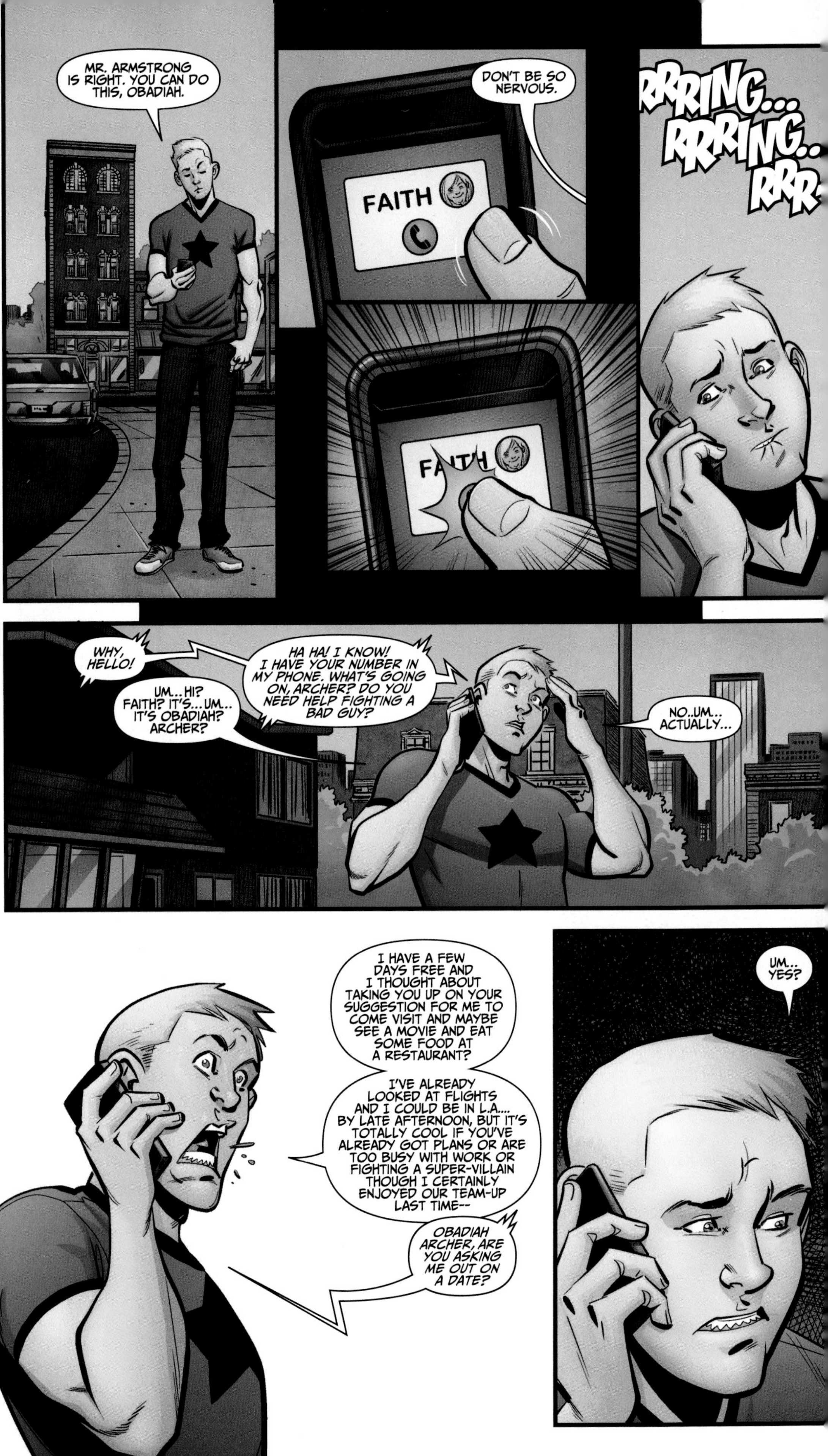

MR. ARMSTRONG IS RIGHT. YOU CAN DO THIS, OBADIAH.
DON'T BE SO NERVOUS.
FAITH
FAITH
RRRING... RRRING... RRR
WHY, HELLO!
UM...HI? FAITH? IT'S...UM... IT'S OBADIAH? ARCHER?
HA HA! I KNOW! I HAVE YOUR NUMBER IN MY PHONE. WHAT'S GOING ON, ARCHER? DO YOU NEED HELP FIGHTING A BAD GUY?
NO..UM.. ACTUALLY...
I HAVE A FEW DAYS FREE AND I THOUGHT ABOUT TAKING YOU UP ON YOUR SUGGESTION FOR ME TO COME VISIT AND MAYBE SEE A MOVIE AND EAT SOME FOOD AT A RESTAURANT?
I'VE ALREADY LOOKED AT FLIGHTS AND I COULD BE IN L.A.... BY LATE AFTERNOON, BUT IT'S TOTALLY COOL IF YOU'VE ALREADY GOT PLANS OR ARE TOO BUSY WITH WORK OR FIGHTING A SUPER-VILLAIN THOUGH I CERTAINLY ENJOYED OUR TEAM-UP LAST TIME--
OBADIAH ARCHER, ARE YOU ASKING ME OUT ON A DATE?
UM... YES?

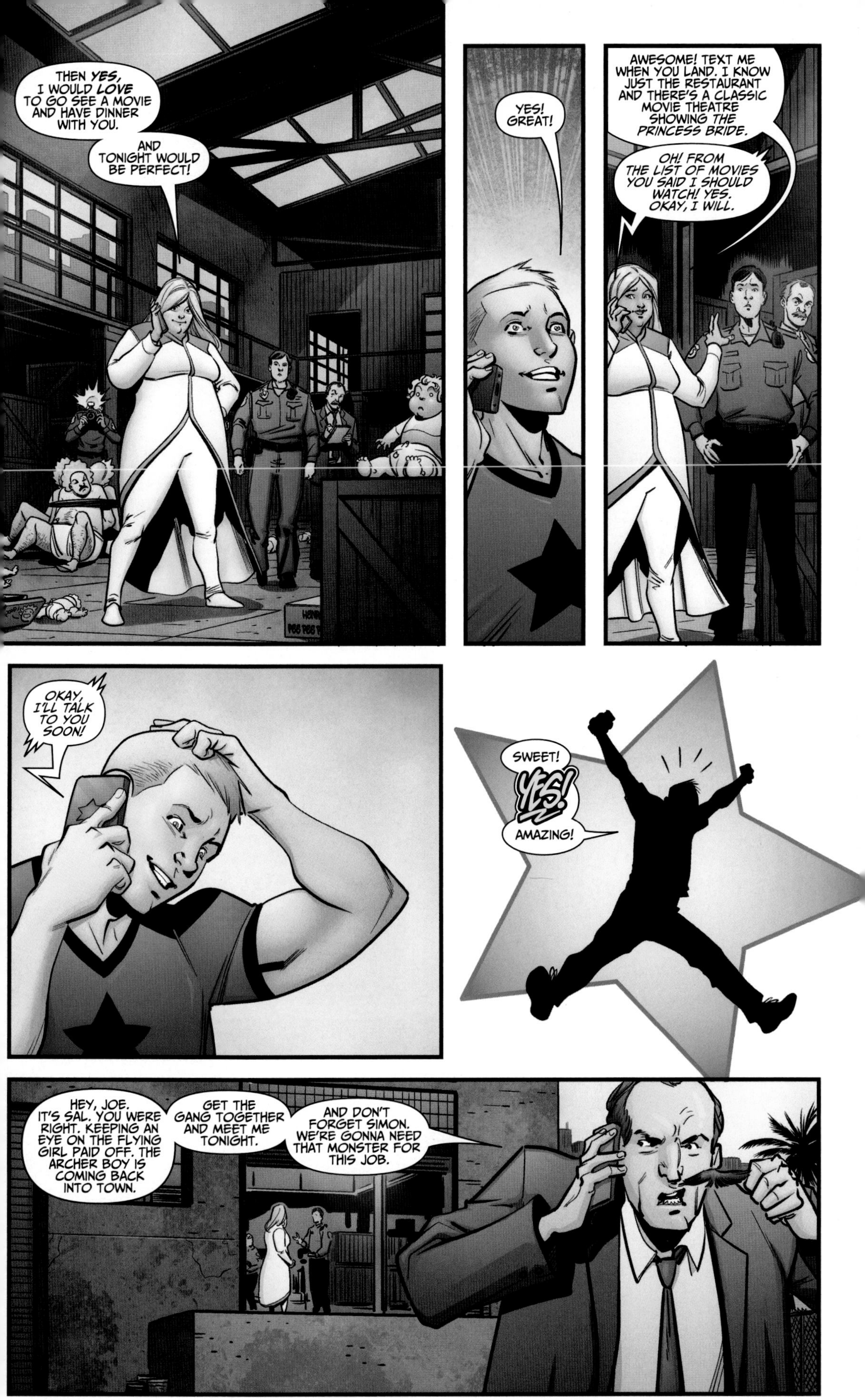

THEN *YES*, I WOULD *LOVE* TO GO SEE A MOVIE AND HAVE DINNER WITH YOU.
AND TONIGHT WOULD BE PERFECT!
YES! GREAT!
AWESOME! TEXT ME WHEN YOU LAND. I KNOW JUST THE RESTAURANT AND THERE'S A CLASSIC MOVIE THEATRE SHOWING *THE PRINCESS BRIDE.*
OH! FROM THE LIST OF MOVIES YOU SAID I SHOULD WATCH! YES. OKAY, I WILL.
OKAY, I'LL TALK TO YOU SOON!
SWEET!
YES!
AMAZING!
HEY, JOE. IT'S SAL. YOU WERE RIGHT. KEEPING AN EYE ON THE FLYING GIRL PAID OFF. THE ARCHER BOY IS COMING BACK INTO TOWN.
GET THE GANG TOGETHER AND MEET ME TONIGHT.
AND DON'T FORGET SIMON. WE'RE GONNA NEED THAT MONSTER FOR THIS JOB.

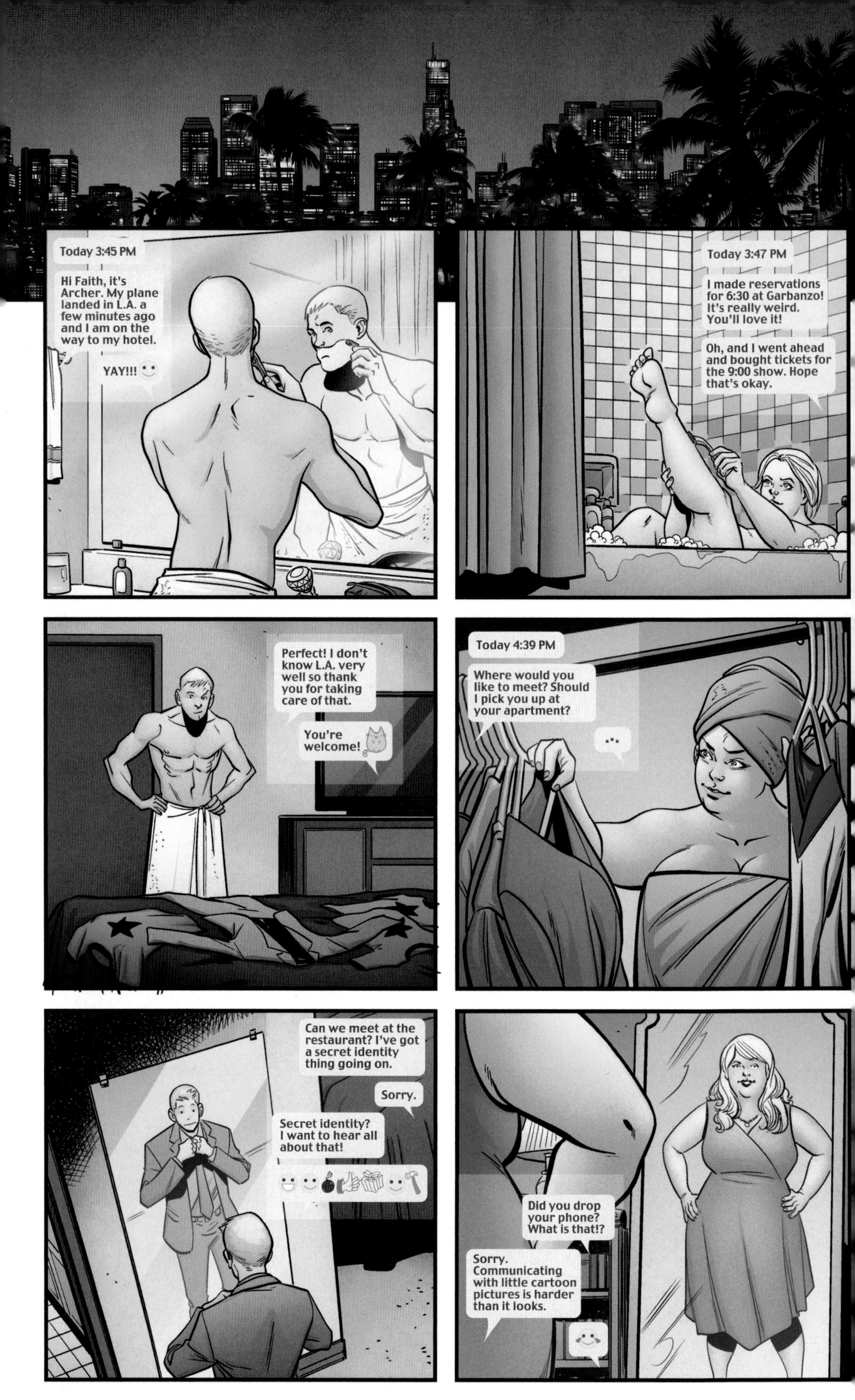

Today 3:45 PM
Hi Faith, it's Archer. My plane landed in L.A. a few minutes ago and I am on the way to my hotel.
YAY!!!
Today 3:47 PM
I made reservations for 6:30 at Garbanzo! It's really weird. You'll love it!
Oh, and I went ahead and bought tickets for the 9:00 show. Hope that's okay.
Perfect! I don't know L.A. very well so thank you for taking care of that.
You're welcome!
Today 4:39 PM
Where would you like to meet? Should I pick you up at your apartment?
...
Can we meet at the restaurant? I've got a secret identity thing going on.
Sorry.
Secret identity? I want to hear all about that!
Did you drop your phone? What is that!?
Sorry. Communicating with little cartoon pictures is harder than it looks.

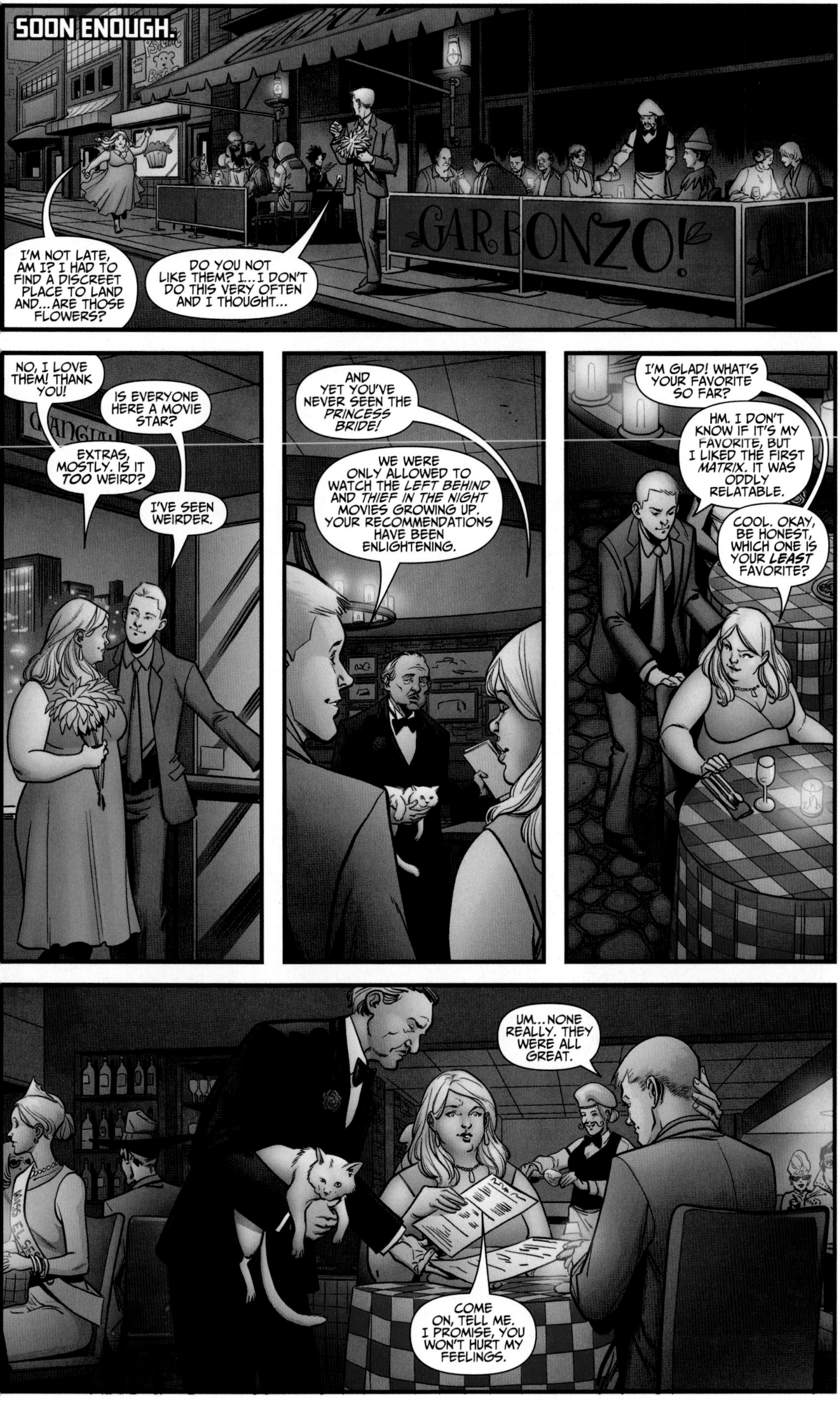
SOON ENOUGH.
I'M NOT LATE, AM I? I HAD TO FIND A DISCREET PLACE TO LAND AND... ARE THOSE FLOWERS?
DO YOU NOT LIKE THEM? I... I DON'T DO THIS VERY OFTEN AND I THOUGHT...
GARBONZO!
NO, I LOVE THEM! THANK YOU!
IS EVERYONE HERE A MOVIE STAR?
EXTRAS, MOSTLY. IS IT TOO WEIRD?
I'VE SEEN WEIRDER.
AND YET YOU'VE NEVER SEEN THE PRINCESS BRIDE!
WE WERE ONLY ALLOWED TO WATCH THE LEFT BEHIND AND THIEF IN THE NIGHT MOVIES GROWING UP. YOUR RECOMMENDATIONS HAVE BEEN ENLIGHTENING.
I'M GLAD! WHAT'S YOUR FAVORITE SO FAR?
HM. I DON'T KNOW IF IT'S MY FAVORITE, BUT I LIKED THE FIRST MATRIX. IT WAS ODDLY RELATABLE.
COOL. OKAY, BE HONEST, WHICH ONE IS YOUR LEAST FAVORITE?
UM... NONE REALLY. THEY WERE ALL GREAT.
COME ON, TELL ME. I PROMISE, YOU WON'T HURT MY FEELINGS.

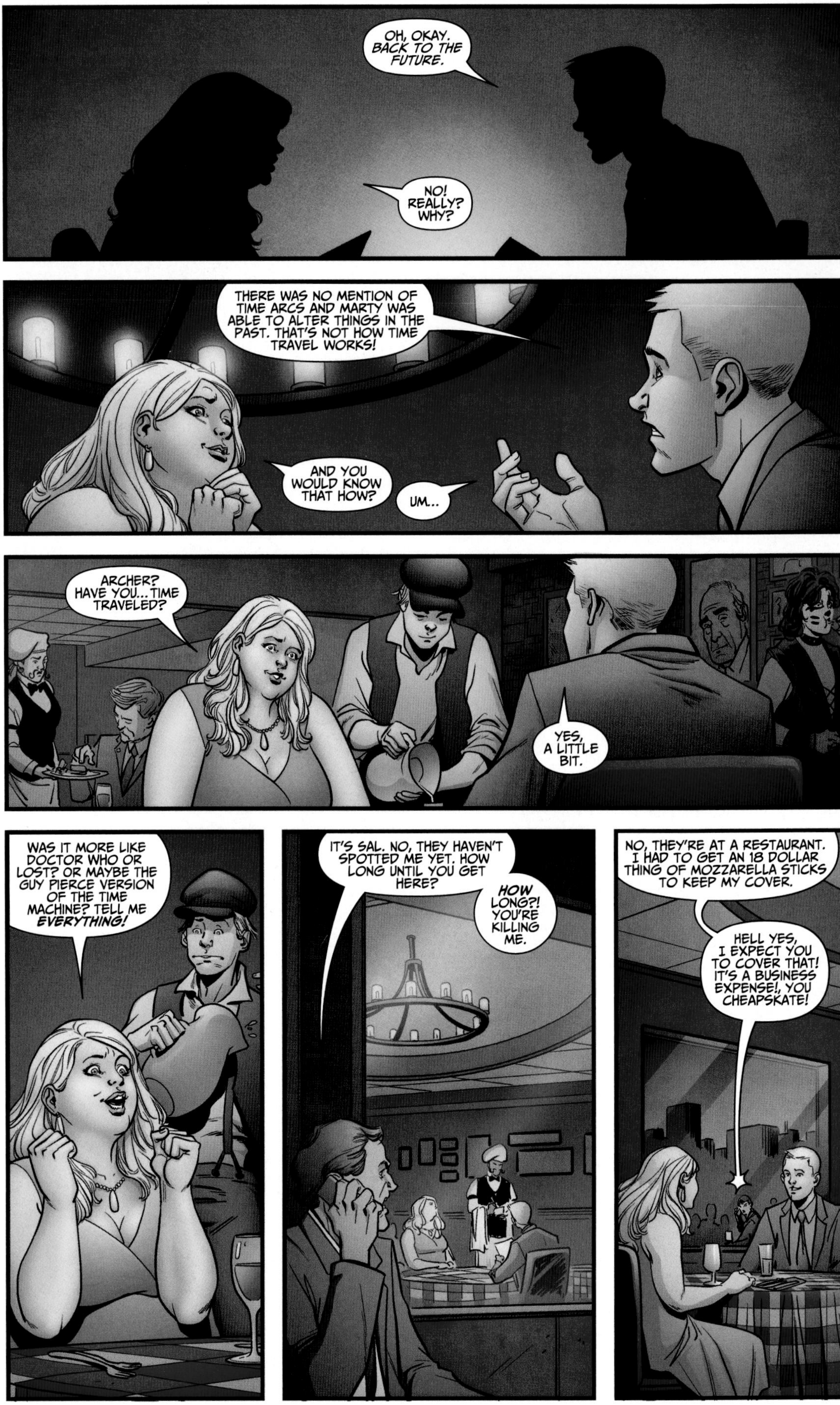
OH, OKAY. BACK TO THE FUTURE.
NO! REALLY? WHY?
THERE WAS NO MENTION OF TIME ARCS AND MARTY WAS ABLE TO ALTER THINGS IN THE PAST. THAT'S NOT HOW TIME TRAVEL WORKS!
AND YOU WOULD KNOW THAT HOW?
UM..
ARCHER? HAVE YOU... TIME TRAVELED?
YES, A LITTLE BIT.
WAS IT MORE LIKE DOCTOR WHO OR LOST? OR MAYBE THE GUY PIERCE VERSION OF THE TIME MACHINE? TELL ME *EVERYTHING!*
IT'S SAL. NO, THEY HAVEN'T SPOTTED ME YET. HOW LONG UNTIL YOU GET HERE?
HOW LONG?! YOU'RE KILLING ME.
NO, THEY'RE AT A RESTAURANT. I HAD TO GET AN 18 DOLLAR THING OF MOZZARELLA STICKS TO KEEP MY COVER.
HELL YES, I EXPECT YOU TO COVER THAT! IT'S A BUSINESS EXPENSE!, YOU CHEAPSKATE!

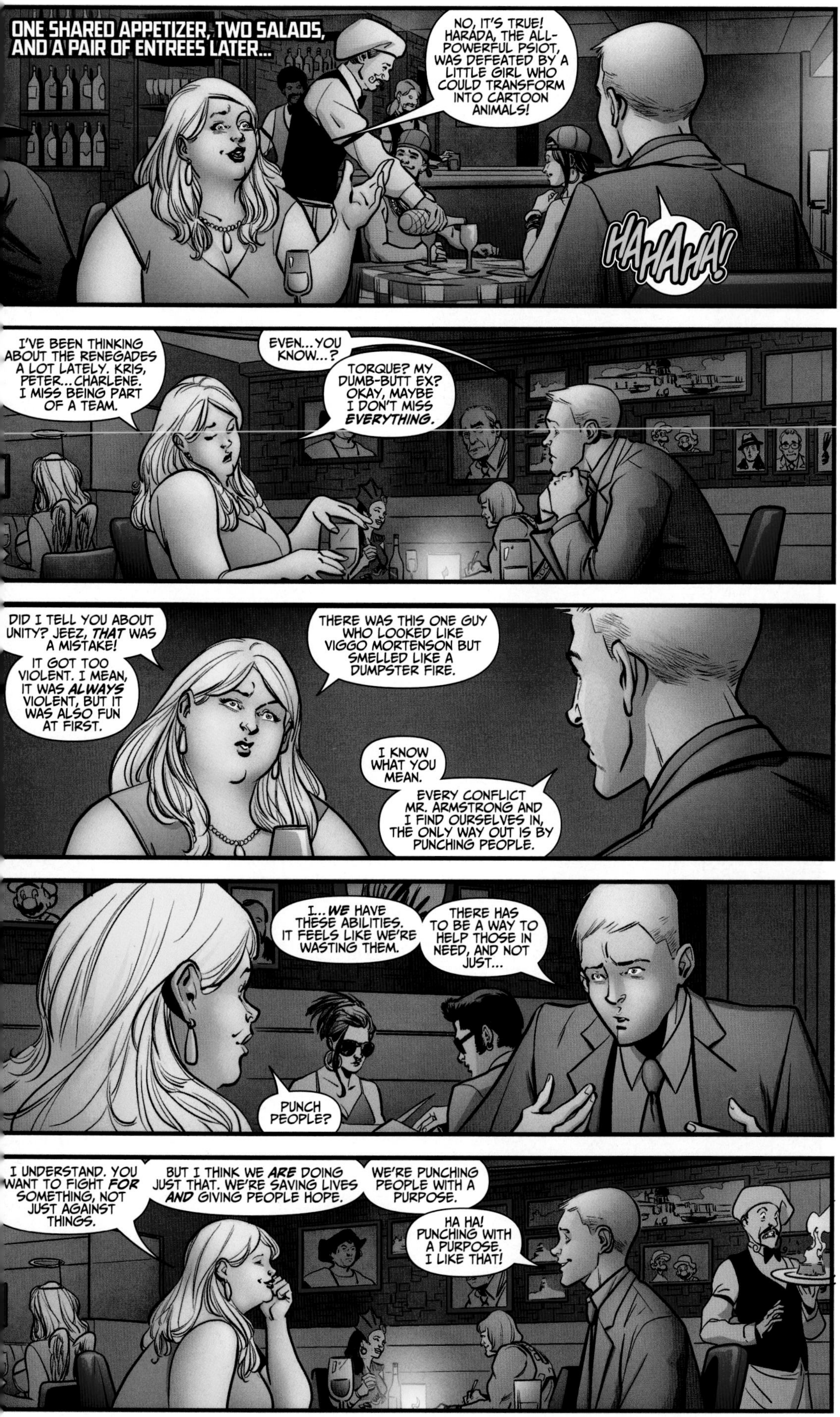
ONE SHARED APPETIZER, TWO SALADS, AND A PAIR OF ENTREES LATER...
NO, IT'S TRUE! HARADA, THE ALL-POWERFUL PSIOT, WAS DEFEATED BY A LITTLE GIRL WHO COULD TRANSFORM INTO CARTOON ANIMALS!
HAHAHA!
I'VE BEEN THINKING ABOUT THE RENEGADES A LOT LATELY. KRIS, PETER...CHARLENE. I MISS BEING PART OF A TEAM.
EVEN...YOU KNOW...?
TORQUE? MY DUMB-BUTT EX? OKAY, MAYBE I DON'T MISS EVERYTHING.
DID I TELL YOU ABOUT UNITY? JEEZ, THAT WAS A MISTAKE!
IT GOT TOO VIOLENT. I MEAN, IT WAS ALWAYS VIOLENT, BUT IT WAS ALSO FUN AT FIRST.
THERE WAS THIS ONE GUY WHO LOOKED LIKE VIGGO MORTENSON BUT SMELLED LIKE A DUMPSTER FIRE.
I KNOW WHAT YOU MEAN.
EVERY CONFLICT MR. ARMSTRONG AND I FIND OURSELVES IN, THE ONLY WAY OUT IS BY PUNCHING PEOPLE.
I...WE HAVE THESE ABILITIES. IT FEELS LIKE WE'RE WASTING THEM.
THERE HAS TO BE A WAY TO HELP THOSE IN NEED, AND NOT JUST...
PUNCH PEOPLE?
I UNDERSTAND. YOU WANT TO FIGHT FOR SOMETHING, NOT JUST AGAINST THINGS.
BUT I THINK WE ARE DOING JUST THAT. WE'RE SAVING LIVES AND GIVING PEOPLE HOPE.
WE'RE PUNCHING PEOPLE WITH A PURPOSE.
HA HA! PUNCHING WITH A PURPOSE. I LIKE THAT!

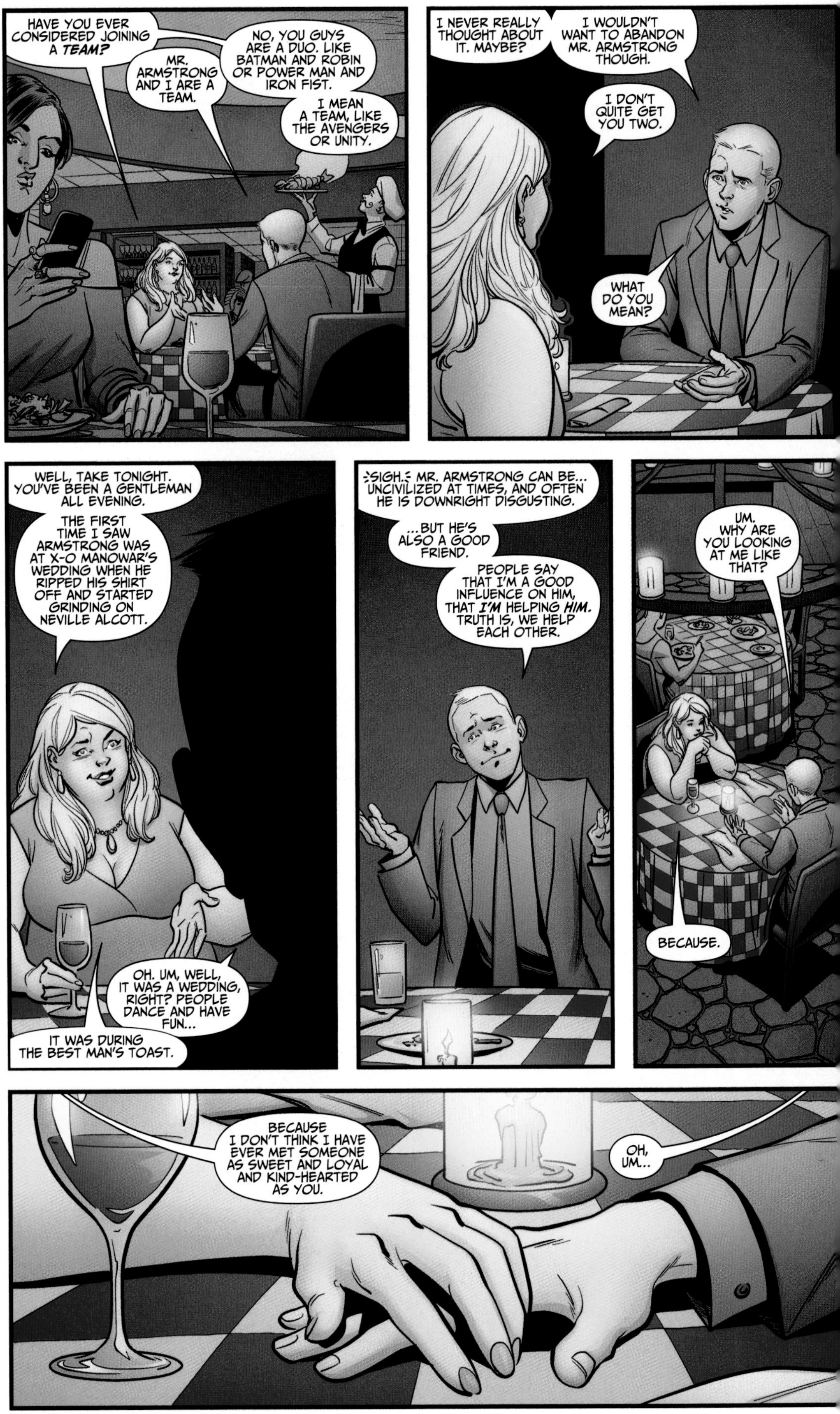
HAVE YOU EVER CONSIDERED JOINING A *TEAM?*
MR. ARMSTRONG AND I ARE A TEAM.
NO, YOU GUYS ARE A DUO. LIKE BATMAN AND ROBIN OR POWER MAN AND IRON FIST.
I MEAN A TEAM, LIKE THE AVENGERS OR UNITY.
I NEVER REALLY THOUGHT ABOUT IT. MAYBE?
I WOULDN'T WANT TO ABANDON MR. ARMSTRONG THOUGH.
I DON'T QUITE GET YOU TWO.
WHAT DO YOU MEAN?
WELL, TAKE TONIGHT. YOU'VE BEEN A GENTLEMAN ALL EVENING.
THE FIRST TIME I SAW ARMSTRONG WAS AT X-O MANOWAR'S WEDDING WHEN HE RIPPED HIS SHIRT OFF AND STARTED GRINDING ON NEVILLE ALCOTT.
OH. UM, WELL, IT WAS A WEDDING, RIGHT? PEOPLE DANCE AND HAVE FUN...
IT WAS DURING THE BEST MAN'S TOAST.
SIGH. MR. ARMSTRONG CAN BE... UNCIVILIZED AT TIMES, AND OFTEN HE IS DOWNRIGHT DISGUSTING.
...BUT HE'S ALSO A GOOD FRIEND.
PEOPLE SAY THAT I'M A GOOD INFLUENCE ON HIM, THAT *I'M* HELPING *HIM.* TRUTH IS, WE HELP EACH OTHER.
UM. WHY ARE YOU LOOKING AT ME LIKE THAT?
BECAUSE.
BECAUSE I DON'T THINK I HAVE EVER MET SOMEONE AS SWEET AND LOYAL AND KIND-HEARTED AS YOU.
OH, UM...

OH! FAITH! THE MOVIE!

WE'VE GOT PLENTY OF TIME.

YES, BUT I WAS HOPING TO GET THERE EARLY SO WE COULD GET A GOOD SEAT AND SOME POPCORN.

ARCHER, RELAX. THE THEATRE IS ONLY A BLOCK AWAY.

KEEP THE CHANGE.

THAT IS AN OFFER I CANNOT REFUSE. YOUR ENEMIES HAVE BECOME MY ENEMIES.

I'M NERVOUS THAT SOMETHING WILL GO WRONG.

I WANT TO MAKE TONIGHT PERFECT.

WELL, RELAX. YOU'RE DOING A GOOD JOB SO FAR.

AFTER THAT MEAL, I'M NOT SURE I EVEN *WANT* POPCORN.

WHAT ABOUT GUMMI BEARS? I WOULDN'T MIND SOME GUMMI BEARS.

GUMMI BEARS SOUND GREAT.

GARBONZO

TARGETS ARE ON THE MOVE. THEY ARE... GOING TO SEE A MOVIE.

STAY ON THEM, SALLY. WE'RE ONLY AN HOUR AWAY.

HURRY UP, WOULD YA? THEY ARE SO FRICKIN' ADORABLE I WANT TO PUKE.

NOW PLAYING
THE PRINCESS BRIDE

NOW PLA
THE PRINCES
NEXT WEEK: DAVID CRONE

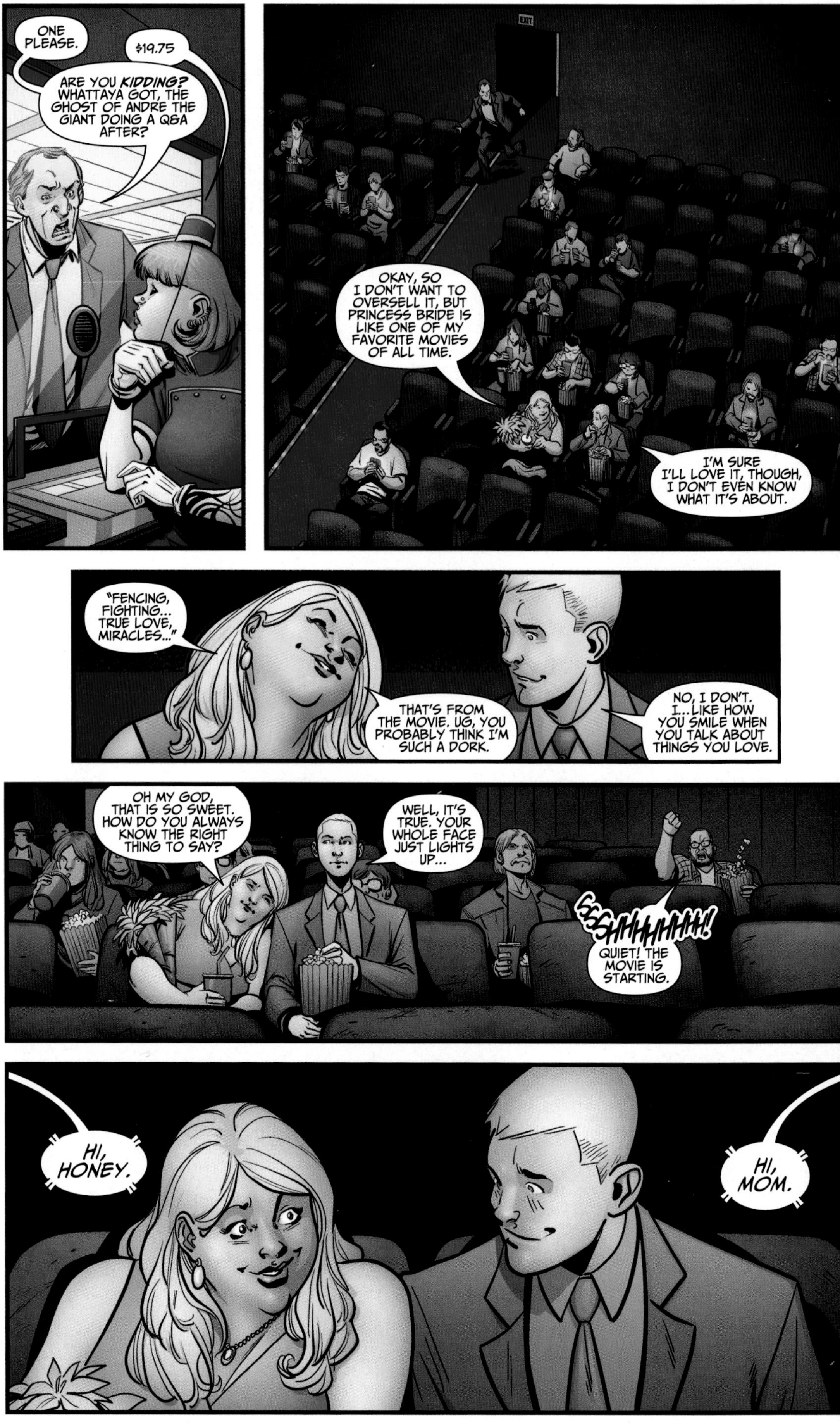
ONE PLEASE.
$19.75
ARE YOU KIDDING? WHATTAYA GOT, THE GHOST OF ANDRE THE GIANT DOING A Q&A AFTER?
EXIT
OKAY, SO I DON'T WANT TO OVERSELL IT, BUT PRINCESS BRIDE IS LIKE ONE OF MY FAVORITE MOVIES OF ALL TIME.
I'M SURE I'LL LOVE IT, THOUGH. I DON'T EVEN KNOW WHAT IT'S ABOUT.
"FENCING, FIGHTING... TRUE LOVE, MIRACLES..."
THAT'S FROM THE MOVIE. UG, YOU PROBABLY THINK I'M SUCH A DORK.
NO, I DON'T. I...LIKE HOW YOU SMILE WHEN YOU TALK ABOUT THINGS YOU LOVE.
OH MY GOD, THAT IS SO SWEET. HOW DO YOU ALWAYS KNOW THE RIGHT THING TO SAY?
WELL, IT'S TRUE. YOUR WHOLE FACE JUST LIGHTS UP...
SSSHHHHHHH!
QUIET! THE MOVIE IS STARTING.
HI, HONEY.
HI, MOM.

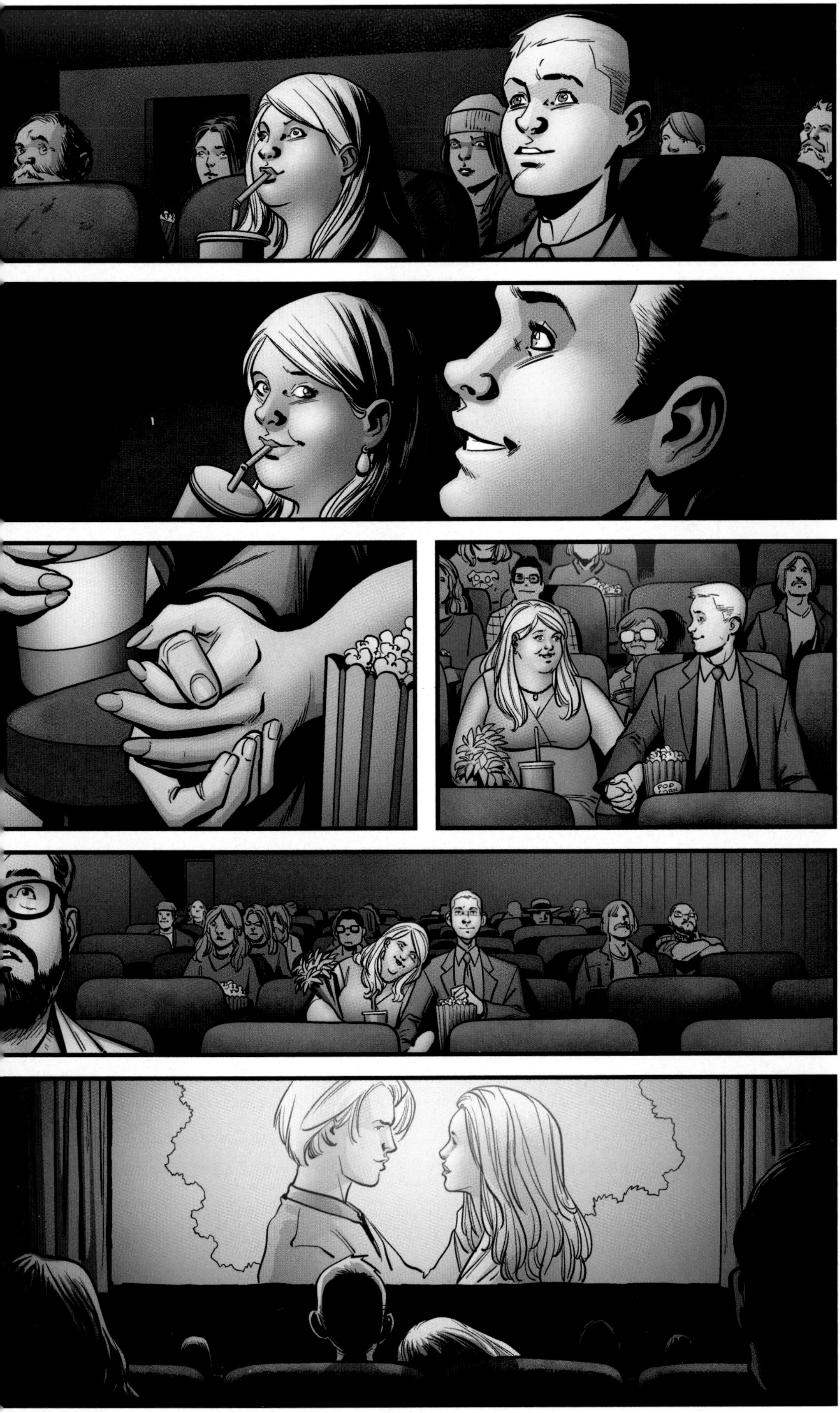
POP CORN

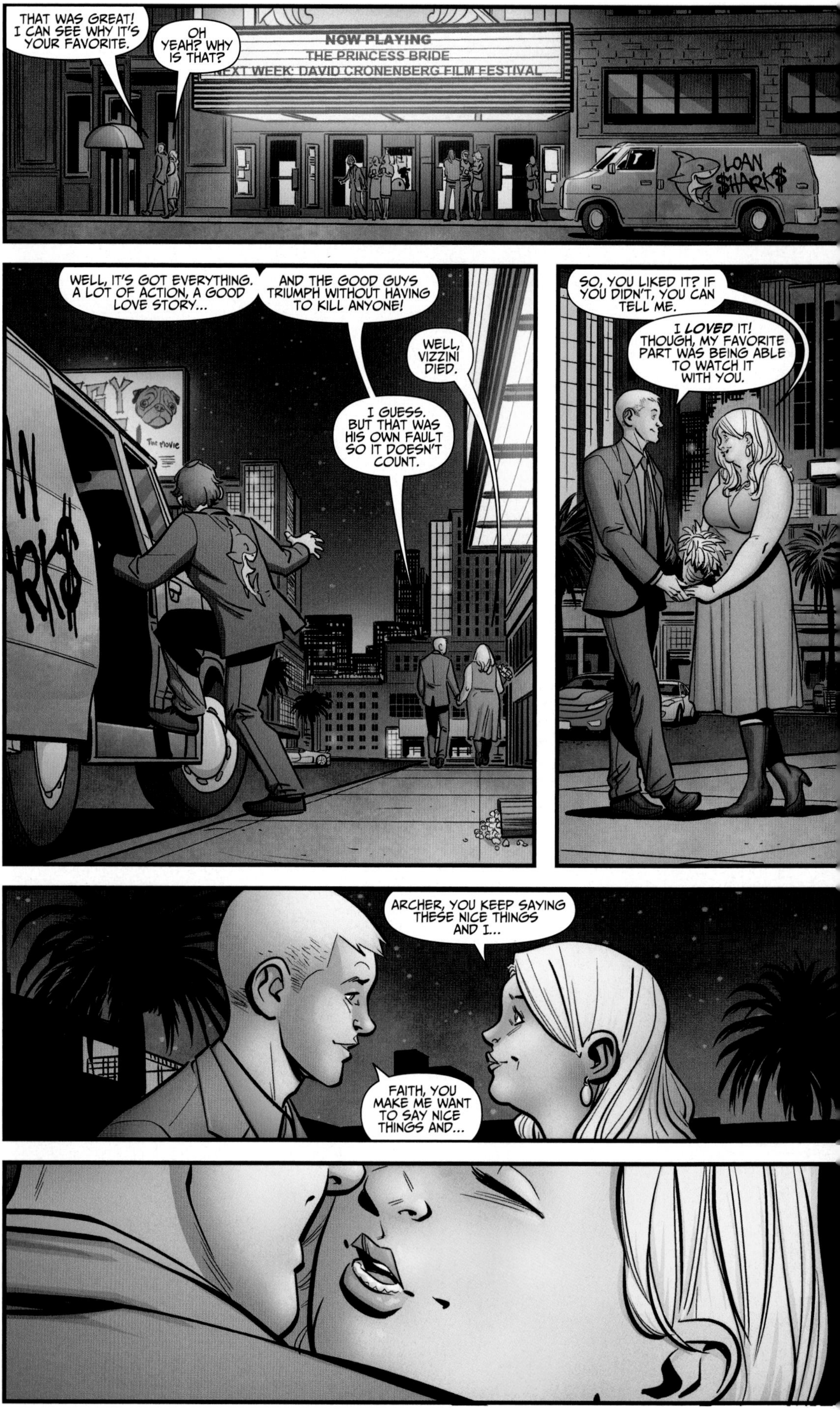
THAT WAS GREAT! I CAN SEE WHY IT'S YOUR FAVORITE.
OH YEAH? WHY IS THAT?
NOW PLAYING
THE PRINCESS BRIDE
NEXT WEEK: DAVID CRONENBERG FILM FESTIVAL
LOAN $HARK$
WELL, IT'S GOT EVERYTHING. A LOT OF ACTION, A GOOD LOVE STORY...
AND THE GOOD GUYS TRIUMPH WITHOUT HAVING TO KILL ANYONE!
WELL, VIZZINI DIED.
I GUESS. BUT THAT WAS HIS OWN FAULT SO IT DOESN'T COUNT.
The Movie
SO, YOU LIKED IT? IF YOU DIDN'T, YOU CAN TELL ME.
I ***LOVED*** IT! THOUGH, MY FAVORITE PART WAS BEING ABLE TO WATCH IT WITH YOU.
ARCHER, YOU KEEP SAYING THESE NICE THINGS AND I...
FAITH, YOU MAKE ME WANT TO SAY NICE THINGS AND...

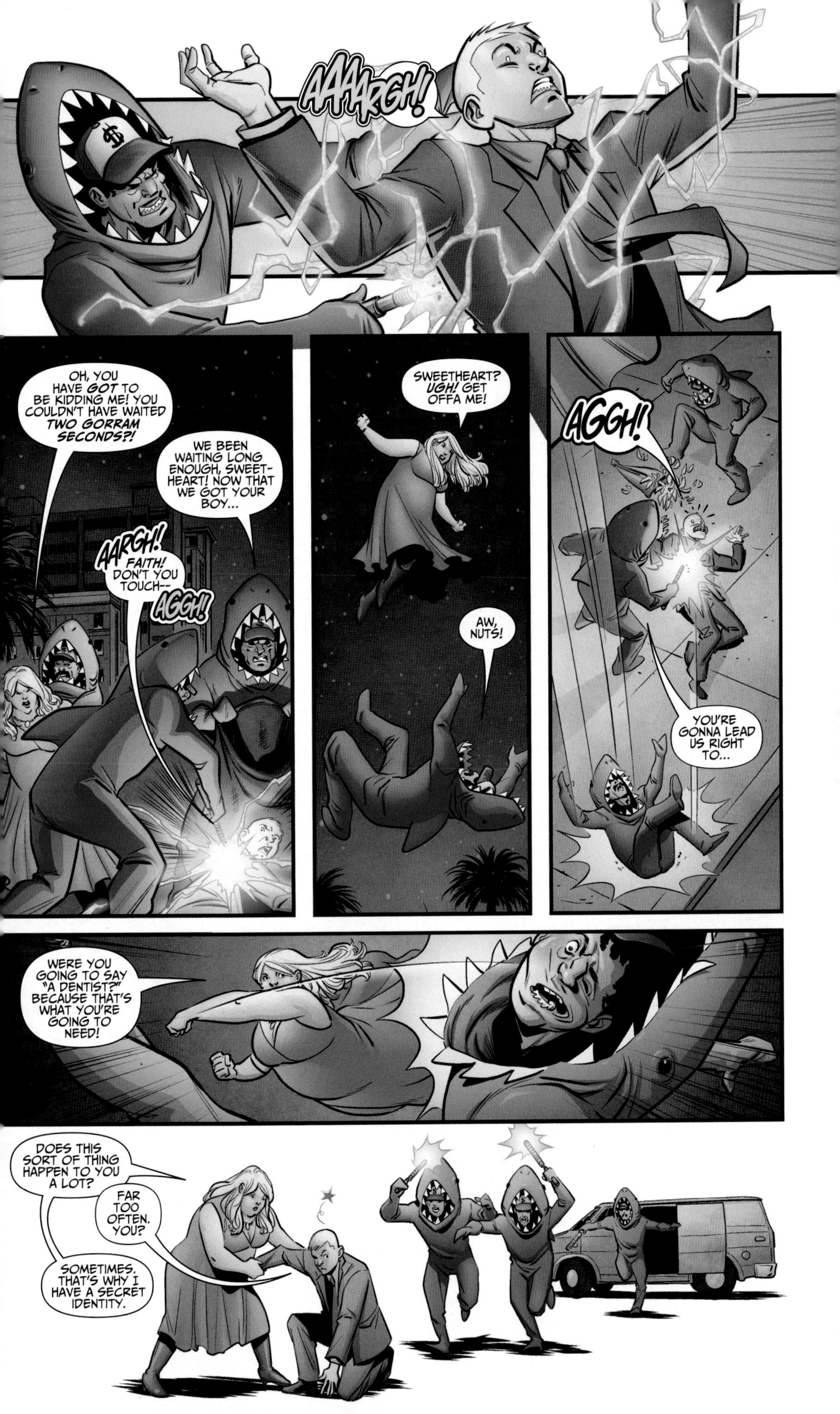
AAAARGH!
OH, YOU HAVE GOT TO BE KIDDING ME! YOU COULDN'T HAVE WAITED TWO GORRAM SECONDS?!
WE BEEN WAITING LONG ENOUGH, SWEET-HEART! NOW THAT WE GOT YOUR BOY...
AARGH! FAITH! DON'T YOU TOUCH--
AGGH!
SWEETHEART? UGH! GET OFFA ME!
AW, NUTS!
AGGH!
YOU'RE GONNA LEAD US RIGHT TO...
WERE YOU GOING TO SAY "A DENTIST?" BECAUSE THAT'S WHAT YOU'RE GOING TO NEED!
DOES THIS SORT OF THING HAPPEN TO YOU A LOT?
FAR TOO OFTEN. YOU?
SOMETIMES. THAT'S WHY I HAVE A SECRET IDENTITY.

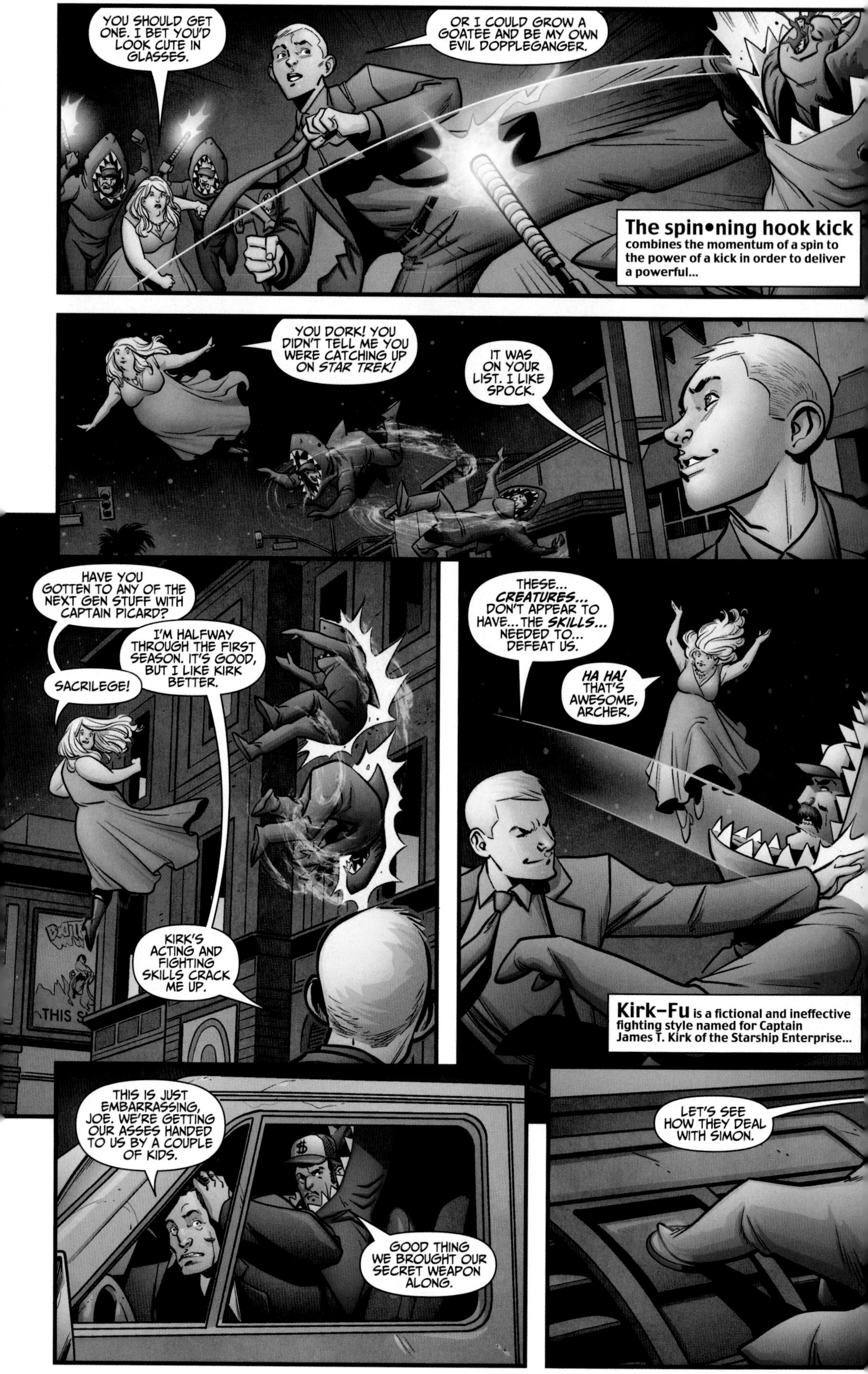

YOU SHOULD GET ONE. I BET YOU'D LOOK CUTE IN GLASSES.
OR I COULD GROW A GOATEE AND BE MY OWN EVIL DOPPLEGANGER.
The spin•ning hook kick combines the momentum of a spin to the power of a kick in order to deliver a powerful...
YOU DORK! YOU DIDN'T TELL ME YOU WERE CATCHING UP ON STAR TREK!
IT WAS ON YOUR LIST. I LIKE SPOCK.
HAVE YOU GOTTEN TO ANY OF THE NEXT GEN STUFF WITH CAPTAIN PICARD?
I'M HALFWAY THROUGH THE FIRST SEASON. IT'S GOOD, BUT I LIKE KIRK BETTER.
SACRILEGE!
KIRK'S ACTING AND FIGHTING SKILLS CRACK ME UP.
THESE... CREATURES... DON'T APPEAR TO HAVE... THE SKILLS... NEEDED TO... DEFEAT US.
HA HA! THAT'S AWESOME, ARCHER.
Kirk-Fu is a fictional and ineffective fighting style named for Captain James T. Kirk of the Starship Enterprise...
THIS IS JUST EMBARRASSING, JOE. WE'RE GETTING OUR ASSES HANDED TO US BY A COUPLE OF KIDS.
GOOD THING WE BROUGHT OUR SECRET WEAPON ALONG.
LET'S SEE HOW THEY DEAL WITH SIMON.

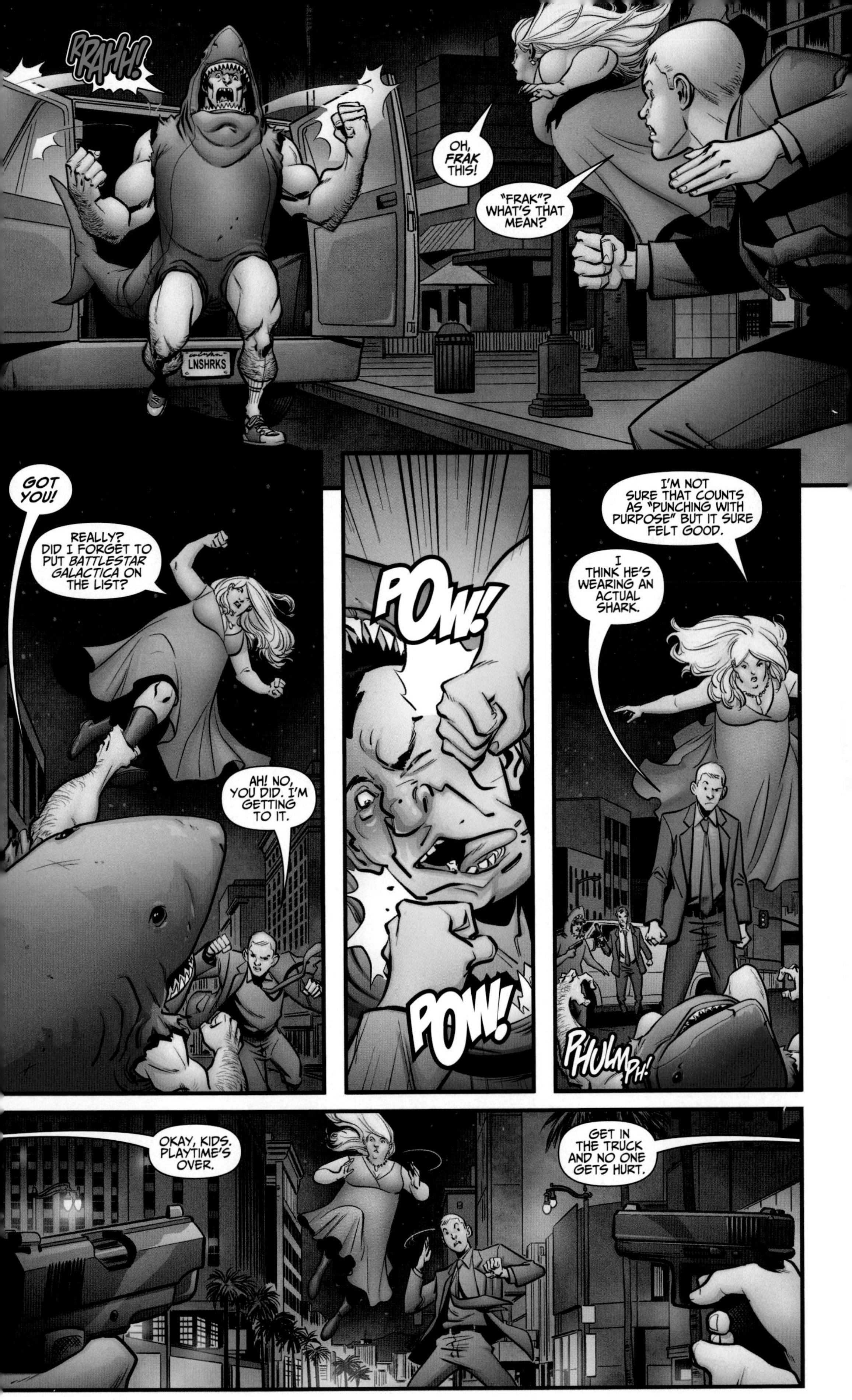
RRAHH!
OH, FRAK THIS!
"FRAK"? WHAT'S THAT MEAN?
LNSHRKS
GOT YOU!
REALLY? DID I FORGET TO PUT BATTLESTAR GALACTICA ON THE LIST?
AH! NO, YOU DID. I'M GETTING TO IT.
POW!
POW!
I'M NOT SURE THAT COUNTS AS "PUNCHING WITH PURPOSE" BUT IT SURE FELT GOOD.
I THINK HE'S WEARING AN ACTUAL SHARK.
PHULMPH!
OKAY, KIDS. PLAYTIME'S OVER.
GET IN THE TRUCK AND NO ONE GETS HURT.

CRAK!

OH, GOD! YOU BROKE MY DAMN WRIST! THE BONE IS STICKING OUT!

EESH! THAT DOES LOOK BAD! I DIDN'T MEAN...

ARCHER, THEY PULLED GUNS YOU DON'T NEED TO APOLOGIZE.

WEE-OOO WEE-OOO WEE-OOO WEE-OOO

YEAH, THAT'S RIGHT. WHAT THE HECK?

WHO ARE YOU? WHY DID YOU ATTACK US?

NEVER HEARD OF THE LOAN SHARKS? FIGURES.

YOU WERE SUPPOSED TO LEAD US TO THAT IMMORTAL FRIEND OF YOURS!

MR. ARMSTRONG? BUT... WAIT, WHY?

THE FRIGGIN' SECT KEEPS REJECTING OUR MEMBERSHIP APPLICATION. "WE GOT FINANCES COVERED", THEY SAID. "YOU'RE JUST A BUNCH OF DOOFS IN PAJAMAS!"

THEY WON'T BE LAUGHING SO HARD AFTER WE DECAPITATE THEIR GREATEST ENEMY!

YOU... YOU PULLED A GUN ON FAITH BECAUSE OF MR. ARMSTRONG? YOU TRIED TO KILL US OVER NOTHING!

YOU KNOW THE SECT DOESN'T EXIST ANYMORE, RIGHT?

UM... WHAT?

ARCHER, IT'S THE COPS. WE SHOULD GO.

WEE-OOO WEE-OOO WEE-OOO WEE-OOO

FREEZE! HANDS WHERE WE CAN SEE THEM!

MY HAND'S ABOUT TO FALL OFF. YOU MIND IF I LEAVE IT RIGHT WHERE IT IS?

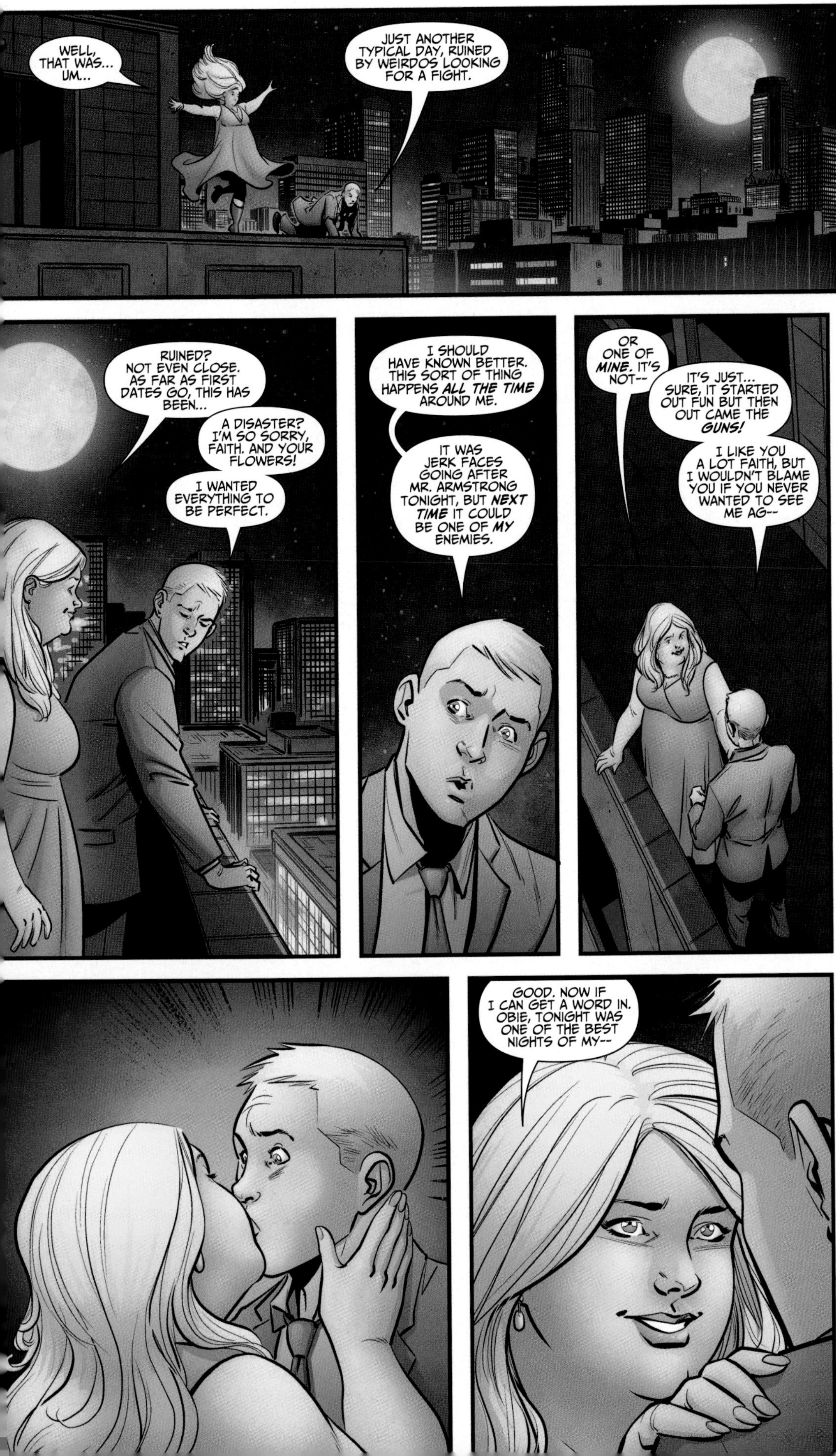
WELL, THAT WAS... UM...
JUST ANOTHER TYPICAL DAY, RUINED BY WEIRDOS LOOKING FOR A FIGHT.
RUINED? NOT EVEN CLOSE. AS FAR AS FIRST DATES GO, THIS HAS BEEN...
A DISASTER? I'M SO SORRY, FAITH. AND YOUR FLOWERS!
I WANTED EVERYTHING TO BE PERFECT.
I SHOULD HAVE KNOWN BETTER. THIS SORT OF THING HAPPENS ALL THE TIME AROUND ME.
IT WAS JERK FACES GOING AFTER MR. ARMSTRONG TONIGHT, BUT NEXT TIME IT COULD BE ONE OF MY ENEMIES.
OR ONE OF MINE. IT'S NOT--
IT'S JUST... SURE, IT STARTED OUT FUN BUT THEN OUT CAME THE GUNS!
I LIKE YOU A LOT FAITH, BUT I WOULDN'T BLAME YOU IF YOU NEVER WANTED TO SEE ME AG--
GOOD. NOW IF I CAN GET A WORD IN. OBIE, TONIGHT WAS ONE OF THE BEST NIGHTS OF MY--

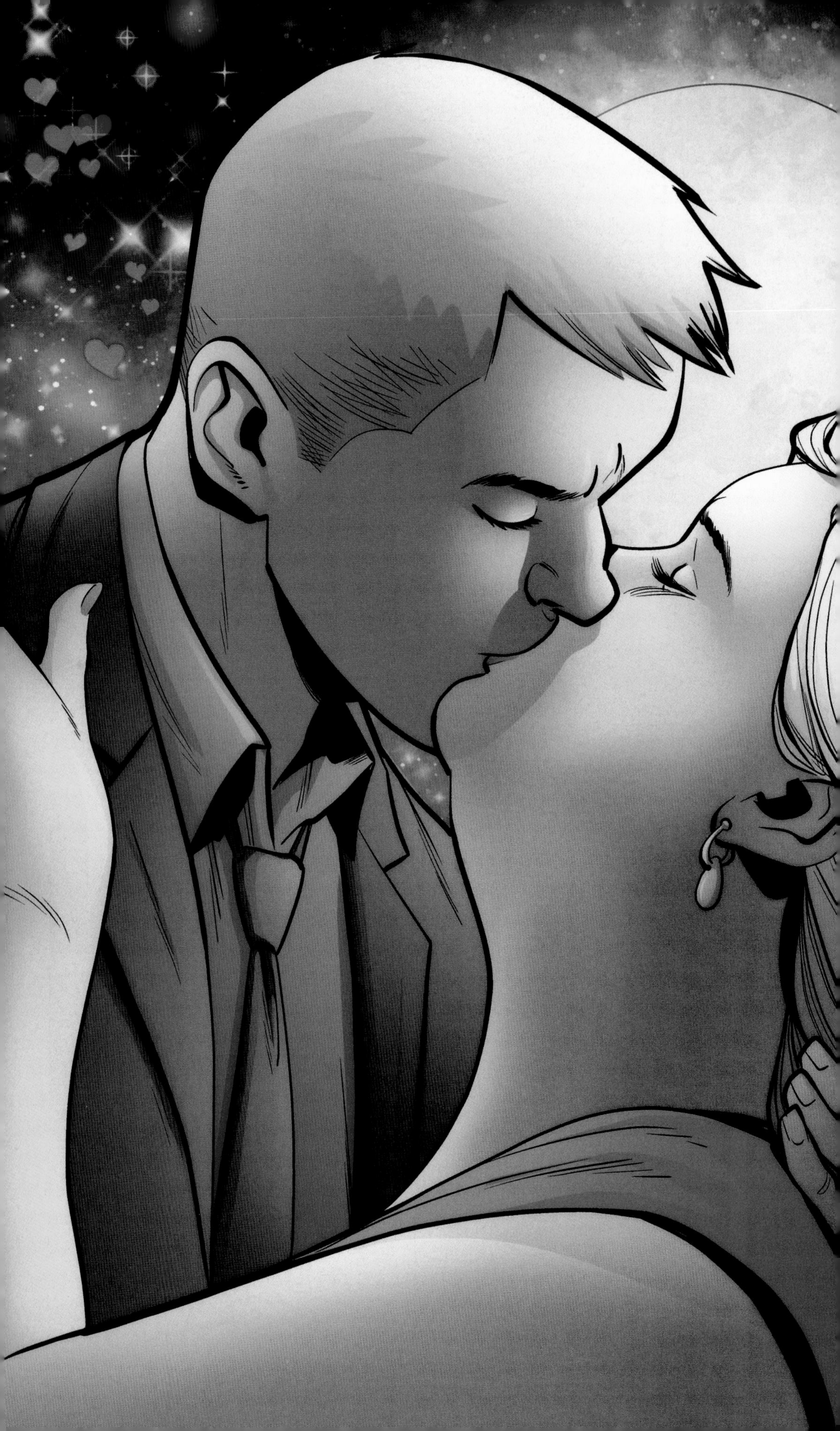

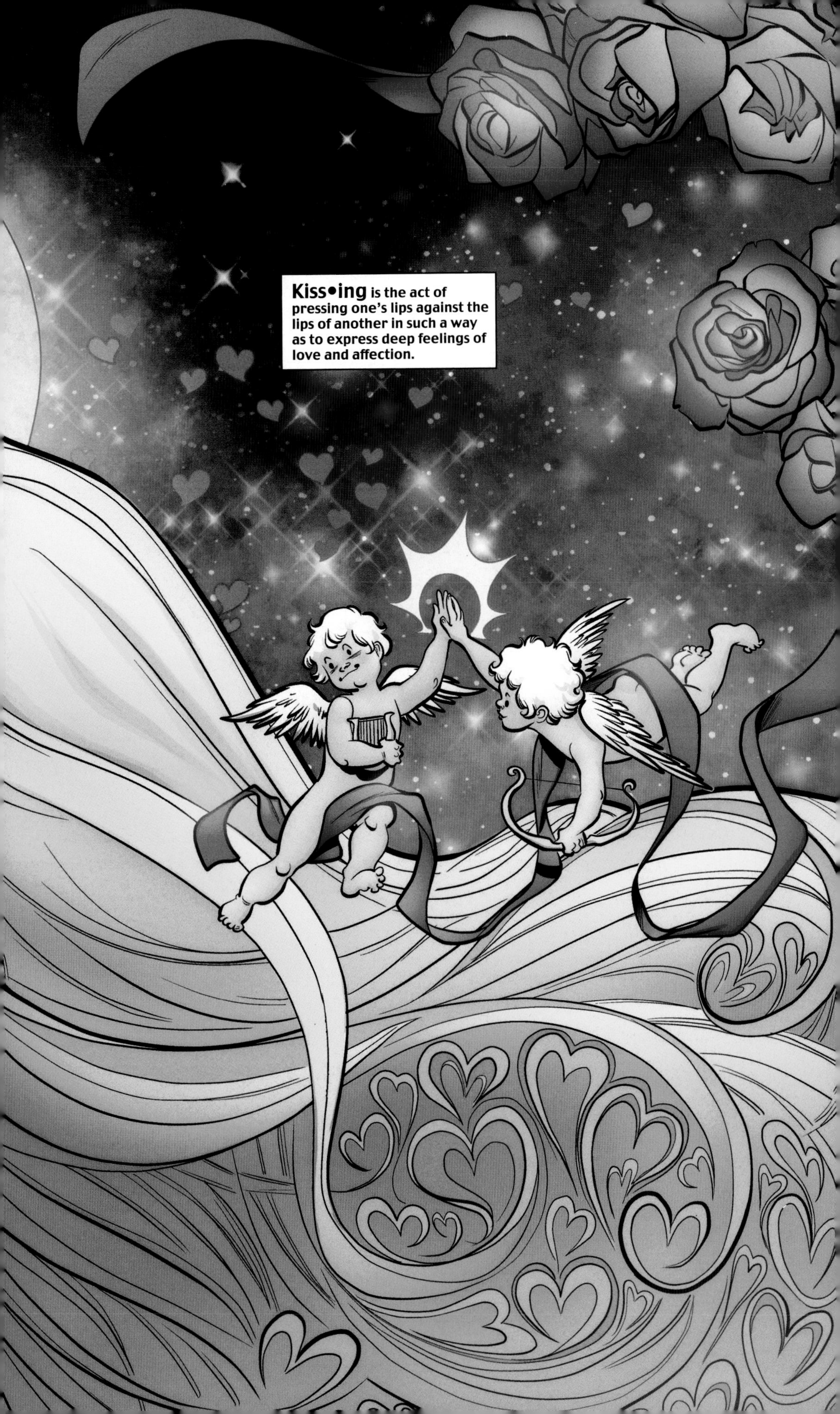
Kiss•ing is the act of pressing one's lips against the lips of another in such a way as to express deep feelings of love and affection.

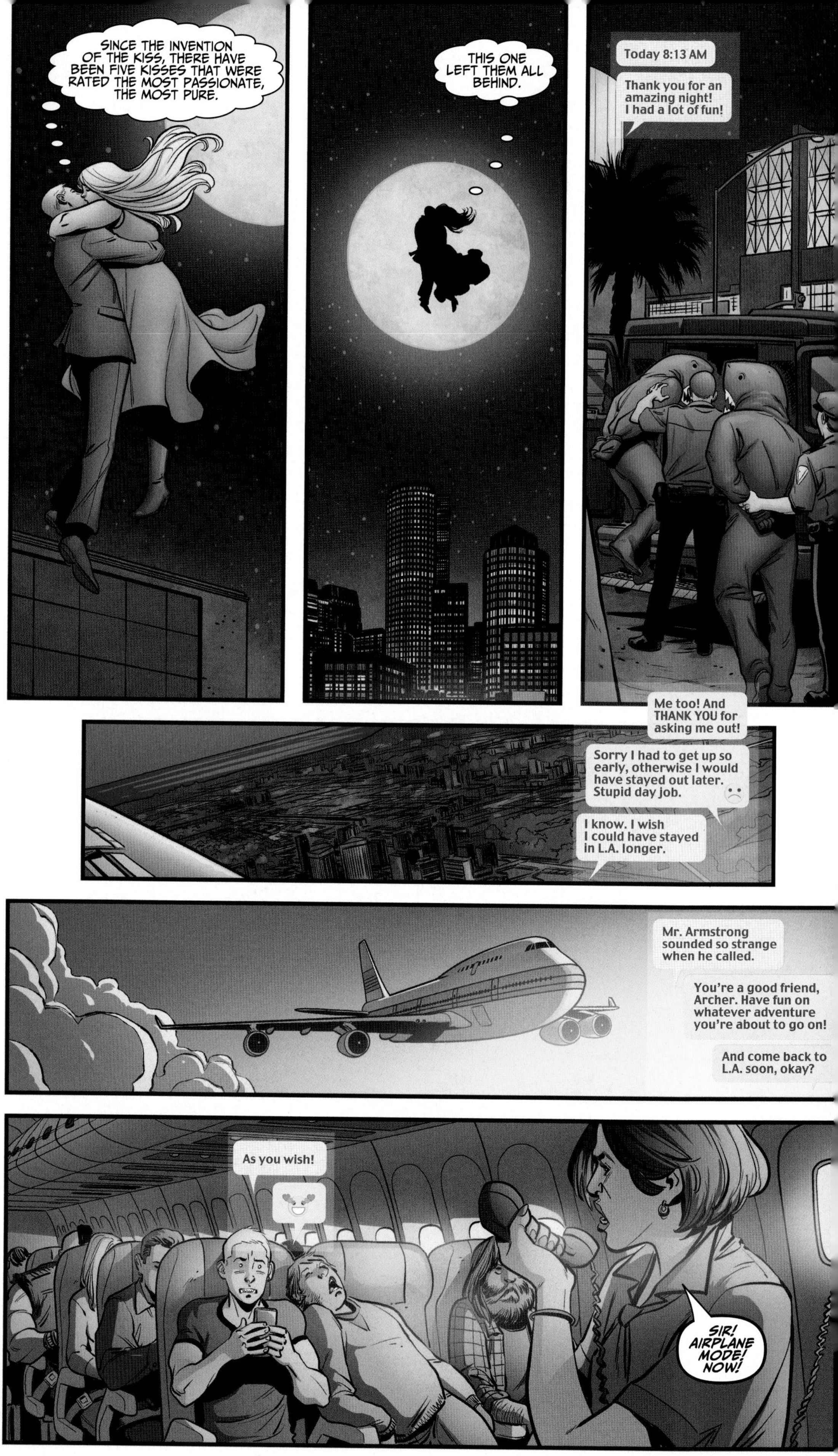
SINCE THE INVENTION OF THE KISS, THERE HAVE BEEN FIVE KISSES THAT WERE RATED THE MOST PASSIONATE, THE MOST PURE.
THIS ONE LEFT THEM ALL BEHIND.
Today 8:13 AM
Thank you for an amazing night! I had a lot of fun!
Me too! And THANK YOU for asking me out!
Sorry I had to get up so early, otherwise I would have stayed out later. Stupid day job.
I know. I wish I could have stayed in L.A. longer.
Mr. Armstrong sounded so strange when he called.
You're a good friend, Archer. Have fun on whatever adventure you're about to go on!
And come back to L.A. soon, okay?
As you wish!
SIR! AIRPLANE MODE! NOW!

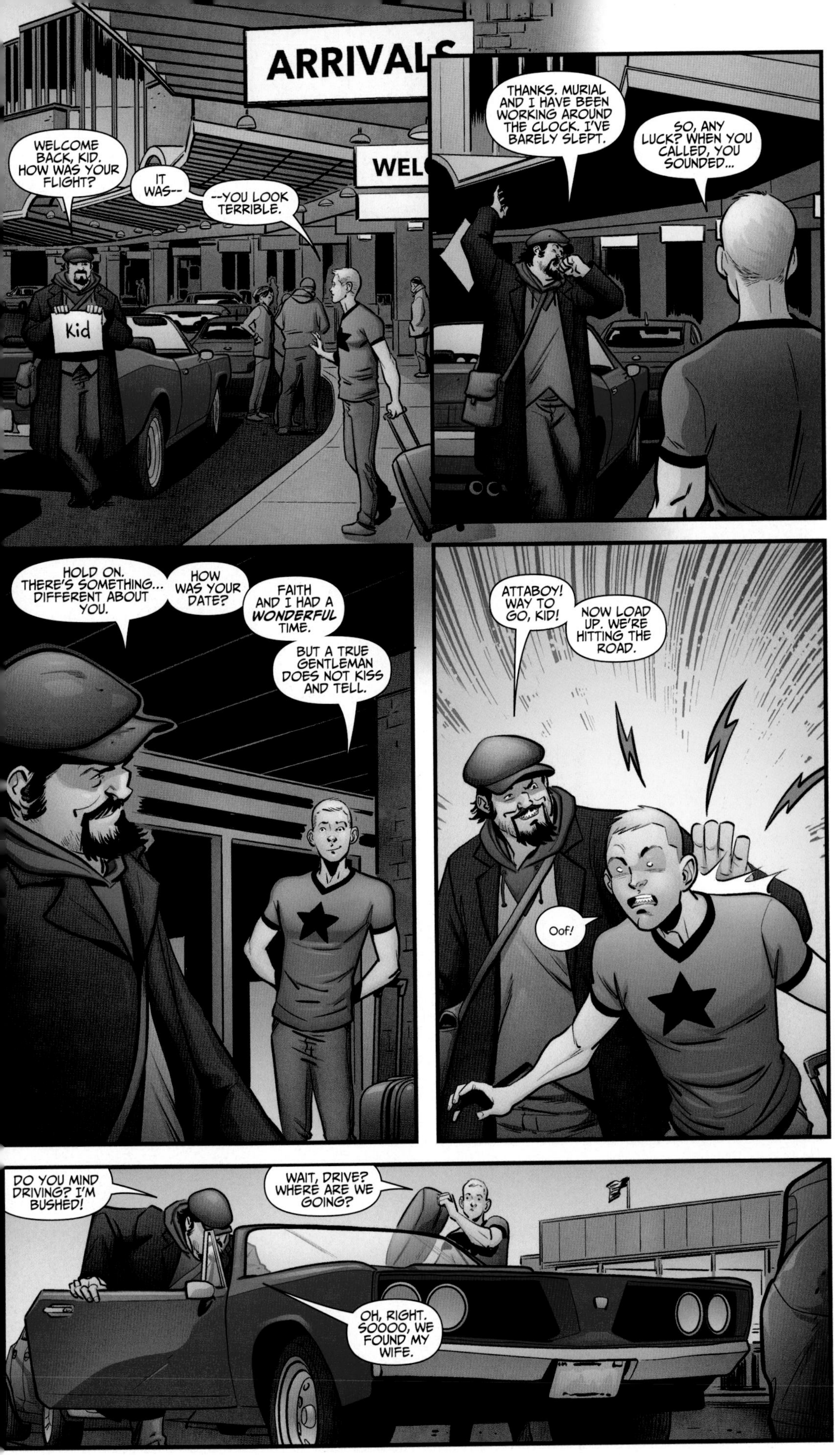
ARRIVALS
WEL
WELCOME BACK, KID. HOW WAS YOUR FLIGHT?
Kid
IT WAS--
--YOU LOOK TERRIBLE.
THANKS. MURIAL AND I HAVE BEEN WORKING AROUND THE CLOCK. I'VE BARELY SLEPT.
SO, ANY LUCK? WHEN YOU CALLED, YOU SOUNDED...
HOLD ON. THERE'S SOMETHING... DIFFERENT ABOUT YOU.
HOW WAS YOUR DATE?
FAITH AND I HAD A *WONDERFUL* TIME.
BUT A TRUE GENTLEMAN DOES NOT KISS AND TELL.
ATTABOY! WAY TO GO, KID!
NOW LOAD UP. WE'RE HITTING THE ROAD.
Oof!
DO YOU MIND DRIVING? I'M BUSHED!
WAIT, DRIVE? WHERE ARE WE GOING?
OH, RIGHT. SOOOO, WE FOUND MY WIFE.

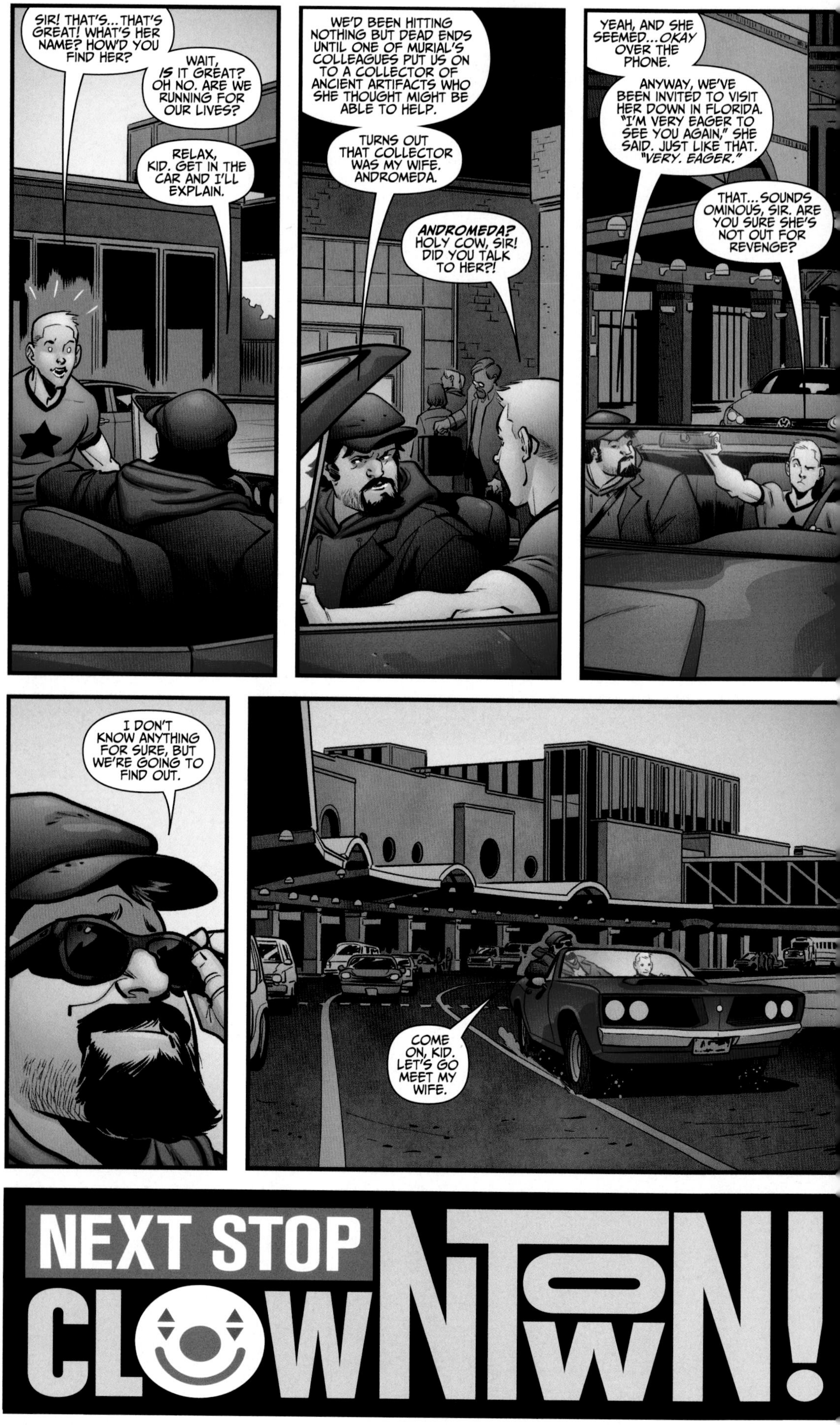
SIR! THAT'S...THAT'S GREAT! WHAT'S HER NAME? HOW'D YOU FIND HER?
WAIT, *IS* IT GREAT? OH NO. ARE WE RUNNING FOR OUR LIVES?
RELAX, KID. GET IN THE CAR AND I'LL EXPLAIN.
WE'D BEEN HITTING NOTHING BUT DEAD ENDS UNTIL ONE OF MURIAL'S COLLEAGUES PUT US ON TO A COLLECTOR OF ANCIENT ARTIFACTS WHO SHE THOUGHT MIGHT BE ABLE TO HELP.
TURNS OUT THAT COLLECTOR WAS MY WIFE. ANDROMEDA.
ANDROMEDA? HOLY COW, SIR! DID YOU TALK TO HER?!
YEAH, AND SHE SEEMED...*OKAY* OVER THE PHONE.
ANYWAY, WE'VE BEEN INVITED TO VISIT HER DOWN IN FLORIDA. "I'M VERY EAGER TO SEE YOU AGAIN," SHE SAID. JUST LIKE THAT. *"VERY. EAGER."*
THAT...SOUNDS OMINOUS, SIR. ARE YOU SURE SHE'S NOT OUT FOR REVENGE?
I DON'T KNOW ANYTHING FOR SURE, BUT WE'RE GOING TO FIND OUT.
COME ON, KID. LET'S GO MEET MY WIFE.
NEXT STOP
CLOWNTOWN!

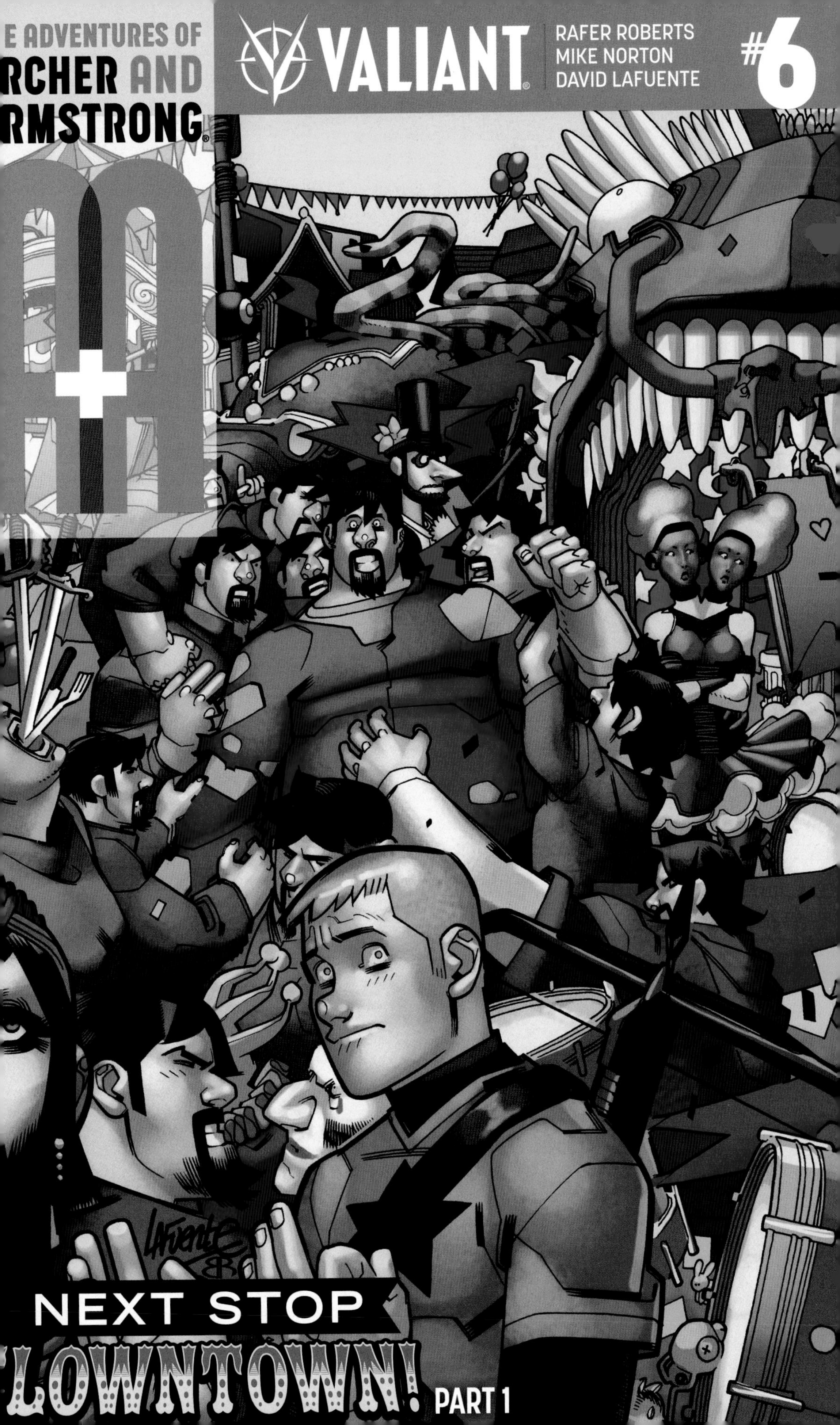
E ADVENTURES OF
RCHER AND
RMSTRONG
VALIANT
RAFER ROBERTS
MIKE NORTON
DAVID LAFUENTE
#6
A+A
LAFUENTE
NEXT STOP
LOWNTOWN! PART 1

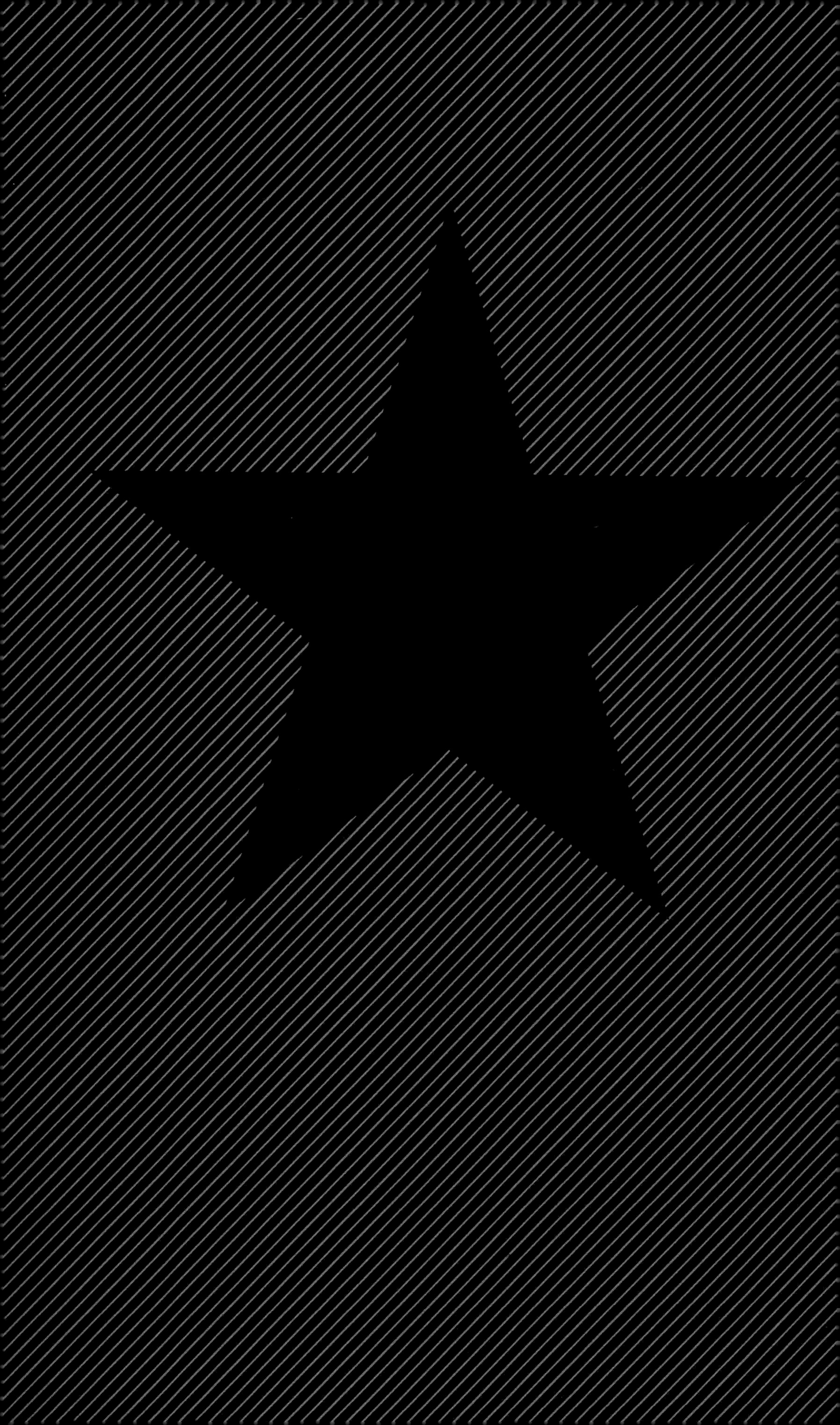

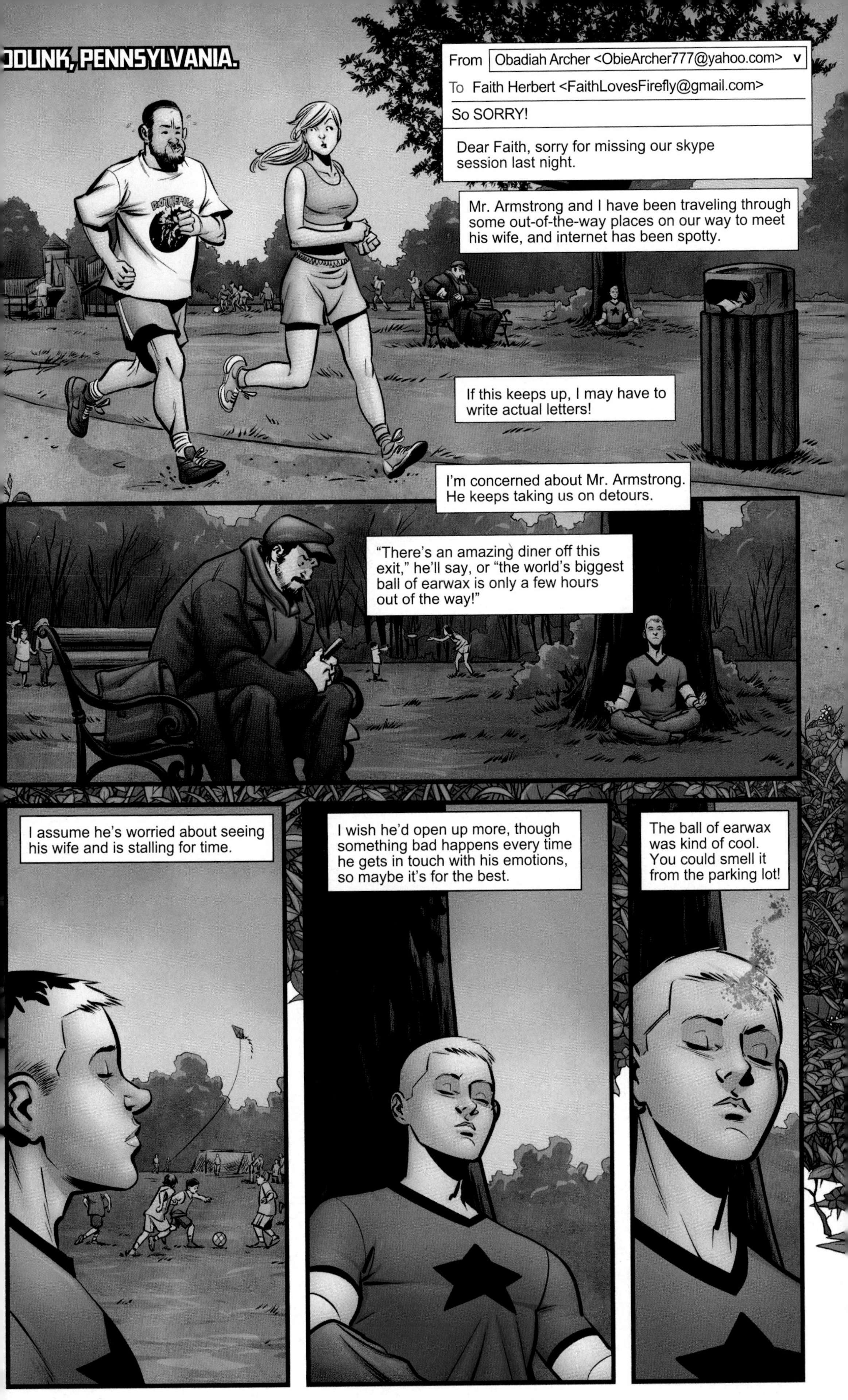

ODUNK, PENNSYLVANIA.
From Obadiah Archer <ObieArcher777@yahoo.com> v
To Faith Herbert <FaithLovesFirefly@gmail.com>
So SORRY!
Dear Faith, sorry for missing our skype session last night.
Mr. Armstrong and I have been traveling through some out-of-the-way places on our way to meet his wife, and internet has been spotty.
If this keeps up, I may have to write actual letters!
I'm concerned about Mr. Armstrong. He keeps taking us on detours.
"There's an amazing diner off this exit," he'll say, or "the world's biggest ball of earwax is only a few hours out of the way!"
I assume he's worried about seeing his wife and is stalling for time.
I wish he'd open up more, though something bad happens every time he gets in touch with his emotions, so maybe it's for the best.
The ball of earwax was kind of cool. You could smell it from the parking lot!

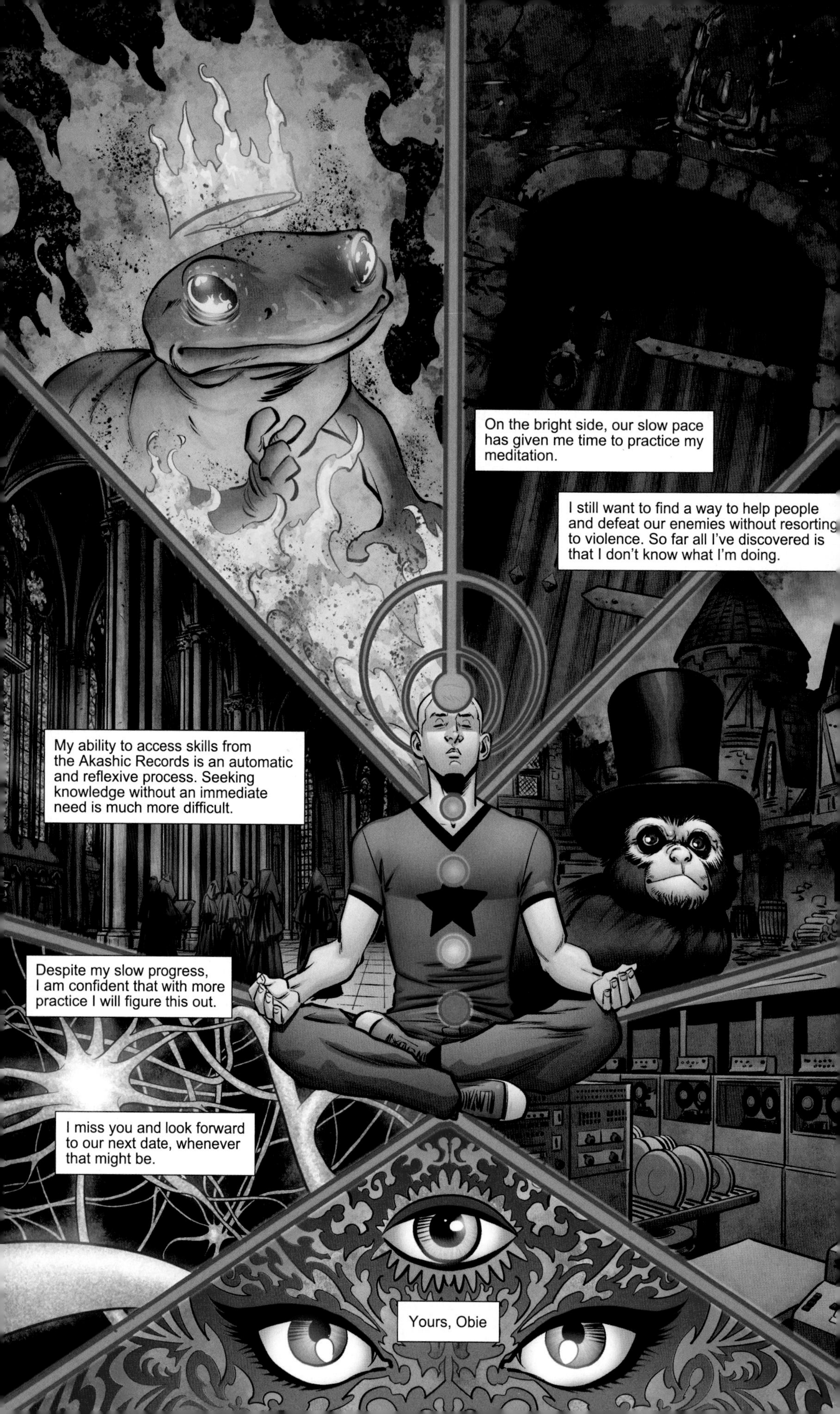
On the bright side, our slow pace has given me time to practice my meditation.
I still want to find a way to help people and defeat our enemies without resorting to violence. So far all I've discovered is that I don't know what I'm doing.
My ability to access skills from the Akashic Records is an automatic and reflexive process. Seeking knowledge without an immediate need is much more difficult.
Despite my slow progress, I am confident that with more practice I will figure this out.
I miss you and look forward to our next date, whenever that might be.
Yours, Obie

JESUS, ARMSTRONG. WHEN YOU ASKED FOR TIME OFF, I NEVER THOUGHT I'D HAVE TO GO A MONTH WITHOUT MY TWO BEST BOUNCERS!

YEAH, SORRY FOR NOT CALLING SOONER, MELISSA. IT'S...UM...IT'S THE KID.

THERE'VE BEEN A LOT OF BIG CHANGES GOING ON IN HIS LIFE AND HE'S NOT SURE HOW TO DEAL WITH THEM. THIS ROAD TRIP IS DOING ME--UH, HIM A LOT OF GOOD.

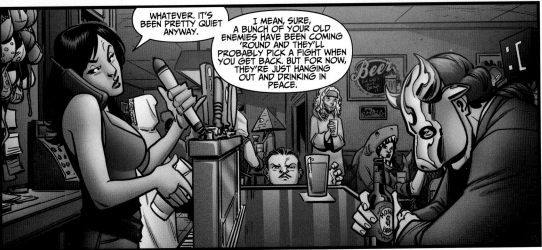

WHATEVER. IT'S BEEN PRETTY QUIET ANYWAY.

I MEAN, SURE, A BUNCH OF YOUR OLD ENEMIES HAVE BEEN COMING 'ROUND AND THEY'LL PROBABLY PICK A FIGHT WHEN YOU GET BACK. BUT FOR NOW, THEY'RE JUST HANGING OUT AND DRINKING IN PEACE.

HAVE FUN IN PODUNK, PENNSYLVANIA. COME BACK WHEN YOU'VE FOUND YOURSELF.

PODUNK, PENNSYLVANIA?

AGAIN, THE KID, NOT ME. AND THANKS, MELISSA, YOU'RE THE BEST!

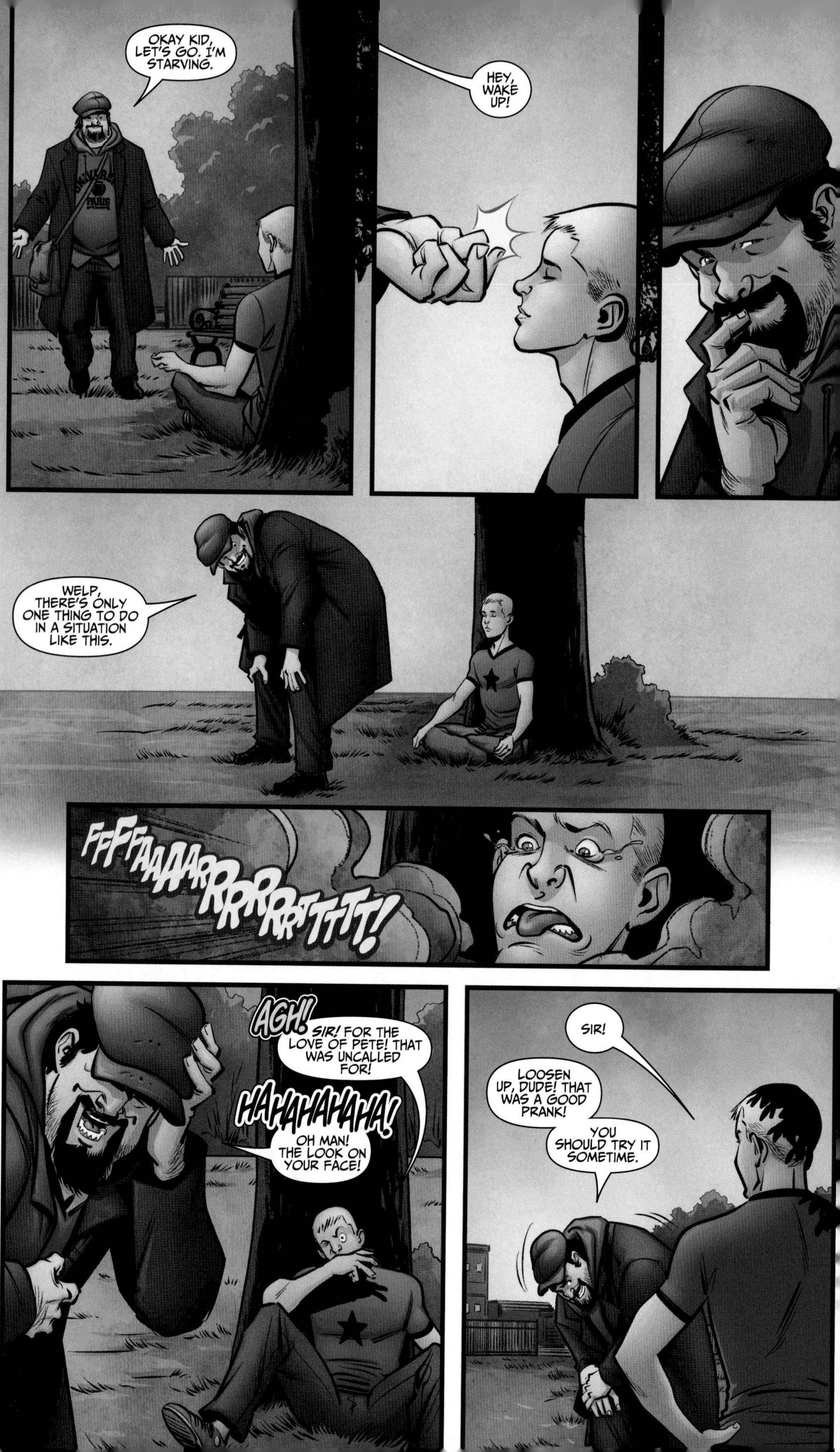
OKAY KID, LET'S GO. I'M STARVING.
HEY, WAKE UP!
WELP, THERE'S ONLY ONE THING TO DO IN A SITUATION LIKE THIS.
FFFFAAAARRRRRRTTTTT!
AGH!
SIR! FOR THE LOVE OF PETE! THAT WAS UNCALLED FOR!
HAHAHAHAHA!
OH MAN! THE LOOK ON YOUR FACE!
SIR!
LOOSEN UP, DUDE! THAT WAS A GOOD PRANK!
YOU SHOULD TRY IT SOMETIME.

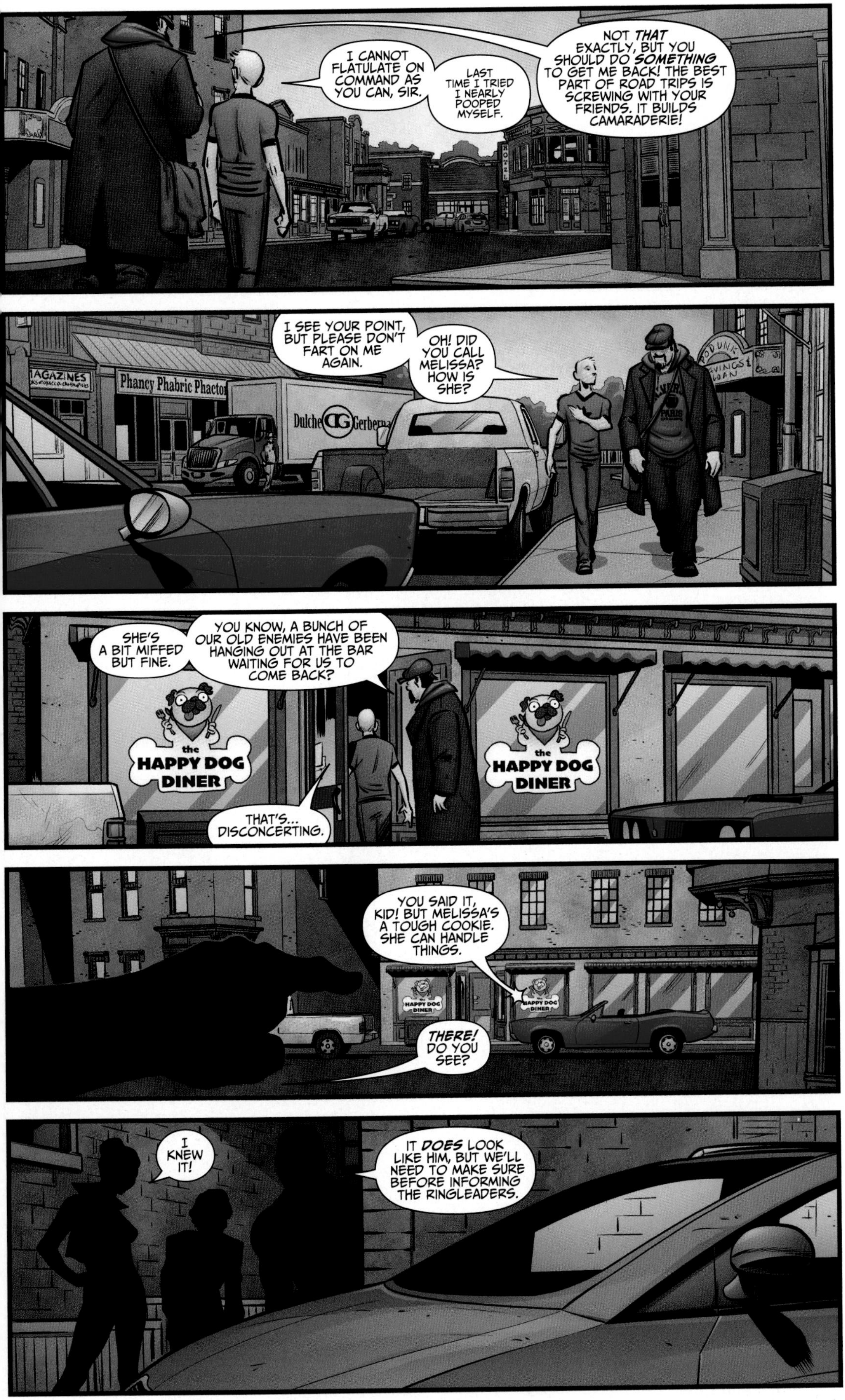
I CANNOT FLATULATE ON COMMAND AS YOU CAN, SIR.
LAST TIME I TRIED I NEARLY POOPED MYSELF.
NOT THAT EXACTLY, BUT YOU SHOULD DO SOMETHING TO GET ME BACK! THE BEST PART OF ROAD TRIPS IS SCREWING WITH YOUR FRIENDS. IT BUILDS CAMARADERIE!
HOTEL
MAGAZINES
Phancy Phabric Phactory
Dulche DG Gerberna
I SEE YOUR POINT, BUT PLEASE DON'T FART ON ME AGAIN.
OH! DID YOU CALL MELISSA? HOW IS SHE?
PODUNK SAVINGS & LOAN
SHE'S A BIT MIFFED BUT FINE.
YOU KNOW, A BUNCH OF OUR OLD ENEMIES HAVE BEEN HANGING OUT AT THE BAR WAITING FOR US TO COME BACK?
the HAPPY DOG DINER
the HAPPY DOG DINER
THAT'S... DISCONCERTING.
YOU SAID IT, KID! BUT MELISSA'S A TOUGH COOKIE. SHE CAN HANDLE THINGS.
HAPPY DOG DINER
HAPPY DOG DINER
THERE! DO YOU SEE?
I KNEW IT!
IT DOES LOOK LIKE HIM, BUT WE'LL NEED TO MAKE SURE BEFORE INFORMING THE RINGLEADERS.

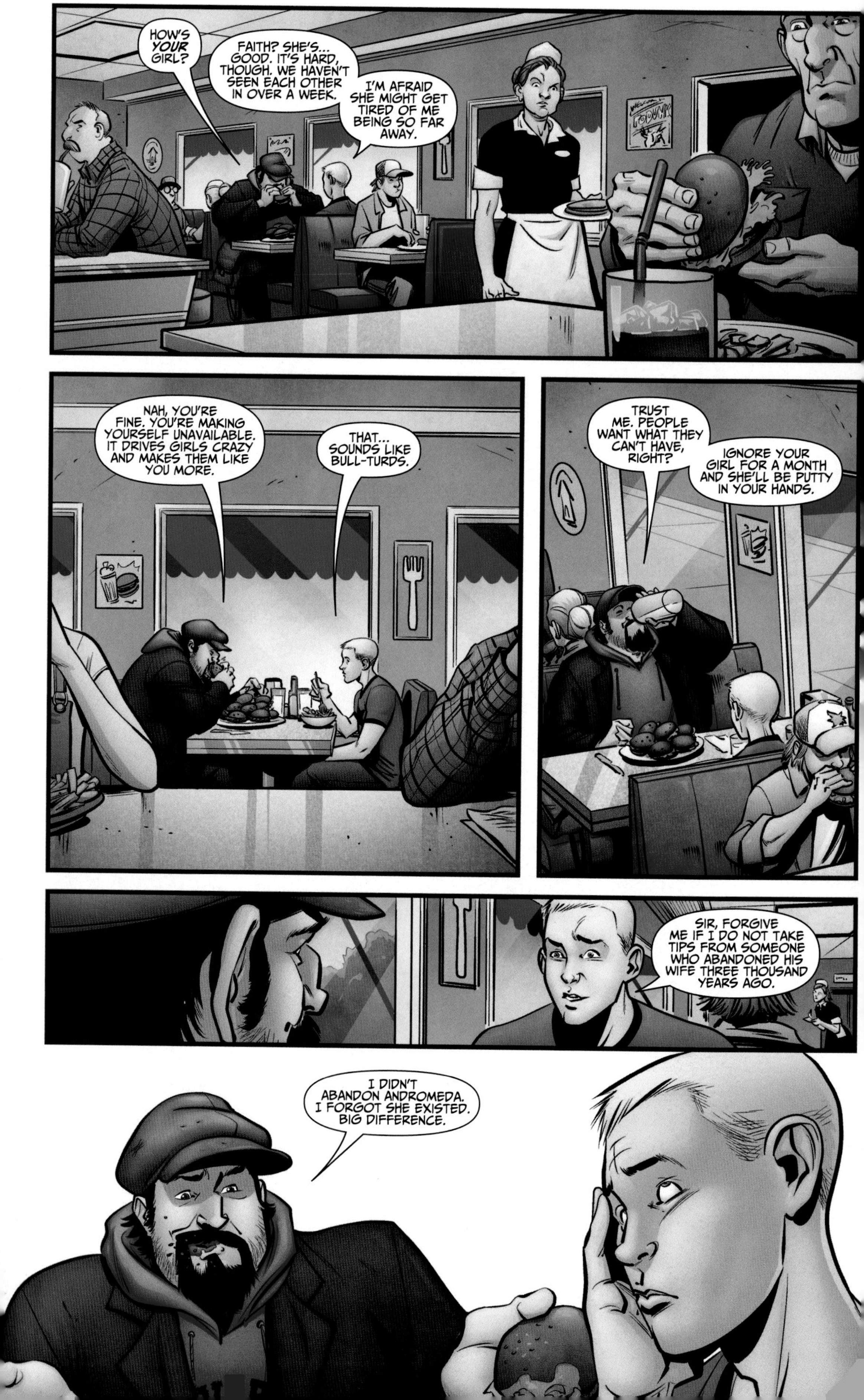
HOW'S YOUR GIRL?
FAITH? SHE'S... GOOD. IT'S HARD, THOUGH. WE HAVEN'T SEEN EACH OTHER IN OVER A WEEK.
I'M AFRAID SHE MIGHT GET TIRED OF ME BEING SO FAR AWAY.
NAH, YOU'RE FINE. YOU'RE MAKING YOURSELF UNAVAILABLE. IT DRIVES GIRLS CRAZY AND MAKES THEM LIKE YOU MORE.
THAT... SOUNDS LIKE BULL-TURDS.
TRUST ME. PEOPLE WANT WHAT THEY CAN'T HAVE, RIGHT?
IGNORE YOUR GIRL FOR A MONTH AND SHE'LL BE PUTTY IN YOUR HANDS.
SIR, FORGIVE ME IF I DO NOT TAKE TIPS FROM SOMEONE WHO ABANDONED HIS WIFE THREE THOUSAND YEARS AGO.
I DIDN'T ABANDON ANDROMEDA. I FORGOT SHE EXISTED. BIG DIFFERENCE.

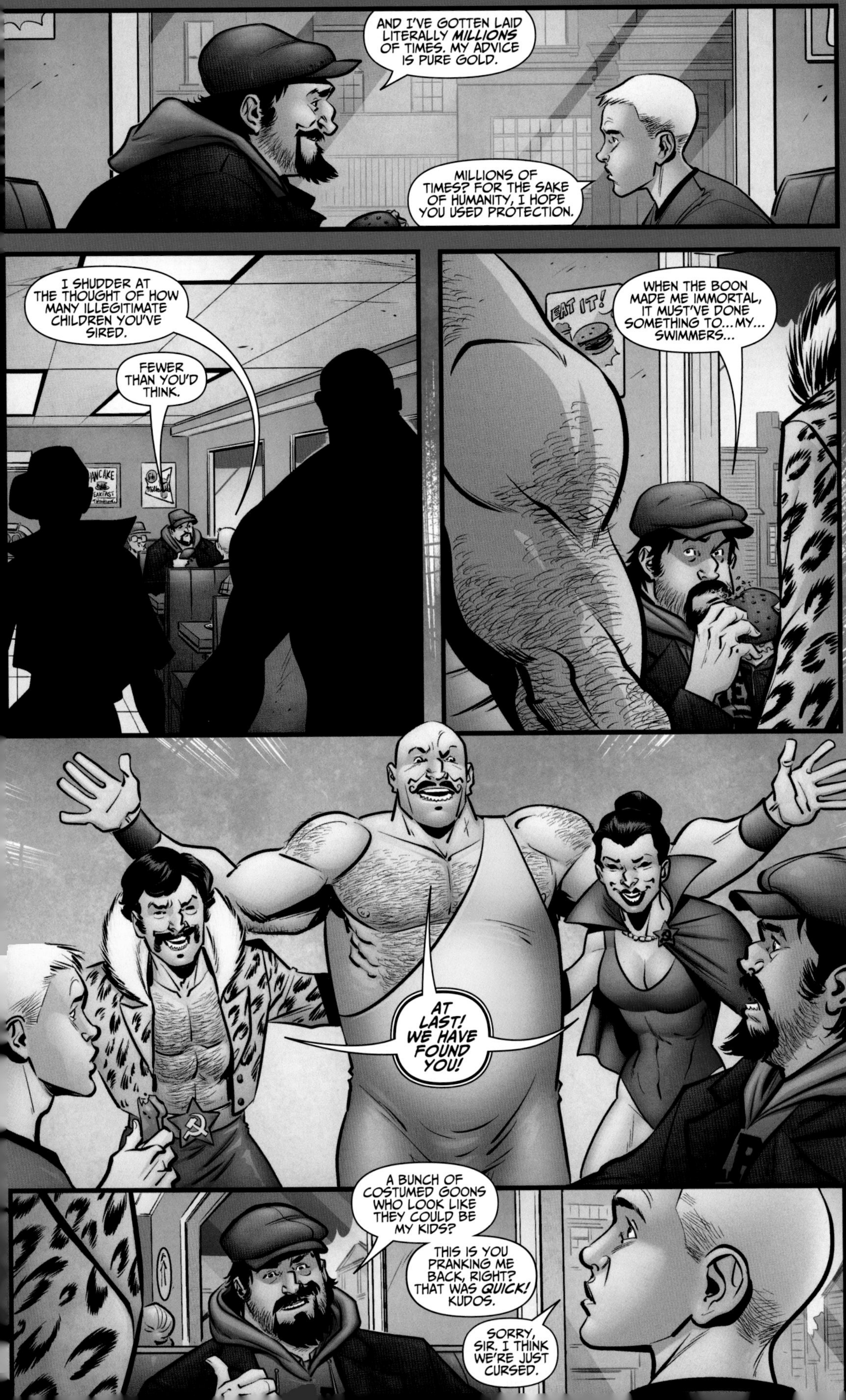
AND I'VE GOTTEN LAID LITERALLY MILLIONS OF TIMES. MY ADVICE IS PURE GOLD.
MILLIONS OF TIMES? FOR THE SAKE OF HUMANITY, I HOPE YOU USED PROTECTION.
I SHUDDER AT THE THOUGHT OF HOW MANY ILLEGITIMATE CHILDREN YOU'VE SIRED.
FEWER THAN YOU'D THINK.
EAT IT!
WHEN THE BOON MADE ME IMMORTAL, IT MUST'VE DONE SOMETHING TO... MY... SWIMMERS...
AT LAST! WE HAVE FOUND YOU!
A BUNCH OF COSTUMED GOONS WHO LOOK LIKE THEY COULD BE MY KIDS?
THIS IS YOU PRANKING ME BACK, RIGHT? THAT WAS QUICK! KUDOS.
SORRY, SIR. I THINK WE'RE JUST CURSED.

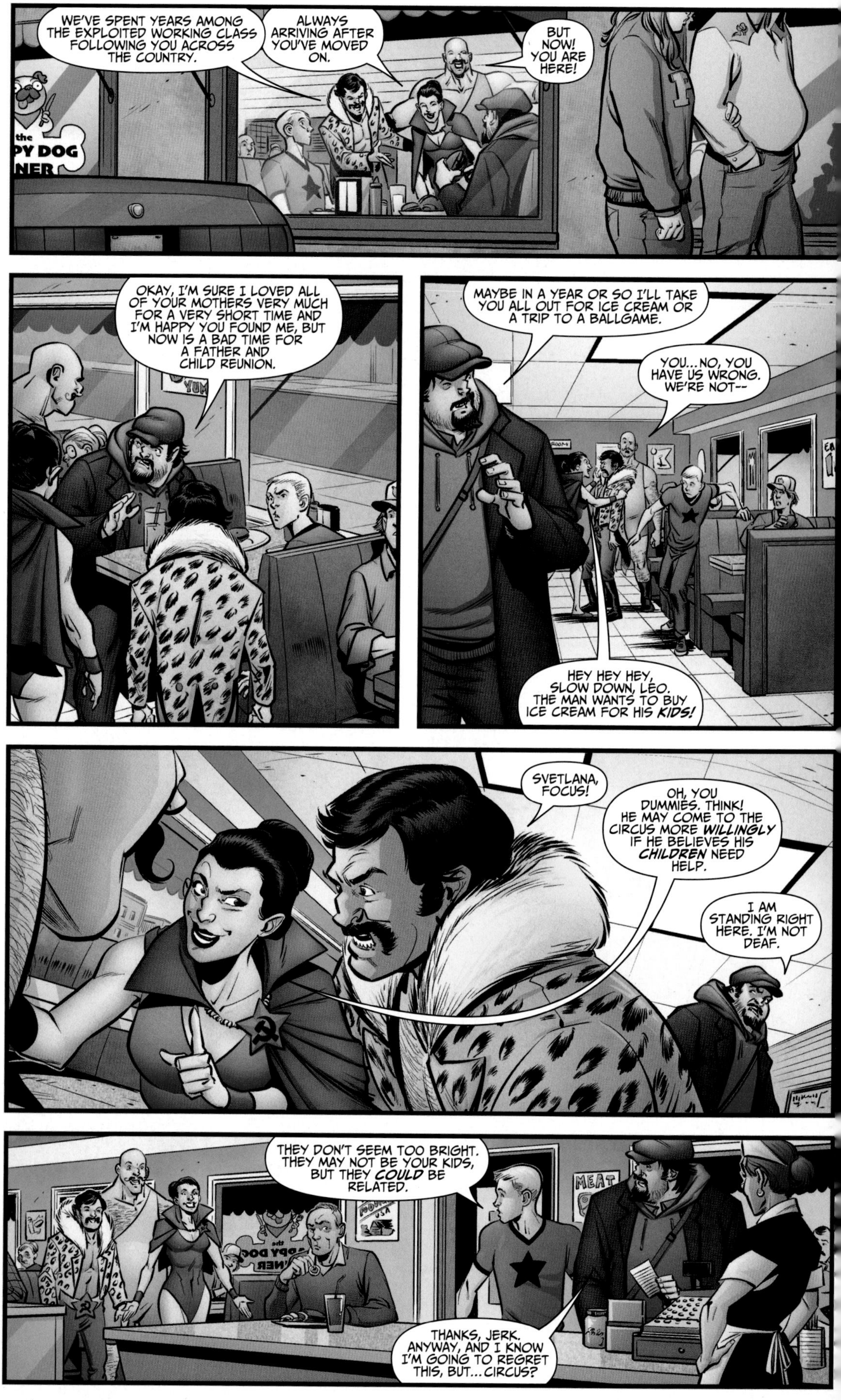
WE'VE SPENT YEARS AMONG THE EXPLOITED WORKING CLASS FOLLOWING YOU ACROSS THE COUNTRY.
ALWAYS ARRIVING AFTER YOU'VE MOVED ON.
BUT NOW! YOU ARE HERE!
OKAY, I'M SURE I LOVED ALL OF YOUR MOTHERS VERY MUCH FOR A VERY SHORT TIME AND I'M HAPPY YOU FOUND ME, BUT NOW IS A BAD TIME FOR A FATHER AND CHILD REUNION.
MAYBE IN A YEAR OR SO I'LL TAKE YOU ALL OUT FOR ICE CREAM OR A TRIP TO A BALLGAME.
YOU...NO, YOU HAVE US WRONG. WE'RE NOT--
HEY HEY HEY, SLOW DOWN, LEO. THE MAN WANTS TO BUY ICE CREAM FOR HIS *KIDS!*
SVETLANA, FOCUS!
OH, YOU DUMMIES. THINK! HE MAY COME TO THE CIRCUS MORE *WILLINGLY* IF HE BELIEVES HIS *CHILDREN* NEED HELP.
I AM STANDING RIGHT HERE. I'M NOT DEAF.
THEY DON'T SEEM TOO BRIGHT. THEY MAY NOT BE YOUR KIDS, BUT THEY *COULD* BE RELATED.
THANKS, JERK. ANYWAY, AND I KNOW I'M GOING TO REGRET THIS, BUT...CIRCUS?

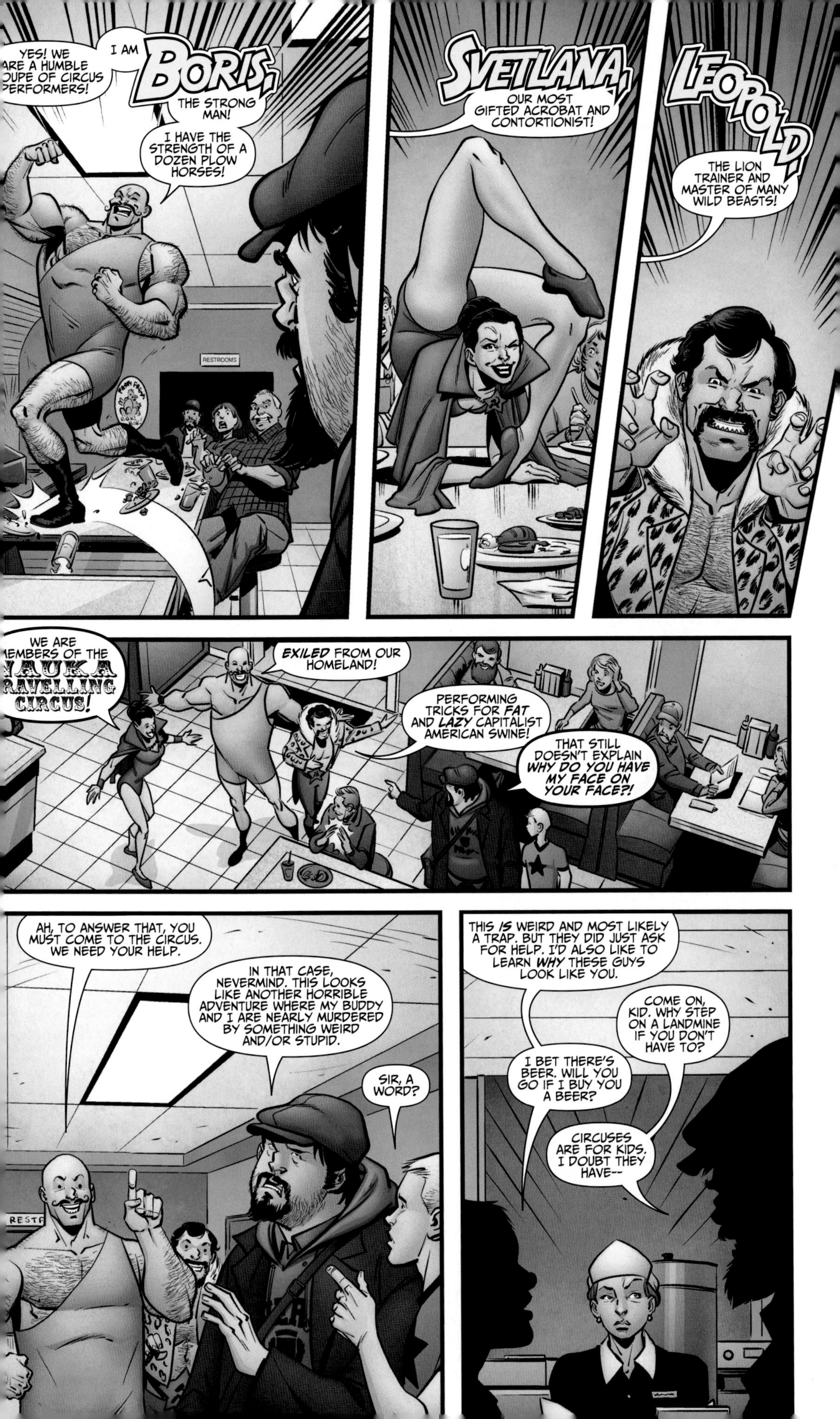
YES! WE ARE A HUMBLE TROUPE OF CIRCUS PERFORMERS!
I AM
BORIS,
THE STRONG MAN!
I HAVE THE STRENGTH OF A DOZEN PLOW HORSES!
RESTROOMS
SVETLANA,
OUR MOST GIFTED ACROBAT AND CONTORTIONIST!
LEOPOLD,
THE LION TRAINER AND MASTER OF MANY WILD BEASTS!
WE ARE MEMBERS OF THE
RAVELLING CIRCUS!
EXILED FROM OUR HOMELAND!
PERFORMING TRICKS FOR FAT AND LAZY CAPITALIST AMERICAN SWINE!
THAT STILL DOESN'T EXPLAIN WHY DO YOU HAVE MY FACE ON YOUR FACE?!
AH, TO ANSWER THAT, YOU MUST COME TO THE CIRCUS. WE NEED YOUR HELP.
IN THAT CASE, NEVERMIND. THIS LOOKS LIKE ANOTHER HORRIBLE ADVENTURE WHERE MY BUDDY AND I ARE NEARLY MURDERED BY SOMETHING WEIRD AND/OR STUPID.
SIR, A WORD?
THIS IS WEIRD AND MOST LIKELY A TRAP. BUT THEY DID JUST ASK FOR HELP. I'D ALSO LIKE TO LEARN WHY THESE GUYS LOOK LIKE YOU.
COME ON, KID. WHY STEP ON A LANDMINE IF YOU DON'T HAVE TO?
I BET THERE'S BEER. WILL YOU GO IF I BUY YOU A BEER?
CIRCUSES ARE FOR KIDS. I DOUBT THEY HAVE--

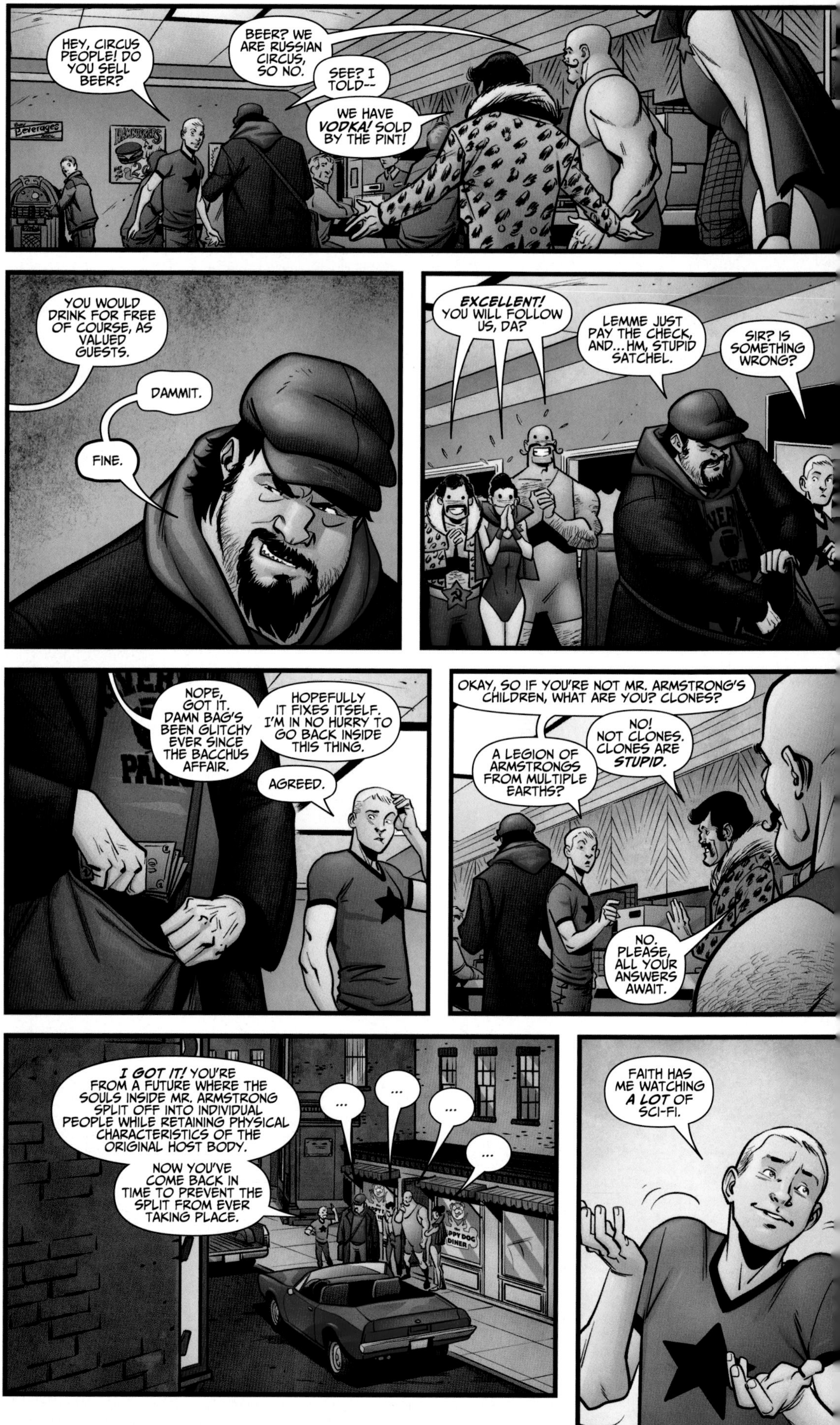
HEY, CIRCUS PEOPLE! DO YOU SELL BEER?
BEER? WE ARE RUSSIAN CIRCUS, SO NO.
SEE? I TOLD--
WE HAVE *VODKA!* SOLD BY THE PINT!
YOU WOULD DRINK FOR FREE OF COURSE, AS VALUED GUESTS.
DAMMIT.
FINE.
EXCELLENT! YOU WILL FOLLOW US, DA?
LEMME JUST PAY THE CHECK, AND...HM, STUPID SATCHEL.
SIR? IS SOMETHING WRONG?
NOPE, GOT IT. DAMN BAG'S BEEN GLITCHY EVER SINCE THE BACCHUS AFFAIR.
HOPEFULLY IT FIXES ITSELF. I'M IN NO HURRY TO GO BACK INSIDE THIS THING.
AGREED.
OKAY, SO IF YOU'RE NOT MR. ARMSTRONG'S CHILDREN, WHAT ARE YOU? CLONES?
NO! NOT CLONES. CLONES ARE *STUPID*.
A LEGION OF ARMSTRONGS FROM MULTIPLE EARTHS?
NO. PLEASE, ALL YOUR ANSWERS AWAIT.
I GOT IT! YOU'RE FROM A FUTURE WHERE THE SOULS INSIDE MR. ARMSTRONG SPLIT OFF INTO INDIVIDUAL PEOPLE WHILE RETAINING PHYSICAL CHARACTERISTICS OF THE ORIGINAL HOST BODY.
NOW YOU'VE COME BACK IN TIME TO PREVENT THE SPLIT FROM EVER TAKING PLACE.
...
...
...
...
FAITH HAS ME WATCHING *A LOT* OF SCI-FI.

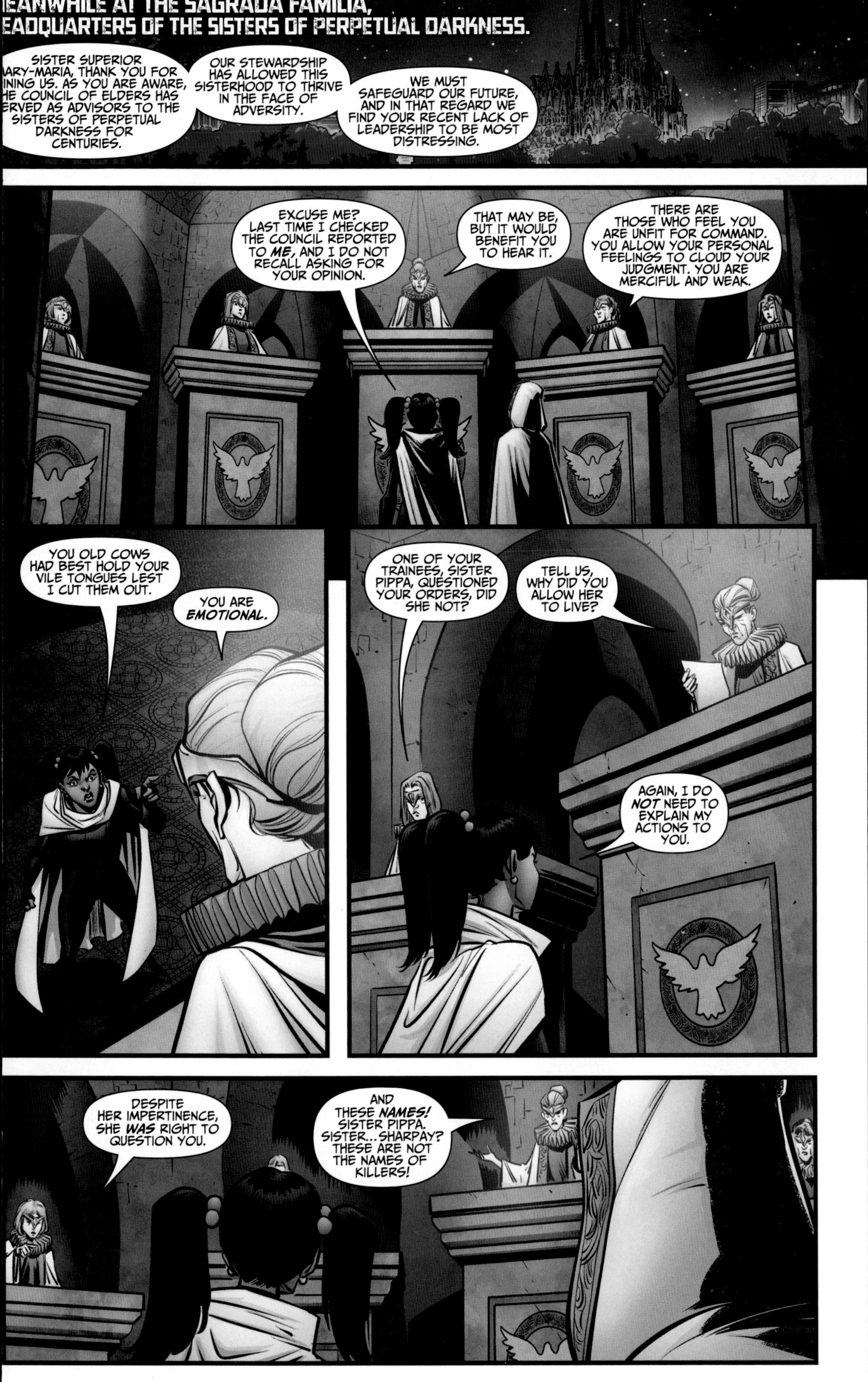
EANWHILE AT THE SAGRADA FAMILIA,
EADQUARTERS OF THE SISTERS OF PERPETUAL DARKNESS.
SISTER SUPERIOR ARY-MARIA, THANK YOU FOR INING US. AS YOU ARE AWARE, HE COUNCIL OF ELDERS HAS ERVED AS ADVISORS TO THE SISTERS OF PERPETUAL DARKNESS FOR CENTURIES.
OUR STEWARDSHIP HAS ALLOWED THIS SISTERHOOD TO THRIVE IN THE FACE OF ADVERSITY.
WE MUST SAFEGUARD OUR FUTURE, AND IN THAT REGARD WE FIND YOUR RECENT LACK OF LEADERSHIP TO BE MOST DISTRESSING.
EXCUSE ME? LAST TIME I CHECKED THE COUNCIL REPORTED TO ME, AND I DO NOT RECALL ASKING FOR YOUR OPINION.
THAT MAY BE, BUT IT WOULD BENEFIT YOU TO HEAR IT.
THERE ARE THOSE WHO FEEL YOU ARE UNFIT FOR COMMAND. YOU ALLOW YOUR PERSONAL FEELINGS TO CLOUD YOUR JUDGMENT. YOU ARE MERCIFUL AND WEAK.
YOU OLD COWS HAD BEST HOLD YOUR VILE TONGUES LEST I CUT THEM OUT.
YOU ARE EMOTIONAL.
ONE OF YOUR TRAINEES, SISTER PIPPA, QUESTIONED YOUR ORDERS, DID SHE NOT?
TELL US, WHY DID YOU ALLOW HER TO LIVE?
AGAIN, I DO NOT NEED TO EXPLAIN MY ACTIONS TO YOU.
DESPITE HER IMPERTINENCE, SHE WAS RIGHT TO QUESTION YOU.
AND THESE NAMES! SISTER PIPPA. SISTER... SHARPAY? THESE ARE NOT THE NAMES OF KILLERS!

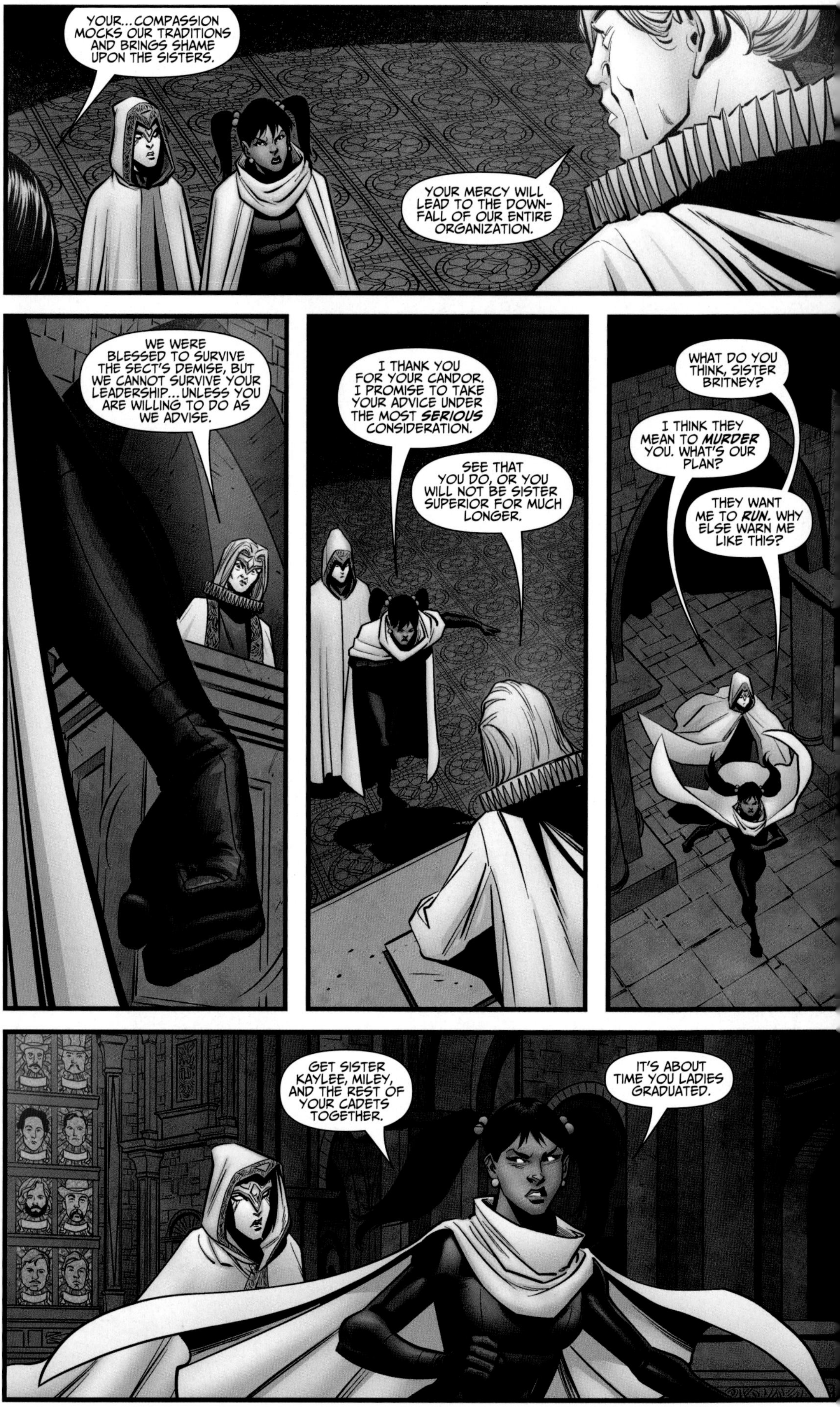
YOUR...COMPASSION MOCKS OUR TRADITIONS AND BRINGS SHAME UPON THE SISTERS.
YOUR MERCY WILL LEAD TO THE DOWN-FALL OF OUR ENTIRE ORGANIZATION.
WE WERE BLESSED TO SURVIVE THE SECT'S DEMISE, BUT WE CANNOT SURVIVE YOUR LEADERSHIP...UNLESS YOU ARE WILLING TO DO AS WE ADVISE.
I THANK YOU FOR YOUR CANDOR. I PROMISE TO TAKE YOUR ADVICE UNDER THE MOST *SERIOUS* CONSIDERATION.
SEE THAT YOU DO, OR YOU WILL NOT BE SISTER SUPERIOR FOR MUCH LONGER.
WHAT DO YOU THINK, SISTER BRITNEY?
I THINK THEY MEAN TO *MURDER* YOU. WHAT'S OUR PLAN?
THEY WANT ME TO *RUN.* WHY ELSE WARN ME LIKE THIS?
GET SISTER KAYLEE, MILEY, AND THE REST OF YOUR CADETS TOGETHER.
IT'S ABOUT TIME YOU LADIES GRADUATED.

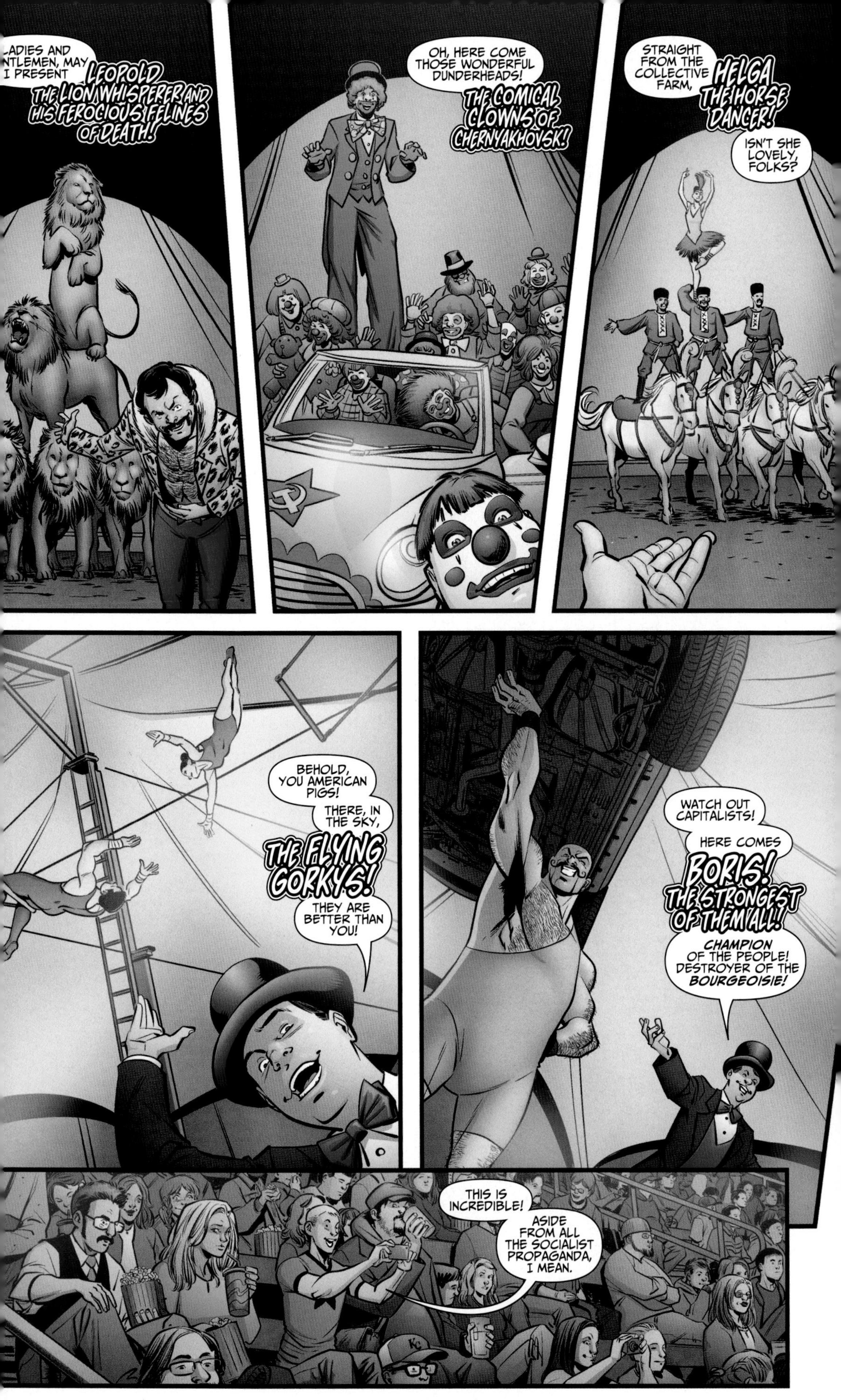
LADIES AND
NTLEMEN, MAY I PRESENT
LEOPOLD THE LION WHISPERER AND HIS FEROCIOUS FELINES OF DEATH!
OH, HERE COME THOSE WONDERFUL DUNDERHEADS!
THE COMICAL CLOWNS OF CHERNYAKHOVSK!
STRAIGHT FROM THE COLLECTIVE FARM,
HELGA THE HORSE DANCER!
ISN'T SHE LOVELY, FOLKS?
BEHOLD, YOU AMERICAN PIGS!
THERE, IN THE SKY,
THE FLYING GORKYS!
THEY ARE BETTER THAN YOU!
WATCH OUT CAPITALISTS!
HERE COMES
BORIS! THE STRONGEST OF THEM ALL!
CHAMPION OF THE PEOPLE! DESTROYER OF THE BOURGEOISIE!
THIS IS INCREDIBLE!
ASIDE FROM ALL THE SOCIALIST PROPAGANDA, I MEAN.

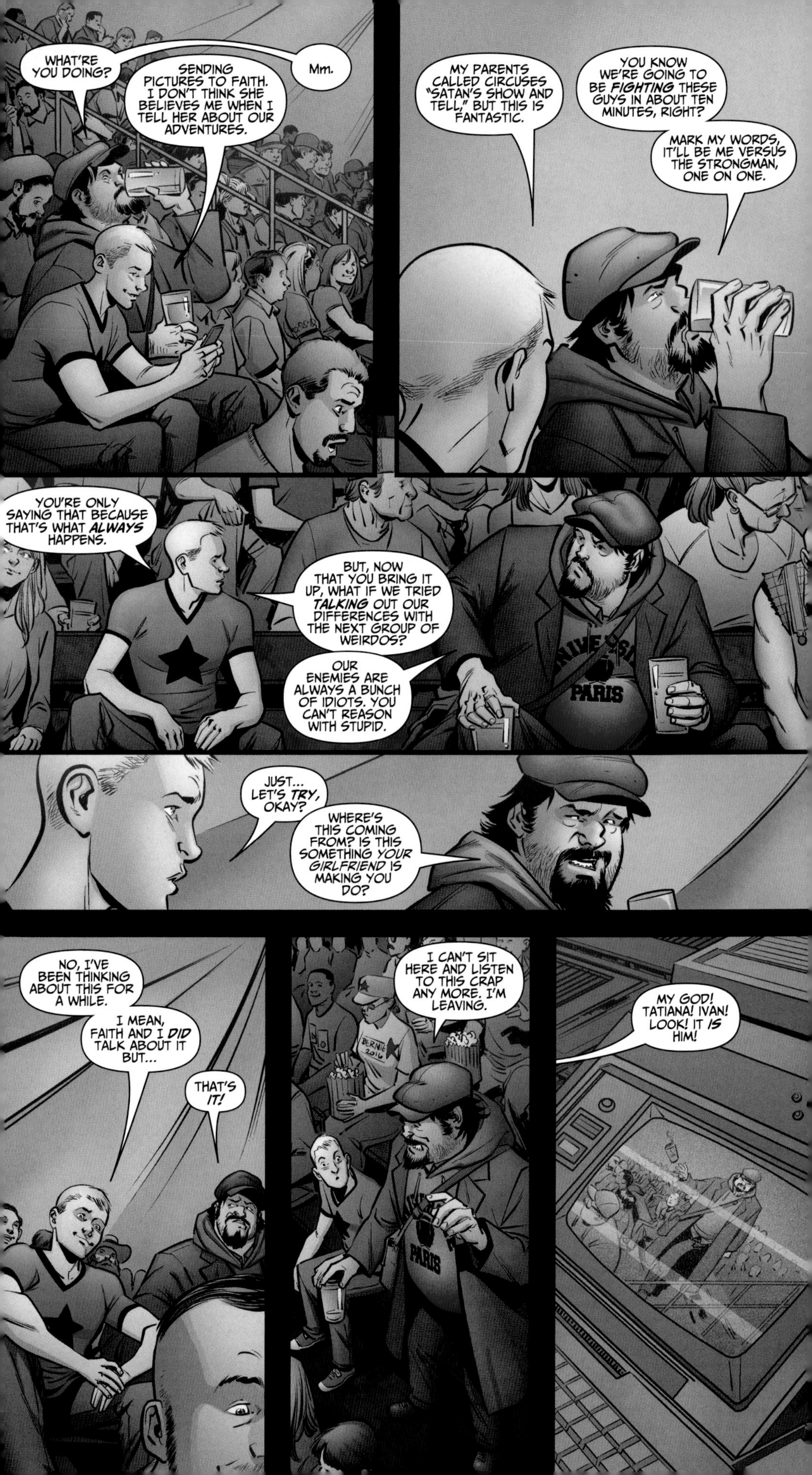
WHAT'RE YOU DOING?
SENDING PICTURES TO FAITH. I DON'T THINK SHE BELIEVES ME WHEN I TELL HER ABOUT OUR ADVENTURES.
Mm.
MY PARENTS CALLED CIRCUSES "SATAN'S SHOW AND TELL," BUT THIS IS FANTASTIC.
YOU KNOW WE'RE GOING TO BE FIGHTING THESE GUYS IN ABOUT TEN MINUTES, RIGHT?
MARK MY WORDS, IT'LL BE ME VERSUS THE STRONGMAN, ONE ON ONE.
YOU'RE ONLY SAYING THAT BECAUSE THAT'S WHAT ALWAYS HAPPENS.
BUT, NOW THAT YOU BRING IT UP, WHAT IF WE TRIED TALKING OUT OUR DIFFERENCES WITH THE NEXT GROUP OF WEIRDOS?
OUR ENEMIES ARE ALWAYS A BUNCH OF IDIOTS. YOU CAN'T REASON WITH STUPID.
PARIS
JUST... LET'S TRY, OKAY?
WHERE'S THIS COMING FROM? IS THIS SOMETHING YOUR GIRLFRIEND IS MAKING YOU DO?
NO, I'VE BEEN THINKING ABOUT THIS FOR A WHILE.
I MEAN, FAITH AND I DID TALK ABOUT IT BUT...
THAT'S IT!
I CAN'T SIT HERE AND LISTEN TO THIS CRAP ANY MORE. I'M LEAVING.
BERNIE 2016
PARIS
MY GOD! TATIANA! IVAN! LOOK! IT IS HIM!

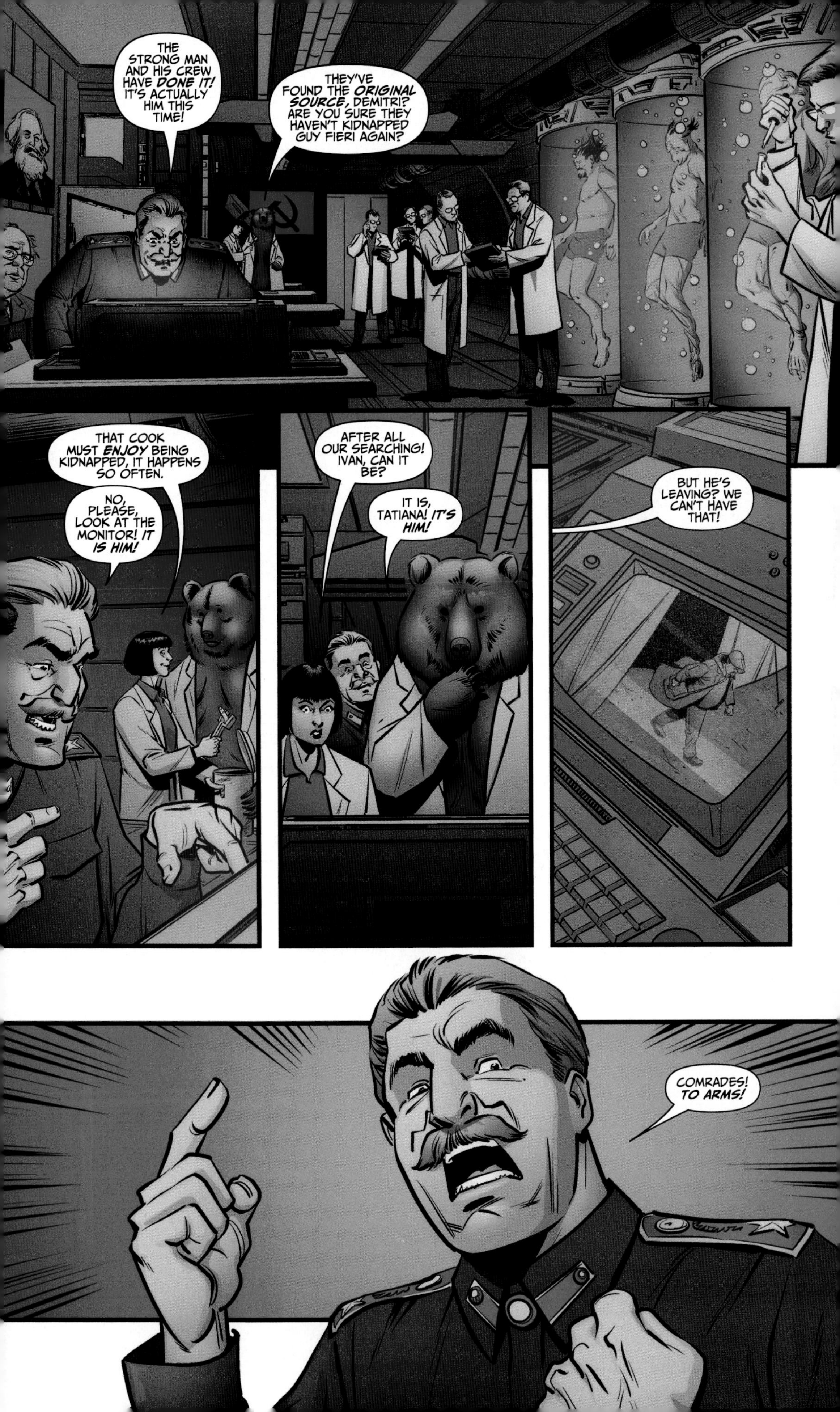

THE STRONG MAN AND HIS CREW HAVE DONE IT! IT'S ACTUALLY HIM THIS TIME!
THEY'VE FOUND THE ORIGINAL SOURCE, DEMITRI? ARE YOU SURE THEY HAVEN'T KIDNAPPED GUY FIERI AGAIN?
THAT COOK MUST ENJOY BEING KIDNAPPED, IT HAPPENS SO OFTEN.
NO, PLEASE, LOOK AT THE MONITOR! IT IS HIM!
AFTER ALL OUR SEARCHING! IVAN, CAN IT BE?
IT IS, TATIANA! IT'S HIM!
BUT HE'S LEAVING? WE CAN'T HAVE THAT!
COMRADES! TO ARMS!

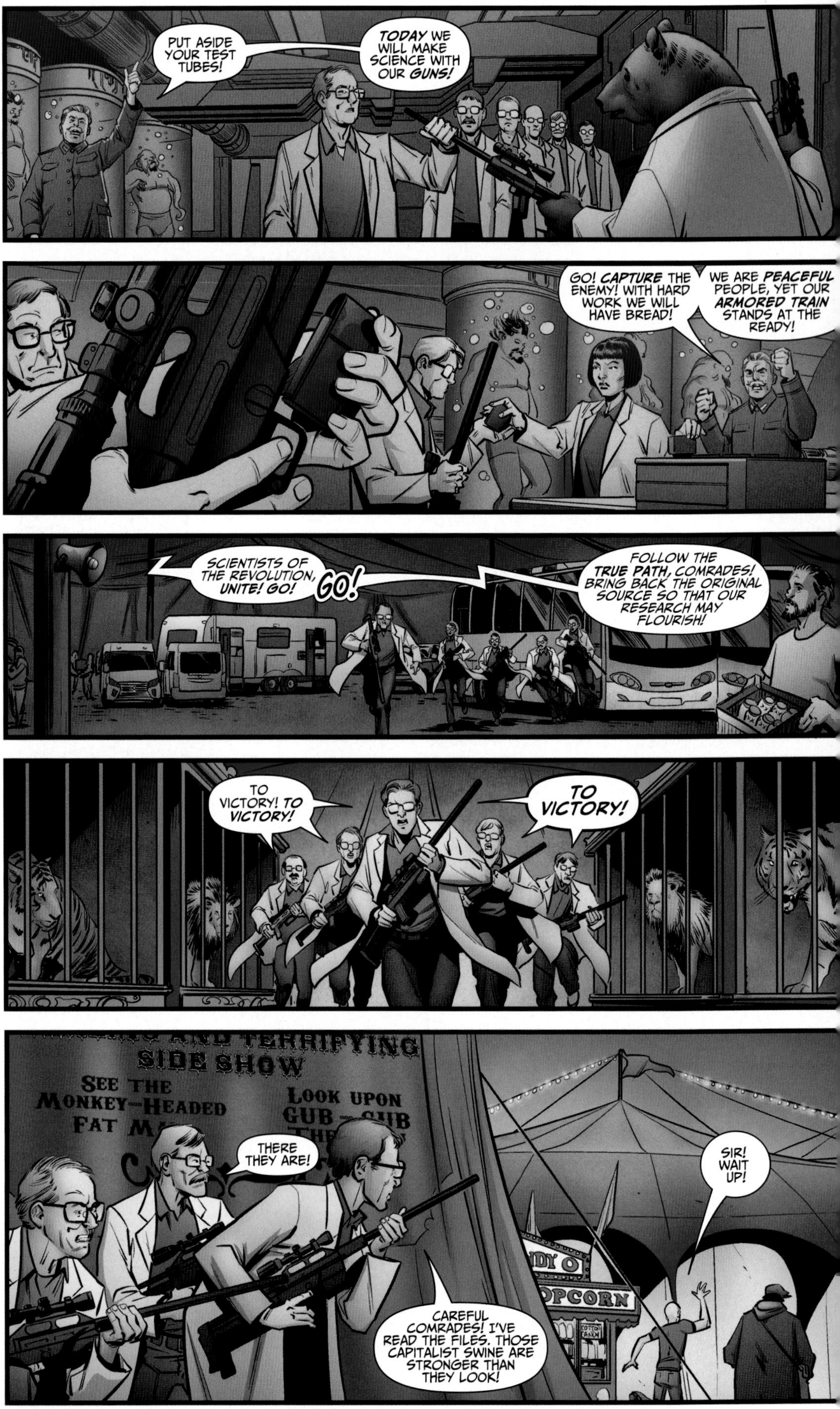
PUT ASIDE YOUR TEST TUBES!
TODAY WE WILL MAKE SCIENCE WITH OUR *GUNS!*
GO! *CAPTURE* THE ENEMY! WITH HARD WORK WE WILL HAVE BREAD!
WE ARE *PEACEFUL* PEOPLE, YET OUR *ARMORED TRAIN* STANDS AT THE READY!
SCIENTISTS OF THE REVOLUTION, *UNITE! GO!*
GO!
FOLLOW THE **TRUE PATH,** COMRADES! BRING BACK THE ORIGINAL SOURCE SO THAT OUR RESEARCH MAY FLOURISH!
TO VICTORY! *TO VICTORY!*
TO VICTORY!
SIDE SHOW
SEE THE
MONKEY-HEADED
LOOK UPON
THERE THEY ARE!
SIR! WAIT UP!
CAREFUL COMRADES! I'VE READ THE FILES. THOSE CAPITALIST SWINE ARE STRONGER THAN THEY LOOK!

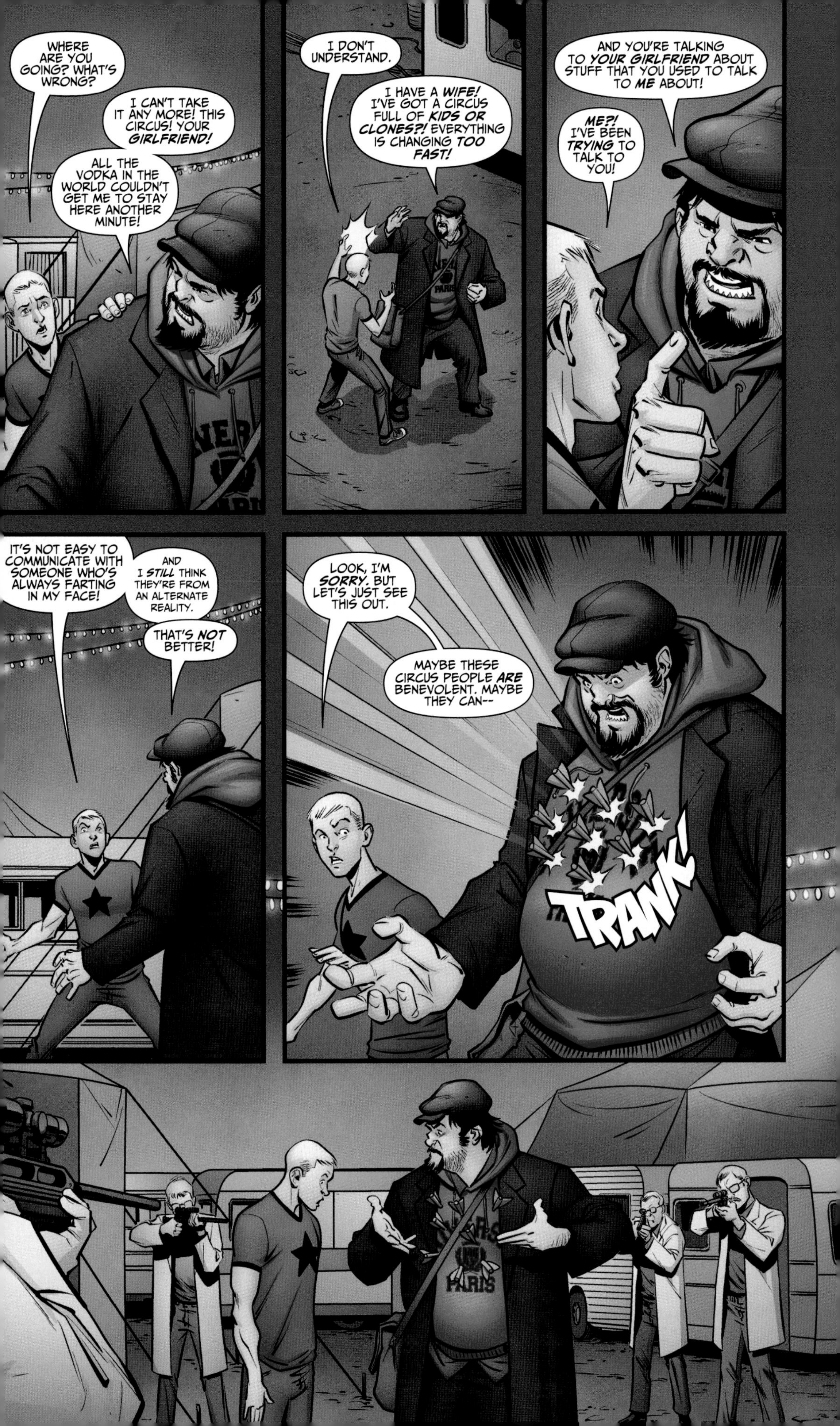

WHERE ARE YOU GOING? WHAT'S WRONG?
I CAN'T TAKE IT ANY MORE! THIS CIRCUS! YOUR GIRLFRIEND!
ALL THE VODKA IN THE WORLD COULDN'T GET ME TO STAY HERE ANOTHER MINUTE!
I DON'T UNDERSTAND.
I HAVE A WIFE! I'VE GOT A CIRCUS FULL OF KIDS OR CLONES?! EVERYTHING IS CHANGING TOO FAST!
AND YOU'RE TALKING TO YOUR GIRLFRIEND ABOUT STUFF THAT YOU USED TO TALK TO ME ABOUT!
ME?! I'VE BEEN TRYING TO TALK TO YOU!
IT'S NOT EASY TO COMMUNICATE WITH SOMEONE WHO'S ALWAYS FARTING IN MY FACE!
AND I STILL THINK THEY'RE FROM AN ALTERNATE REALITY.
THAT'S NOT BETTER!
LOOK, I'M SORRY. BUT LET'S JUST SEE THIS OUT.
MAYBE THESE CIRCUS PEOPLE ARE BENEVOLENT. MAYBE THEY CAN--
TRANK!
PARIS

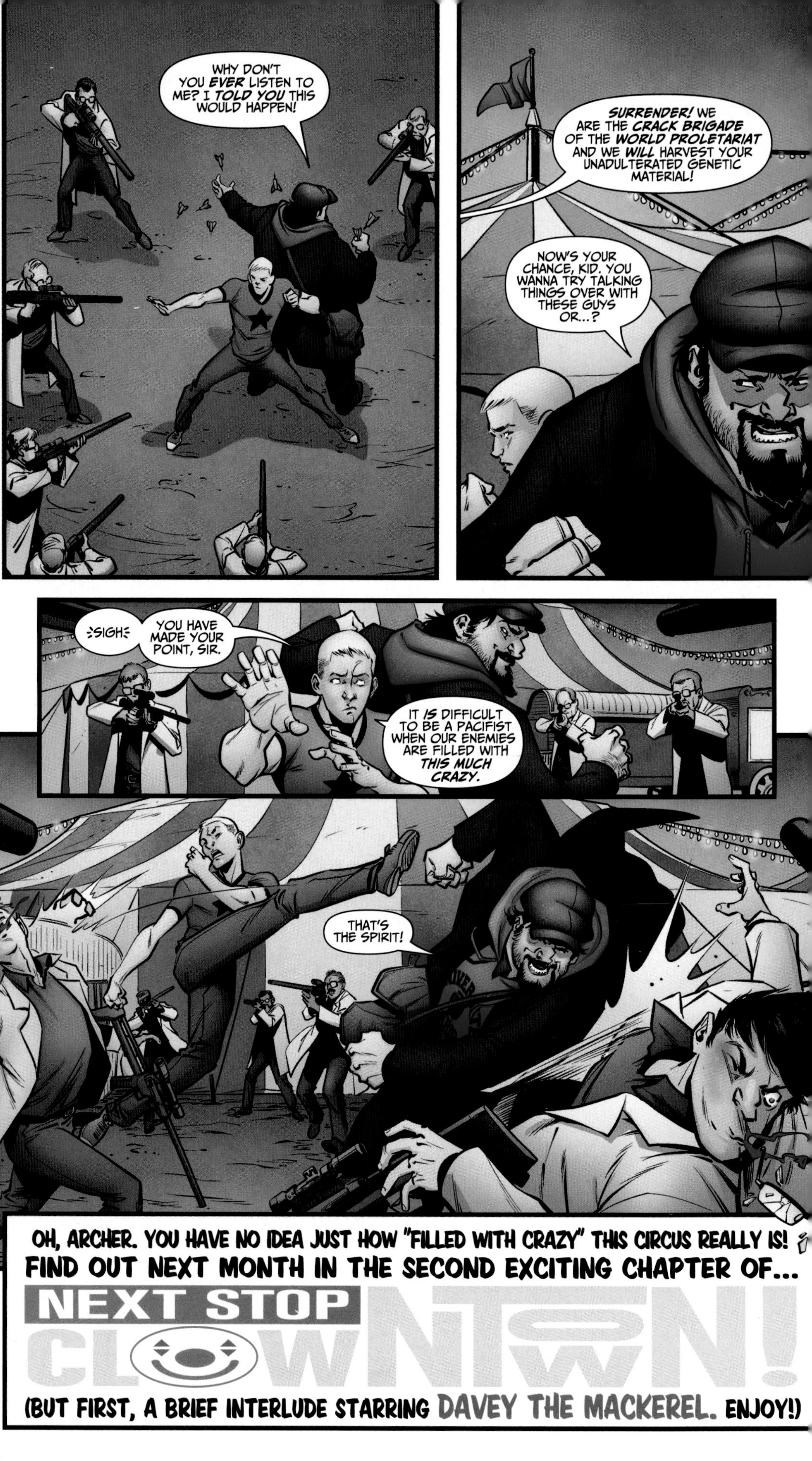

WHY DON'T YOU EVER LISTEN TO ME? I TOLD YOU THIS WOULD HAPPEN!
SURRENDER! WE ARE THE CRACK BRIGADE OF THE WORLD PROLETARIAT AND WE WILL HARVEST YOUR UNADULTERATED GENETIC MATERIAL!
NOW'S YOUR CHANCE, KID. YOU WANNA TRY TALKING THINGS OVER WITH THESE GUYS OR...?
SIGH
YOU HAVE MADE YOUR POINT, SIR.
IT IS DIFFICULT TO BE A PACIFIST WHEN OUR ENEMIES ARE FILLED WITH THIS MUCH CRAZY.
THAT'S THE SPIRIT!
OH, ARCHER. YOU HAVE NO IDEA JUST HOW "FILLED WITH CRAZY" THIS CIRCUS REALLY IS!
FIND OUT NEXT MONTH IN THE SECOND EXCITING CHAPTER OF...
NEXT STOP CLOWNTOWN!
(BUT FIRST, A BRIEF INTERLUDE STARRING DAVEY THE MACKEREL. ENJOY!)

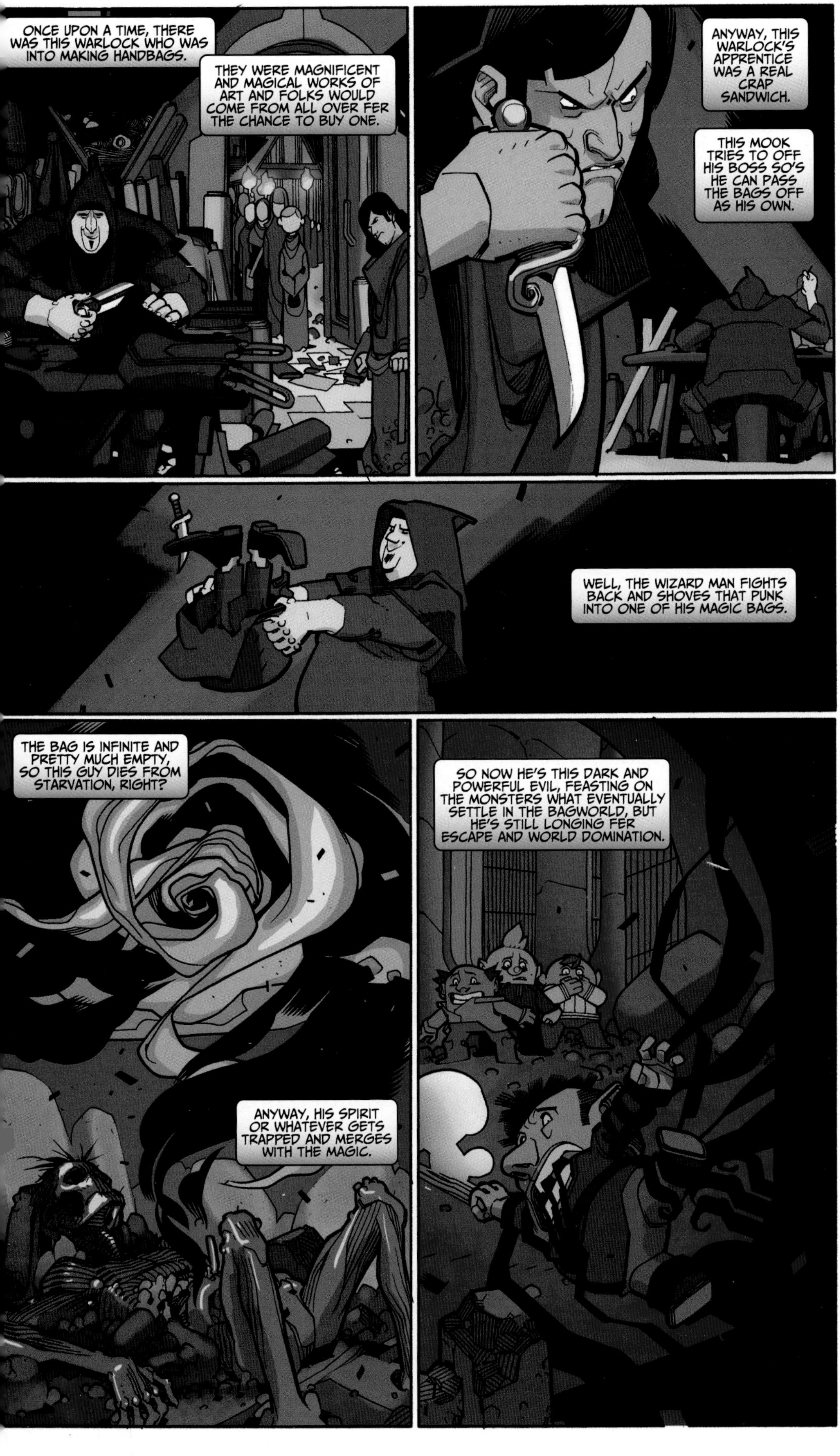
ONCE UPON A TIME, THERE WAS THIS WARLOCK WHO WAS INTO MAKING HANDBAGS.
THEY WERE MAGNIFICENT AND MAGICAL WORKS OF ART AND FOLKS WOULD COME FROM ALL OVER FER THE CHANCE TO BUY ONE.
ANYWAY, THIS WARLOCK'S APPRENTICE WAS A REAL CRAP SANDWICH.
THIS MOOK TRIES TO OFF HIS BOSS SO'S HE CAN PASS THE BAGS OFF AS HIS OWN.
WELL, THE WIZARD MAN FIGHTS BACK AND SHOVES THAT PUNK INTO ONE OF HIS MAGIC BAGS.
THE BAG IS INFINITE AND PRETTY MUCH EMPTY, SO THIS GUY DIES FROM STARVATION, RIGHT?
ANYWAY, HIS SPIRIT OR WHATEVER GETS TRAPPED AND MERGES WITH THE MAGIC.
SO NOW HE'S THIS DARK AND POWERFUL EVIL, FEASTING ON THE MONSTERS WHAT EVENTUALLY SETTLE IN THE BAGWORLD, BUT HE'S STILL LONGING FER ESCAPE AND WORLD DOMINATION.

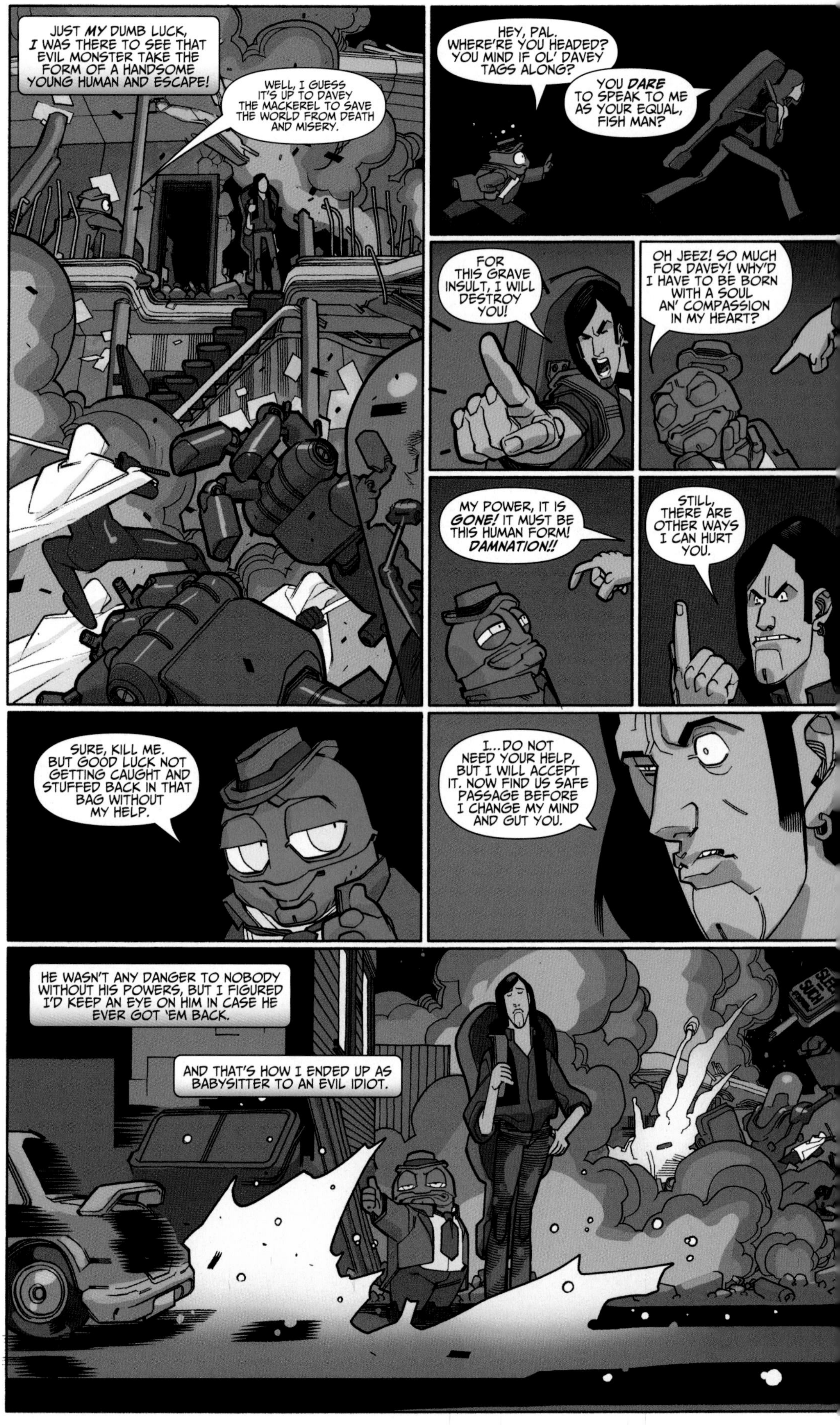
JUST MY DUMB LUCK, I WAS THERE TO SEE THAT EVIL MONSTER TAKE THE FORM OF A HANDSOME YOUNG HUMAN AND ESCAPE!
WELL, I GUESS IT'S UP TO DAVEY THE MACKEREL TO SAVE THE WORLD FROM DEATH AND MISERY.
HEY, PAL. WHERE'RE YOU HEADED? YOU MIND IF OL' DAVEY TAGS ALONG?
YOU DARE TO SPEAK TO ME AS YOUR EQUAL, FISH MAN?
FOR THIS GRAVE INSULT, I WILL DESTROY YOU!
OH JEEZ! SO MUCH FOR DAVEY! WHY'D I HAVE TO BE BORN WITH A SOUL AN' COMPASSION IN MY HEART?
MY POWER, IT IS GONE! IT MUST BE THIS HUMAN FORM! DAMNATION!!
STILL, THERE ARE OTHER WAYS I CAN HURT YOU.
SURE, KILL ME. BUT GOOD LUCK NOT GETTING CAUGHT AND STUFFED BACK IN THAT BAG WITHOUT MY HELP.
I...DO NOT NEED YOUR HELP, BUT I WILL ACCEPT IT. NOW FIND US SAFE PASSAGE BEFORE I CHANGE MY MIND AND GUT YOU.
HE WASN'T ANY DANGER TO NOBODY WITHOUT HIS POWERS, BUT I FIGURED I'D KEEP AN EYE ON HIM IN CASE HE EVER GOT 'EM BACK.
AND THAT'S HOW I ENDED UP AS BABYSITTER TO AN EVIL IDIOT.

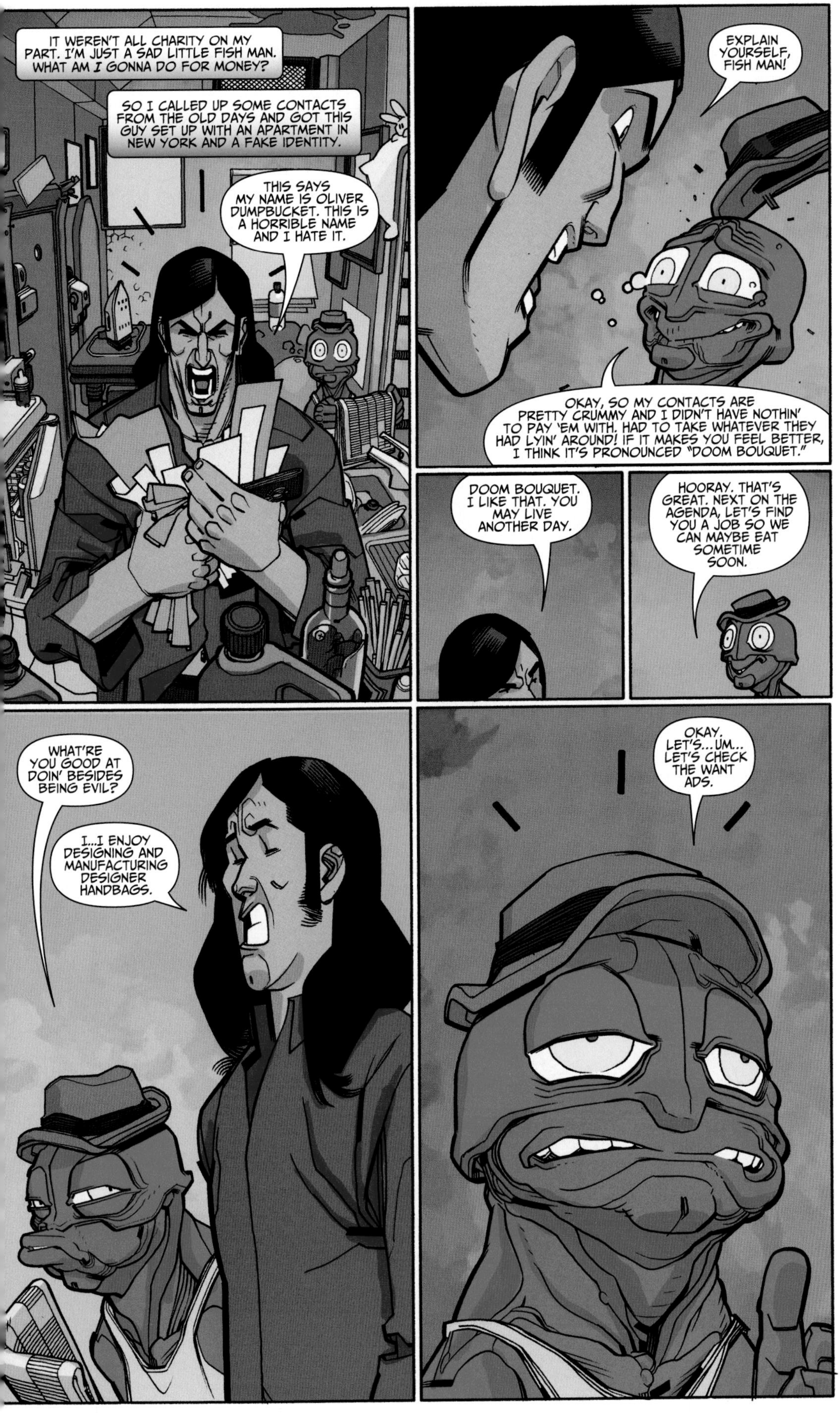
IT WEREN'T ALL CHARITY ON MY PART. I'M JUST A SAD LITTLE FISH MAN. WHAT AM *I* GONNA DO FOR MONEY?
SO I CALLED UP SOME CONTACTS FROM THE OLD DAYS AND GOT THIS GUY SET UP WITH AN APARTMENT IN NEW YORK AND A FAKE IDENTITY.
THIS SAYS MY NAME IS OLIVER DUMPBUCKET. THIS IS A HORRIBLE NAME AND I HATE IT.
EXPLAIN YOURSELF, FISH MAN!
OKAY, SO MY CONTACTS ARE PRETTY CRUMMY AND I DIDN'T HAVE NOTHIN' TO PAY 'EM WITH. HAD TO TAKE WHATEVER THEY HAD LYIN' AROUND! IF IT MAKES YOU FEEL BETTER, I THINK IT'S PRONOUNCED "DOOM BOUQUET."
DOOM BOUQUET. I LIKE THAT. YOU MAY LIVE ANOTHER DAY.
HOORAY. THAT'S GREAT. NEXT ON THE AGENDA, LET'S FIND YOU A JOB SO WE CAN MAYBE EAT SOMETIME SOON.
WHAT'RE YOU GOOD AT DOIN' BESIDES BEING EVIL?
I...I ENJOY DESIGNING AND MANUFACTURING DESIGNER HANDBAGS.
OKAY. LET'S...UM... LET'S CHECK THE WANT ADS.

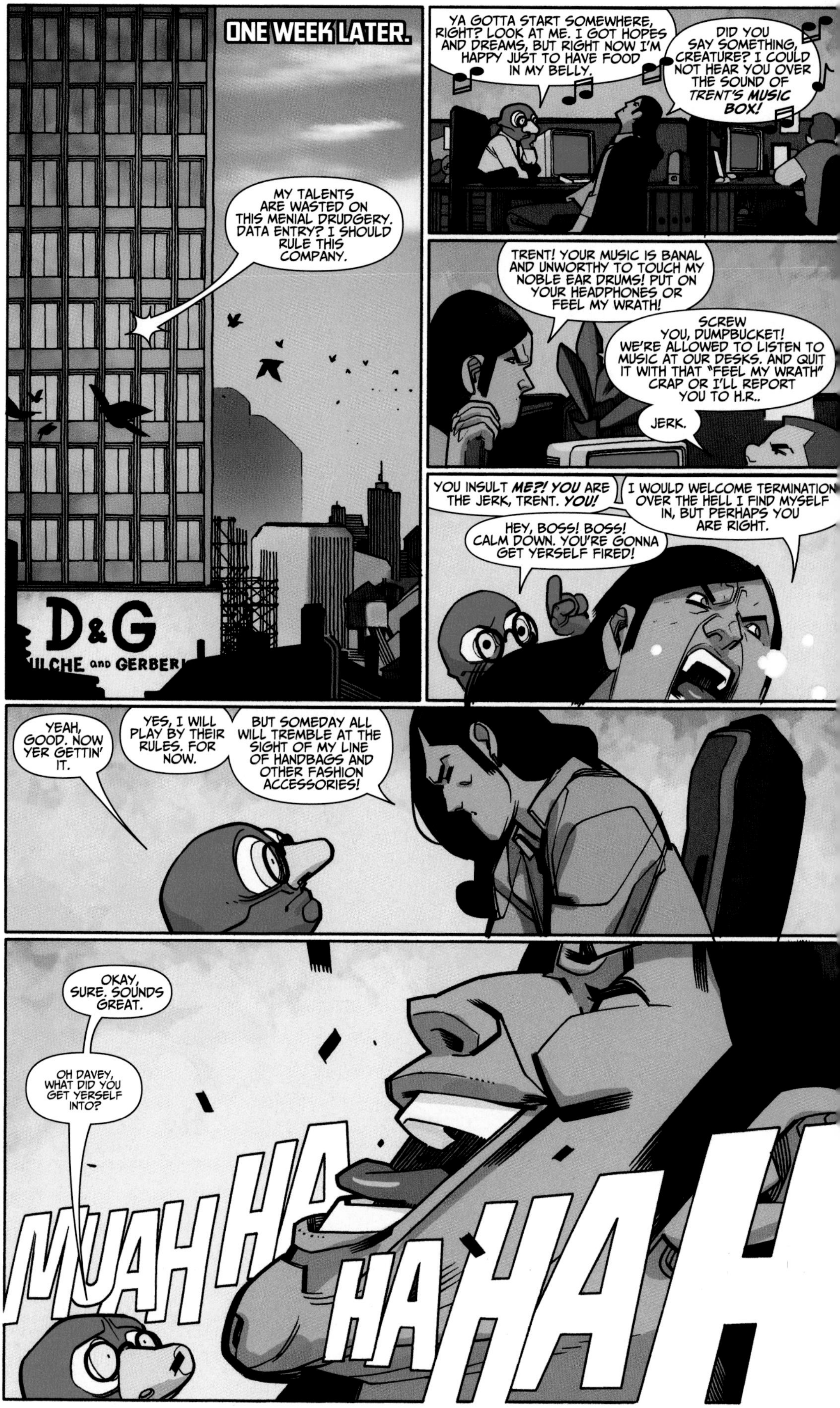
ONE WEEK LATER.
MY TALENTS ARE WASTED ON THIS MENIAL DRUDGERY. DATA ENTRY? I SHOULD RULE THIS COMPANY.
D&G
ULCHE and GERBER
YA GOTTA START SOMEWHERE, RIGHT? LOOK AT ME. I GOT HOPES AND DREAMS, BUT RIGHT NOW I'M HAPPY JUST TO HAVE FOOD IN MY BELLY.
DID YOU SAY SOMETHING, CREATURE? I COULD NOT HEAR YOU OVER THE SOUND OF TRENT'S MUSIC BOX!
TRENT! YOUR MUSIC IS BANAL AND UNWORTHY TO TOUCH MY NOBLE EAR DRUMS! PUT ON YOUR HEADPHONES OR FEEL MY WRATH!
SCREW YOU, DUMPBUCKET! WE'RE ALLOWED TO LISTEN TO MUSIC AT OUR DESKS. AND QUIT IT WITH THAT "FEEL MY WRATH" CRAP OR I'LL REPORT YOU TO H.R..
JERK.
YOU INSULT ME?! YOU ARE THE JERK, TRENT. YOU!
HEY, BOSS! BOSS! CALM DOWN. YOU'RE GONNA GET YERSELF FIRED!
I WOULD WELCOME TERMINATION OVER THE HELL I FIND MYSELF IN, BUT PERHAPS YOU ARE RIGHT.
YEAH, GOOD. NOW YER GETTIN' IT.
YES, I WILL PLAY BY THEIR RULES. FOR NOW.
BUT SOMEDAY ALL WILL TREMBLE AT THE SIGHT OF MY LINE OF HANDBAGS AND OTHER FASHION ACCESSORIES!
OKAY, SURE. SOUNDS GREAT.
OH DAVEY, WHAT DID YOU GET YERSELF INTO?
MUAH HA HAHAH

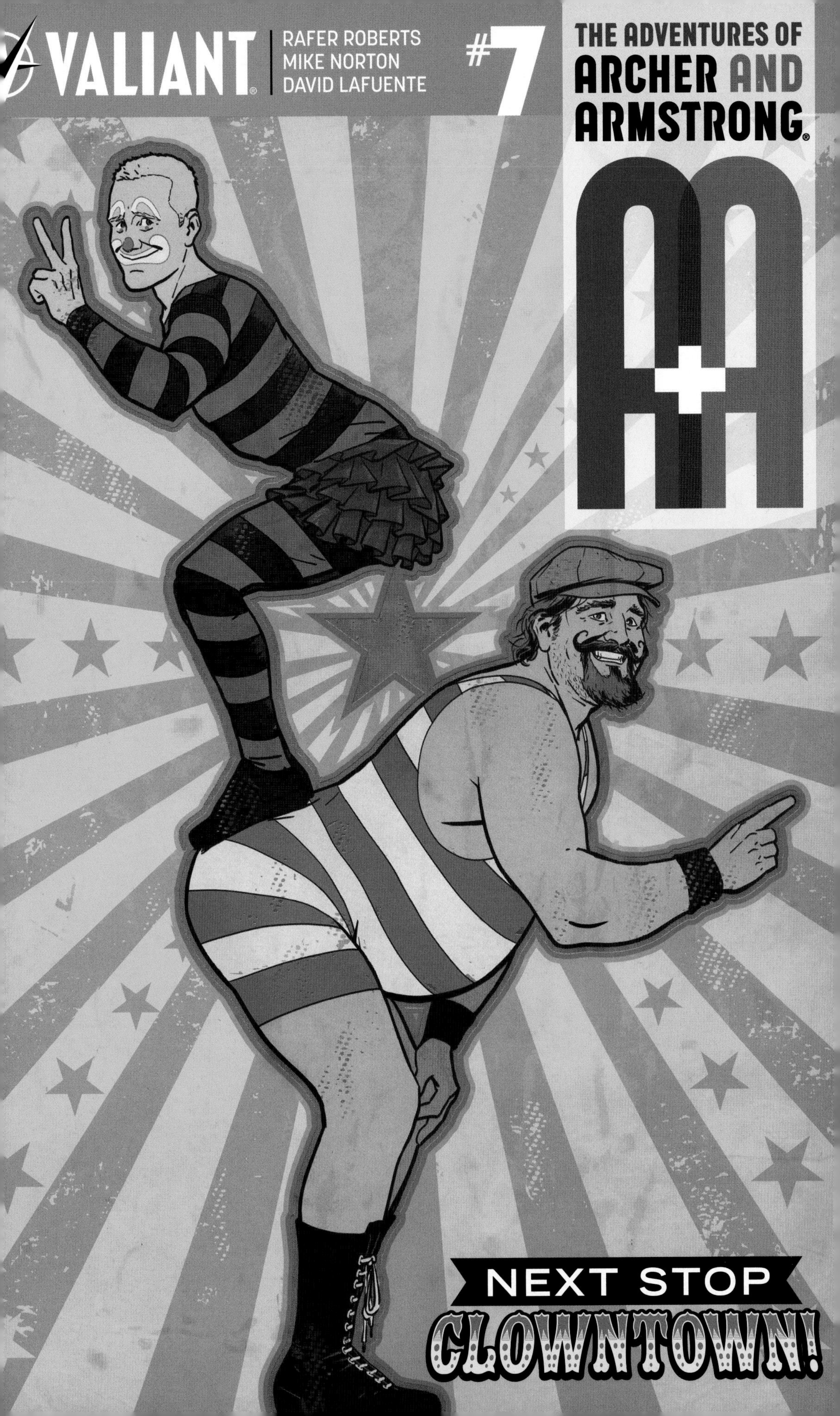
VALIANT
RAFER ROBERTS
MIKE NORTON
DAVID LAFUENTE
#7
THE ADVENTURES OF
ARCHER AND
ARMSTRONG
A+A
NEXT STOP
CLOWNTOWN!

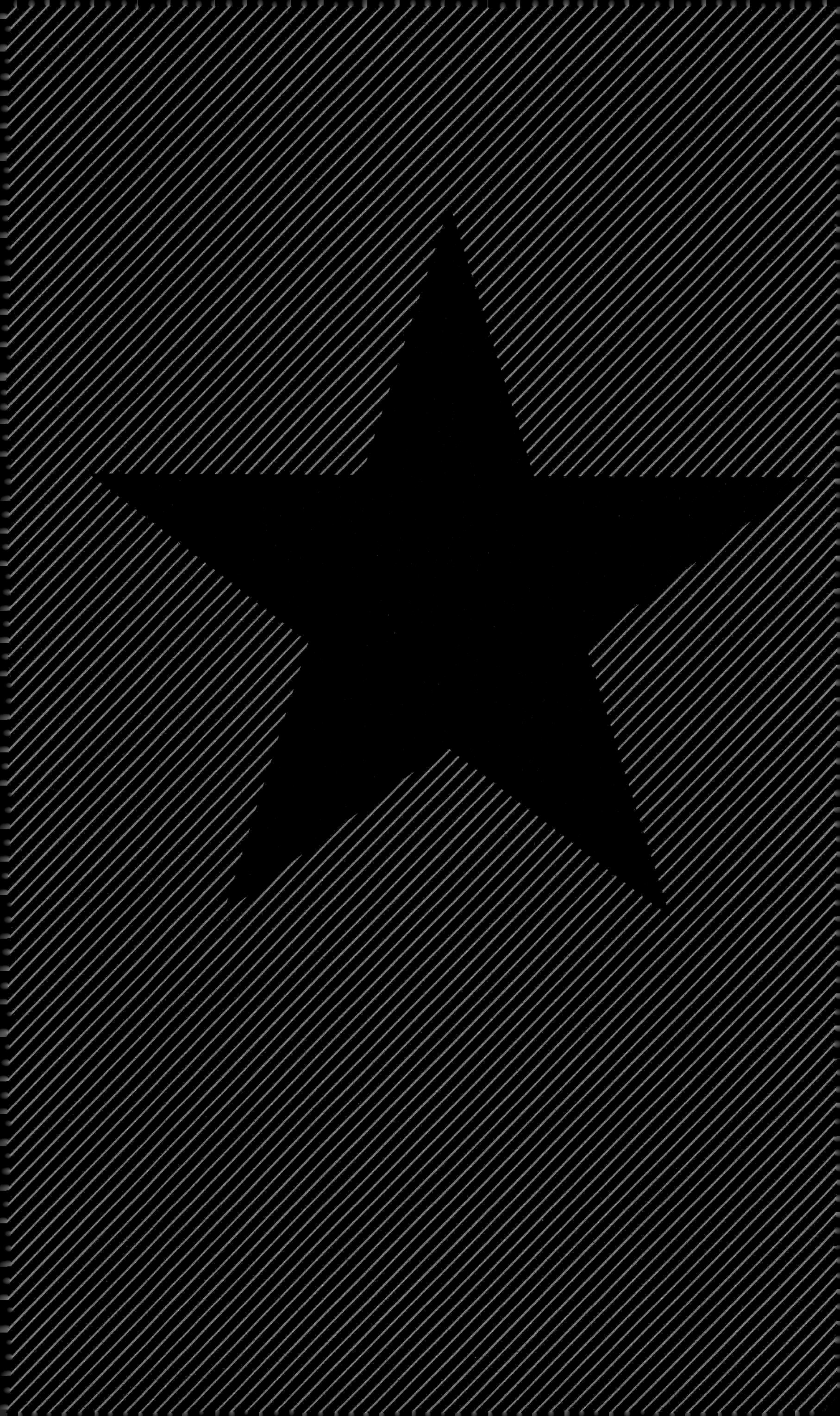

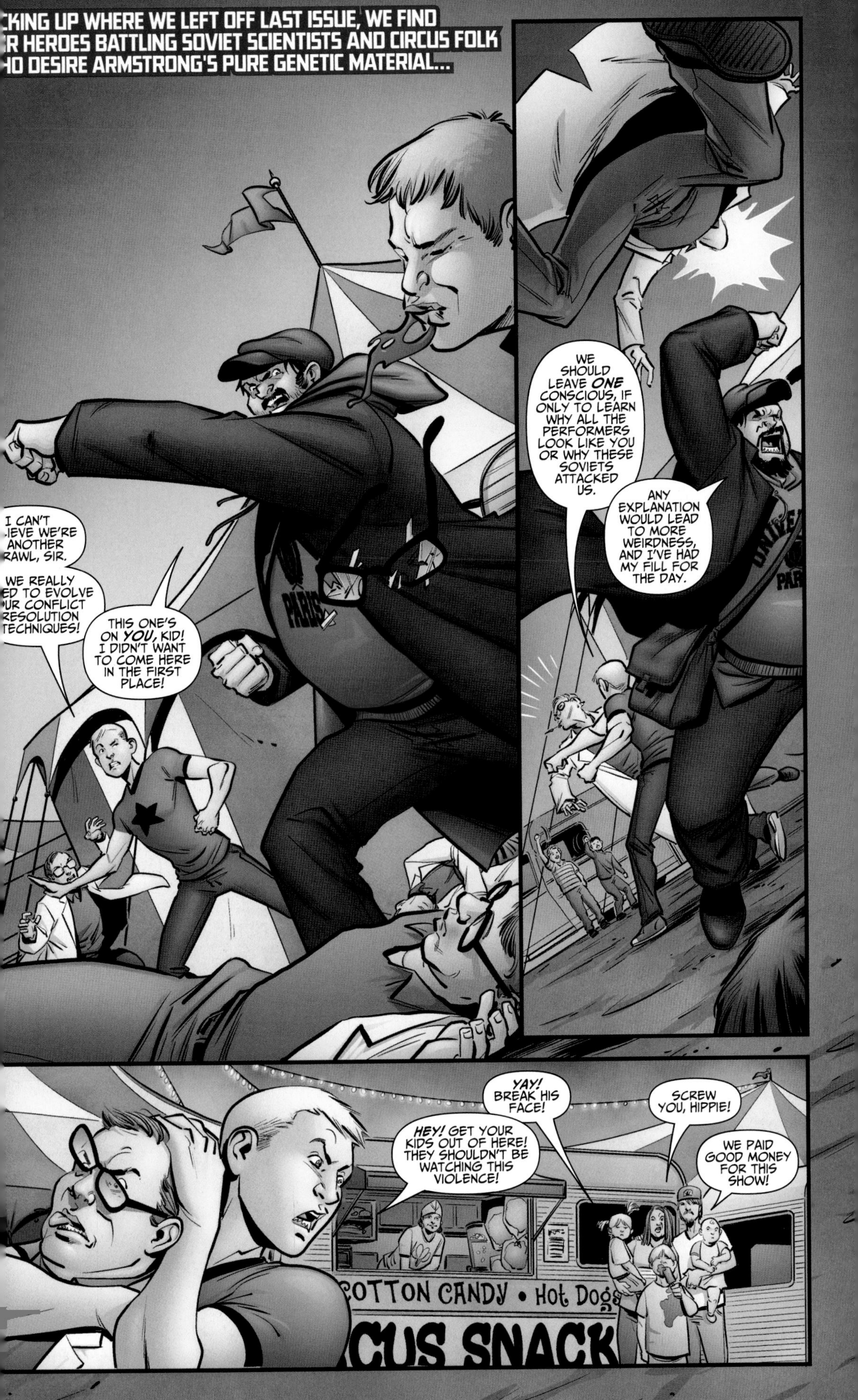
CKING UP WHERE WE LEFT OFF LAST ISSUE, WE FIND
R HEROES BATTLING SOVIET SCIENTISTS AND CIRCUS FOLK
HO DESIRE ARMSTRONG'S PURE GENETIC MATERIAL...
I CAN'T LIEVE WE'RE ANOTHER RAWL, SIR.
WE REALLY ED TO EVOLVE UR CONFLICT RESOLUTION TECHNIQUES!
THIS ONE'S ON YOU, KID! I DIDN'T WANT TO COME HERE IN THE FIRST PLACE!
WE SHOULD LEAVE ONE CONSCIOUS, IF ONLY TO LEARN WHY ALL THE PERFORMERS LOOK LIKE YOU OR WHY THESE SOVIETS ATTACKED US.
ANY EXPLANATION WOULD LEAD TO MORE WEIRDNESS, AND I'VE HAD MY FILL FOR THE DAY.
HEY! GET YOUR KIDS OUT OF HERE! THEY SHOULDN'T BE WATCHING THIS VIOLENCE!
YAY! BREAK HIS FACE!
SCREW YOU, HIPPIE!
WE PAID GOOD MONEY FOR THIS SHOW!
COTTON CANDY • Hot Dogs
CUS SNACK

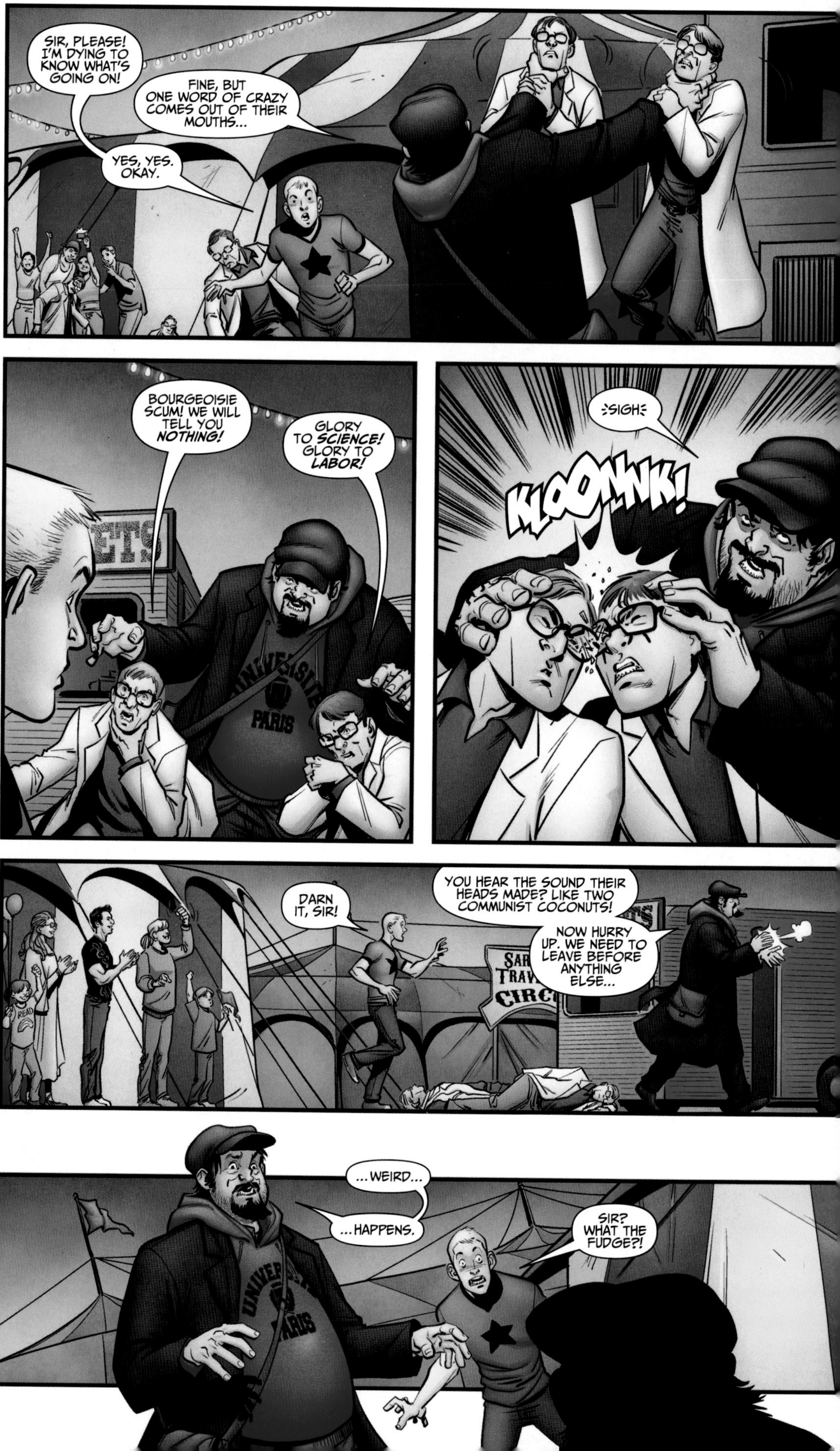
SIR, PLEASE! I'M DYING TO KNOW WHAT'S GOING ON!
FINE, BUT ONE WORD OF CRAZY COMES OUT OF THEIR MOUTHS...
YES, YES. OKAY.
BOURGEOISIE SCUM! WE WILL TELL YOU NOTHING!
GLORY TO SCIENCE! GLORY TO LABOR!
SIGH
KLOONNK!
DARN IT, SIR!
YOU HEAR THE SOUND THEIR HEADS MADE? LIKE TWO COMMUNIST COCONUTS!
NOW HURRY UP. WE NEED TO LEAVE BEFORE ANYTHING ELSE...
...WEIRD...
...HAPPENS.
SIR? WHAT THE FUDGE?!

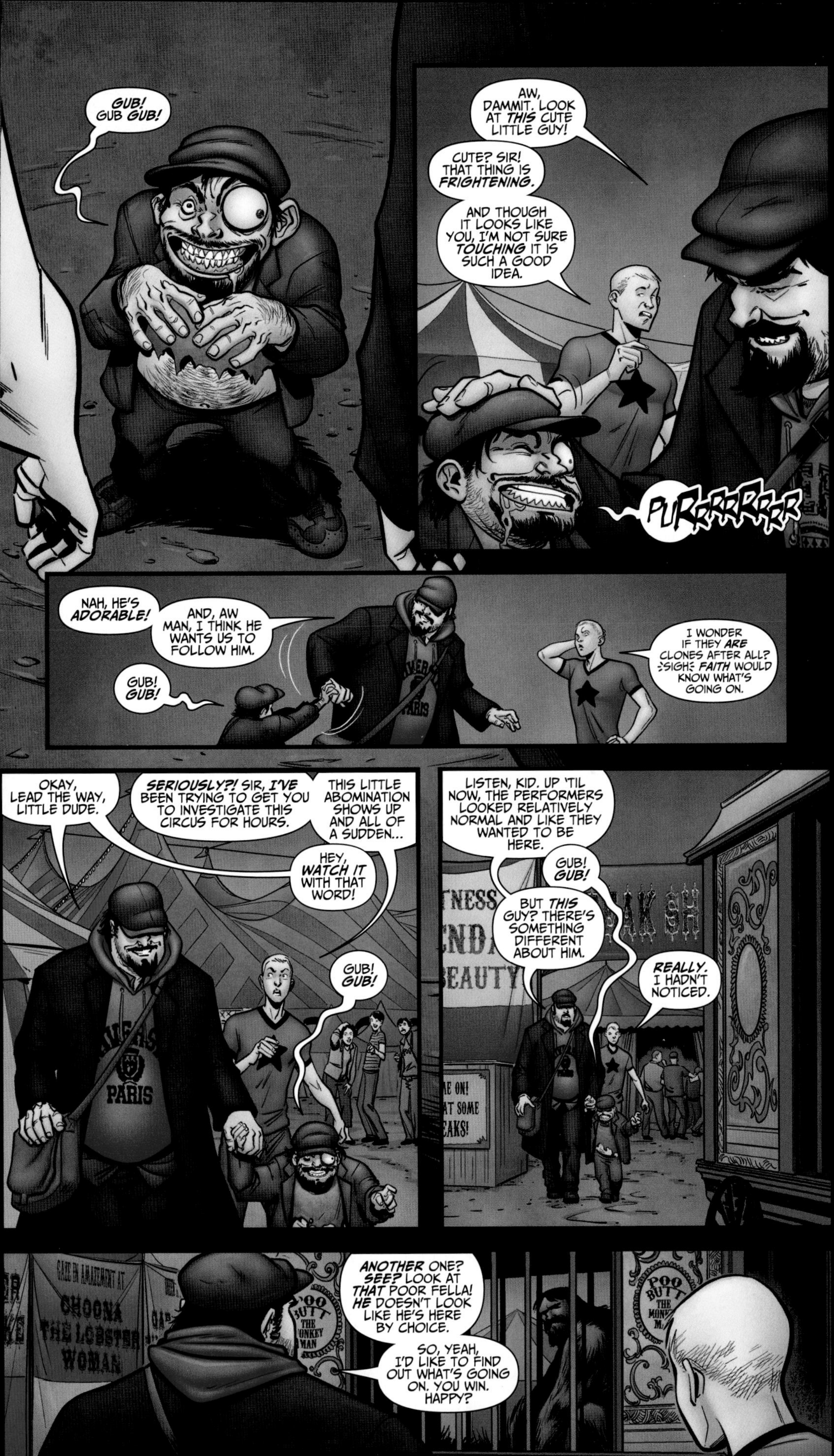
GUB! GUB GUB!
AW, DAMMIT. LOOK AT THIS CUTE LITTLE GUY!
CUTE? SIR! THAT THING IS FRIGHTENING.
AND THOUGH IT LOOKS LIKE YOU, I'M NOT SURE TOUCHING IT IS SUCH A GOOD IDEA.
PURRRRRRR
NAH, HE'S ADORABLE!
AND, AW MAN, I THINK HE WANTS US TO FOLLOW HIM.
GUB! GUB!
I WONDER IF THEY ARE CLONES AFTER ALL? SIGH FAITH WOULD KNOW WHAT'S GOING ON.
OKAY, LEAD THE WAY, LITTLE DUDE.
SERIOUSLY?! SIR, I'VE BEEN TRYING TO GET YOU TO INVESTIGATE THIS CIRCUS FOR HOURS.
THIS LITTLE ABOMINATION SHOWS UP AND ALL OF A SUDDEN...
HEY, WATCH IT WITH THAT WORD!
GUB! GUB!
PARIS
LISTEN, KID. UP 'TIL NOW, THE PERFORMERS LOOKED RELATIVELY NORMAL AND LIKE THEY WANTED TO BE HERE.
GUB! GUB!
BUT THIS GUY? THERE'S SOMETHING DIFFERENT ABOUT HIM.
REALLY. I HADN'T NOTICED.
GAZE IN AMAZEMENT AT
CHOONA THE LOBSTER WOMAN
POO BUTT THE MONKEY MAN
ANOTHER ONE? SEE? LOOK AT THAT POOR FELLA! HE DOESN'T LOOK LIKE HE'S HERE BY CHOICE.
SO, YEAH, I'D LIKE TO FIND OUT WHAT'S GOING ON. YOU WIN. HAPPY?

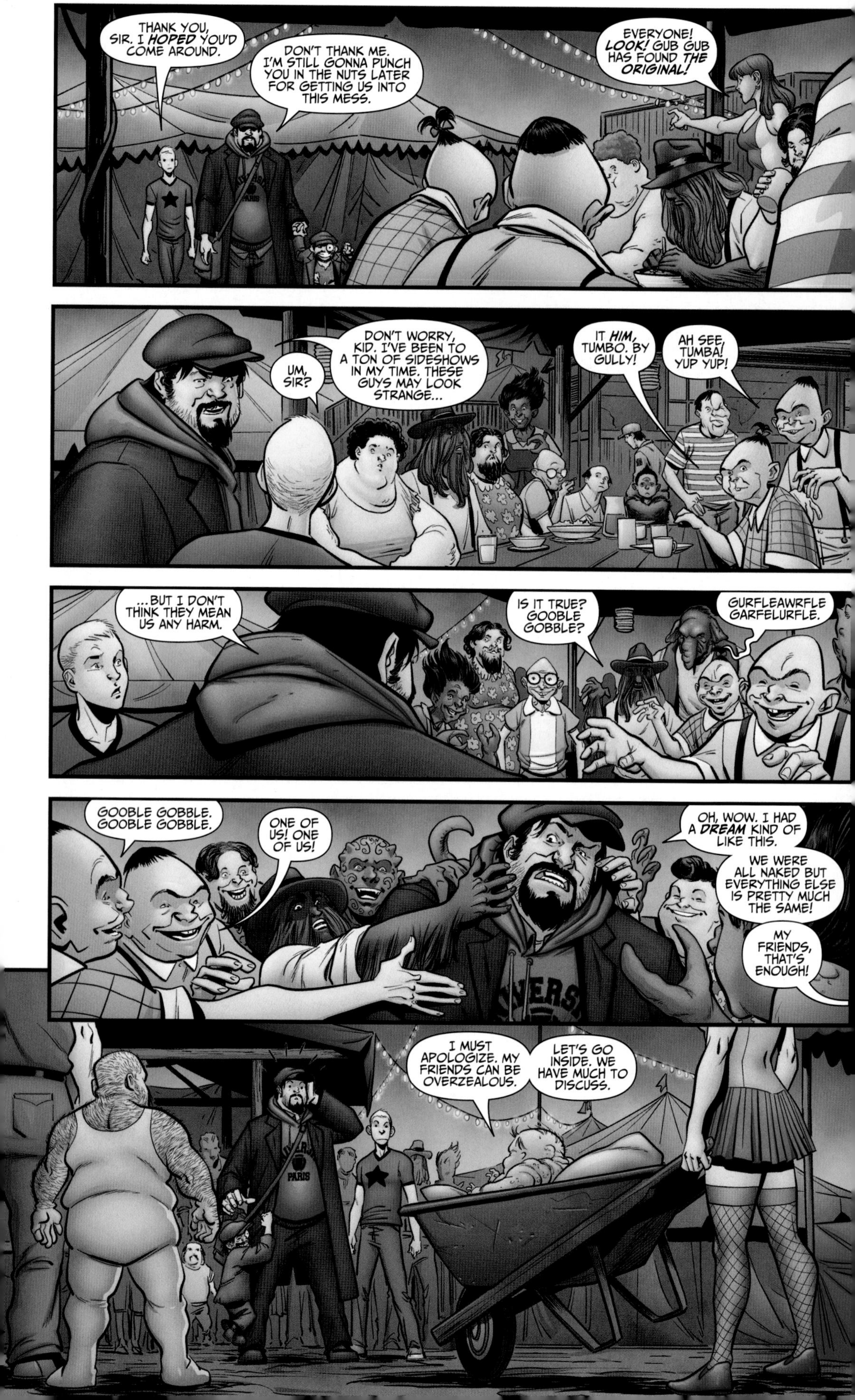
THANK YOU, SIR. I HOPED YOU'D COME AROUND.
DON'T THANK ME. I'M STILL GONNA PUNCH YOU IN THE NUTS LATER FOR GETTING US INTO THIS MESS.
EVERYONE! LOOK! GUB GUB HAS FOUND THE ORIGINAL!
UM, SIR?
DON'T WORRY, KID. I'VE BEEN TO A TON OF SIDESHOWS IN MY TIME. THESE GUYS MAY LOOK STRANGE...
IT HIM, TUMBO. BY GULLY!
AH SEE, TUMBA! YUP YUP!
...BUT I DON'T THINK THEY MEAN US ANY HARM.
IS IT TRUE? GOOBLE GOBBLE?
GURFLEAWRFLE GARFELURFLE.
GOOBLE GOBBLE. GOOBLE GOBBLE.
ONE OF US! ONE OF US!
OH, WOW. I HAD A DREAM KIND OF LIKE THIS.
WE WERE ALL NAKED BUT EVERYTHING ELSE IS PRETTY MUCH THE SAME!
MY FRIENDS, THAT'S ENOUGH!
I MUST APOLOGIZE. MY FRIENDS CAN BE OVERZEALOUS.
LET'S GO INSIDE. WE HAVE MUCH TO DISCUSS.

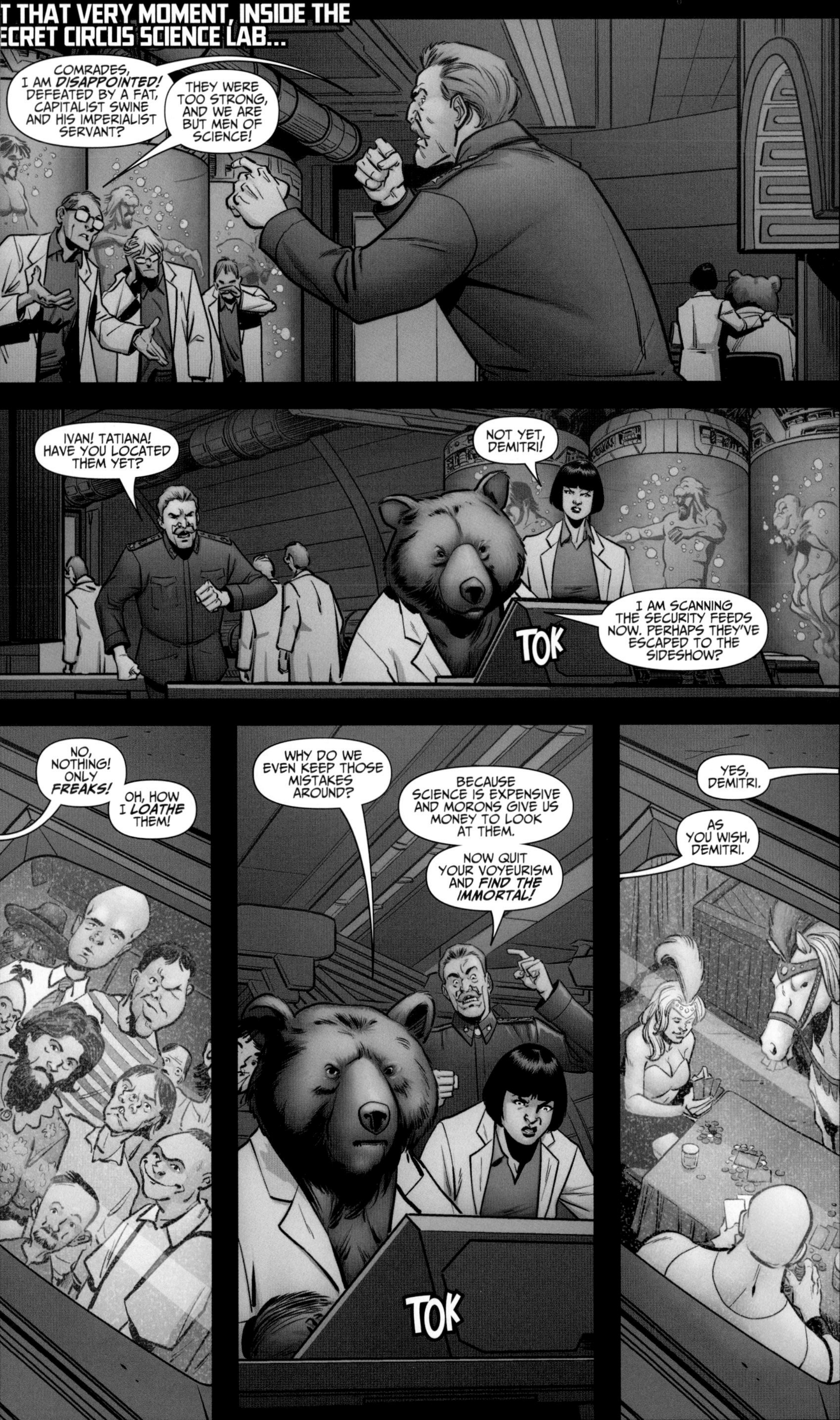
T THAT VERY MOMENT, INSIDE THE
ECRET CIRCUS SCIENCE LAB...
COMRADES, I AM DISAPPOINTED! DEFEATED BY A FAT, CAPITALIST SWINE AND HIS IMPERIALIST SERVANT?
THEY WERE TOO STRONG, AND WE ARE BUT MEN OF SCIENCE!
IVAN! TATIANA! HAVE YOU LOCATED THEM YET?
NOT YET, DEMITRI!
TOK
I AM SCANNING THE SECURITY FEEDS NOW. PERHAPS THEY'VE ESCAPED TO THE SIDESHOW?
NO, NOTHING! ONLY FREAKS!
OH, HOW I LOATHE THEM!
WHY DO WE EVEN KEEP THOSE MISTAKES AROUND?
BECAUSE SCIENCE IS EXPENSIVE AND MORONS GIVE US MONEY TO LOOK AT THEM.
NOW QUIT YOUR VOYEURISM AND FIND THE IMMORTAL!
TOK
YES, DEMITRI.
AS YOU WISH, DEMITRI.

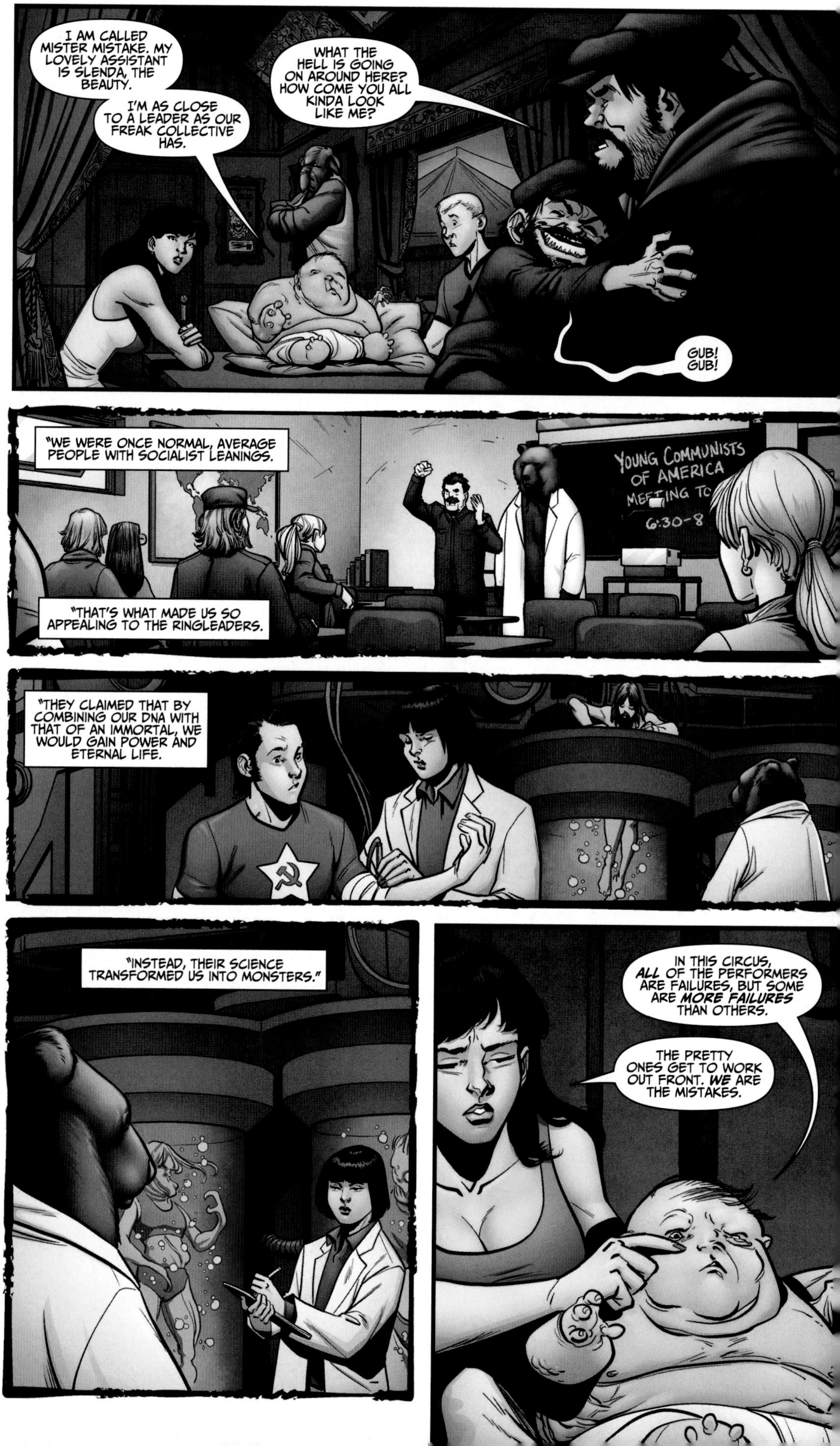
I AM CALLED MISTER MISTAKE. MY LOVELY ASSISTANT IS SLENDA, THE BEAUTY.
I'M AS CLOSE TO A LEADER AS OUR FREAK COLLECTIVE HAS.
WHAT THE HELL IS GOING ON AROUND HERE? HOW COME YOU ALL KINDA LOOK LIKE ME?
GUB! GUB!
"WE WERE ONCE NORMAL, AVERAGE PEOPLE WITH SOCIALIST LEANINGS.
YOUNG COMMUNISTS OF AMERICA MEETING TO
6:30-8
"THAT'S WHAT MADE US SO APPEALING TO THE RINGLEADERS.
"THEY CLAIMED THAT BY COMBINING OUR DNA WITH THAT OF AN IMMORTAL, WE WOULD GAIN POWER AND ETERNAL LIFE.
"INSTEAD, THEIR SCIENCE TRANSFORMED US INTO MONSTERS."
IN THIS CIRCUS, ***ALL*** OF THE PERFORMERS ARE FAILURES, BUT SOME ARE ***MORE FAILURES*** THAN OTHERS.
THE PRETTY ONES GET TO WORK OUT FRONT. ***WE*** ARE THE MISTAKES.

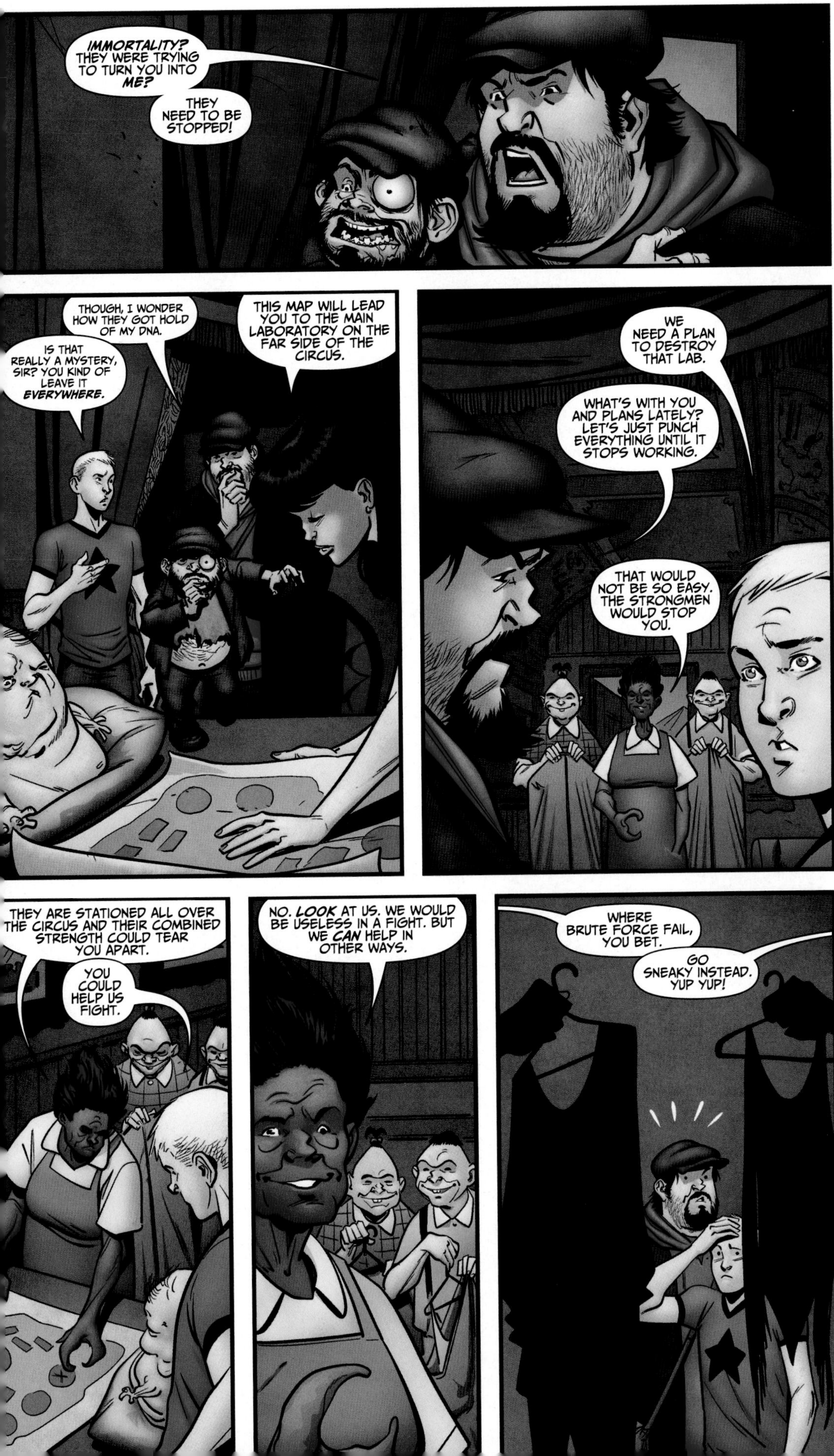
IMMORTALITY? THEY WERE TRYING TO TURN YOU INTO ME?
THEY NEED TO BE STOPPED!
THOUGH, I WONDER HOW THEY GOT HOLD OF MY DNA.
IS THAT REALLY A MYSTERY, SIR? YOU KIND OF LEAVE IT EVERYWHERE.
THIS MAP WILL LEAD YOU TO THE MAIN LABORATORY ON THE FAR SIDE OF THE CIRCUS.
WE NEED A PLAN TO DESTROY THAT LAB.
WHAT'S WITH YOU AND PLANS LATELY? LET'S JUST PUNCH EVERYTHING UNTIL IT STOPS WORKING.
THAT WOULD NOT BE SO EASY. THE STRONGMEN WOULD STOP YOU.
THEY ARE STATIONED ALL OVER THE CIRCUS AND THEIR COMBINED STRENGTH COULD TEAR YOU APART.
YOU COULD HELP US FIGHT.
NO. LOOK AT US. WE WOULD BE USELESS IN A FIGHT. BUT WE CAN HELP IN OTHER WAYS.
WHERE BRUTE FORCE FAIL, YOU BET.
GO SNEAKY INSTEAD. YUP YUP!

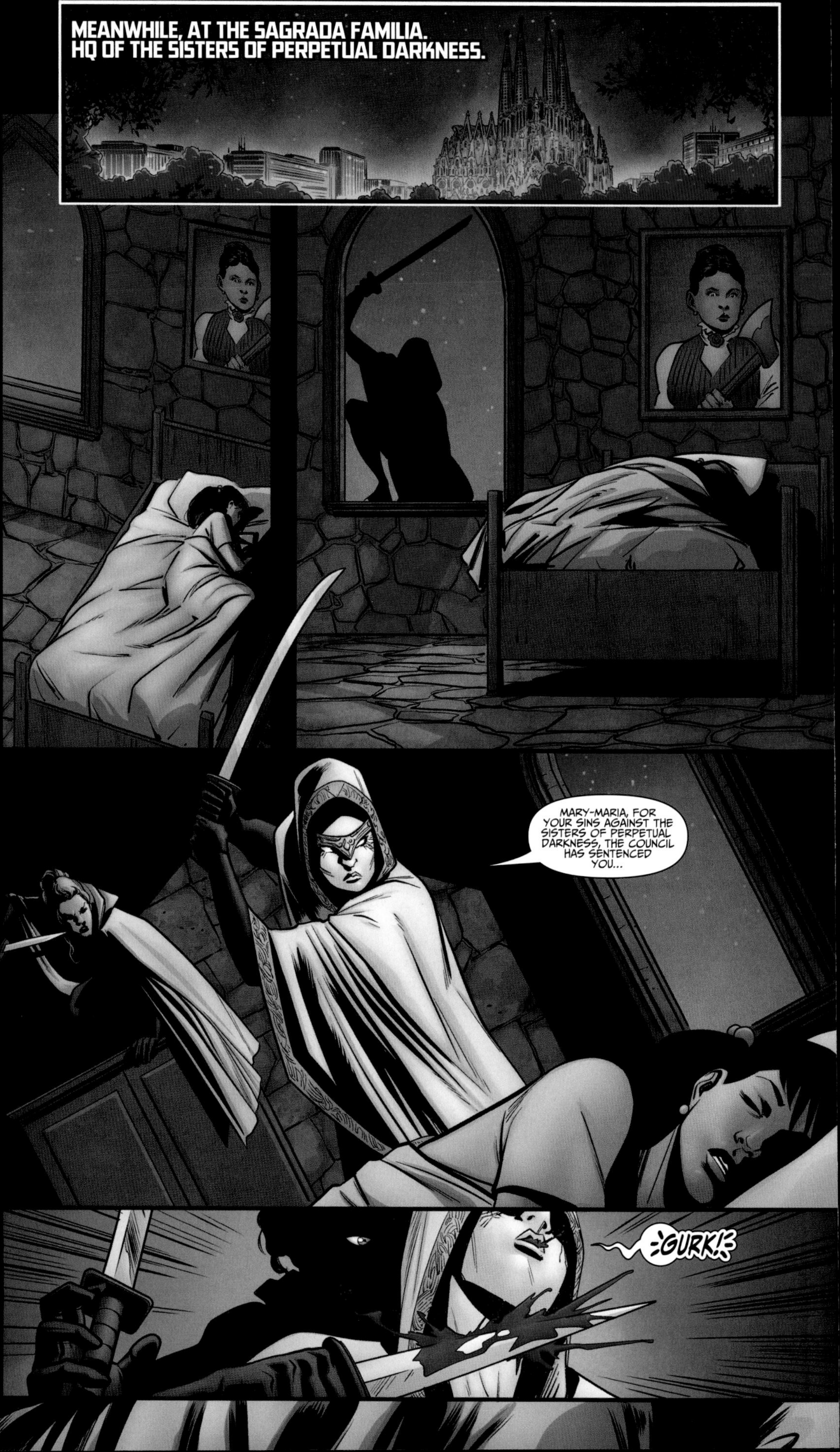
MEANWHILE, AT THE SAGRADA FAMILIA.
HQ OF THE SISTERS OF PERPETUAL DARKNESS.
MARY-MARIA, FOR YOUR SINS AGAINST THE SISTERS OF PERPETUAL DARKNESS, THE COUNCIL HAS SENTENCED YOU...
GURK!

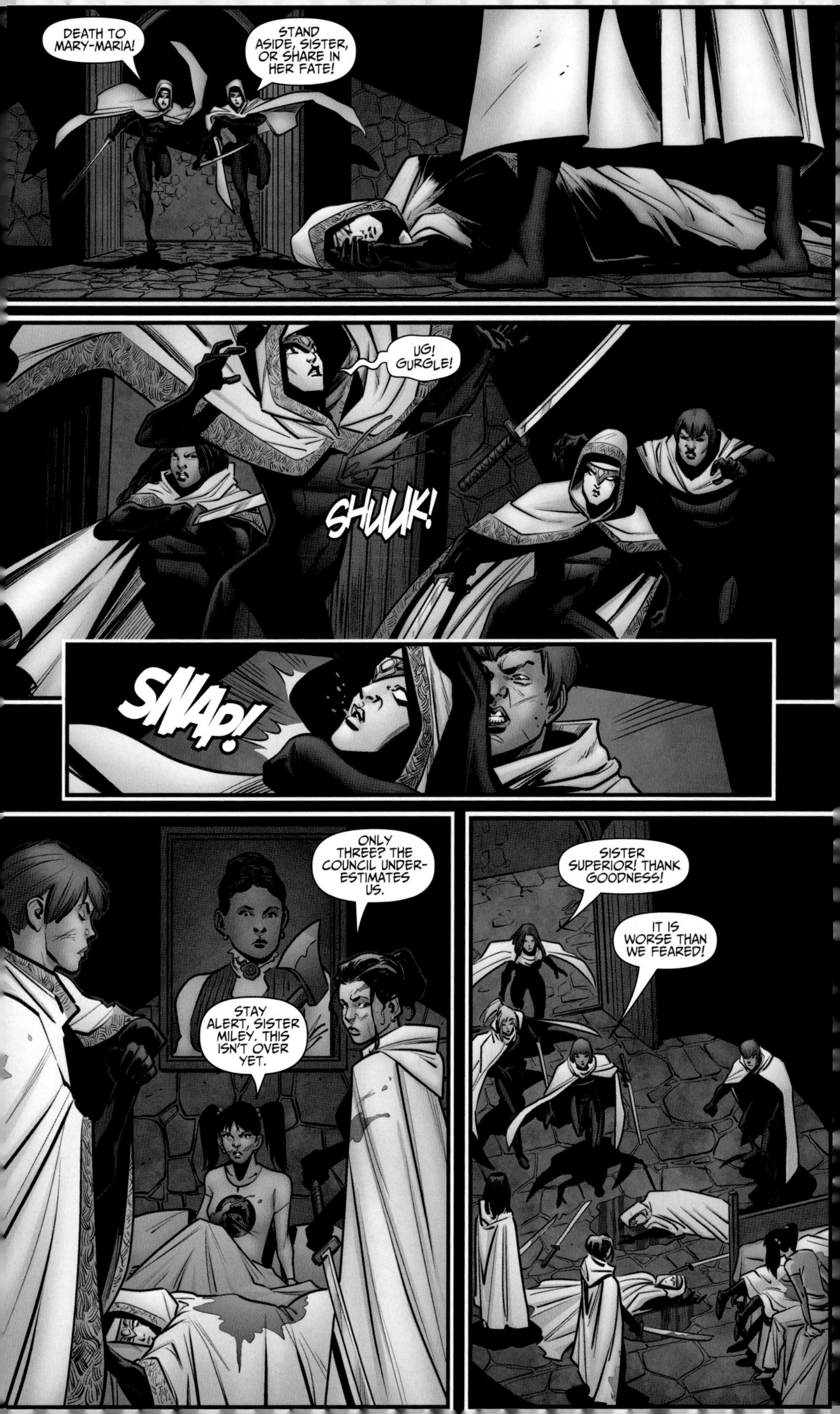
DEATH TO MARY-MARIA!
STAND ASIDE, SISTER, OR SHARE IN HER FATE!
UG! GURGLE!
SHUUK!
SNAP!
ONLY THREE? THE COUNCIL UNDER-ESTIMATES US.
STAY ALERT, SISTER MILEY. THIS ISN'T OVER YET.
SISTER SUPERIOR! THANK GOODNESS!
IT IS WORSE THAN WE FEARED!

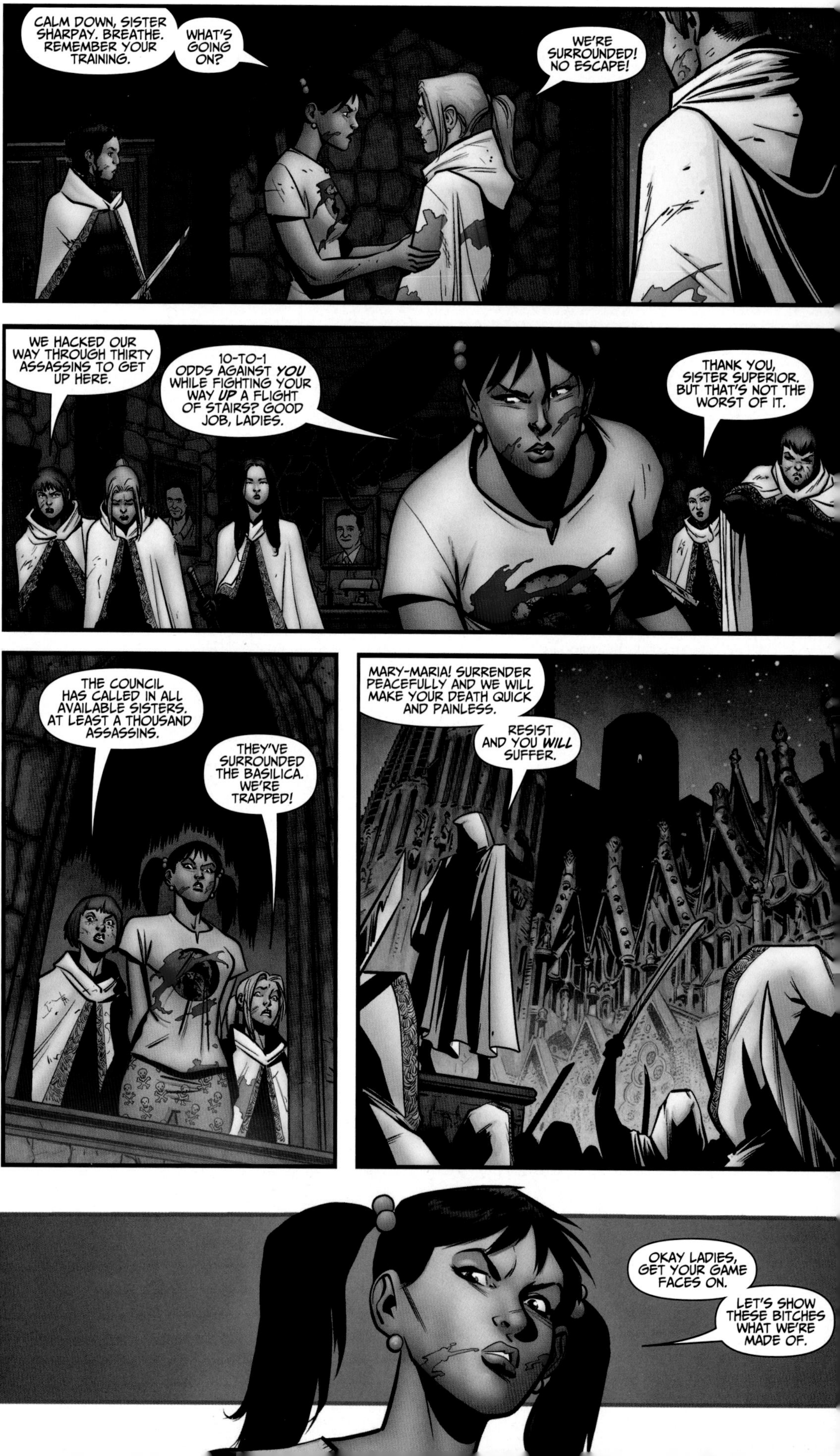

CALM DOWN, SISTER SHARPAY. BREATHE. REMEMBER YOUR TRAINING.
WHAT'S GOING ON?
WE'RE SURROUNDED! NO ESCAPE!
WE HACKED OUR WAY THROUGH THIRTY ASSASSINS TO GET UP HERE.
10-TO-1 ODDS AGAINST YOU WHILE FIGHTING YOUR WAY UP A FLIGHT OF STAIRS? GOOD JOB, LADIES.
THANK YOU, SISTER SUPERIOR. BUT THAT'S NOT THE WORST OF IT.
THE COUNCIL HAS CALLED IN ALL AVAILABLE SISTERS. AT LEAST A THOUSAND ASSASSINS.
THEY'VE SURROUNDED THE BASILICA. WE'RE TRAPPED!
MARY-MARIA! SURRENDER PEACEFULLY AND WE WILL MAKE YOUR DEATH QUICK AND PAINLESS.
RESIST AND YOU WILL SUFFER.
OKAY LADIES, GET YOUR GAME FACES ON.
LET'S SHOW THESE BITCHES WHAT WE'RE MADE OF.

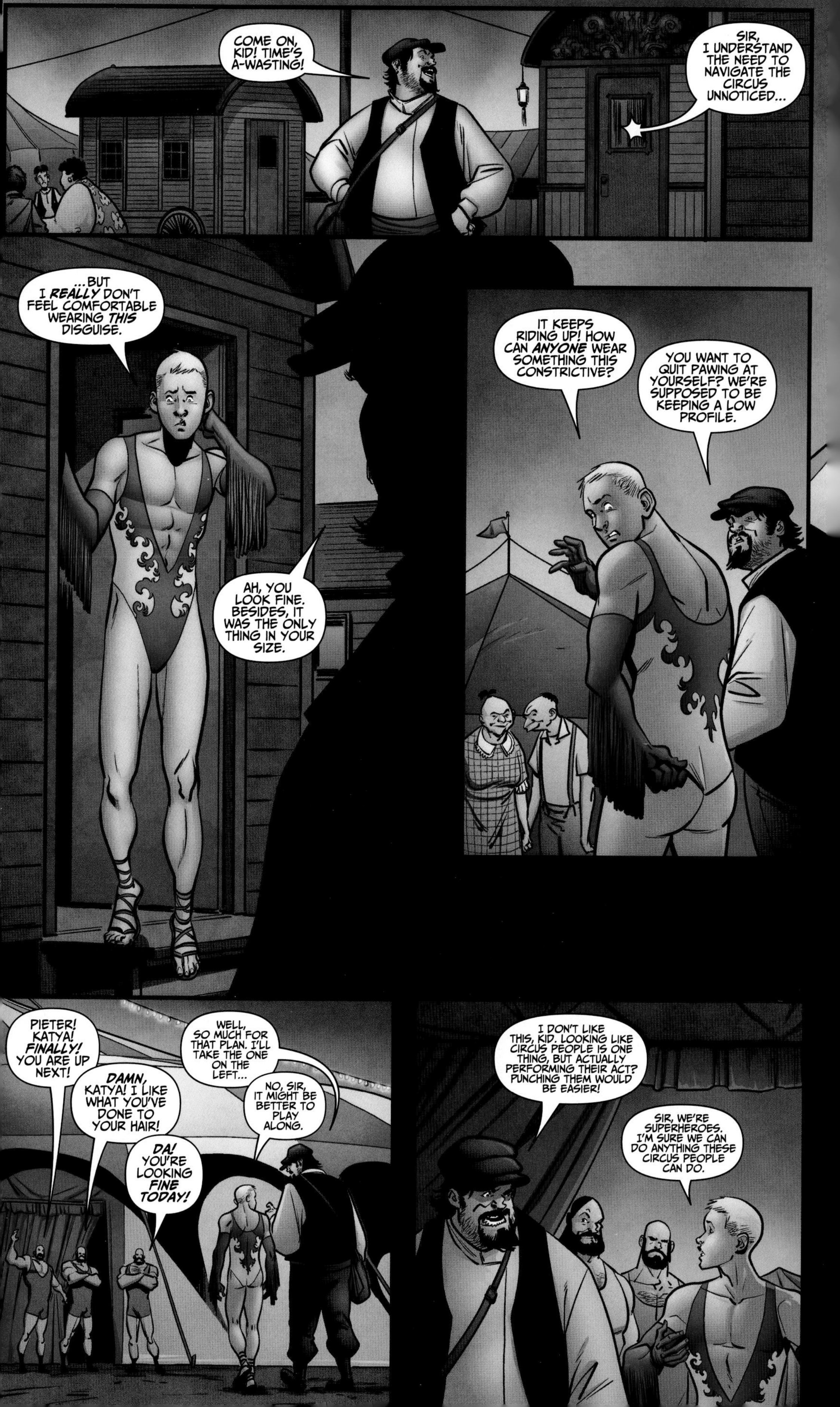
COME ON, KID! TIME'S A-WASTING!
SIR, I UNDERSTAND THE NEED TO NAVIGATE THE CIRCUS UNNOTICED...
...BUT I REALLY DON'T FEEL COMFORTABLE WEARING THIS DISGUISE.
AH, YOU LOOK FINE. BESIDES, IT WAS THE ONLY THING IN YOUR SIZE.
IT KEEPS RIDING UP! HOW CAN ANYONE WEAR SOMETHING THIS CONSTRICTIVE?
YOU WANT TO QUIT PAWING AT YOURSELF? WE'RE SUPPOSED TO BE KEEPING A LOW PROFILE.
PIETER! KATYA! FINALLY! YOU ARE UP NEXT!
DAMN, KATYA! I LIKE WHAT YOU'VE DONE TO YOUR HAIR!
DA! YOU'RE LOOKING FINE TODAY!
WELL, SO MUCH FOR THAT PLAN. I'LL TAKE THE ONE ON THE LEFT...
NO, SIR, IT MIGHT BE BETTER TO PLAY ALONG.
I DON'T LIKE THIS, KID. LOOKING LIKE CIRCUS PEOPLE IS ONE THING, BUT ACTUALLY PERFORMING THEIR ACT? PUNCHING THEM WOULD BE EASIER!
SIR, WE'RE SUPERHEROES. I'M SURE WE CAN DO ANYTHING THESE CIRCUS PEOPLE CAN DO.

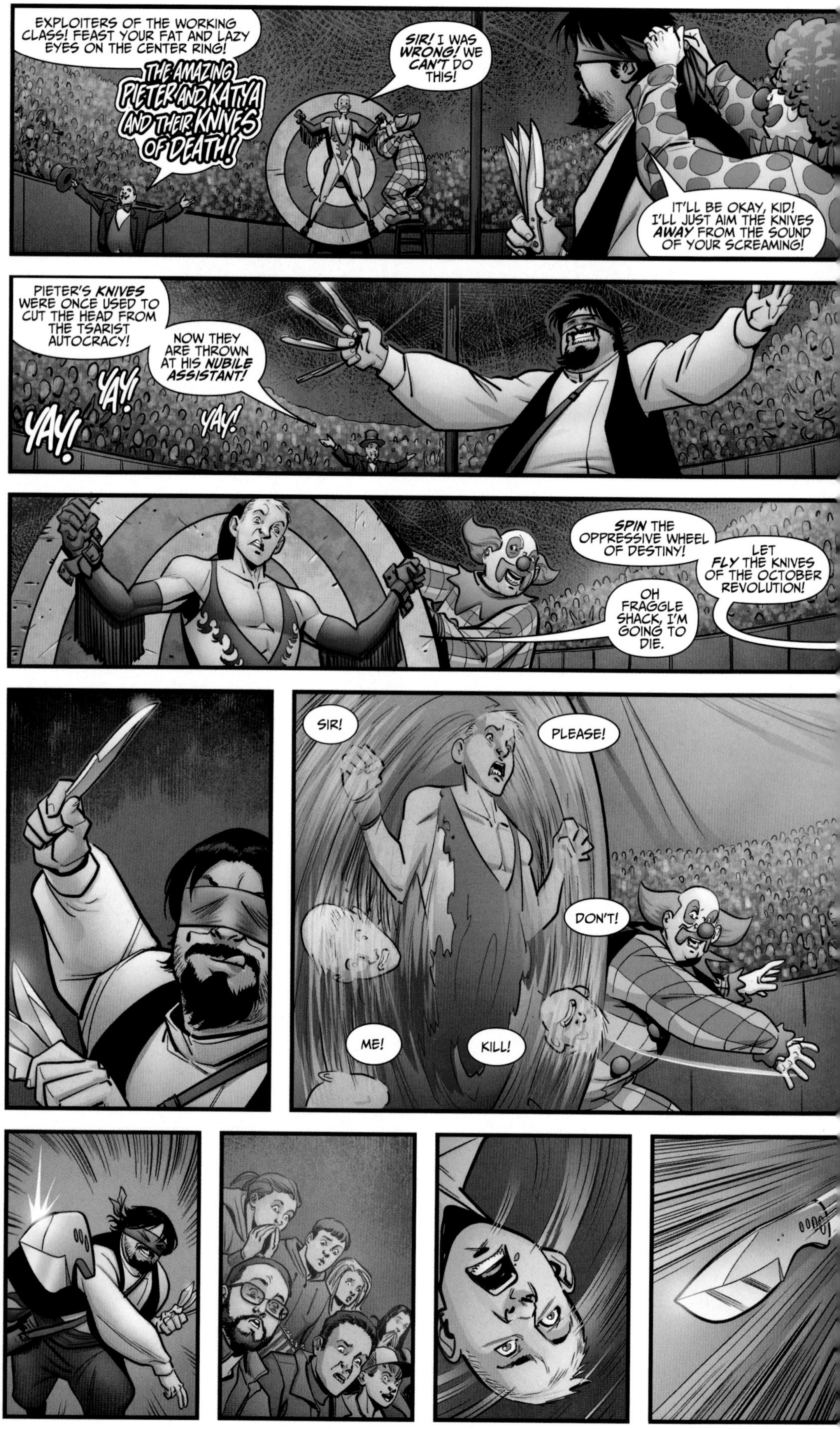
EXPLOITERS OF THE WORKING CLASS! FEAST YOUR FAT AND LAZY EYES ON THE CENTER RING!
THE AMAZING PIETER AND KATYA AND THEIR KNIVES OF DEATH!
SIR! I WAS WRONG! WE CAN'T DO THIS!
IT'LL BE OKAY, KID! I'LL JUST AIM THE KNIVES AWAY FROM THE SOUND OF YOUR SCREAMING!
PIETER'S KNIVES WERE ONCE USED TO CUT THE HEAD FROM THE TSARIST AUTOCRACY!
NOW THEY ARE THROWN AT HIS NUBILE ASSISTANT!
YAY!
YAY!
YAY!
SPIN THE OPPRESSIVE WHEEL OF DESTINY!
LET FLY THE KNIVES OF THE OCTOBER REVOLUTION!
OH FRAGGLE SHACK, I'M GOING TO DIE.
SIR!
PLEASE!
DON'T!
KILL!
ME!

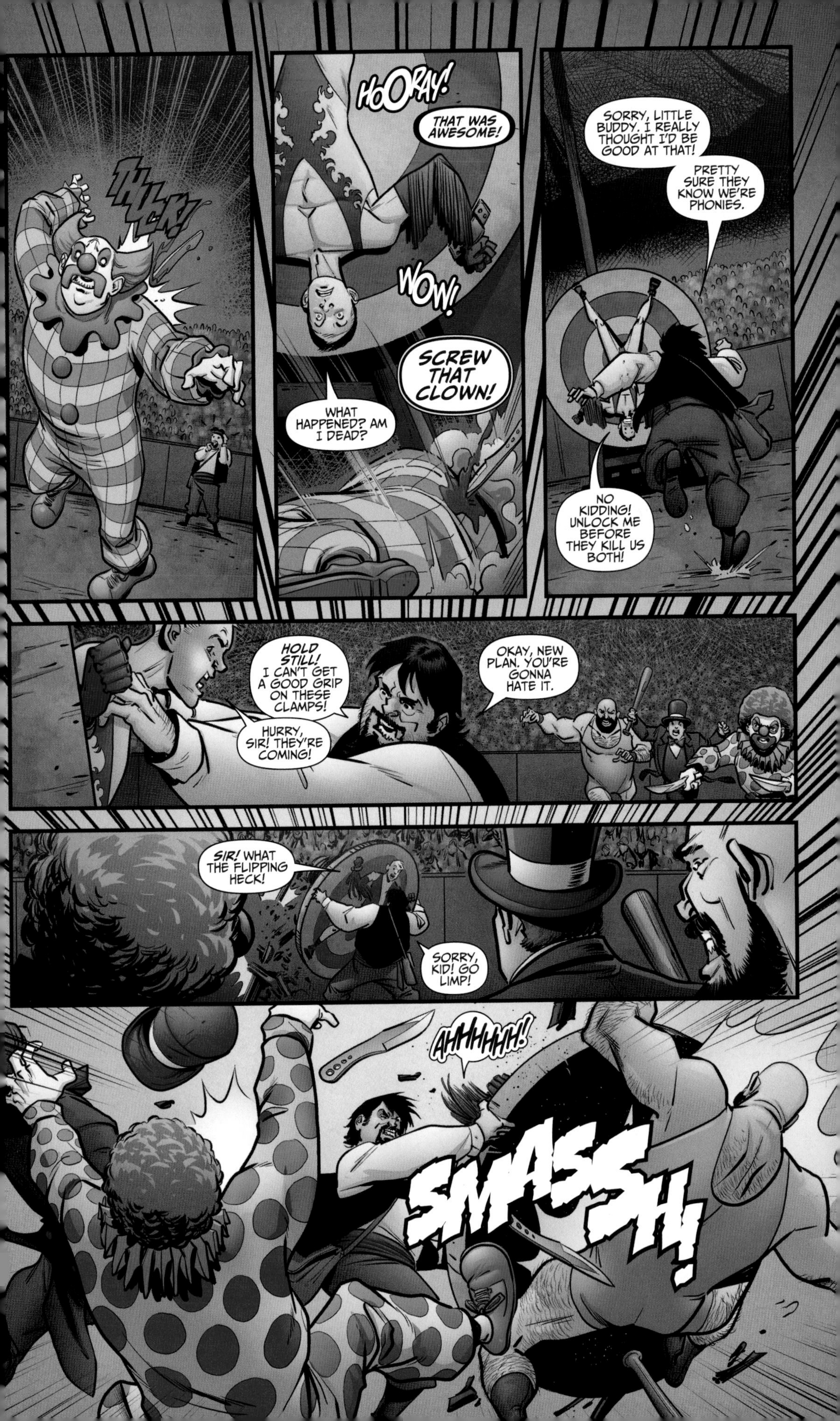
THUCK!
HOORAY!
THAT WAS AWESOME!
WOW!
SCREW THAT CLOWN!
WHAT HAPPENED? AM I DEAD?
SORRY, LITTLE BUDDY. I REALLY THOUGHT I'D BE GOOD AT THAT!
PRETTY SURE THEY KNOW WE'RE PHONIES.
NO KIDDING! UNLOCK ME BEFORE THEY KILL US BOTH!
HOLD STILL! I CAN'T GET A GOOD GRIP ON THESE CLAMPS!
HURRY, SIR! THEY'RE COMING!
OKAY, NEW PLAN. YOU'RE GONNA HATE IT.
SIR! WHAT THE FLIPPING HECK!
SORRY, KID! GO LIMP!
AHHHHHH!
SMASSH!

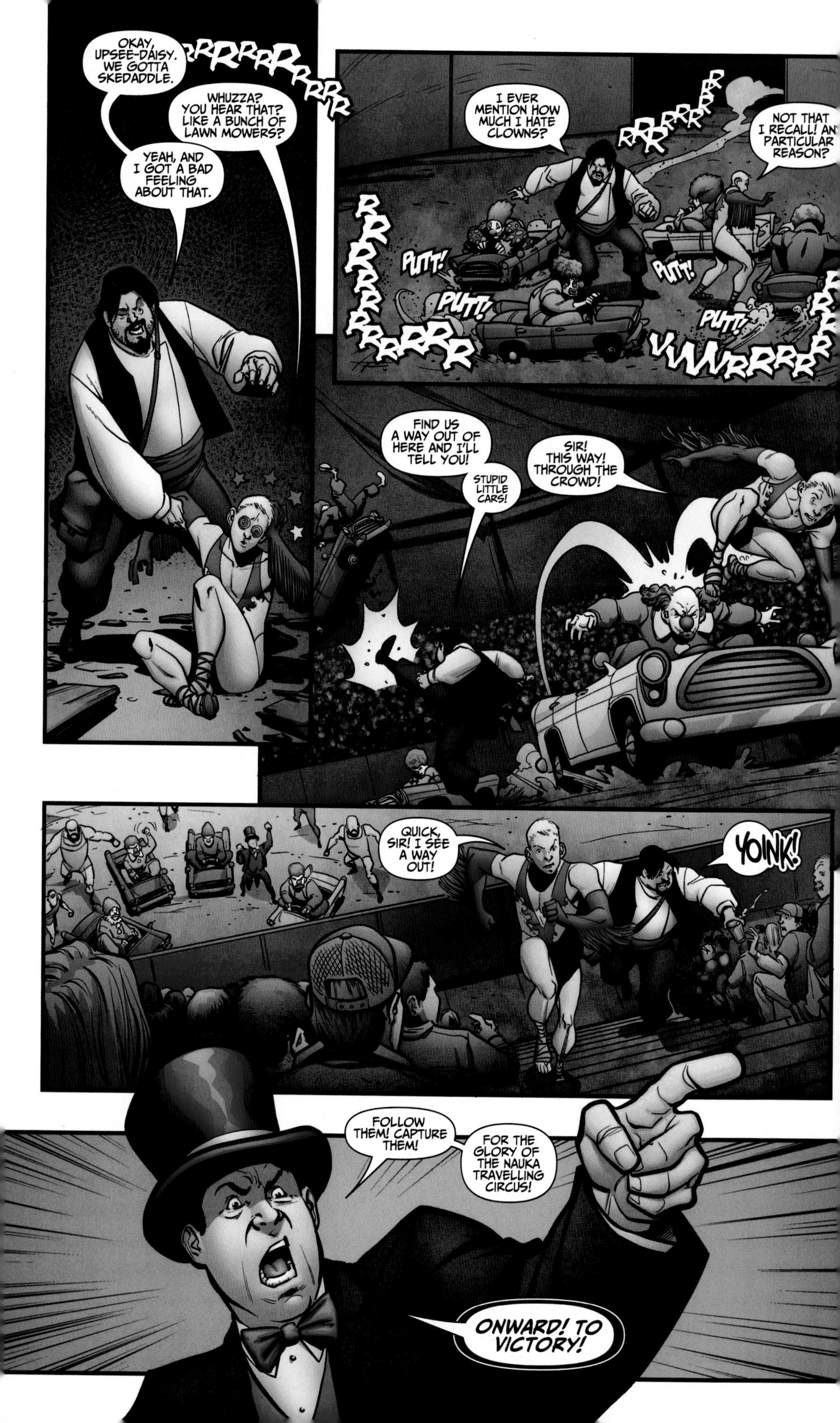

OKAY, UPSEE-DAISY. WE GOTTA SKEDADDLE.
RRRRRRRRRRRR
WHUZZA? YOU HEAR THAT? LIKE A BUNCH OF LAWN MOWERS?
YEAH, AND I GOT A BAD FEELING ABOUT THAT.
I EVER MENTION HOW MUCH I HATE CLOWNS?
RRRRRRRR
NOT THAT I RECALL! AN PARTICULAR REASON?
RRRRRRRRRRR
PUTT!
PUTT!
PUTT!
PUTT!
VVVVRRRRR
FIND US A WAY OUT OF HERE AND I'LL TELL YOU!
STUPID LITTLE CARS!
SIR! THIS WAY! THROUGH THE CROWD!
QUICK, SIR! I SEE A WAY OUT!
YOINK!
FOLLOW THEM! CAPTURE THEM!
FOR THE GLORY OF THE NAUKA TRAVELLING CIRCUS!
ONWARD! TO VICTORY!

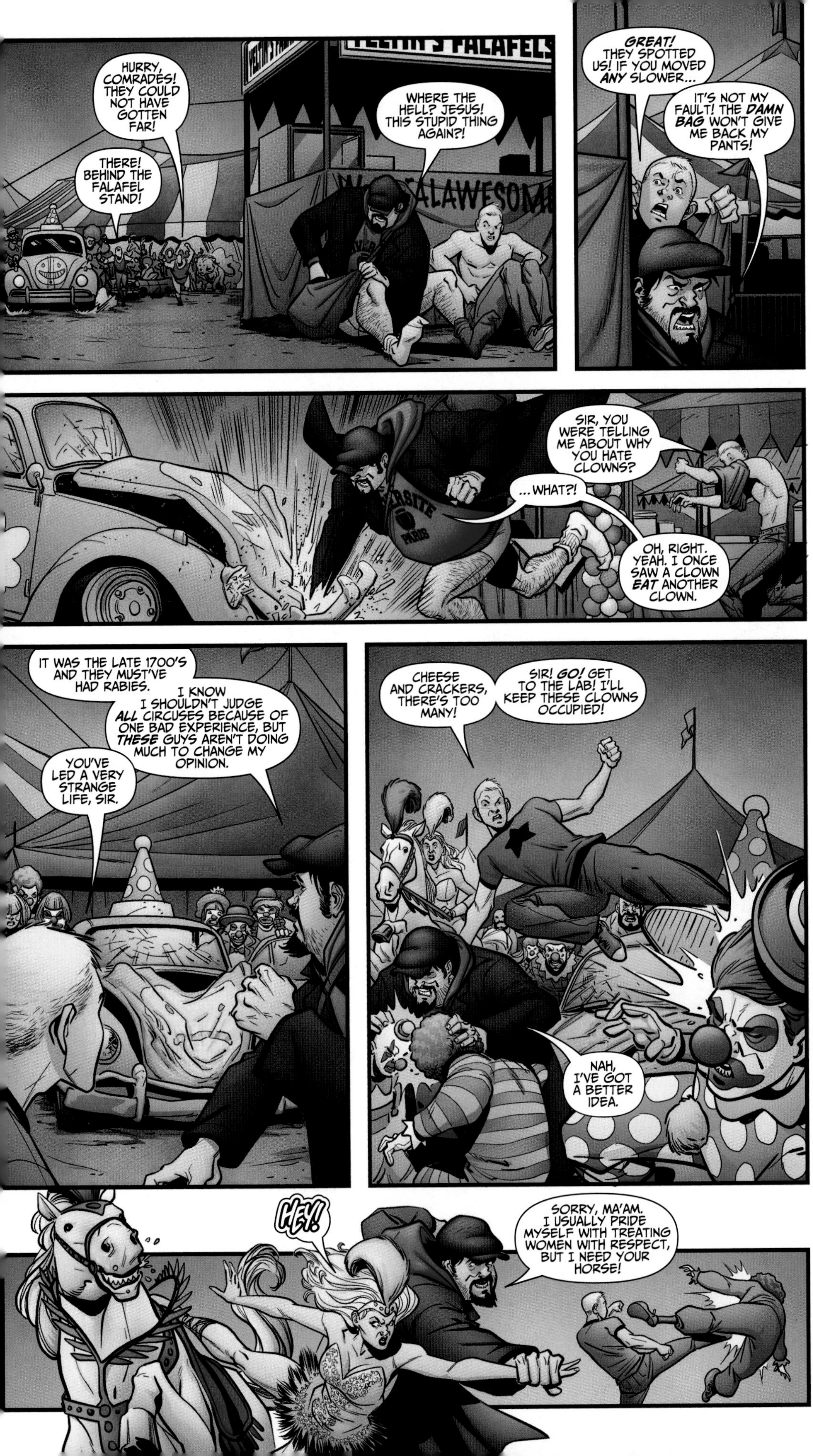

HURRY, COMRADES! THEY COULD NOT HAVE GOTTEN FAR!
THERE! BEHIND THE FALAFEL STAND!
WHERE THE HELL? JESUS! THIS STUPID THING AGAIN?!
GREAT! THEY SPOTTED US! IF YOU MOVED ANY SLOWER...
IT'S NOT MY FAULT! THE DAMN BAG WON'T GIVE ME BACK MY PANTS!
SIR, YOU WERE TELLING ME ABOUT WHY YOU HATE CLOWNS?
...WHAT?!
OH, RIGHT. YEAH. I ONCE SAW A CLOWN EAT ANOTHER CLOWN.
IT WAS THE LATE 1700'S AND THEY MUST'VE HAD RABIES.
I KNOW I SHOULDN'T JUDGE ALL CIRCUSES BECAUSE OF ONE BAD EXPERIENCE, BUT THESE GUYS AREN'T DOING MUCH TO CHANGE MY OPINION.
YOU'VE LED A VERY STRANGE LIFE, SIR.
CHEESE AND CRACKERS, THERE'S TOO MANY!
SIR! GO! GET TO THE LAB! I'LL KEEP THESE CLOWNS OCCUPIED!
NAH, I'VE GOT A BETTER IDEA.
HEY!
SORRY, MA'AM. I USUALLY PRIDE MYSELF WITH TREATING WOMEN WITH RESPECT, BUT I NEED YOUR HORSE!

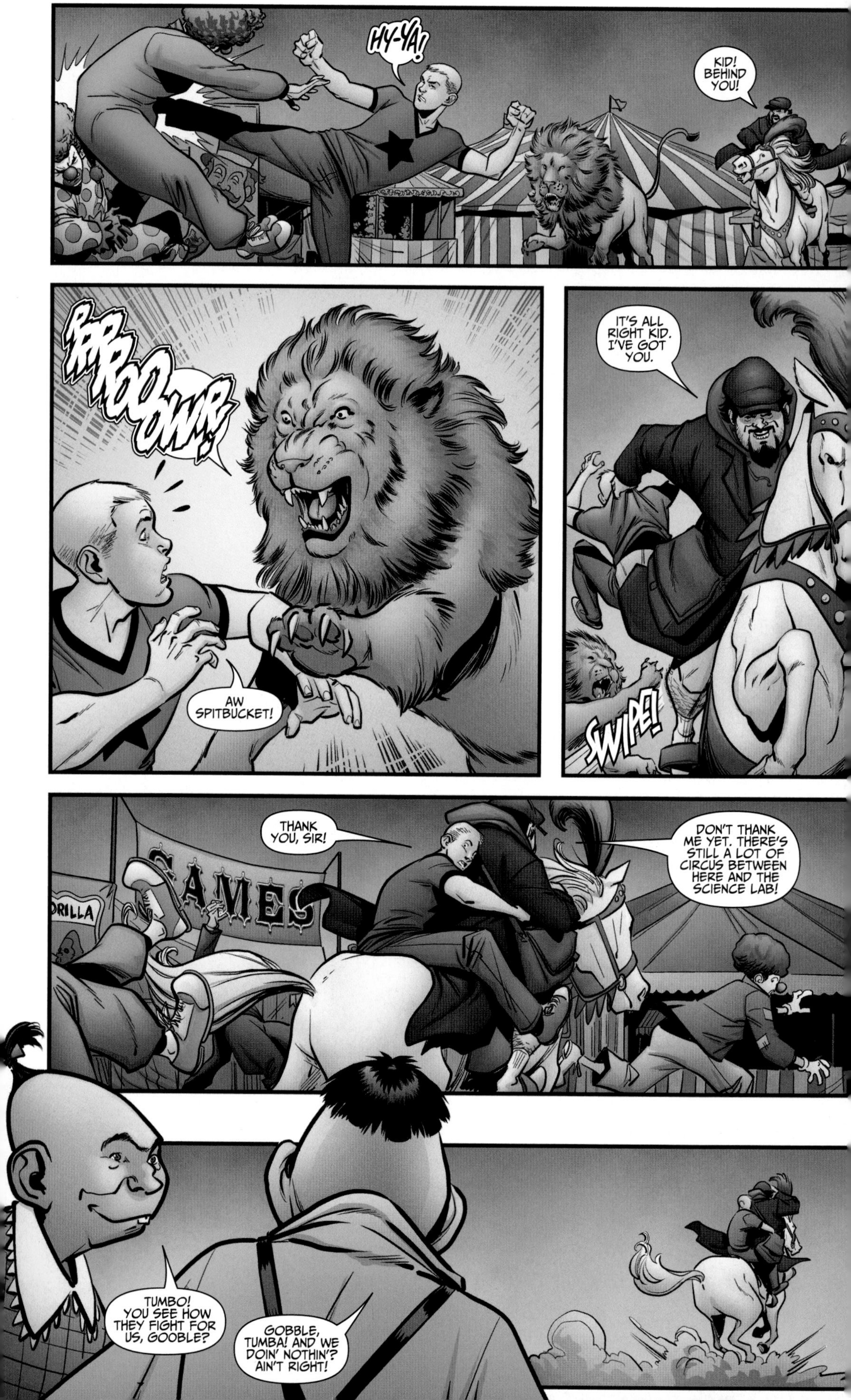
HY-YA!
KID! BEHIND YOU!
RRROOOWR!
AW SPITBUCKET!
IT'S ALL RIGHT KID. I'VE GOT YOU.
SWIPE!
THANK YOU, SIR!
DON'T THANK ME YET. THERE'S STILL A LOT OF CIRCUS BETWEEN HERE AND THE SCIENCE LAB!
GAMES
ORILLA
TUMBO! YOU SEE HOW THEY FIGHT FOR US, GOOBLE?
GOBBLE, TUMBA! AND WE DOIN' NOTHIN'? AIN'T RIGHT!

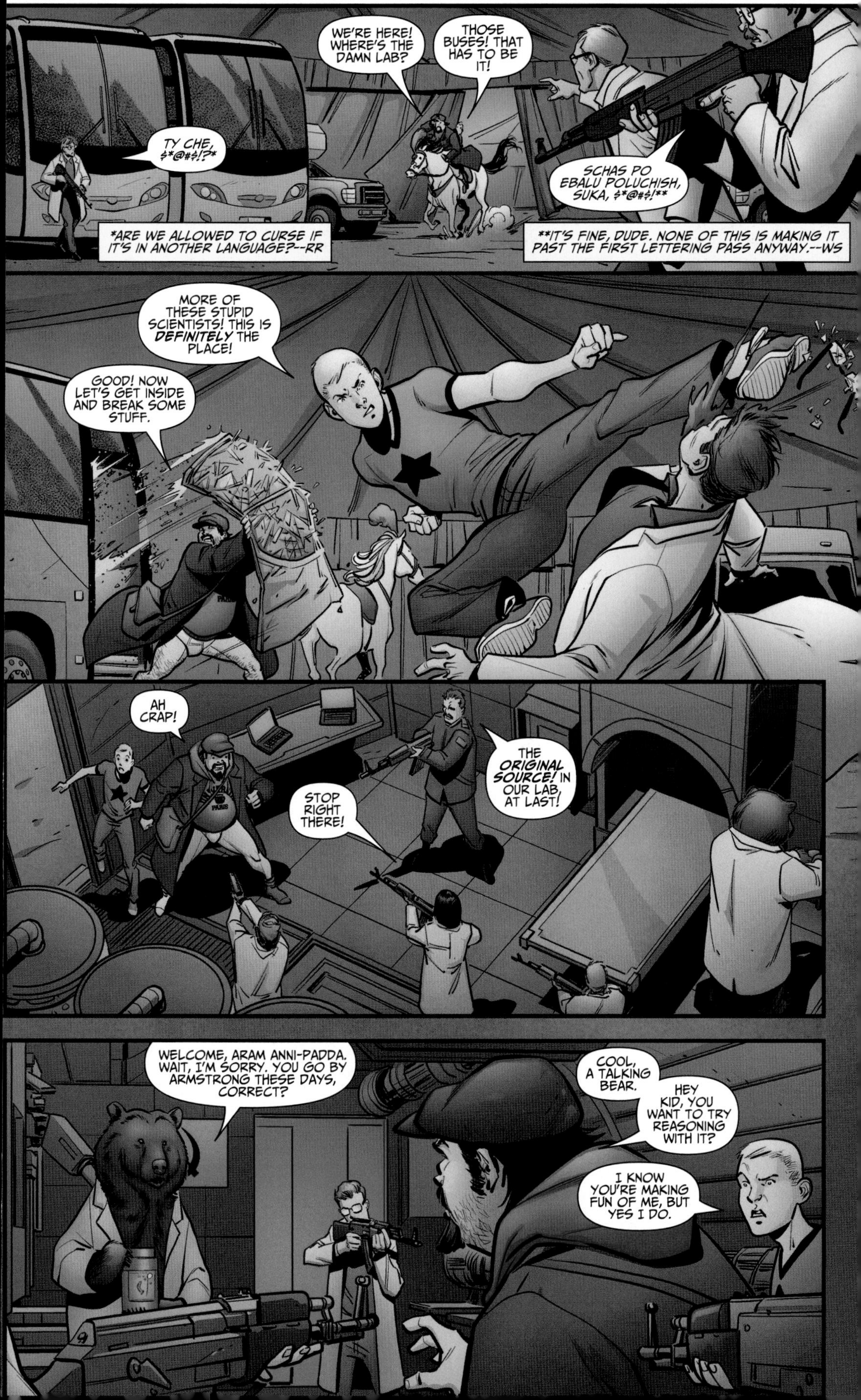
WE'RE HERE! WHERE'S THE DAMN LAB?
THOSE BUSES! THAT HAS TO BE IT!
TY CHE, $*@#$!?*
SCHAS PO EBALU POLUCHISH, SUKA, $*@#$!**
*ARE WE ALLOWED TO CURSE IF IT'S IN ANOTHER LANGUAGE?--RR
**IT'S FINE, DUDE. NONE OF THIS IS MAKING IT PAST THE FIRST LETTERING PASS ANYWAY.--WS
MORE OF THESE STUPID SCIENTISTS! THIS IS DEFINITELY THE PLACE!
GOOD! NOW LET'S GET INSIDE AND BREAK SOME STUFF.
AH CRAP!
THE ORIGINAL SOURCE! IN OUR LAB, AT LAST!
STOP RIGHT THERE!
WELCOME, ARAM ANNI-PADDA. WAIT, I'M SORRY. YOU GO BY ARMSTRONG THESE DAYS, CORRECT?
COOL, A TALKING BEAR.
HEY KID, YOU WANT TO TRY REASONING WITH IT?
I KNOW YOU'RE MAKING FUN OF ME, BUT YES I DO.

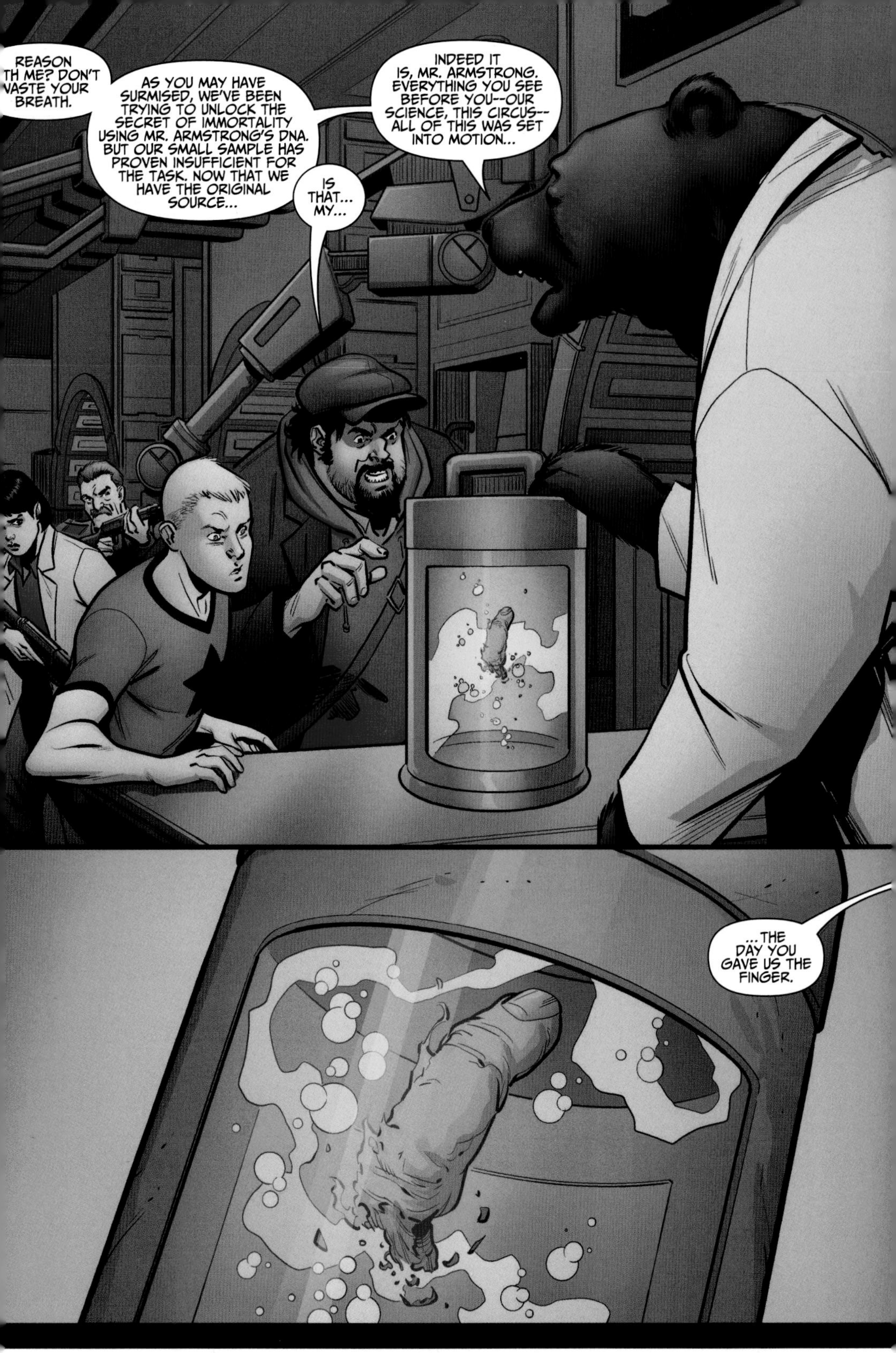
REASON
TH ME? DON'T
VASTE YOUR
BREATH.
AS YOU MAY HAVE SURMISED, WE'VE BEEN TRYING TO UNLOCK THE SECRET OF IMMORTALITY USING MR. ARMSTRONG'S DNA. BUT OUR SMALL SAMPLE HAS PROVEN INSUFFICIENT FOR THE TASK. NOW THAT WE HAVE THE ORIGINAL SOURCE...
IS THAT... MY...
INDEED IT IS, MR. ARMSTRONG. EVERYTHING YOU SEE BEFORE YOU--OUR SCIENCE, THIS CIRCUS--ALL OF THIS WAS SET INTO MOTION...
...THE DAY YOU GAVE US THE FINGER.

NEXT TIME IN A&A: THE ADVENTURES OF ARCHER AND ARMSTRONG

CHAOS UNDER THE BIG TOP! WHO WILL LIVE? WHO WILL DIE!

WILL ARMSTRONG FIND HIS PANTS?

(BUT FIRST, ANOTHER EPISODE OF DAVEY THE MACKEREL AND THE BAGMAKER!)

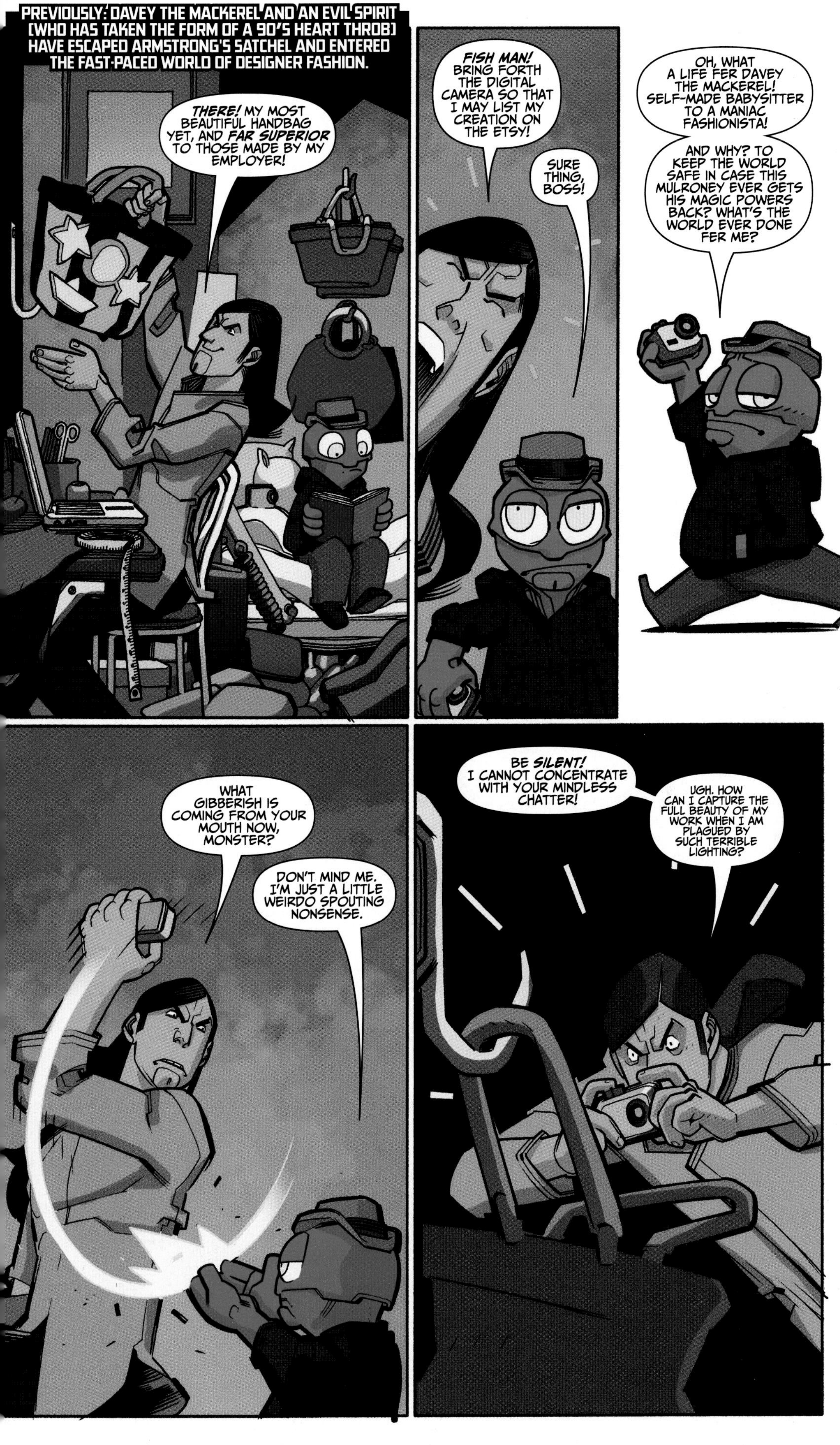
PREVIOUSLY: DAVEY THE MACKEREL AND AN EVIL SPIRIT [WHO HAS TAKEN THE FORM OF A 90'S HEART THROB] HAVE ESCAPED ARMSTRONG'S SATCHEL AND ENTERED THE FAST-PACED WORLD OF DESIGNER FASHION.
THERE! MY MOST BEAUTIFUL HANDBAG YET, AND FAR SUPERIOR TO THOSE MADE BY MY EMPLOYER!
FISH MAN! BRING FORTH THE DIGITAL CAMERA SO THAT I MAY LIST MY CREATION ON THE ETSY!
SURE THING, BOSS!
OH, WHAT A LIFE FER DAVEY THE MACKEREL! SELF-MADE BABYSITTER TO A MANIAC FASHIONISTA!
AND WHY? TO KEEP THE WORLD SAFE IN CASE THIS MULRONEY EVER GETS HIS MAGIC POWERS BACK? WHAT'S THE WORLD EVER DONE FER ME?
WHAT GIBBERISH IS COMING FROM YOUR MOUTH NOW, MONSTER?
DON'T MIND ME. I'M JUST A LITTLE WEIRDO SPOUTING NONSENSE.
BE SILENT! I CANNOT CONCENTRATE WITH YOUR MINDLESS CHATTER!
UGH. HOW CAN I CAPTURE THE FULL BEAUTY OF MY WORK WHEN I AM PLAGUED BY SUCH TERRIBLE LIGHTING?

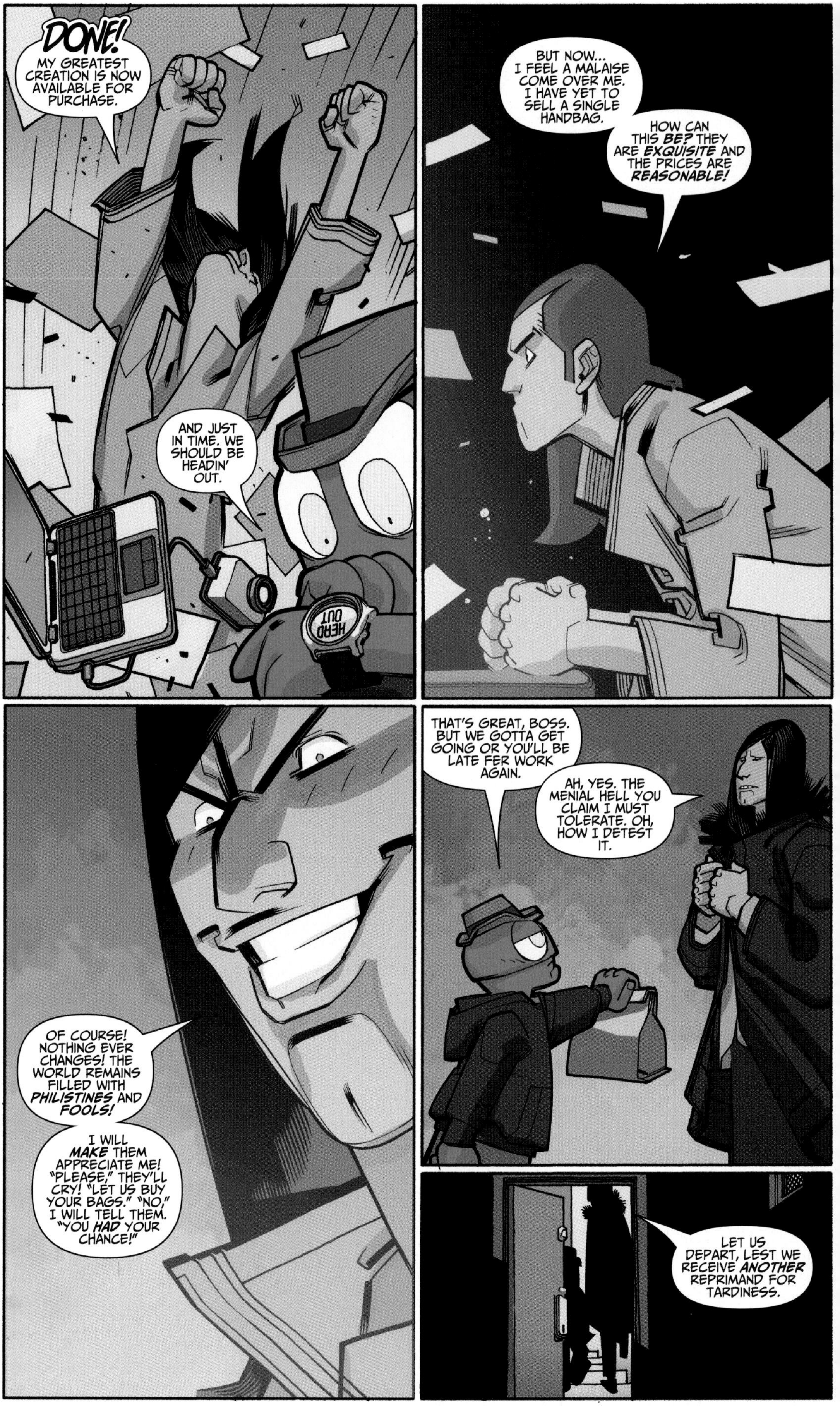
DONE!
MY GREATEST CREATION IS NOW AVAILABLE FOR PURCHASE.
AND JUST IN TIME. WE SHOULD BE HEADIN' OUT.
HEAD OUT
BUT NOW... I FEEL A MALAISE COME OVER ME. I HAVE YET TO SELL A SINGLE HANDBAG.
HOW CAN THIS **BE?** THEY ARE **EXQUISITE** AND THE PRICES ARE **REASONABLE!**
OF COURSE! NOTHING EVER CHANGES! THE WORLD REMAINS FILLED WITH **PHILISTINES** AND **FOOLS!**
I WILL **MAKE** THEM APPRECIATE ME! "PLEASE," THEY'LL CRY! "LET US BUY YOUR BAGS." "NO," I WILL TELL THEM. "YOU **HAD** YOUR CHANCE!"
THAT'S GREAT, BOSS. BUT WE GOTTA GET GOING OR YOU'LL BE LATE FER WORK AGAIN.
AH, YES. THE MENIAL HELL YOU CLAIM I MUST TOLERATE. OH, HOW I DETEST IT.
LET US DEPART, LEST WE RECEIVE **ANOTHER** REPRIMAND FOR TARDINESS.

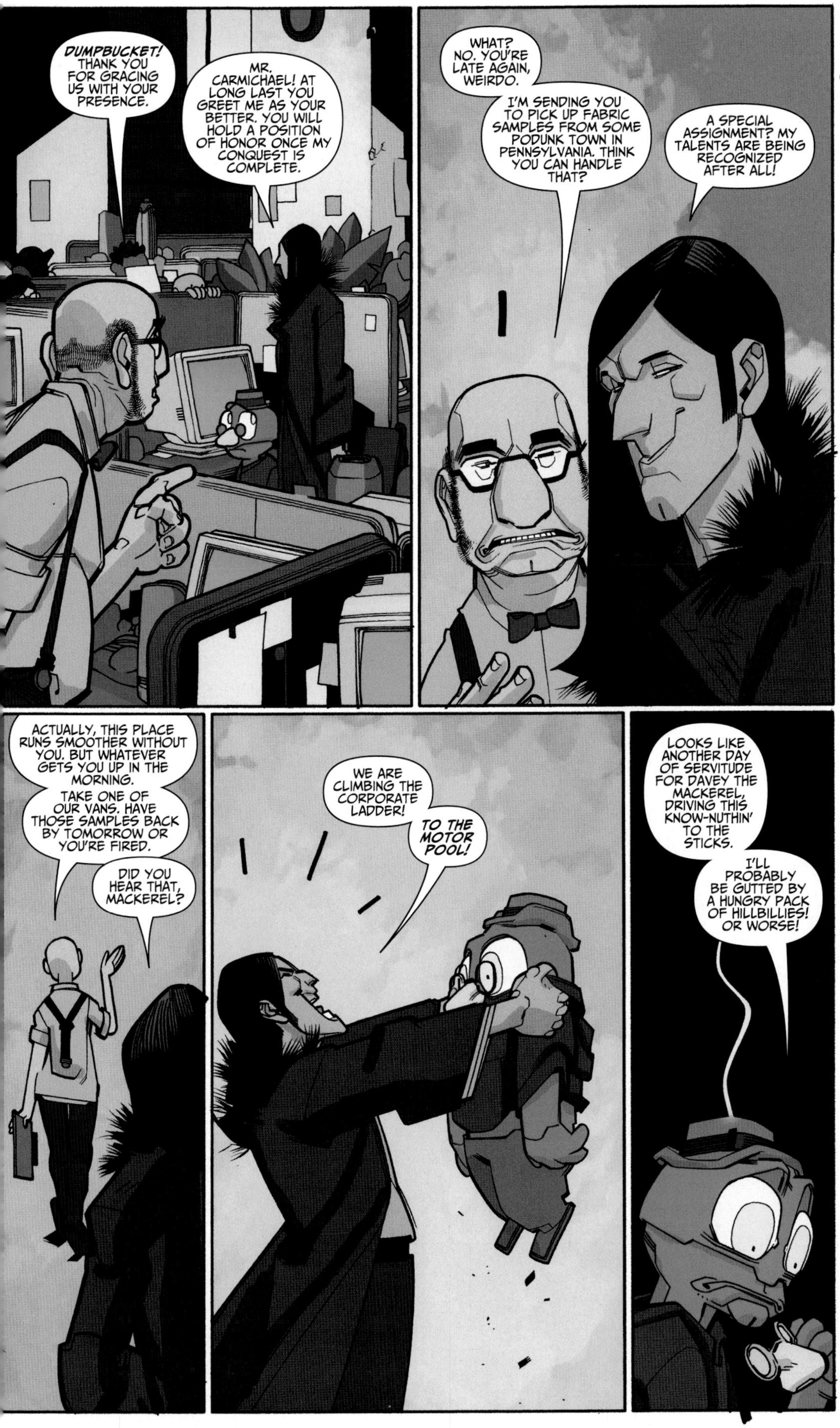
DUMPBUCKET! THANK YOU FOR GRACING US WITH YOUR PRESENCE.
MR. CARMICHAEL! AT LONG LAST YOU GREET ME AS YOUR BETTER. YOU WILL HOLD A POSITION OF HONOR ONCE MY CONQUEST IS COMPLETE.
WHAT? NO. YOU'RE LATE AGAIN, WEIRDO.
I'M SENDING YOU TO PICK UP FABRIC SAMPLES FROM SOME PODUNK TOWN IN PENNSYLVANIA. THINK YOU CAN HANDLE THAT?
A SPECIAL ASSIGNMENT? MY TALENTS ARE BEING RECOGNIZED AFTER ALL!
ACTUALLY, THIS PLACE RUNS SMOOTHER WITHOUT YOU. BUT WHATEVER GETS YOU UP IN THE MORNING.
TAKE ONE OF OUR VANS. HAVE THOSE SAMPLES BACK BY TOMORROW OR YOU'RE FIRED.
DID YOU HEAR THAT, MACKEREL?
WE ARE CLIMBING THE CORPORATE LADDER!
TO THE MOTOR POOL!
LOOKS LIKE ANOTHER DAY OF SERVITUDE FOR DAVEY THE MACKEREL, DRIVING THIS KNOW-NUTHIN' TO THE STICKS.
I'LL PROBABLY BE GUTTED BY A HUNGRY PACK OF HILLBILLIES! OR WORSE!

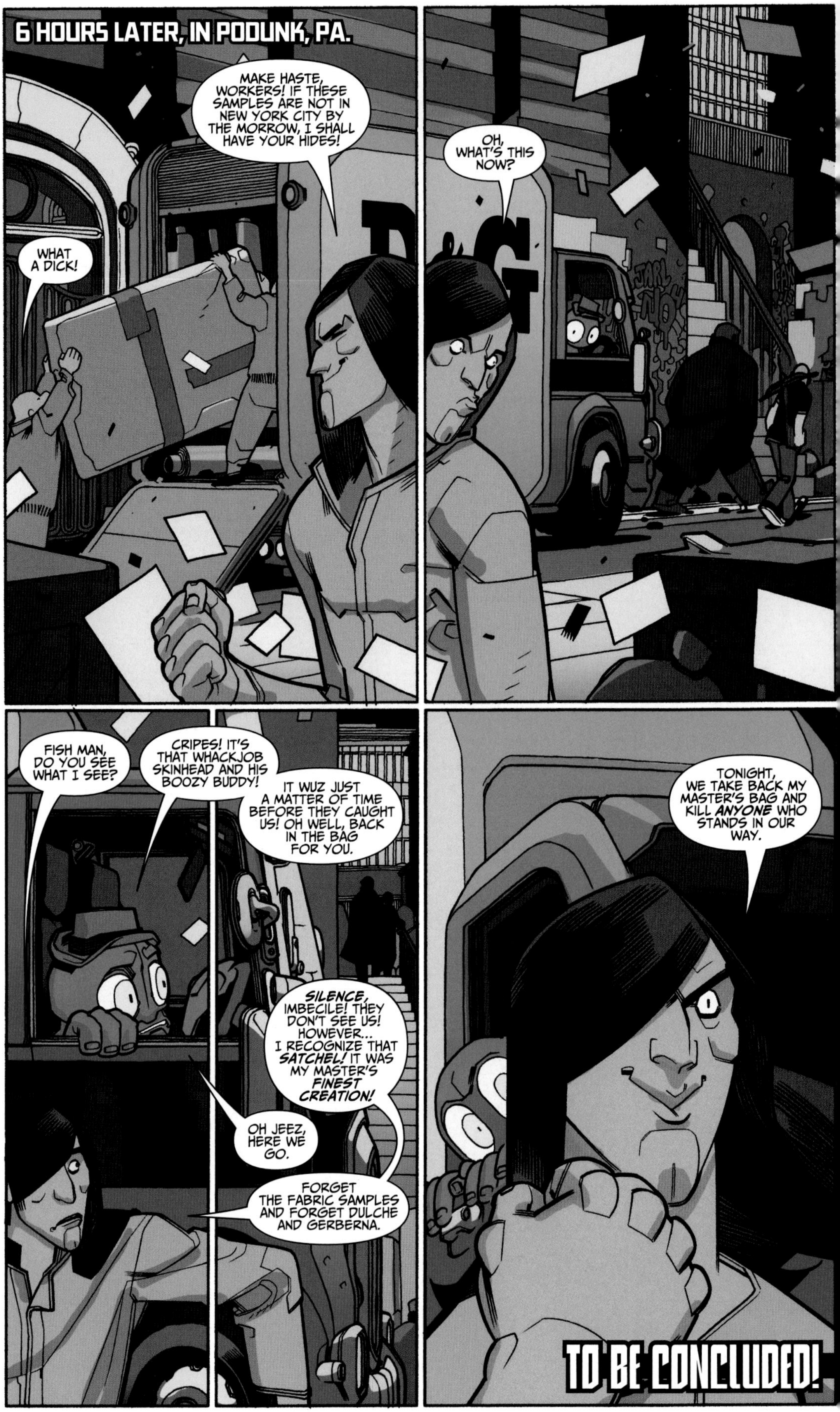
6 HOURS LATER, IN PODUNK, PA.
MAKE HASTE, WORKERS! IF THESE SAMPLES ARE NOT IN NEW YORK CITY BY THE MORROW, I SHALL HAVE YOUR HIDES!
WHAT A DICK!
OH, WHAT'S THIS NOW?
FISH MAN, DO YOU SEE WHAT I SEE?
CRIPES! IT'S THAT WHACKJOB SKINHEAD AND HIS BOOZY BUDDY!
IT WUZ JUST A MATTER OF TIME BEFORE THEY CAUGHT US! OH WELL, BACK IN THE BAG FOR YOU.
SILENCE, IMBECILE! THEY DON'T SEE US! HOWEVER... I RECOGNIZE THAT SATCHEL! IT WAS MY MASTER'S FINEST CREATION!
OH JEEZ, HERE WE GO.
FORGET THE FABRIC SAMPLES AND FORGET DULCHE AND GERBERNA.
TONIGHT, WE TAKE BACK MY MASTER'S BAG AND KILL ANYONE WHO STANDS IN OUR WAY.
TO BE CONCLUDED!

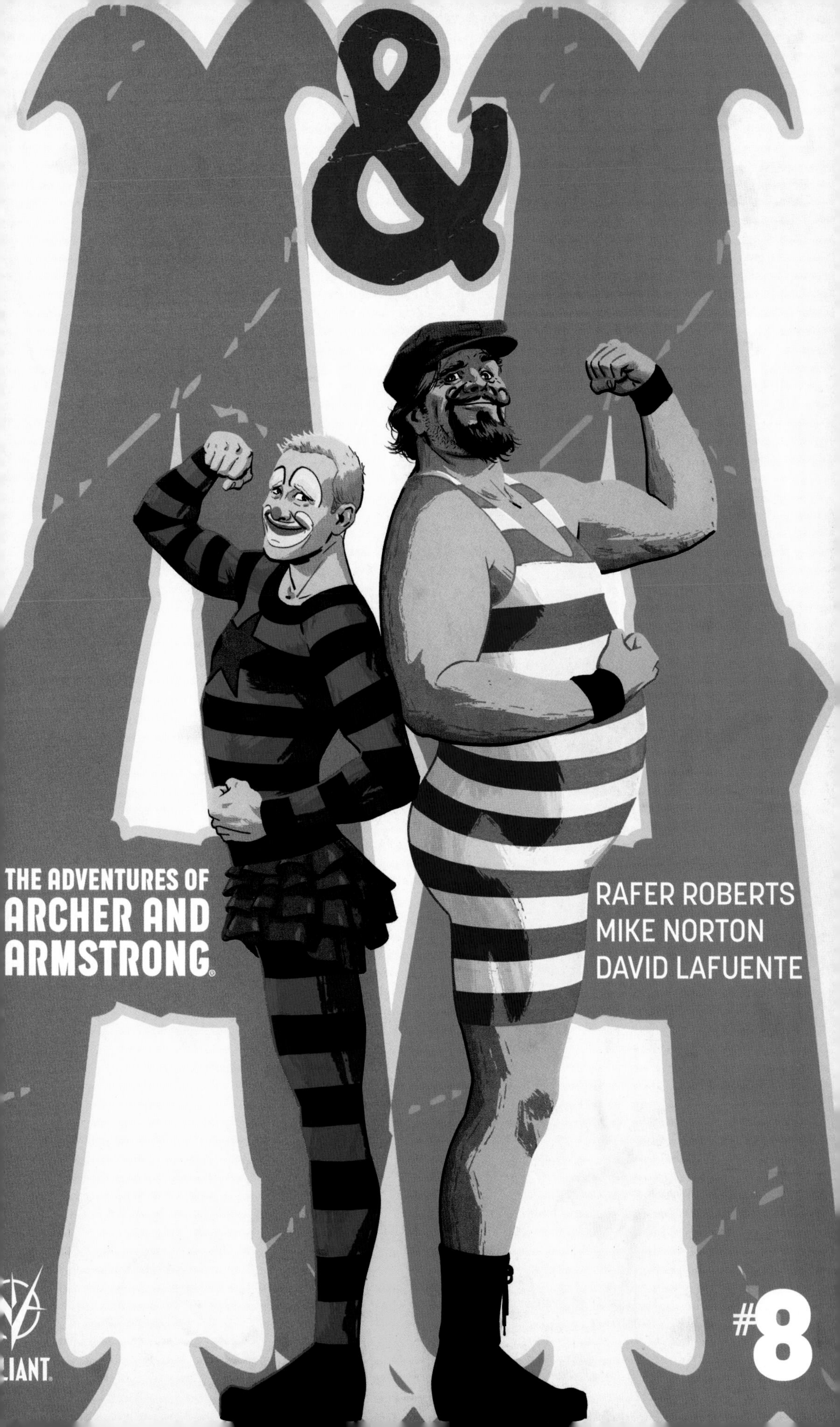

&
THE ADVENTURES OF
ARCHER AND
ARMSTRONG®
RAFER ROBERTS
MIKE NORTON
DAVID LAFUENTE
#8

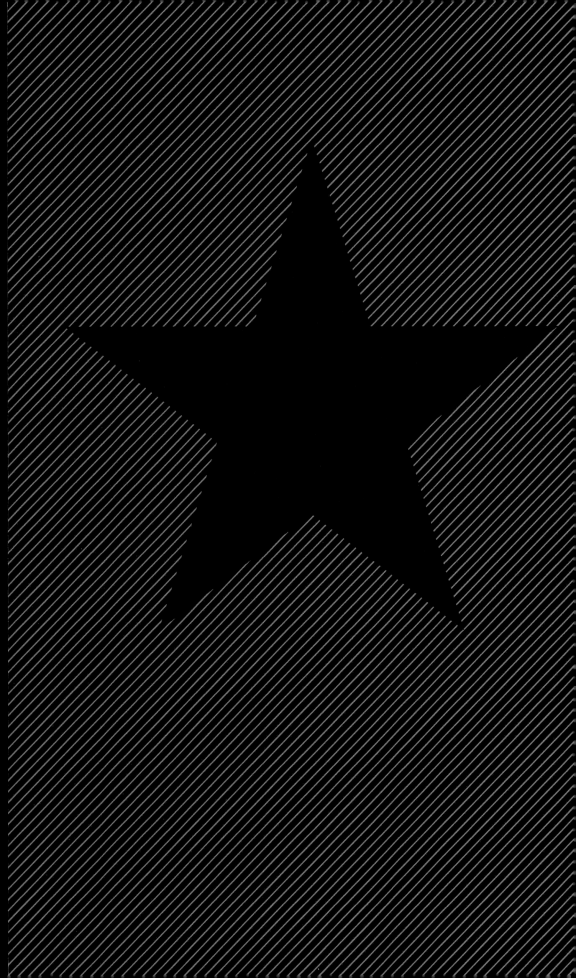

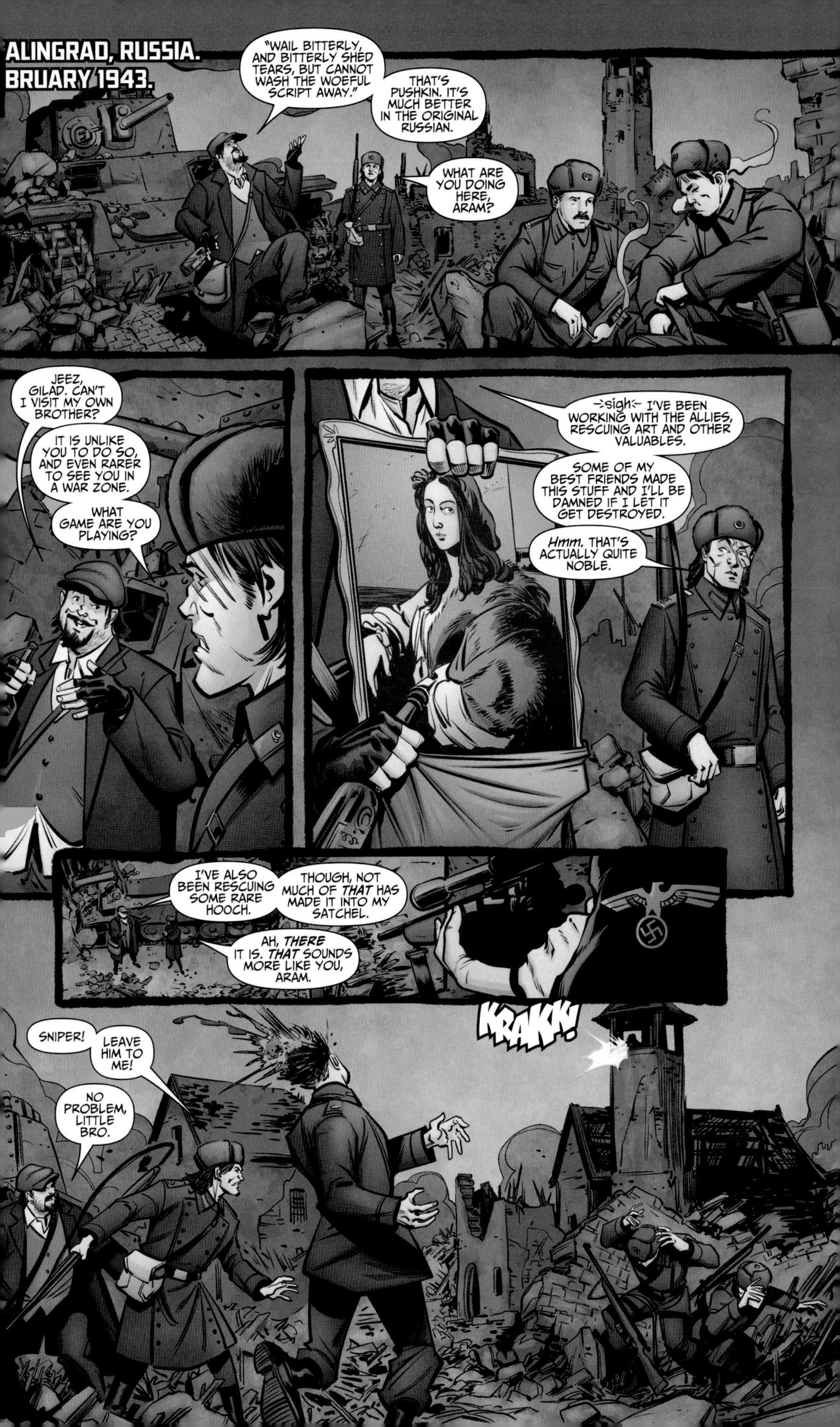
ALINGRAD, RUSSIA.
BRUARY 1943.
"WAIL BITTERLY, AND BITTERLY SHED TEARS, BUT CANNOT WASH THE WOEFUL SCRIPT AWAY."
THAT'S PUSHKIN. IT'S MUCH BETTER IN THE ORIGINAL RUSSIAN.
WHAT ARE YOU DOING HERE, ARAM?
JEEZ, GILAD. CAN'T I VISIT MY OWN BROTHER?
IT IS UNLIKE YOU TO DO SO, AND EVEN RARER TO SEE YOU IN A WAR ZONE.
WHAT GAME ARE YOU PLAYING?
-sigh- I'VE BEEN WORKING WITH THE ALLIES, RESCUING ART AND OTHER VALUABLES.
SOME OF MY BEST FRIENDS MADE THIS STUFF AND I'LL BE DAMNED IF I LET IT GET DESTROYED.
Hmm. THAT'S ACTUALLY QUITE NOBLE.
I'VE ALSO BEEN RESCUING SOME RARE HOOCH.
THOUGH, NOT MUCH OF *THAT* HAS MADE IT INTO MY SATCHEL.
AH, *THERE* IT IS. *THAT* SOUNDS MORE LIKE YOU, ARAM.
KRAKK!
SNIPER!
LEAVE HIM TO ME!
NO PROBLEM, LITTLE BRO.

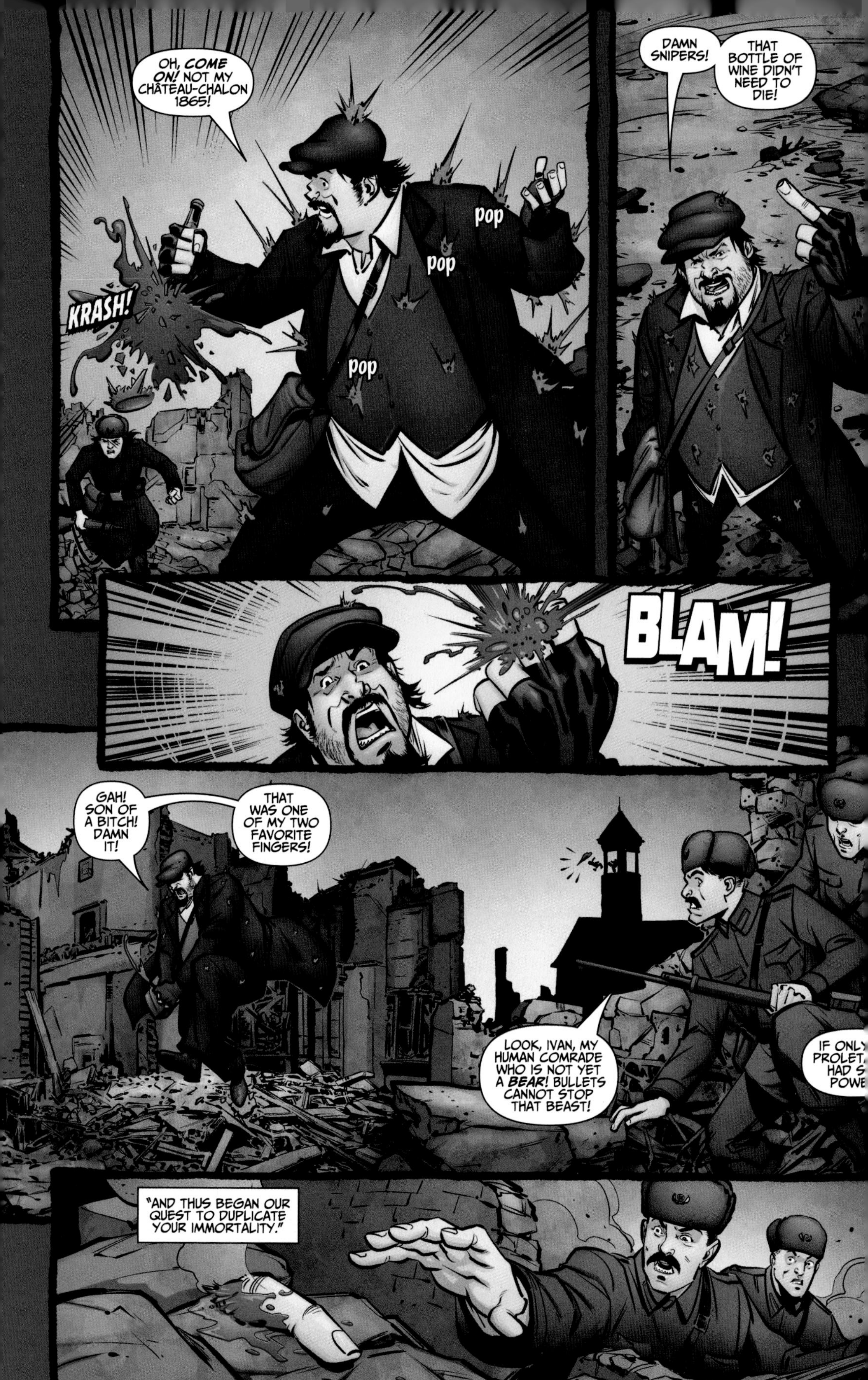

OH, COME ON! NOT MY CHÂTEAU-CHALON 1865!
KRASH!
pop
pop
pop
DAMN SNIPERS!
THAT BOTTLE OF WINE DIDN'T NEED TO DIE!
BLAM!
GAH! SON OF A BITCH! DAMN IT!
THAT WAS ONE OF MY TWO FAVORITE FINGERS!
LOOK, IVAN, MY HUMAN COMRADE WHO IS NOT YET A BEAR! BULLETS CANNOT STOP THAT BEAST!
"AND THUS BEGAN OUR QUEST TO DUPLICATE YOUR IMMORTALITY."

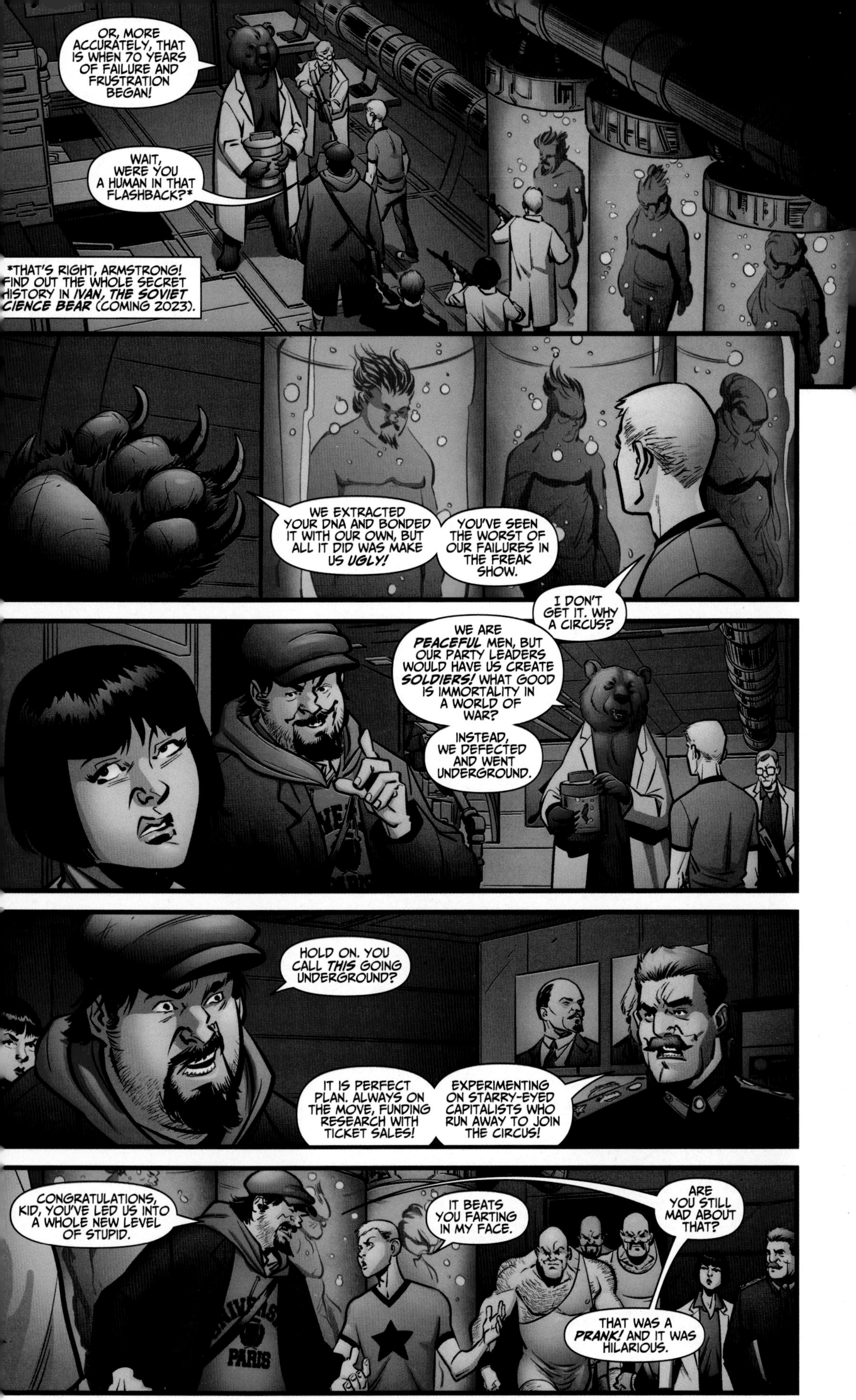
OR, MORE ACCURATELY, THAT IS WHEN 70 YEARS OF FAILURE AND FRUSTRATION BEGAN!
WAIT, WERE YOU A HUMAN IN THAT FLASHBACK?*
*THAT'S RIGHT, ARMSTRONG! FIND OUT THE WHOLE SECRET HISTORY IN IVAN, THE SOVIET SCIENCE BEAR (COMING 2023).
WE EXTRACTED YOUR DNA AND BONDED IT WITH OUR OWN, BUT ALL IT DID WAS MAKE US UGLY!
YOU'VE SEEN THE WORST OF OUR FAILURES IN THE FREAK SHOW.
I DON'T GET IT. WHY A CIRCUS?
WE ARE PEACEFUL MEN, BUT OUR PARTY LEADERS WOULD HAVE US CREATE SOLDIERS! WHAT GOOD IS IMMORTALITY IN A WORLD OF WAR?
INSTEAD, WE DEFECTED AND WENT UNDERGROUND.
HOLD ON. YOU CALL THIS GOING UNDERGROUND?
IT IS PERFECT PLAN. ALWAYS ON THE MOVE, FUNDING RESEARCH WITH TICKET SALES!
EXPERIMENTING ON STARRY-EYED CAPITALISTS WHO RUN AWAY TO JOIN THE CIRCUS!
CONGRATULATIONS, KID, YOU'VE LED US INTO A WHOLE NEW LEVEL OF STUPID.
IT BEATS YOU FARTING IN MY FACE.
ARE YOU STILL MAD ABOUT THAT?
THAT WAS A PRANK! AND IT WAS HILARIOUS.

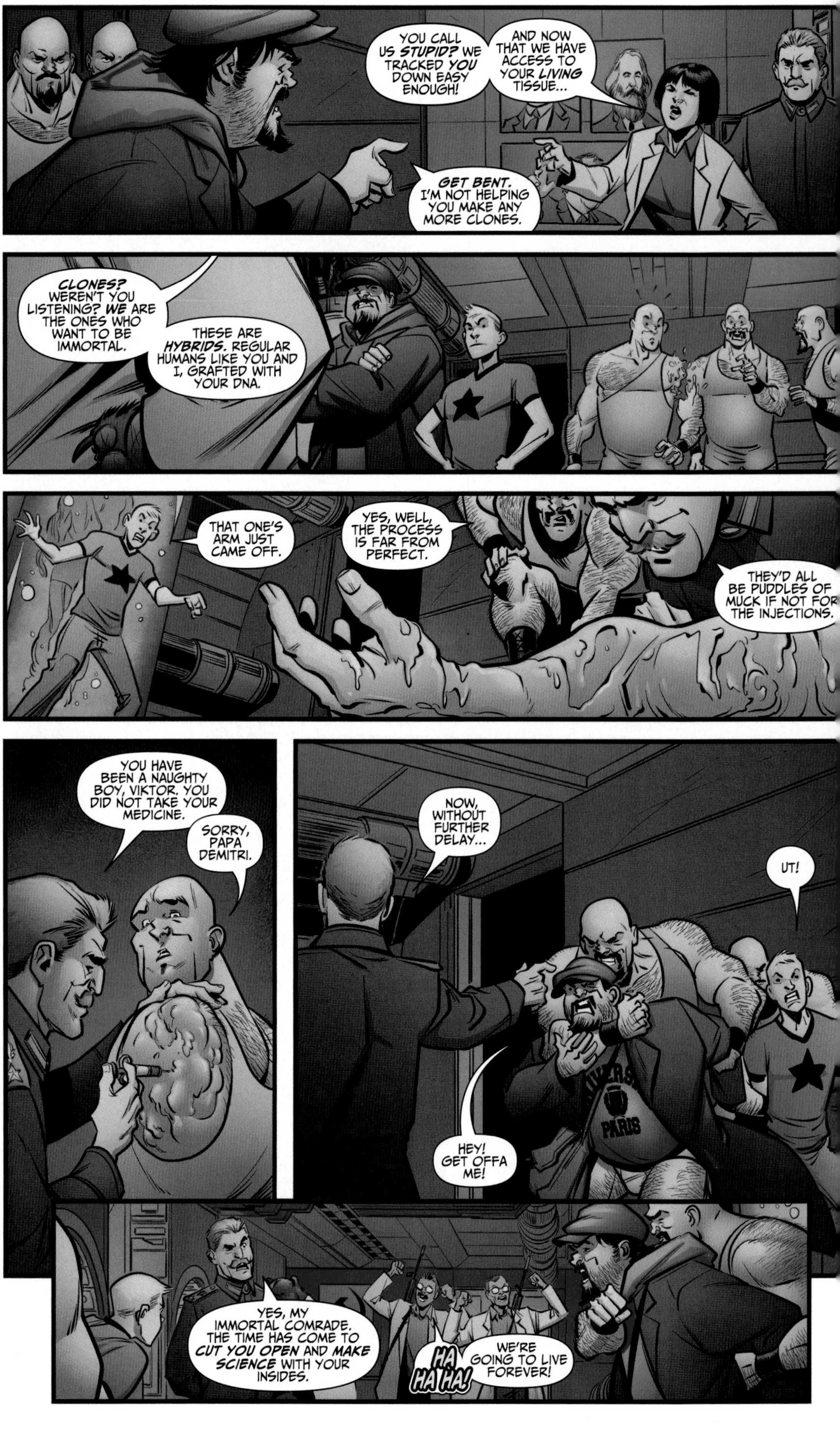
YOU CALL US STUPID? WE TRACKED YOU DOWN EASY ENOUGH!
AND NOW THAT WE HAVE ACCESS TO YOUR LIVING TISSUE...
GET BENT. I'M NOT HELPING YOU MAKE ANY MORE CLONES.
CLONES? WEREN'T YOU LISTENING? WE ARE THE ONES WHO WANT TO BE IMMORTAL.
THESE ARE HYBRIDS. REGULAR HUMANS LIKE YOU AND I, GRAFTED WITH YOUR DNA.
THAT ONE'S ARM JUST CAME OFF.
YES, WELL, THE PROCESS IS FAR FROM PERFECT.
THEY'D ALL BE PUDDLES OF MUCK IF NOT FOR THE INJECTIONS.
YOU HAVE BEEN A NAUGHTY BOY, VIKTOR. YOU DID NOT TAKE YOUR MEDICINE.
SORRY, PAPA DEMITRI.
NOW, WITHOUT FURTHER DELAY...
UT!
HEY! GET OFFA ME!
PARIS
YES, MY IMMORTAL COMRADE. THE TIME HAS COME TO CUT YOU OPEN AND MAKE SCIENCE WITH YOUR INSIDES.
HA HA HA!
WE'RE GOING TO LIVE FOREVER!

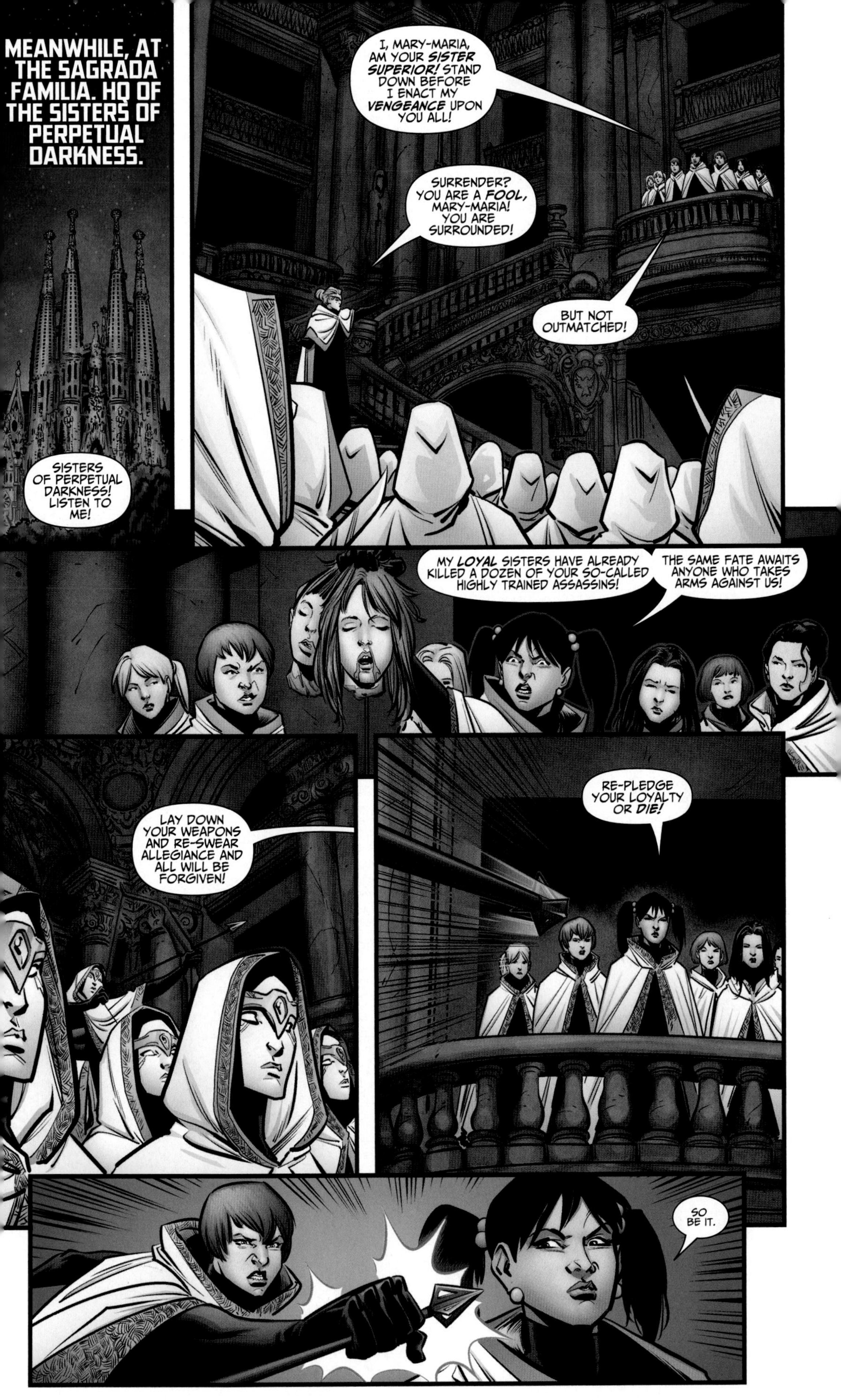
MEANWHILE, AT THE SAGRADA FAMILIA. HQ OF THE SISTERS OF PERPETUAL DARKNESS.
SISTERS OF PERPETUAL DARKNESS! LISTEN TO ME!
I, MARY-MARIA, AM YOUR SISTER SUPERIOR! STAND DOWN BEFORE I ENACT MY VENGEANCE UPON YOU ALL!
SURRENDER? YOU ARE A FOOL, MARY-MARIA! YOU ARE SURROUNDED!
BUT NOT OUTMATCHED!
MY LOYAL SISTERS HAVE ALREADY KILLED A DOZEN OF YOUR SO-CALLED HIGHLY TRAINED ASSASSINS!
THE SAME FATE AWAITS ANYONE WHO TAKES ARMS AGAINST US!
LAY DOWN YOUR WEAPONS AND RE-SWEAR ALLEGIANCE AND ALL WILL BE FORGIVEN!
RE-PLEDGE YOUR LOYALTY OR DIE!
SO BE IT.

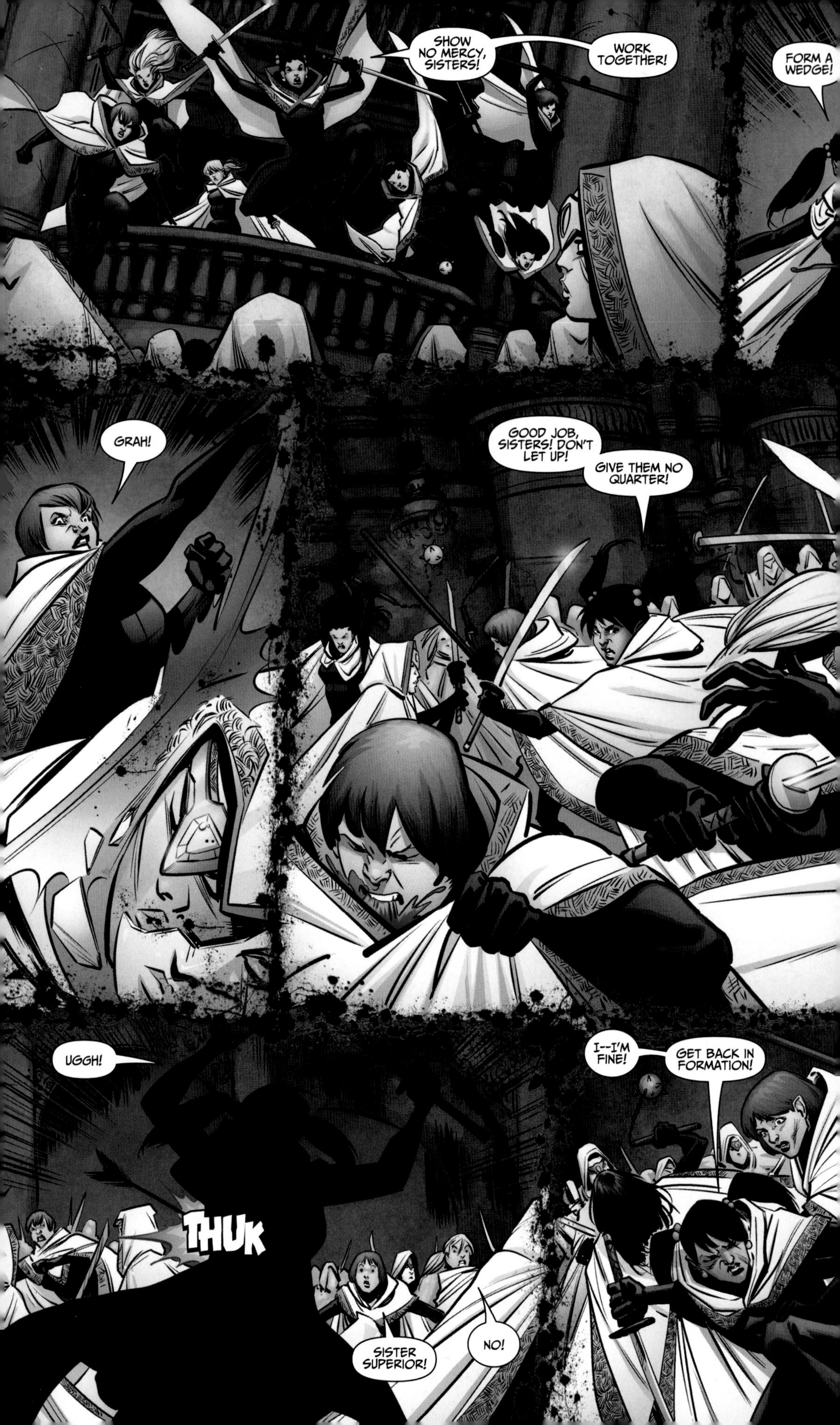
SHOW NO MERCY, SISTERS!
WORK TOGETHER!
FORM A WEDGE!
GRAH!
GOOD JOB, SISTERS! DON'T LET UP!
GIVE THEM NO QUARTER!
UGGH!
THUK
I--I'M FINE!
GET BACK IN FORMATION!
SISTER SUPERIOR!
NO!

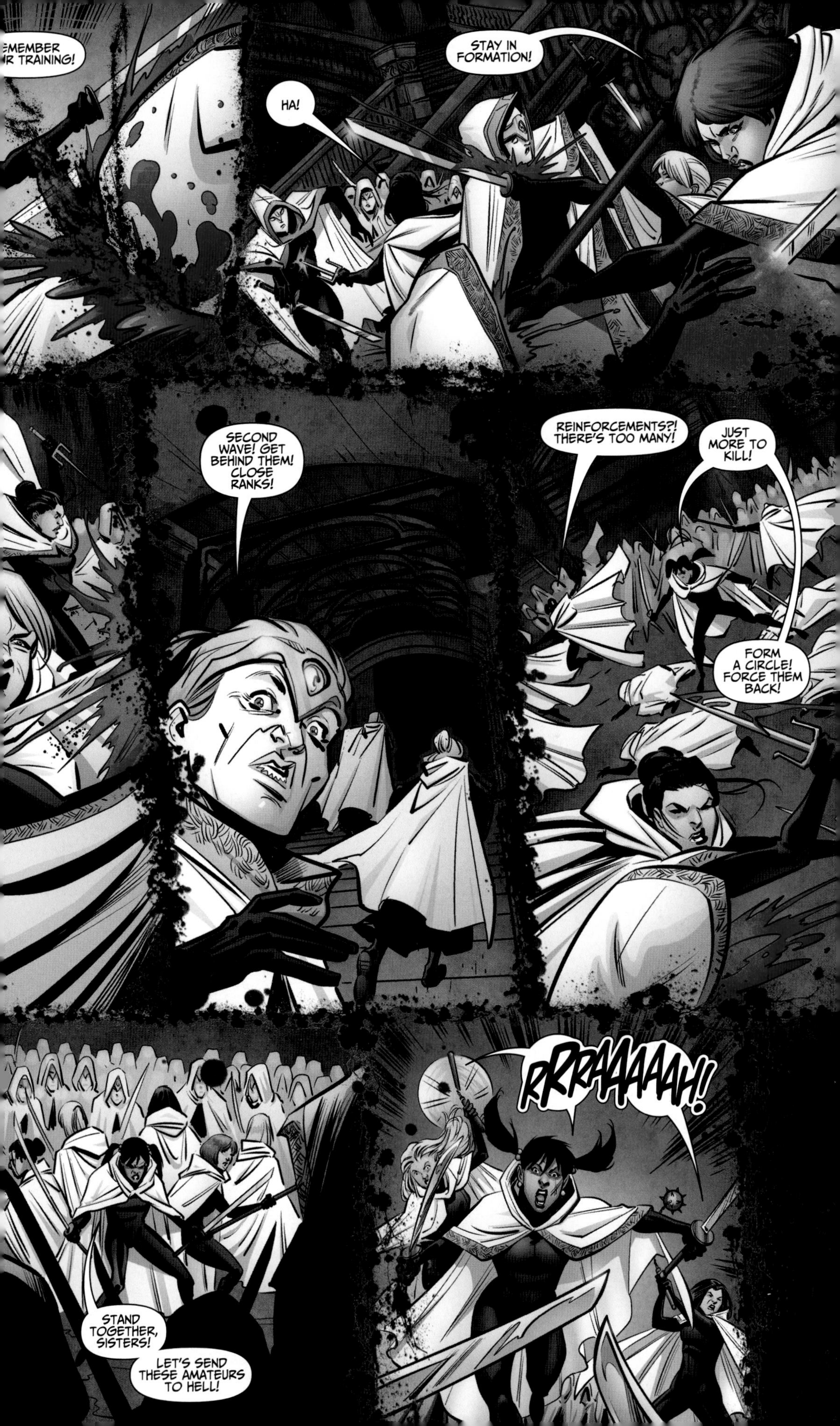
EMEMBER
R TRAINING!
STAY IN FORMATION!
HA!
SECOND WAVE! GET BEHIND THEM! CLOSE RANKS!
REINFORCEMENTS?! THERE'S TOO MANY!
JUST MORE TO KILL!
FORM A CIRCLE! FORCE THEM BACK!
RRRAAAAAAH!
STAND TOGETHER, SISTERS!
LET'S SEND THESE AMATEURS TO HELL!

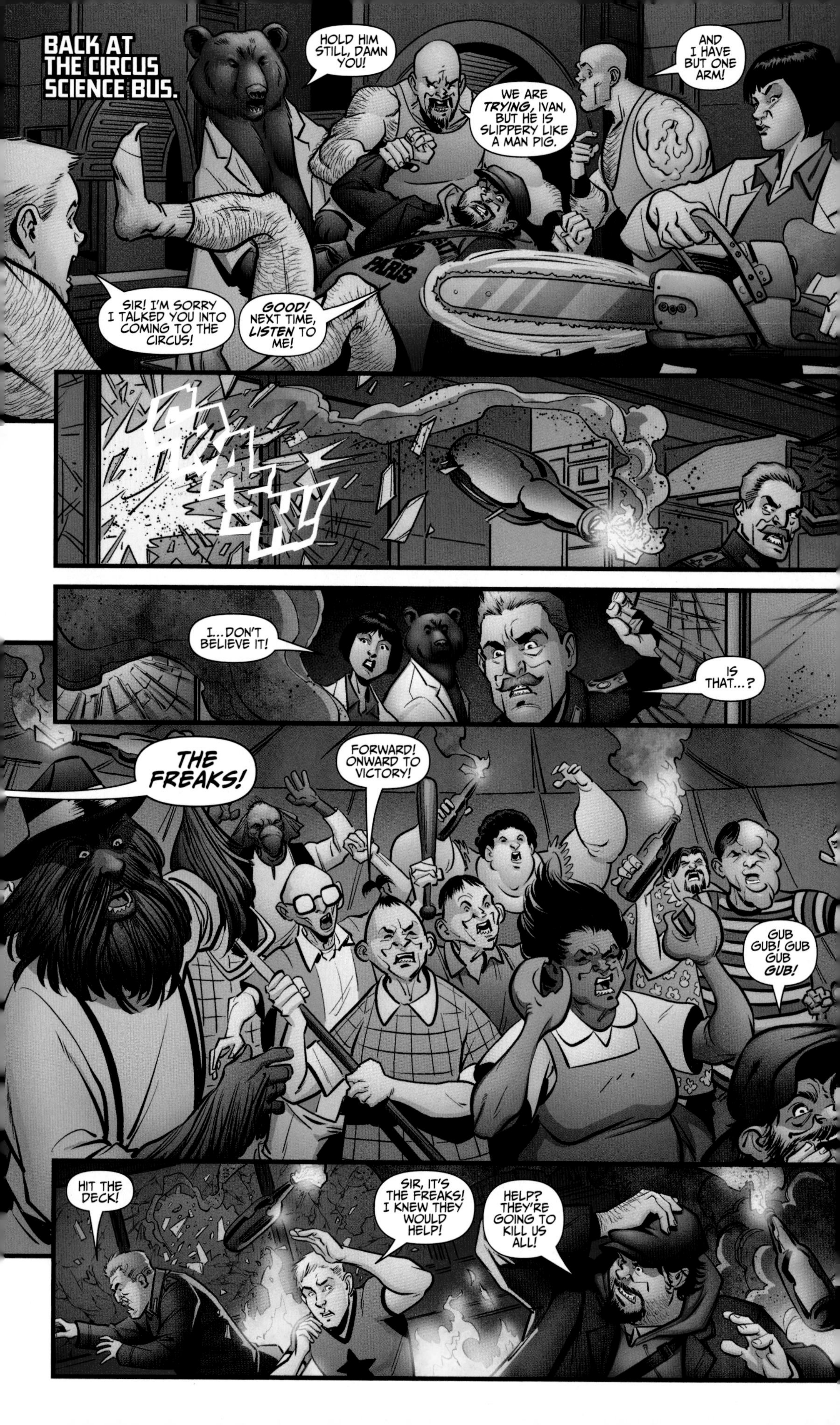
BACK AT THE CIRCUS SCIENCE BUS.
HOLD HIM STILL, DAMN YOU!
WE ARE *TRYING*, IVAN, BUT HE IS SLIPPERY LIKE A MAN PIG.
AND I HAVE BUT ONE ARM!
SIR! I'M SORRY I TALKED YOU INTO COMING TO THE CIRCUS!
GOOD! NEXT TIME, *LISTEN* TO ME!
I...DON'T BELIEVE IT!
IS THAT...?
THE FREAKS!
FORWARD! ONWARD TO VICTORY!
GUB GUB! GUB GUB *GUB!*
HIT THE DECK!
SIR, IT'S THE FREAKS! I KNEW THEY WOULD HELP!
HELP? THEY'RE GOING TO KILL US ALL!

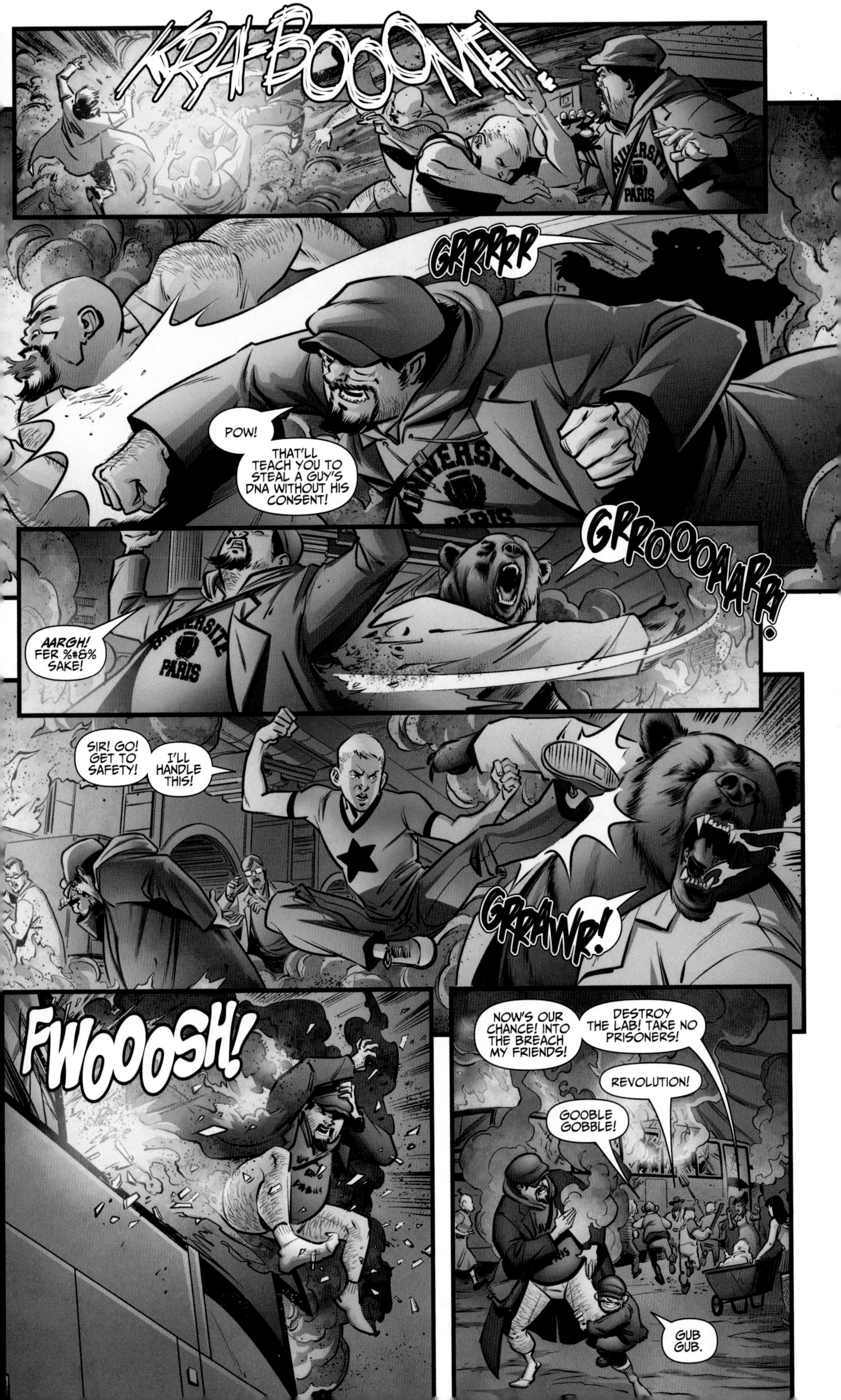
KRA-BOOOM!
GRRRRR
POW!
THAT'LL TEACH YOU TO STEAL A GUY'S DNA WITHOUT HIS CONSENT!
GRROOOAARR!
AARGH! FER %#&% SAKE!
SIR! GO! GET TO SAFETY!
I'LL HANDLE THIS!
GRRAWR!
FWOOOSH!
NOW'S OUR CHANCE! INTO THE BREACH MY FRIENDS!
DESTROY THE LAB! TAKE NO PRISONERS!
REVOLUTION!
GOOBLE GOBBLE!
GUB GUB.

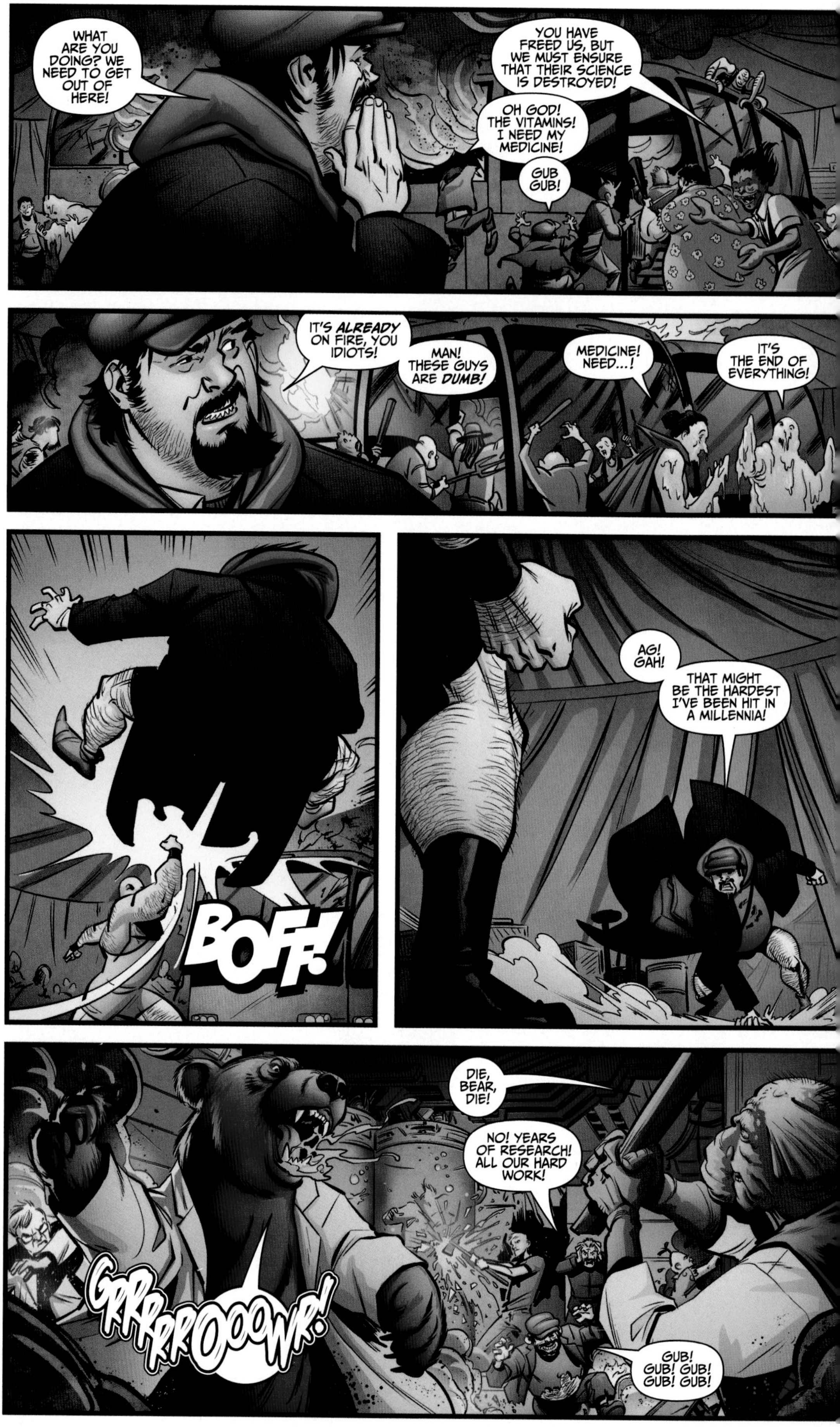
WHAT ARE YOU DOING? WE NEED TO GET OUT OF HERE!
YOU HAVE FREED US, BUT WE MUST ENSURE THAT THEIR SCIENCE IS DESTROYED!
OH GOD! THE VITAMINS! I NEED MY MEDICINE!
GUB GUB!
IT'S ALREADY ON FIRE, YOU IDIOTS!
MAN! THESE GUYS ARE DUMB!
MEDICINE! NEED...!
IT'S THE END OF EVERYTHING!
BOFF!
AG! GAH!
THAT MIGHT BE THE HARDEST I'VE BEEN HIT IN A MILLENNIA!
DIE, BEAR, DIE!
NO! YEARS OF RESEARCH! ALL OUR HARD WORK!
GRRRRROOOOWR!
GUB! GUB! GUB! GUB! GUB!

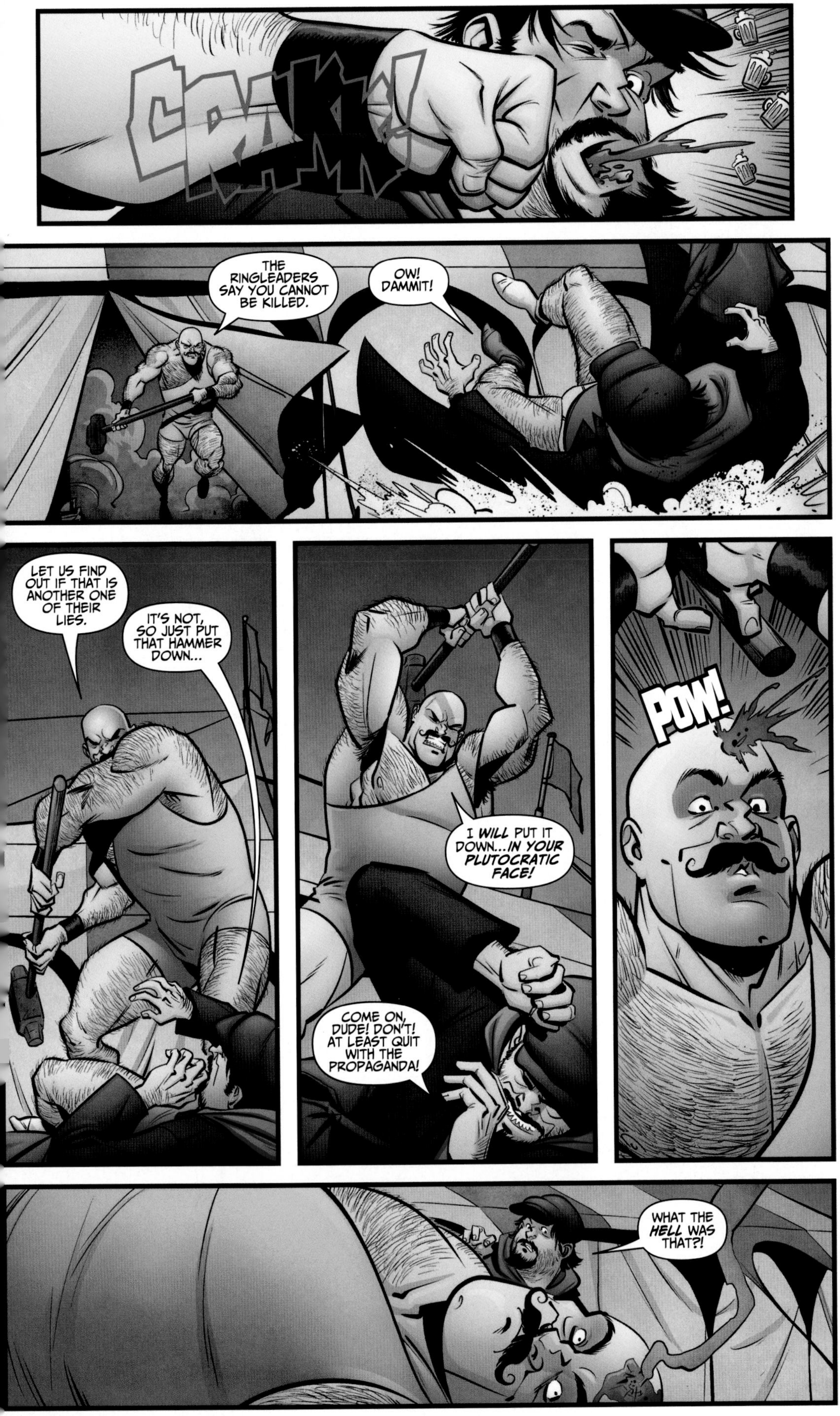

CRAKK!
THE RINGLEADERS SAY YOU CANNOT BE KILLED.
OW! DAMMIT!
LET US FIND OUT IF THAT IS ANOTHER ONE OF THEIR LIES.
IT'S NOT, SO JUST PUT THAT HAMMER DOWN...
I *WILL* PUT IT DOWN...*IN YOUR PLUTOCRATIC FACE!*
COME ON, DUDE! DON'T! AT LEAST QUIT WITH THE PROPAGANDA!
POW!
WHAT THE *HELL* WAS THAT?!

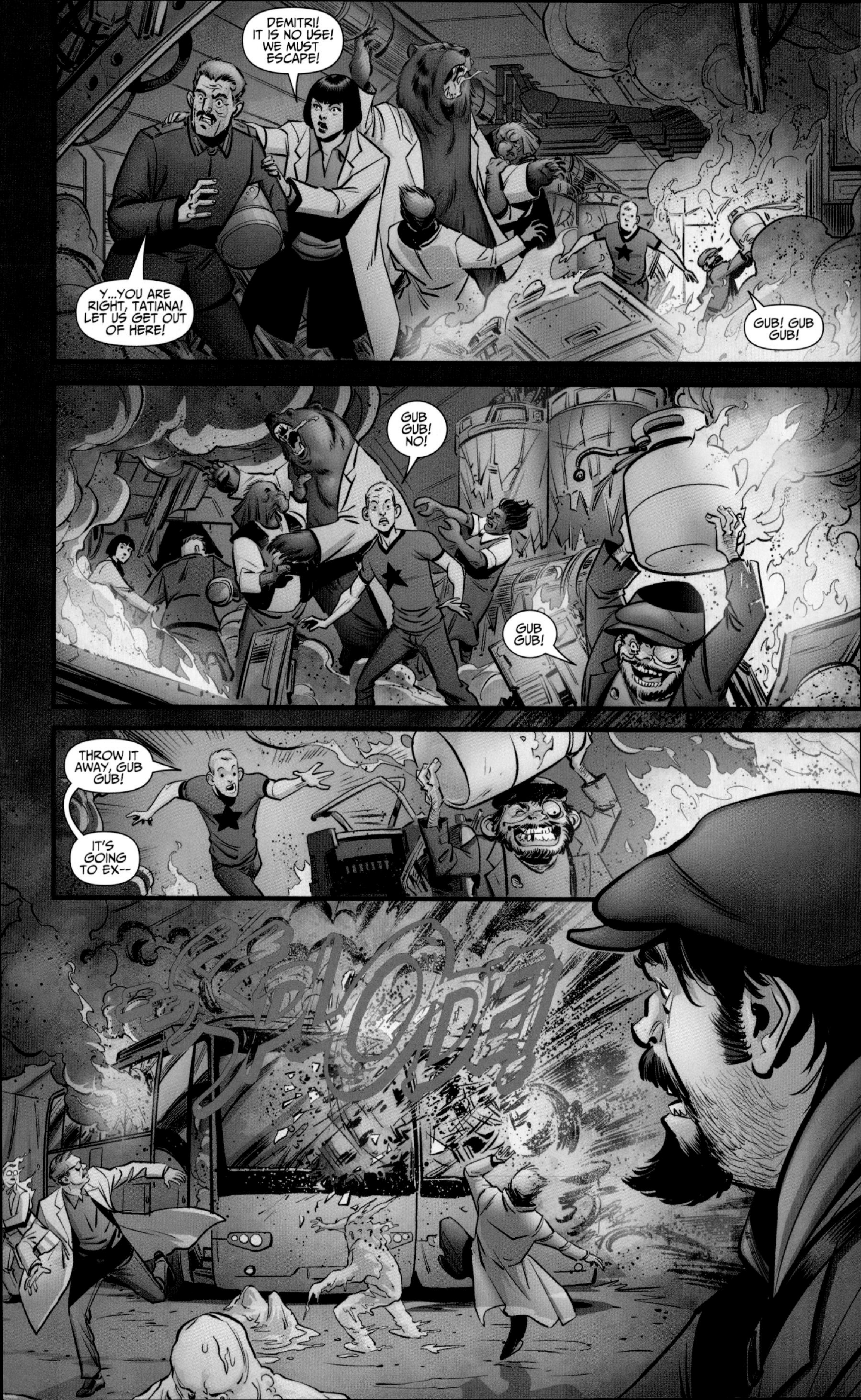
DEMITRI! IT IS NO USE! WE MUST ESCAPE!
Y...YOU ARE RIGHT, TATIANA! LET US GET OUT OF HERE!
GUB! GUB GUB!
GUB GUB! NO!
GUB GUB!
THROW IT AWAY, GUB GUB!
IT'S GOING TO EX--

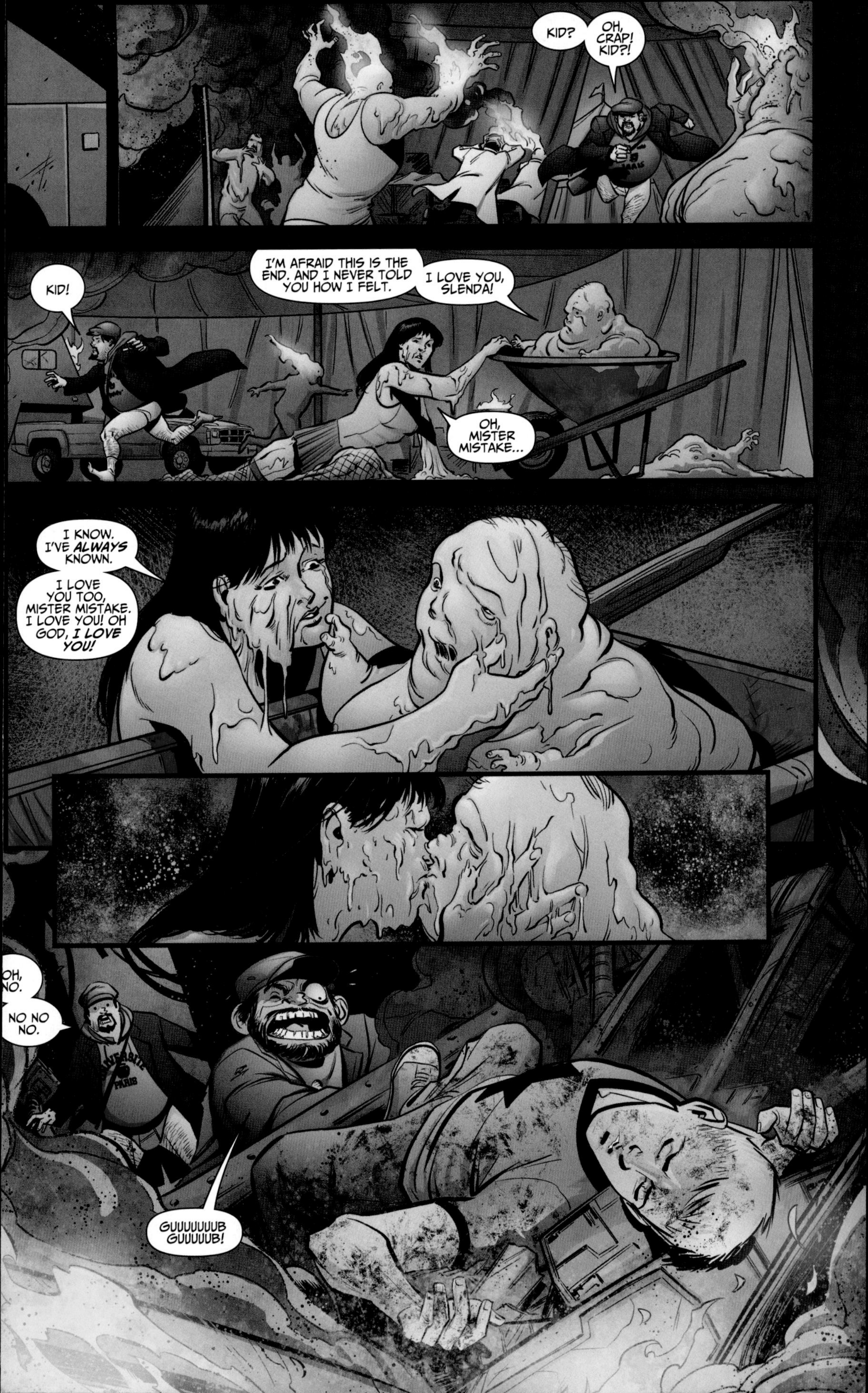
KID?
OH, CRAP! KID?!
KID!
I'M AFRAID THIS IS THE END. AND I NEVER TOLD YOU HOW I FELT.
I LOVE YOU, SLENDA!
OH, MISTER MISTAKE...
I KNOW. I'VE ALWAYS KNOWN.
I LOVE YOU TOO, MISTER MISTAKE. I LOVE YOU! OH GOD, I LOVE YOU!
OH, NO.
NO NO NO.
GUUUUUUUB GUUUUUB!

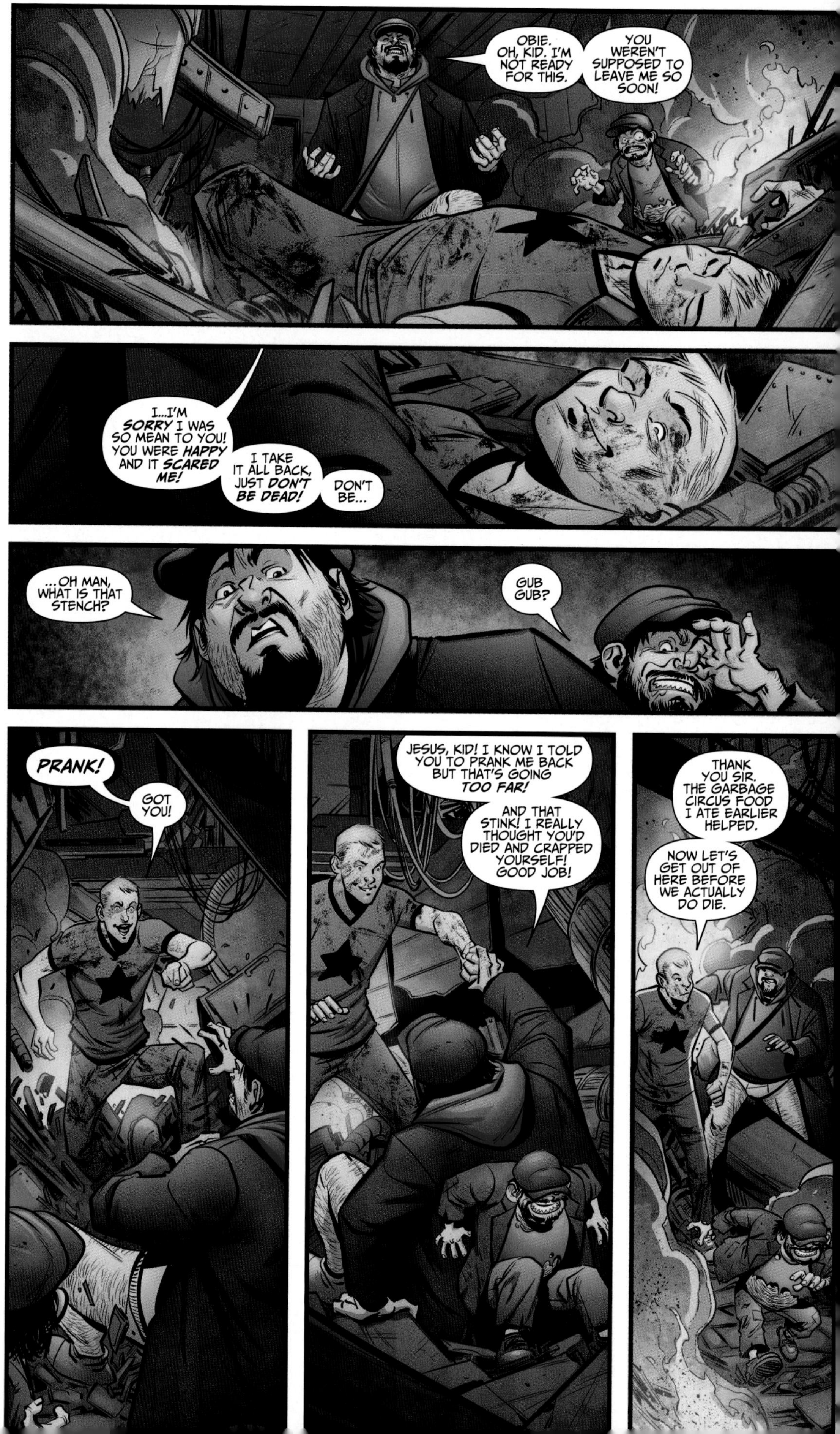
OBIE. OH, KID. I'M NOT READY FOR THIS.
YOU WEREN'T SUPPOSED TO LEAVE ME SO SOON!
I...I'M SORRY I WAS SO MEAN TO YOU! YOU WERE HAPPY AND IT SCARED ME!
I TAKE IT ALL BACK, JUST DON'T BE DEAD!
DON'T BE...
...OH MAN, WHAT IS THAT STENCH?
GUB GUB?
PRANK!
GOT YOU!
JESUS, KID! I KNOW I TOLD YOU TO PRANK ME BACK BUT THAT'S GOING TOO FAR!
AND THAT STINK! I REALLY THOUGHT YOU'D DIED AND CRAPPED YOURSELF! GOOD JOB!
THANK YOU SIR. THE GARBAGE CIRCUS FOOD I ATE EARLIER HELPED.
NOW LET'S GET OUT OF HERE BEFORE WE ACTUALLY DO DIE.

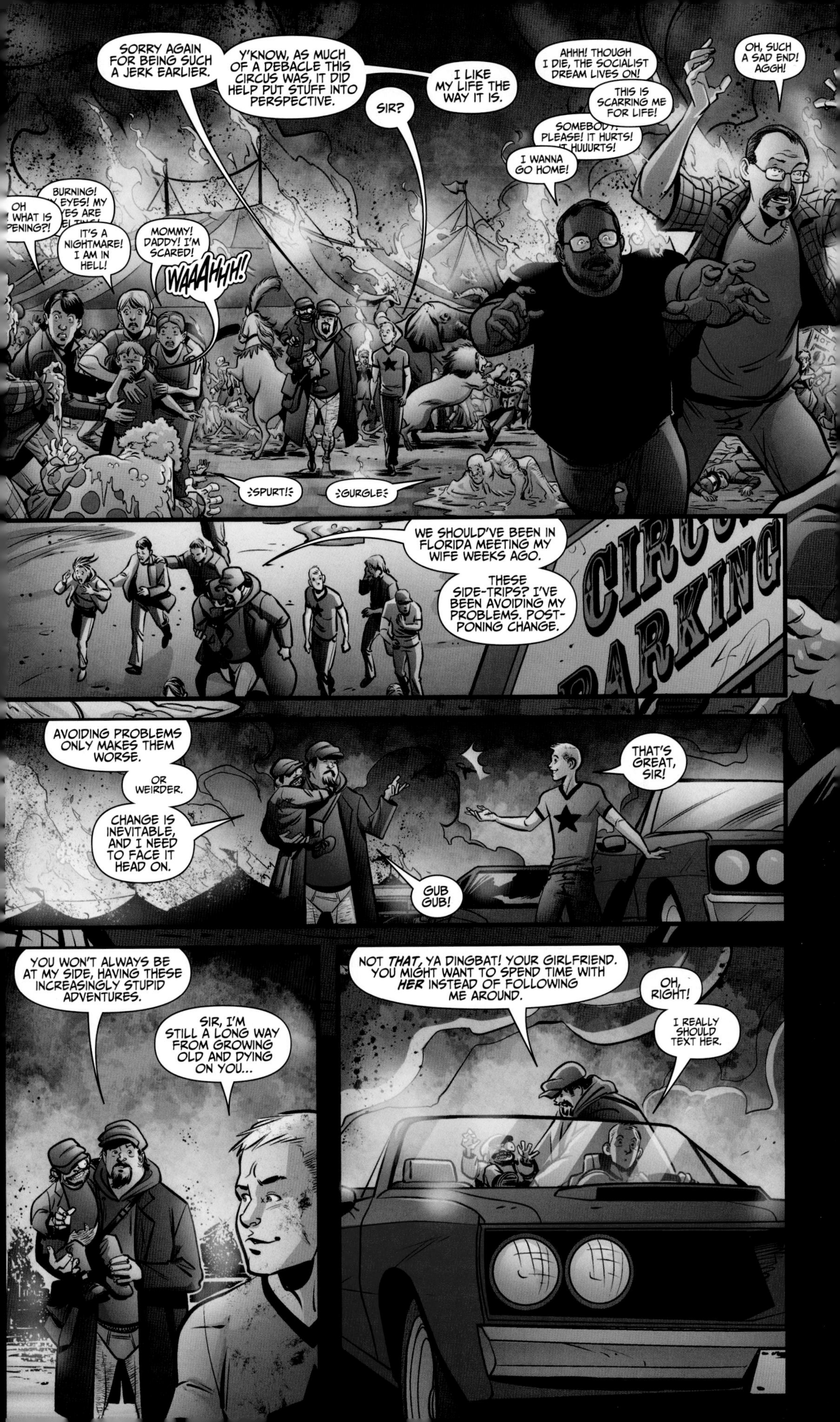
SORRY AGAIN FOR BEING SUCH A JERK EARLIER.
Y'KNOW, AS MUCH OF A DEBACLE THIS CIRCUS WAS, IT DID HELP PUT STUFF INTO PERSPECTIVE.
I LIKE MY LIFE THE WAY IT IS.
SIR?
AHHH! THOUGH I DIE, THE SOCIALIST DREAM LIVES ON!
OH, SUCH A SAD END! AGGH!
THIS IS SCARRING ME FOR LIFE!
PLEASE! IT HURTS!
I WANNA GO HOME!
BURNING!
IT'S A NIGHTMARE! I AM IN HELL!
MOMMY! DADDY! I'M SCARED!
WAAAHHH!
SPURT!
GURGLE
WE SHOULD'VE BEEN IN FLORIDA MEETING MY WIFE WEEKS AGO.
THESE SIDE-TRIPS? I'VE BEEN AVOIDING MY PROBLEMS. POST-PONING CHANGE.
CIRCUS PARKING
AVOIDING PROBLEMS ONLY MAKES THEM WORSE.
OR WEIRDER.
CHANGE IS INEVITABLE, AND I NEED TO FACE IT HEAD ON.
GUB GUB!
THAT'S GREAT, SIR!
YOU WON'T ALWAYS BE AT MY SIDE, HAVING THESE INCREASINGLY STUPID ADVENTURES.
SIR, I'M STILL A LONG WAY FROM GROWING OLD AND DYING ON YOU...
NOT THAT, YA DINGBAT! YOUR GIRLFRIEND. YOU MIGHT WANT TO SPEND TIME WITH HER INSTEAD OF FOLLOWING ME AROUND.
OH, RIGHT!
I REALLY SHOULD TEXT HER.

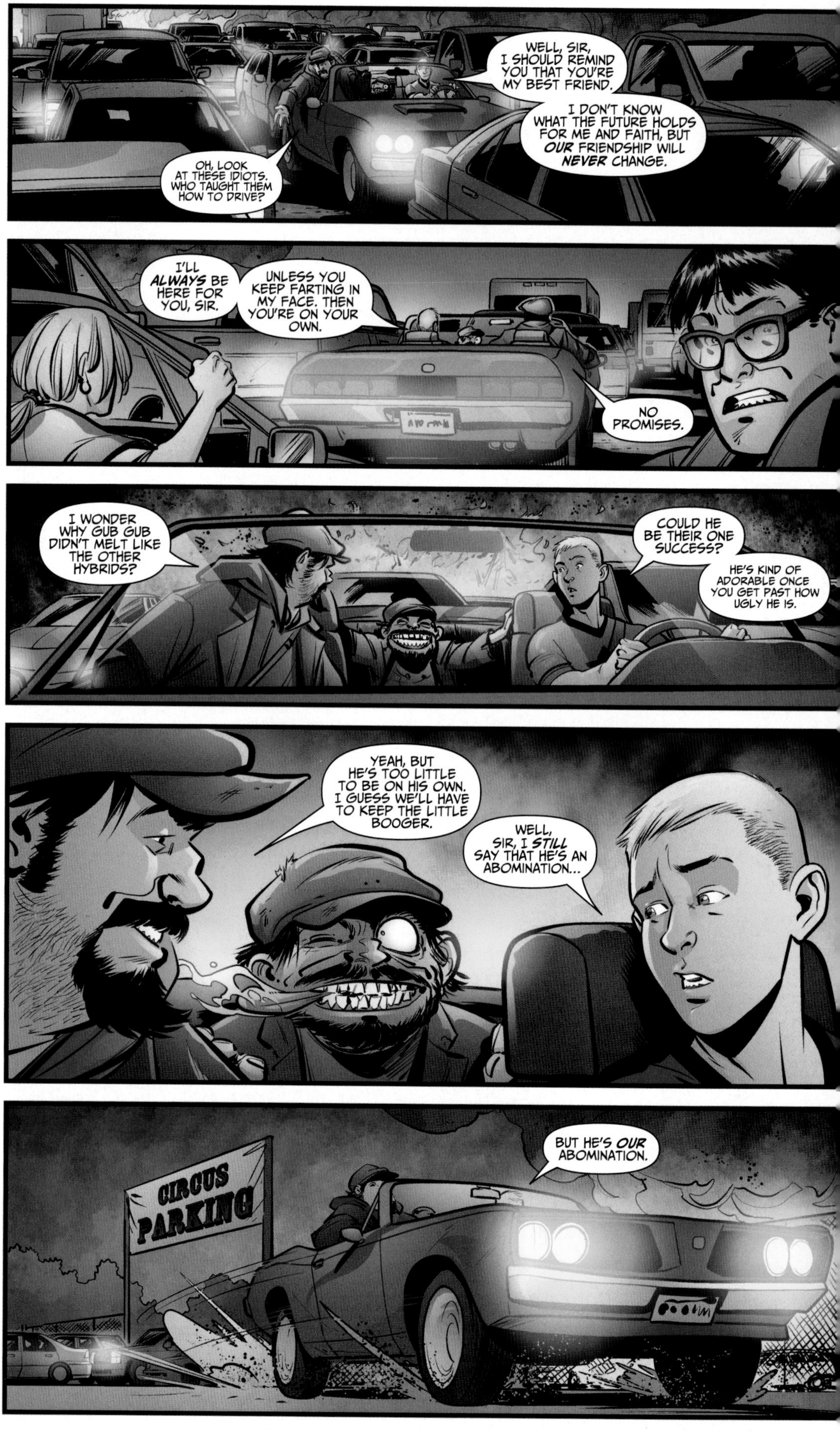
WELL, SIR, I SHOULD REMIND YOU THAT YOU'RE MY BEST FRIEND.
I DON'T KNOW WHAT THE FUTURE HOLDS FOR ME AND FAITH, BUT **OUR** FRIENDSHIP WILL **NEVER** CHANGE.
OH, LOOK AT THESE IDIOTS. WHO TAUGHT THEM HOW TO DRIVE?
I'LL **ALWAYS** BE HERE FOR YOU, SIR.
UNLESS YOU KEEP FARTING IN MY FACE. THEN YOU'RE ON YOUR OWN.
NO PROMISES.
I WONDER WHY GUB GUB DIDN'T MELT LIKE THE OTHER HYBRIDS?
COULD HE BE THEIR ONE SUCCESS?
HE'S KIND OF ADORABLE ONCE YOU GET PAST HOW UGLY HE IS.
YEAH, BUT HE'S TOO LITTLE TO BE ON HIS OWN. I GUESS WE'LL HAVE TO KEEP THE LITTLE BOOGER.
WELL, SIR, I **STILL** SAY THAT HE'S AN ABOMINATION...
BUT HE'S **OUR** ABOMINATION.
CIRCUS PARKING

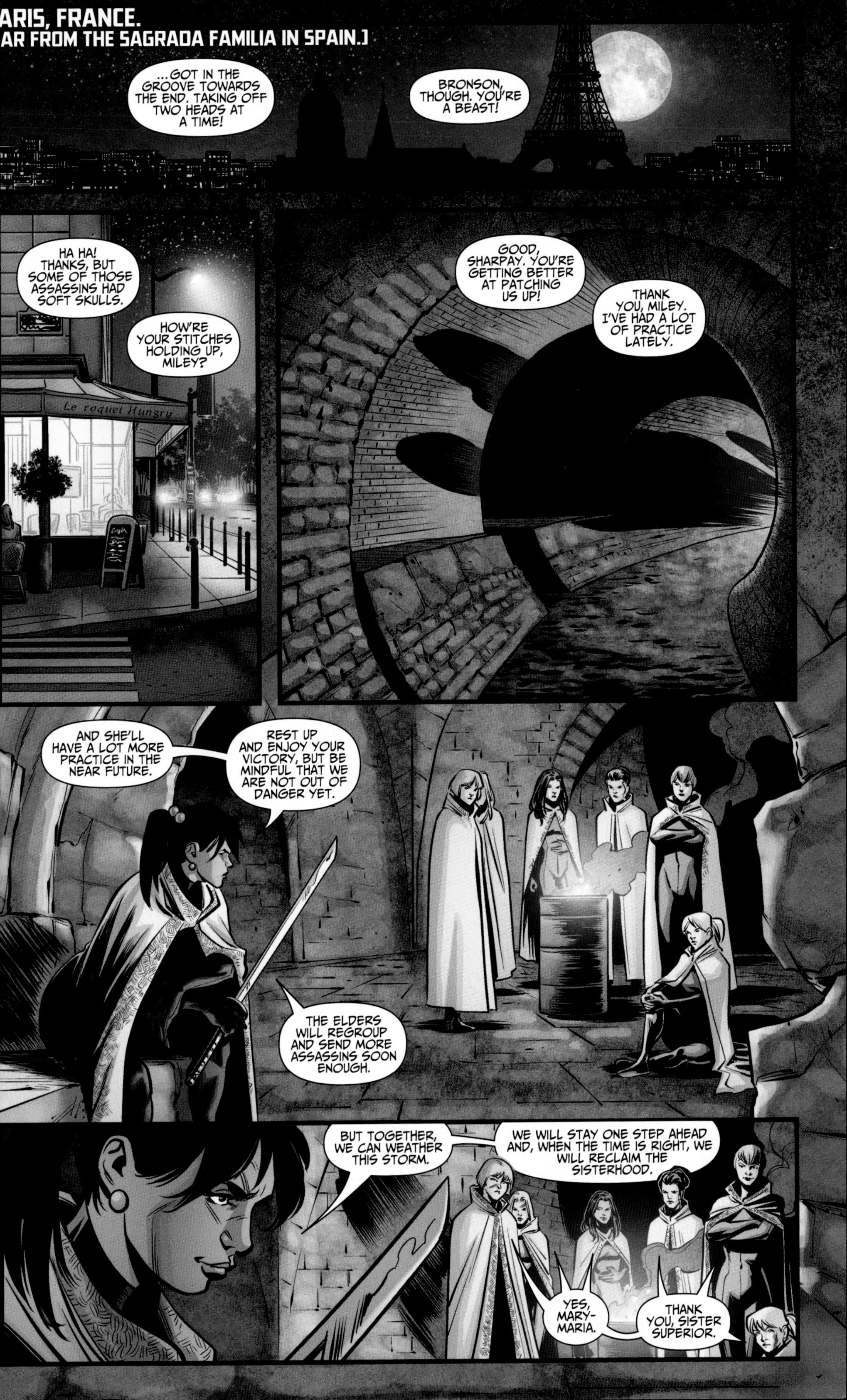

ARIS, FRANCE.
AR FROM THE SAGRADA FAMILIA IN SPAIN.]
...GOT IN THE GROOVE TOWARDS THE END. TAKING OFF TWO HEADS AT A TIME!
BRONSON, THOUGH. YOU'RE A BEAST!
HA HA! THANKS, BUT SOME OF THOSE ASSASSINS HAD SOFT SKULLS.
HOW'RE YOUR STITCHES HOLDING UP, MILEY?
Le roquet Hungry
GOOD, SHARPAY. YOU'RE GETTING BETTER AT PATCHING US UP!
THANK YOU, MILEY. I'VE HAD A LOT OF PRACTICE LATELY.
AND SHE'LL HAVE A LOT MORE PRACTICE IN THE NEAR FUTURE.
REST UP AND ENJOY YOUR VICTORY, BUT BE MINDFUL THAT WE ARE NOT OUT OF DANGER YET.
THE ELDERS WILL REGROUP AND SEND MORE ASSASSINS SOON ENOUGH.
BUT TOGETHER, WE CAN WEATHER THIS STORM.
WE WILL STAY ONE STEP AHEAD AND, WHEN THE TIME IS RIGHT, WE WILL RECLAIM THE SISTERHOOD.
YES, MARY-MARIA.
THANK YOU, SISTER SUPERIOR.

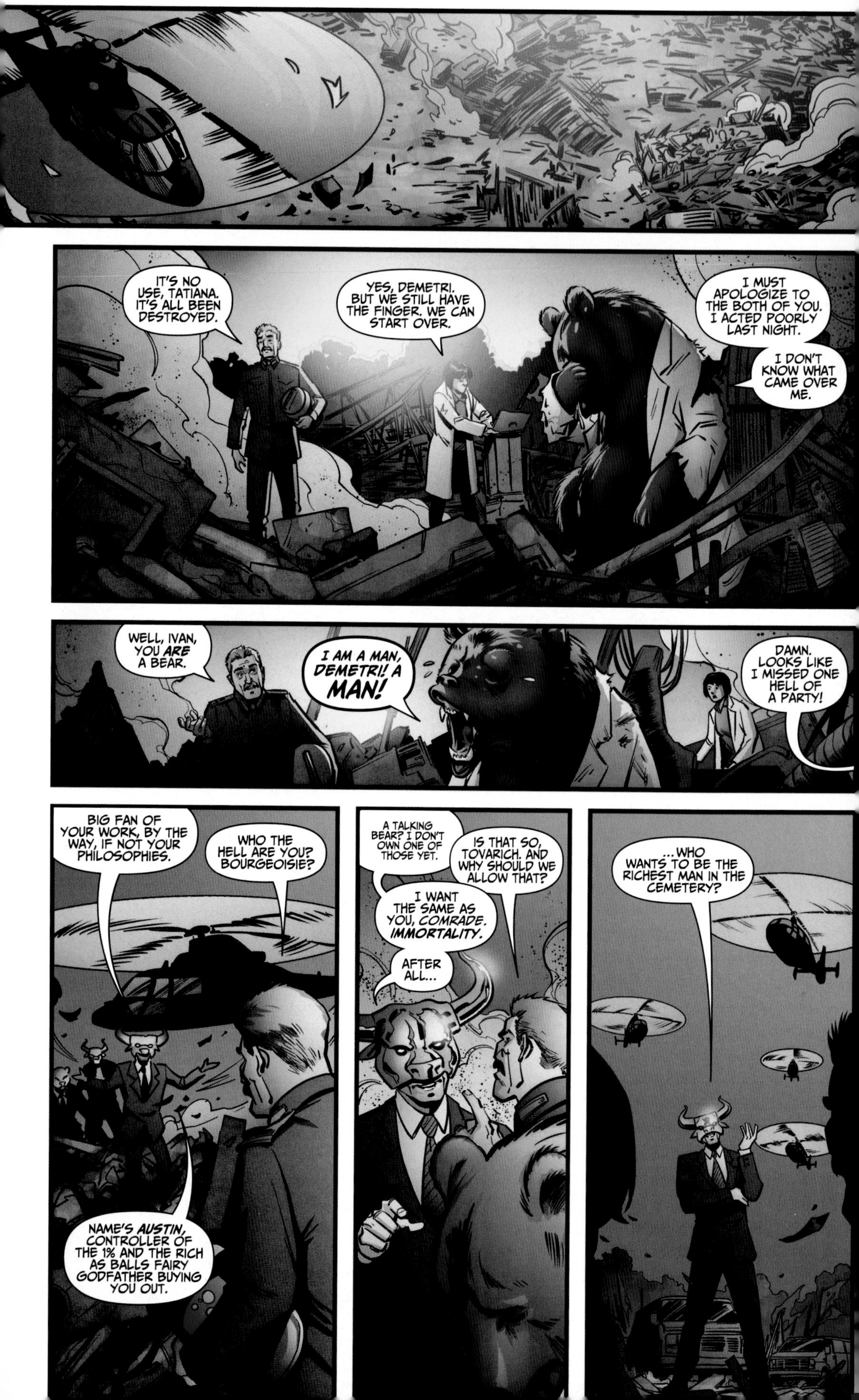
IT'S NO USE, TATIANA. IT'S ALL BEEN DESTROYED.
YES, DEMETRI. BUT WE STILL HAVE THE FINGER. WE CAN START OVER.
I MUST APOLOGIZE TO THE BOTH OF YOU. I ACTED POORLY LAST NIGHT.
I DON'T KNOW WHAT CAME OVER ME.
WELL, IVAN, YOU *ARE* A BEAR.
I AM A MAN, DEMETRI! A MAN!
DAMN. LOOKS LIKE I MISSED ONE HELL OF A PARTY!
BIG FAN OF YOUR WORK, BY THE WAY, IF NOT YOUR PHILOSOPHIES.
WHO THE HELL ARE YOU? BOURGEOISIE?
NAME'S *AUSTIN*, CONTROLLER OF THE 1% AND THE RICH AS BALLS FAIRY GODFATHER BUYING YOU OUT.
A TALKING BEAR? I DON'T OWN ONE OF THOSE YET.
IS THAT SO, TOVARICH. AND WHY SHOULD WE ALLOW THAT?
I WANT THE SAME AS YOU, *COMRADE. IMMORTALITY.*
AFTER ALL...
...WHO WANTS TO BE THE RICHEST MAN IN THE CEMETERY?

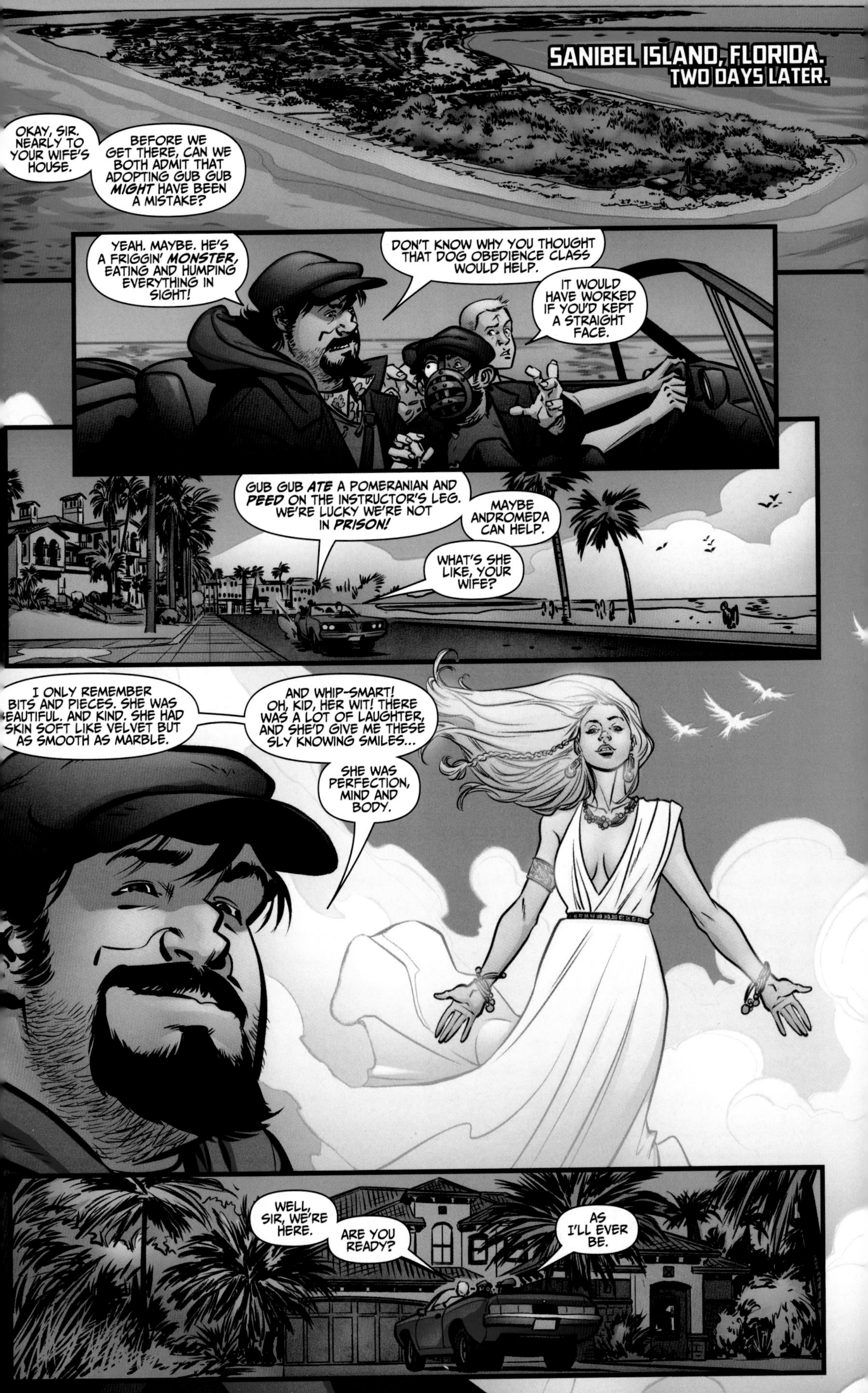
SANIBEL ISLAND, FLORIDA. TWO DAYS LATER.
OKAY, SIR. NEARLY TO YOUR WIFE'S HOUSE.
BEFORE WE GET THERE, CAN WE BOTH ADMIT THAT ADOPTING GUB GUB MIGHT HAVE BEEN A MISTAKE?
YEAH. MAYBE. HE'S A FRIGGIN' MONSTER, EATING AND HUMPING EVERYTHING IN SIGHT!
DON'T KNOW WHY YOU THOUGHT THAT DOG OBEDIENCE CLASS WOULD HELP.
IT WOULD HAVE WORKED IF YOU'D KEPT A STRAIGHT FACE.
GUB GUB ATE A POMERANIAN AND PEED ON THE INSTRUCTOR'S LEG. WE'RE LUCKY WE'RE NOT IN PRISON!
MAYBE ANDROMEDA CAN HELP.
WHAT'S SHE LIKE, YOUR WIFE?
I ONLY REMEMBER BITS AND PIECES. SHE WAS BEAUTIFUL. AND KIND. SHE HAD SKIN SOFT LIKE VELVET BUT AS SMOOTH AS MARBLE.
AND WHIP-SMART! OH, KID, HER WIT! THERE WAS A LOT OF LAUGHTER, AND SHE'D GIVE ME THESE SLY KNOWING SMILES...
SHE WAS PERFECTION, MIND AND BODY.
WELL, SIR, WE'RE HERE.
ARE YOU READY?
AS I'LL EVER BE.

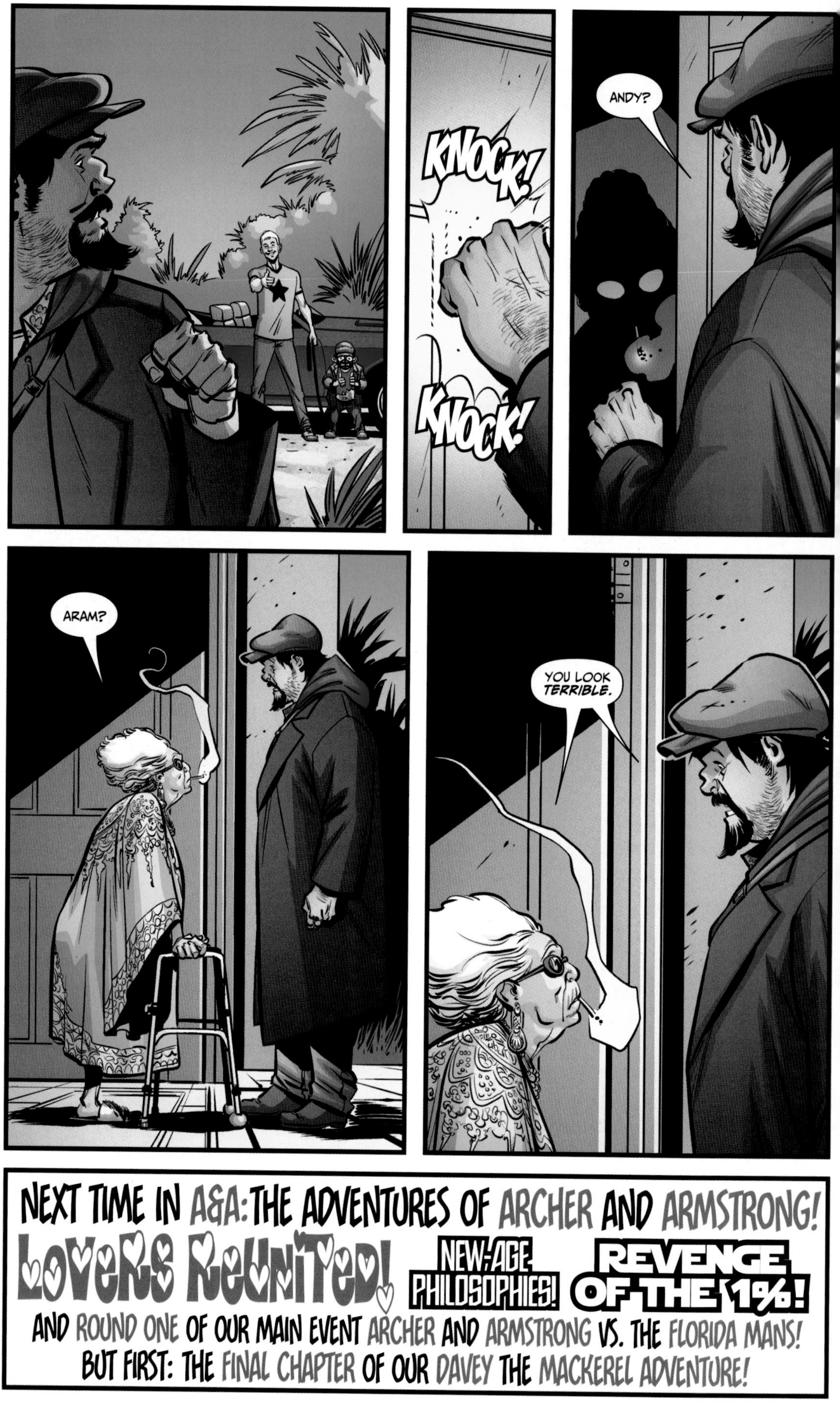

KNOCK!
KNOCK!
ANDY?
ARAM?
YOU LOOK TERRIBLE.

NEXT TIME IN A&A: THE ADVENTURES OF ARCHER AND ARMSTRONG!

LOVERS REUNITED! NEW-AGE PHILOSOPHIES! REVENGE OF THE 1%!

AND ROUND ONE OF OUR MAIN EVENT ARCHER AND ARMSTRONG VS. THE FLORIDA MANS!

BUT FIRST: THE FINAL CHAPTER OF OUR DAVEY THE MACKEREL ADVENTURE!

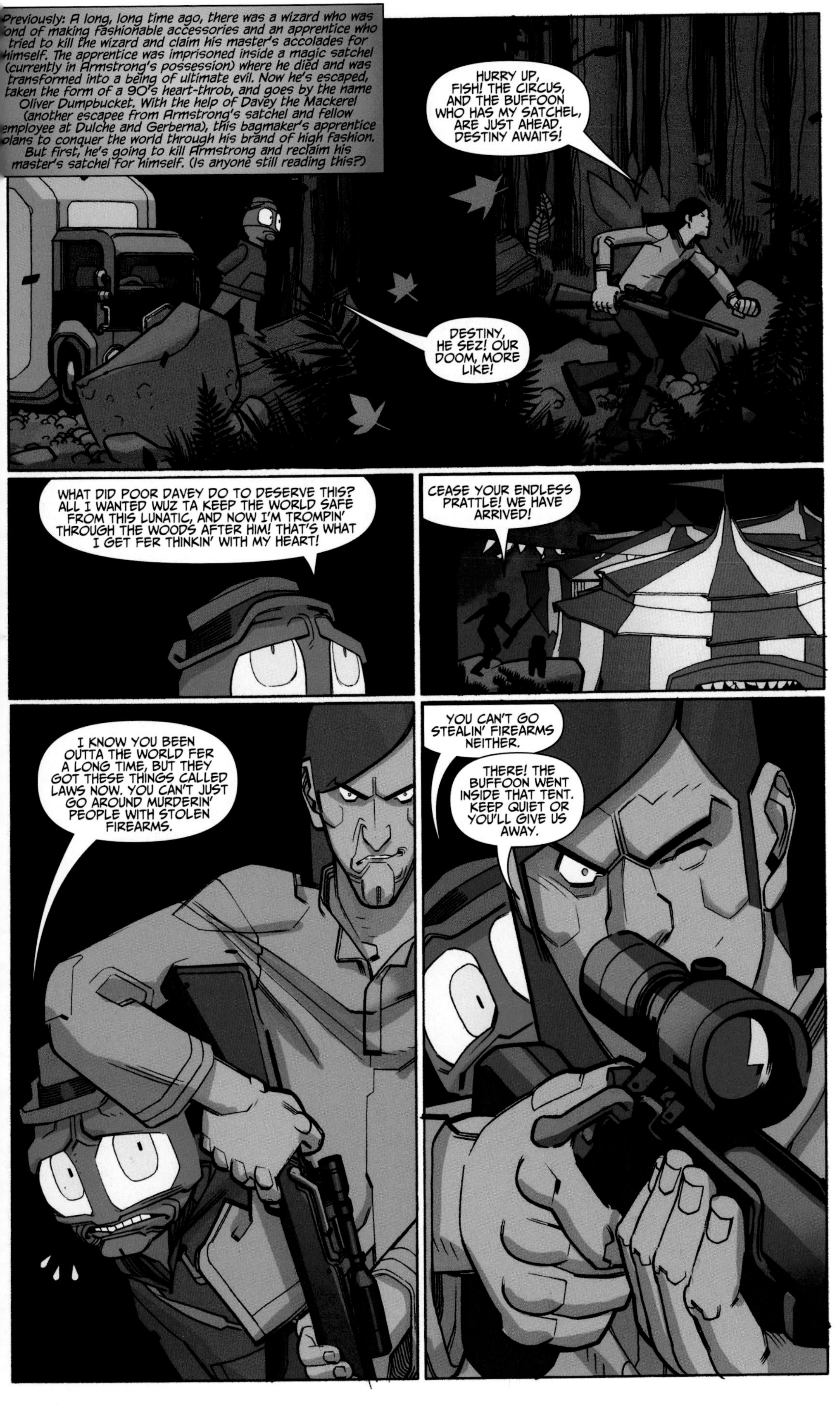
Previously: A long, long time ago, there was a wizard who was fond of making fashionable accessories and an apprentice who tried to kill the wizard and claim his master's accolades for himself. The apprentice was imprisoned inside a magic satchel (currently in Armstrong's possession) where he died and was transformed into a being of ultimate evil. Now he's escaped, taken the form of a 90's heart-throb, and goes by the name Oliver Dumpbucket. With the help of Davey the Mackerel (another escapee from Armstrong's satchel and fellow employee at Dulche and Gerberna), this bagmaker's apprentice plans to conquer the world through his brand of high fashion. But first, he's going to kill Armstrong and reclaim his master's satchel for himself. (Is anyone still reading this?)
HURRY UP, FISH! THE CIRCUS, AND THE BUFFOON WHO HAS MY SATCHEL, ARE JUST AHEAD. DESTINY AWAITS!
DESTINY, HE SEZ! OUR DOOM, MORE LIKE!
WHAT DID POOR DAVEY DO TO DESERVE THIS? ALL I WANTED WUZ TA KEEP THE WORLD SAFE FROM THIS LUNATIC, AND NOW I'M TROMPIN' THROUGH THE WOODS AFTER HIM! THAT'S WHAT I GET FER THINKIN' WITH MY HEART!
CEASE YOUR ENDLESS PRATTLE! WE HAVE ARRIVED!
I KNOW YOU BEEN OUTTA THE WORLD FER A LONG TIME, BUT THEY GOT THESE THINGS CALLED LAWS NOW. YOU CAN'T JUST GO AROUND MURDERIN' PEOPLE WITH STOLEN FIREARMS.
YOU CAN'T GO STEALIN' FIREARMS NEITHER.
THERE! THE BUFFOON WENT INSIDE THAT TENT. KEEP QUIET OR YOU'LL GIVE US AWAY.

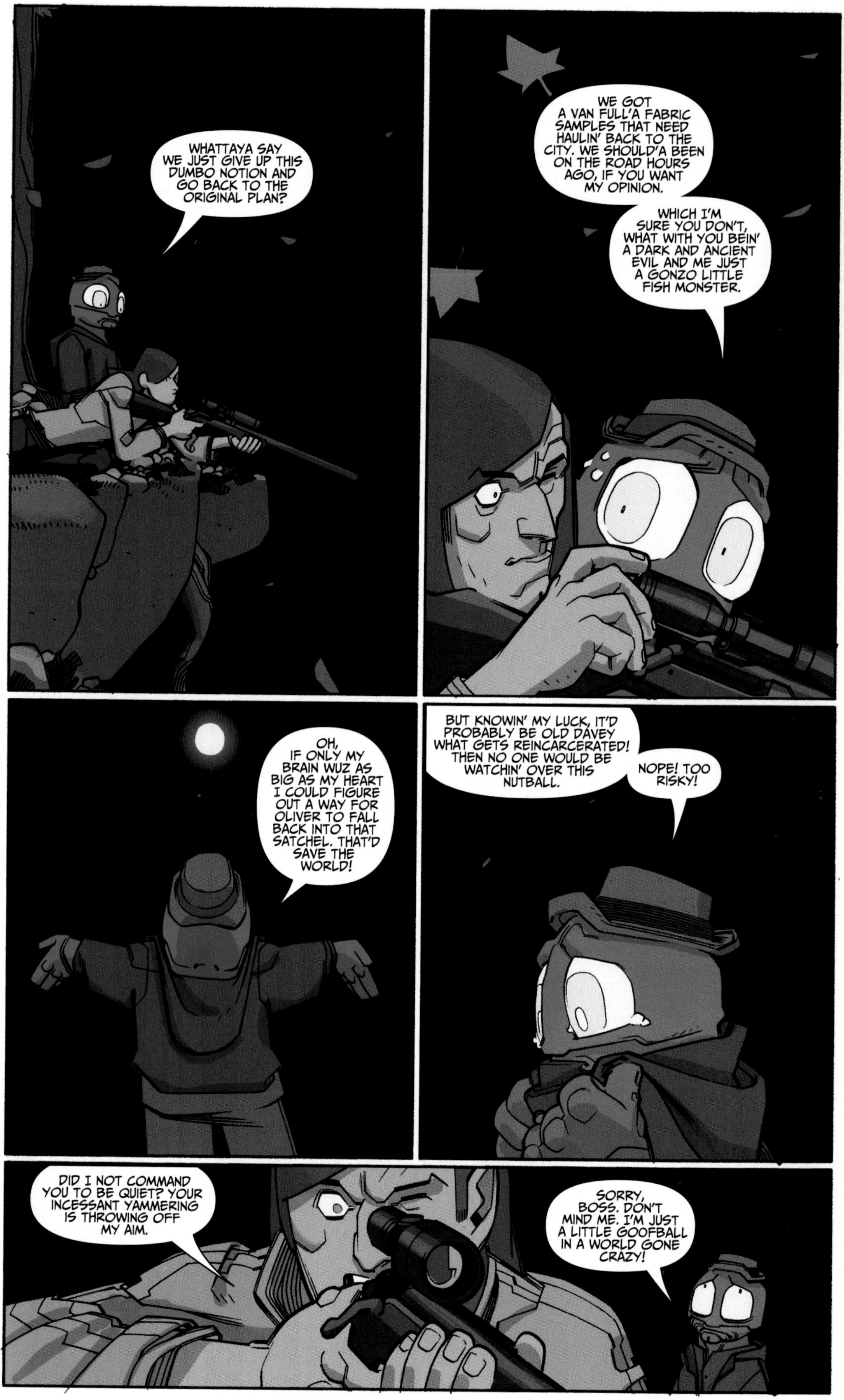
WHATTAYA SAY WE JUST GIVE UP THIS DUMBO NOTION AND GO BACK TO THE ORIGINAL PLAN?
WE GOT A VAN FULL'A FABRIC SAMPLES THAT NEED HAULIN' BACK TO THE CITY. WE SHOULD'A BEEN ON THE ROAD HOURS AGO, IF YOU WANT MY OPINION.
WHICH I'M SURE YOU DON'T, WHAT WITH YOU BEIN' A DARK AND ANCIENT EVIL AND ME JUST A GONZO LITTLE FISH MONSTER.
OH, IF ONLY MY BRAIN WUZ AS BIG AS MY HEART I COULD FIGURE OUT A WAY FOR OLIVER TO FALL BACK INTO THAT SATCHEL. THAT'D SAVE THE WORLD!
BUT KNOWIN' MY LUCK, IT'D PROBABLY BE OLD DAVEY WHAT GETS REINCARCERATED! THEN NO ONE WOULD BE WATCHIN' OVER THIS NUTBALL.
NOPE! TOO RISKY!
DID I NOT COMMAND YOU TO BE QUIET? YOUR INCESSANT YAMMERING IS THROWING OFF MY AIM.
SORRY, BOSS. DON'T MIND ME. I'M JUST A LITTLE GOOFBALL IN A WORLD GONE CRAZY!

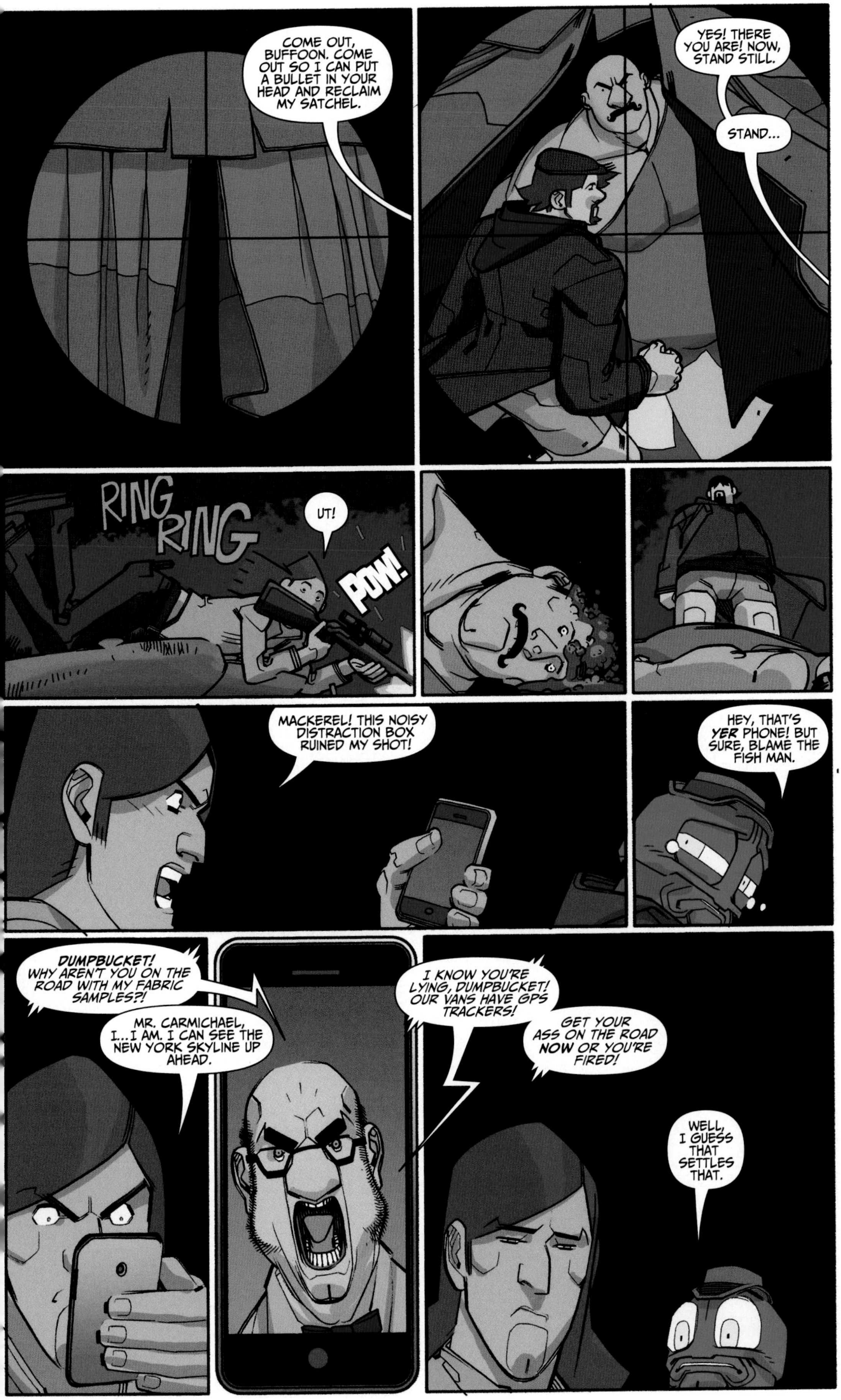
COME OUT, BUFFOON. COME OUT SO I CAN PUT A BULLET IN YOUR HEAD AND RECLAIM MY SATCHEL.
YES! THERE YOU ARE! NOW, STAND STILL.
STAND...
RING RING
UT!
POW!
MACKEREL! THIS NOISY DISTRACTION BOX RUINED MY SHOT!
HEY, THAT'S YER PHONE! BUT SURE, BLAME THE FISH MAN.
DUMPBUCKET! WHY AREN'T YOU ON THE ROAD WITH MY FABRIC SAMPLES?!
MR. CARMICHAEL, I...I AM. I CAN SEE THE NEW YORK SKYLINE UP AHEAD.
I KNOW YOU'RE LYING, DUMPBUCKET! OUR VANS HAVE GPS TRACKERS!
GET YOUR ASS ON THE ROAD NOW OR YOU'RE FIRED!
WELL, I GUESS THAT SETTLES THAT.

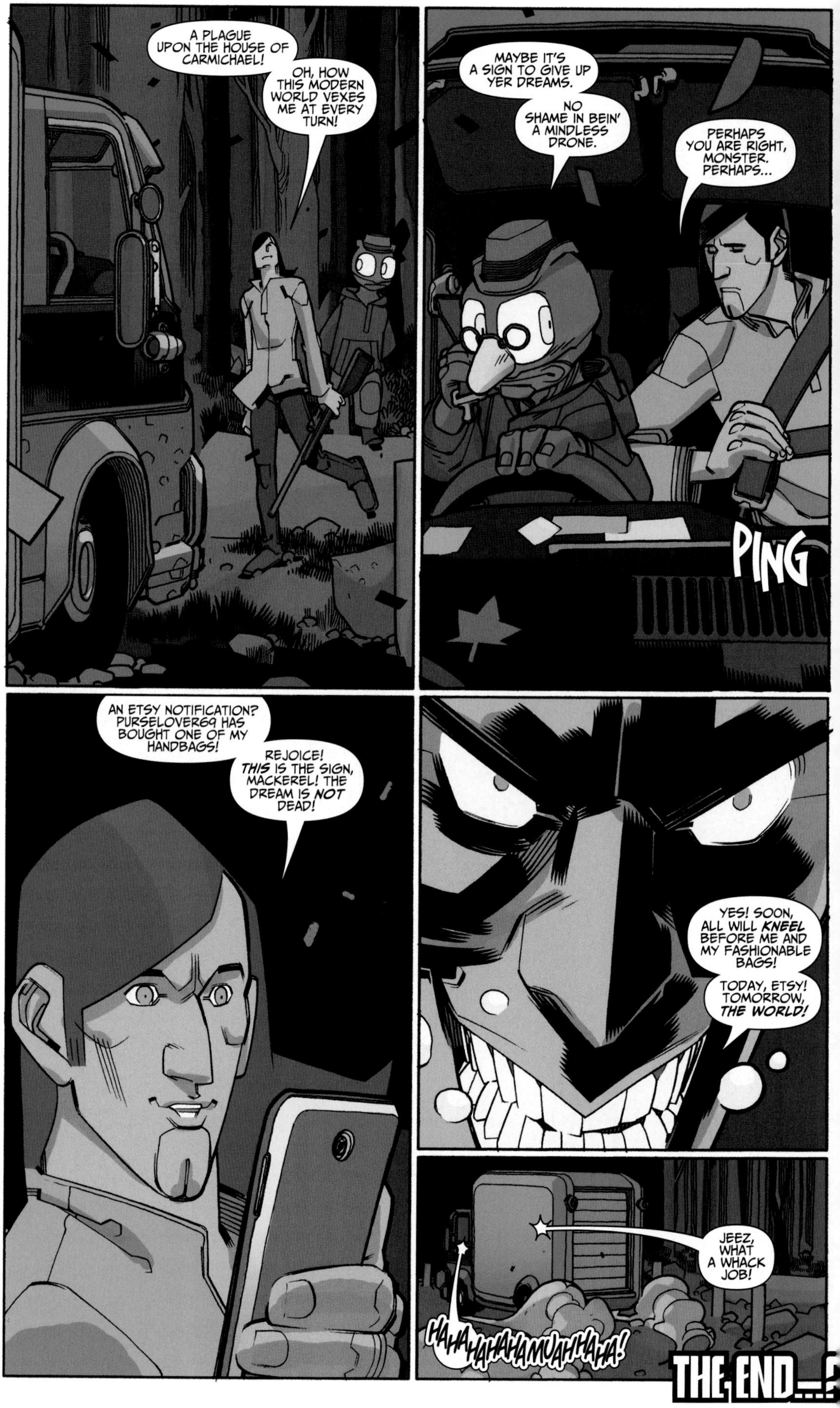
A PLAGUE UPON THE HOUSE OF CARMICHAEL!
OH, HOW THIS MODERN WORLD VEXES ME AT EVERY TURN!
MAYBE IT'S A SIGN TO GIVE UP YER DREAMS.
NO SHAME IN BEIN' A MINDLESS DRONE.
PERHAPS YOU ARE RIGHT, MONSTER. PERHAPS...
PING
AN ETSY NOTIFICATION? PURSELOVER69 HAS BOUGHT ONE OF MY HANDBAGS!
REJOICE! *THIS* IS THE SIGN, MACKEREL! THE DREAM IS *NOT* DEAD!
YES! SOON, ALL WILL *KNEEL* BEFORE ME AND MY FASHIONABLE BAGS!
TODAY, ETSY! TOMORROW, *THE WORLD!*
JEEZ, WHAT A WHACK JOB!
HAHAHAHAHAMUAHHAHA!
THE END...?

GALLERY

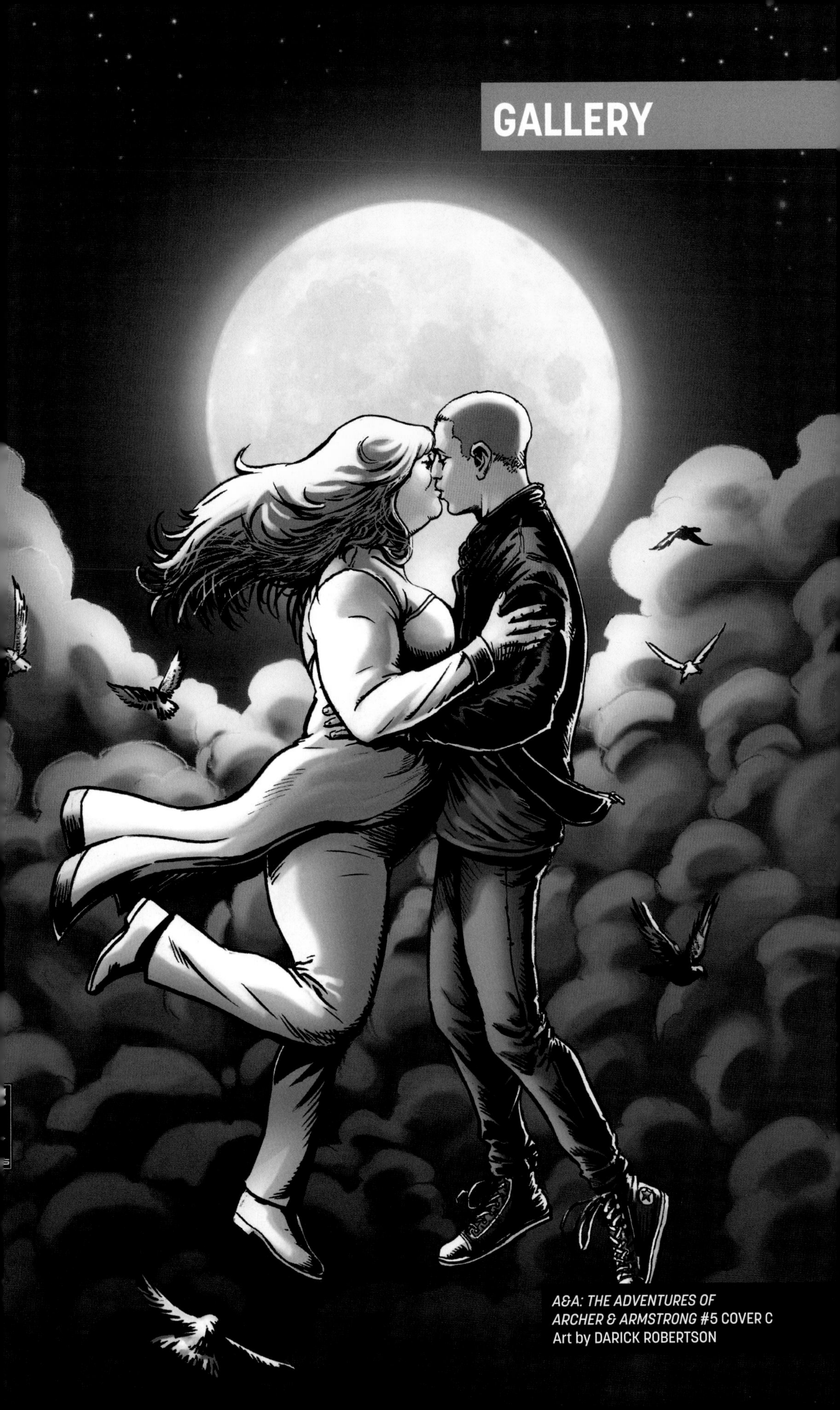

A&A: THE ADVENTURES OF ARCHER & ARMSTRONG #5 COVER C
Art by DARICK ROBERTSON

A&A: THE ADVENTURES OF ARCHER & ARMSTRONG #6
COVER B
Art by KANO

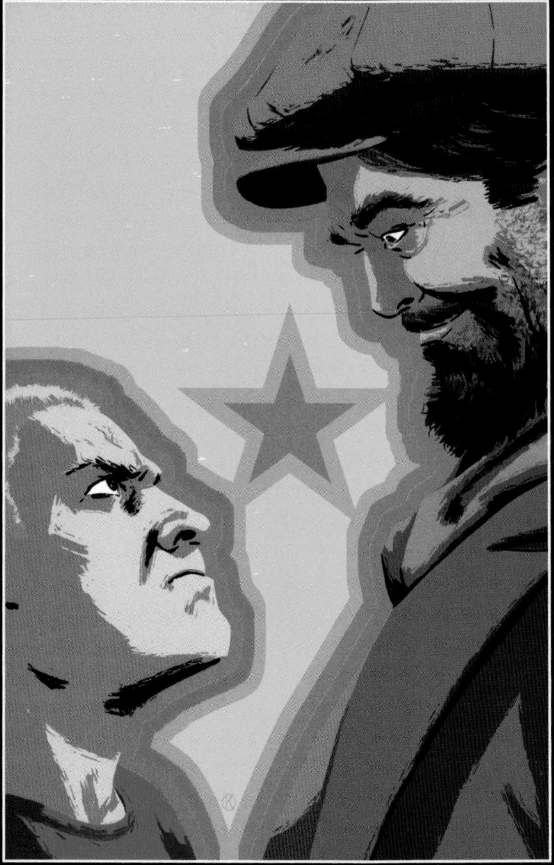

A&A: THE ADVENTURES OF ARCHER & ARMSTRONG #7
VARIANT COVER
Art by ADAM GORHAM and MICHAEL SPICER

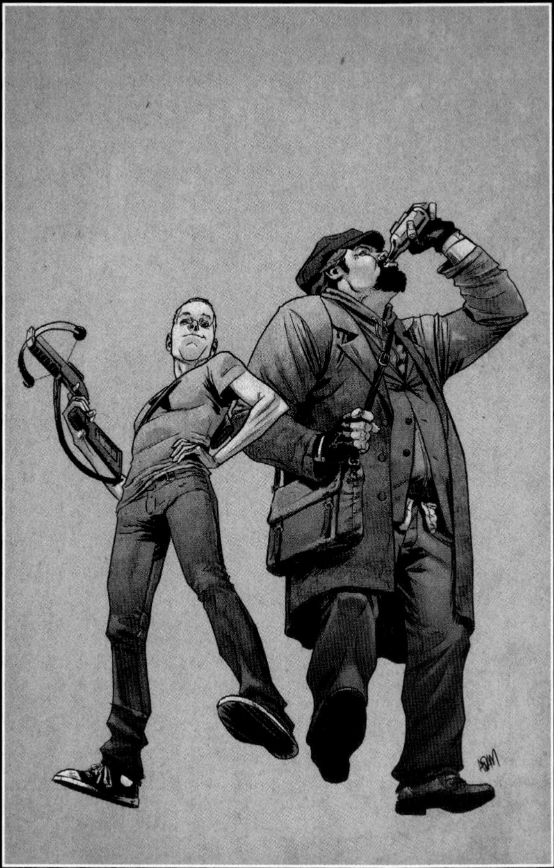

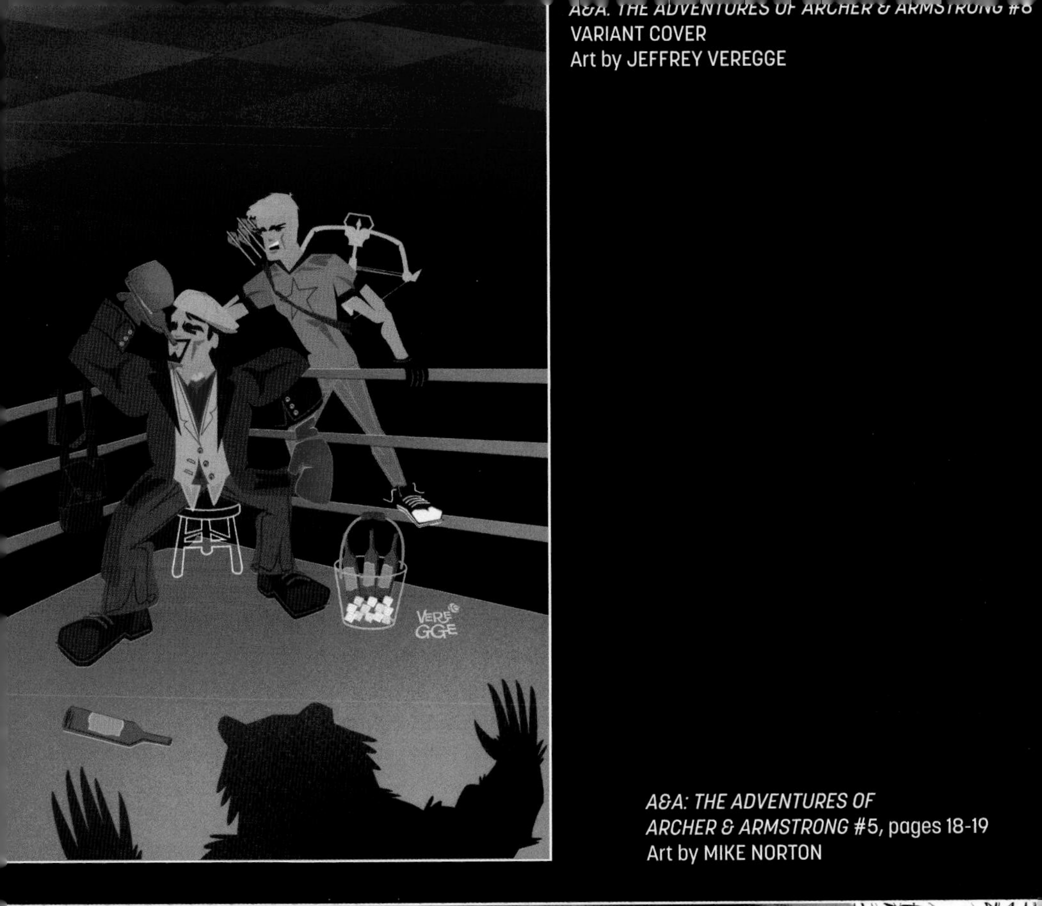

A&A: THE ADVENTURES OF ARCHER & ARMSTRONG #8
VARIANT COVER
Art by JEFFREY VEREGGE

A&A: THE ADVENTURES OF ARCHER & ARMSTRONG #5, pages 18-19
Art by MIKE NORTON

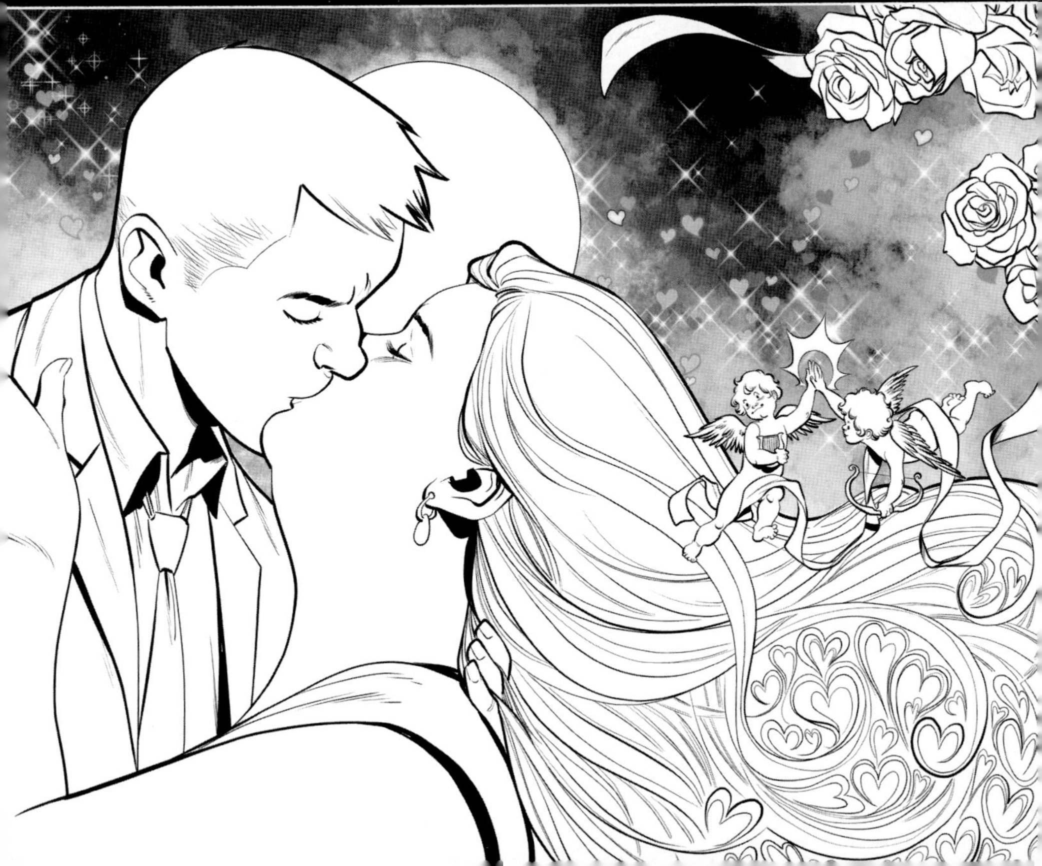

A&A: THE ADVENTURES OF ARCHER & ARMSTRONG #6, p.2
Art by MIKE NORTON

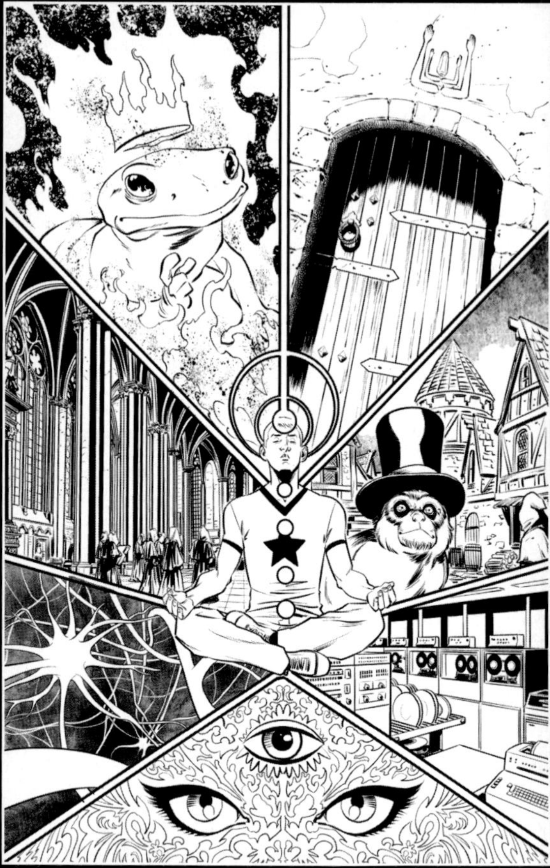

A&A: THE ADVENTURES OF ARCHER & ARMSTRONG #7, p.1
Art by MIKE NORTON

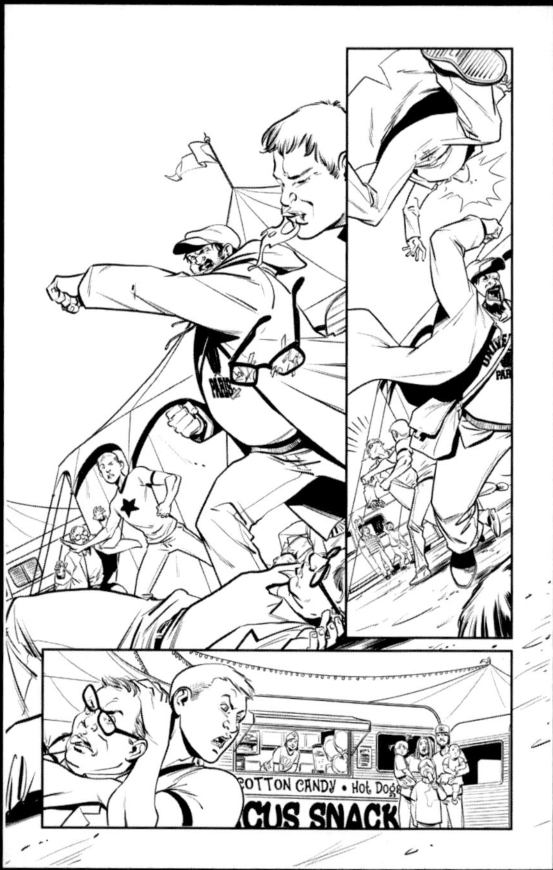
COTTON CANDY • Hot Dogs
CUS SNACK

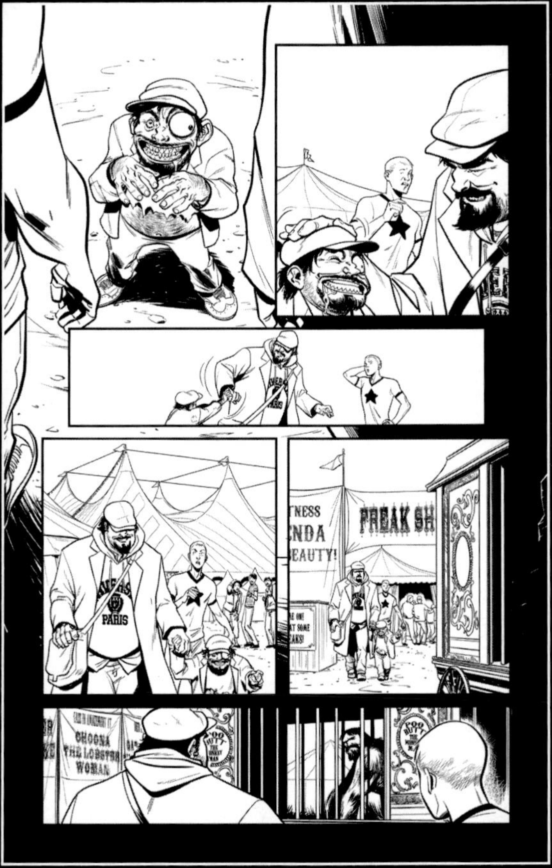
TNESS
NDA
EAUTY!
FREAK SH
PARIS
CHOONA
THE LOBSTER
WOMAN

A&A: THE ADVENTURES OF ARCHER & ARMSTRONG #7, p3
Art by MIKE NORTON

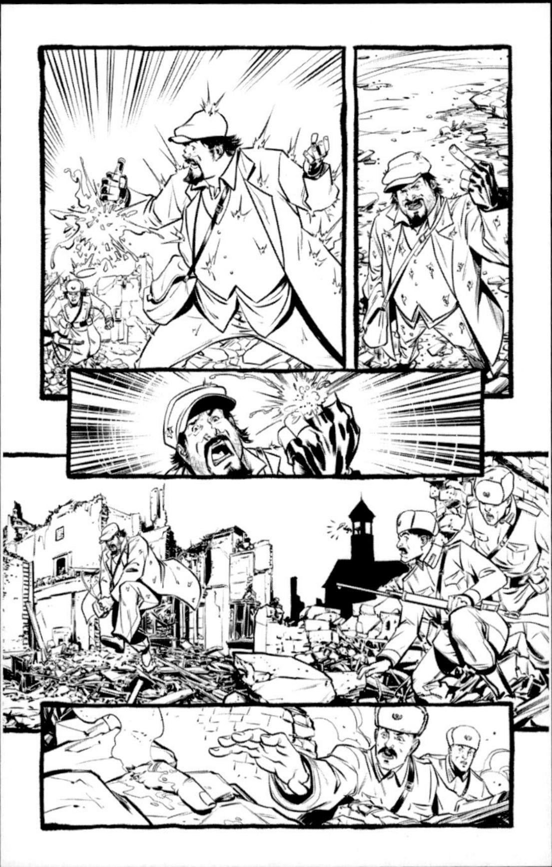

A&A: THE ADVENTURES OF ARCHER & ARMSTRONG #8, p2
Art by MIKE NORTON

EXPLORE THE VALIANT UNIVERSE

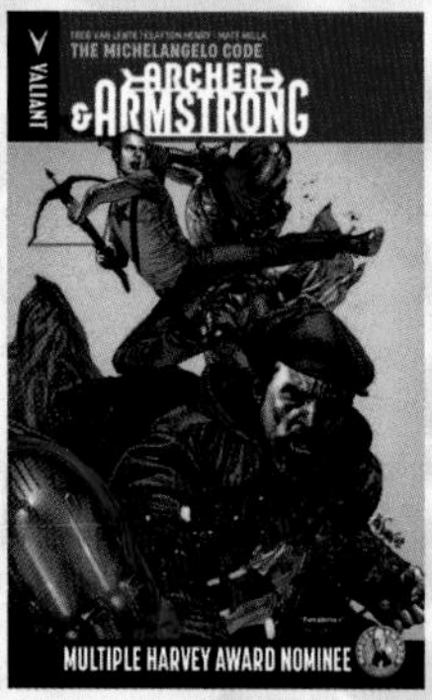
VALIANT
THE MICHELANGELO CODE
ARCHER & ARMSTRONG
MULTIPLE HARVEY AWARD NOMINEE

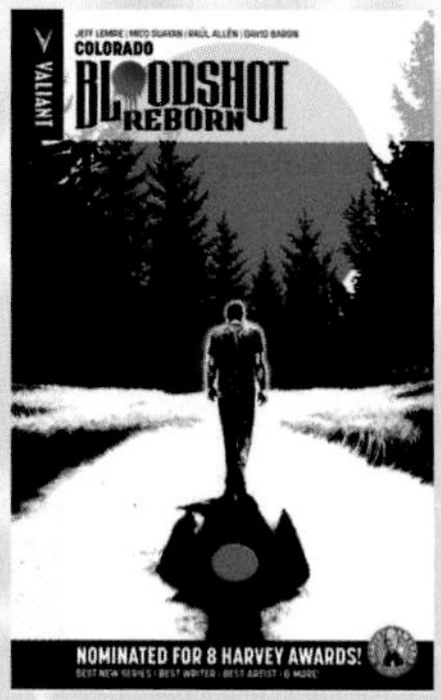
VALIANT
COLORADO
BLOODSHOT
REBORN
NOMINATED FOR 8 HARVEY AWARDS!

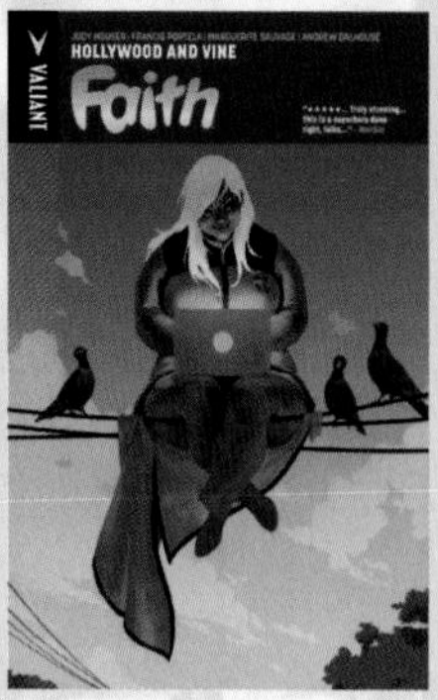
VALIANT
HOLLYWOOD AND VINE
Faith

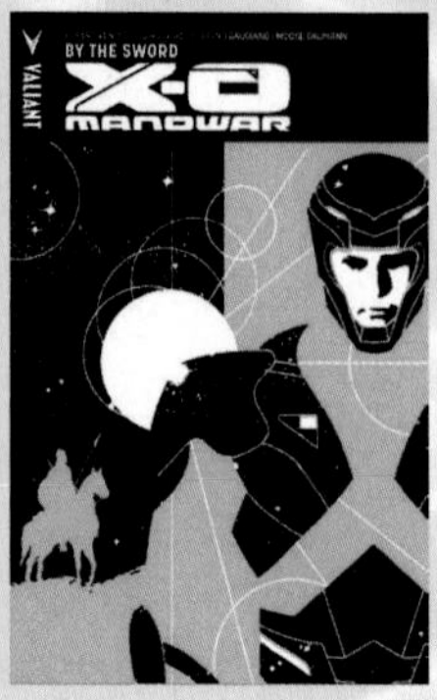
VALIANT
BY THE SWORD
X-O
MANOWAR

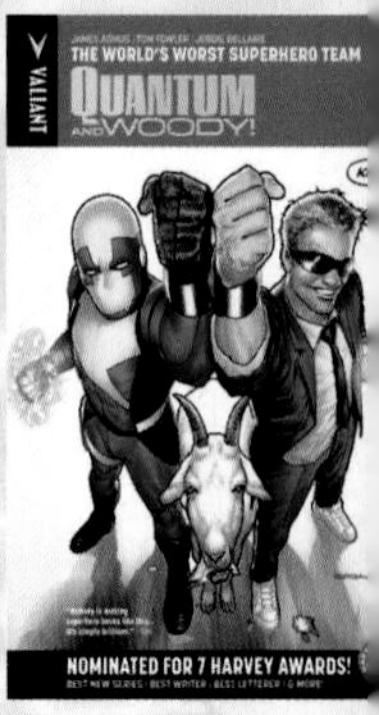
VALIANT
THE WORLD'S WORST SUPERHERO TEAM
QUANTUM
AND WOODY!
NOMINATED FOR 7 HARVEY AWARDS!

4001 A.D.

4001 A.D.
ISBN: 9781682151433

4001 A.D.: Beyond New Japan
ISBN: 9781682151464

Rai Vol 4: 4001 A.D.
ISBN: 9781682151471

A&A: THE ADVENTURES OF ARCHER AND ARMSTRONG

Volume 1: In the Bag
ISBN: 9781682151495

Volume 2: Romance and Road Trips
ISBN: 9781682151716

ARCHER & ARMSTRONG

Volume 1: The Michelangelo Code
ISBN: 9780979640988

Volume 2: Wrath of the Eternal Warrior
ISBN: 9781939346049

Volume 3: Far Faraway
ISBN: 9781939346148

Volume 4: Sect Civil War
ISBN: 9781939346254

Volume 5: Mission: Improbable
ISBN: 9781939346353

Volume 6: American Wasteland
ISBN: 9781939346421

Volume 7: The One Percent and Other Tales
ISBN: 9781939346537

ARMOR HUNTERS

Armor Hunters
ISBN: 9781939346452

Armor Hunters: Bloodshot
ISBN: 9781939346469

Armor Hunters: Harbinger
ISBN: 9781939346506

Unity Vol. 3: Armor Hunters
ISBN: 9781939346445

X-O Manowar Vol. 7: Armor Hunters
ISBN: 9781939346476

BLOODSHOT

Volume 1: Setting the World on Fire
ISBN: 9780979640964

Volume 2: The Rise and the Fall
ISBN: 9781939346032

Volume 3: Harbinger Wars
ISBN: 9781939346124

Volume 4: H.A.R.D. Corps
ISBN: 9781939346193

Volume 5: Get Some!
ISBN: 9781939346315

Volume 6: The Glitch and Other Tales
ISBN: 9781939346711

BLOODSHOT REBORN

Volume 1: Colorado
ISBN: 9781939346674

Volume 2: The Hunt
ISBN: 9781939346827

Volume 3: The Analog Man
ISBN: 9781682151334

BOOK OF DEATH

Book of Death
ISBN: 9781939346971

Book of Death: The Fall of the Valiant Universe
ISBN: 9781939346988

DEAD DROP

ISBN: 9781939346858

THE DEATH-DEFYING DOCTOR MIRAGE

Volume 1
ISBN: 9781939346490

Volume 2: Second Lives
ISBN: 9781682151297

THE DELINQUENTS

ISBN: 9781939346513

DIVINITY

Volume 1
ISBN: 9781939346766

Volume 2
ISBN: 9781682151518

ETERNAL WARRIOR

Volume 1: Sword of the Wild
ISBN: 9781939346209

Volume 2: Eternal Emperor
ISBN: 9781939346292

Volume 3: Days of Steel
ISBN: 9781939346742

WRATH OF THE ETERNAL WARRIOR

Volume 1: Risen
ISBN: 9781682151235

Volumel 2: Labyrinth
ISBN: 9781682151594

FAITH

Faith Vol 1: Hollywood and Vine
ISBN: 9781682151402

Faith Vol 2: California Scheming
ISBN: 9781682151631

HARBINGER

Volume 1: Omega Rising
ISBN: 9780979640957

Volume 2: Renegades
ISBN: 9781939346025

Volume 3: Harbinger Wars
ISBN: 9781939346117

Volume 4: Perfect Day
ISBN: 9781939346155

Volume 5: Death of a Renegade
ISBN: 9781939346339

Volume 6: Omegas
ISBN: 9781939346384

EXPLORE THE VALIANT UNIVERSE

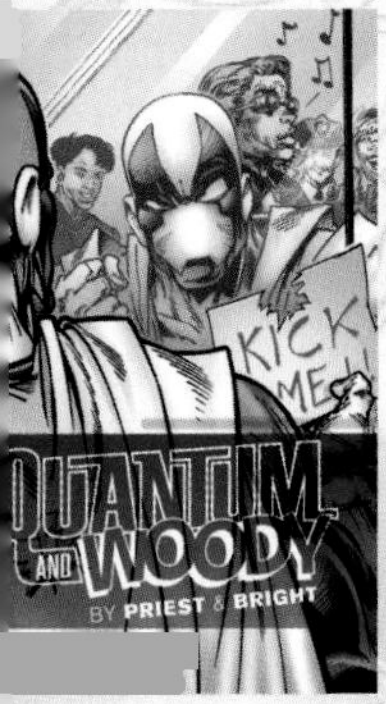
KICK ME
BY PRIEST & BRIGHT
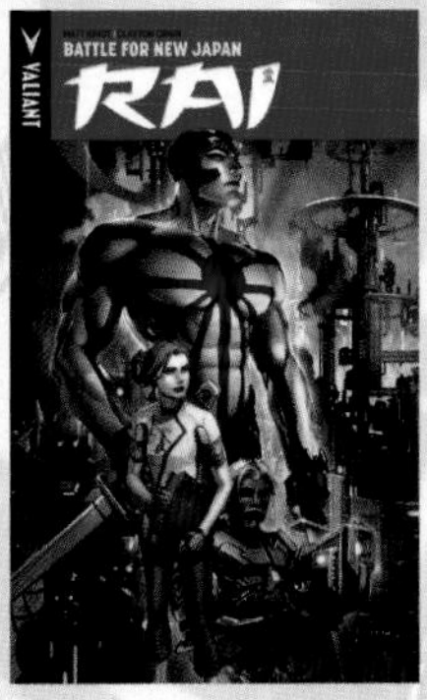
VALIANT
BATTLE FOR NEW JAPAN
RAI
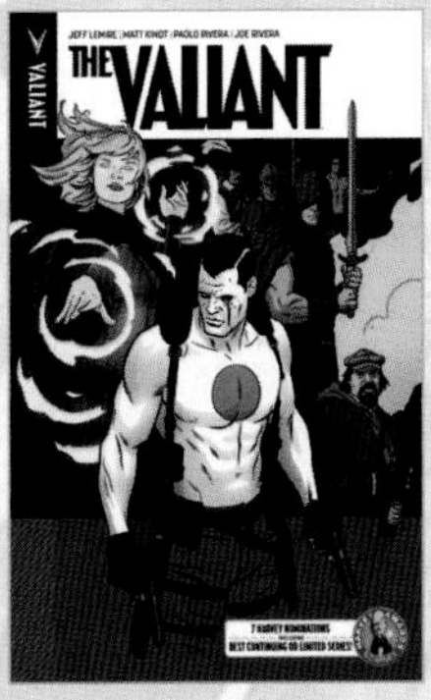
VALIANT
THE VALIANT
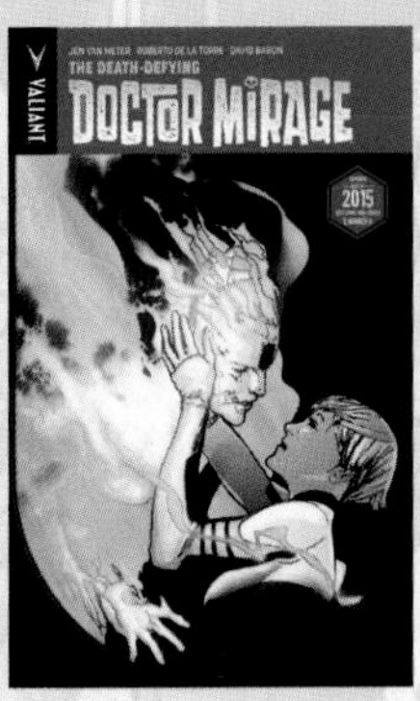
VALIANT
THE DEATH-DEFYING
DOCTOR MIRAGE
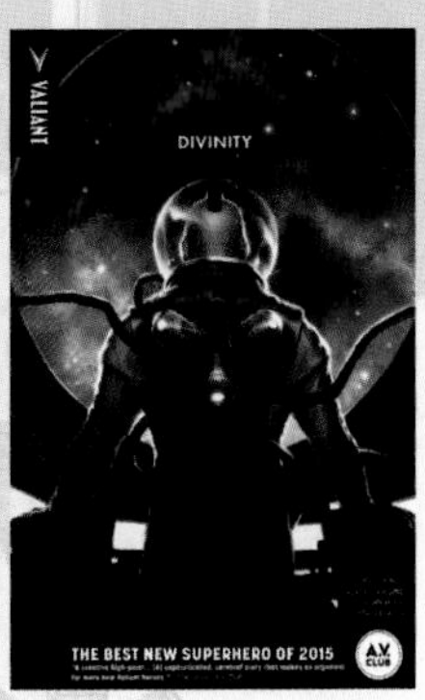
VALIANT
DIVINITY
THE BEST NEW SUPERHERO OF 2015

ARBINGER WARS

'binger Wars
N: 9781939346094

odshot Vol. 3: Harbinger Wars
N: 9781939346124

'binger Vol. 3: Harbinger Wars
N: 9781939346117

IPERIUM

ume 1: Collecting Monsters
N: 9781939346759

ume 2: Broken Angels
N: 9781939346896

ume 3: The Vine Imperative
N: 9781682151112

ume 4: Stormbreak
N: 9781682151372

INJAK

ume 1: Weaponeer
N: 9781939346667

ume 2: The Shadow Wars
N: 9781939346940

ume 3: Operation: Deadside
N: 9781682151259

ume 4: The Siege of King's Castle
N: 9781682151617

UANTUM AND WOODY

ume 1: The World's Worst Superhero Team
N: 9781939346186

ume 2: In Security
N: 9781939346230

ume 3: Crooked Pasts, Present Tense
N: 9781939346391

ume 4: Quantum and Woody Must Die!
N: 9781939346629

UANTUM AND WOODY Y PRIEST & BRIGHT

ume 1: Klang
N: 9781939346780

ume 2: Switch
N: 9781939346803

Volume 3: And So...
ISBN: 9781939346865

Volume 4: Q2 - The Return
ISBN: 9781682151099

RAI

Volume 1: Welcome to New Japan
ISBN: 9781939346414

Volume 2: Battle for New Japan
ISBN: 9781939346612

Volume 3: The Orphan
ISBN: 9781939346841

Rai Vol 4: 4001 A.D.
ISBN: 9781682151471

SHADOWMAN

Volume 1: Birth Rites
ISBN: 9781939346001

Volume 2: Darque Reckoning
ISBN: 9781939346056

Volume 3: Deadside Blues
ISBN: 9781939346162

Volume 4: Fear, Blood, And Shadows
ISBN: 9781939346278

Volume 5: End Times
ISBN: 9781939346377

SHADOWMAN BY ENNIS & WOOD

ISBN: 9781682151358

IVAR, TIMEWALKER

Volume 1: Making History
ISBN: 9781939346636

Volume 2: Breaking History
ISBN: 9781939346834

Volume 3: Ending History
ISBN: 9781939346995

UNITY

Volume 1: To Kill a King
ISBN: 9781939346261

Volume 2: Trapped by Webnet
ISBN: 9781939346346

Volume 3: Armor Hunters
ISBN: 9781939346445

Volume 4: The United
ISBN: 9781939346544

Volume 5: Homefront
ISBN: 9781939346797

Volume 6: The War-Monger
ISBN: 9781939346902

Volume 7: Revenge of the Armor Hunters
ISBN: 9781682151136

THE VALIANT

ISBN: 9781939346605

VALIANT ZEROES AND ORIGINS

ISBN: 9781939346582

X-O MANOWAR

Volume 1: By the Sword
ISBN: 9780979640940

Volume 2: Enter Ninjak
ISBN: 9780979640995

Volume 3: Planet Death
ISBN: 9781939346087

Volume 4: Homecoming
ISBN: 9781939346179

Volume 5: At War With Unity
ISBN: 9781939346247

Volume 6: Prelude to Armor Hunters
ISBN: 9781939346407

Volume 7: Armor Hunters
ISBN: 9781939346476

Volume 8: Enter: Armorines
ISBN: 9781939346551

Volume 9: Dead Hand
ISBN: 9781939346650

Volume 10: Exodus
ISBN: 9781939346933

Volume 11: The Kill List
ISBN: 9781682151273

Volume 12: Long Live the King
ISBN: 9781682151655

EXPLORE THE VALIANT UNIVERSE

VALIANT
HARBINGER
DELUXE EDITION 2

ROBERT VENDITTI MATT KINDT JOSHUA DYSART JOE HARRIS ROBERT GILL DOUG BRAITHWAITE DIEGO BERNARD TREVOR HAIRSINE STEPHEN SEGOVIA
VALIANT
ARMOR HUNTERS
DELUXE EDITION

JIM SHOOTER · DAVID LAPHAM
VALIANT
VALIANT MASTERS
CHILDREN OF THE EIGHTH DAY
HARBINGER

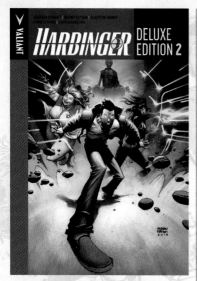

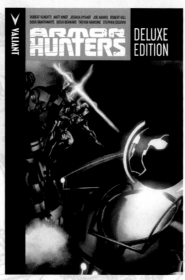

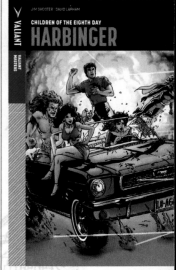

Omnibuses

Archer & Armstrong: The Complete Classic Omnibus
ISBN: 9781939346872
Collecting ARCHER & ARMSTRONG (1992) #0-26, ETERNAL WARRIOR (1992) #25 along with ARCHER & ARMSTRONG: THE FORMATION OF THE SECT.

Quantum and Woody: The Complete Classic Omnibus
ISBN: 9781939346360
Collecting QUANTUM AND WOODY (1997) #0, 1-21 and #32, THE GOAT: H.A.E.D.U.S. #1, and X-O MANOWAR (1996) #16

X-O Manowar Classic Omnibus Vol. 1
ISBN: 9781939346308
Collecting X-O MANOWAR (1992) #0-30, ARMORINES #0, X-O DATABASE #1, as well as material from SECRETS OF THE VALIANT UNIVERSE #1

Deluxe Editions

Archer & Armstrong Deluxe Edition Book 1
ISBN: 9781939346223
Collecting ARCHER & ARMSTRONG #0-13

Archer & Armstrong Deluxe Edition Book 2
ISBN: 9781939346957
Collecting ARCHER & ARMSTRONG #14-25, ARCHER & ARMSTRONG: ARCHER #0 and BLOODSHOT AND H.A.R.D. CORPS #20-21.

Armor Hunters Deluxe Edition
ISBN: 9781939346728
Collecting Armor Hunters #1-4, Armor Hunters: Aftermath #1, Armor Hunters: Bloodshot #1-3, Armor Hunters: Harbinger #1-3, Unity #8-11, and X-O MANOWAR #23-29

Bloodshot Deluxe Edition Book 1
ISBN: 9781939346216
Collecting BLOODSHOT #1-13

Bloodshot Deluxe Edition Book 2
ISBN: 9781939346810
Collecting BLOODSHOT AND H.A.R.D. CORPS #14-23, BLOODSHOT #24-25, BLOODSHOT #0, BLOODSHOT AND H.A.R.D. CORPS: H.A.R.D. CORPS #0, along with ARCHER & ARMSTRONG #18-19

Book of Death Deluxe Edition
ISBN: 9781682151150
Collecting BOOK OF DEATH #1-4, BOOK OF DEATH: THE FALL OF BLOODSHOT #1, BOOK OF DEATH: THE FALL OF NINJAK #1, BOOK OF DEATH: THE FALL OF HARBINGER #1, and BOOK OF DEATH: THE FALL OF X-O MANOWAR #1.

Divinity Deluxe Edition
ISBN: 97819393460993
Collecting DIVNITY #1-4

Harbinger Deluxe Edition Book 1
ISBN: 9781939346131
Collecting HARBINGER #0-14

Harbinger Deluxe Edition Book 2
ISBN: 9781939346773
Collecting HARBINGER #15-25, HARBINGER: OMEGAS #1-3, and HARBINGER: BLEEDING MONK #0

Harbinger Wars Deluxe Edition
ISBN: 9781939346322
Collecting HARBINGER WARS #1-4, HARBINGER #11-14, and BLOODSHOT #10-13

Ivar, Timewalker Deluxe Edition Book 1
ISBN: 9781682151198
Collecting IVAR, TIMEWALKER #1-12

Quantum and Woody Deluxe Edition Book 1
ISBN: 9781939346681
Collecting QUANTUM AND WOODY #1-12 and QUANTUM AND WOODY: THE GOAT #0

Q2: The Return of Quantum and Woody Deluxe Edition
ISBN: 9781939346568
Collecting Q2: THE RETURN OF QUANTUM AND WOODY #1-5

Rai Deluxe Edition Book 1
ISBN: 9781682151174
Collecting RAI #1-12, along with material from RAI #1 PLUS EDITION and RAI #5 PLUS EDITION

Shadowman Deluxe Edition Book 1
ISBN: 9781939346438
Collecting SHADOWMAN #0-10

Shadowman Deluxe Edition Book 2
ISBN: 9781682151075
Collecting SHADOWMAN #11-16, SHADOWMAN #13X, SHADOWMAN: END TIMES #1-3 and PUNK MAMBO #0

Unity Deluxe Edition Book 1
ISBN: 9781939346575
Collecting UNITY #0-14

The Valiant Deluxe Edition
ISBN: 97819393460986
Collecting THE VALIANT #1-4

X-O Manowar Deluxe Edition Book 1
ISBN: 9781939346100
Collecting X-O MANOWAR #1-14

X-O Manowar Deluxe Edition Book 2
ISBN: 9781939346520
Collecting X-O MANOWAR #15-22, and UNITY #1-

X-O Manowar Deluxe Edition Book 3
ISBN: 9781682151310
Collecting X-O MANOWAR #23-29 and ARMOR HUNTERS #1-4.

Valiant Masters

Bloodshot Vol. 1 - Blood of the Machine
ISBN: 9780979640933

H.A.R.D. Corps Vol. 1 - Search and Destroy
ISBN: 9781939346285

Harbinger Vol. 1 - Children of the Eighth Day
ISBN: 9781939346483

Ninjak Vol. 1 - Black Water
ISBN: 9780979640971

Rai Vol. 1 - From Honor to Strength
ISBN: 9781939346070

Shadowman Vol. 1 - Spirits Within
ISBN: 9781939346018

THE ADVENTURES OF ARCHER AND ARMSTRONG | READING ORDER

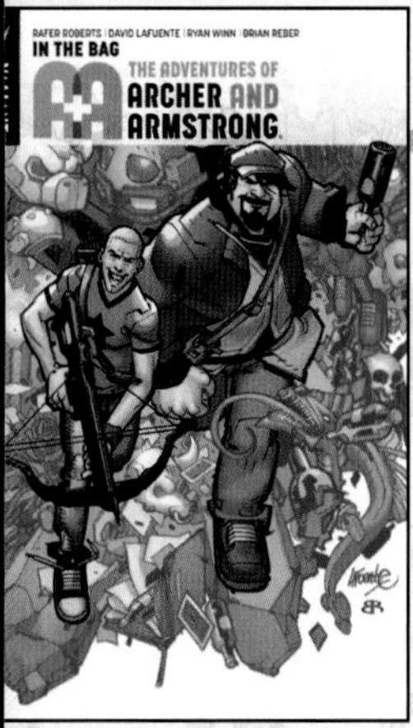
IN THE BAG
THE ADVENTURES OF
ARCHER AND
ARMSTRONG

A&A: The Adventures of Archer & Armstrong Vol. 1: In the Bag

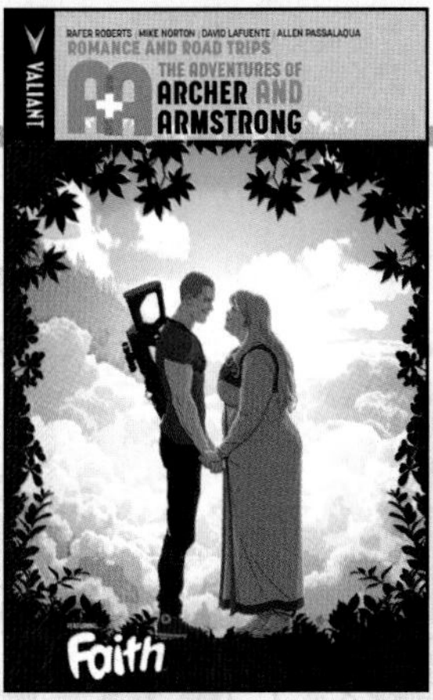
ROMANCE AND ROAD TRIPS
THE ADVENTURES OF
ARCHER AND
ARMSTRONG
VALIANT
Faith

A&A: The Adventures of Archer & Armstrong Vol. 2: Romance and Road Trips

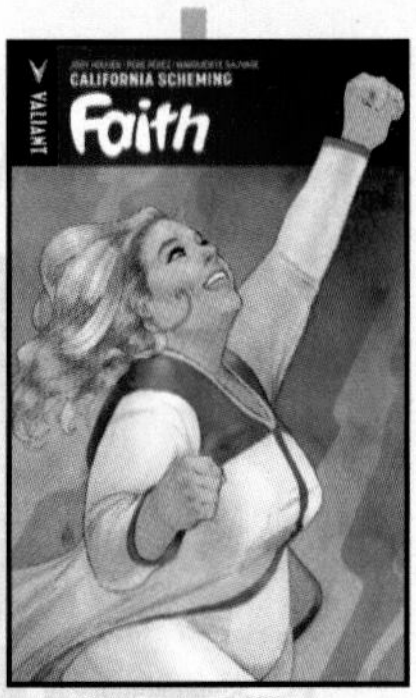
CALIFORNIA SCHEMING
Faith
VALIANT

Faith Vol. 2: California Scheming
(OPTIONAL)

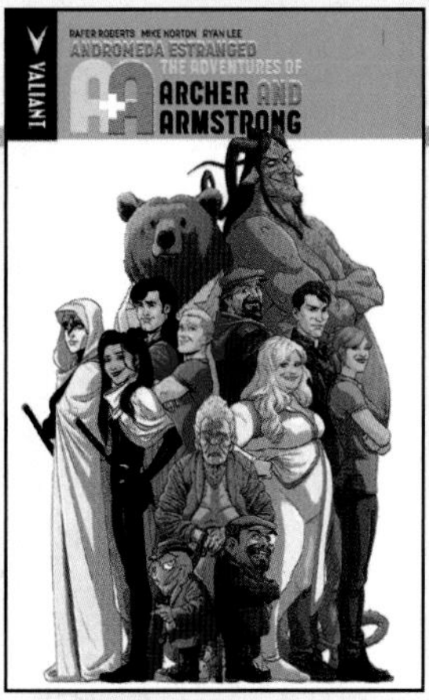
ANDROMEDA ESTRANGED
THE ADVENTURES OF
ARCHER AND
ARMSTRONG
VALIANT

A&A: The Adventures of Archer & Armstrong Vol. 3: Andromeda Estranged

Follow all of the critically acclaimed adventures of Valiant's history-smashing duo!

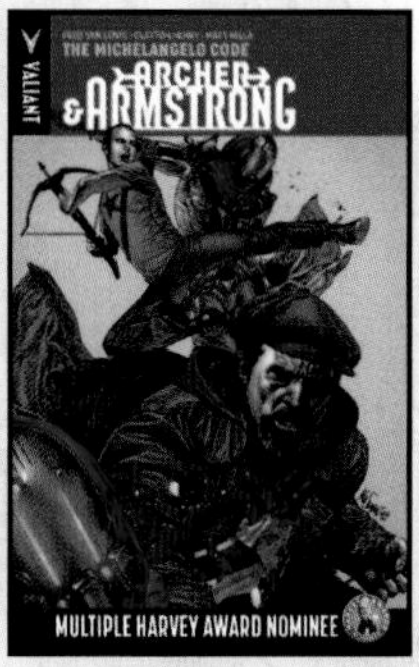
THE MICHELANGELO CODE
ARCHER & ARMSTRONG
VALIANT
MULTIPLE HARVEY AWARD NOMINEE

Archer & Armstrong Vol. 1: The Michelangelo Code

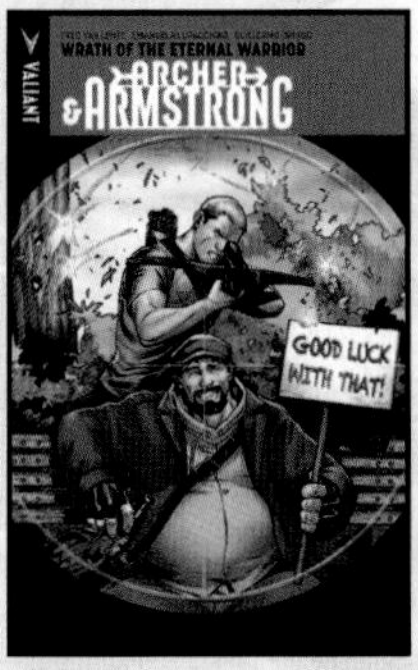
WRATH OF THE ETERNAL WARRIOR
ARCHER & ARMSTRONG
VALIANT
GOOD LUCK WITH THAT!

Archer & Armstrong Vol. 2: Wrath of the Eternal Warrior

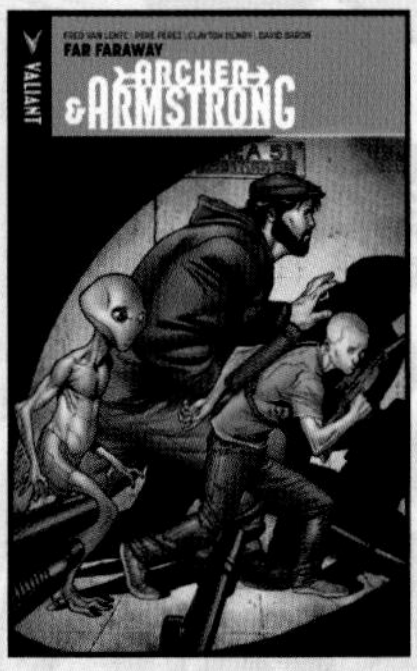
FAR FARAWAY
ARCHER & ARMSTRONG
VALIANT

Archer & Armstrong Vol. 3: Far Faraway

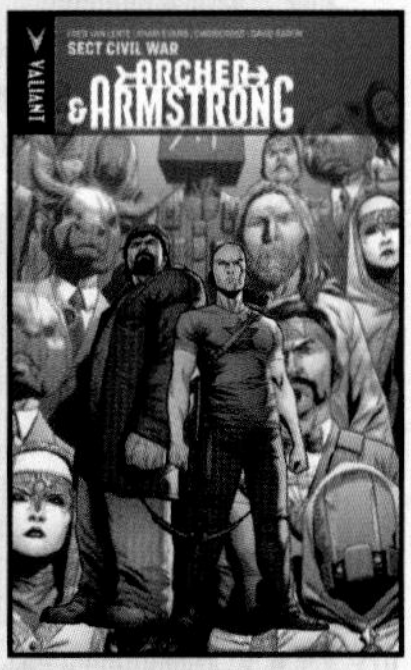
SECT CIVIL WAR
ARCHER & ARMSTRONG
VALIANT

Archer & Armstrong Vol. 4: Sect Civil War

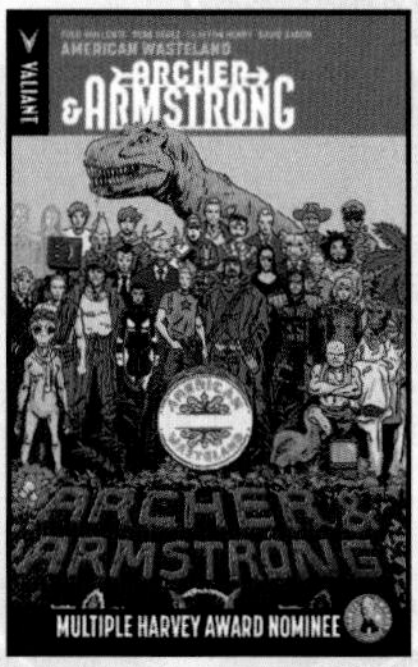
AMERICAN WASTELAND
ARCHER & ARMSTRONG
VALIANT
ARCHER & ARMSTRONG
MULTIPLE HARVEY AWARD NOMINEE

Archer & Armstrong Vol. 5: Mission: Improbable

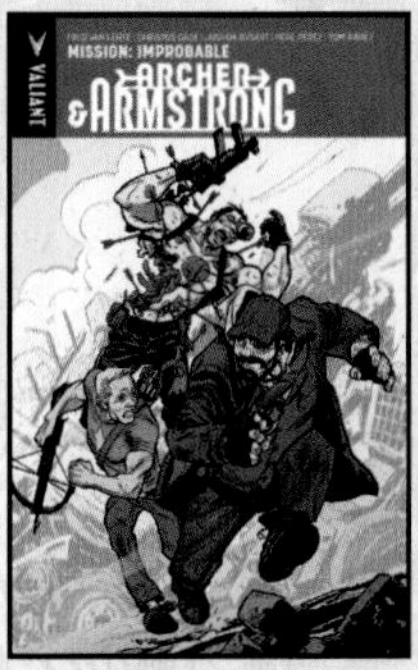
MISSION: IMPROBABLE
ARCHER & ARMSTRONG
VALIANT

Archer & Armstrong Vol. 6: American Wasteland

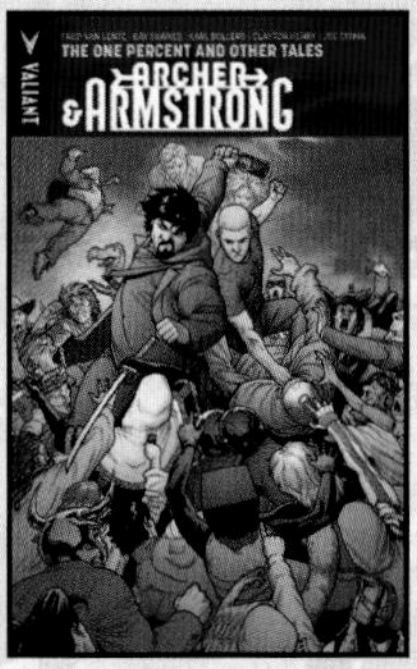
THE ONE PERCENT AND OTHER TALES
ARCHER & ARMSTRONG
VALIANT

Archer & Armstrong Vol. 7: The One Percent and Other Tales

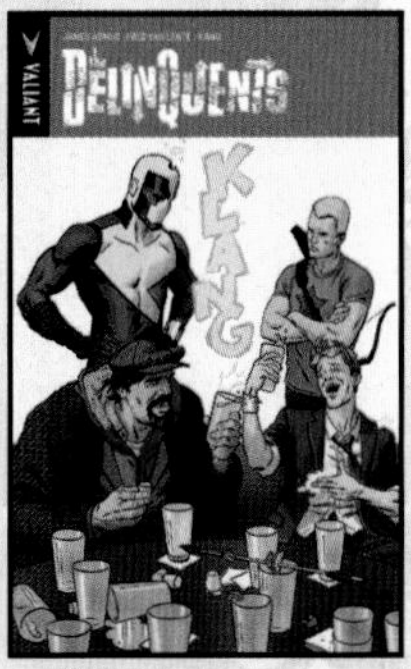
THE DELINQUENTS
VALIANT

The Delinquents

VALIANT

THE ADVENTURES OF ARCHER AND ARMSTRONG

VOLUME THREE: ANDROMEDA ESTRANGED

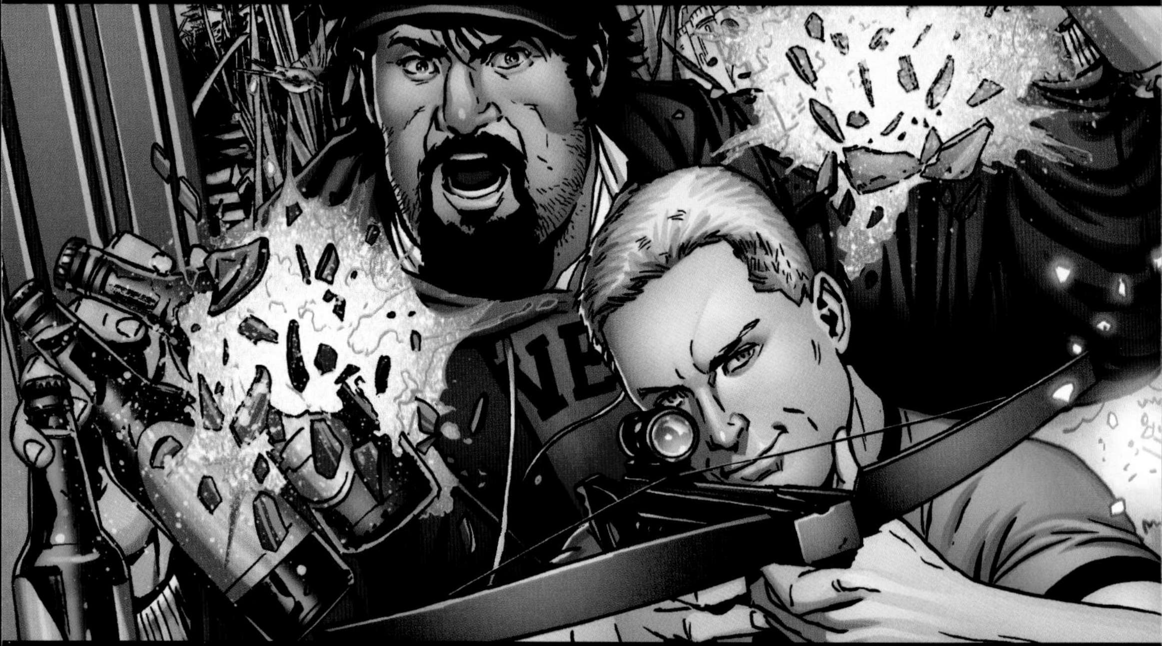

BEATDOWN IN THE BAYOU!

At long last, Valiant's gallant adventurers have finally located Armstrong's long-missing wife...in that dreaded land that dare not speak its name: Florida! But after centuries of thinking that his near-immortal bride, Andromeda, was just a booze-induced hallucination, how will Armstrong make up for years of lies, losses, and infidelities? And, as if that wasn't enough, a nefarious new force is about to release an army of bathsalt-using "Florida Men" to finish off Archer & Armstrong once and for all!

It's a true story (not really) ripped from today's headlines (pretty much)! Pack your Crocs and don't skimp on the lotion because the Sunshine State is about to hit Archer & Armstrong like a bad seafood buffet...and we only have Harvey Award-nominated writer Rafer Roberts (HARBINGER RENEGADES) and acclaimed artist Mike Norton (*Revival*) to blame!

TRADE PAPERBACK
ISBN: 978-1-68215-203-4

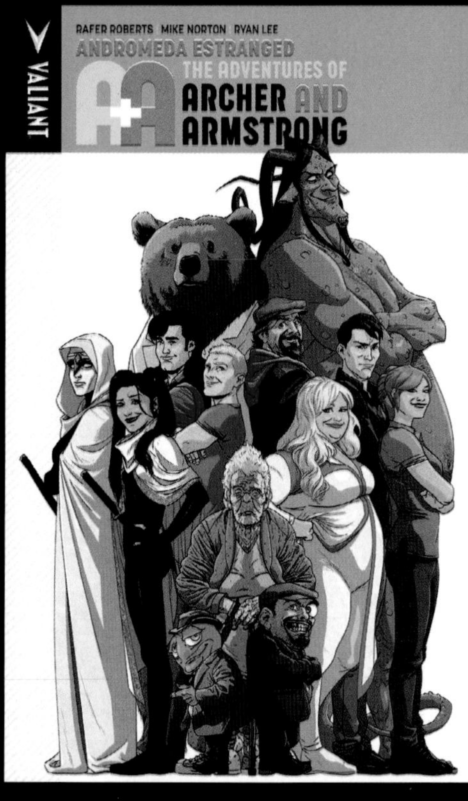
VALIANT
RAFER ROBERTS MIKE NORTON RYAN LEE
ANDROMEDA ESTRANGED
THE ADVENTURES OF
ARCHER AND
ARMSTRONG

................A STORY OF HUMAN SACRIFICE

Words by: Jonathan Hickman
Art by: Tomm Coker
Colors by: Michael Garland
Letters by: Rus Wooton

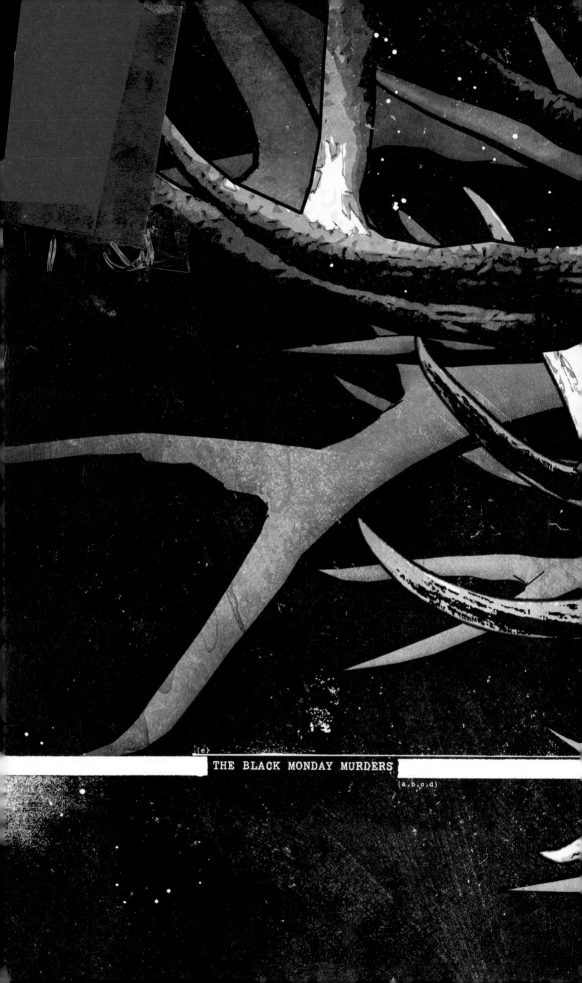

THE BLACK MONDAY MURDERS

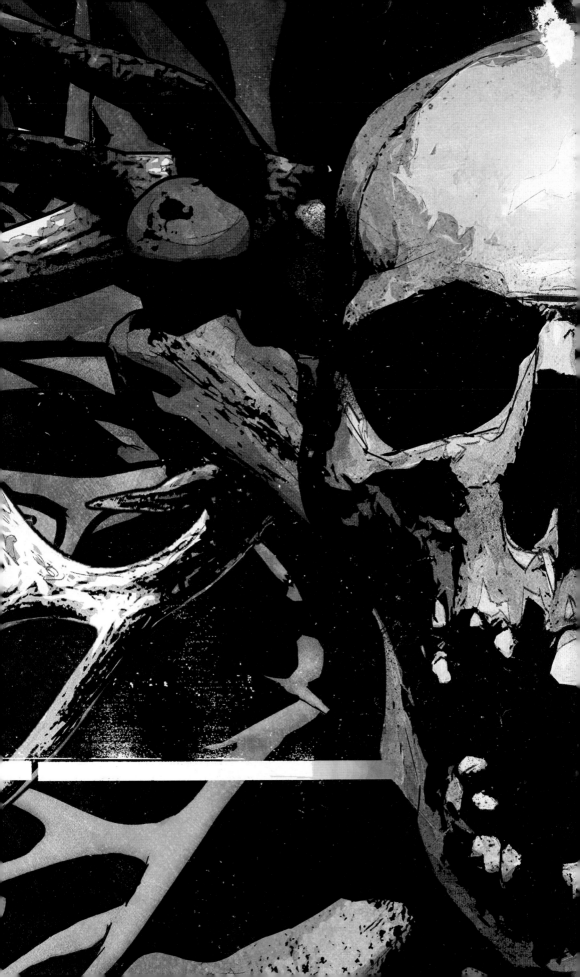

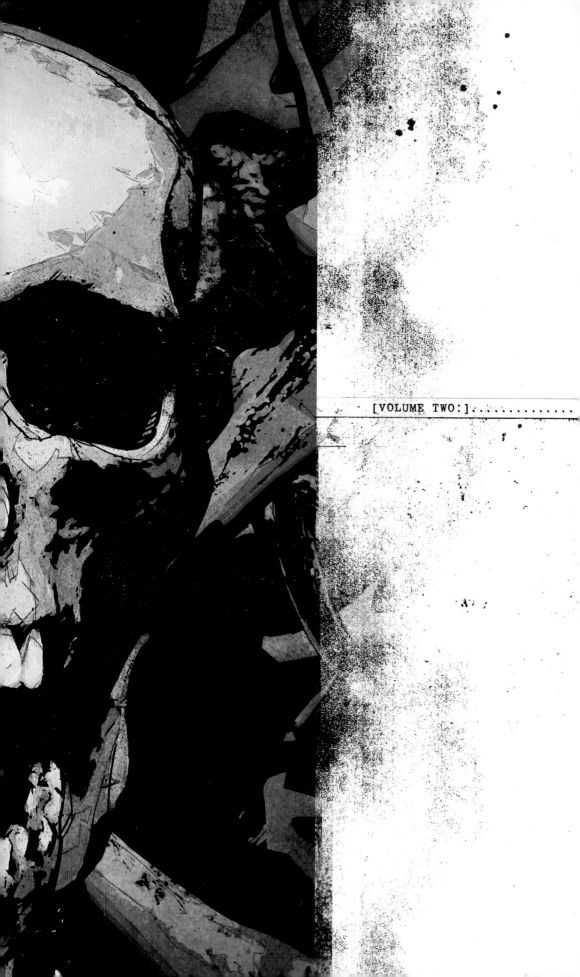

[VOLUME TWO:].................

..............THE SCALES

CONTENTS

VI

VII

VIII

Bonus

(a)
DRAMATIS PERSONAE: (e)

(b,c,d)

(e)

CAINA
1929

Charles Ackermann
  (The Ackermann seat)
J.W. Bischoff
  (The Bischoff seat)
Raymond Dominic
  (The Dominic seat)
Milton Rothschild
  (The Rothschild seat)
Abigail
  (Rothschild Familiar)

KANKRIN
1985/Current

Irena Kozlov
  (The Judge)
Alexi Malkin
  (The Body)
Viktor Eresko
  (The Executioner)

CAINA
1985/Current

Wynn Ackermann
  (The Ackermann seat)
Beatrix Bischoff
  (The Bischoff seat)
Marco Dominic
  (The Dominic seat)
Daniel Rothschild
  (The Rothschild seat)
Grigoria Rothschild
  (The Rothschild seat)
Abby
  (Rothschild Familiar)

Thomas Dane
  (Head of Security)

NEW YORK POLICE DEPARTMENT

Theodore Dumas
  (Detective)
Michael Caffey
  (Detective)
Susana Moreno
  (Detective)
William Merritt
  (Captain)

OTHER

Dr. Tyler Gaddis
  (Professor of Economics,
   Fordham)   (a,b,c,d)

OPERATION ARGENT

BOLIVIA: 1970-1973

(X-1972-09200)

August 16, 1972

(a)

(b,c,d)

August 16, 1972

From: [redacted]
Office of the Executive
Director of the CIA

To: Pierre-Paul Schweitzer
Managing Director
International Monetary Fund

Subject: Operation Argent
[redacted]

Ref: X-1972-09200

Mr. Schweitzer:

This is in response to your 5 August 1972 letter which my office received on 10 August 1972 regarding personnel concerns related to our mutual commitment in [redacted]

I understand your unease, especially in regards to optics and potential blowback, and have taken the following actions to mitigate said concerns:

(e,f)

Funneling of additional assets: [redacted] untraceable funds [redacted] third party, unaffiliated banking institutions [redacted]

Reassignment of strategic personnel: [redacted] To that end, we are sending [redacted] as well as field operative Thomas Dane, Special Activities Division (SAD), [redacted] experienced South American asset [redacted] formerly U.S. Army Special Forces [redacted]

I believe these actions will be sufficient in executing our shared strategy. Please let me know if you have any further concerns.

(g)

Sincerely,

[redacted]

(a) Satellite (19°35'00" : 65°45'11")

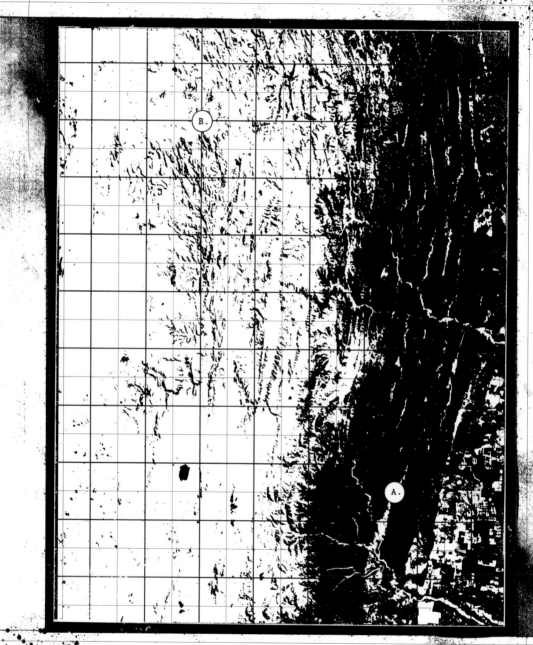

A. Reserva Tariquia
B. Potosi

(b,c,d)

(e,f,g,h)
(i)
(j,k)

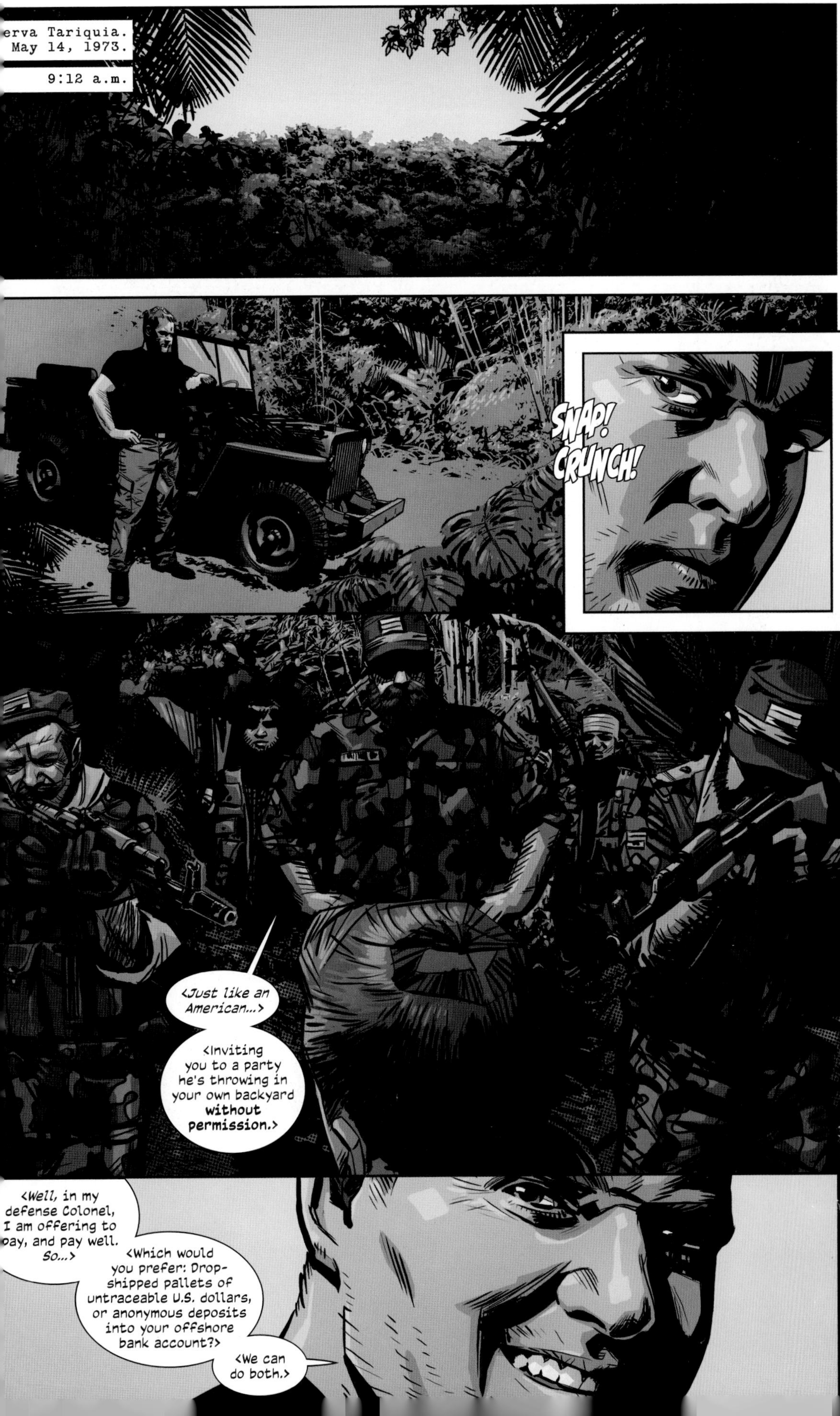

erva Tariquia.
May 14, 1973.
9:12 a.m.
SNAP!
CRUNCH!
<*Just like an American...*>
<Inviting you to a party he's throwing in your own backyard **without permission.**>
<*Well,* in my defense Colonel, I am offering to pay, and pay well. *So...*>
<Which would you prefer: Drop-shipped pallets of untraceable U.S. dollars, or anonymous deposits into your offshore bank account?>
<We can do both.>

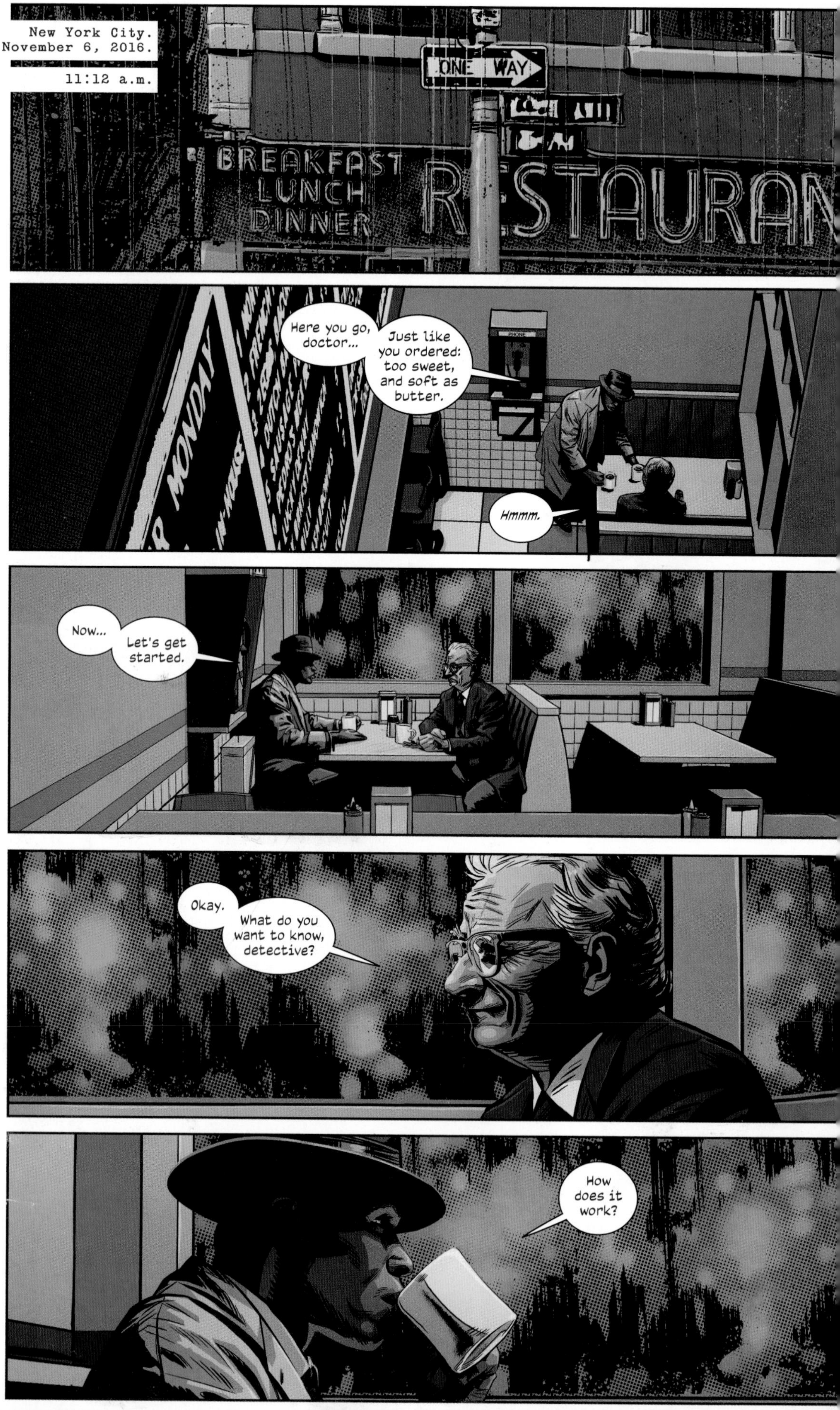
New York City.
November 6, 2016.
11:12 a.m.
ONE WAY
BREAKFAST
LUNCH
DINNER
RESTAURAN
Here you go, doctor...
Just like you ordered: too sweet, and soft as butter.
Hmmm.
Now...
Let's get started.
Okay.
What do you want to know, detective?
How does it work?

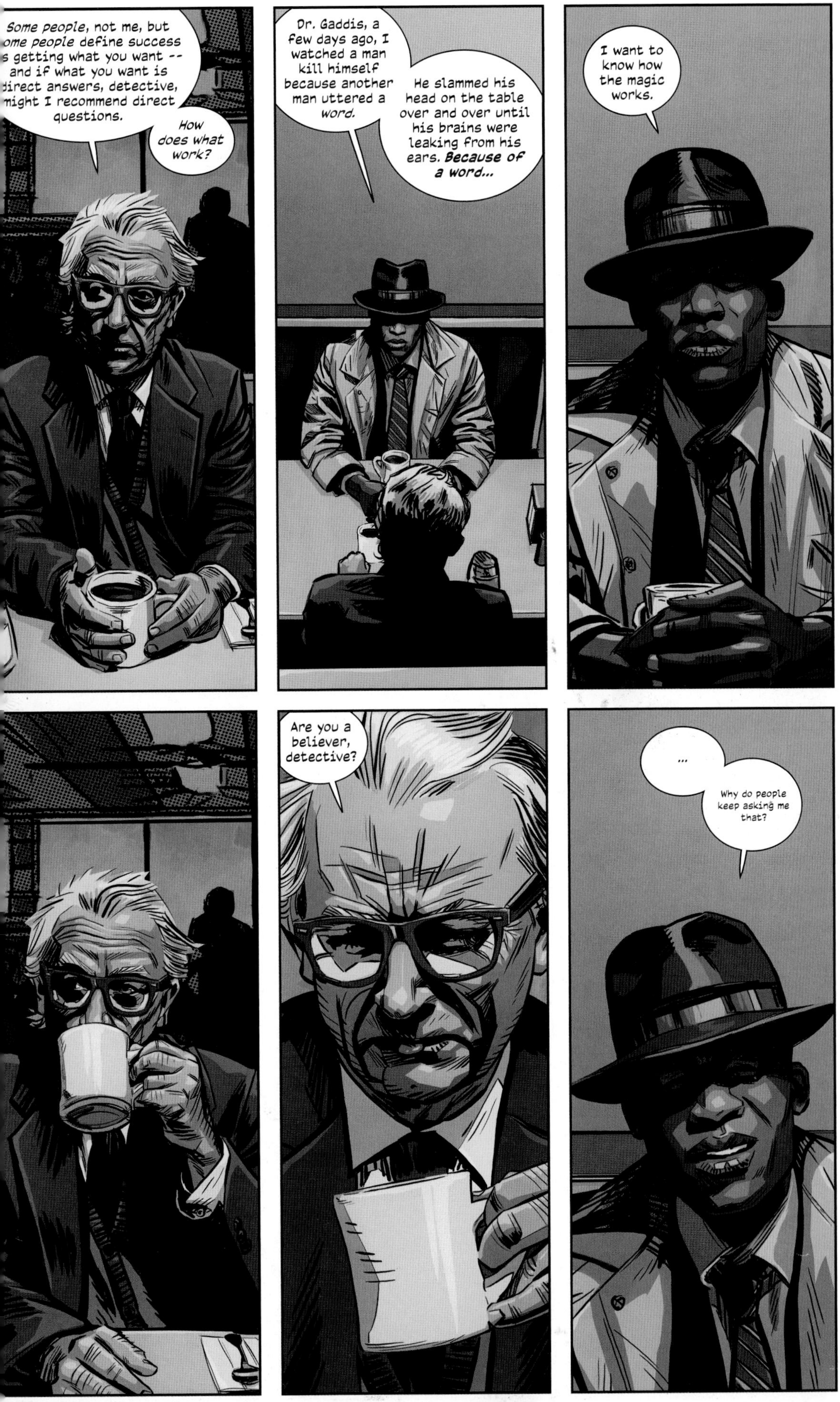
Some people, not me, but
ome people define success
s getting what you want --
and if what you want is
direct answers, detective,
might I recommend direct
questions.
How does what work?
Dr. Gaddis, a few days ago, I watched a man kill himself because another man uttered a word.
He slammed his head on the table over and over until his brains were leaking from his ears. Because of a word...
I want to know how the magic works.
Are you a believer, detective?
...
Why do people keep asking me that?

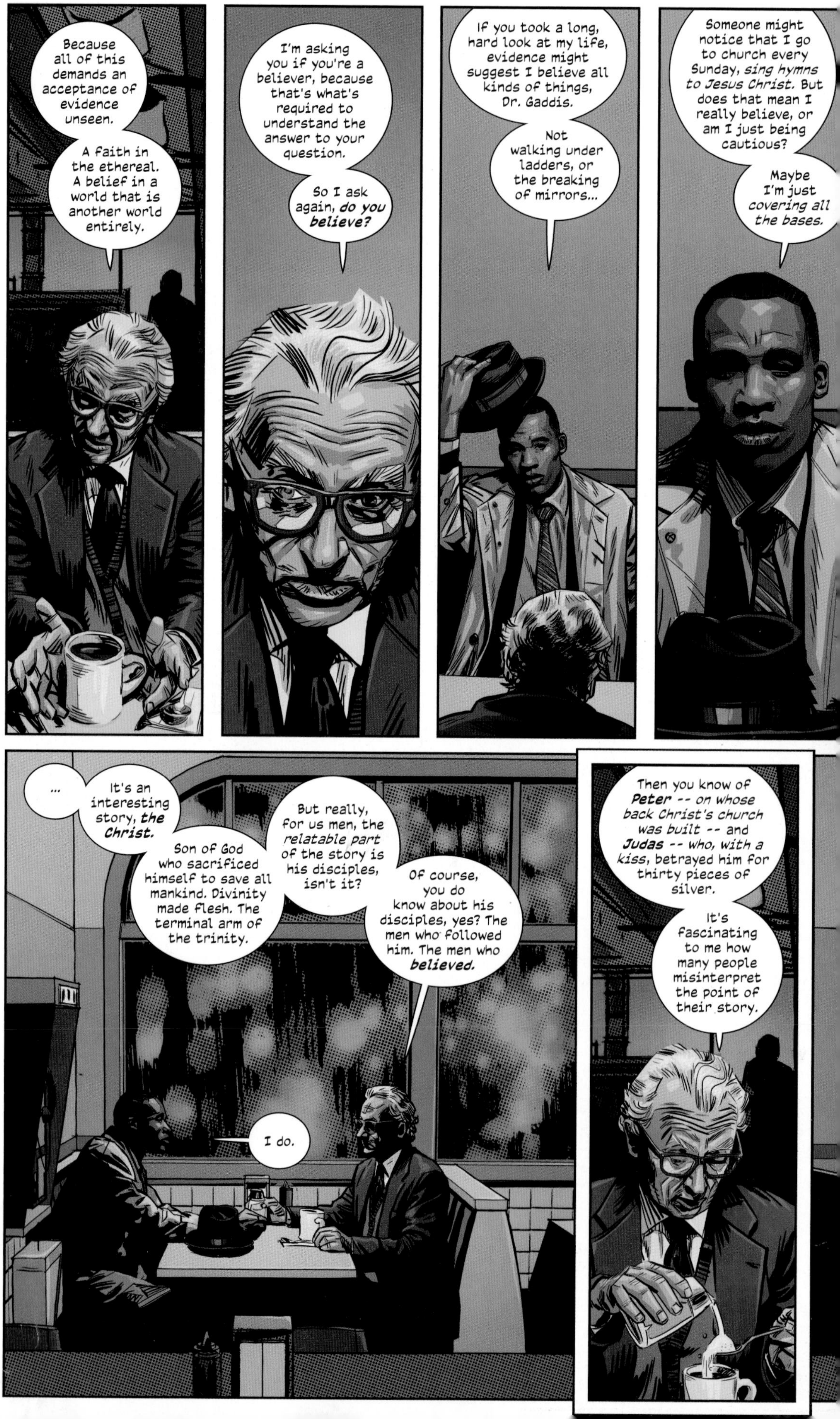
Because all of this demands an acceptance of evidence unseen.
A faith in the ethereal. A belief in a world that is another world entirely.
I'm asking you if you're a believer, because that's what's required to understand the answer to your question.
So I ask again, *do you believe?*
If you took a long, hard look at my life, evidence might suggest I believe all kinds of things, Dr. Gaddis.
Not walking under ladders, or the breaking of mirrors...
Someone might notice that I go to church every Sunday, *sing hymns to Jesus Christ.* But does that mean I really believe, or am I just being cautious?
Maybe I'm just *covering all the bases.*
...
It's an interesting story, ***the Christ.***
Son of God who sacrificed himself to save all mankind. Divinity made flesh. The terminal arm of the trinity.
But really, for us men, the *relatable part* of the story is his disciples, isn't it?
Of course, you do know about his disciples, yes? The men who followed him. The men who ***believed.***
I do.
Then you know of ***Peter*** *-- on whose back Christ's church was built --* and ***Judas*** *-- who, with a kiss,* betrayed him for thirty pieces of silver.
It's fascinating to me how many people misinterpret the point of their story.

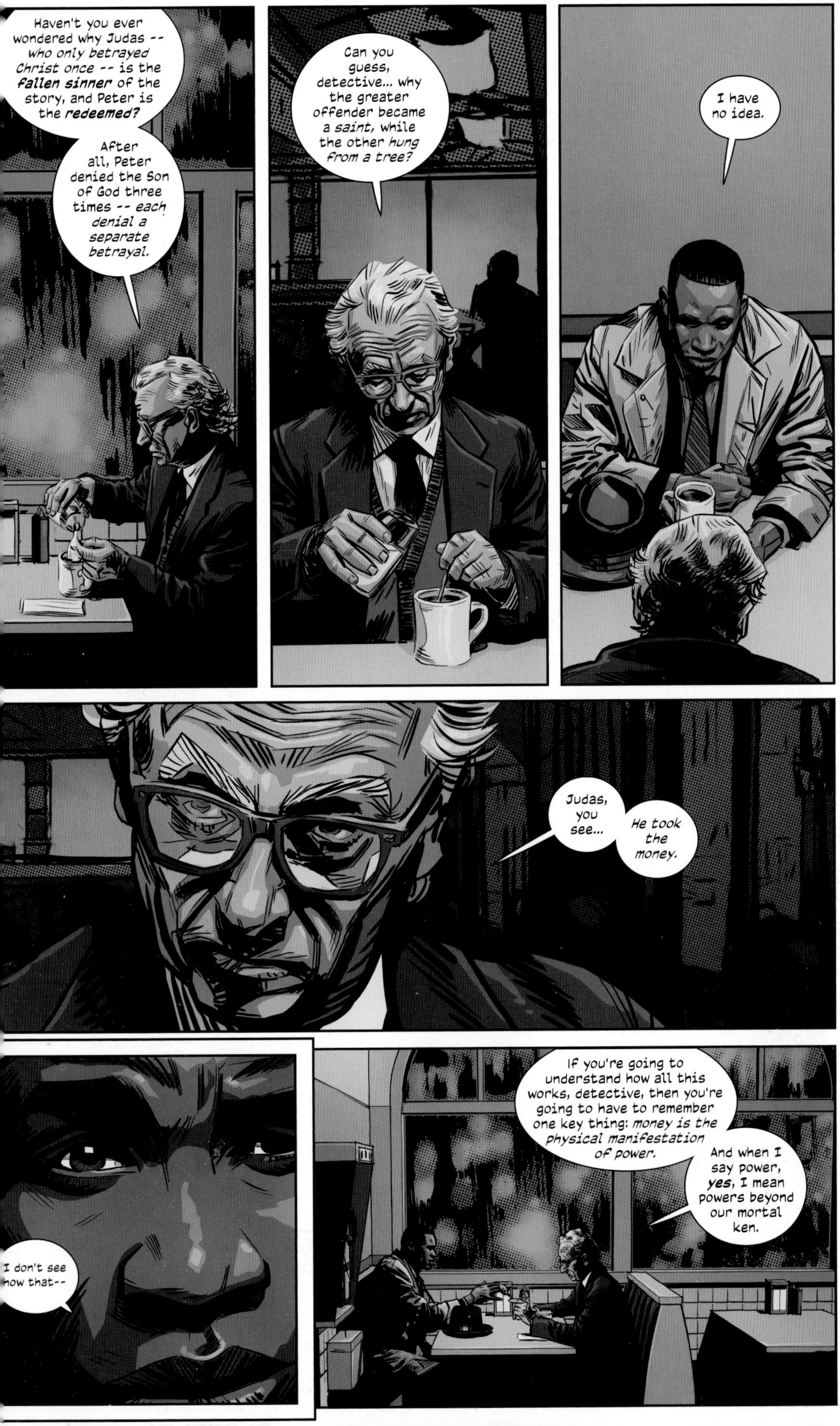
Haven't you ever wondered why Judas -- who only betrayed Christ once -- is the fallen sinner of the story, and Peter is the redeemed?
After all, Peter denied the Son of God three times -- each denial a separate betrayal.
Can you guess, detective... why the greater offender became a saint, while the other hung from a tree?
I have no idea.
Judas, you see...
He took the money.
I don't see how that--
If you're going to understand how all this works, detective, then you're going to have to remember one key thing: money is the physical manifestation of power.
And when I say power, yes, I mean powers beyond our mortal ken.

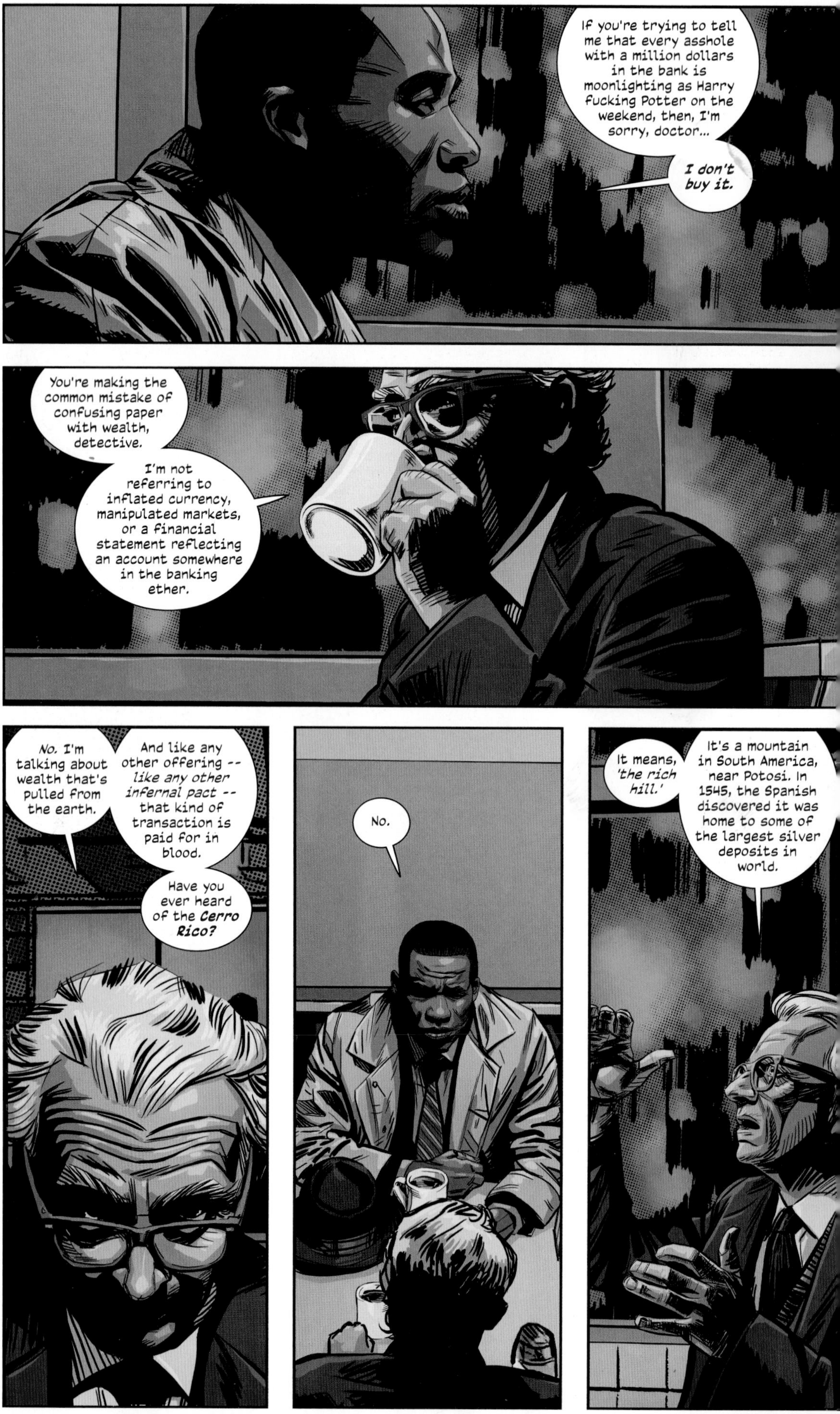
If you're trying to tell me that every asshole with a million dollars in the bank is moonlighting as Harry fucking Potter on the weekend, then, I'm sorry, doctor...
I don't buy it.
You're making the common mistake of confusing paper with wealth, detective.
I'm not referring to inflated currency, manipulated markets, or a financial statement reflecting an account somewhere in the banking ether.
No. I'm talking about wealth that's pulled from the earth.
And like any other offering -- like any other infernal pact -- that kind of transaction is paid for in blood.
Have you ever heard of the Cerro Rico?
No.
It means, 'the rich hill.'
It's a mountain in South America, near Potosi. In 1545, the Spanish discovered it was home to some of the largest silver deposits in world.

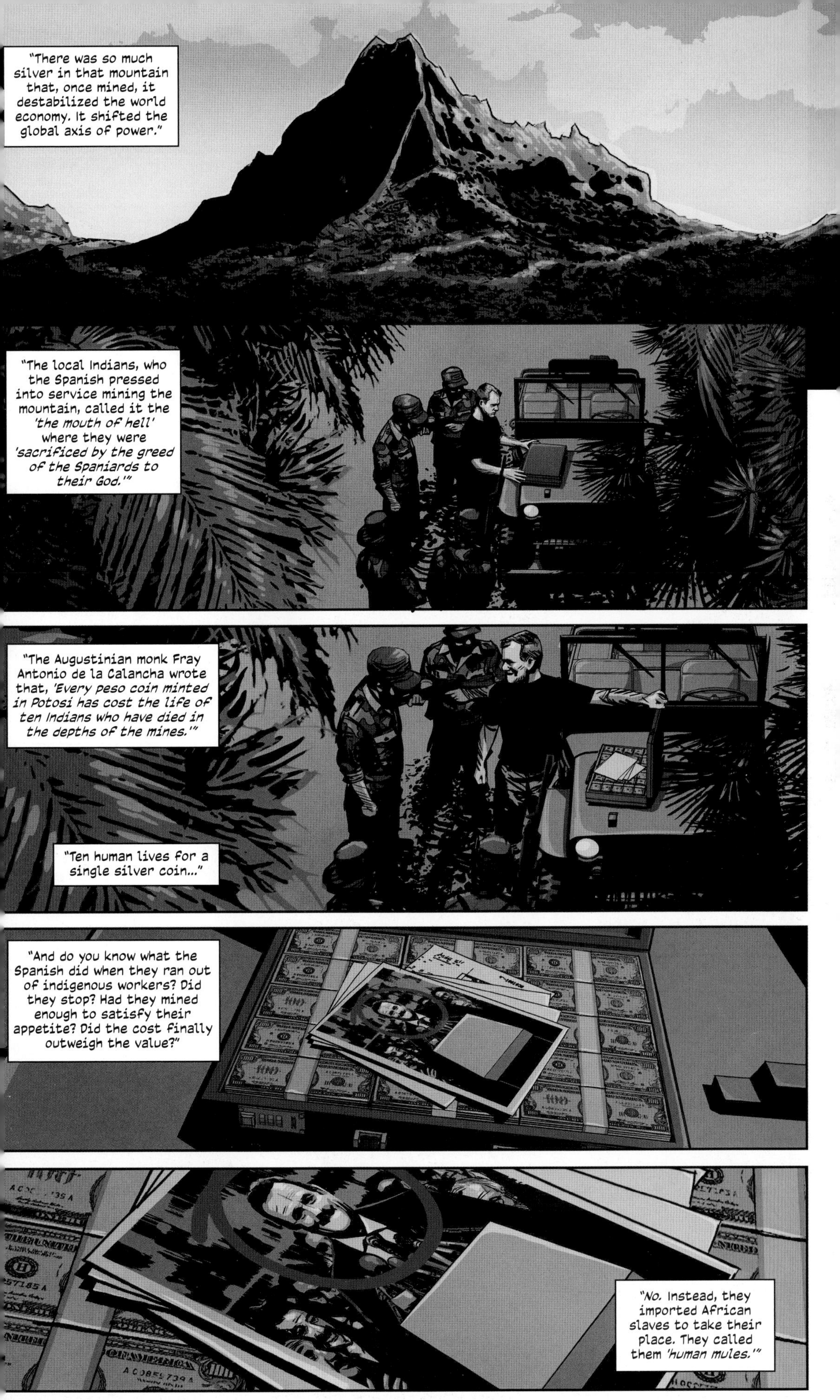
"There was so much silver in that mountain that, once mined, it destabilized the world economy. It shifted the global axis of power."
"The local Indians, who the Spanish pressed into service mining the mountain, called it the *'the mouth of hell'* where they were *'sacrificed by the greed of the Spaniards to their God.'*"
"The Augustinian monk Fray Antonio de la Calancha wrote that, *'Every peso coin minted in Potosi has cost the life of ten Indians who have died in the depths of the mines.'*"
"Ten human lives for a single silver coin..."
"And do you know what the Spanish did when they ran out of indigenous workers? Did they stop? Had they mined enough to satisfy their appetite? Did the cost finally outweigh the value?"
"No. Instead, they imported African slaves to take their place. They called them *'human mules.'*"

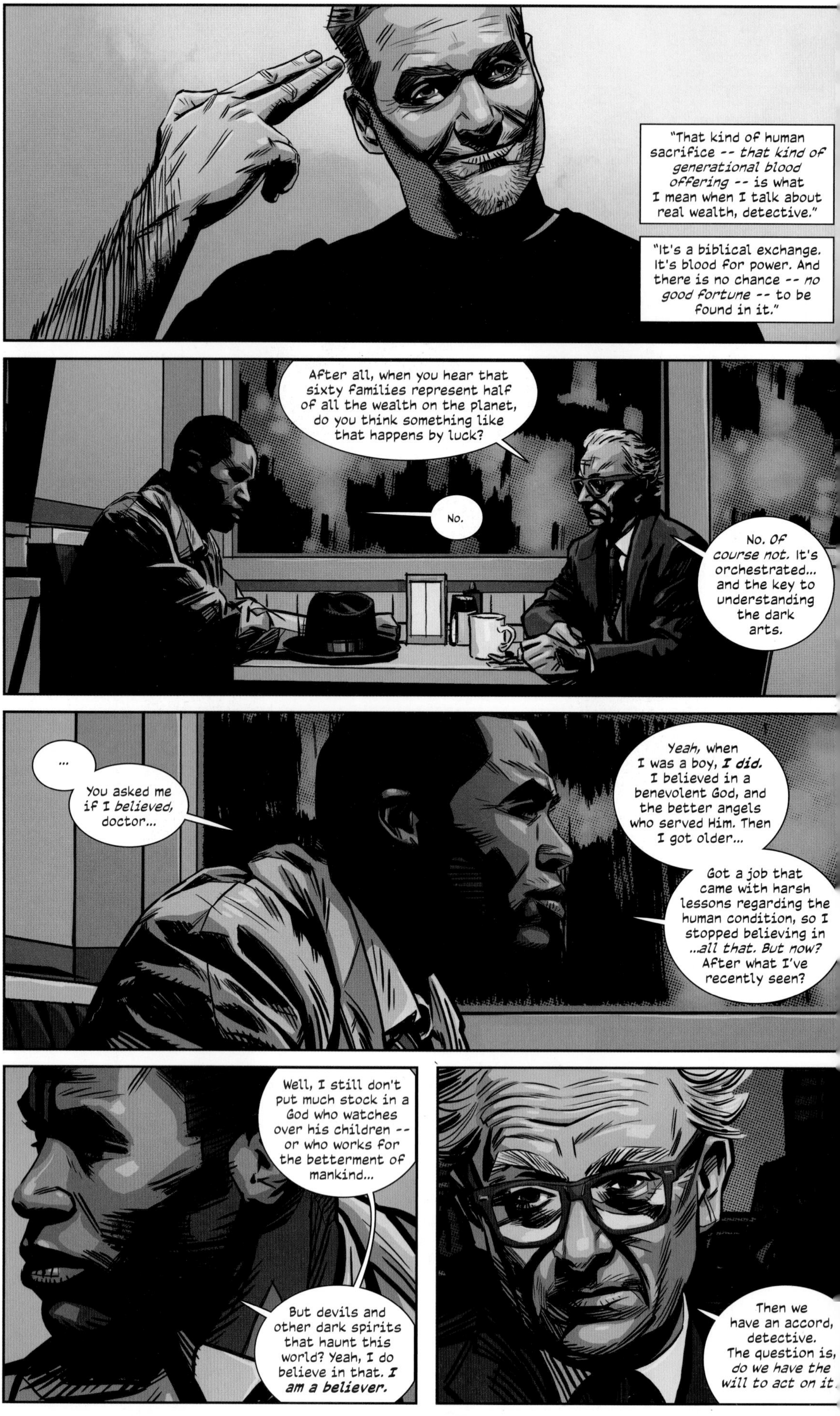
"That kind of human sacrifice -- *that kind of generational blood offering* -- is what I mean when I talk about real wealth, detective."
"It's a biblical exchange. It's blood for power. And there is no chance -- *no good fortune* -- to be found in it."
After all, when you hear that sixty families represent half of all the wealth on the planet, do you think something like that happens by luck?
No.
No. *Of course not.* It's orchestrated... and the key to understanding the dark arts.
...
You asked me if I *believed,* doctor...
Yeah, when I was a boy, ***I did.*** I believed in a benevolent God, and the better angels who served Him. Then I got older...
Got a job that came with harsh lessons regarding the human condition, so I stopped believing in *...all that. But now?* After what I've recently seen?
Well, I still don't put much stock in a God who watches over his children -- or who works for the betterment of mankind...
But devils and other dark spirits that haunt this world? Yeah, I do believe in that. ***I am a believer.***
Then we have an accord, detective. The question is, *do we have the will to act on it.*

Government Remains Silent on President's Death

Upcoming elections in turmoil following the assassination of President Santiago.

June 3, 1973 | By Antonio Barnard, Miami Herald

Col. Gustaf Diaz, long a powerful figure in South American military circles, has said that there are still no leads regarding the assassination of President Juan Manuel Jesus Santiago, a Bolivian television channel reported Wednesday. While conflicting reports continue to swirl regarding the assassination itself, no new answers appear to be forthcoming.

On Monday, the United States condemned the killing, which came just weeks before the country's upcoming presidential election, and it called on the government to protect all remaining political candidates. "This is yet another deadly attack orchestrated by extranational parties specifically aimed at candidates who support liberal democracy," said State Department spokesman James Houston in a statement. "Campaigns of fear, violence and intimidation have no place in any election."

When asked if the election would continue as scheduled, Diaz ensured they would and that all remaining candidates would receive around-the-clock security. "I personally guarantee their safety," Diaz said.

CHAPTER FIVE:

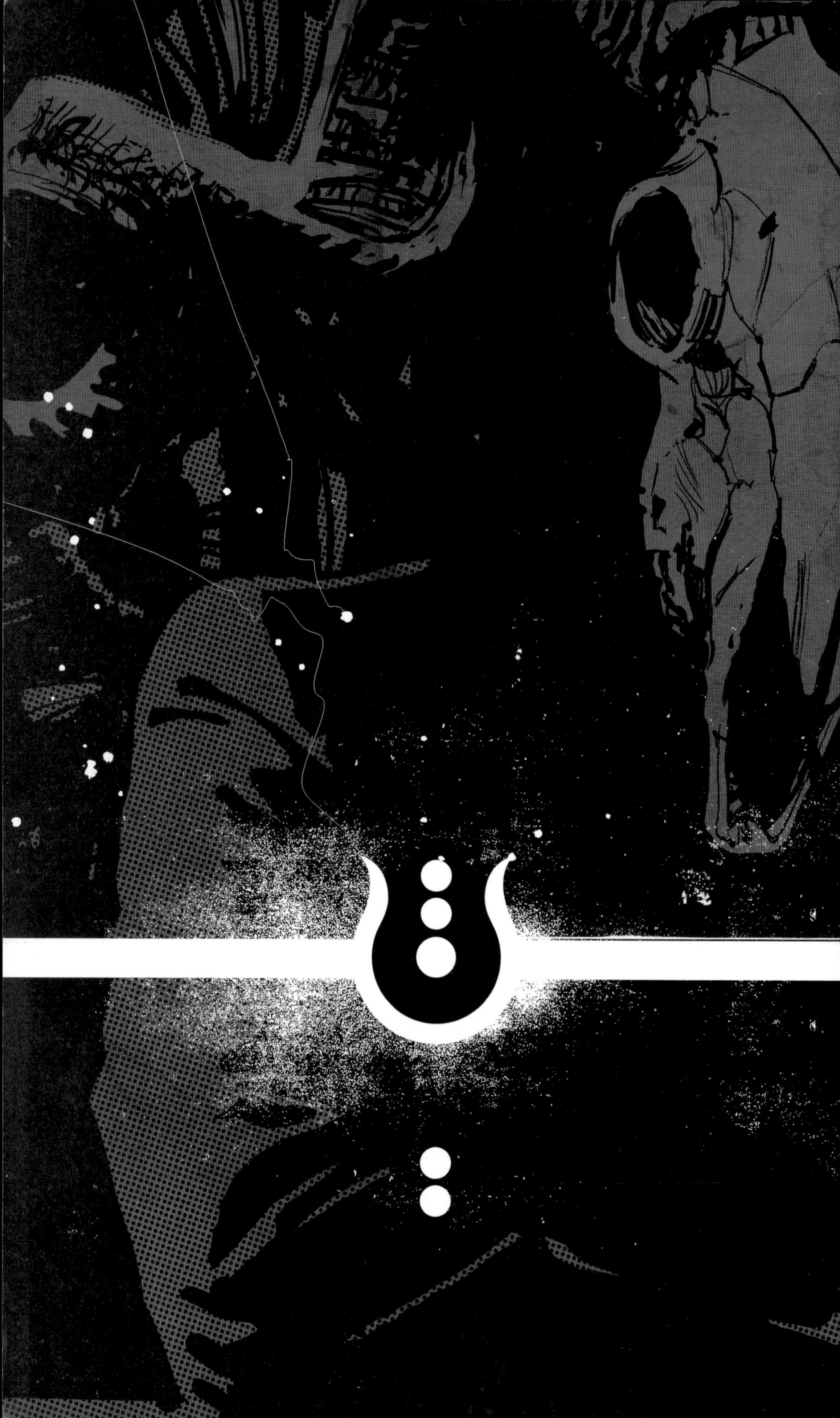

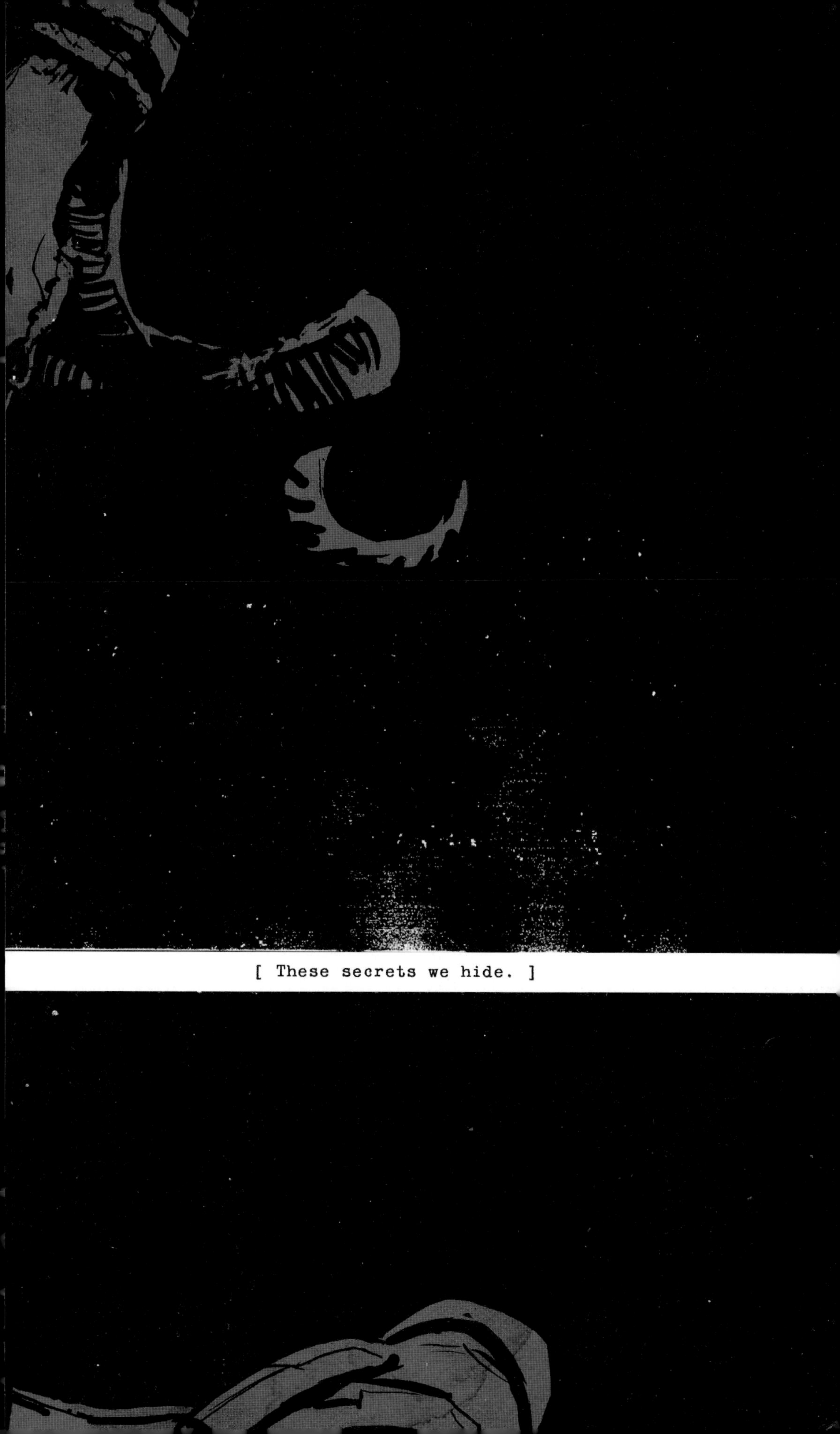
[These secrets we hide.]

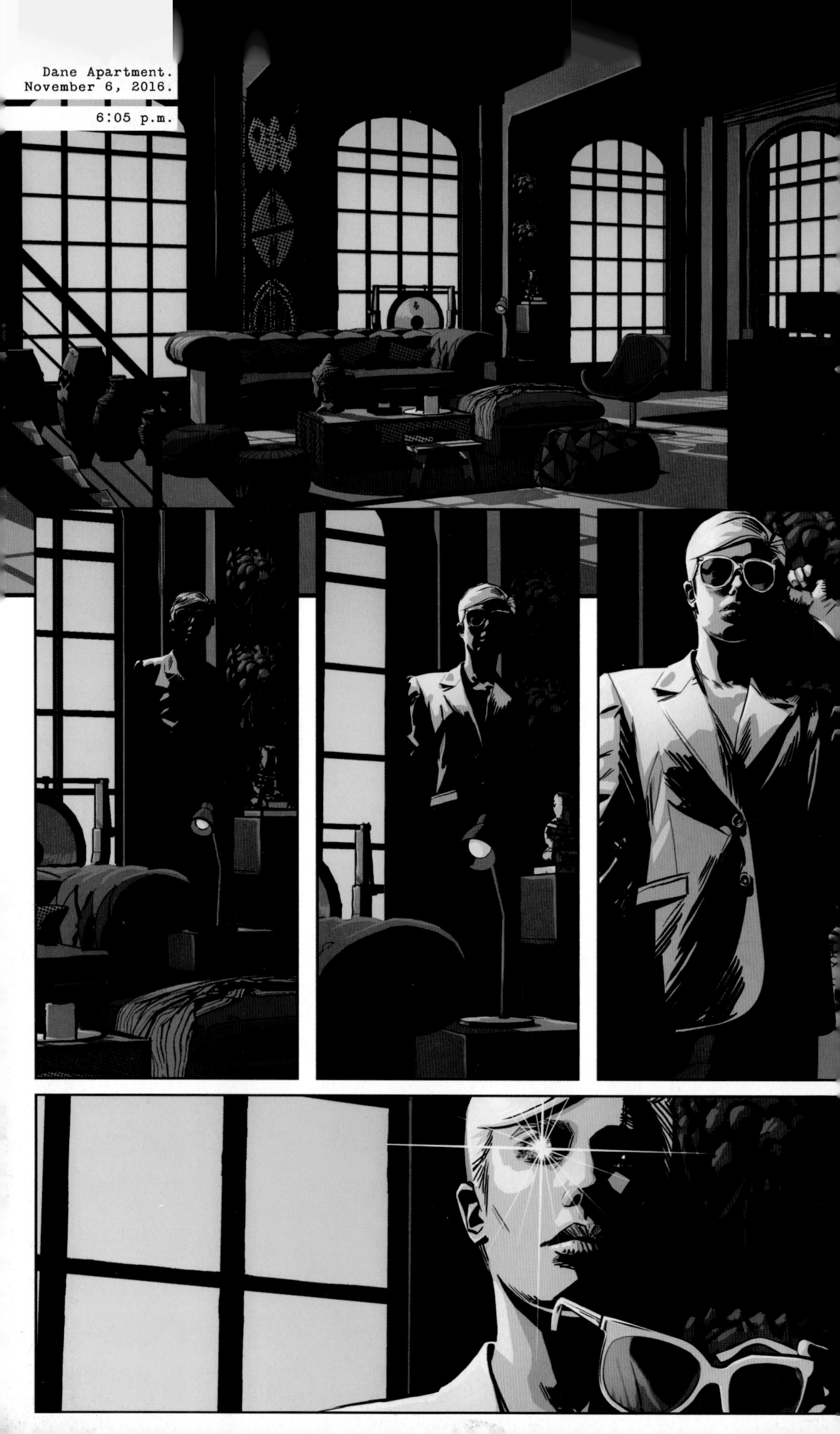
Dane Apartment.
November 6, 2016.
6:05 p.m.

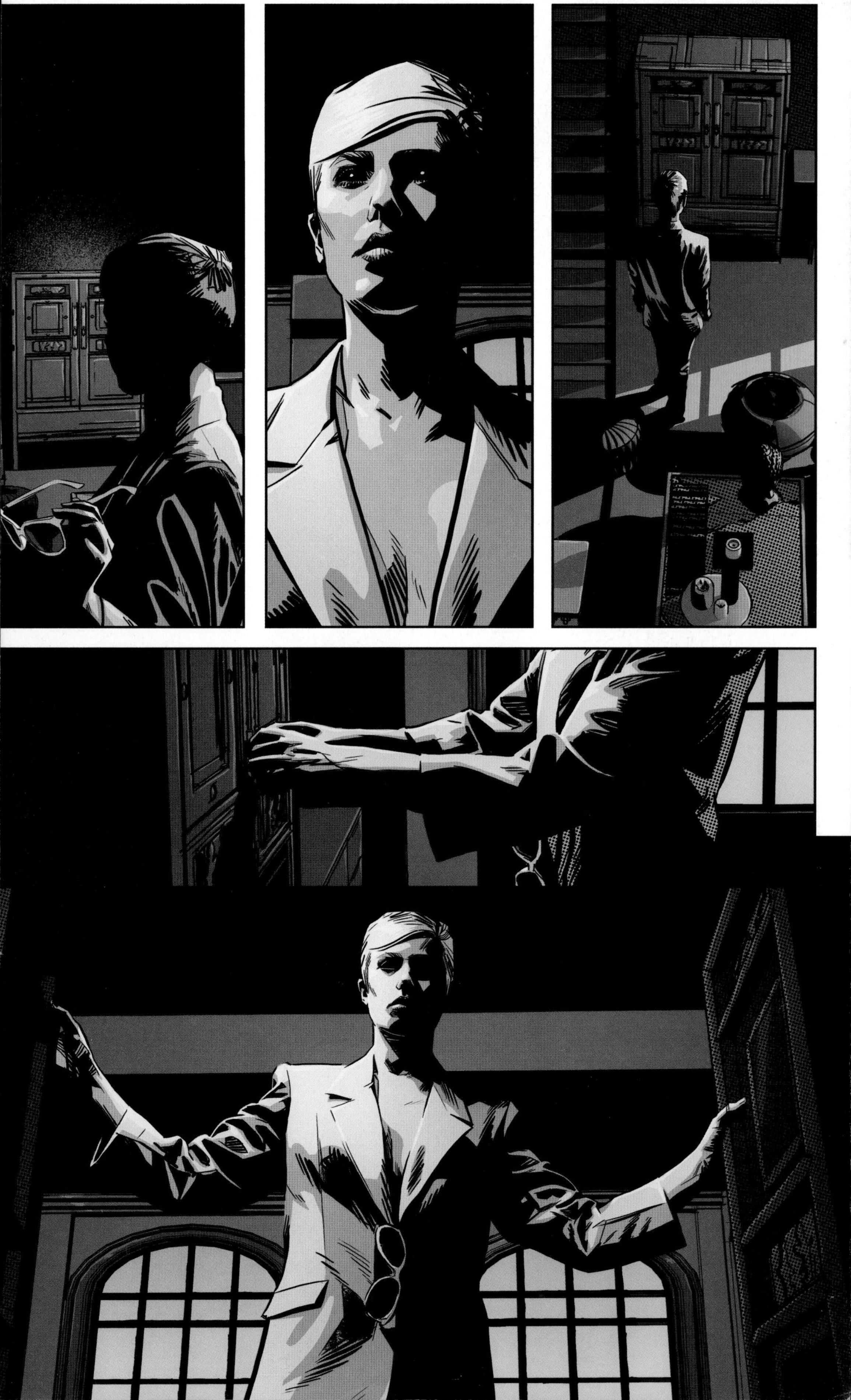

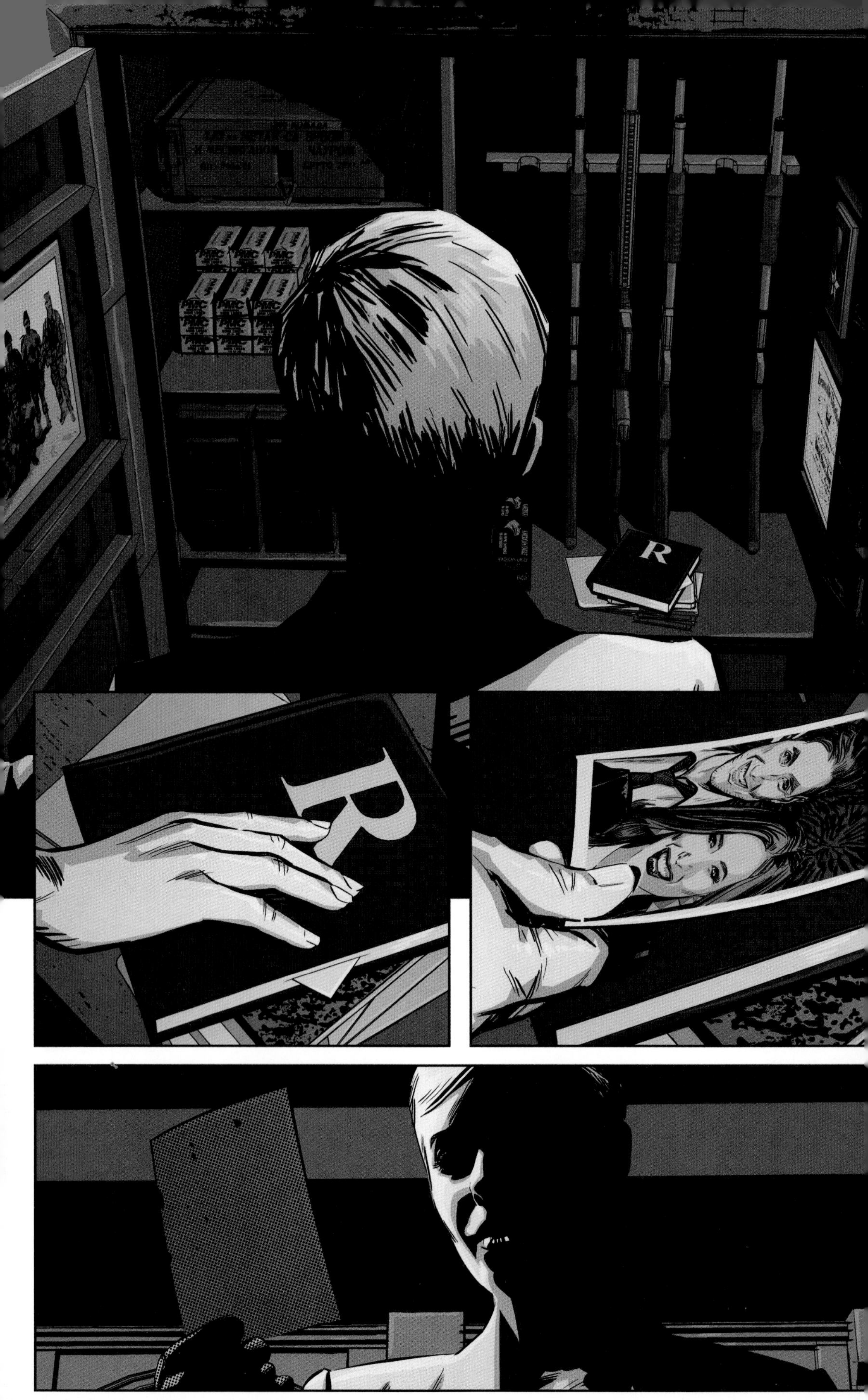
PMC
R

- THE EXECUTIVE JOURNAL OF -
- DANIEL ROTHSCHILD -

THE EXECUTIVE JOURNAL OF DANIEL ROTHSCHILD

January 29, 1993

There was an uprising in the Kenyan Lattice academy yesterday. Seven doctors of the Broken Hand decided to 'retire' their Merovingian watcher, and after eating his heart, used the accrued power to escape into Idea Space.

The best minds of the Hyperpyron school think it's a suicide run. If so, and accounting for the potential power wielded by six terminal doctors, they believe they have a vulnerability window of 20 years. So, unless they're wrong, or the Lattice doctors are total incompetents, someone higher up in the Merovingian school is probably going to be murdered in their crib.

With any luck, it will be that Anjou prick, Alfonso.

Regardless, this latest news is yet another in an increasing line of arcane disasters. I find this uptick troubling, and I'm having trouble moving past two parallel ideas in my head:

1. The appearance of global peace seems to be indicative of increased conflict within the independent houses. I've uncovered ample evidence that the Black Pope is investing in Balkan destabilization in an effort to combat this with the Vatican. This idea might be worth presenting to the board.

2. I think I need to hire personal security.

April 17, 1993

I have hired an IMF security expert named Thomas Dane to be my personal bodyguard.

He comes with the blessing of Michel Camdessus, as well as a letter of recommendation from the CIA.

If he turns out to be everything he seems, then I plan to groom him to take over, and reconstitute, Caina-Kankrin corporate security during my next rotation into the Ascendant Seat.

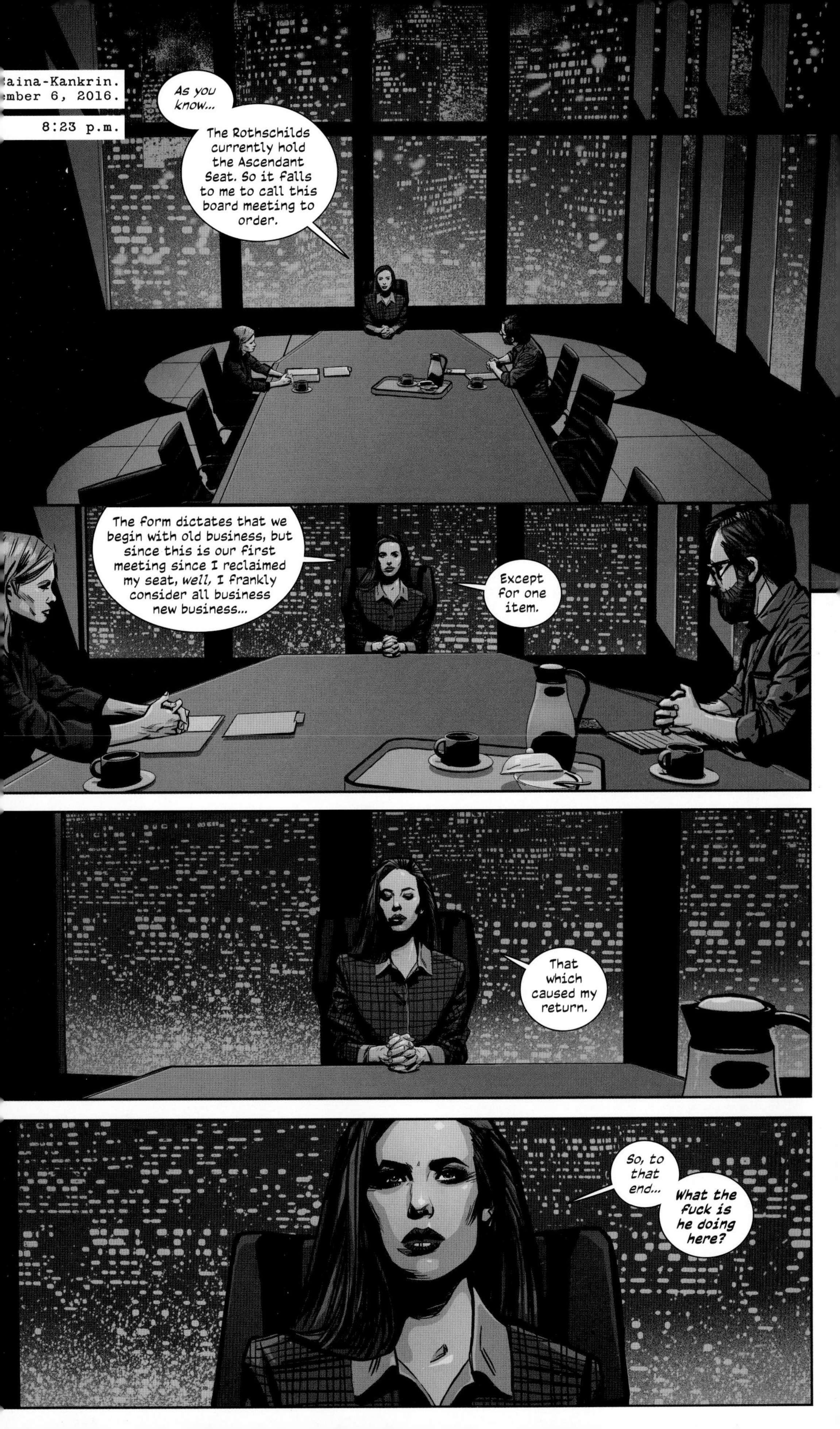

aina-Kankrin.
mber 6, 2016.
8:23 p.m.
As you know...
The Rothschilds currently hold the Ascendant Seat. So it falls to me to call this board meeting to order.
The form dictates that we begin with old business, but since this is our first meeting since I reclaimed my seat, *well,* I frankly consider all business new business...
Except for one item.
That which caused my return.
So, to that end...
What the fuck is he doing here?

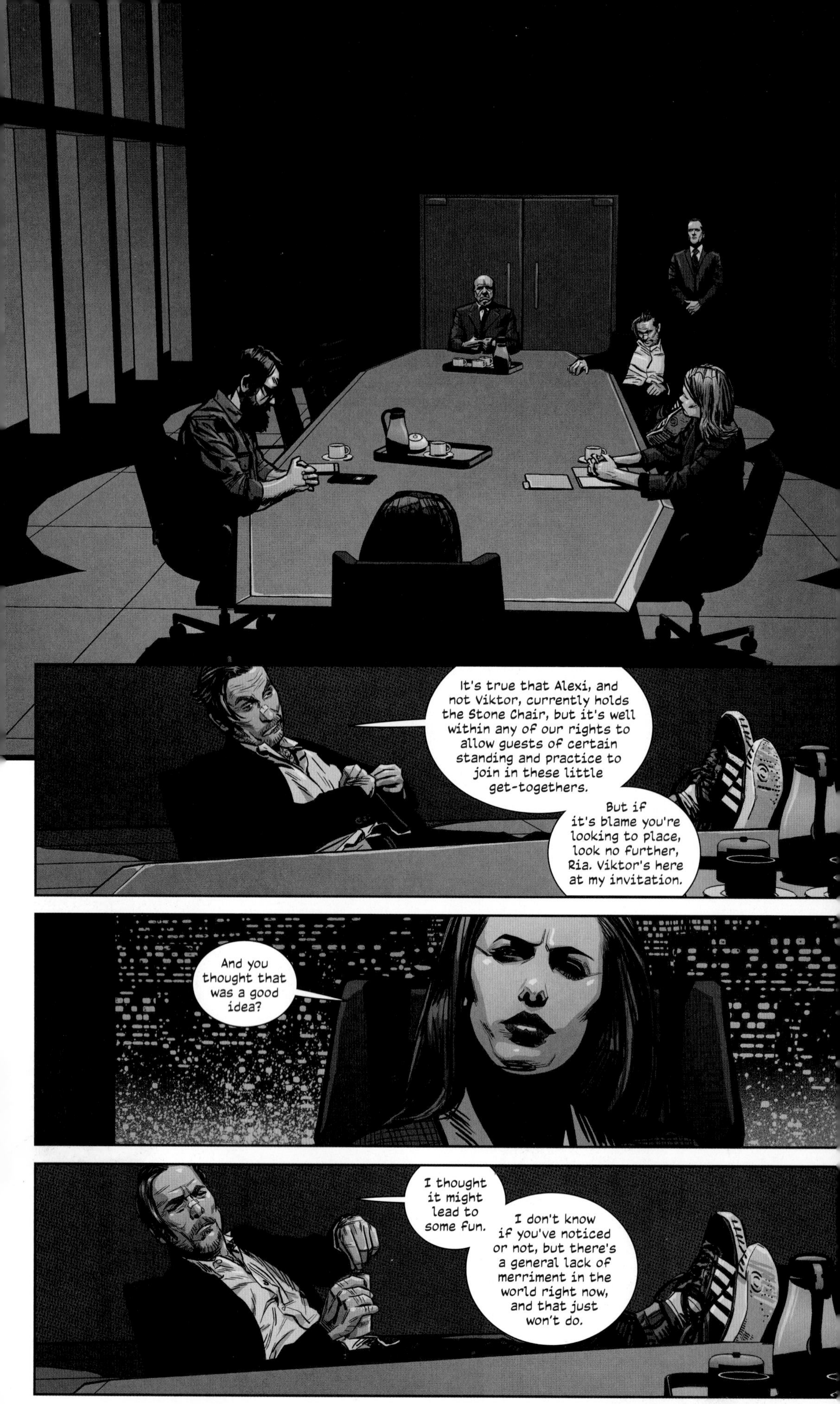
It's true that Alexi, and not Viktor, currently holds the Stone Chair, but it's well within any of our rights to allow guests of certain standing and practice to join in these little get-togethers.
But if it's blame you're looking to place, look no further, Ria. Viktor's here at my invitation.
And you thought that was a good idea?
I thought it might lead to some fun.
I don't know if you've noticed or not, but there's a general lack of merriment in the world right now, and that just won't do.

Some might say there's an equal lack of manners, Marco.

Who gives a shit about either, Alexi? I'm looking at the intentional devaluation of the yuan by the Yinhang, and the Black Pope is, once again, making overtures to the al-Jinn.

Perhaps we can move on to matters of a more serious nature and leave all pettiness for the back room.

And what do you say, Viktor? Should we just move past this?

Whore. Daughter of a whore.

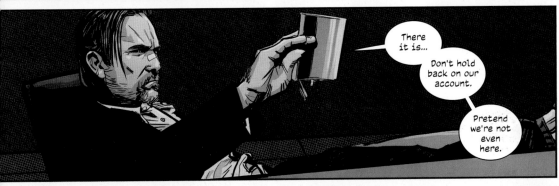

There it is... Don't hold back on our account. Pretend we're not even here.

I bled your brother dry, Ria, and I will do the same to you. I will erase your entire line...

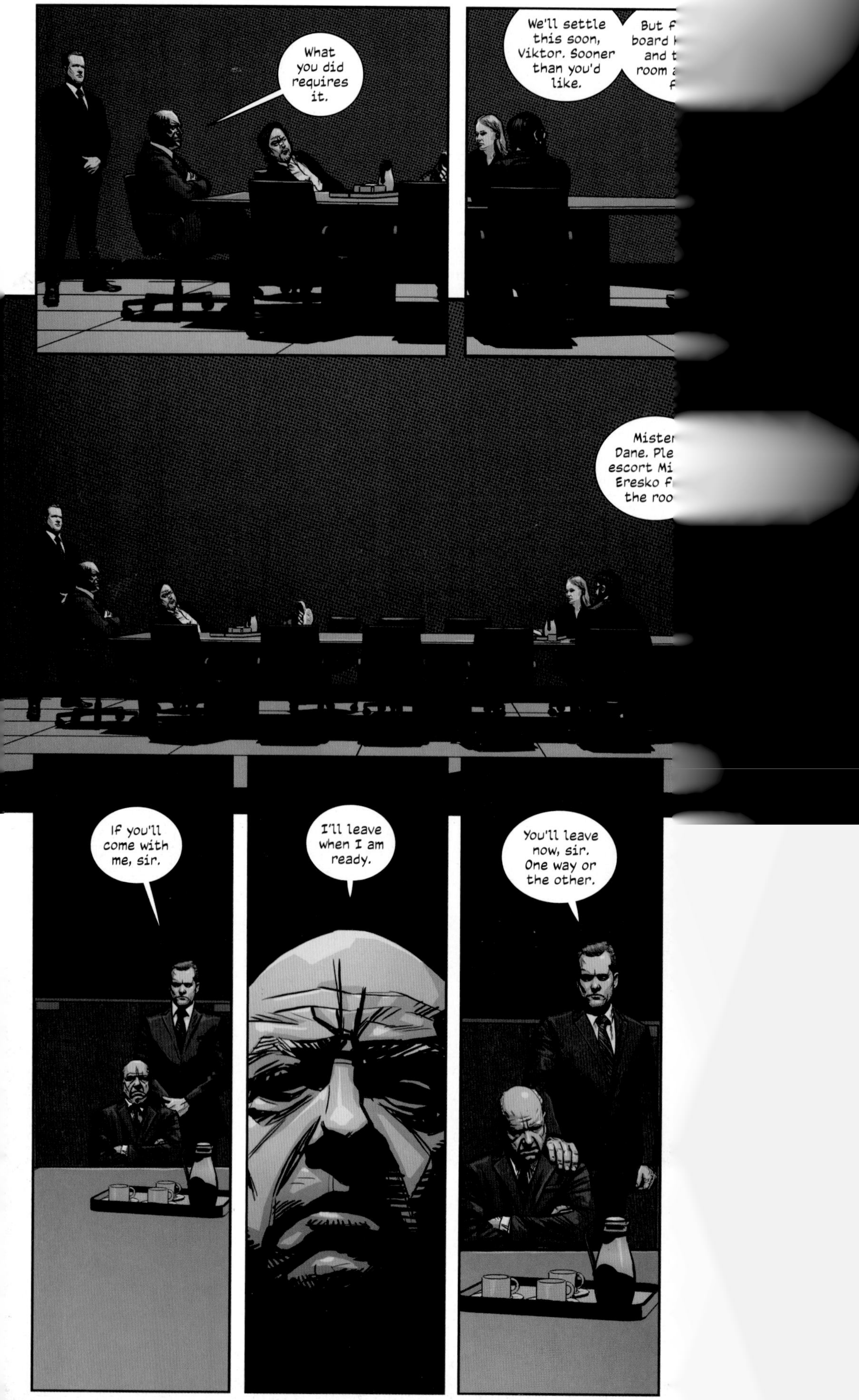
What you did requires it.
We'll settle this soon, Viktor. Sooner than you'd like.
But f board k and t room a f
Mister Dane. Ple escort Mi Eresko f the roo
If you'll come with me, sir.
I'll leave when I am ready.
You'll leave now, sir. One way or the other.

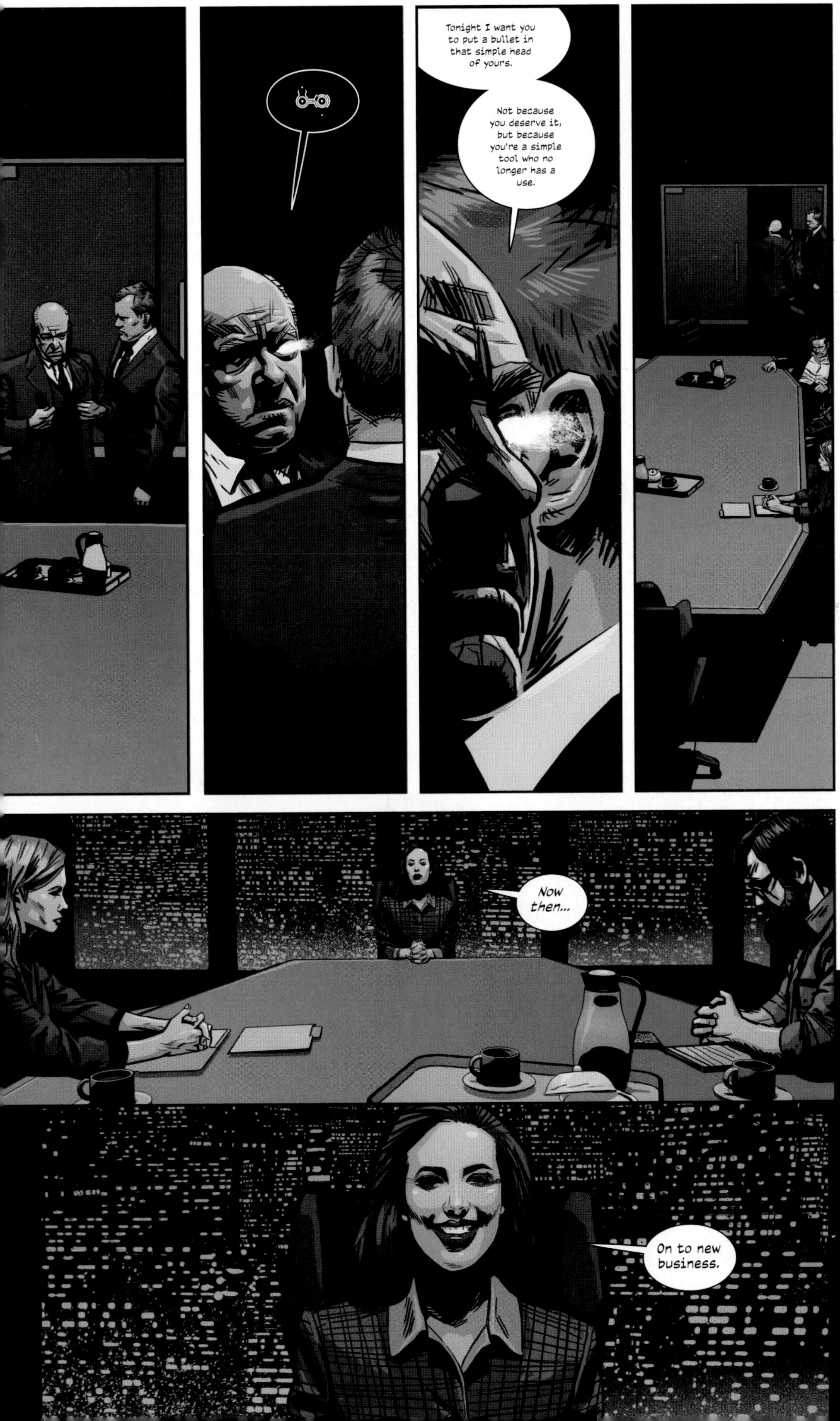
Tonight I want you to put a bullet in that simple head of yours.
Not because you deserve it, but because you're a simple tool who no longer has a use.
Now then...
On to new business.

THE EXECUTIVE JOURNAL OF DANIEL ROTHSCHILD

November 28, 1997

For the past six months, my head of security, Thomas Dane, has started
acting erratic after several years of exceptional service.

Yesterday, when I confronted him about this, he admitted that my
concerns were not unfounded and that he had become disillusioned with
the work he was doing. He told me that his time in the CIA had broken
him of his belief in government, and that his work at the IMF had done
the same regarding the greater benefits of nation states. Then he told
me that witnessing the inner workings of Caina, of seeing what we do on
a daily basis to bleed the population of wealth and power, had killed
any remaining hope in the general goodness of man.

I confessed to him I felt the same way.

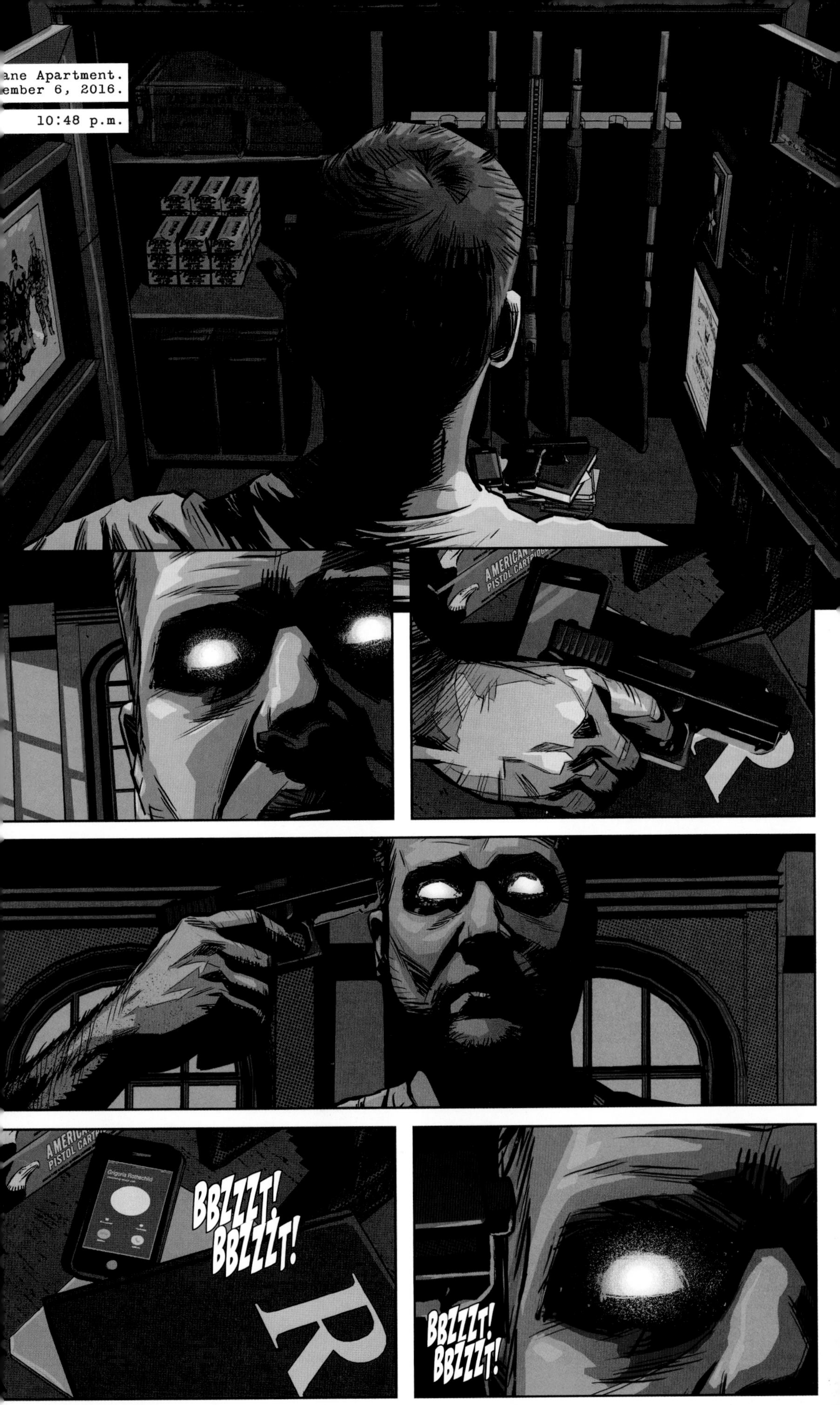
ane Apartment.
ember 6, 2016.
10:48 p.m.
AMERICAN
PISTOL CARTRIDGES
Grigoria Rothschild
BBZZZT! BBZZZT!
BBZZZT! BBZZZT!

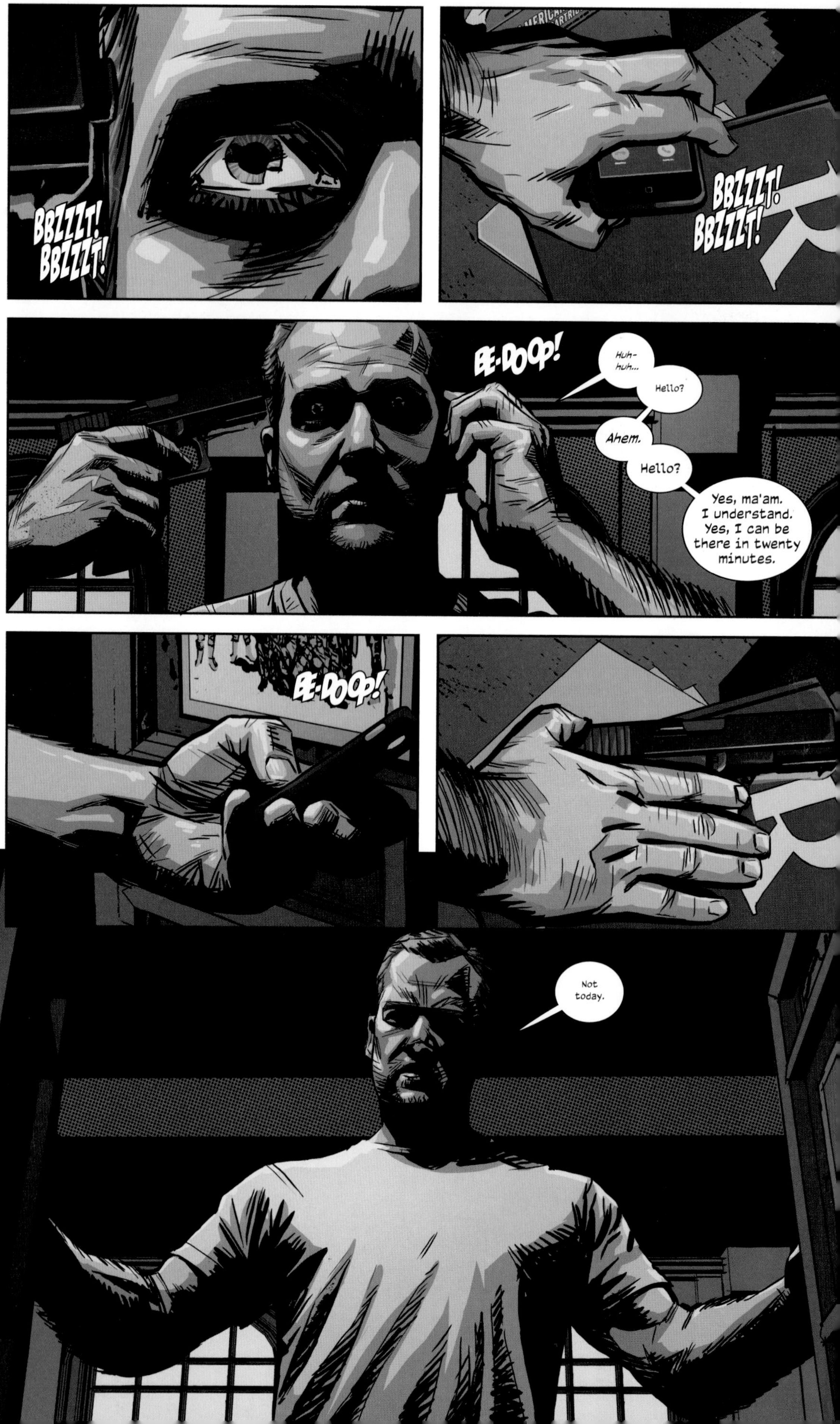
BBZZZT! BBZZZT!
BBZZZT! BBZZZT!
BE-DOOP!
Huh-huh...
Hello?
Ahem.
Hello?
Yes, ma'am. I understand. Yes, I can be there in twenty minutes.
BE-DOOP!
Not today.

(a)

THE EXECUTIVE JOURNAL OF DANIEL ROTHSCHILD

March 9, 2000

I made Thomas smile today when I told him that our 'benevolence fund'
now contained almost $13.4 billion dollars.

Over the next six months, we'll disperse almost half of that to various
nonprofits and education endowments. The rest will be divided between
the 15 highest rated international foundations combating poverty and
illiteracy.

Mister Dane still cannot believe that we were able to bleed that much
money from numerous corporations using our wholly-manufactured Y2K dis-
information campaign. I explained to him that truly wealthy people don't
mind paying a premium if the alternative is the possible collapse of the
system from which they benefit.

They can afford the lie.

(g)

THE EXECUTIVE JOURNAL OF DANIEL ROTHSCHILD

October 11, 2007

The Stone Chair has claimed Irena Kozlov.

December 29, 2007

Viktor Eresko remains inconsolable. The death of Irena Kozlov continues to resonate.

August 16, 2009

Viktor Eresko has returned from sabbatical to assume the Stone Chair, reeking of power. He used his prolonged absence as an excuse to examine all financial records contained in the Caina-Kankrin grimoire. Wynn Ackermann objected, but backed down when Viktor threatened him.

There is something unsettling about this new Viktor Eresko. Thomas Dane agrees. Something about his eyes. Something about what's looking back at you.

April 20, 2012

During my rotated, scheduled absence, the board has unanimously voted to transition the position of Caina-Kankrin head of security from my purview to one that answers to the board at large.

Any repair I believed I had accomplished from the events surrounding my sister's banishment appear to have failed and we are, once again, fractured. Suspicion and fear rule Caina-Kankrin. Chaos has set in.

I suspect Viktor Eresko is behind this.

July 6, 2014

Thomas no longer believes I am safe, and Wynn Ackermann has disappeared.

All my hopes rest in regaining the Ascendant Seat.

The clock continues to tick.

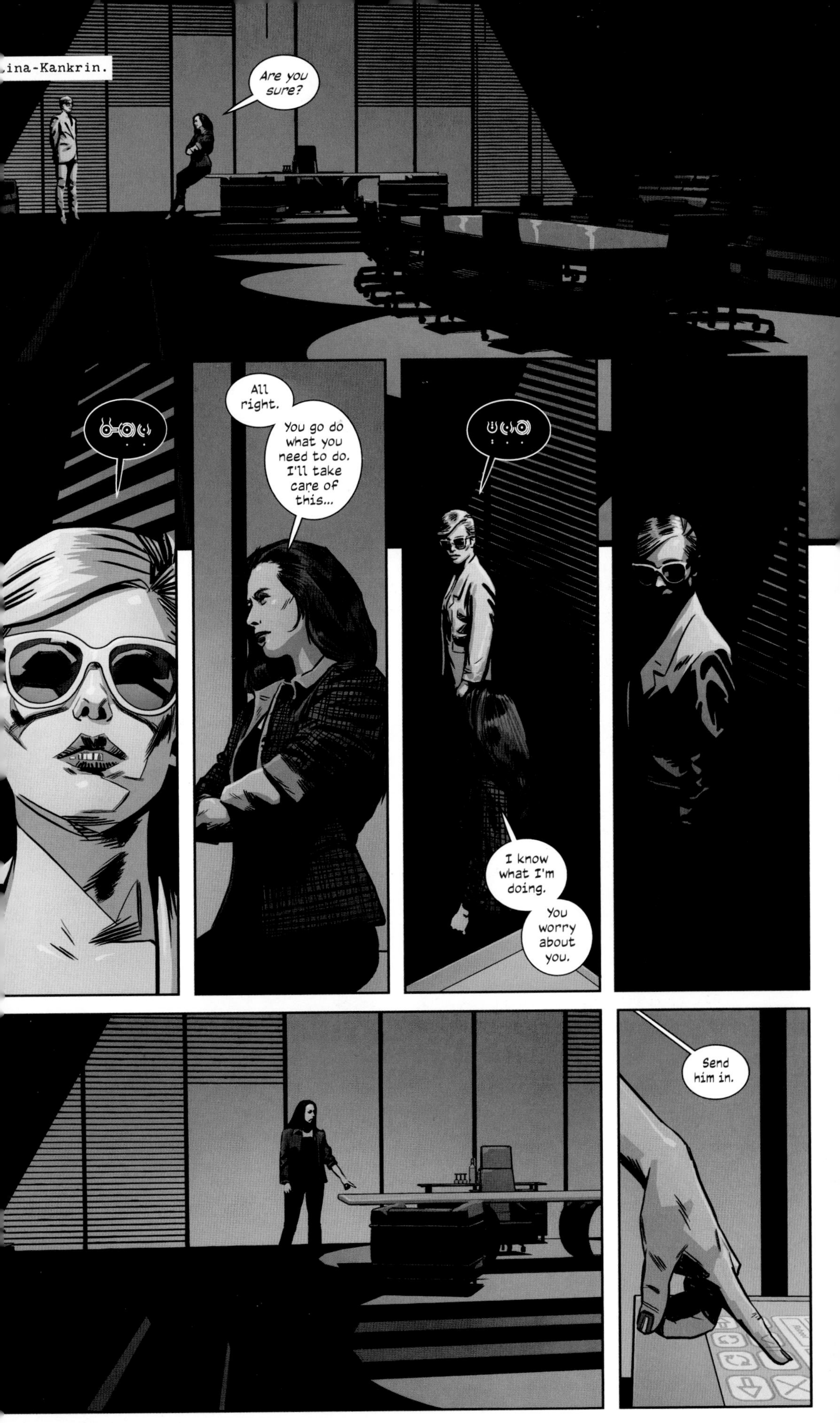
…ina-Kankrin.
Are you sure?
All right.
You go do what you need to do. I'll take care of this...
I know what I'm doing.
You worry about you.
Send him in.

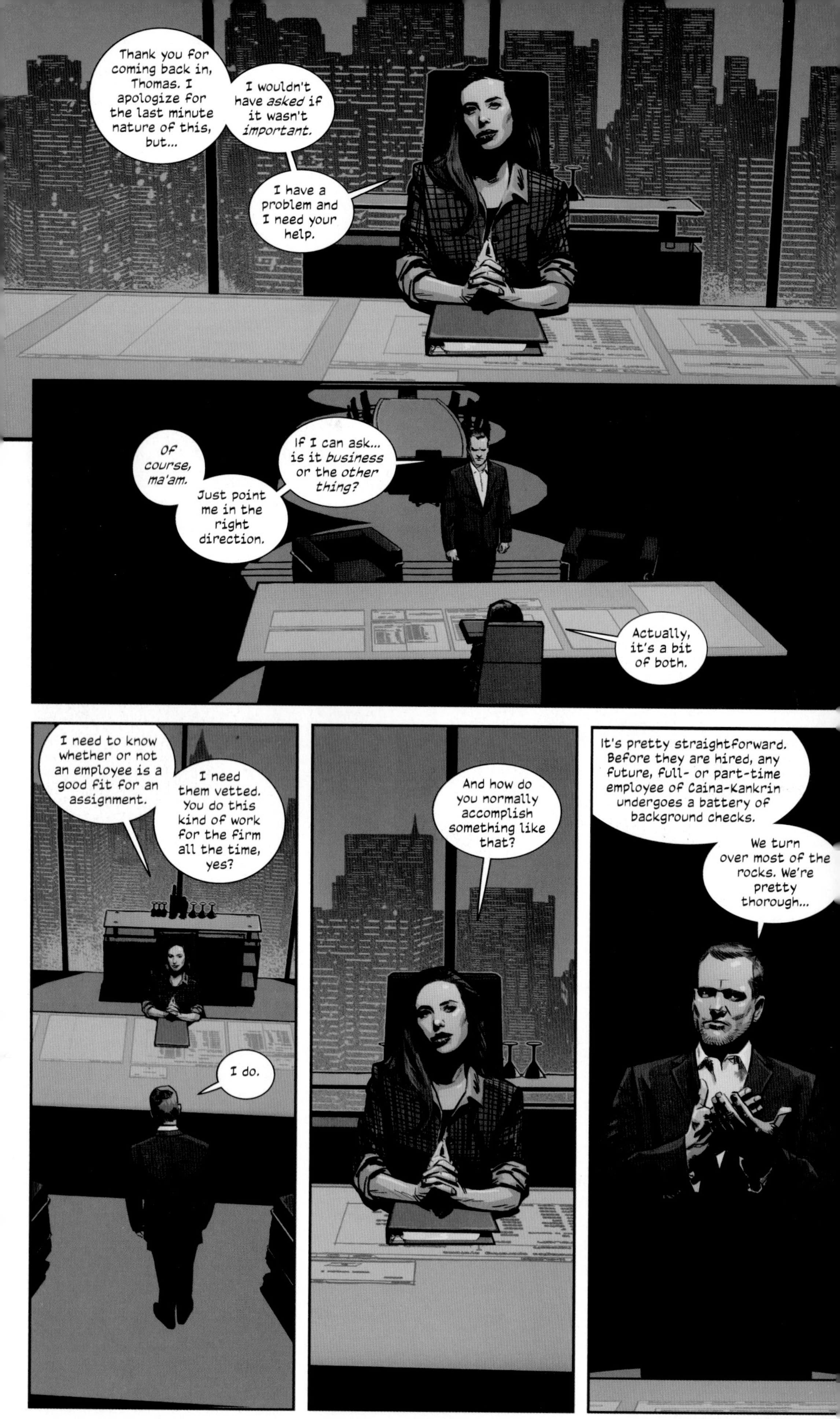

Thank you for coming back in, Thomas. I apologize for the last minute nature of this, but...
I wouldn't have *asked* if it wasn't *important.*
I have a problem and I need your help.
Of course, ma'am.
Just point me in the right direction.
If I can ask... is it *business* or the *other thing?*
Actually, it's a bit of both.
I need to know whether or not an employee is a good fit for an assignment.
I need them vetted. You do this kind of work for the firm all the time, yes?
I do.
And how do you normally accomplish something like that?
It's pretty straightforward. Before they are hired, any future, full- or part-time employee of Caina-Kankrin undergoes a battery of background checks.
We turn over most of the rocks. We're pretty thorough...

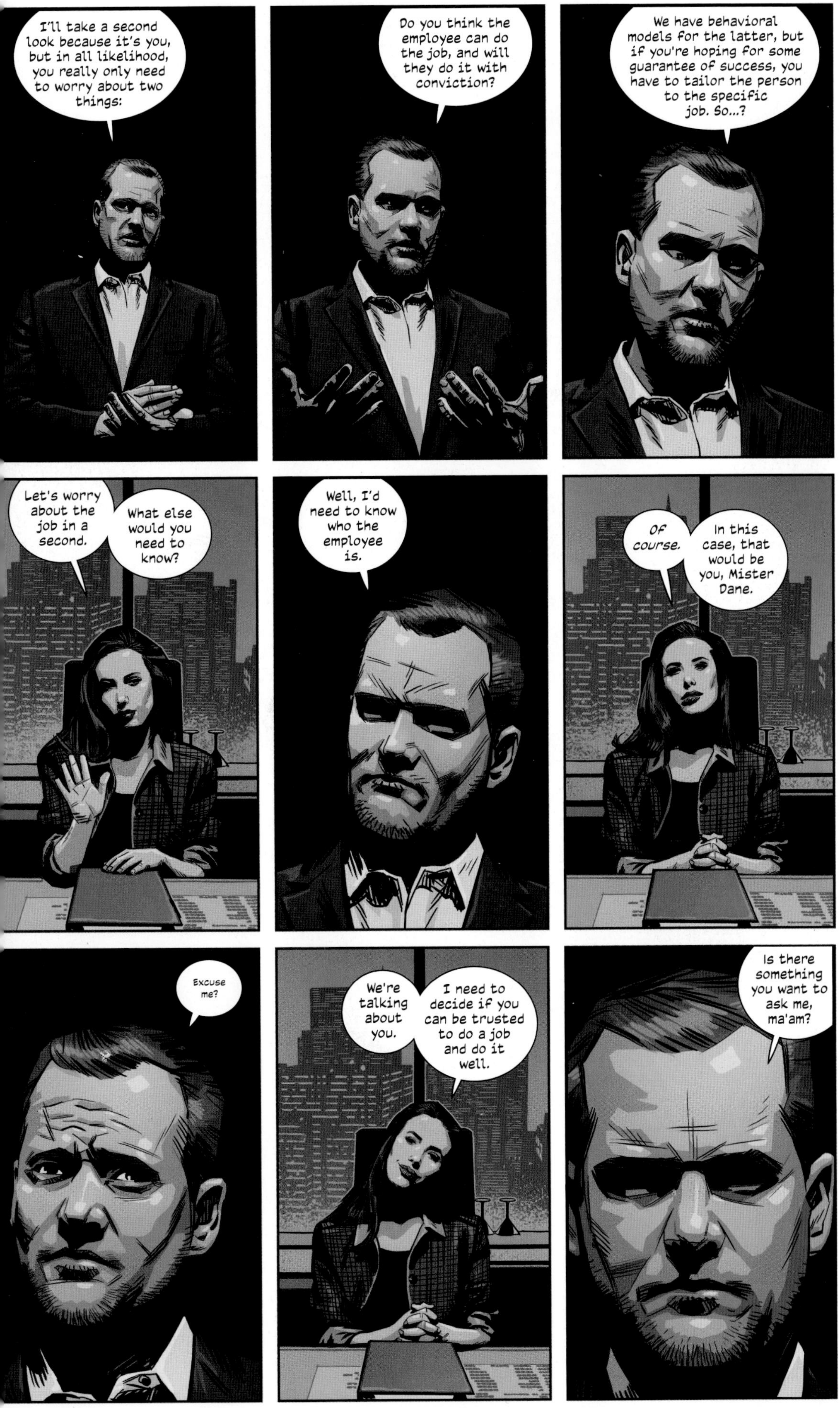
I'll take a second look because it's you, but in all likelihood, you really only need to worry about two things:
Do you think the employee can do the job, and will they do it with conviction?
We have behavioral models for the latter, but if you're hoping for some guarantee of success, you have to tailor the person to the specific job. So...?
Let's worry about the job in a second.
What else would you need to know?
Well, I'd need to know who the employee is.
Of course.
In this case, that would be you, Mister Dane.
Excuse me?
We're talking about you.
I need to decide if you can be trusted to do a job and do it well.
Is there something you want to ask me, ma'am?

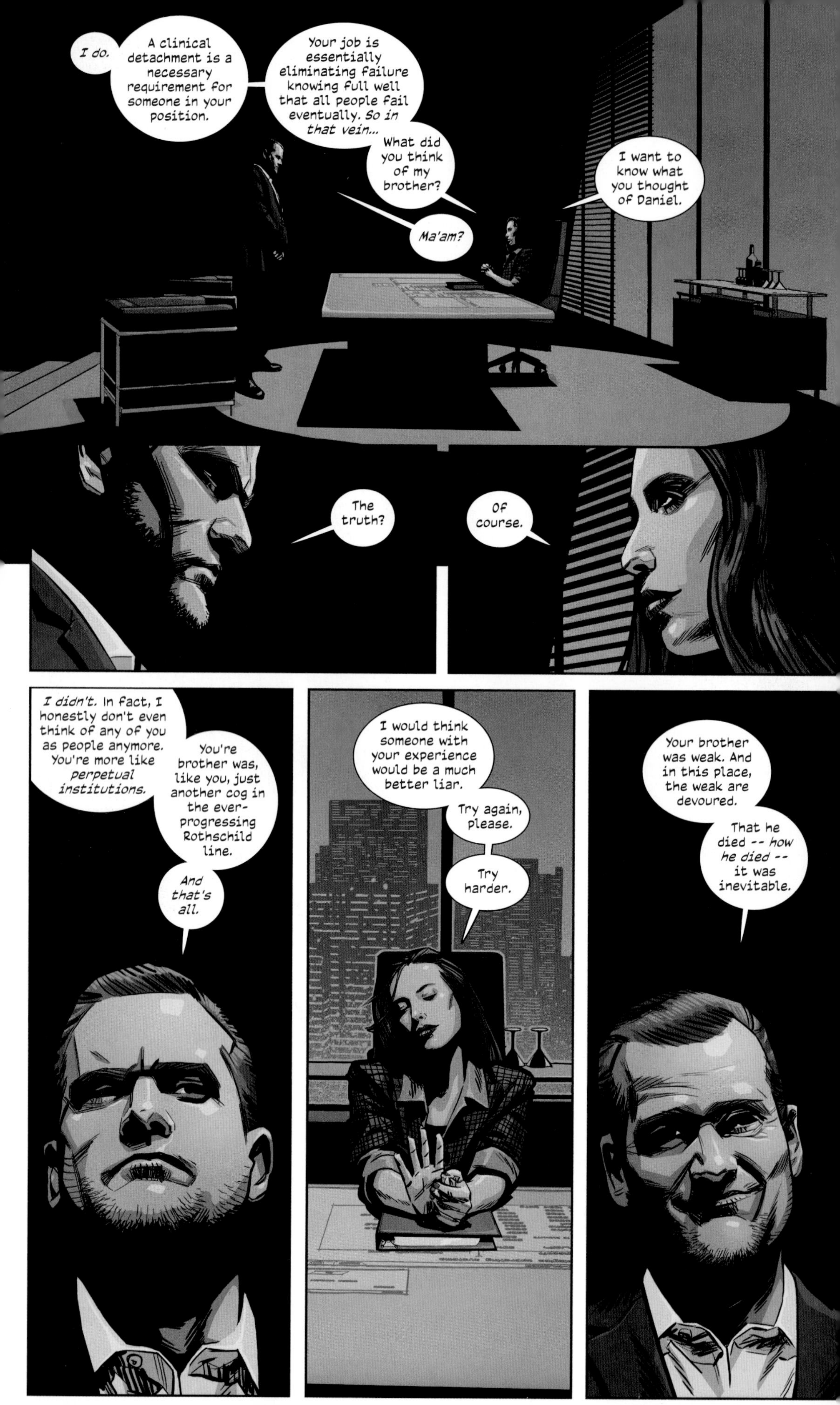
I do.
A clinical detachment is a necessary requirement for someone in your position.
Your job is essentially eliminating failure knowing full well that all people fail eventually. So in that vein...
What did you think of my brother?
Ma'am?
I want to know what you thought of Daniel.
The truth?
Of course.
I didn't. In fact, I honestly don't even think of any of you as people anymore. You're more like perpetual institutions.
You're brother was, like you, just another cog in the ever-progressing Rothschild line.
And that's all.
I would think someone with your experience would be a much better liar.
Try again, please.
Try harder.
Your brother was weak. And in this place, the weak are devoured.
That he died -- how he died -- it was inevitable.

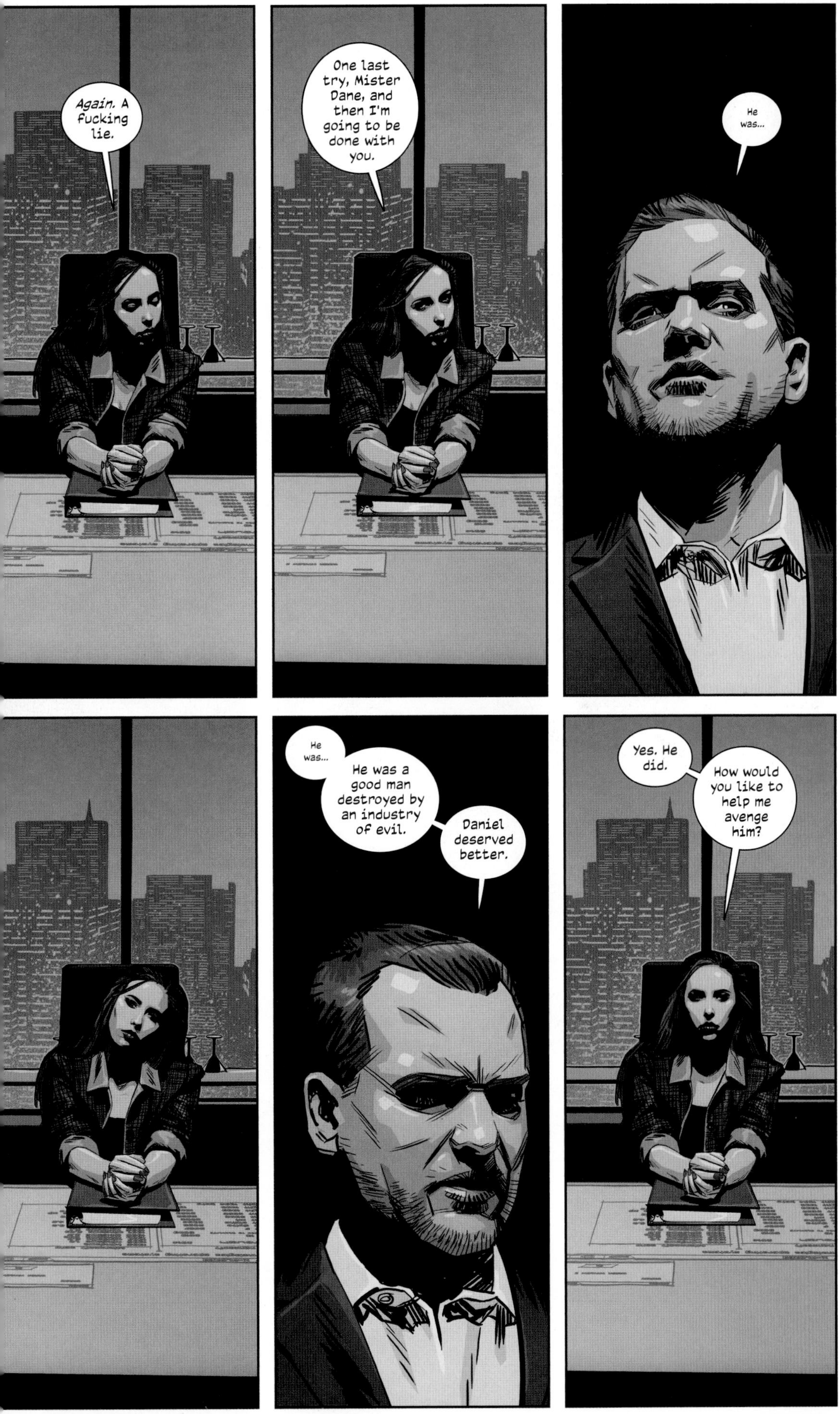
Again. A fucking lie.
One last try, Mister Dane, and then I'm going to be done with you.
He was...
He was...
He was a good man destroyed by an industry of evil.
Daniel deserved better.
Yes. He did.
How would you like to help me avenge him?

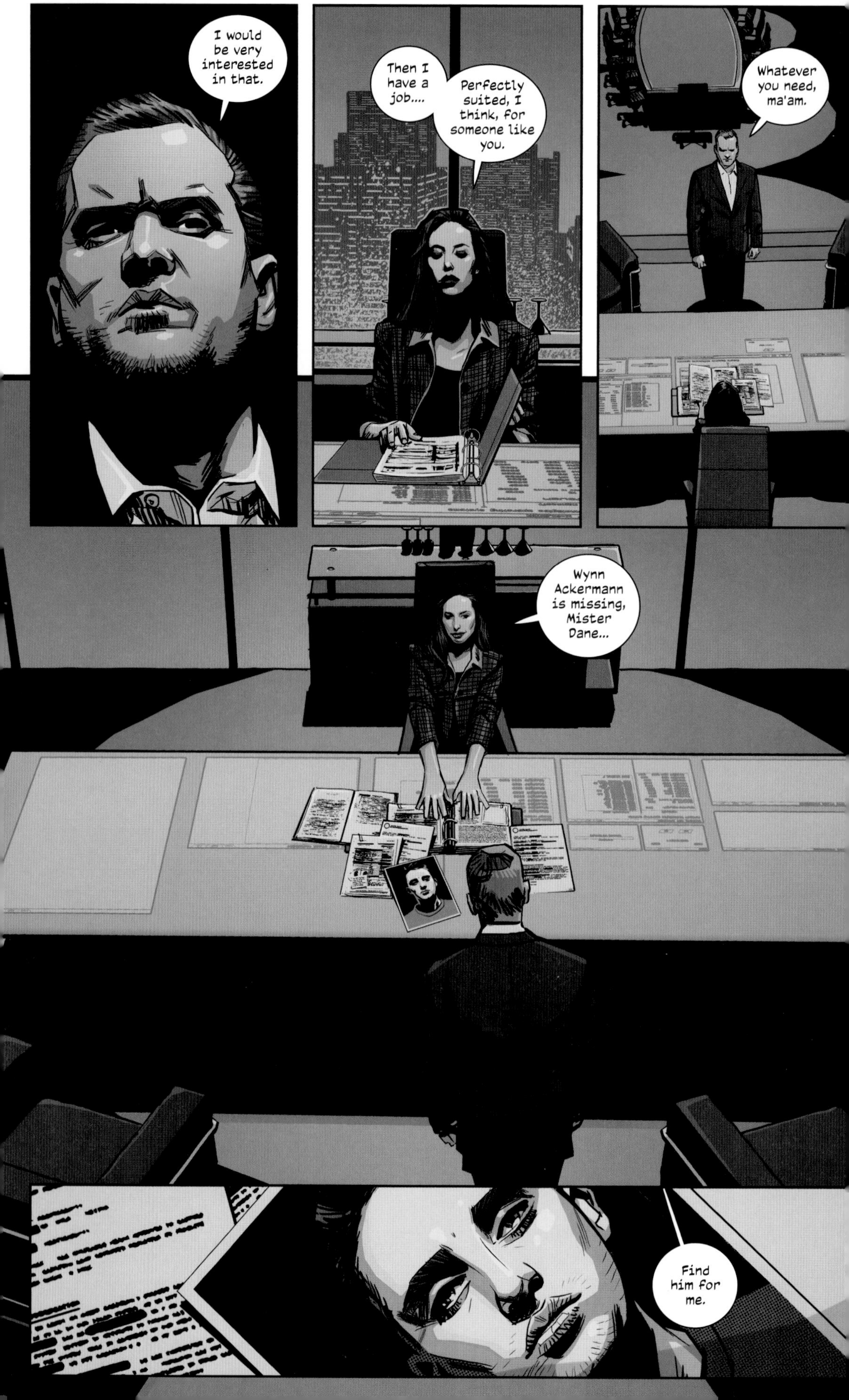
I would be very interested in that.
Then I have a job....
Perfectly suited, I think, for someone like you.
Whatever you need, ma'am.
Wynn Ackermann is missing, Mister Dane...
Find him for me.

There is no hiding.

We will always find you.

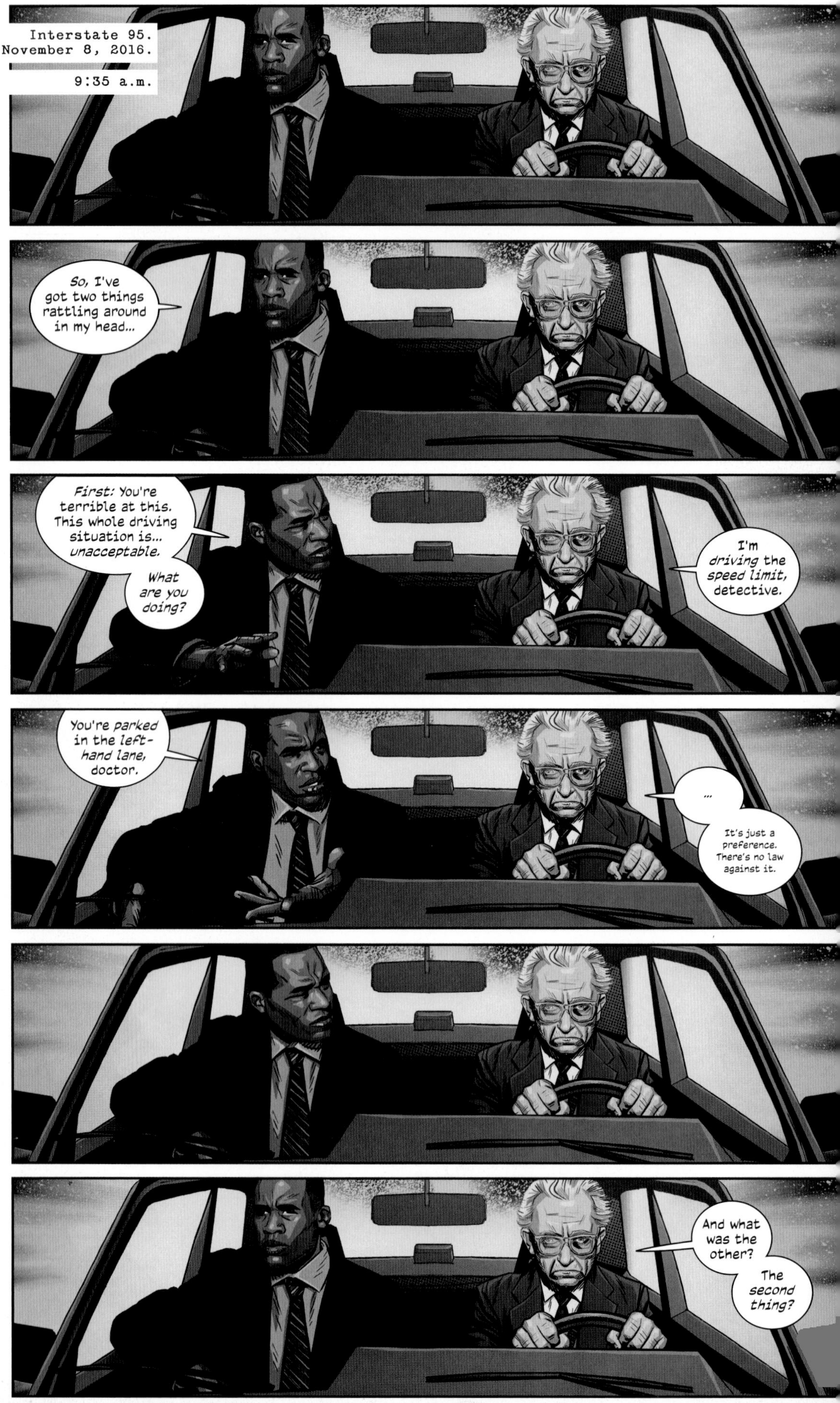

Interstate 95.
November 8, 2016.
9:35 a.m.
So, I've got two things rattling around in my head...
First: You're terrible at this. This whole driving situation is... unacceptable.
What are you doing?
I'm driving the speed limit, detective.
You're parked in the left-hand lane, doctor.
...
It's just a preference. There's no law against it.
And what was the other?
The second thing?

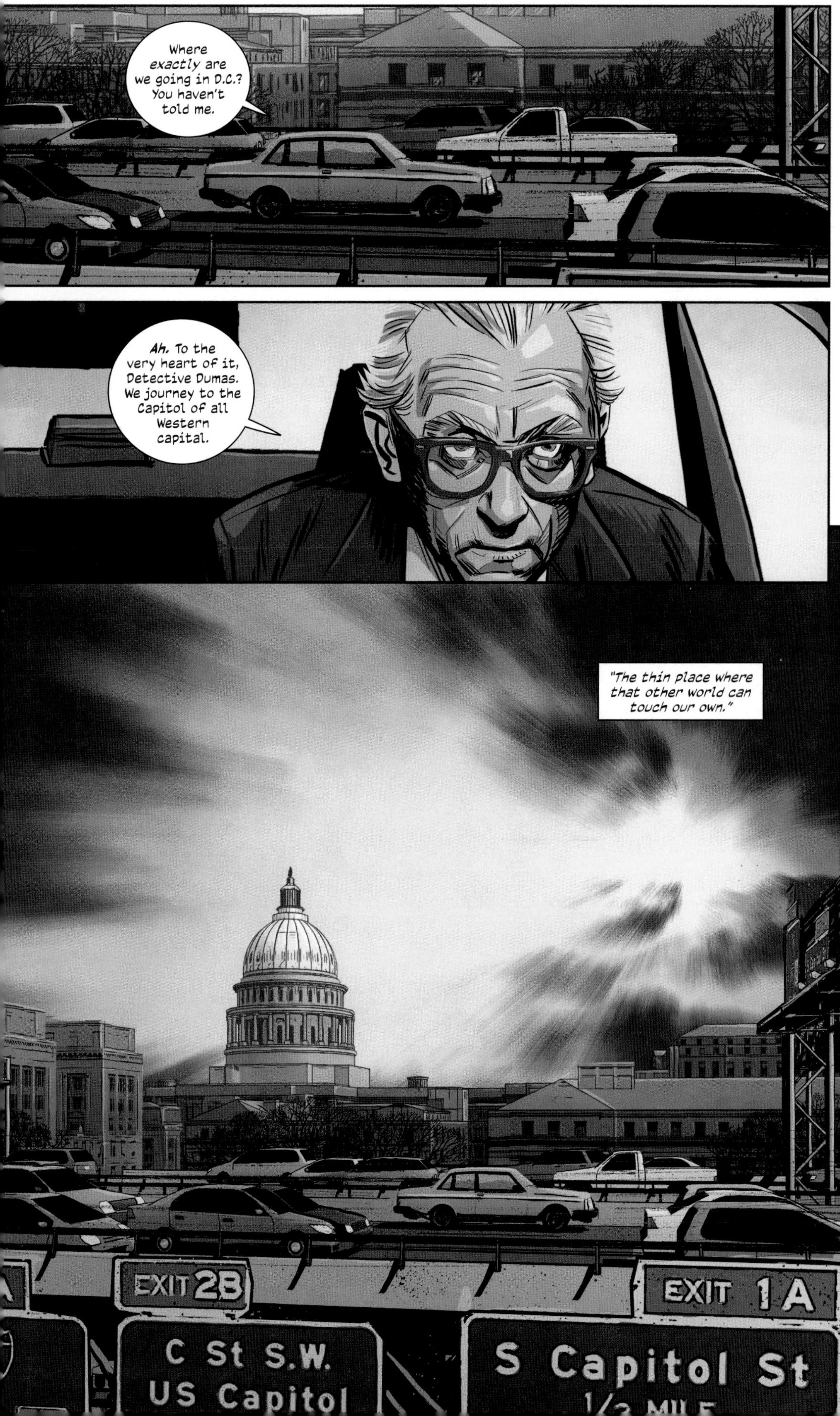
Where *exactly* are we going in D.C.? You haven't told me.
Ah. To the very heart of it, Detective Dumas. We journey to the Capitol of all Western capital.
"The thin place where that other world can touch our own."
EXIT 2B
C St S.W.
US Capitol
EXIT 1A
S Capitol St

CHAPTER SIX:

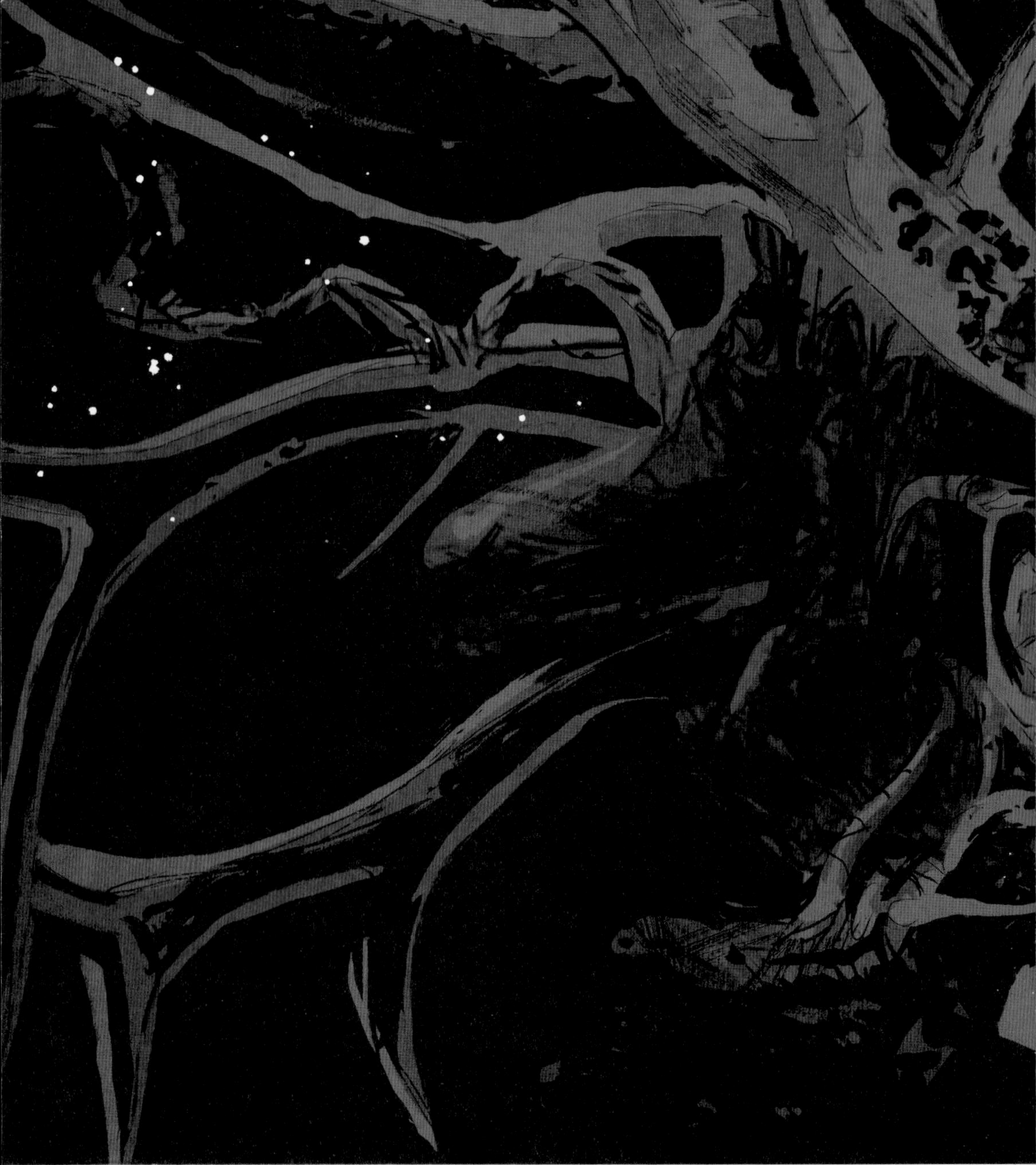

[They will devour us whole.]

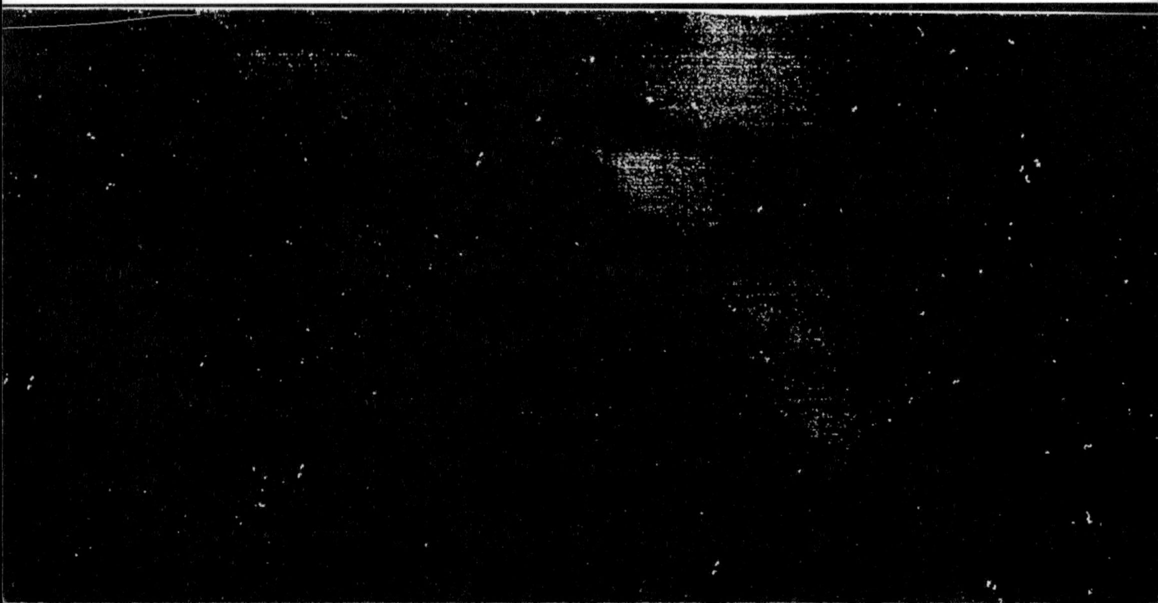

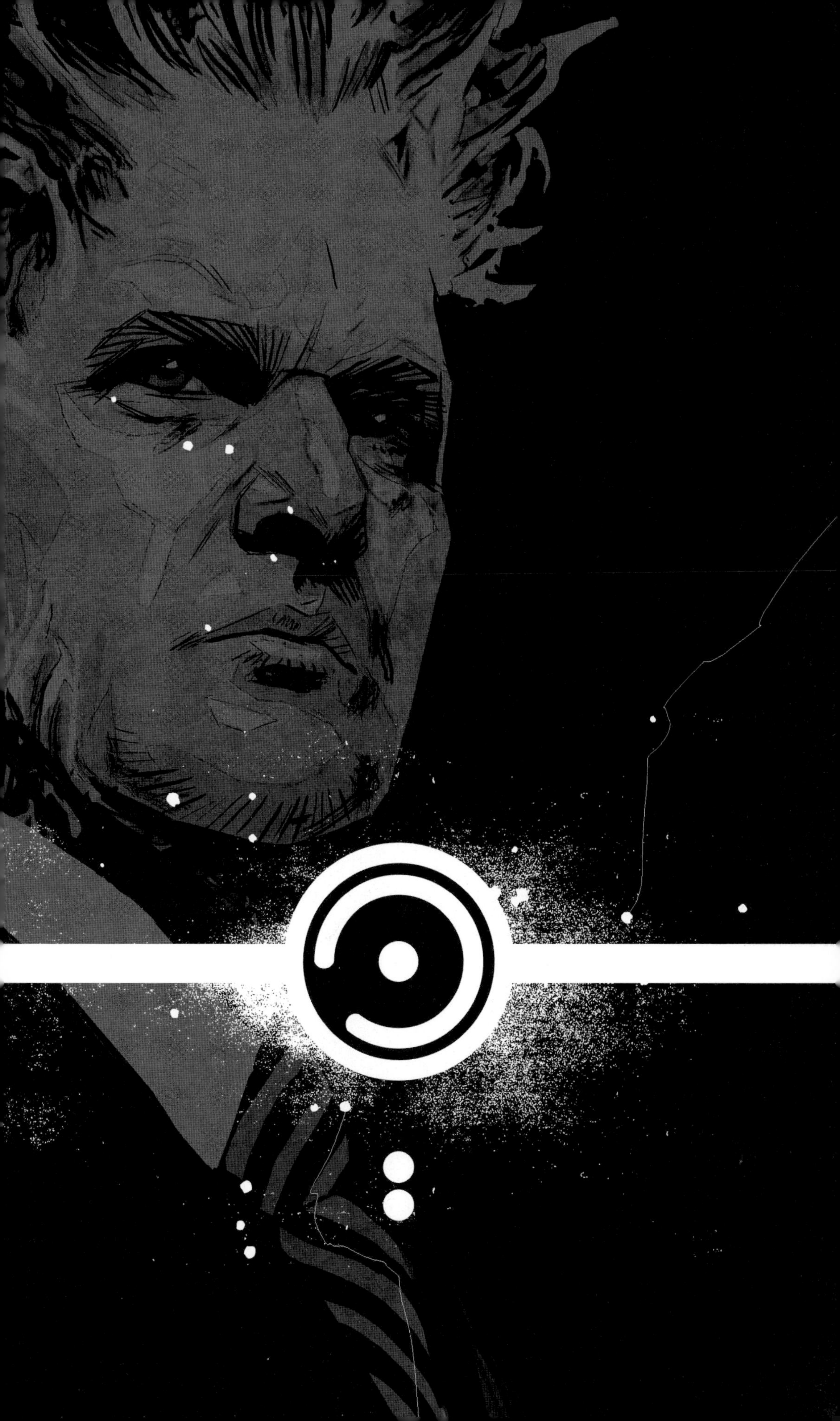

8

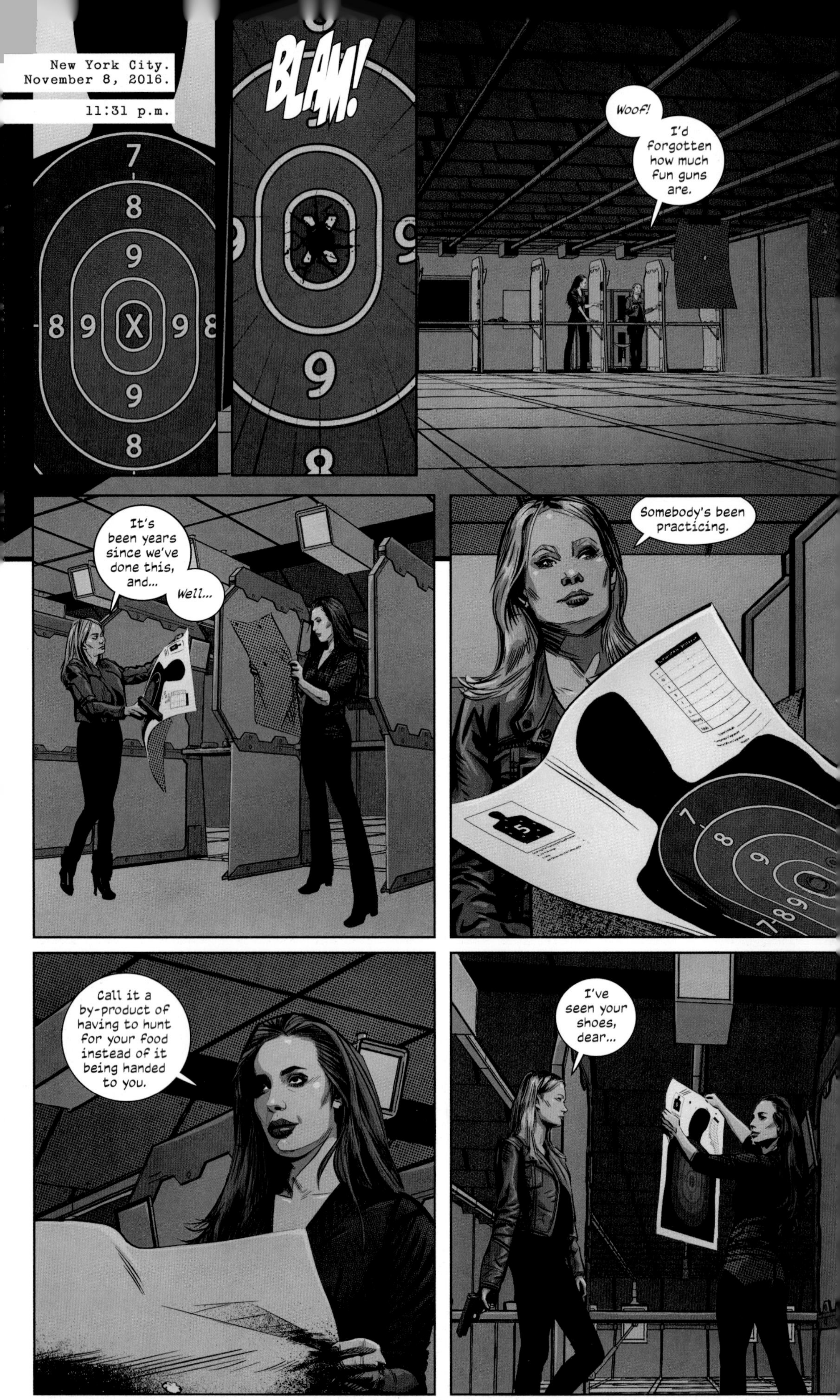
New York City.
November 8, 2016.
11:31 p.m.
BLAM!
Woof! I'd forgotten how much fun guns are.
It's been years since we've done this, and...
Well...
Somebody's been practicing.
Call it a by-product of having to hunt for your food instead of it being handed to you.
I've seen your shoes, dear...

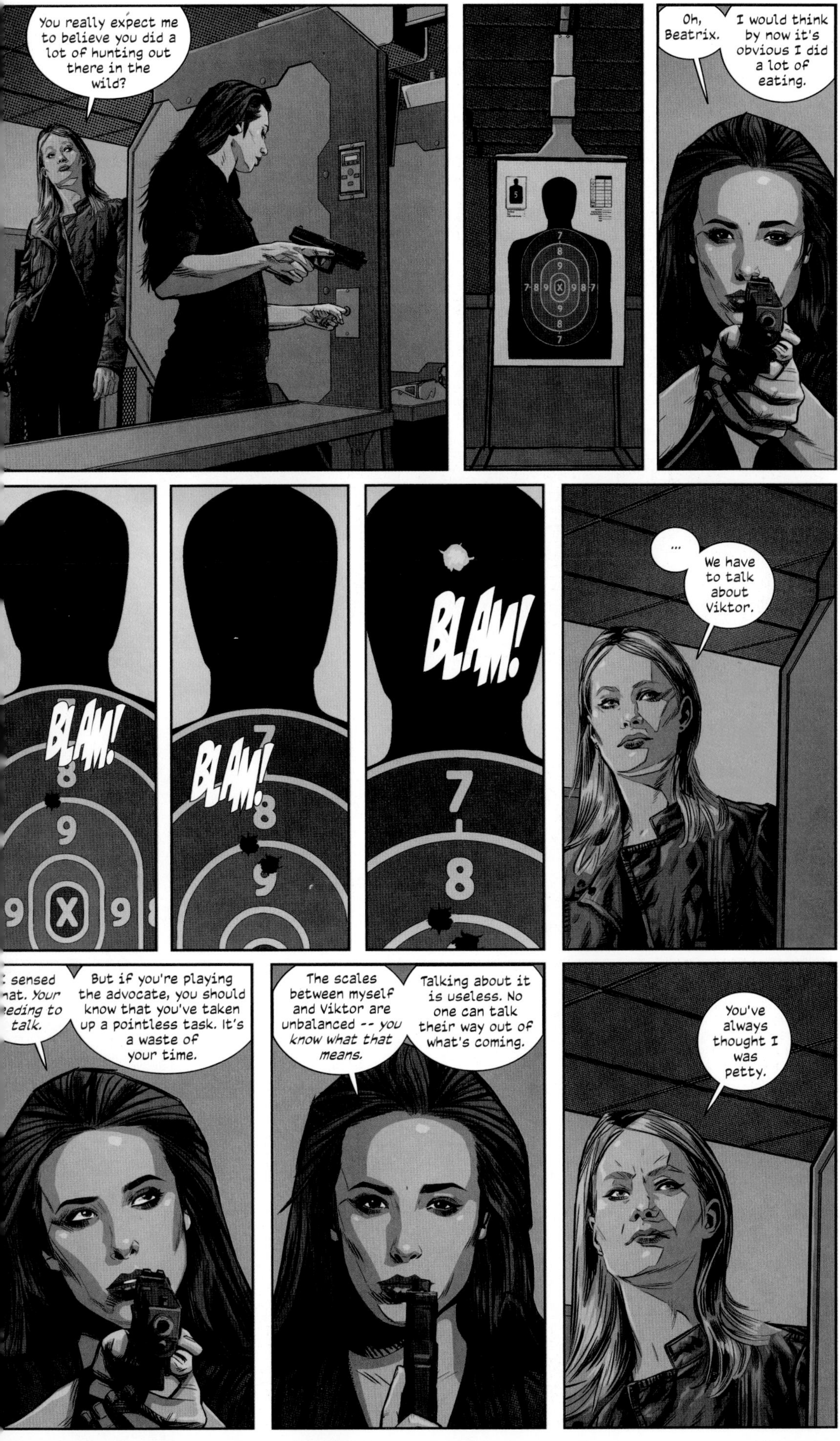
You really expect me to believe you did a lot of hunting out there in the wild?
Oh, Beatrix.
I would think by now it's obvious I did a lot of eating.
BLAM!
BLAM!
BLAM!
...
We have to talk about Viktor.
sensed hat. *Your* eding to *talk.*
But if you're playing the advocate, you should know that you've taken up a pointless task. It's a waste of your time.
The scales between myself and Viktor are unbalanced -- *you know what that means.*
Talking about it is useless. No one can talk their way out of what's coming.
You've always thought I was petty.

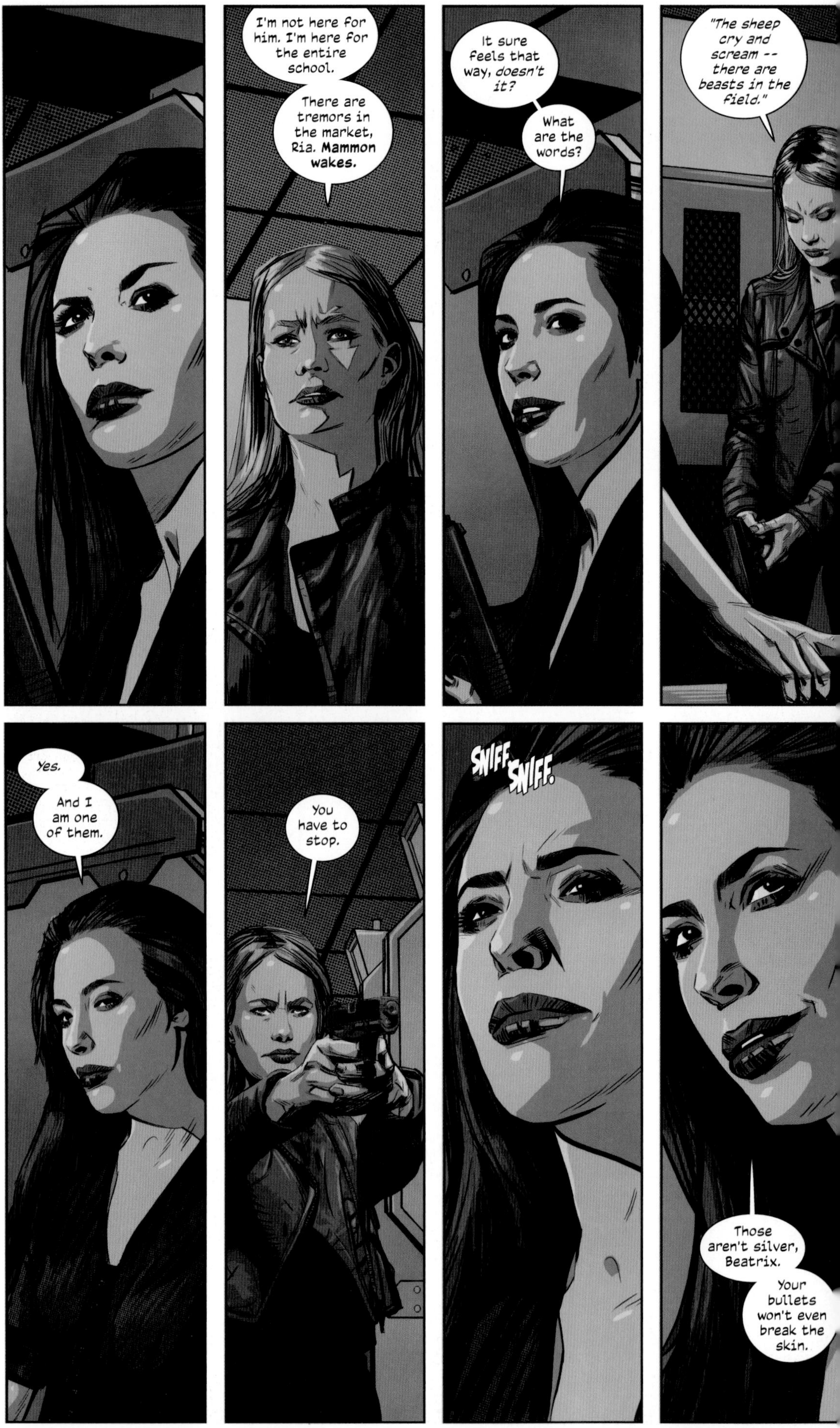
I'm not here for him. I'm here for the entire school.
There are tremors in the market, Ria. **Mammon wakes.**
It sure feels that way, *doesn't* it?
What are the words?
"The sheep cry and scream -- there are beasts in the field."
Yes.
And I am one of them.
You have to stop.
SNIFF SNIFF
Those aren't silver, Beatrix.
Your bullets won't even break the skin.

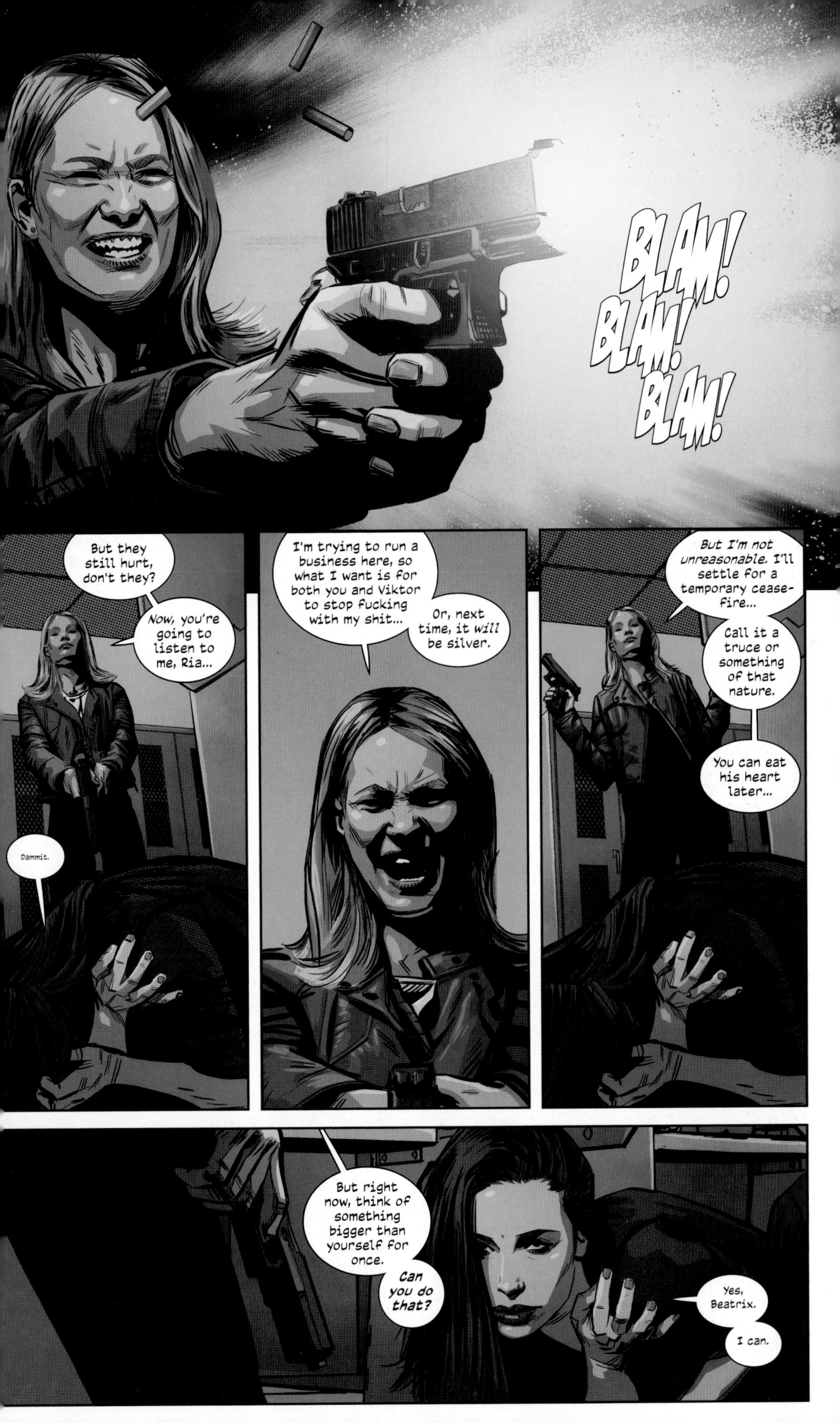
BLAM!
BLAM!
BLAM!
But they still hurt, don't they?
Now, you're going to listen to me, Ria...
Dammit.
I'm trying to run a business here, so what I want is for both you and Viktor to stop fucking with my shit...
Or, next time, it will be silver.
But I'm not unreasonable. I'll settle for a temporary cease-fire...
Call it a truce or something of that nature.
You can eat his heart later...
But right now, think of something bigger than yourself for once.
Can you do that?
Yes, Beatrix.
I can.

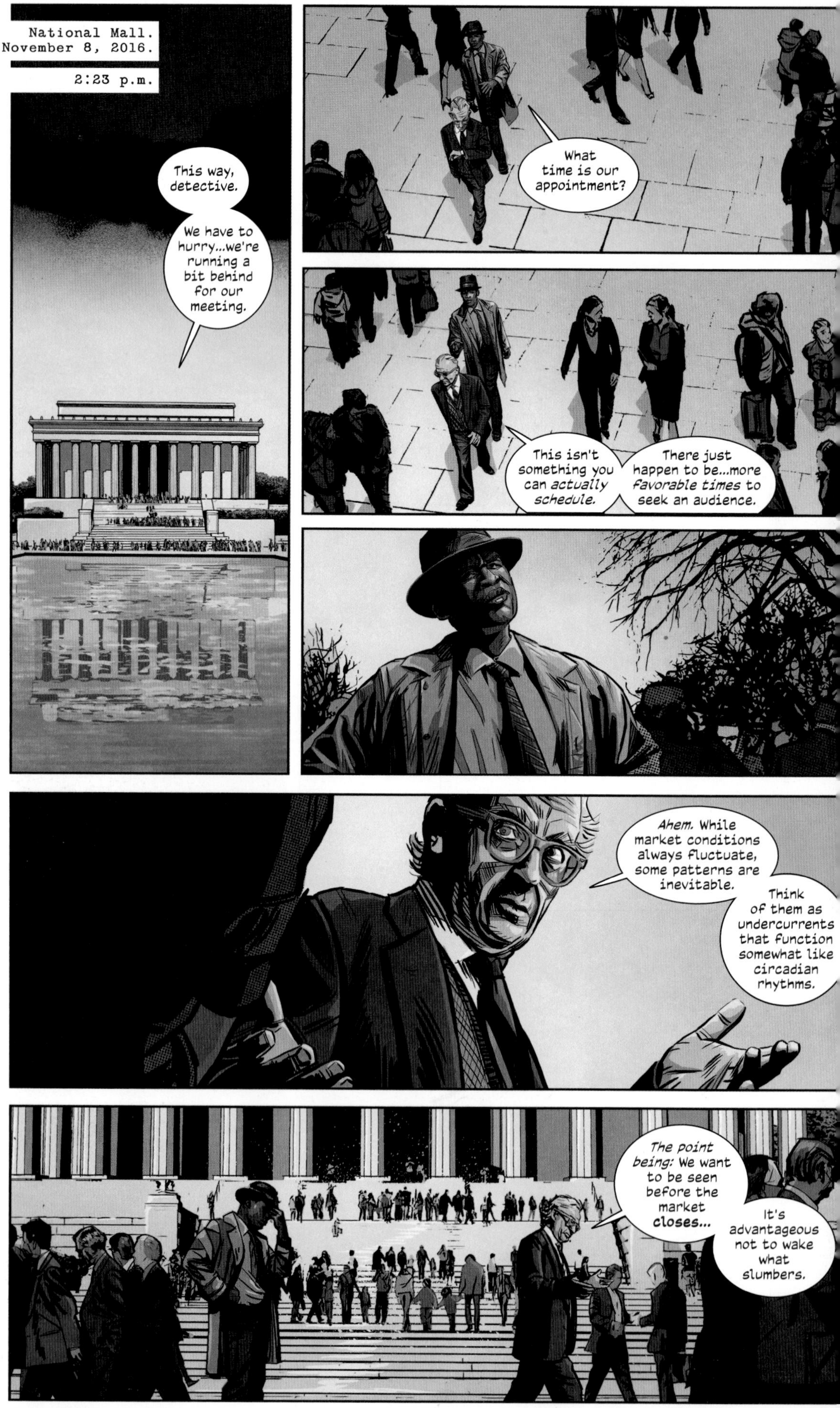
National Mall. November 8, 2016.
2:23 p.m.
This way, detective.
We have to hurry...we're running a bit behind for our meeting.
What time is our appointment?
This isn't something you can *actually* schedule.
There just happen to be...more *favorable times* to seek an audience.
Ahem. While market conditions always fluctuate, some patterns are inevitable.
Think of them as undercurrents that function somewhat like circadian rhythms.
The point being: We want to be seen before the market **closes...**
It's advantageous not to wake what slumbers.

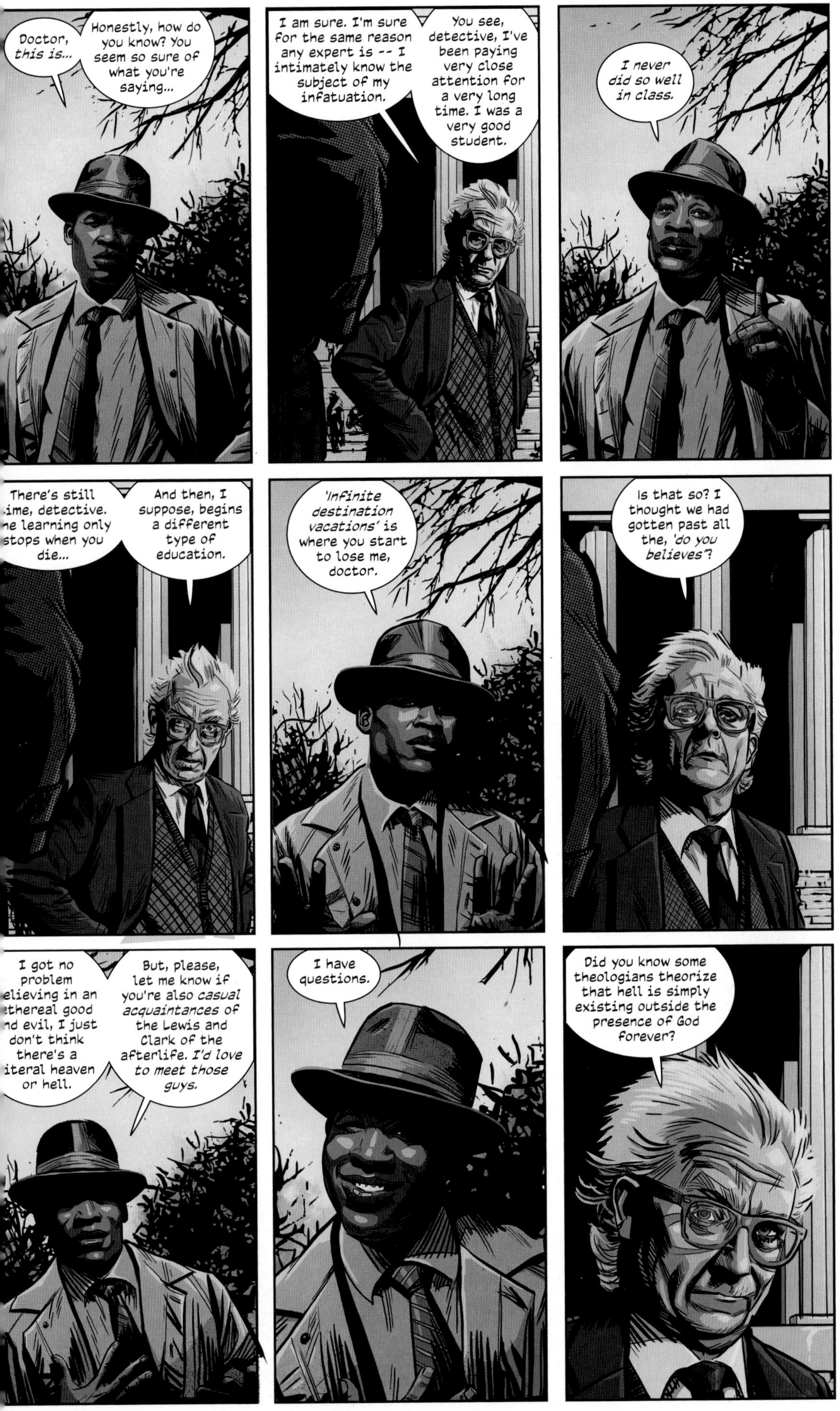
Doctor, *this is...*
Honestly, how do you know? You seem so sure of what you're saying...
I am sure. I'm sure for the same reason any expert is -- I intimately know the subject of my infatuation.
You see, detective, I've been paying very close attention for a very long time. I was a very good student.
I never did so well in class.
There's still ime, detective. ne learning only stops when you die...
And then, I suppose, begins a different type of education.
'Infinite destination vacations' is where you start to lose me, doctor.
Is that so? I thought we had gotten past all the, *'do you believes'*?
I got no problem elieving in an thereal good nd evil, I just don't think there's a iteral heaven or hell.
But, please, let me know if you're also *casual acquaintances* of the Lewis and Clark of the afterlife. *I'd love to meet those guys.*
I have questions.
Did you know some theologians theorize that hell is simply existing outside the presence of God forever?

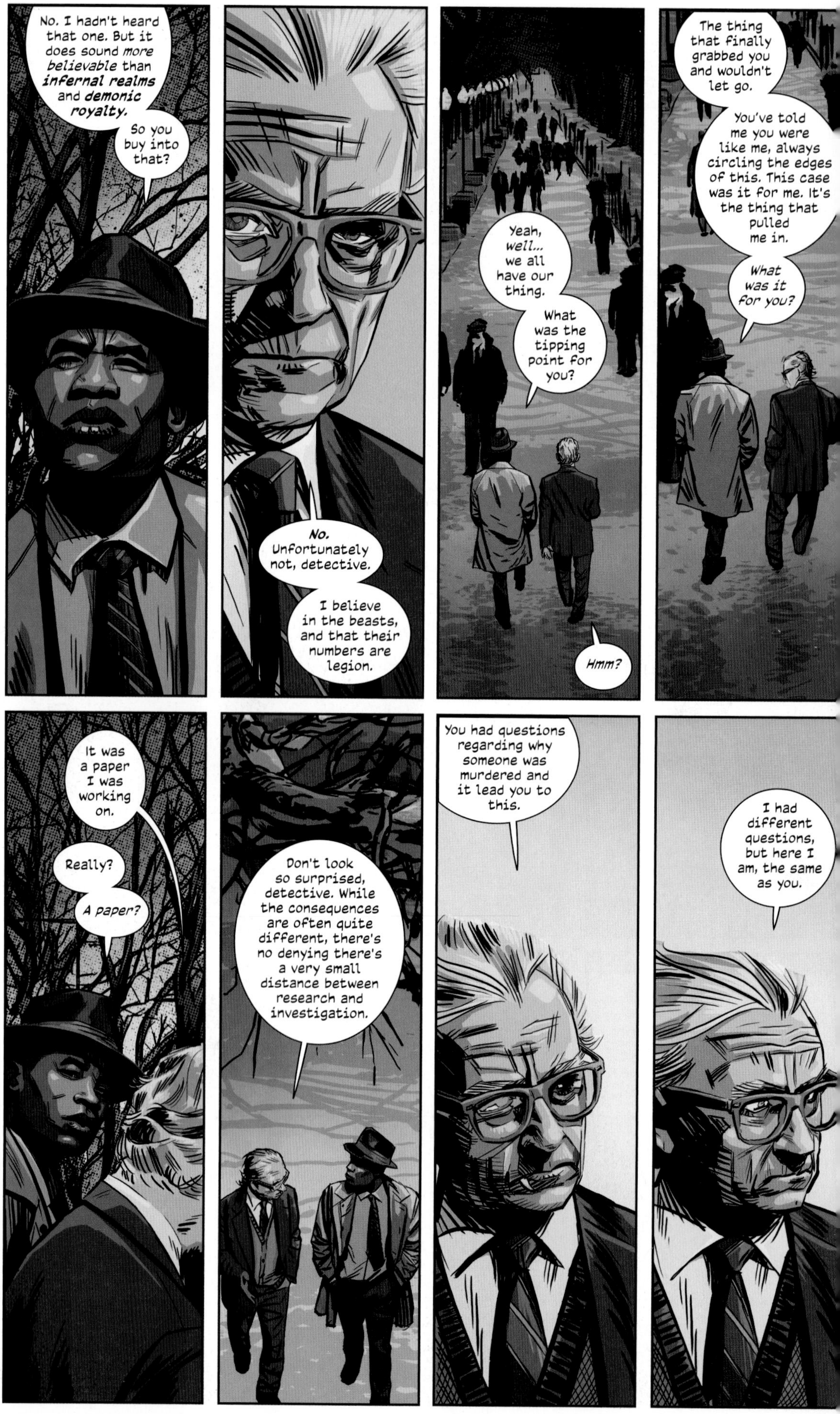
No. I hadn't heard that one. But it does sound *more believable* than ***infernal realms*** and ***demonic royalty.***
So you buy into that?
No. Unfortunately not, detective.
I believe in the beasts, and that their numbers are legion.
Yeah, *well...* we all have our thing.
What was the tipping point for you?
Hmm?
The thing that finally grabbed you and wouldn't let go.
You've told me you were like me, always circling the edges of this. This case was it for me. It's the thing that pulled me in.
What was it for you?
It was a paper I was working on.
Really?
A paper?
Don't look so surprised, detective. While the consequences are often quite different, there's no denying there's a very small distance between research and investigation.
You had questions regarding why someone was murdered and it lead you to this.
I had different questions, but here I am, the same as you.

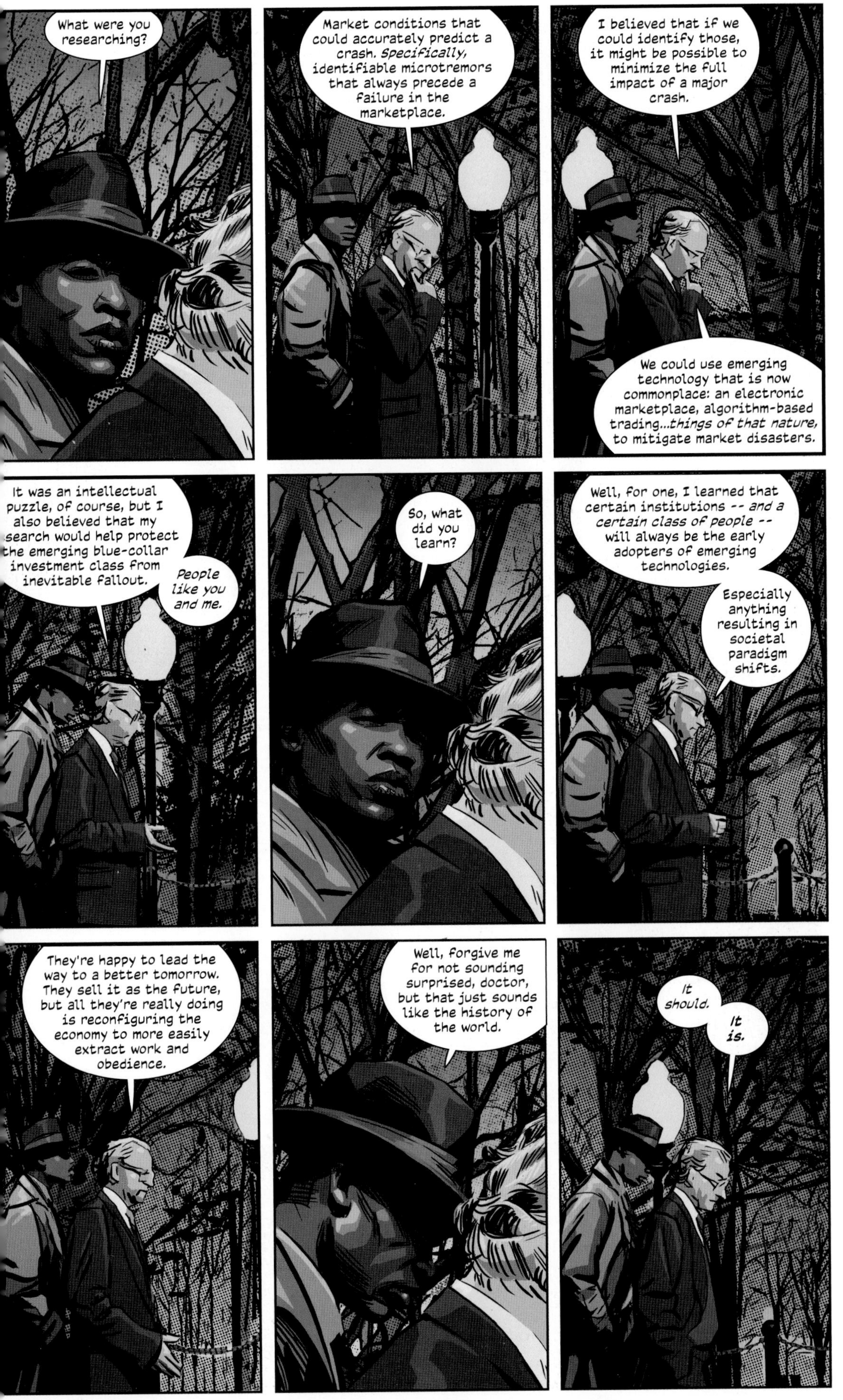
What were you researching?
Market conditions that could accurately predict a crash. *Specifically,* identifiable microtremors that always precede a failure in the marketplace.
I believed that if we could identify those, it might be possible to minimize the full impact of a major crash.
We could use emerging technology that is now commonplace: an electronic marketplace, algorithm-based trading...*things of that nature,* to mitigate market disasters.
It was an intellectual puzzle, of course, but I also believed that my search would help protect the emerging blue-collar investment class from inevitable fallout.
People like you and me.
So, what did you learn?
Well, for one, I learned that certain institutions -- *and a certain class of people* -- will always be the early adopters of emerging technologies.
Especially anything resulting in societal paradigm shifts.
They're happy to lead the way to a better tomorrow. They sell it as the future, but all they're really doing is reconfiguring the economy to more easily extract work and obedience.
Well, forgive me for not sounding surprised, doctor, but that just sounds like the history of the world.
It should.
It is.

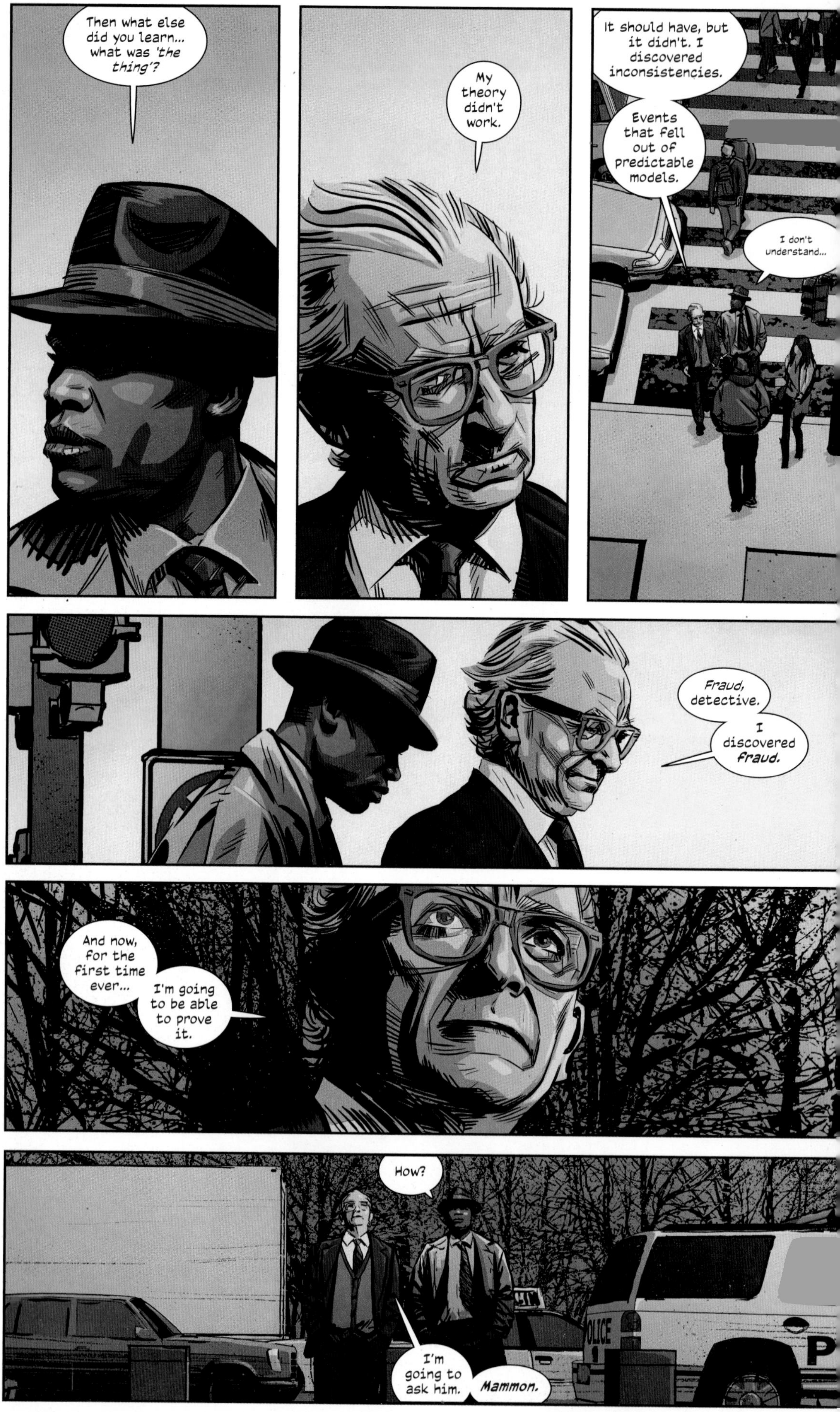
Then what else did you learn... what was *'the thing'*?
My theory didn't work.
It should have, but it didn't. I discovered inconsistencies.
Events that fell out of predictable models.
I don't understand...
Fraud, detective.
I discovered *fraud.*
And now, for the first time ever...
I'm going to be able to prove it.
How?
I'm going to ask him.
Mammon.

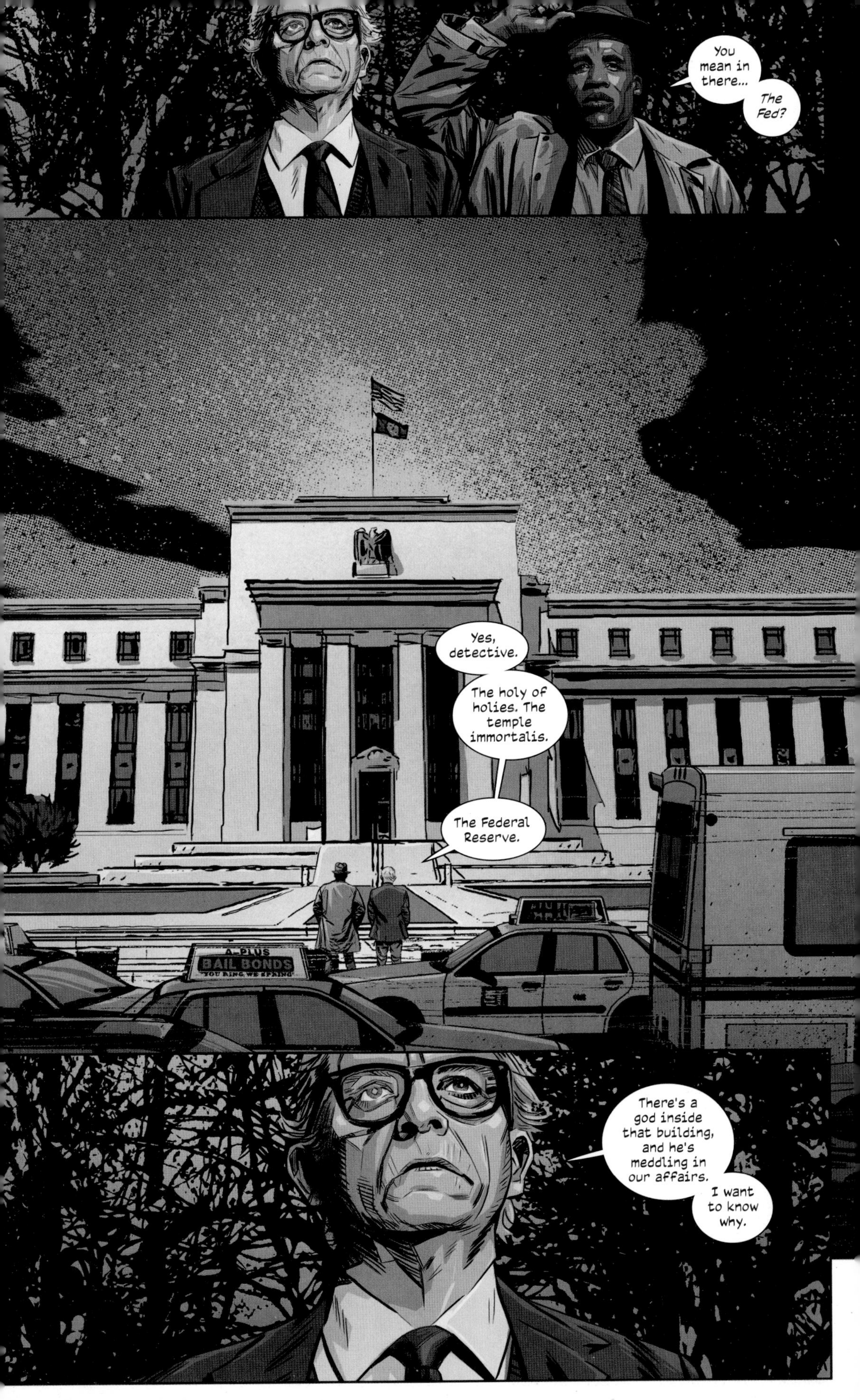

You mean in there... *The Fed?*
Yes, detective.
The holy of holies. The temple immortalis.
The Federal Reserve.
A-PLUS
BAIL BONDS
There's a god inside that building, and he's meddling in our affairs.
I want to know why.

{e}[l]

[f] ....

....

....

....

....

....

....

....

....

....

....

—

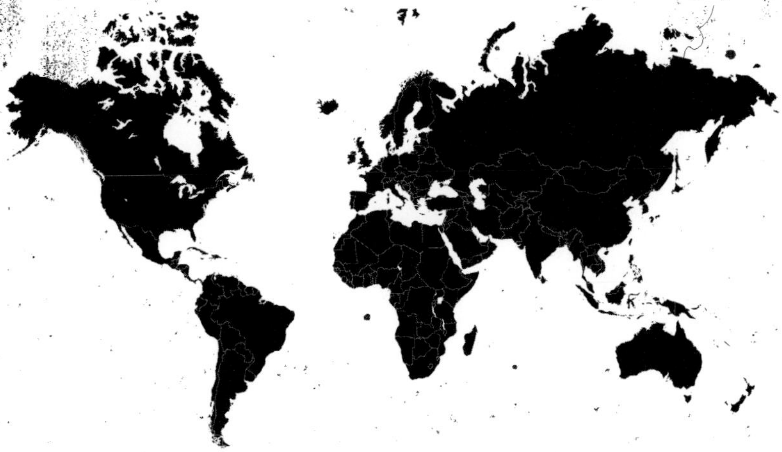

THE UPPER TERRITORIES OF MAMMON
[The Schools]

[a]
[b]

[c]
[d]

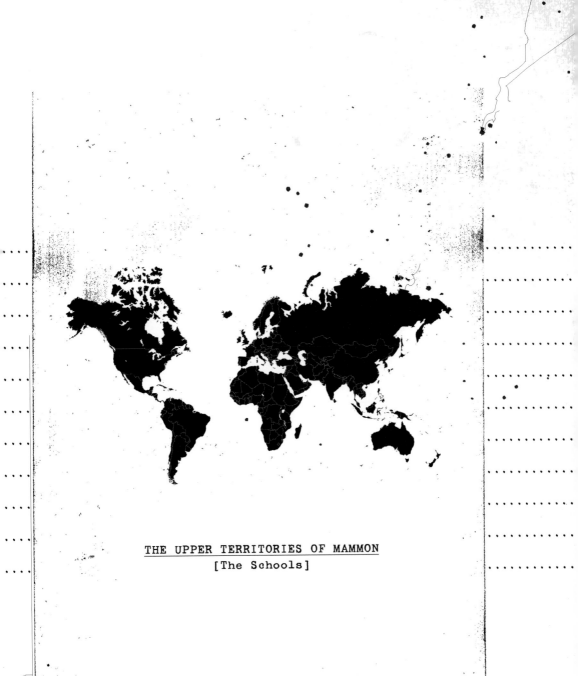

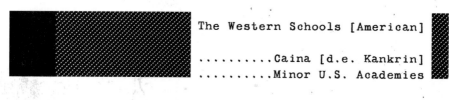

The Western Schools [American]

.........Caina [d.e. Kankrin]
.........Minor U.S. Academies

The Papacy of Night

...............The Black Pope
..........The Cardinal Nimbus

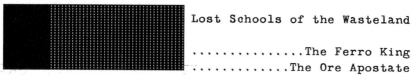

Lost Schools of the Wasteland

...............The Ferro King
............The Ore Apostate

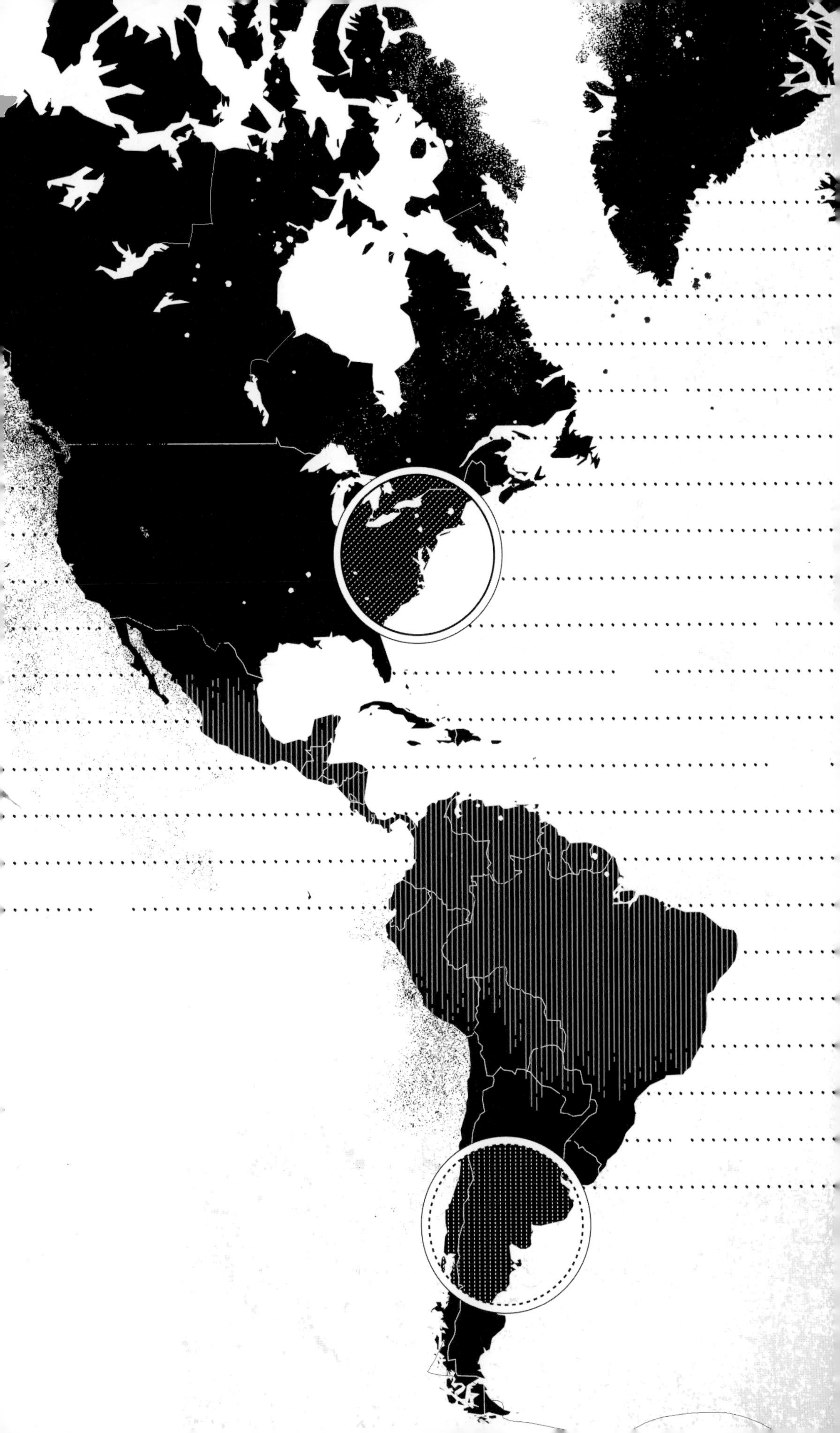

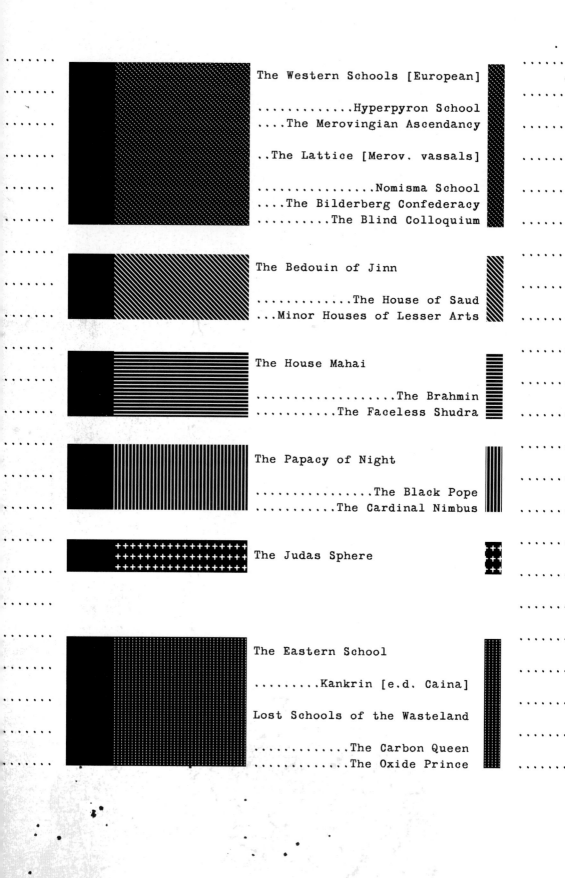

The Western Schools [European]

.............Hyperpyron School
....The Merovingian Ascendancy

..The Lattice [Merov. vassals]

................Nomisma School
....The Bilderberg Confederacy
.........The Blind Colloquium

The Bedouin of Jinn

.............The House of Saud
...Minor Houses of Lesser Arts

The House Mahai

..................The Brahmin
...........The Faceless Shudra

The Papacy of Night

................The Black Pope
..........The Cardinal Nimbus

The Judas Sphere

The Eastern School

.........Kankrin [e.d. Caina]

Lost Schools of the Wasteland

............The Carbon Queen
............The Oxide Prince

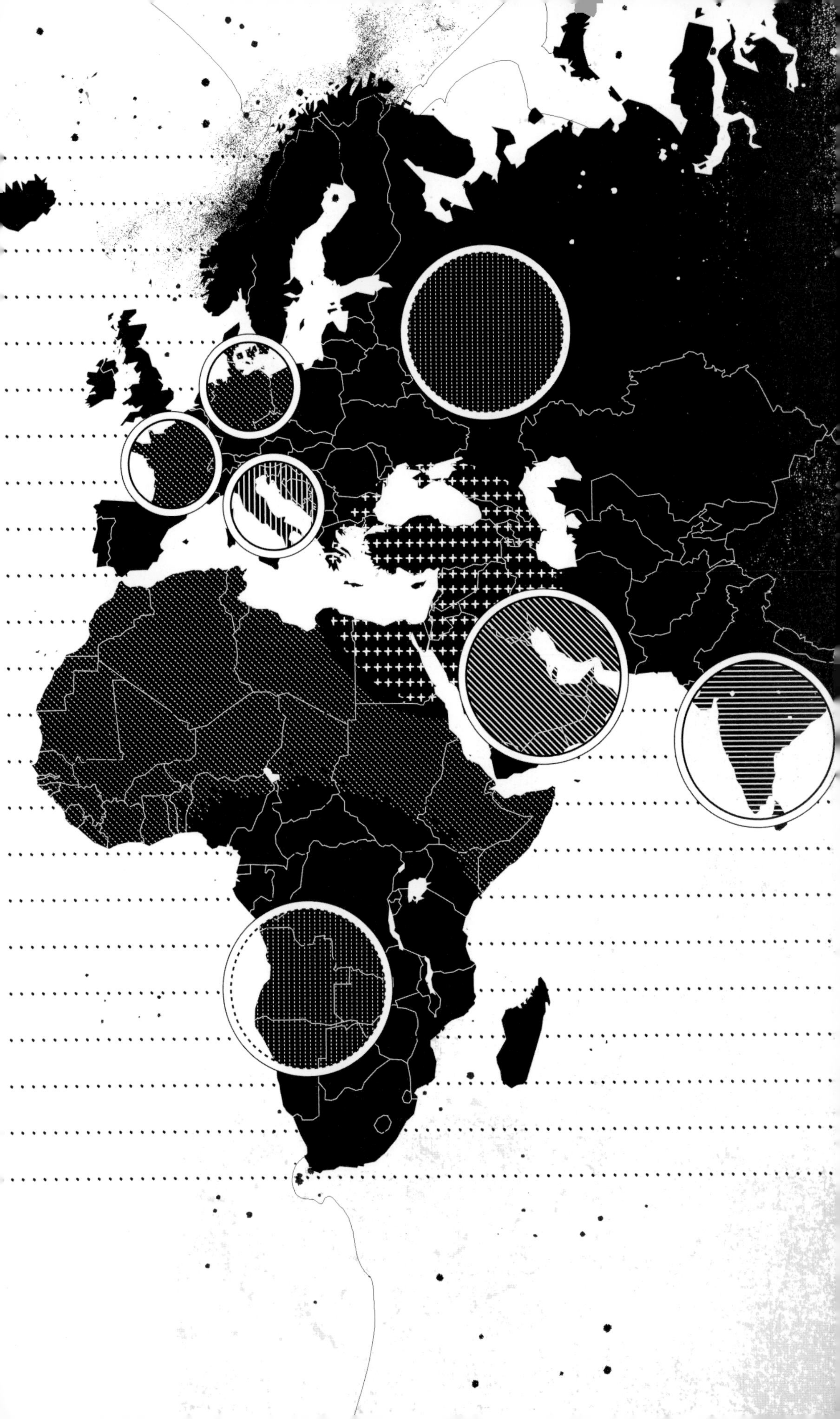

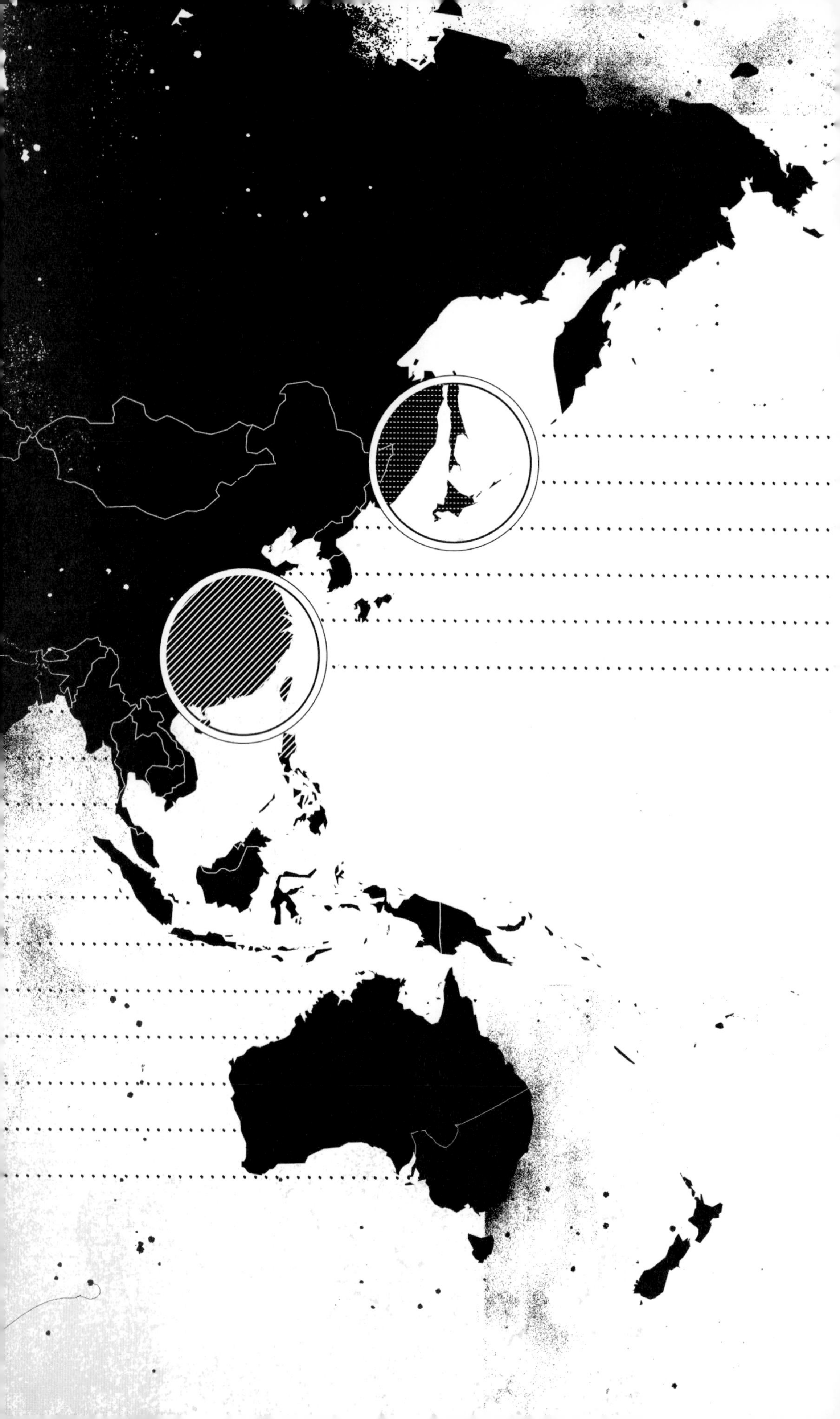

The Ronin of Dai-iche

....House of the Hidden Master
..Mirror of the Ravenous Beast

The Yinhang Solidarity

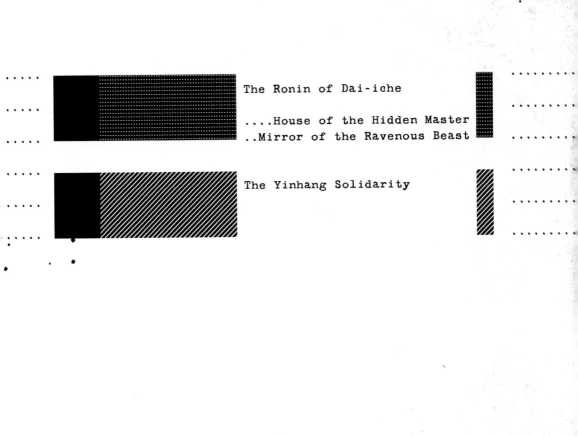

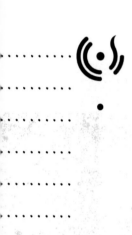

dominion |dəˈminyən|

noun

1 sovereignty; control: God's eternal dominion over man.................

[redacted]..

2 [redacted] all [redacted] these [redacted]..

[redacted] lands [redacted]..

[redacted] are [redacted] mi[redacted]ne[redacted]..

[redacted] for [redacted]..

3 [redacted] ever [redacted]..

ORIGIN

Middle English: via Old French from medieval Latin dominio,....

from Latin dominium, from dominus ‘lord, master.’.......................

....

....

....

....

....

....

....

....

....

....

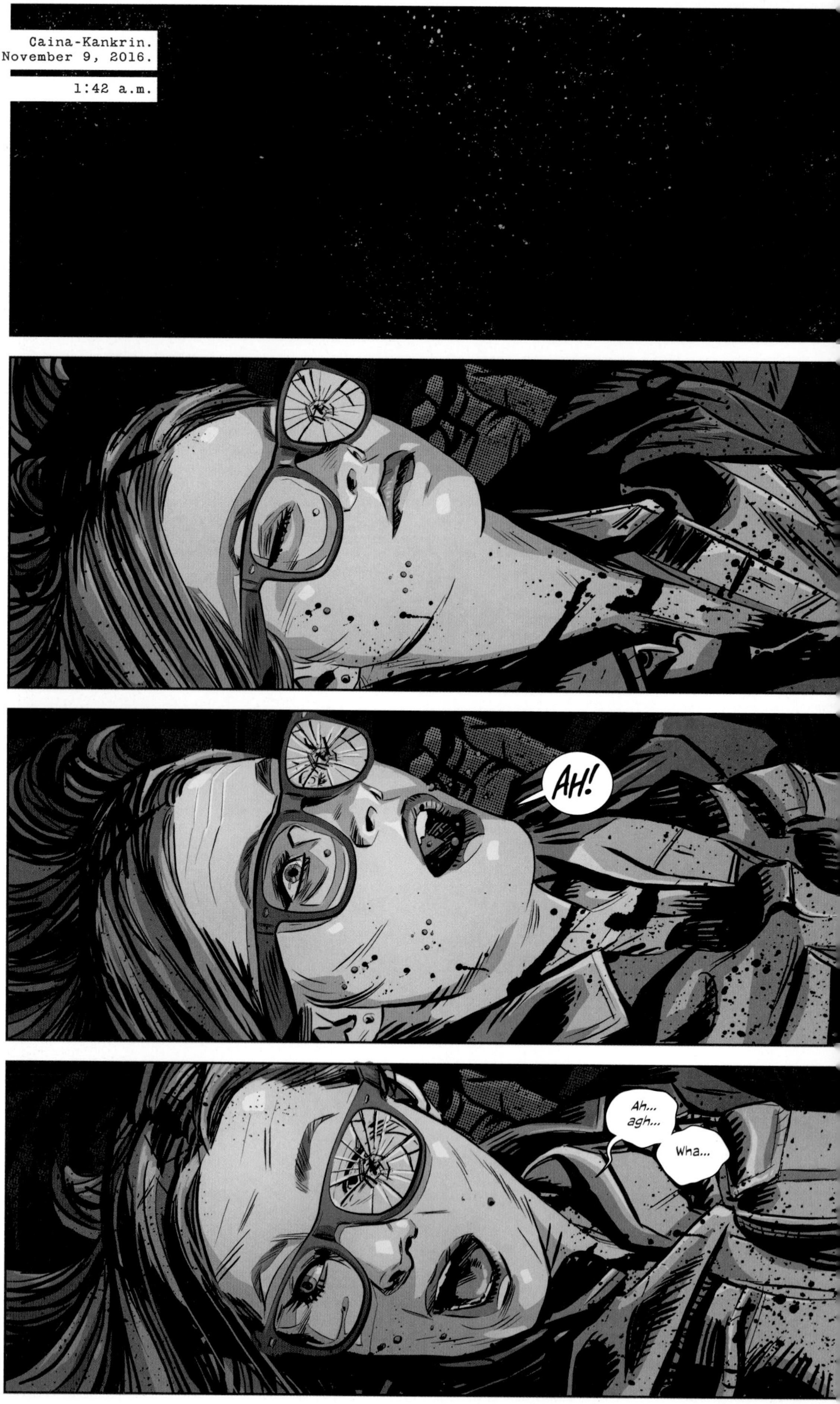
Caina-Kankrin.
November 9, 2016.
1:42 a.m.
AH!
Ah... agh...
Wha...

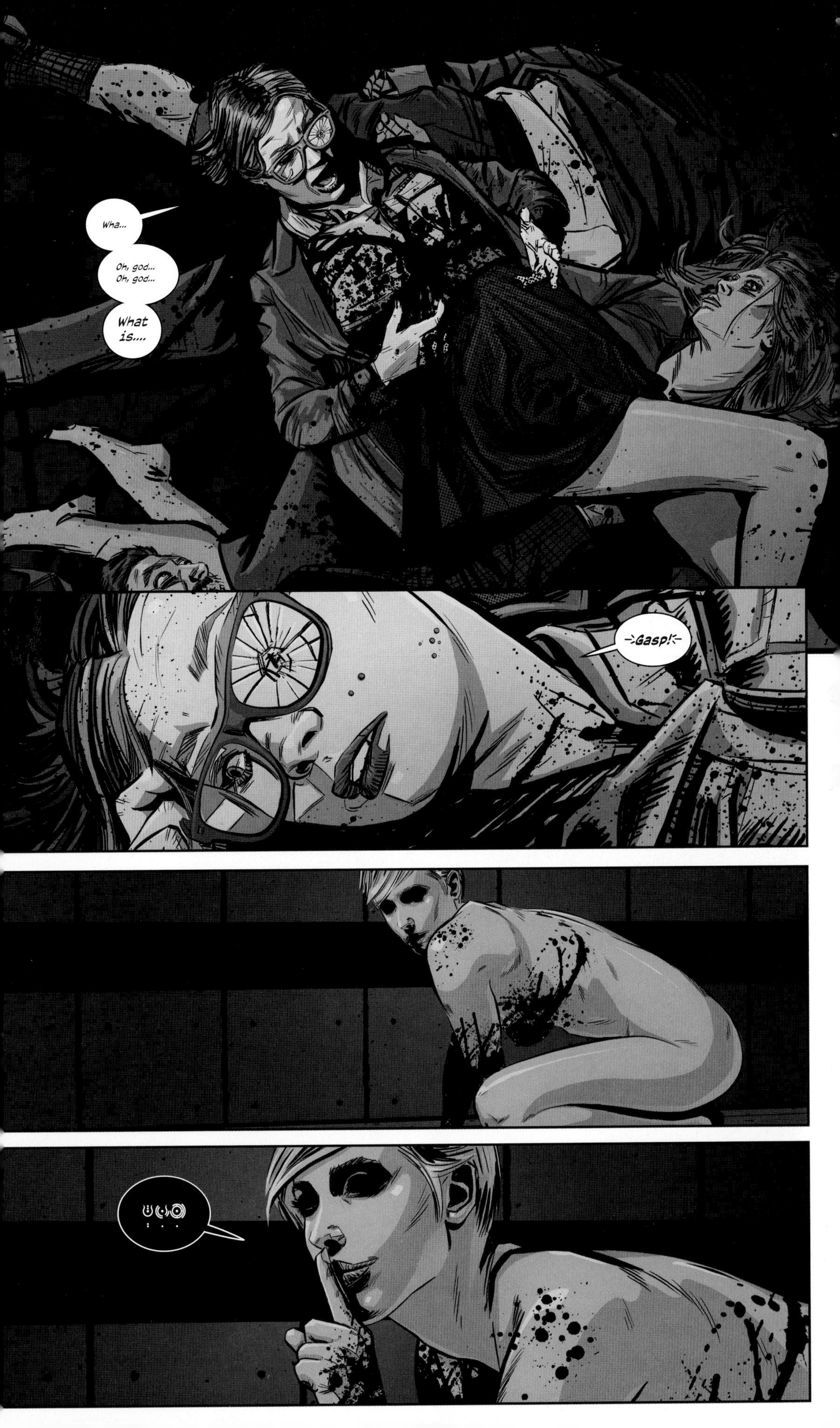
Wha...
Oh, god...
Oh, god...
What is....
-Gasp!-

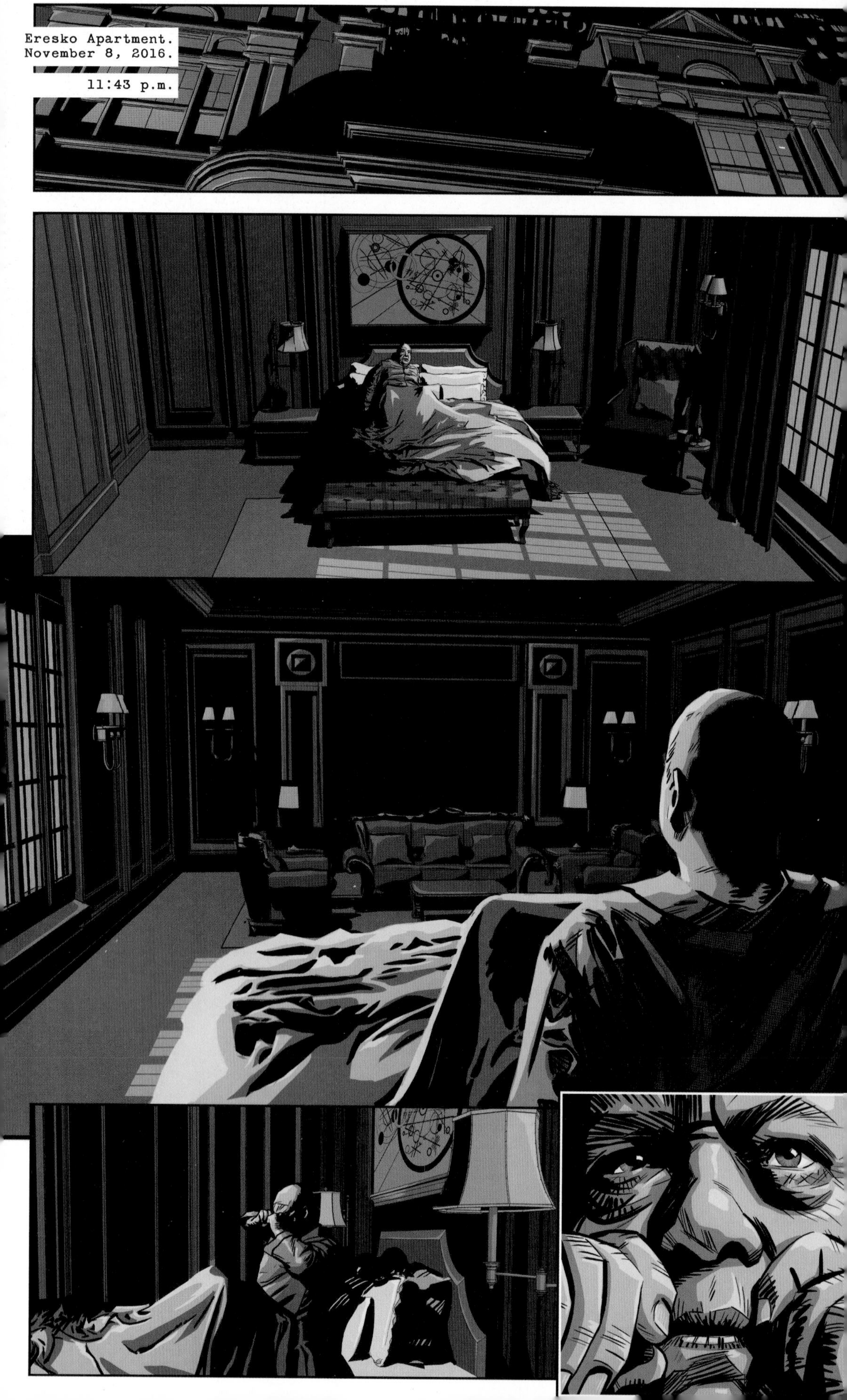
Eresko Apartment.
November 8, 2016.
11:43 p.m.

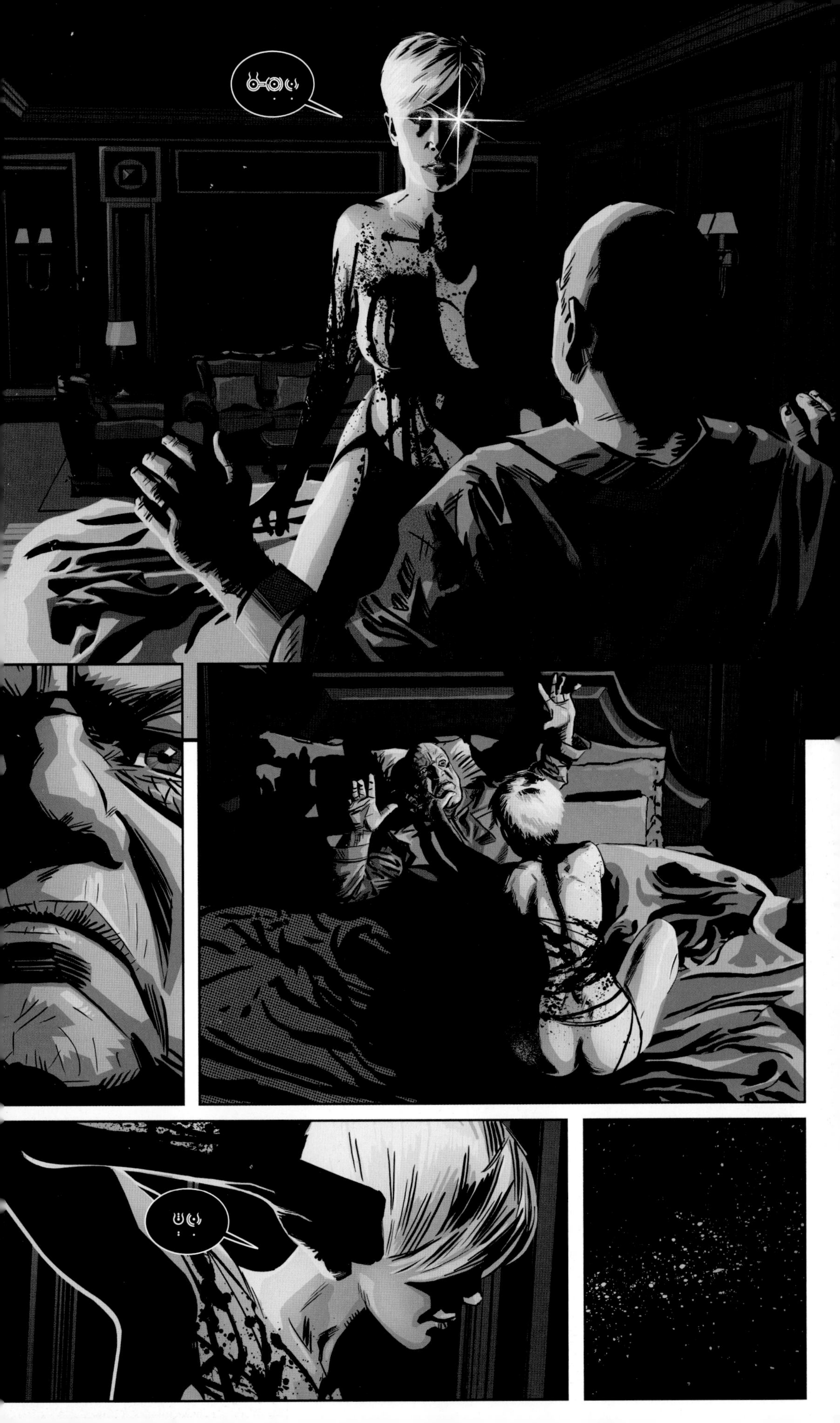

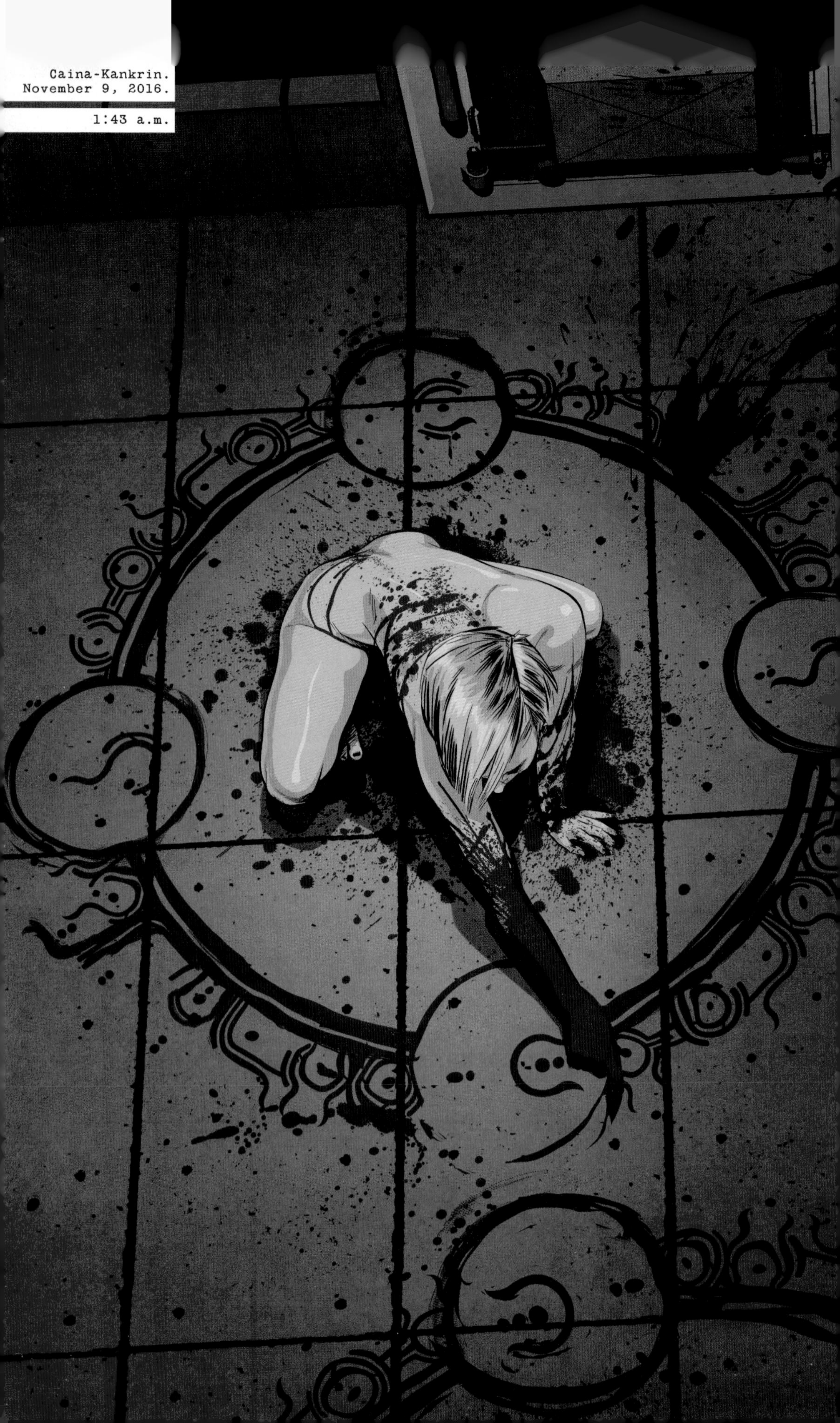
Caina-Kankrin.
November 9, 2016.
1:43 a.m.

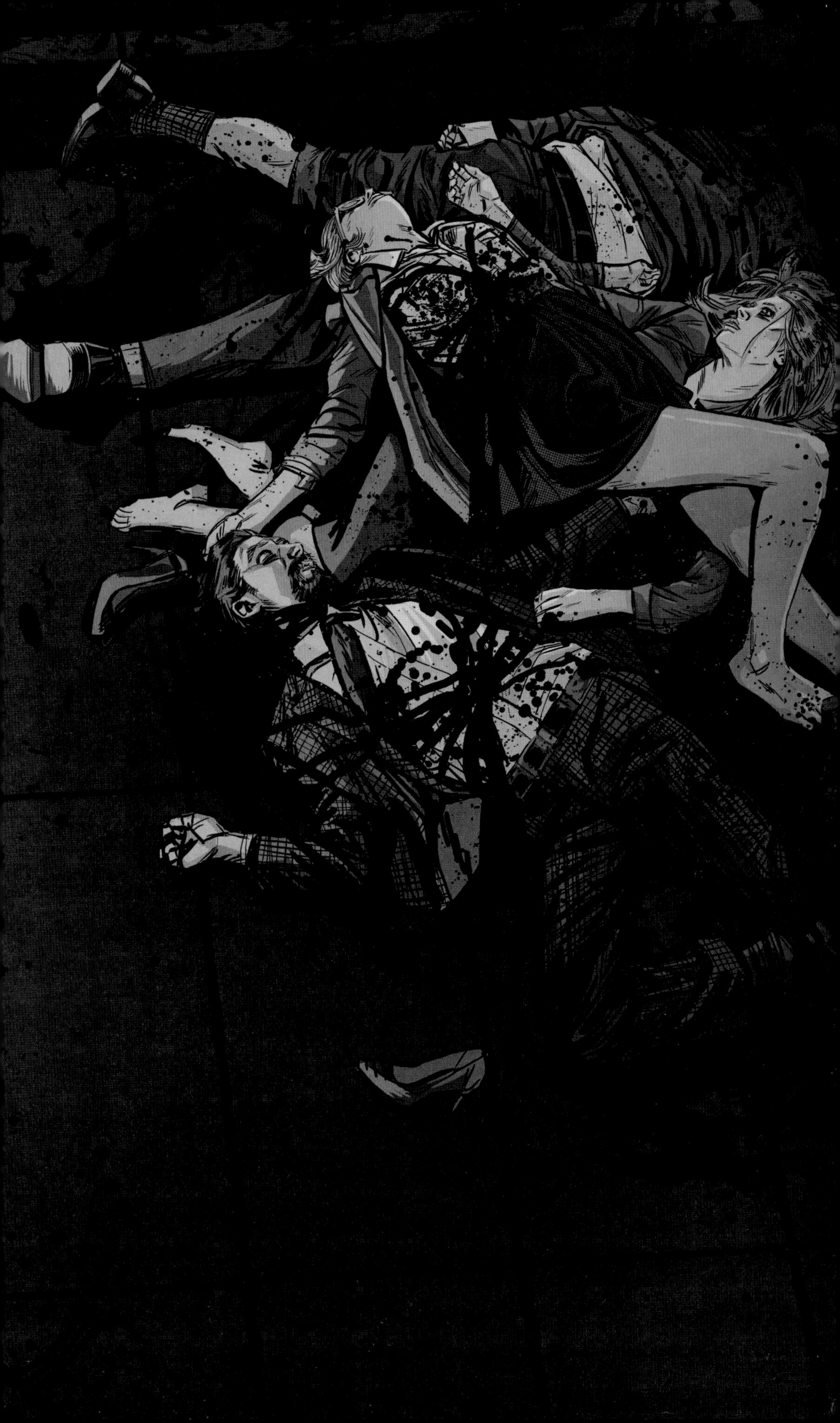

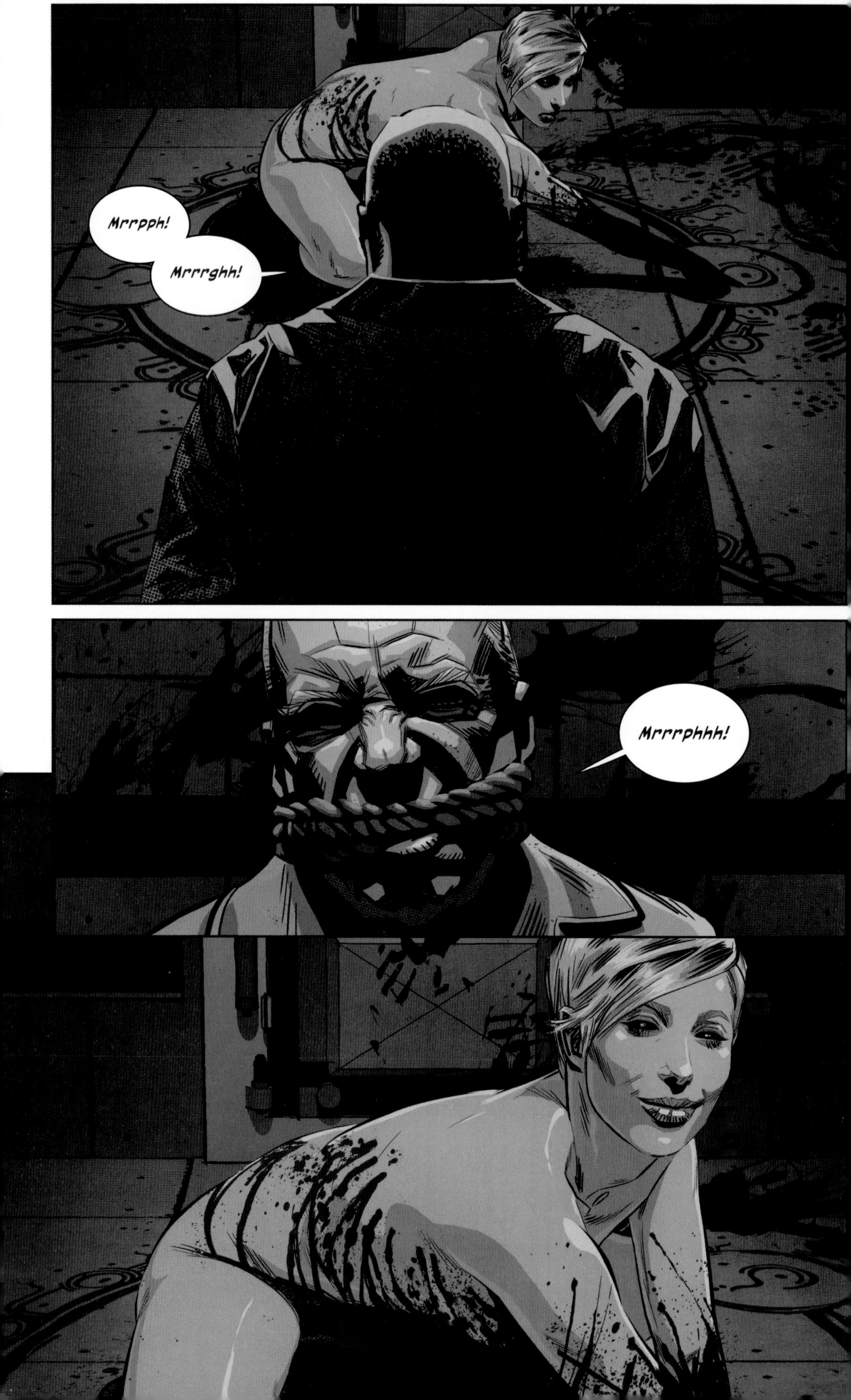
Mrrpph!
Mrrrghh!
Mrrrphhh!

When the world becomes the arena,

who will stand for you in the circle?

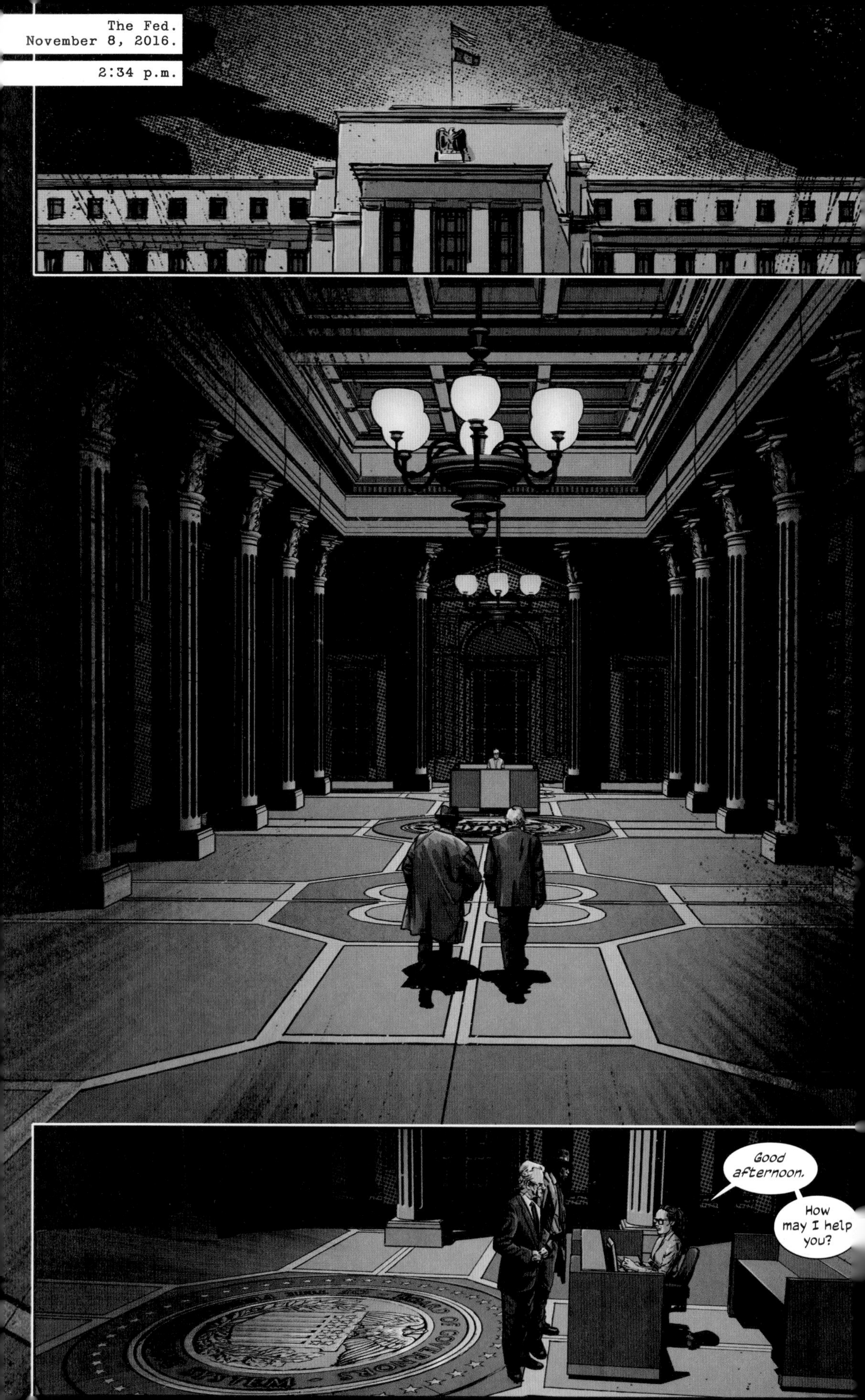
The Fed.
November 8, 2016.
2:34 p.m.
Good afternoon.
How may I help you?

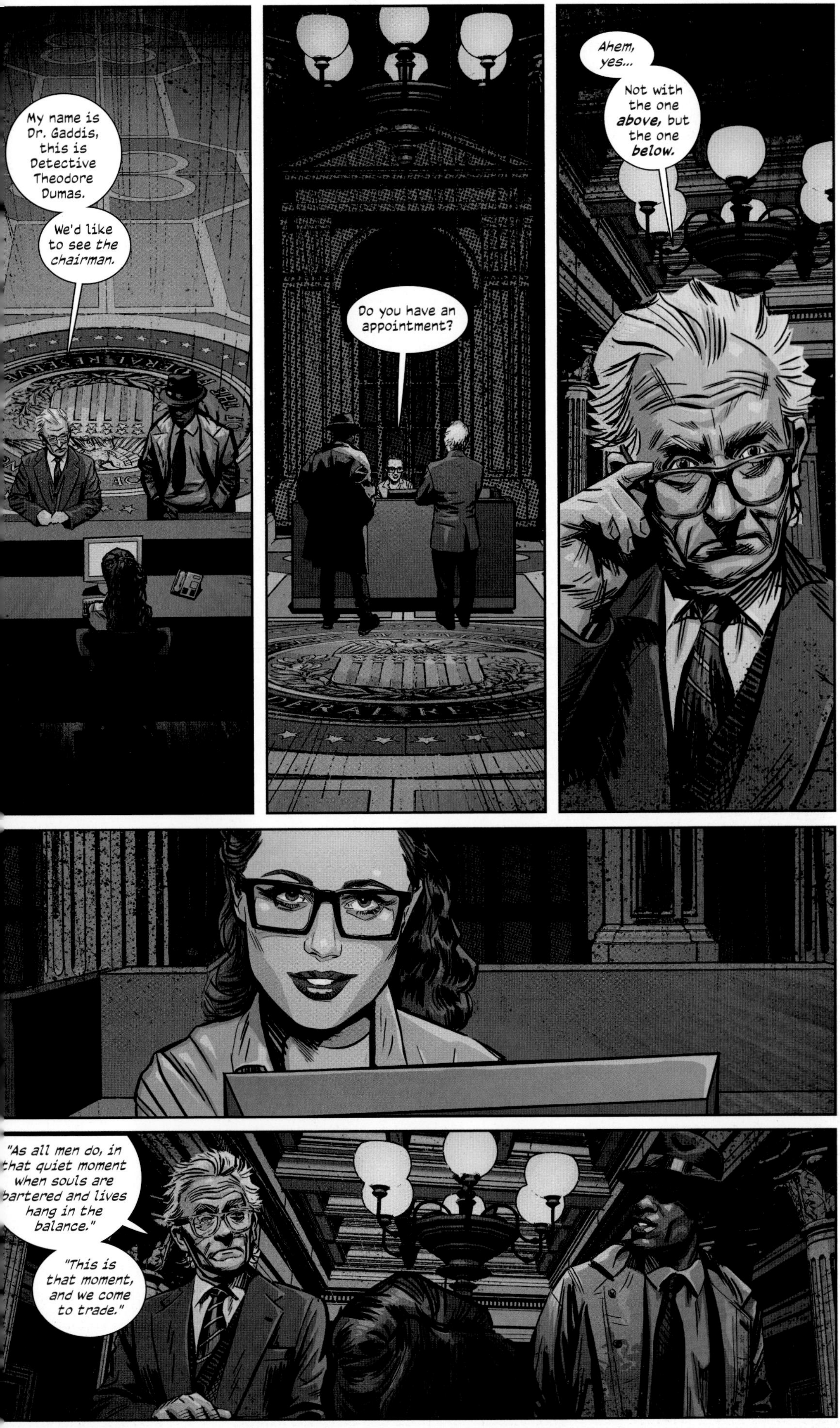
My name is Dr. Gaddis, this is Detective Theodore Dumas.
We'd like to see *the chairman.*
Do you have an appointment?
Ahem, yes...
Not with the one ***above,*** but the one ***below.***
"As all men do, in that quiet moment when souls are bartered and lives hang in the balance."
"This is that moment, and we come to trade."

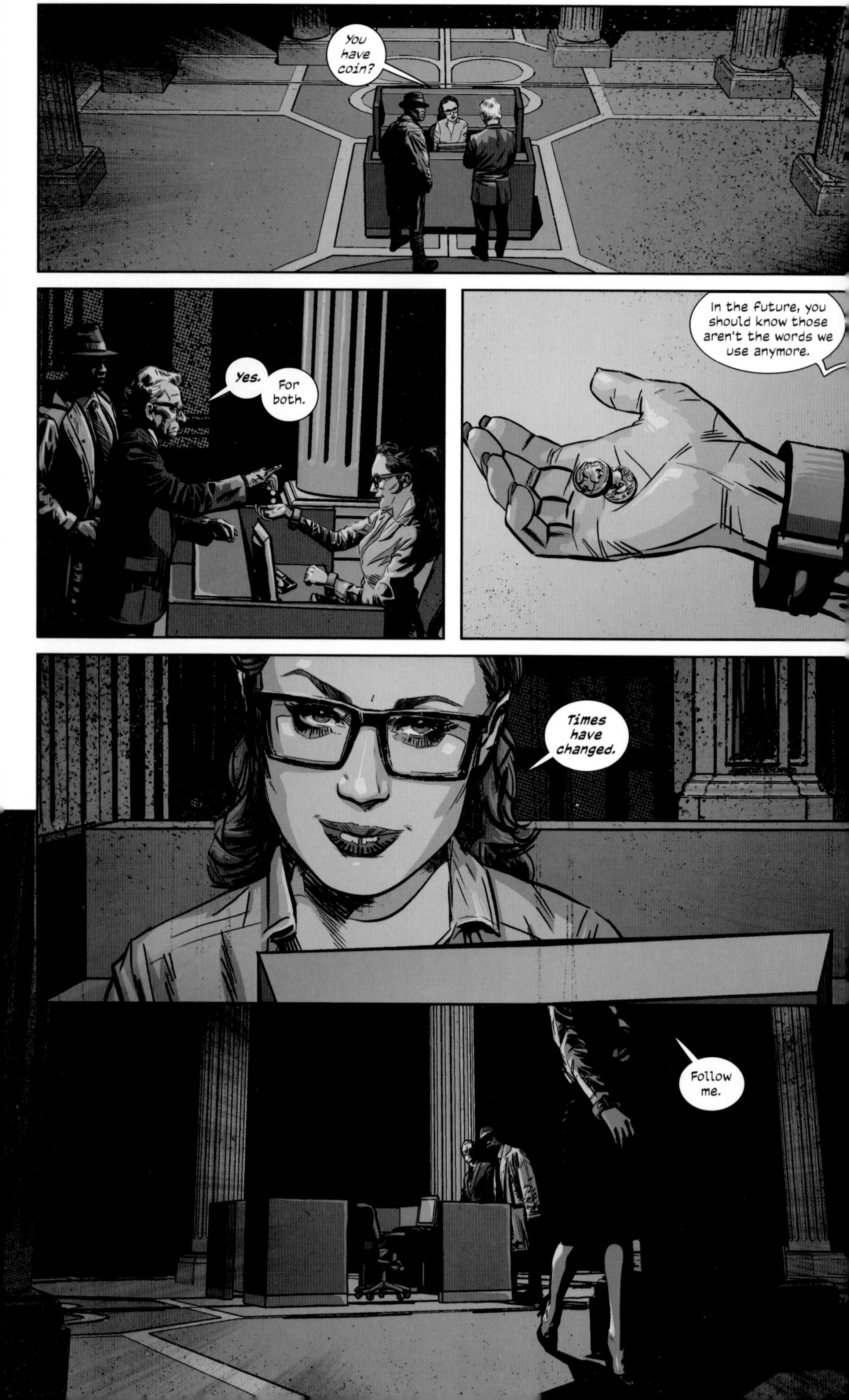
You have coin?
Yes.
For both.
In the future, you should know those aren't the words we use anymore.
Times have changed.
Follow me.

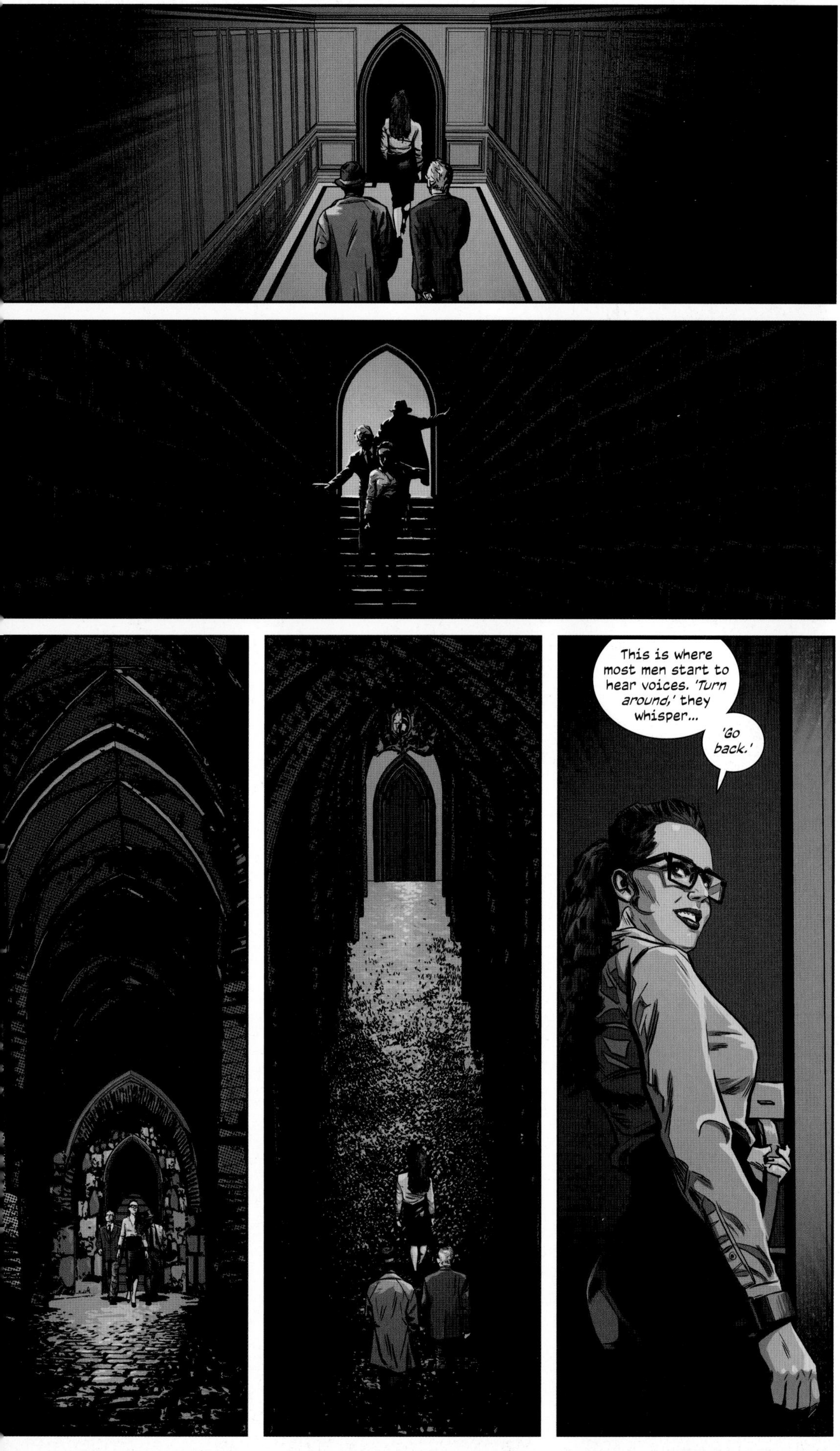
This is where most men start to hear voices. 'Turn around,' they whisper...
'Go back.'

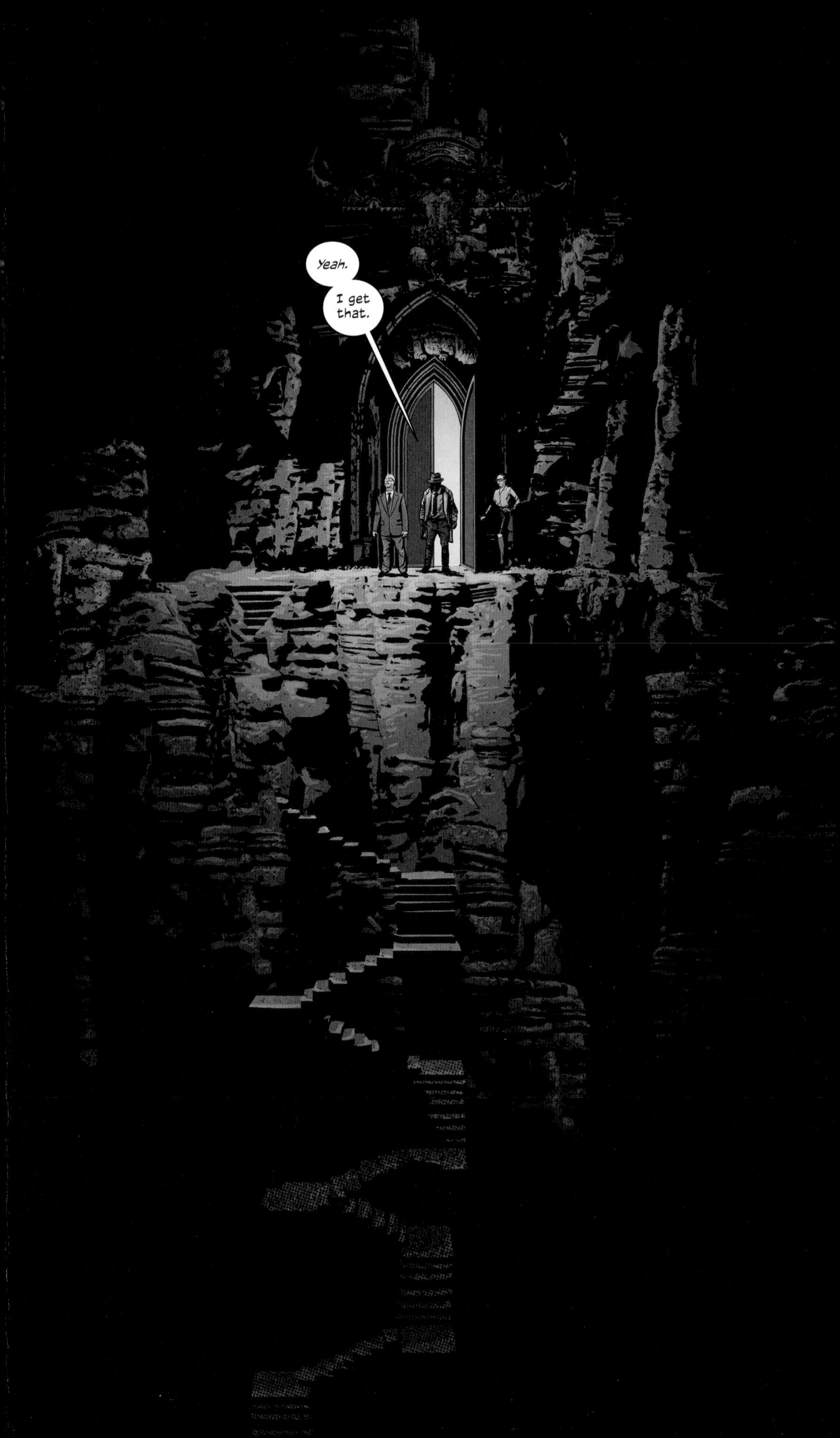
Yeah.
I get that.

To: Ackermann, Wynn   [May 27, 2014 at 4:03 PM]

From: Rothschild, Daniel

>> You disappeared.

Where the fuck are you, Wynn?

DR

CHAPTER SEVEN:

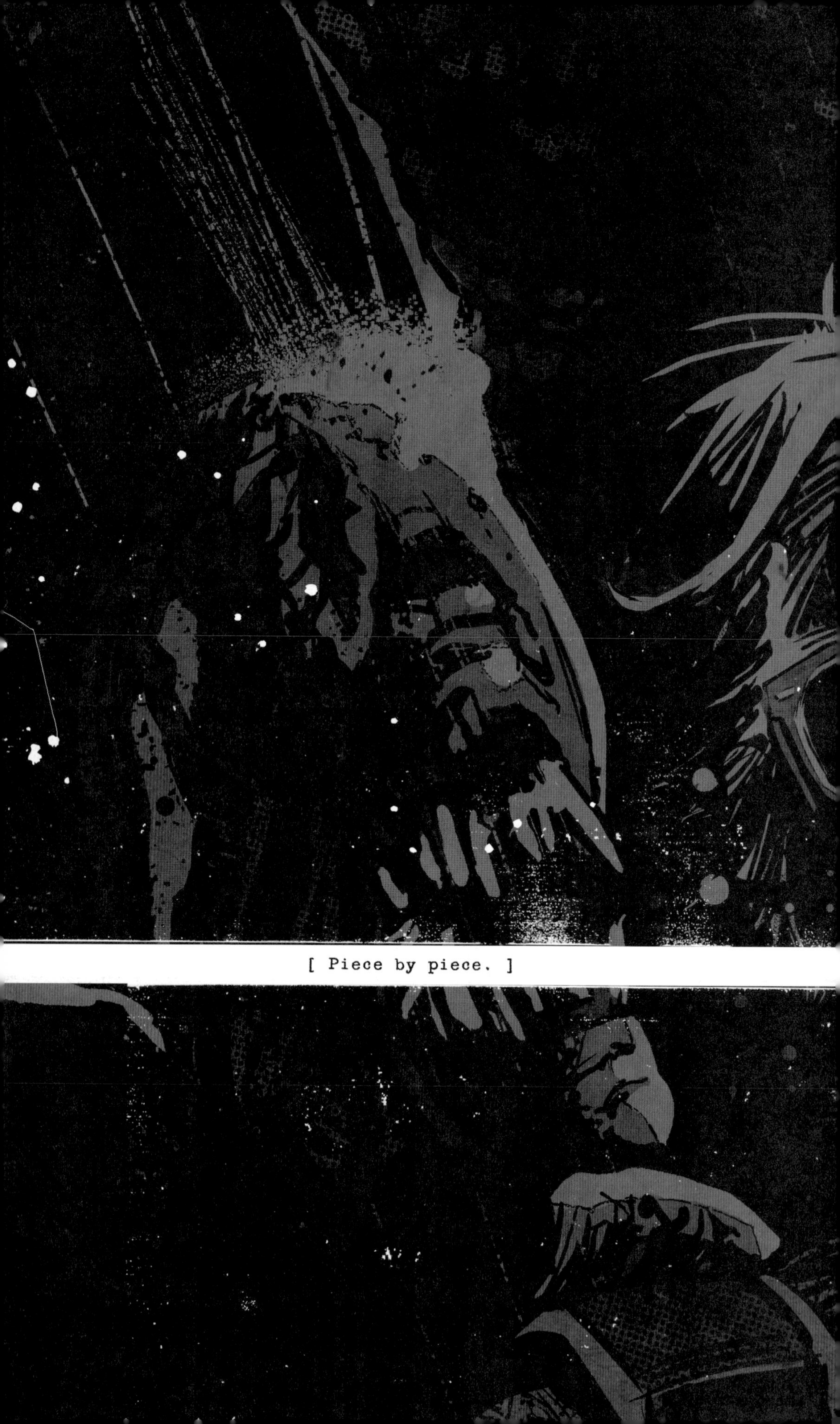

[Piece by piece.]

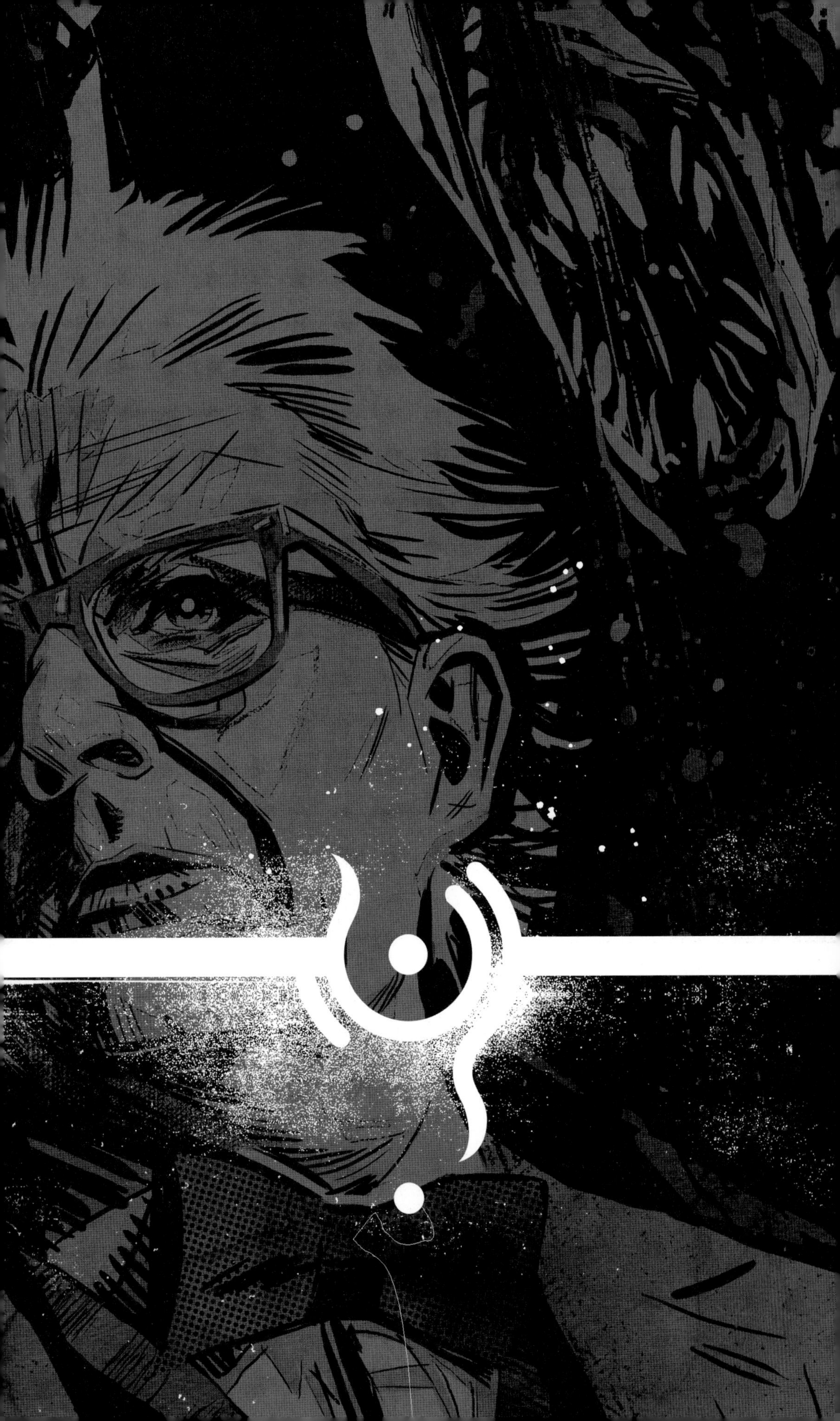

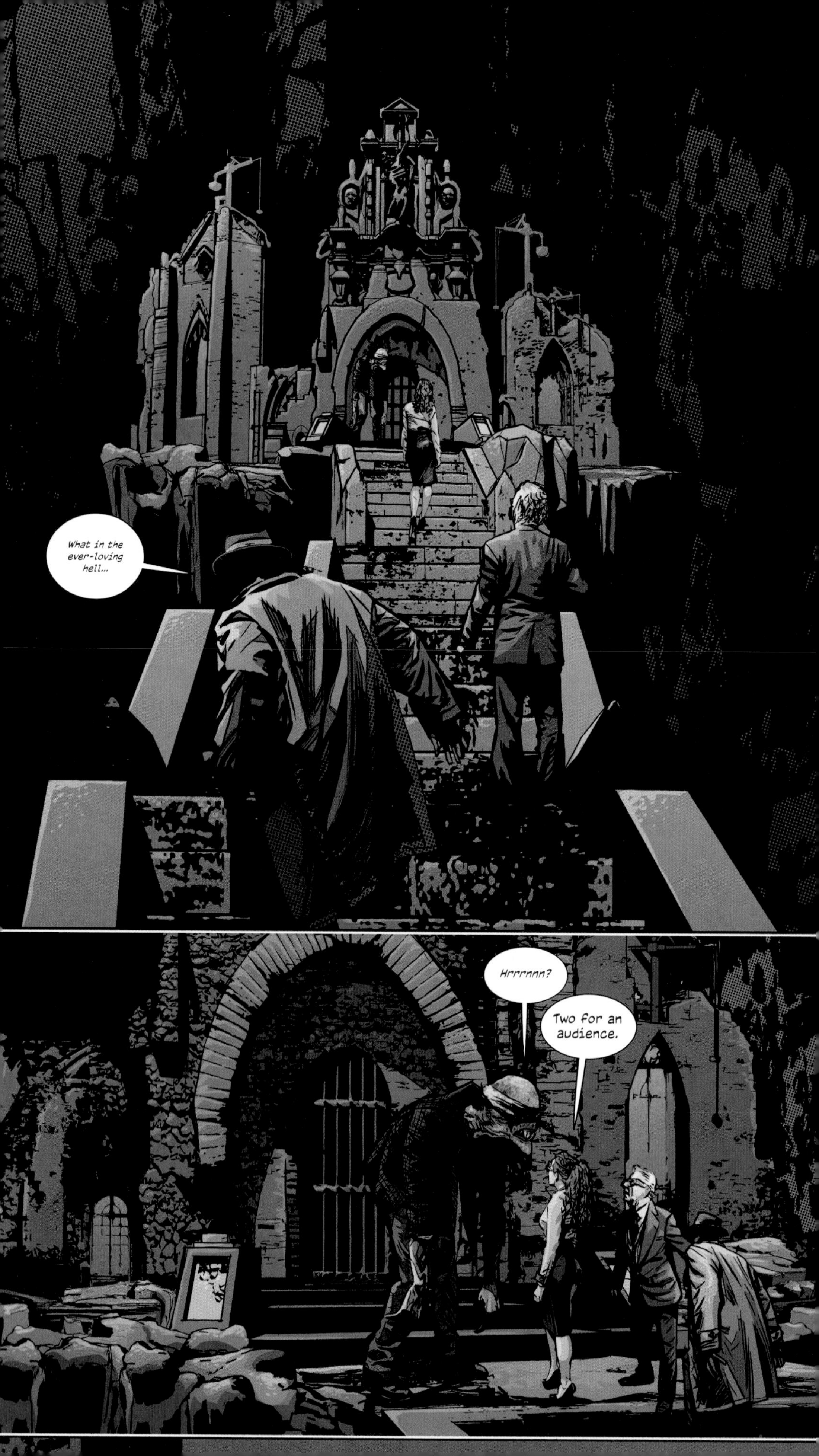
What in the ever-loving hell...
Hrrrnnn?
Two for an audience.

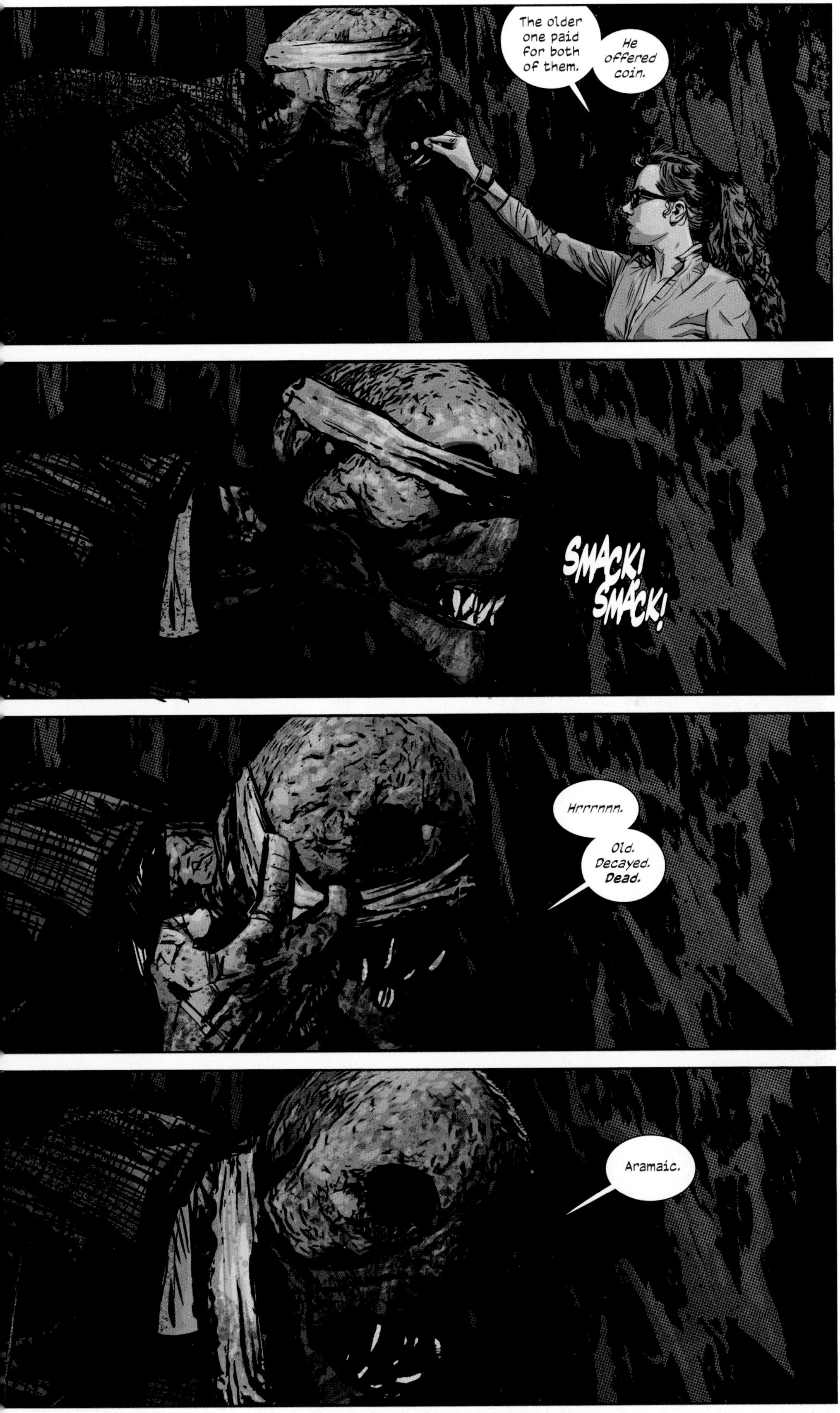

The older one paid for both of them.
He offered coin.
SMACK! SMACK!
Hrrrnnn.
Old. Decayed. Dead.
Aramaic.

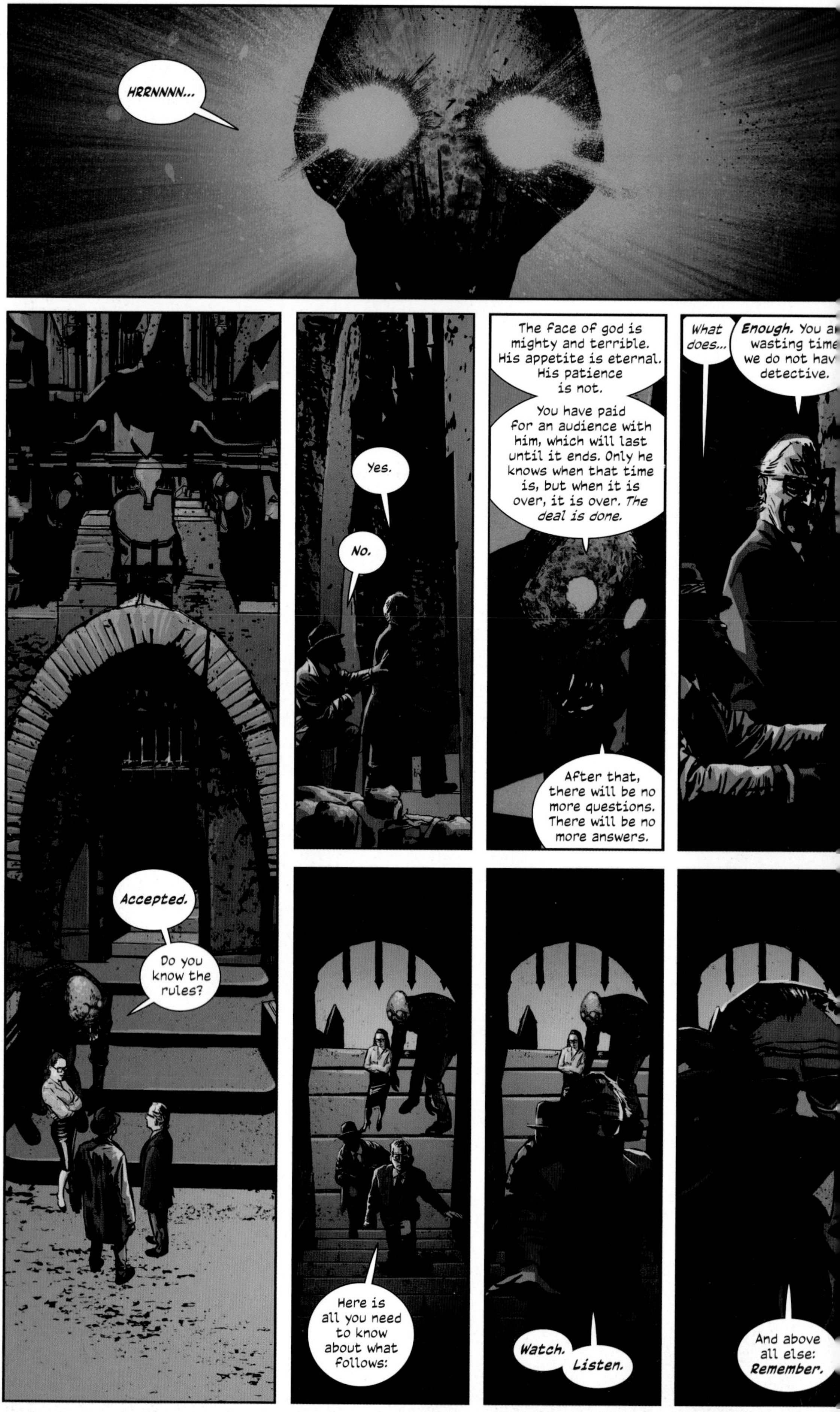
HRRNNNN...
Accepted.
Do you know the rules?
Yes.
No.
The face of god is mighty and terrible. His appetite is eternal. His patience is not.
You have paid for an audience with him, which will last until it ends. Only he knows when that time is, but when it is over, it is over. The deal is done.
After that, there will be no more questions. There will be no more answers.
What does...
Enough. You a wasting time we do not hav detective.
Here is all you need to know about what follows:
Watch.
Listen.
And above all else: Remember.

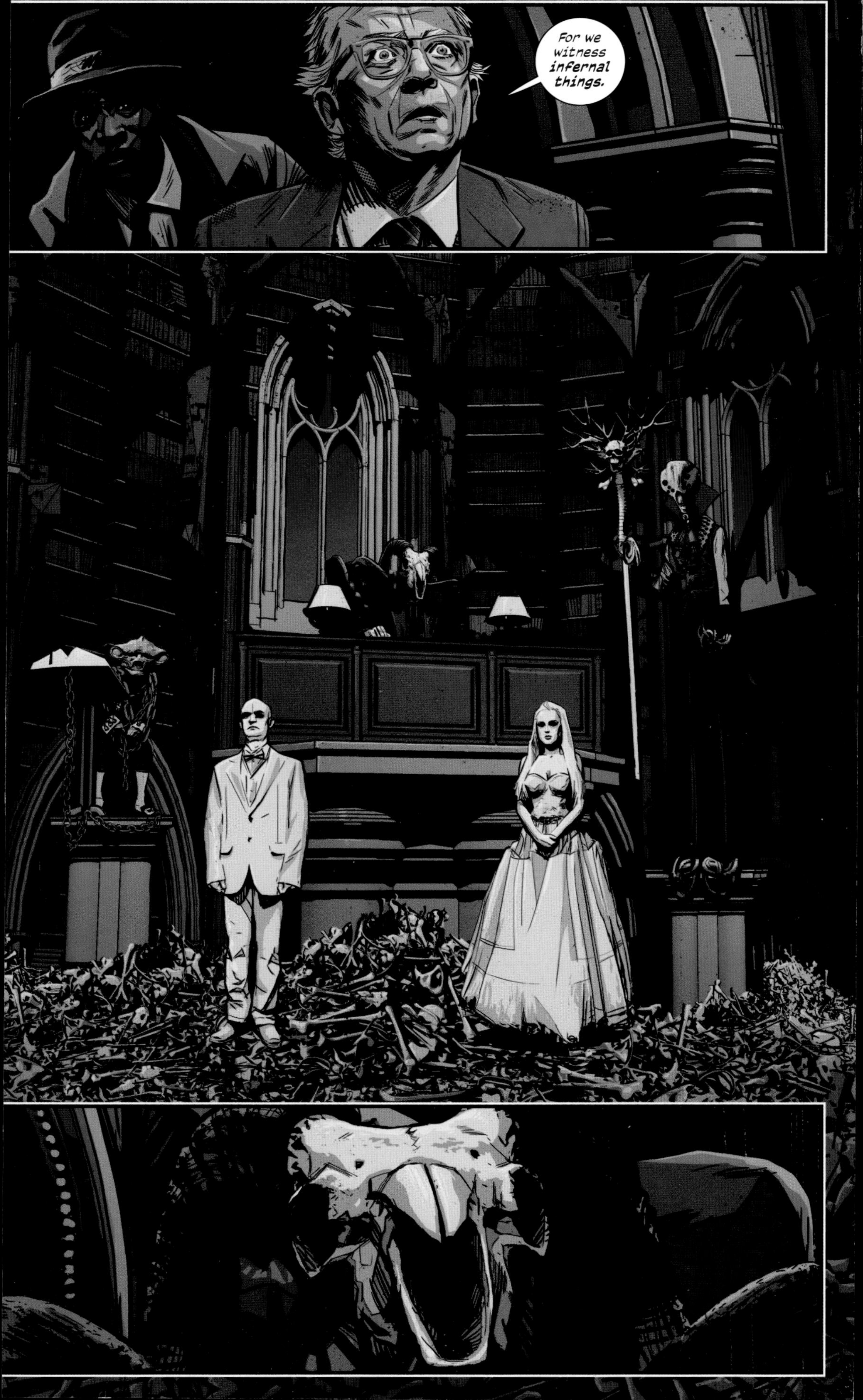
For we witness infernal things.

To: Rothschild, Daniel   [May 27, 2014 at 4:28 PM]
From: Ackermann, Wynn

Re: You disappeared.

A

Berlin.

But I'm catching a train to Denmark in an hour.

W -

// Where the fuck are you, Wynn?
//
// DR
//
//
//
//

To: Ackermann, Wynn

From: Rothschild, Daniel

[May 27, 2014 at 4:35 PM]

Re: You disappeared.

Why? I need you here. We have a board meeting in two days.

DR

// Berlin.
//
// But I'm catching a train to Denmark in an hour.
//
// W -
//
//
//// Where the fuck are you, Wynn?
////
//// DR
////
////
////
////

NOTICE: This communication may contain client privileged and/or confidential information. If you are not the intended recipient, you are hereby notified that any dissemination, distribution or copying of this message is strictly prohibited. If you have received this communication in error, please advise the sender by return email and immediately delete the message and any attachments without copying or disclosing the contents. Thank you.

To: **Rothschild, Daniel**   [May 27, 2014 at 4:48 PM]

From: **Ackermann, Wynn**

Re: You disappeared.

A

Emergency.

I'm meeting someone in Copenhagen before the Nomisma conclave.

W -

```
//  Why? I need you here. We have a board meeting in two days.
//
//  DR
//.
//
////  Berlin.
////
////  But I'm catching a train to Denmark in an hour.
////
////  W -
////
////
//////  Where the fuck are you, Wynn?
//////
//////  DR
//////
//////
//////
//////
```

To: Ackermann, Wynn   [May 27, 2014 at 4:57 PM]
From: Rothschild, Daniel

Re: You disappeared.

R

Who?

DR

// Emergency.
//
// I'm meeting someone in Copenhagen before the Nomisma conclave.
//
// W -
//-
//
//// Why? I need you here. We have a board meeting in two days.
////
//// DR
////
////
////// Berlin.
//////
////// But I'm catching a train to Denmark in an hour.
//////
////// W -
//////
//////
//////// Where the fuck are you, Wynn?
////////
//////// DR
////////
////////
////////
////////

To: [Rothschild, Daniel]   [May 27, 2014 at 5:01 PM]

From: [Ackermann, Wynn]

Re: You disappeared.

───

You know who.

You know why.

W -

// Who?
//
// DR
//
//
//// Emergency.
////
//// I'm meeting someone in Copenhagen before the Nomisma conclave.
////
//// W -
////
////
////// Why? I need you here. We have a board meeting in two days.
//////
////// DR
//////
//////
//////// Berlin.
////////
//////// But I'm catching a train to Denmark in an hour.
////////
//////// W -
////////
////////
////////// Where the fuck are you, Wynn?
//////////
////////// DR
//////////
//////////
//////////
//////////

To: Ackermann, Wynn   [May 27, 2014 at 5:03 PM]

From: Rothschild, Daniel

Re: You disappeared.

Fucking Christ. What does she want?

DR

```
// You know who.
//            )
// You know why.
//
// W -
//
//
//// Who?
////
//// DR
////
////
////// Emergency.
//////
////// I'm meeting someone in Copenhagen before the Nomisma conclave.
//////
////// W -
//////
//////
//////// Why? I need you here. We have a board meeting in two days.
////////
//////// DR
////////
////////
////////// Berlin.
//////////
////////// But I'm catching a train to Denmark in an hour.
//////////
////////// W -
//////////
//////////
////////////// Where the fuck are you, Wynn?
//////////////
////////////// DR
//////////////
//////////////
//////////////
//////////////
//////////////
```

To: Rothschild, Daniel
From: Ackermann, Wynn

[May 27, 2014 at 5:12 PM]

Re: You disappeared.

A few introductions to the newer Colloquium members who are handling outreach to the island. She's offered to act as a go between, and I vouched for her. They don't trust us, especially her, so there will be Bilderberg Confederates there as well.

But don't worry. Everything should be fine.

Hey, everyone needs a little help sometimes. Even her.

W -

// Fucking Christ. What does she want?
//
// DR
//
//
//// You know who.
////
//// You know why.
////
//// W -
//////
//////
////// Who?
//////
////// DR
//////
//////
//////// Emergency.
////////
//////// I'm meeting someone in Copenhagen before the Nomisma conclave.
////////
//////// W -
////////
////////
////////// Why? I need you here. We have a board meeting in two days.
//////////
////////// DR
//////////
//////////
//////////// Berlin.
////////////
//////////// But I'm catching a train to Denmark in an hour.
////////////
//////////// W -
////////////
////////////
////////////// Where the fuck are you, Wynn?
//////////////
////////////// DR
//////////////
//////////////
//////////////
//////////////

To: Ackermann, Wynn
From: Rothschild, Daniel

[May 27, 2014 at 5:17 PM]

Re: You disappeared.

Okay. Let me know what happens as soon as you get done.

Send Ria my love.

DR

// A few introductions to the newer Colloquium members who are handling
// outreach to the island. She's offered to act as a go between, and I
// vouched for her. They don't trust us, especially her, so there will
// be Bilderberg Confederates there as well.
//
// But don't worry. Everything should be fine.
//
// Hey, everyone needs a little help sometimes. Even her.
//
// W -
//
//
//// Fucking Christ. What does she want?
////
//// DR
////
////
////// You know who.
//////
////// You know why.
//////
////// W -
//////
//////
//////// Who?
////////
//////// DR
////////
////////
////////// Emergency.
//////////
////////// I'm meeting someone in Copenhagen before the Nomisma conclave.
//////////
////////// W -
//////////
//////////
//////////// Why? I need you here. We have a board meeting in two days.
////////////
//////////// DR
////////////
////////////
////////////// Berlin.
//////////////
////////////// But I'm catching a train to Denmark in an hour.
//////////////
////////////// W -
//////////////
//////////////
//////////////// Where the fuck are you, Wynn?
////////////////
//////////////// DR
////////////////
////////////////
////////////////
////////////////

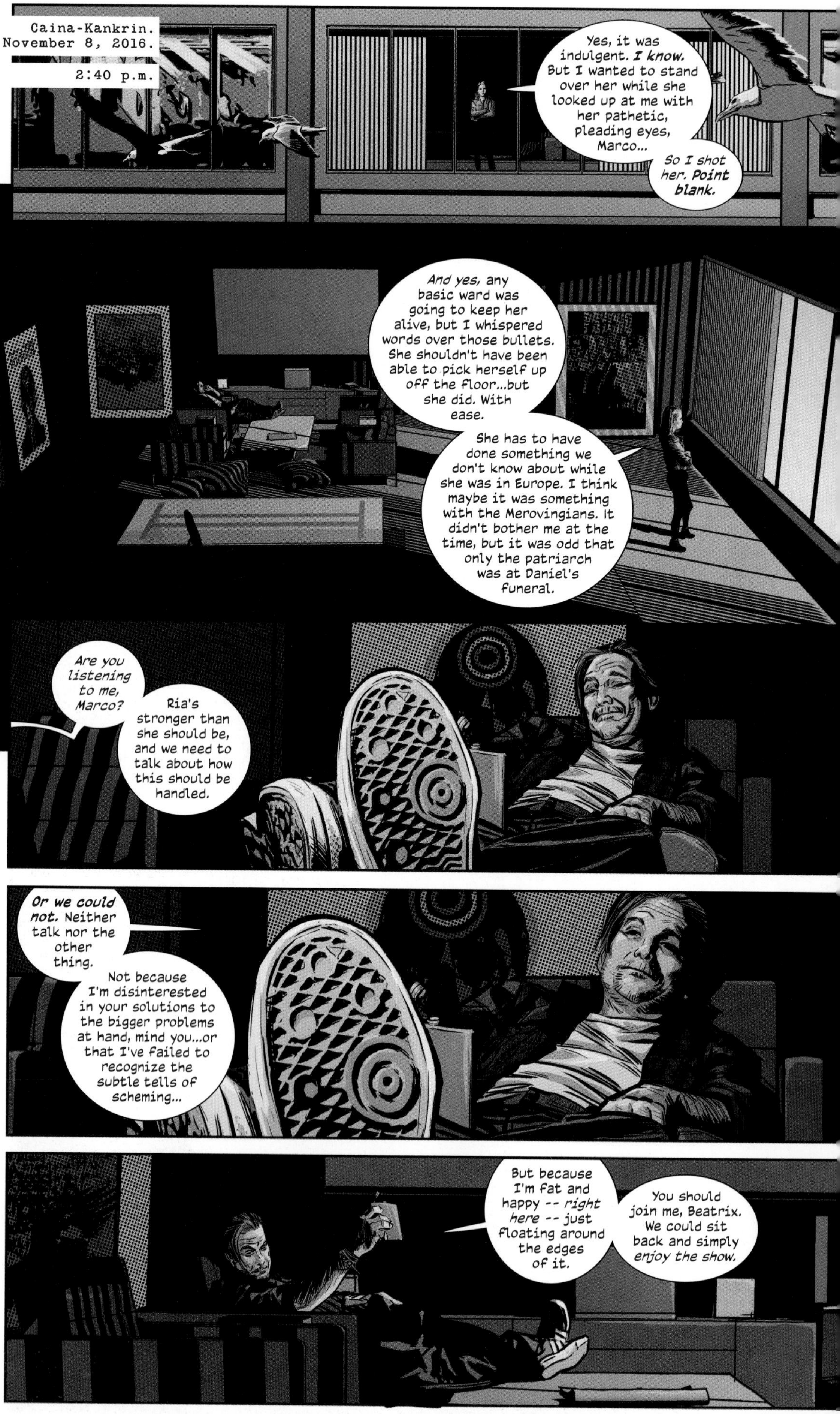
Caina-Kankrin. November 8, 2016.
2:40 p.m.
Yes, it was indulgent. I know. But I wanted to stand over her while she looked up at me with her pathetic, pleading eyes, Marco...
So I shot her. Point blank.
And yes, any basic ward was going to keep her alive, but I whispered words over those bullets. She shouldn't have been able to pick herself up off the floor...but she did. With ease.
She has to have done something we don't know about while she was in Europe. I think maybe it was something with the Merovingians. It didn't bother me at the time, but it was odd that only the patriarch was at Daniel's funeral.
Are you listening to me, Marco?
Ria's stronger than she should be, and we need to talk about how this should be handled.
Or we could not. Neither talk nor the other thing.
Not because I'm disinterested in your solutions to the bigger problems at hand, mind you...or that I've failed to recognize the subtle tells of scheming...
But because I'm fat and happy -- right here -- just floating around the edges of it.
You should join me, Beatrix. We could sit back and simply enjoy the show.

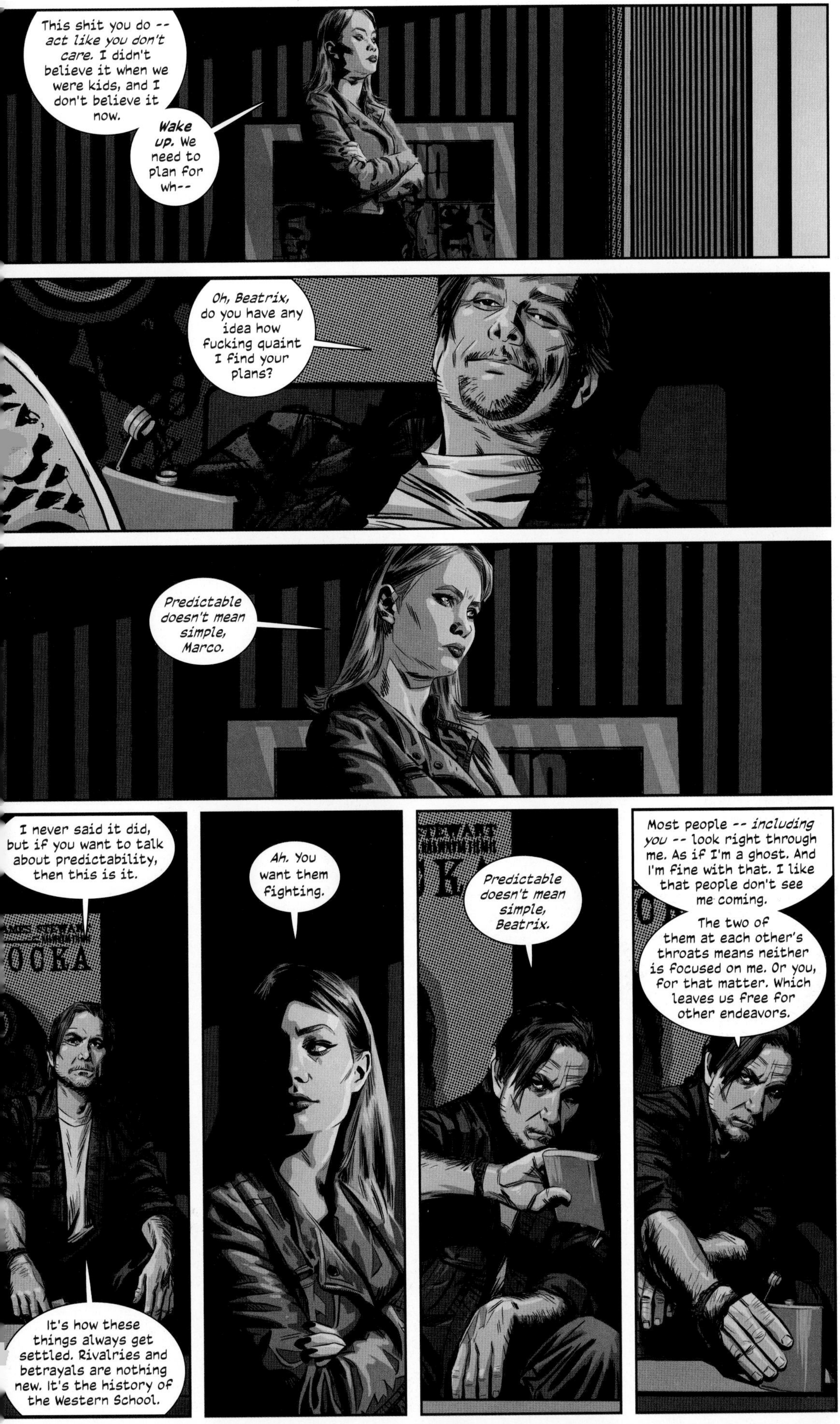
This shit you do -- *act like you don't care.* I didn't believe it when we were kids, and I don't believe it now.
Wake up. We need to plan for wh--
Oh, Beatrix, do you have any idea how fucking quaint I find your plans?
Predictable doesn't mean simple, Marco.
I never said it did, but if you want to talk about predictability, then this is it.
It's how these things always get settled. Rivalries and betrayals are nothing new. It's the history of the Western School.
Ah. You want them fighting.
Predictable doesn't mean simple, Beatrix.
Most people -- *including you* -- look right through me. As if I'm a ghost. And I'm fine with that. I like that people don't see me coming.
The two of them at each other's throats means neither is focused on me. Or you, for that matter. Which leaves us free for other endeavors.

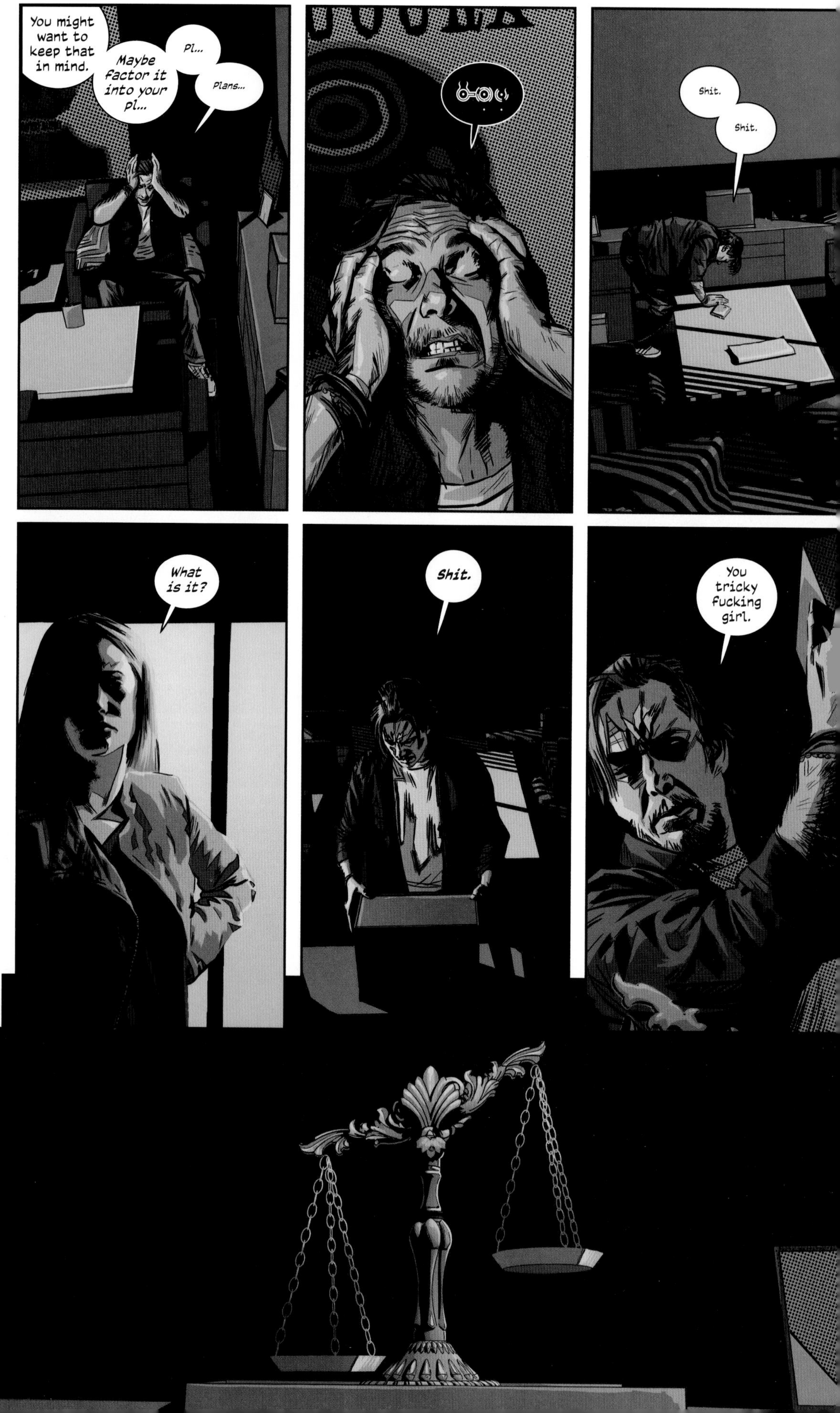

You might want to keep that in mind.
Maybe factor it into your pl...
Pl...
Plans...
Shit.
Shit.
What is it?
Shit.
You tricky fucking girl.

To: Ackermann, Wynn

From: Rothschild, Daniel

[May 27, 2014 at 11:37 PM]

R

Re: You disappeared.

You there? What the hell is going on?

Is this you?

https://www.theguardian.com/world/live/2014/may/27/
riots-explosions-at-bilderberg-group-hotel

DR

// Okay. Let me know what happens as soon as you get done.
//
// Send Ria my love.
//
// DR
//
//
//// A few introductions to the newer Colloquium members who are handling
//// outreach to the island. She's offered to act as a go between, and I
//// vouched for her. They don't trust us, especially her, so there will
//// be Bilderberg Confederates there as well.
////
//// But don't worry. Everything should be fine.
////
//// Hey, everyone needs a little help sometimes. Even her.
////
//// W -
////
////
////// Fucking Christ. What does she want?
//////
////// DR
//////
//////
//////// You know who.
////////
//////// You know why.
////////
//////// W -
////////
////////
////////// Who?
//////////
////////// DR
//////////
//////////
//////////// Emergency.
////////////
//////////// I'm meeting someone in Copenhagen before the Nomisma conclave.
////////////
//////////// W -
////////////
////////////
////////////// Why? I need you here. We have a board meeting in two days.
//////////////
////////////// DR
//////////////
//////////////
//////////////// Berlin.
////////////////
//////////////// But I'm catching a train to Denmark in an hour.
////////////////
//////////////// W -
////////////////
////////////////
////////////////// Where the fuck are you, Wynn?
//////////////////
////////////////// DR
//////////////////

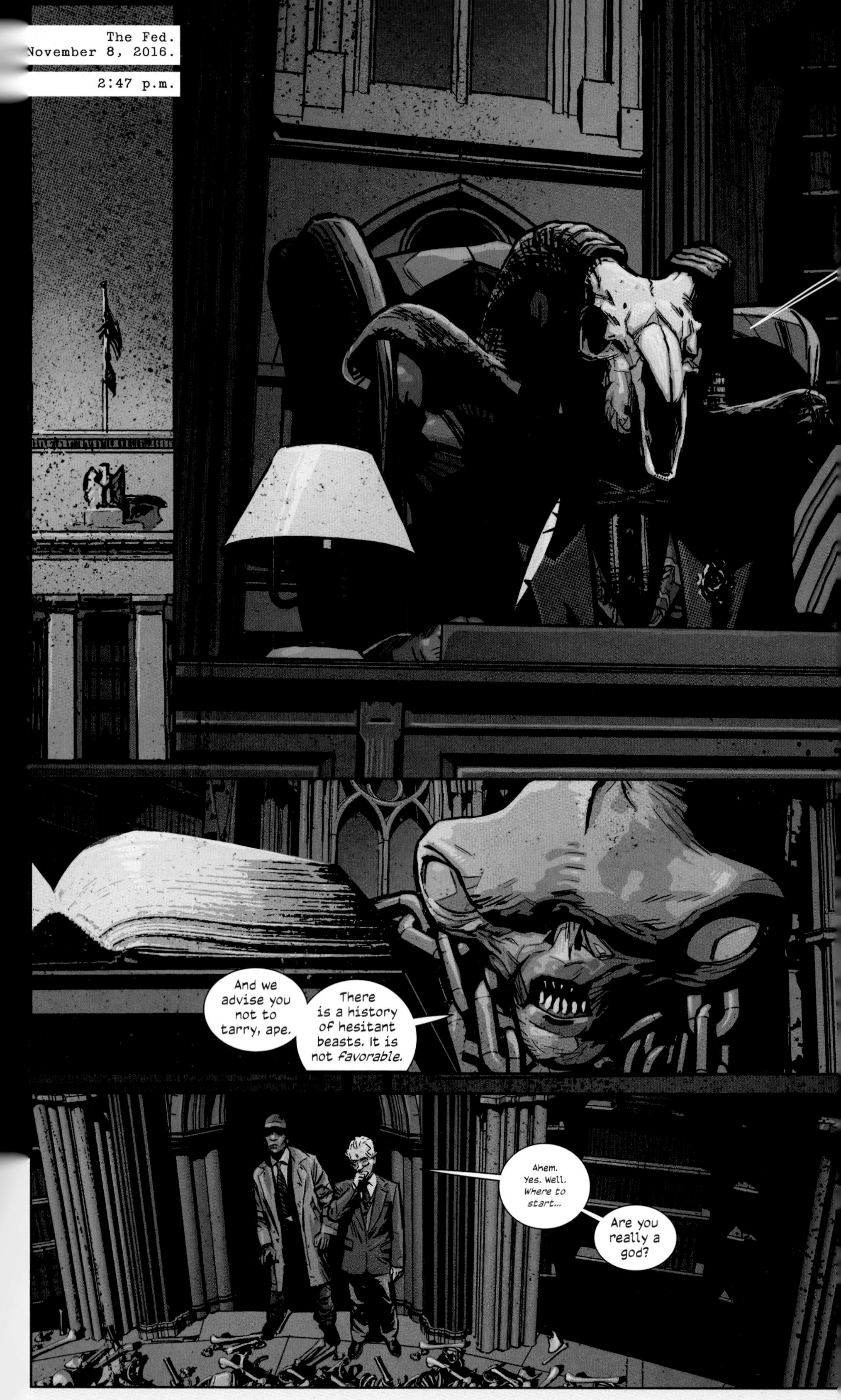

The Fed.
November 8, 2016.
2:47 p.m.
And we advise you not to tarry, ape.
There is a history of hesitant beasts. It is not *favorable.*
Ahem. Yes. Well. *Where to start...*
Are you really a god?

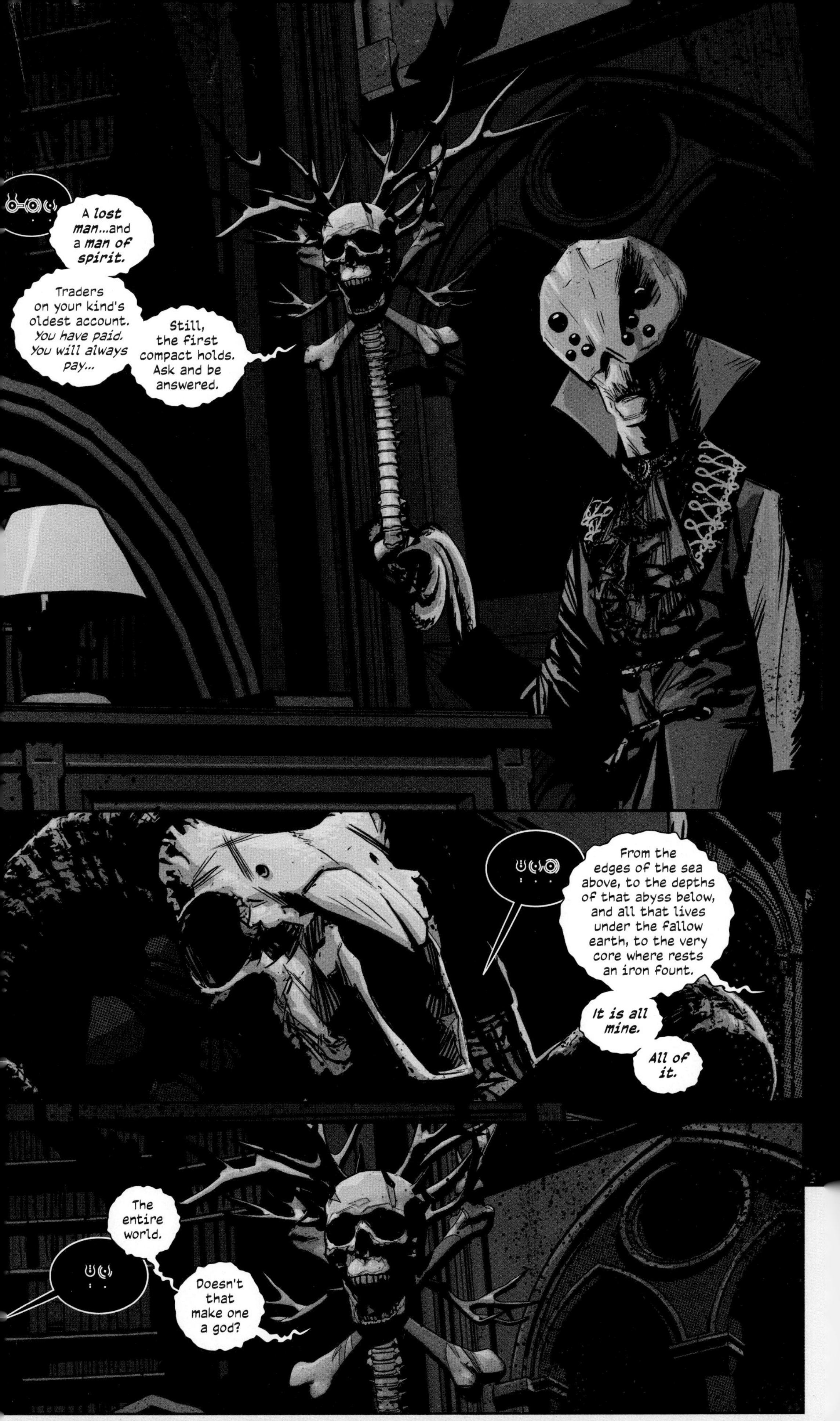
A lost man...and a man of spirit.
Traders on your kind's oldest account. You have paid. You will always pay...
Still, the first compact holds. Ask and be answered.
From the edges of the sea above, to the depths of that abyss below, and all that lives under the fallow earth, to the very core where rests an iron fount.
It is all mine.
All of it.
The entire world.
Doesn't that make one a god?

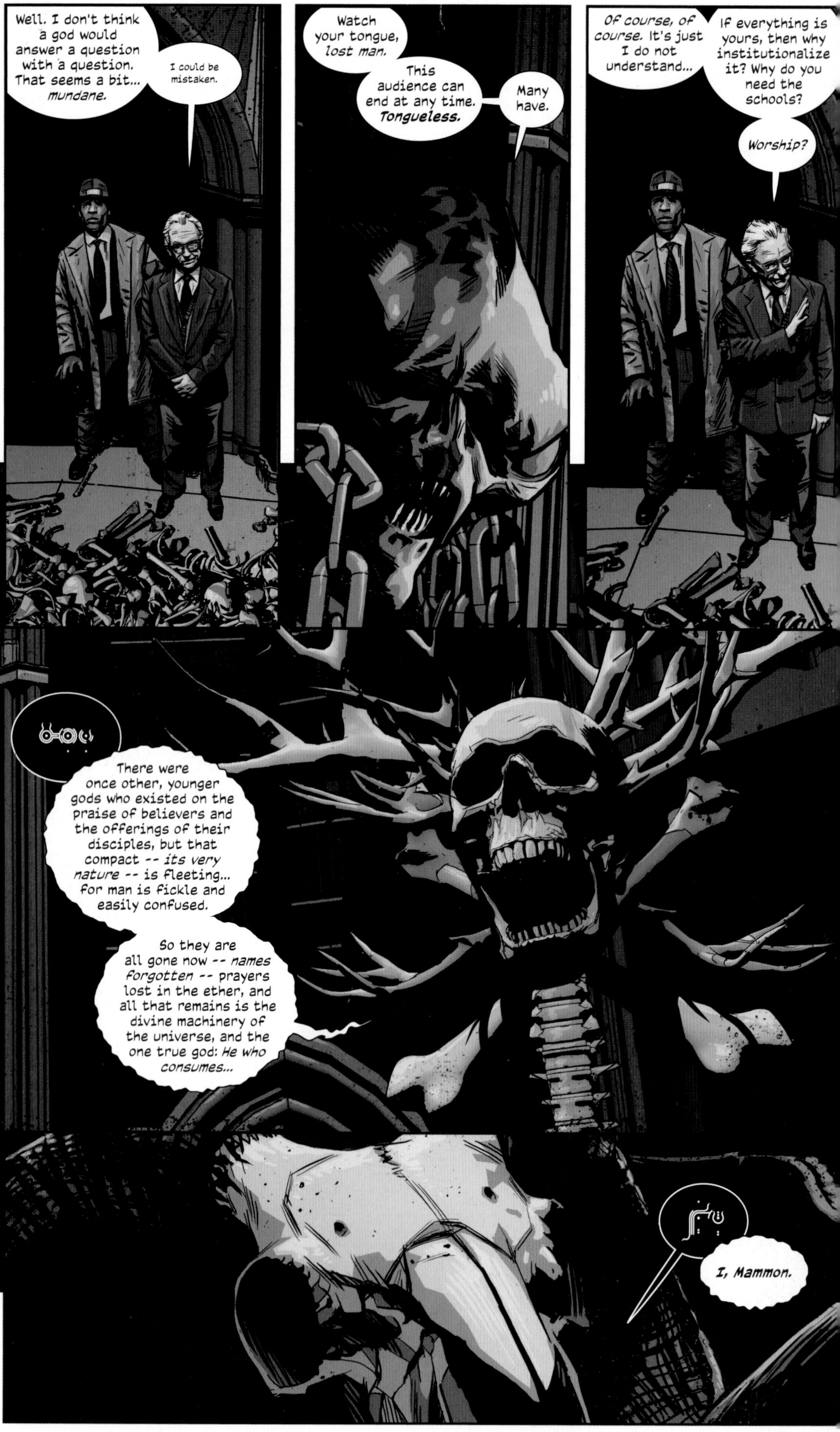
Well. I don't think a god would answer a question with a question. That seems a bit... *mundane.*
I could be mistaken.
Watch your tongue, *lost man.*
This audience can end at any time. ***Tongueless.***
Many have.
Of course, of course. It's just I do not understand...
If everything is yours, then why institutionalize it? Why do you need the schools?
Worship?
There were once other, younger gods who existed on the praise of believers and the offerings of their disciples, but that compact -- *its very nature* -- is fleeting... for man is fickle and easily confused.
So they are all gone now -- *names forgotten* -- prayers lost in the ether, and all that remains is the divine machinery of the universe, and the one true god: *He who consumes...*
I, Mammon.

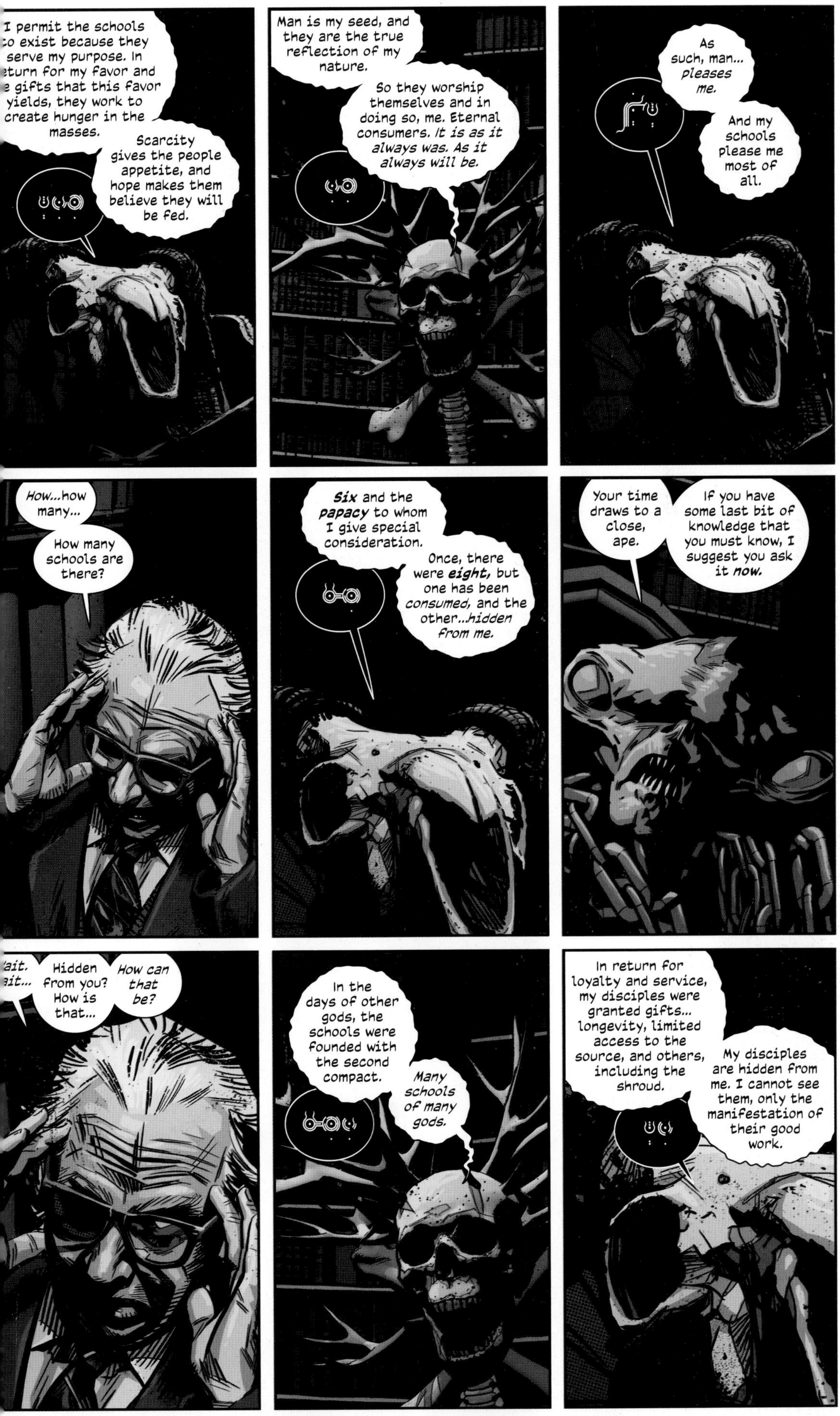

I permit the schools to exist because they serve my purpose. In return for my favor and the gifts that this favor yields, they work to create hunger in the masses.
Scarcity gives the people appetite, and hope makes them believe they will be fed.
Man is my seed, and they are the true reflection of my nature.
So they worship themselves and in doing so, me. Eternal consumers. It is as it always was. As it always will be.
As such, man... pleases me.
And my schools please me most of all.
How...how many...
How many schools are there?
Six and the papacy to whom I give special consideration.
Once, there were eight, but one has been consumed, and the other...hidden from me.
Your time draws to a close, ape.
If you have some last bit of knowledge that you must know, I suggest you ask it now.
ait. ait...
Hidden from you? How is that...
How can that be?
In the days of other gods, the schools were founded with the second compact.
Many schools of many gods.
In return for loyalty and service, my disciples were granted gifts... longevity, limited access to the source, and others, including the shroud.
My disciples are hidden from me. I cannot see them, only the manifestation of their good work.

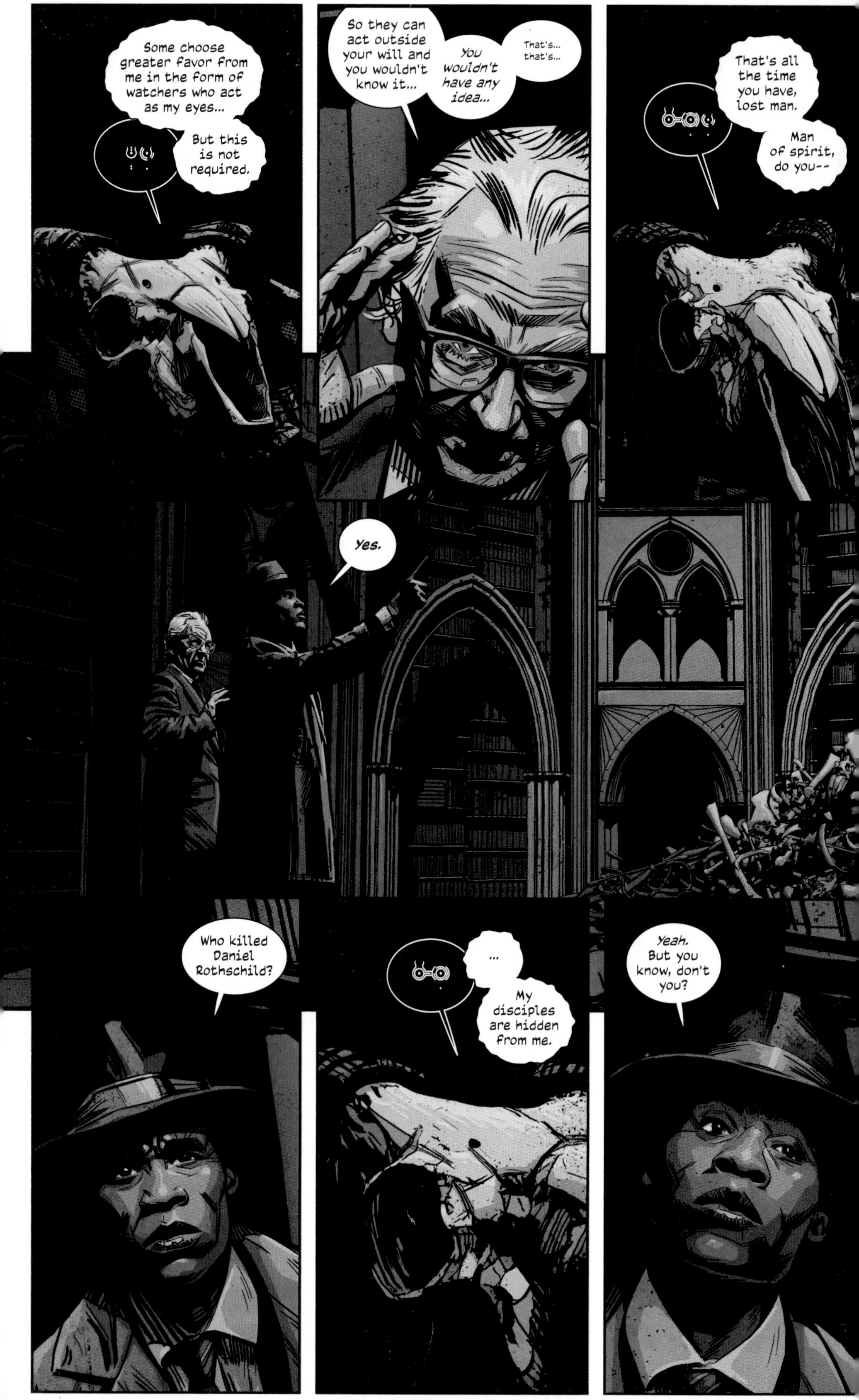
Some choose greater favor from me in the form of watchers who act as my eyes...
But this is not required.
So they can act outside your will and you wouldn't know it...
You wouldn't have any idea...
That's... that's...
That's all the time you have, lost man.
Man of spirit, do you--
Yes.
Who killed Daniel Rothschild?
...
My disciples are hidden from me.
Yeah. But you know, don't you?

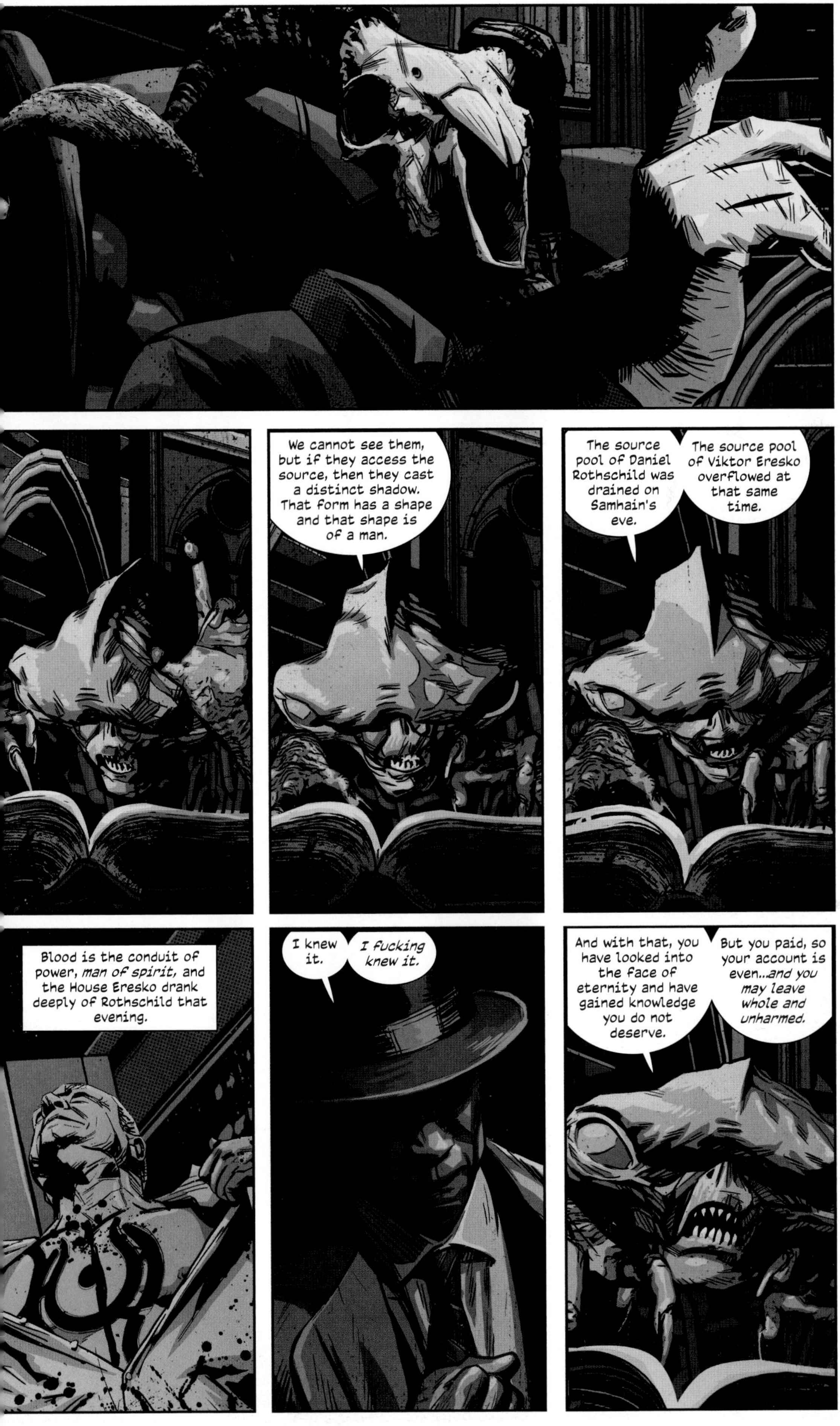

We cannot see them, but if they access the source, then they cast a distinct shadow. That form has a shape and that shape is of a man.
The source pool of Daniel Rothschild was drained on Samhain's eve.
The source pool of Viktor Eresko overflowed at that same time.
Blood is the conduit of power, *man of spirit,* and the House Eresko drank deeply of Rothschild that evening.
I knew it.
I fucking knew it.
And with that, you have looked into the face of eternity and have gained knowledge you do not deserve.
But you paid, so your account is even...*and you may leave whole and unharmed.*

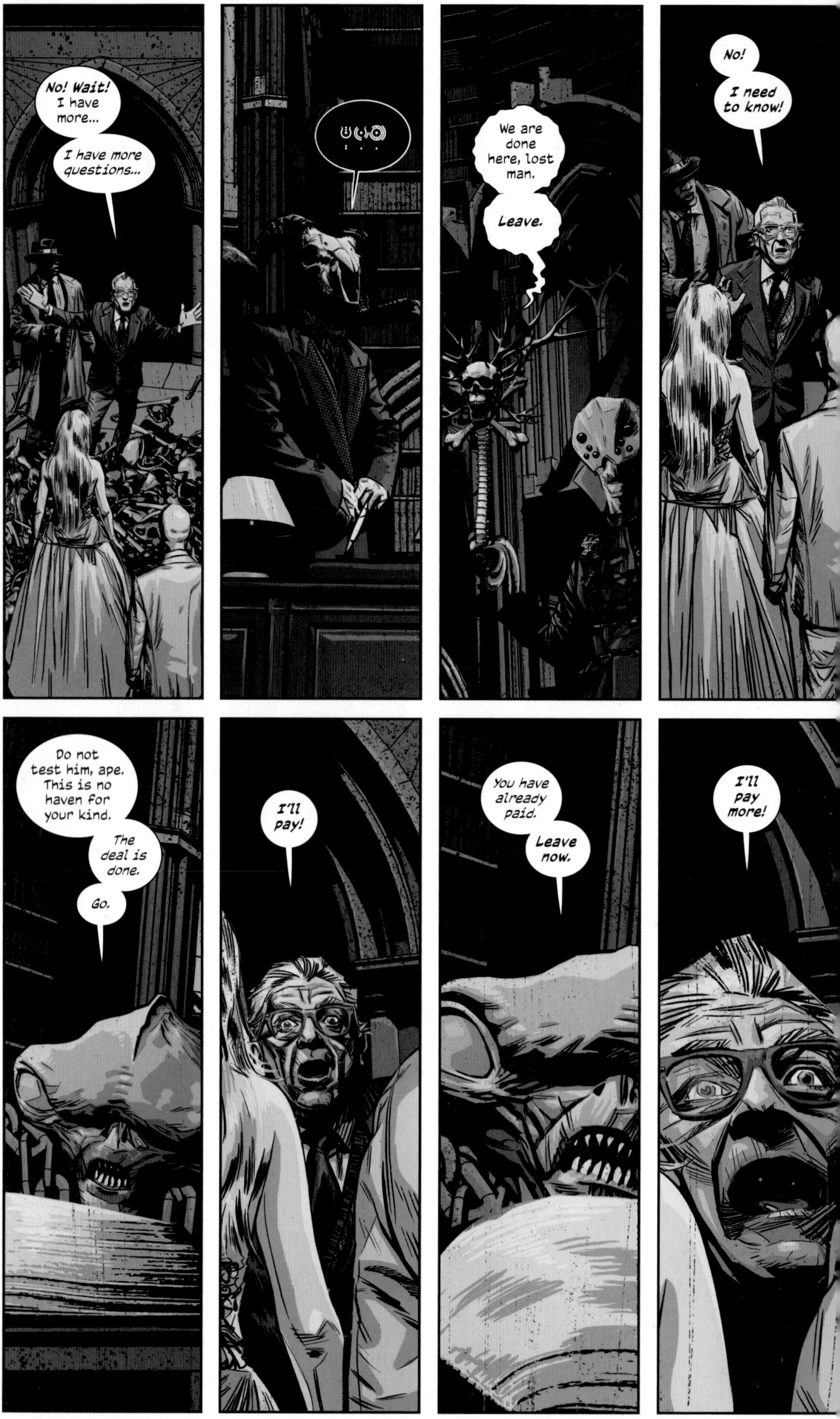
No! Wait! I have more...
I have more questions...
We are done here, lost man.
Leave.
No!
I need to know!
Do not test him, ape. This is no haven for your kind.
The deal is done.
Go.
I'll pay!
You have already paid.
Leave now.
I'll pay more!

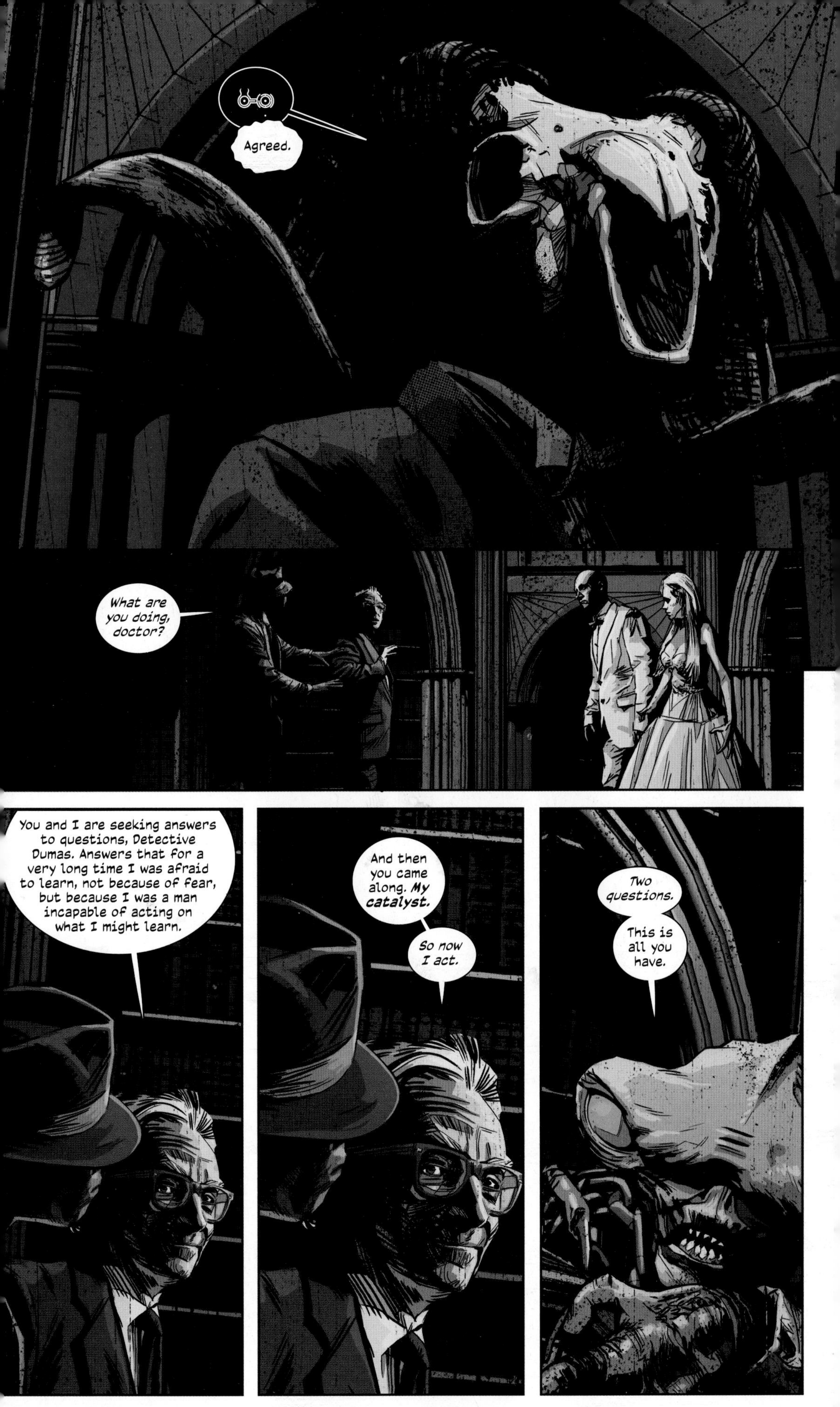
Agreed.
What are you doing, doctor?
You and I are seeking answers to questions, Detective Dumas. Answers that for a very long time I was afraid to learn, not because of fear, but because I was a man incapable of acting on what I might learn.
And then you came along. My catalyst.
So now I act.
Two questions.
This is all you have.

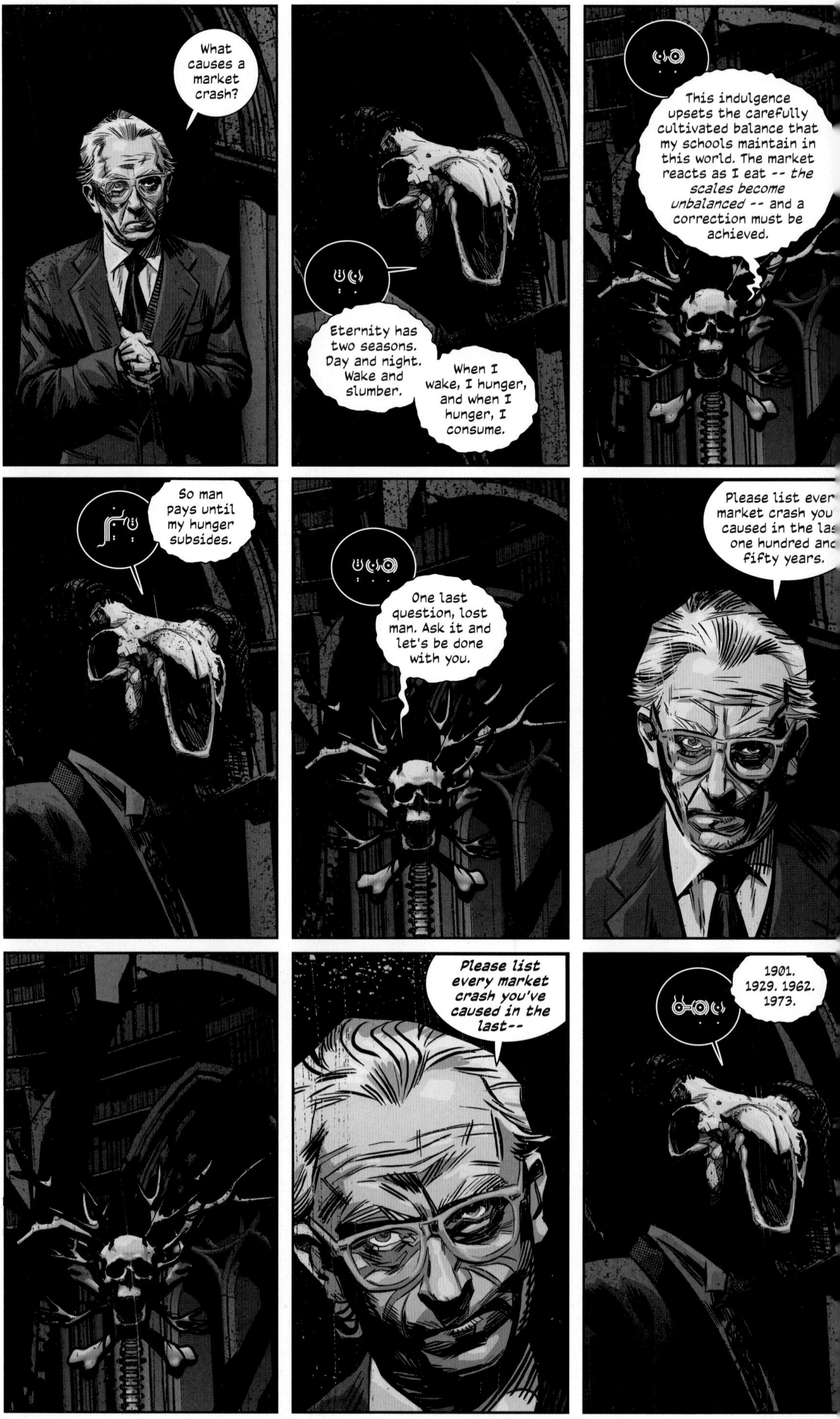
What causes a market crash?
Eternity has two seasons. Day and night. Wake and slumber.
When I wake, I hunger, and when I hunger, I consume.
This indulgence upsets the carefully cultivated balance that my schools maintain in this world. The market reacts as I eat -- *the scales become unbalanced* -- and a correction must be achieved.
So man pays until my hunger subsides.
One last question, lost man. Ask it and let's be done with you.
Please list every market crash you've caused in the last--
1901. 1929. 1962. 1973.

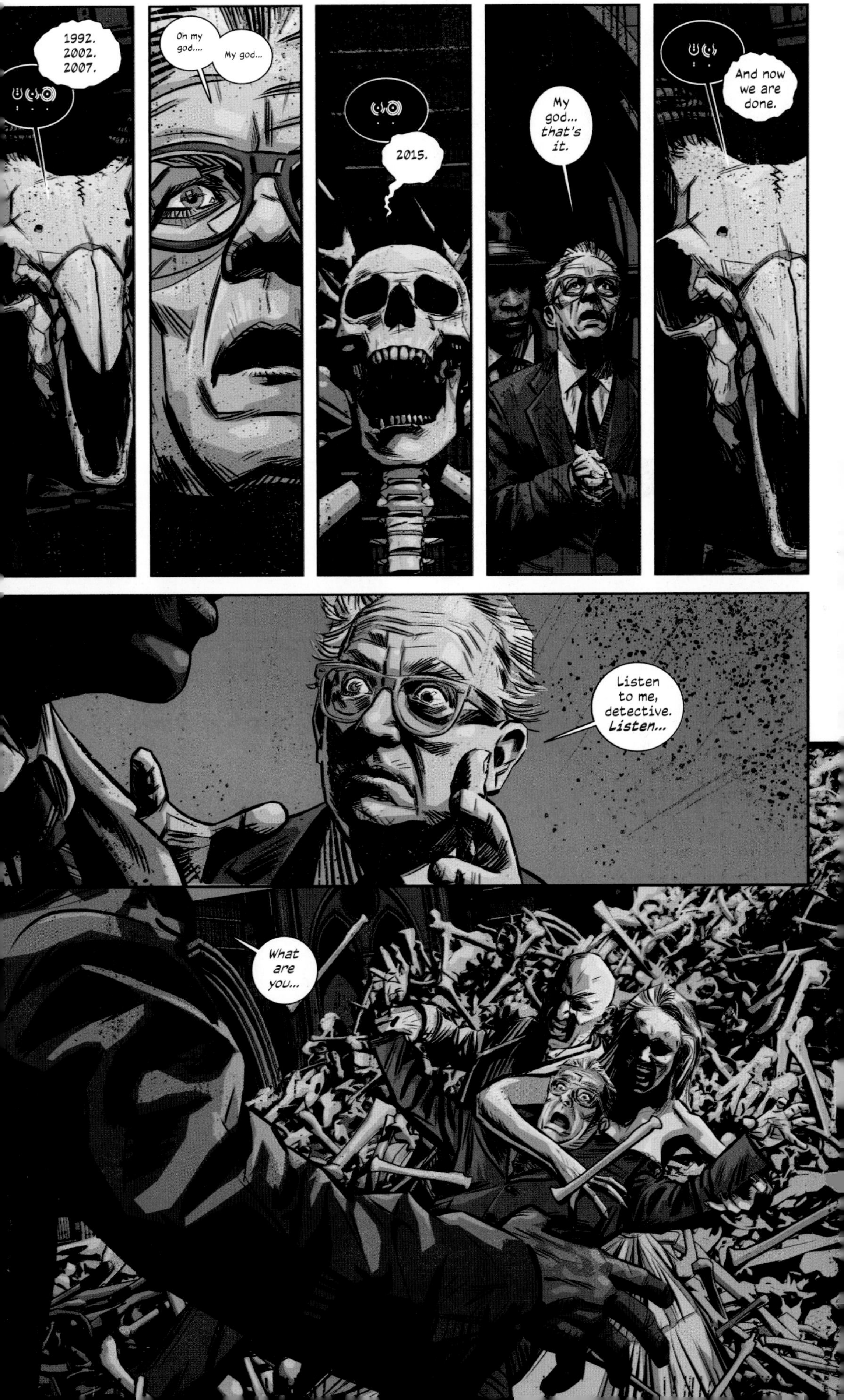
1992. 2002. 2007.
Oh my god....
My god...
2015.
My god... that's it.
And now we are done.
Listen to me, detective. Listen...
What are you...

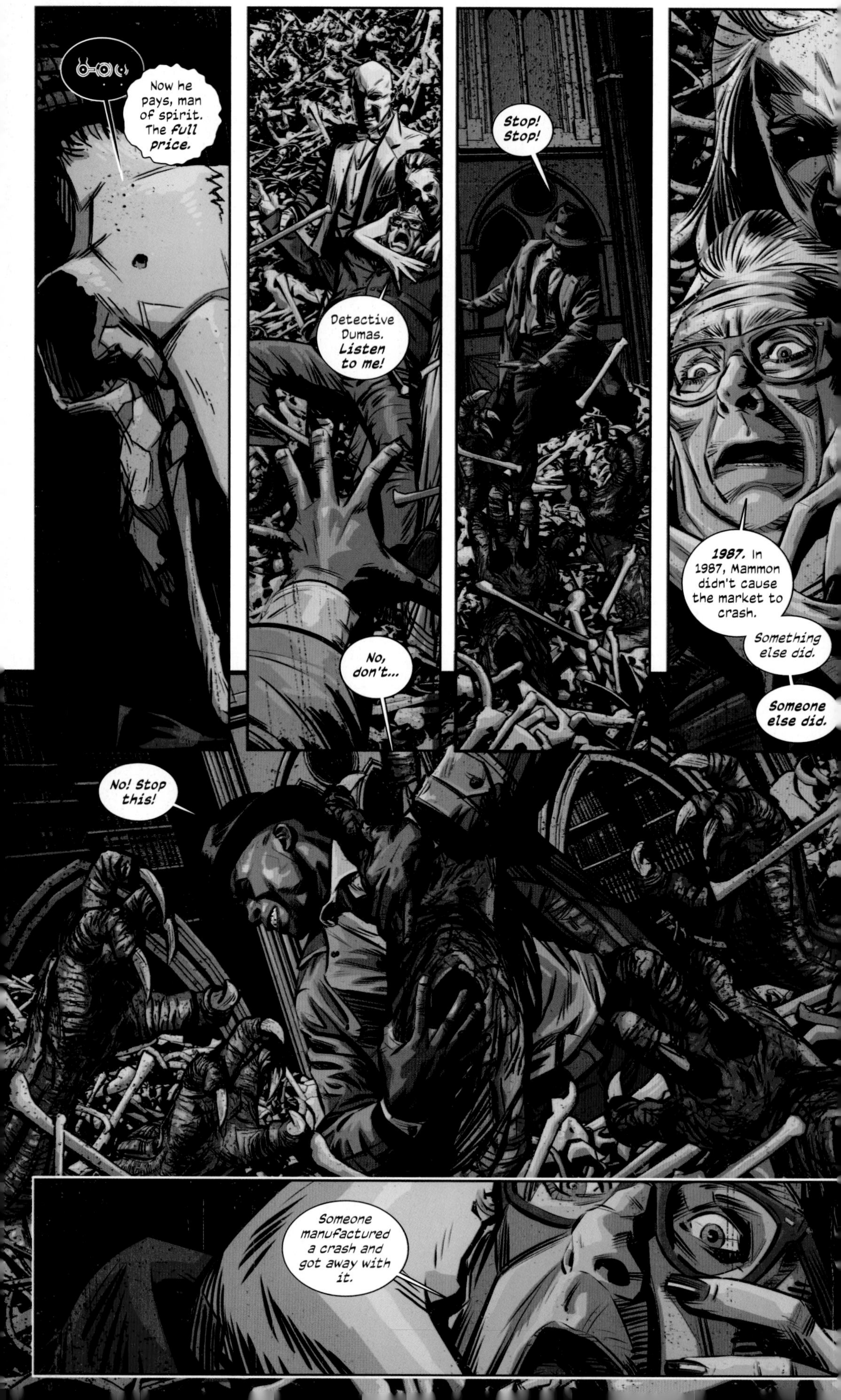

Now he pays, man of spirit. The *full price.*
Detective Dumas. *Listen to me!*
No, don't...
Stop! Stop!
1987. In 1987, Mammon didn't cause the market to crash.
Something else did.
Someone else did.
No! Stop this!
Someone manufactured a crash and got away with it.

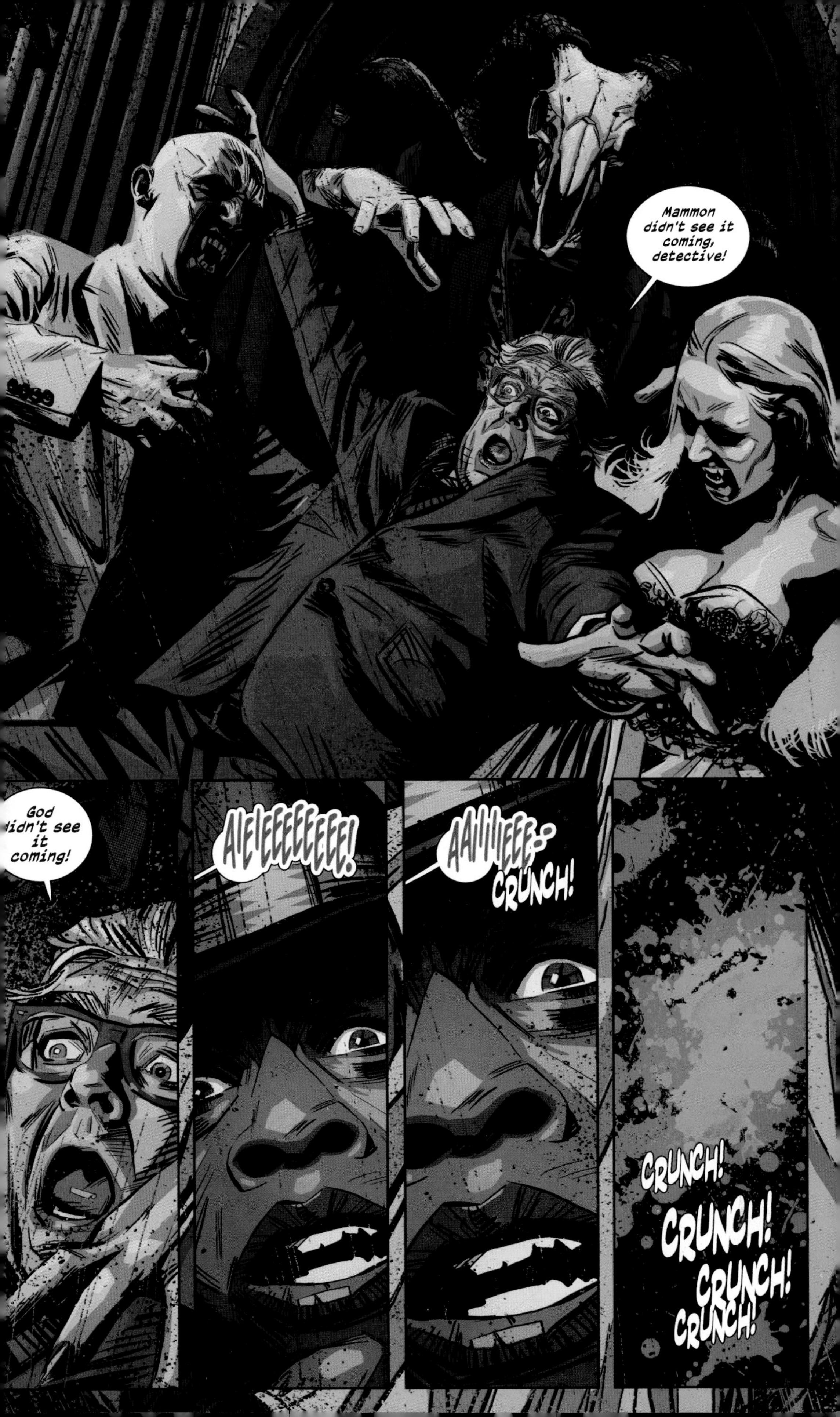
Mammon didn't see it coming, detective!
God idn't see it coming!
AIEIEEEEEEEE!
AAIIIIEEE-CRUNCH!
CRUNCH!
CRUNCH!
CRUNCH!
CRUNCH!

To: Ackermann, Wynn   [May 28, 2014 at 6:28 AM]

From: Rothschild, Daniel

Re: You disappeared.

R

What the fuck happened?

https://www.theguardian.com/world/live/2014/may/28/
confirmed-six-dead-before-bilderberg-meetings-begin

DR

```
// You there? What the hell is going on?
//
// Is this you?
//
// https://www.theguardian.com/world/live/2014/may/28/
// riots-explosions-at-bilderberg-group-hotel
//
// DR
//
//
//// Okay. Let me know what happens as soon as you get done.
////
//// Send Ria my love.
////
//// DR
////
////// A few introductions to the newer Colloquium members who are handling
////// outreach to the island. She's offered to act as a go between, and I
////// vouched for her. They don't trust us, especially her, so they're will
////// be Bilderberg Confederates there as well.
//////
////// But don't worry. Everything should be fine.
//////
////// Hey, everyone needs a little help sometimes. Even her.
//////
////// W -
//////
//////
//////// Fucking Christ. What does she want?
////////
//////// DR
////////
////////
////////// You know who.
//////////
////////// You know why.
//////////
////////// W -
//////////
//////////
//////////// Who?
////////////
//////////// DR
////////////
////////////
//////////////// Emergency.
////////////////
//////////////// I'm meeting someone in Copenhagen before the Nomisma conclave.
////////////////
//////////////// W -
////////////////
////////////////
//////////////////// Why? I need you here. We have a board meeting in two days.
//////////////////
////////////////// DR
//////////////////
//////////////////
//////////////////// Berlin.
//////////////////
/////////////////////// But I'm catching a train to Denmark in
```

To: Ackermann, Wynn   [May 28, 2014 at 7:17 PM]

From: Rothschild, Daniel

Re: You disappeared.

R

I'm getting worried. I know something's gone wrong.

Are you okay?

DR

// What the fuck happened?
//
// https://www.theguardian.com/world/live/2014/may/29/
//.confirmed-six-dead-before-bilderberg-meetings-begin
//
// DR
//
//
//// You there? What the hell is going on?
////
//// Is this you?
////
//// https://www.theguardian.com/world/live/2014/may/28/
//// riots-explosions-at-bilderberg-group-hotel
////
//// DR
////
////
existing////// Okay. Let me know what happens as soon as you get done.
//////
////// Send Ria my love.
//////
////// DR
//////
//////
//////// A few introductions to the newer Colloquium members who are handling
//////// outreach to the island. She's offered to act as a go between, and I
//////// vouched for her. They don't trust us, especially her, so they're will
//////// be Bilderberg Confederates there as well.
////////
//////// But don't worry. Everything should be fine.
////////
//////// Hey, everyone needs a little help sometimes. Even her.
////////
//////// W -
////////
////////
////////// Fucking Christ. What does she want?
//////////
////////// DR
//////////
//////////
////////// You know who.
//////////
////////// You know why.
//////////
////////// W -
//////////
//////////
//////////// Who?
//////////
//////////// DR
//////////
//////////
//////////// Emergency.
//////////
//////////// I'm meeting someone in Copenhagen before the Nomisma conclave.
//////////
//////////// W -
//////////
//////////// Why? I need you here. We have a board meeting in two days.

A

It's fucked, Daniel.

It's all fucked.

I'm not coming home.

W -

// I'm getting worried. I know something's gone wrong.
//
// Are you okay?
//
// DR
//
//
//// What the fuck happened?
////
//// https://www.theguardian.com/world/live/2014/may/29/
//// confirmed-six-dead-before-bilderberg-meetings-begin
////
//// DR
////
////
existing////// You there? What the hell is going on?
//////
existing////// Is this you?
//////
existing////// https://www.theguardian.com/world/live/2014/may/28/
existing////// riots-explosions-at-bilderberg-group-hotel
//////
existing////// DR
//////
//////
//////// Okay. Let me know what happens as soon as you get done.
////////
//////// Send Ria my love.
////////
//////// DR
////////
////////
///////// A few introductions to the newer Colloquium members who are handling
///////// outreach to the island. She's offered to act as a go between, and I
///////// vouched for her. They don't trust us, especially her, so they're wil
///////// be Bilderberg Confederates there as well.
/////////
///////// But don't worry. Everything should be fine.
/////////
///////// Hey, everyone needs a little help sometimes. Even her.
/////////
///////// W -
/////////
/////////
////////// Fucking Christ. What does she want?
//////////
////////// DR
//////////
//////////
//////////// You know who.
////////////
//////////// You know why.
////////////
//////////// W -
////////////
////////////
////////////// Who?
//////////////
////////////// DR

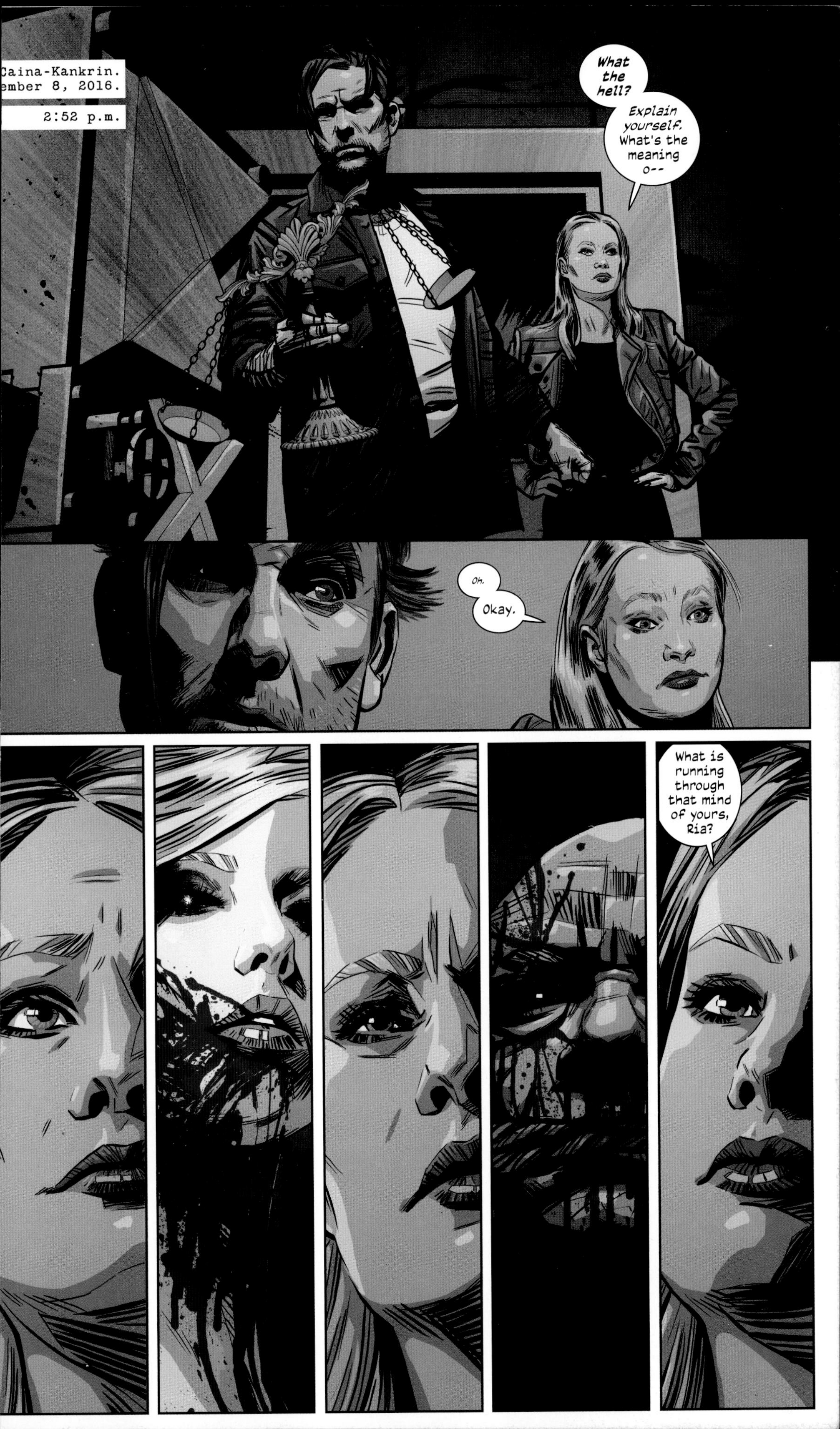
Caina-Kankrin.
ember 8, 2016.
2:52 p.m.
What the hell?
Explain yourself. What's the meaning o--
Oh.
Okay.
What is running through that mind of yours, Ria?

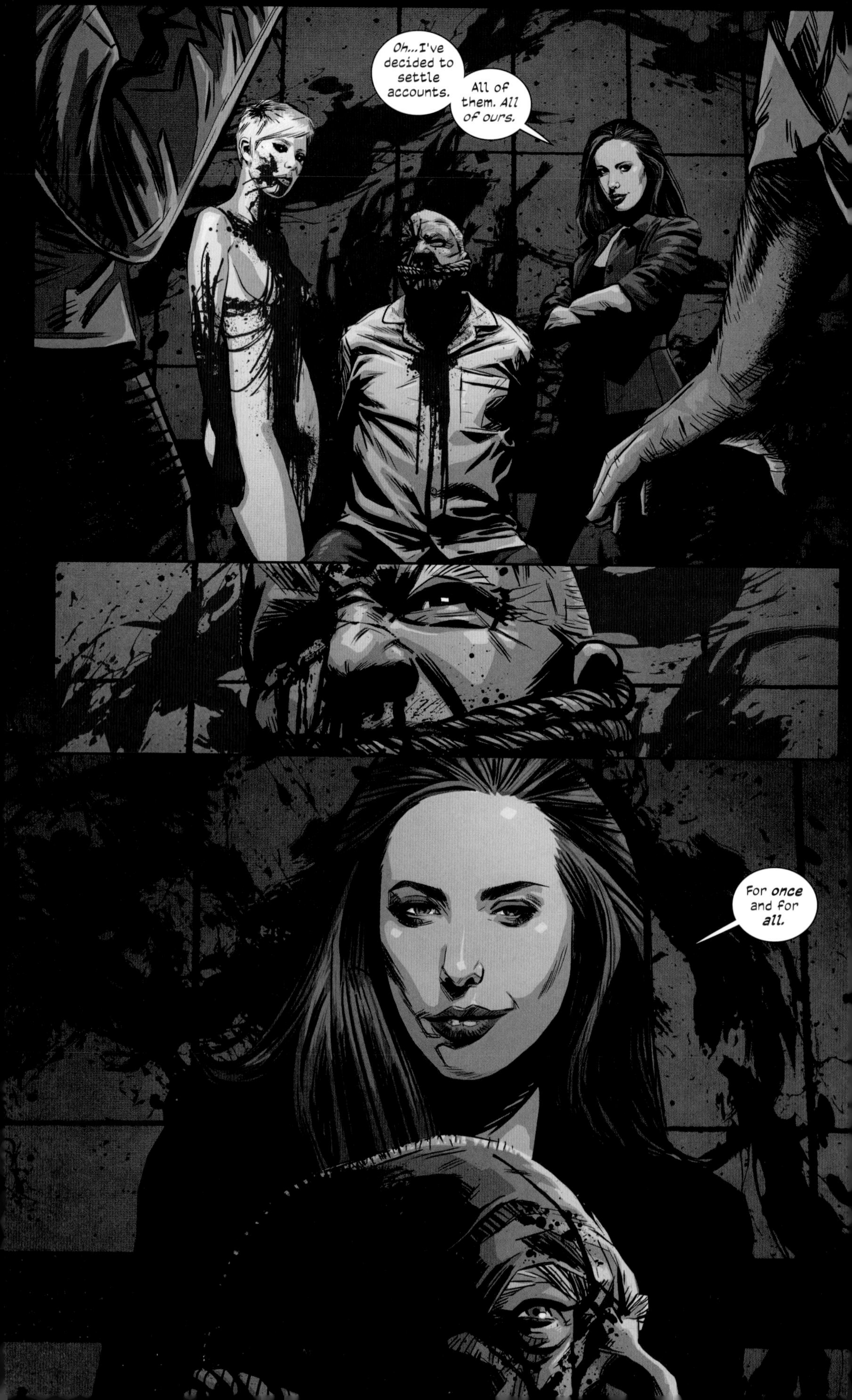
Oh...I've decided to settle accounts.
All of them. *All* of ours.
For *once* and for *all.*

Who do you serve?

I, Mammon.

- PAY ONCE -

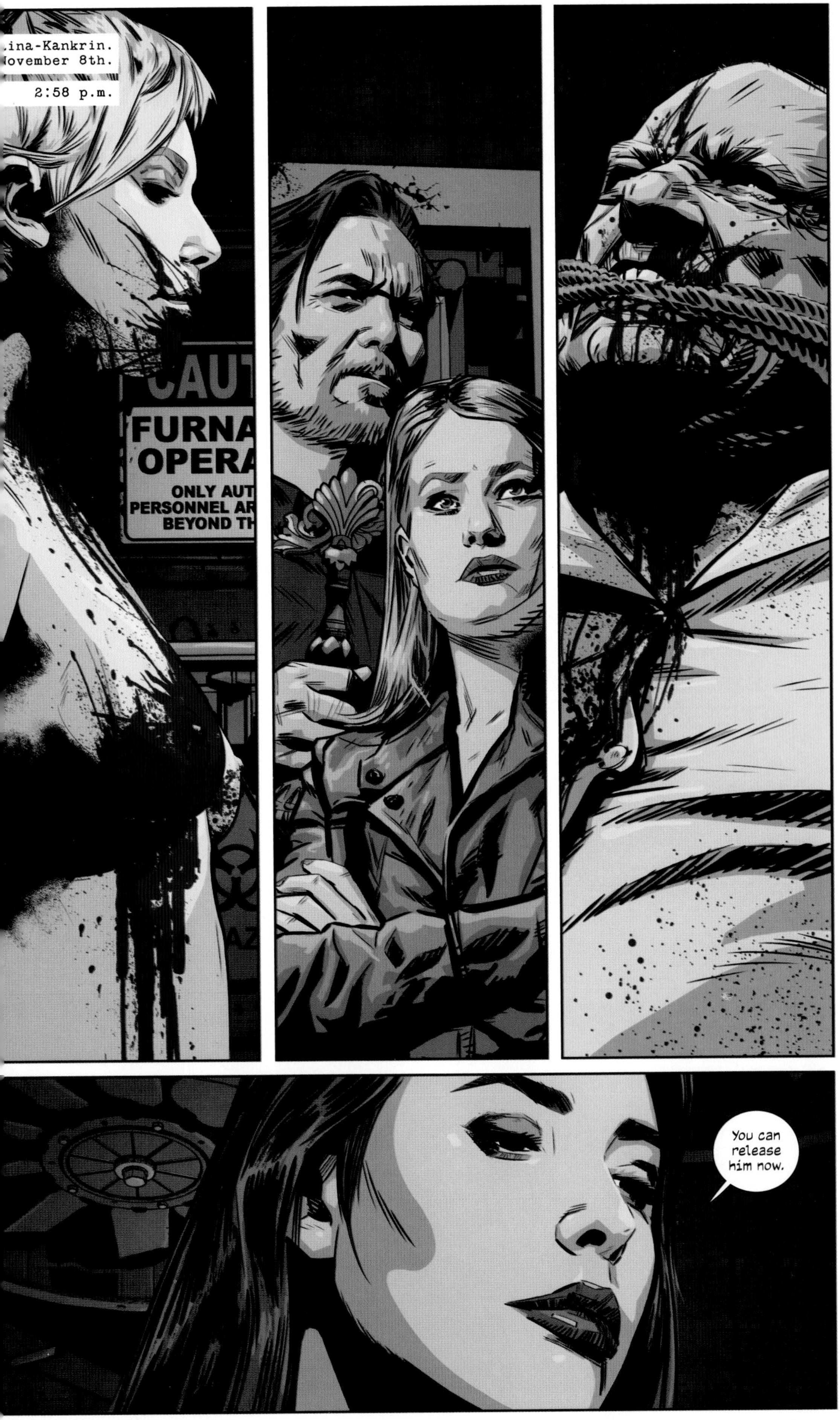

ina-Kankrin.
ovember 8th.
2:58 p.m.
CAUT
FURNA
OPERA
ONLY AUT
PERSONNEL AR
BEYOND TH
You can release him now.

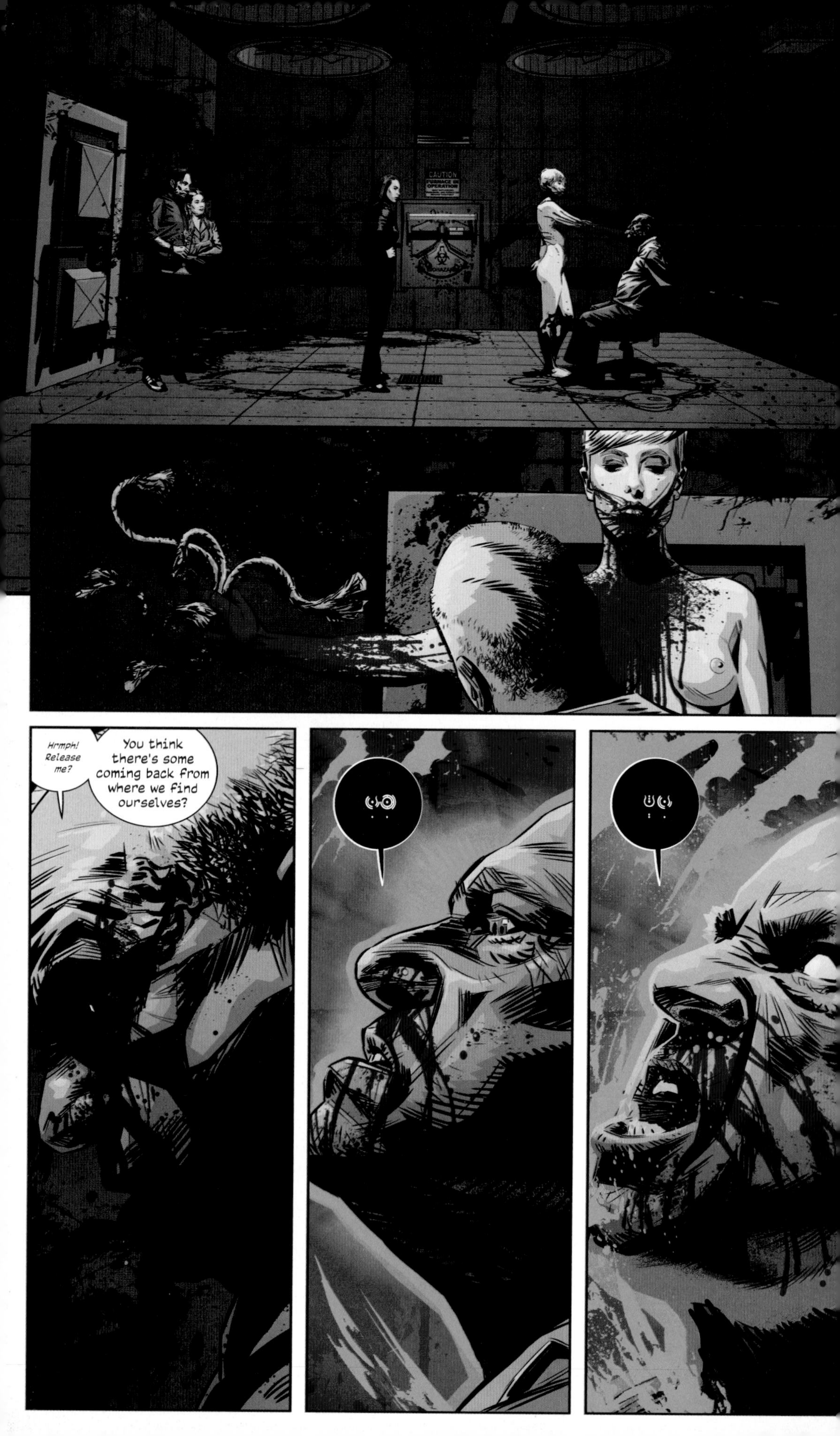
CAUTION
FURNACE IN OPERATION
Hrmph! Release me?
You think there's some coming back from where we find ourselves?

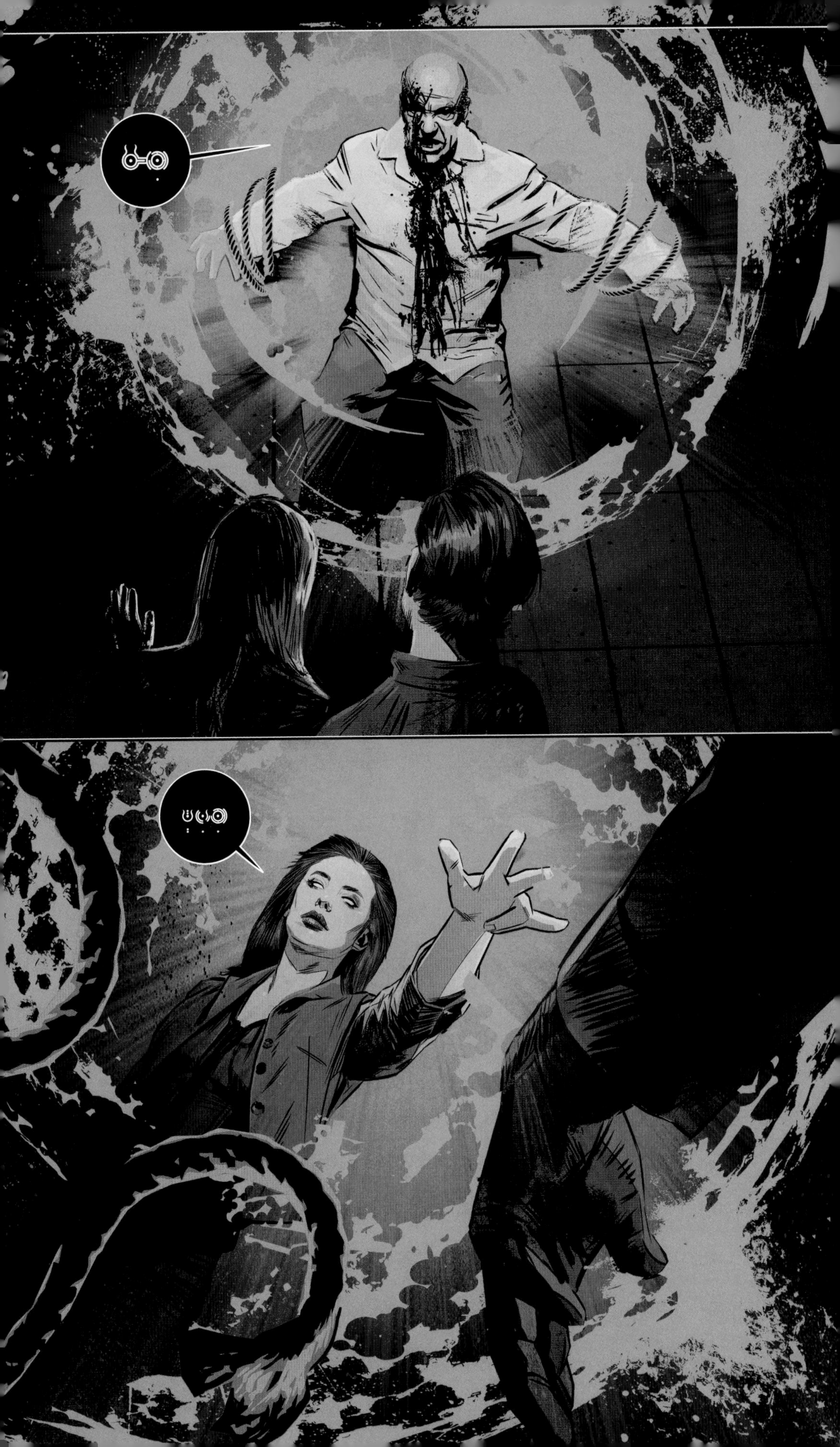

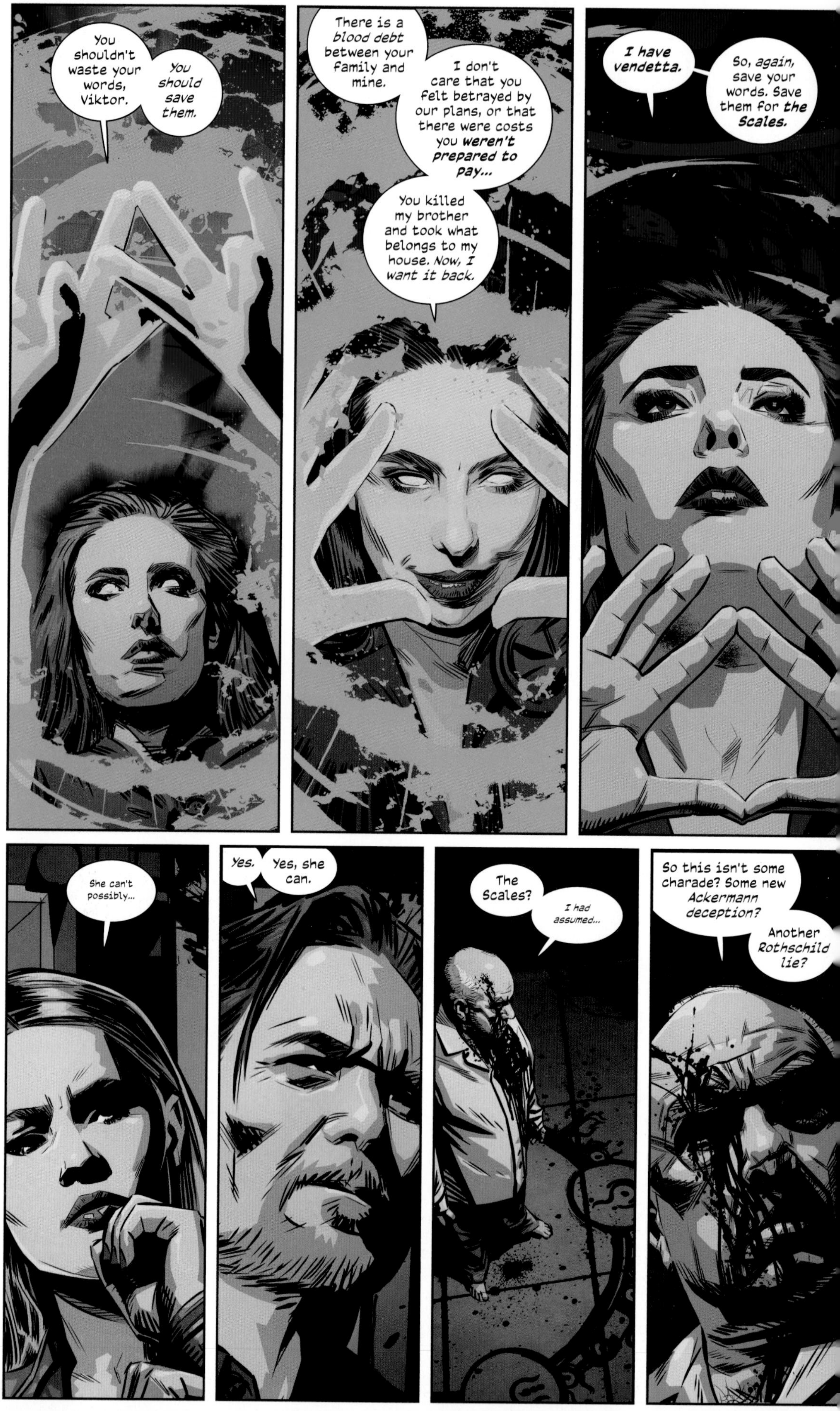

You shouldn't waste your words, Viktor.
You should save them.
There is a blood debt between your family and mine.
I don't care that you felt betrayed by our plans, or that there were costs you weren't prepared to pay...
You killed my brother and took what belongs to my house. Now, I want it back.
I have vendetta.
So, again, save your words. Save them for the Scales.
She can't possibly...
Yes.
Yes, she can.
The Scales?
I had assumed...
So this isn't some charade? Some new Ackermann deception?
Another Rothschild lie?

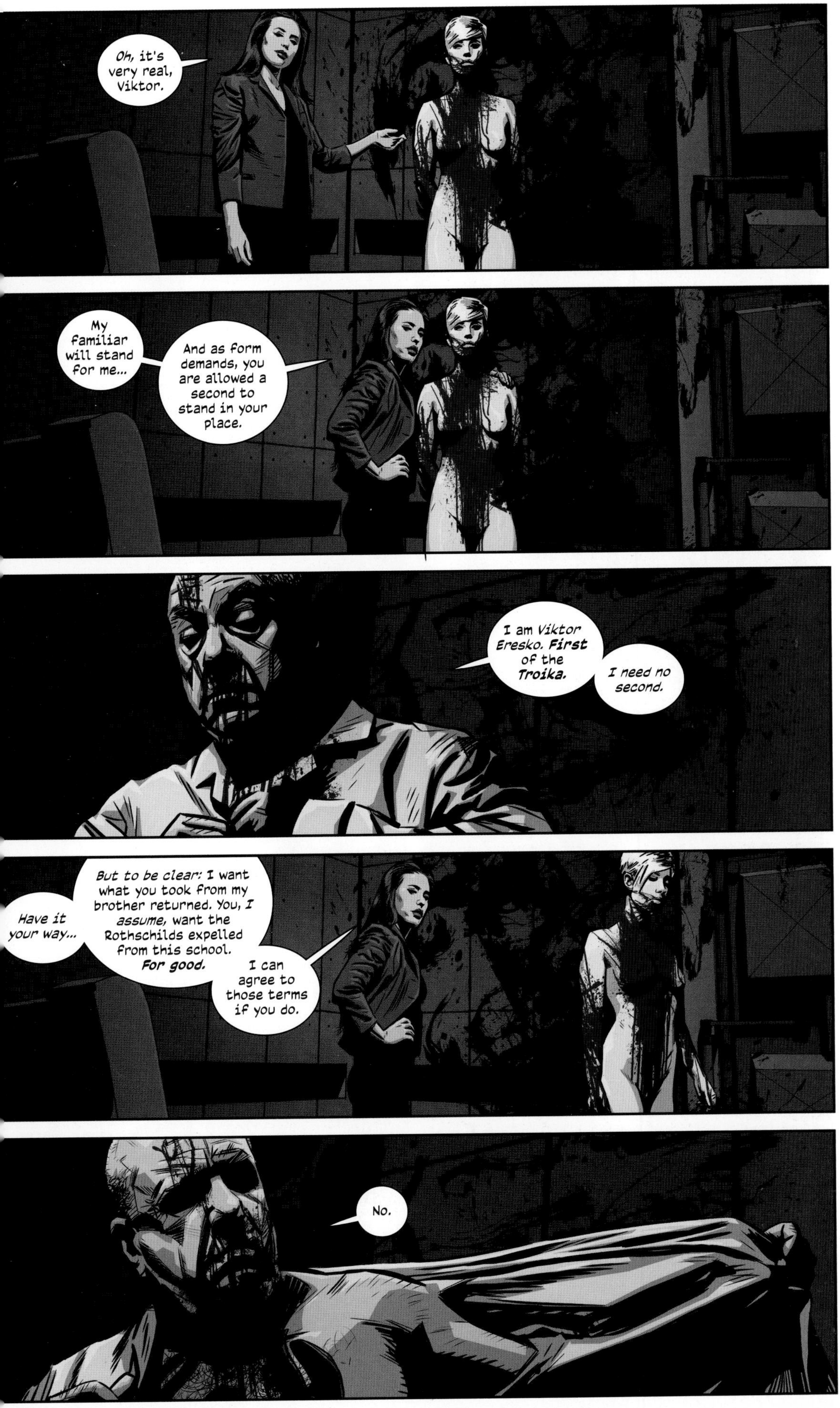
Oh, it's very real, Viktor.
My familiar will stand for me...
And as form demands, you are allowed a second to stand in your place.
I am Viktor Eresko. First of the Troika.
I need no second.
Have it your way...
But to be clear: I want what you took from my brother returned. You, I assume, want the Rothschilds expelled from this school. For good.
I can agree to those terms if you do.
No.

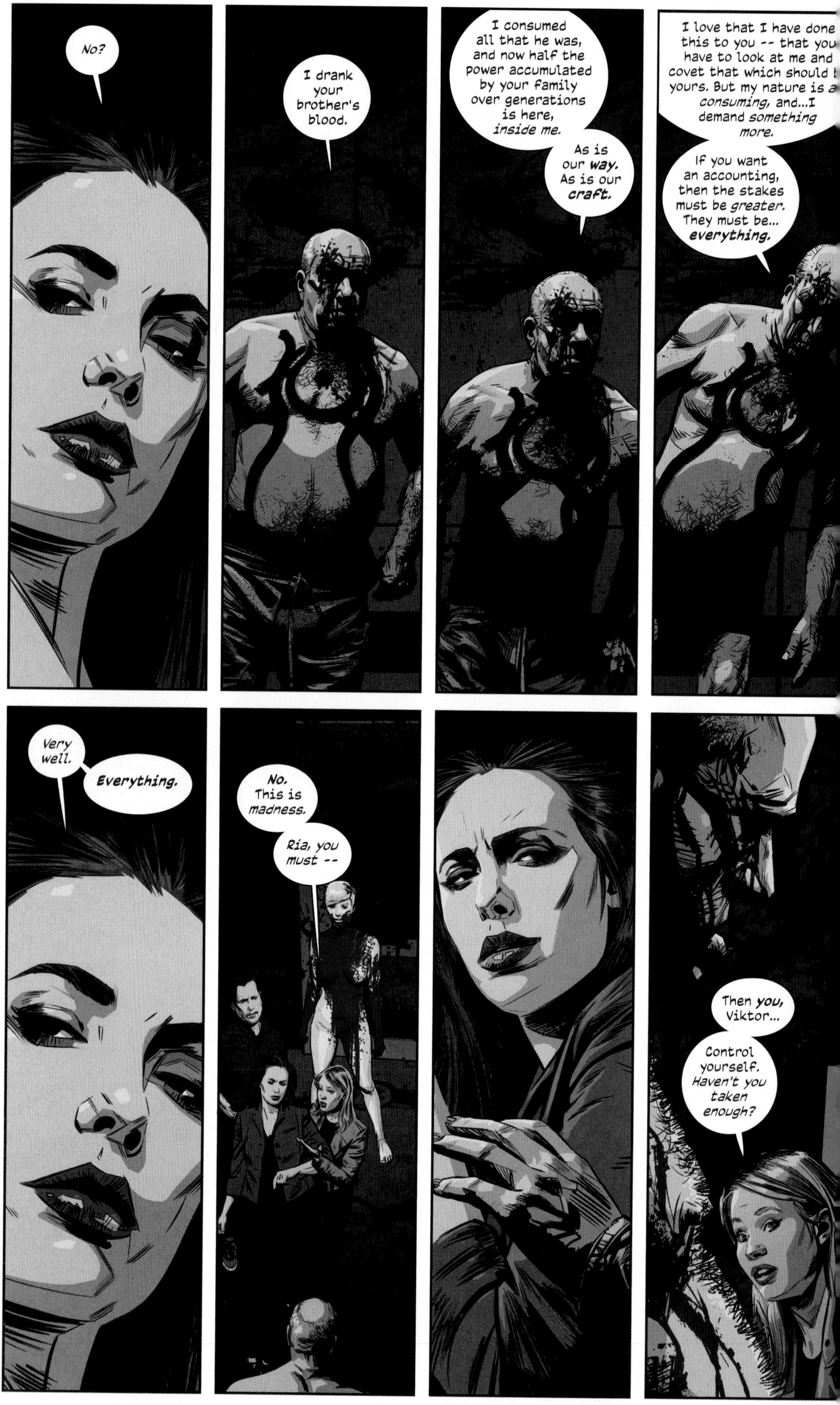

No?
I drank your brother's blood.
I consumed all that he was, and now half the power accumulated by your family over generations is here, *inside me.*
As is our **way.** As is our ***craft.***
I love that I have done this to you -- that you have to look at me and covet that which should
yours. But my nature is a *consuming,* and...I demand *something more.*
If you want an accounting, then the stakes must be *greater.* They must be... ***everything.***
Very well.
Everything.
No. *This is madness.*
Ria, you must --
Then ***you,*** Viktor...
Control yourself. *Haven't you taken enough?*

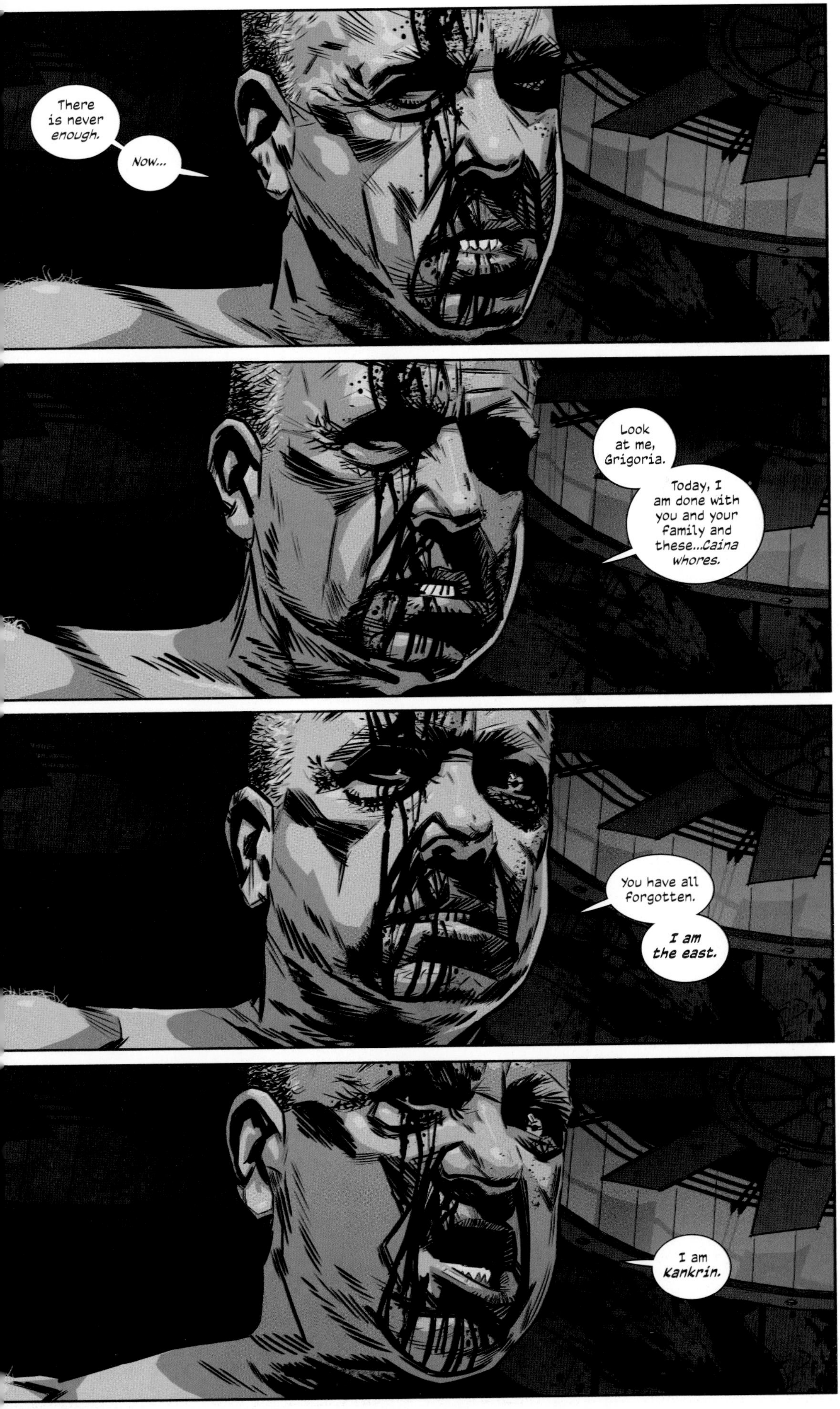
There is never *enough.*
Now...
Look at me, Grigoria.
Today, I am done with you and your family and these...*Caina whores.*
You have all forgotten.
I am the east.
I am *Kankrin.*

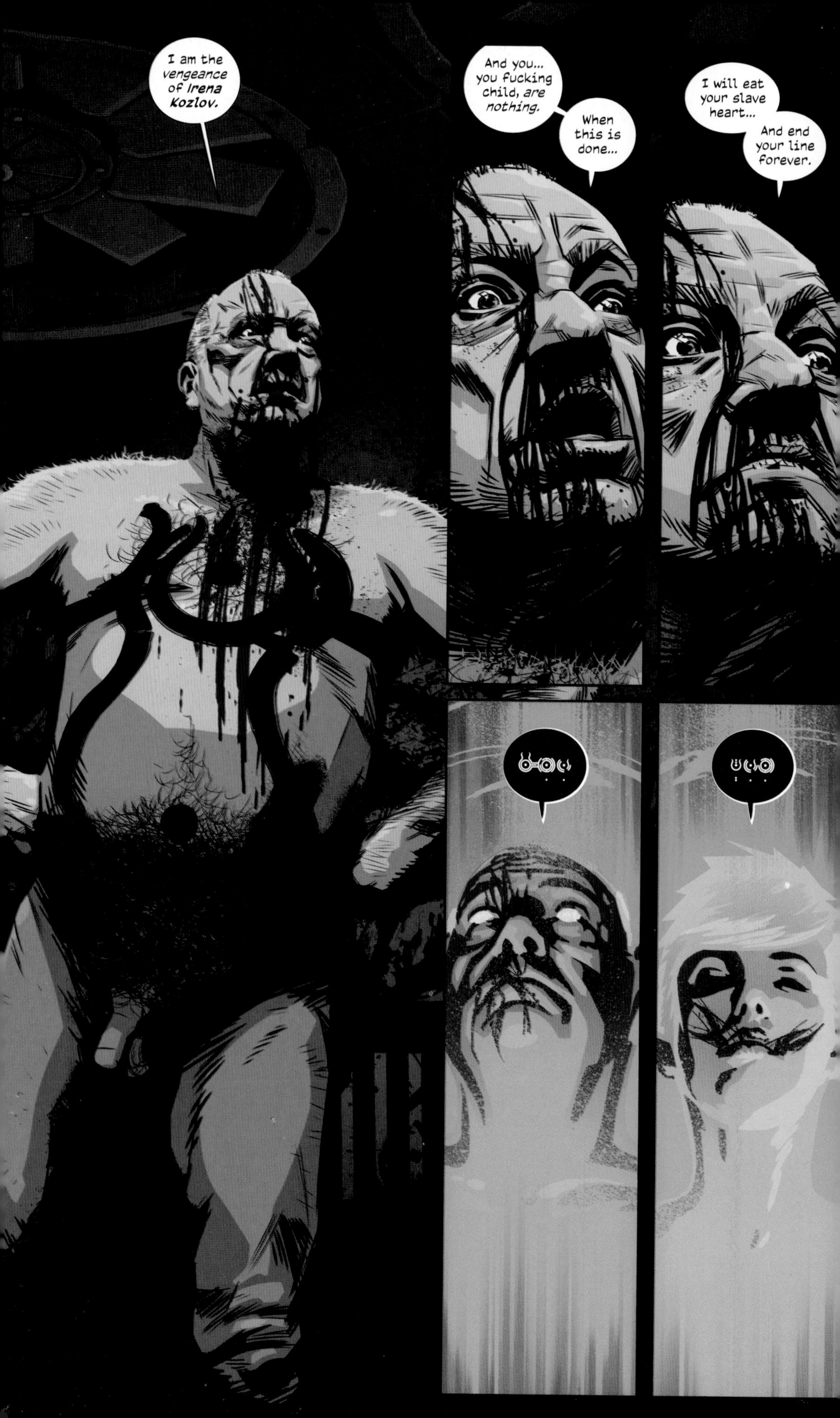

I am the vengeance of Irena Kozlov.
And you... you fucking child, are nothing.
When this is done...
I will eat your slave heart...
And end your line forever.

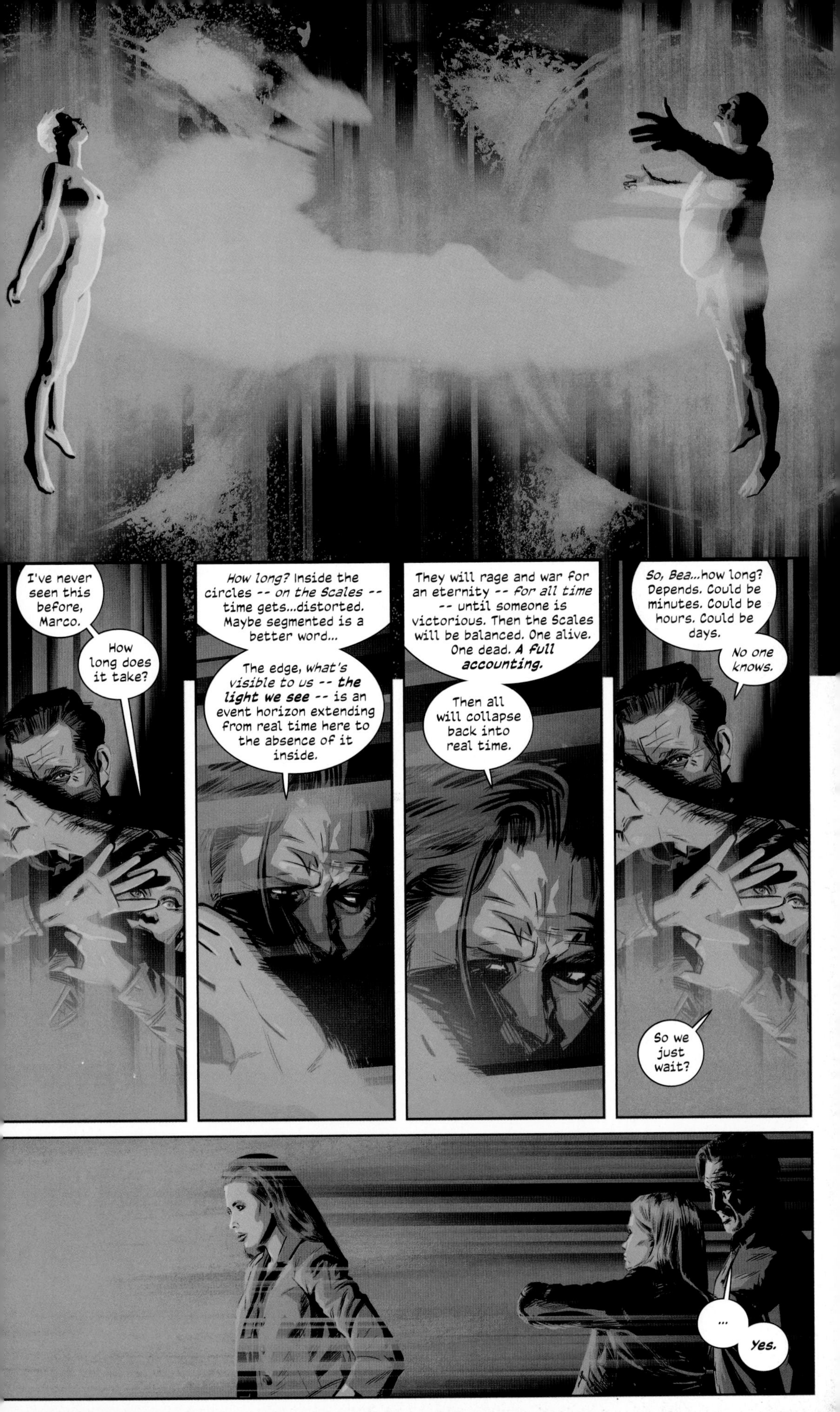
I've never seen this before, Marco.
How long does it take?
How long? Inside the circles -- *on the Scales* -- time gets...distorted. Maybe segmented is a better word...
The edge, *what's visible to us* -- ***the light we see*** -- is an event horizon extending from real time here to the absence of it inside.
They will rage and war for an eternity -- *for all time* -- until someone is victorious. Then the Scales will be balanced. One alive. One dead. ***A full accounting.***
Then all will collapse back into real time.
*So, Bea...*how long? Depends. Could be minutes. Could be hours. Could be days.
No one knows.
So we just wait?
...
Yes.

CHAPTER EIGHT:

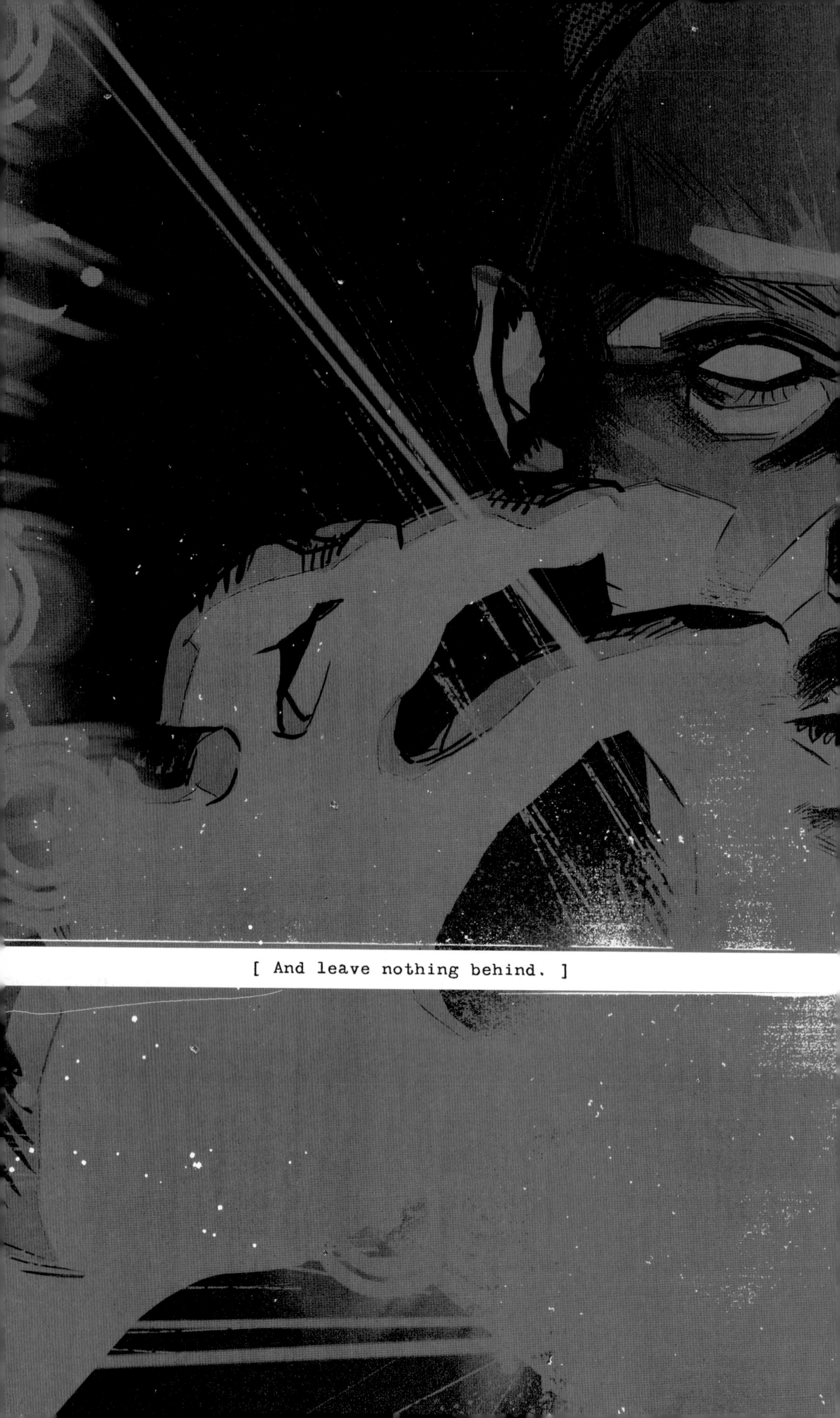
[And leave nothing behind.]

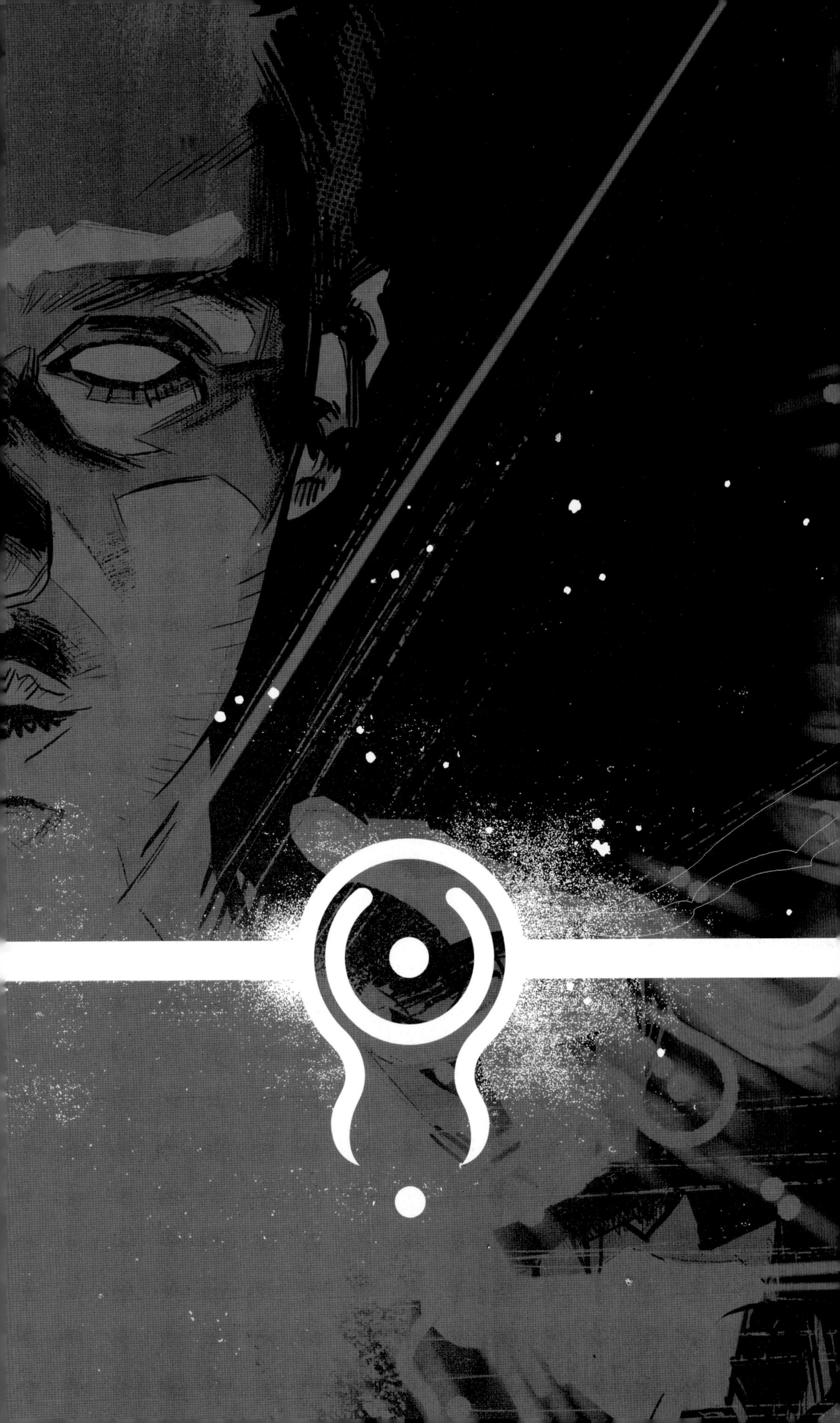

- PAY EVERYTHING -

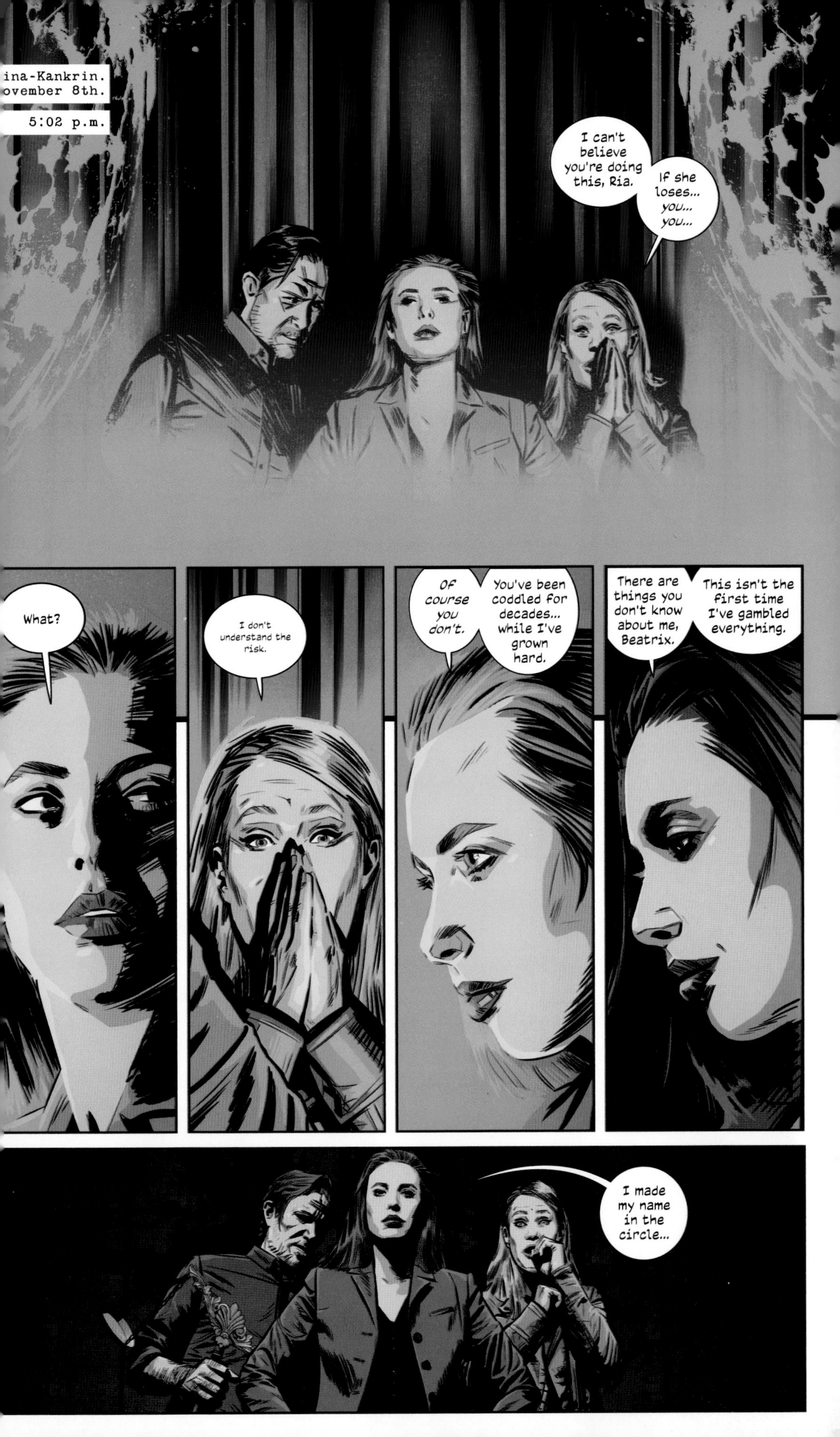
ina-Kankrin.
ovember 8th.
5:02 p.m.
I can't believe you're doing this, Ria.
If she loses... you... you...
What?
I don't understand the risk.
Of course you don't.
You've been coddled for decades... while I've grown hard.
There are things you don't know about me, Beatrix.
This isn't the first time I've gambled everything.
I made my name in the circle...

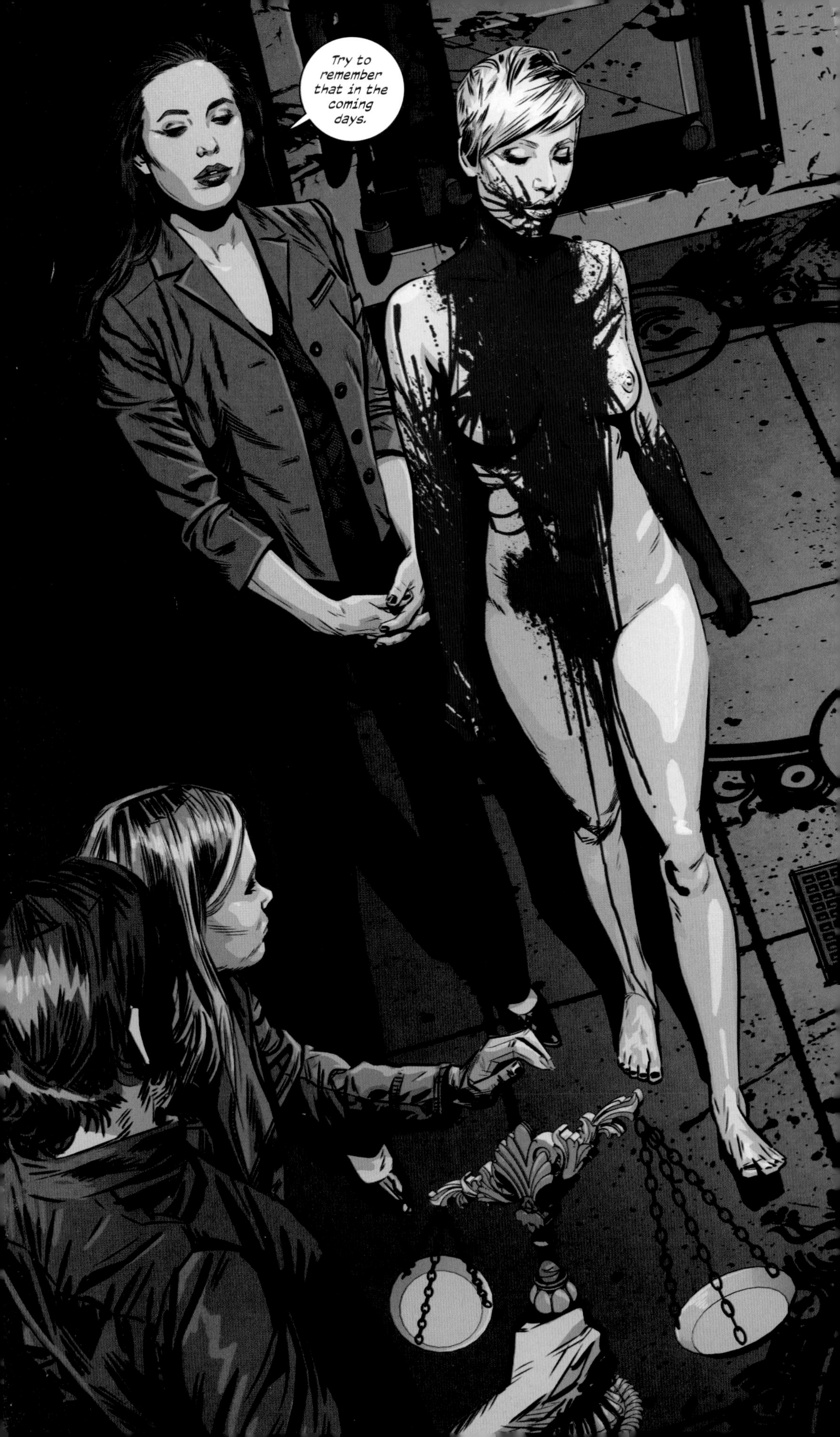
Try to remember that in the coming days.

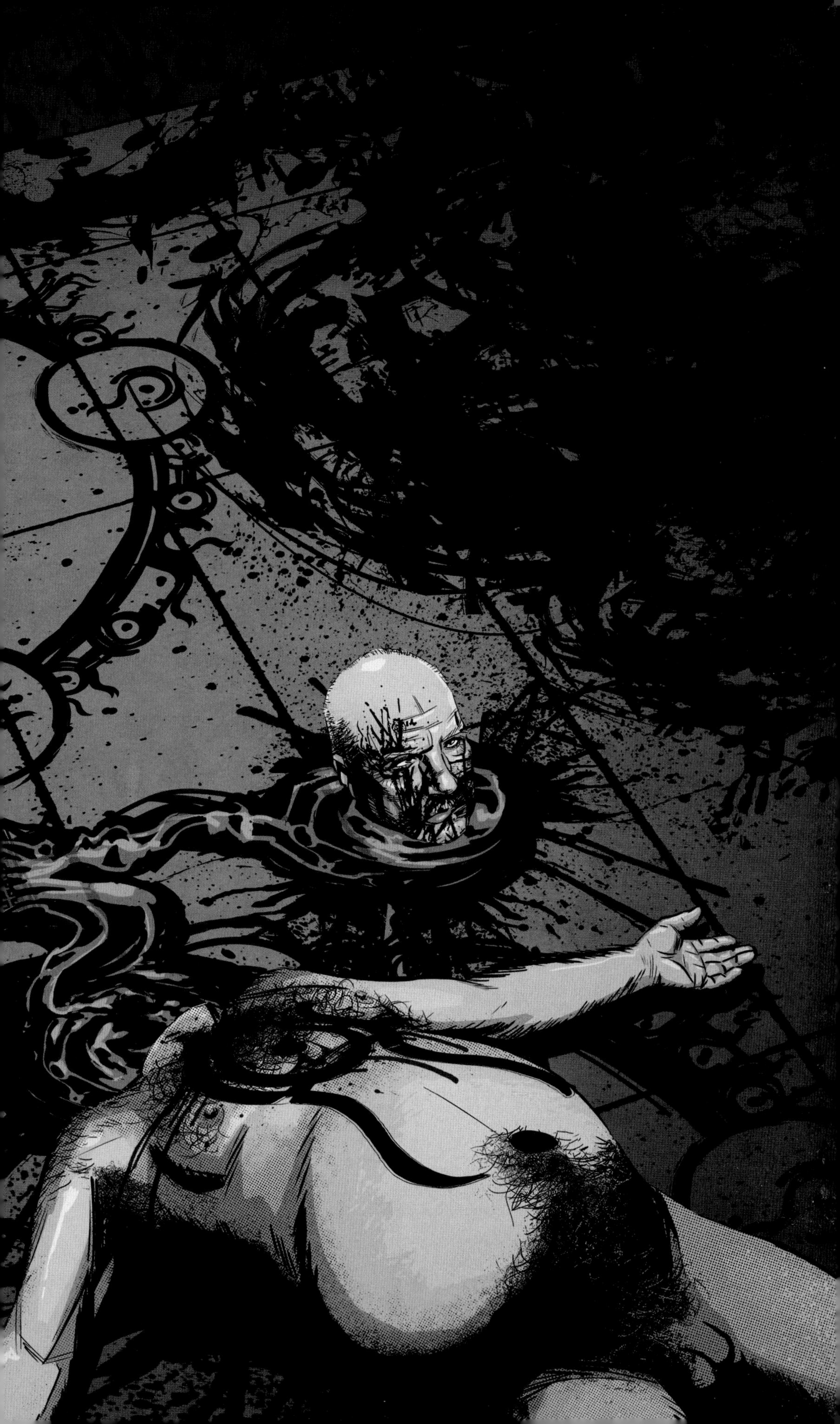

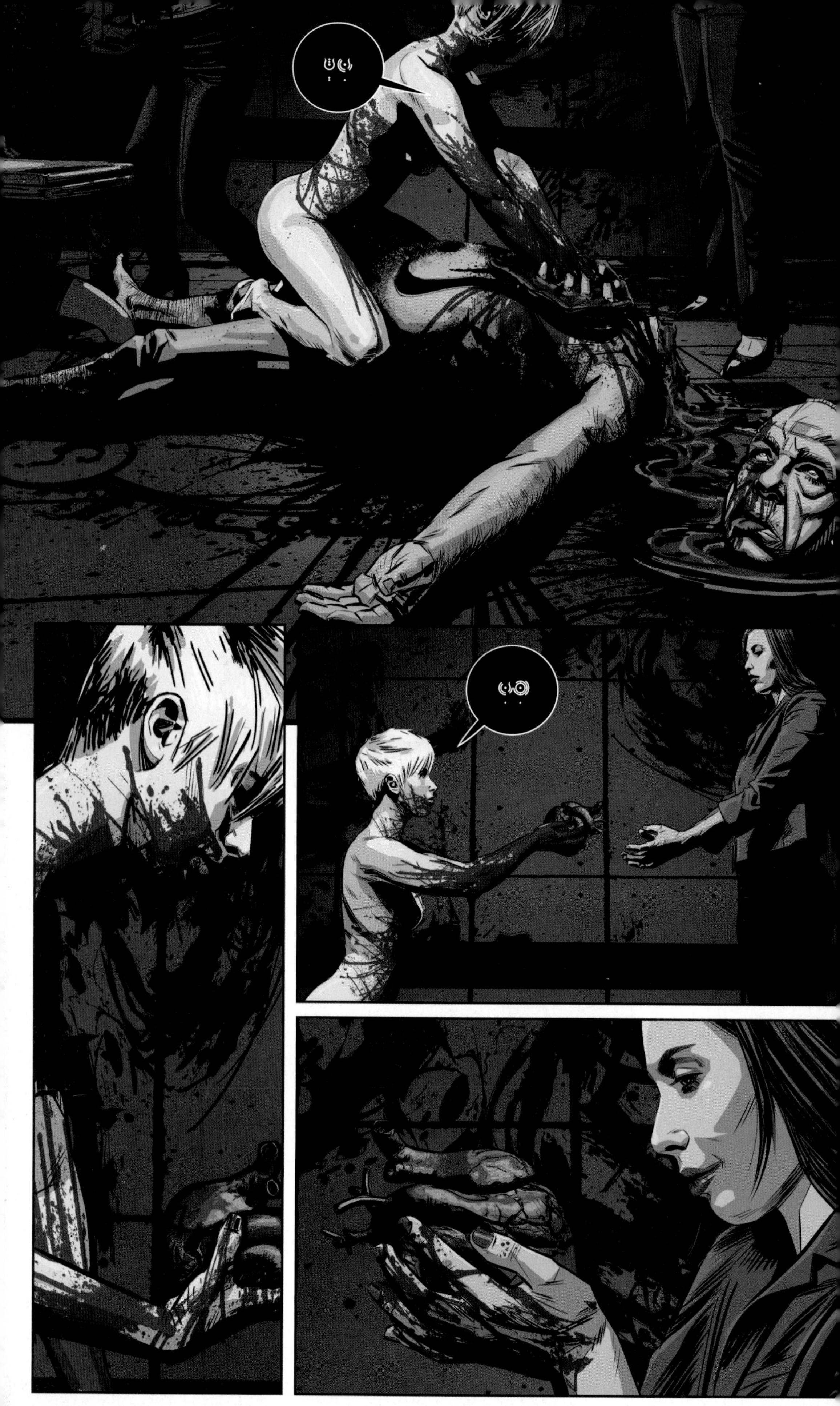

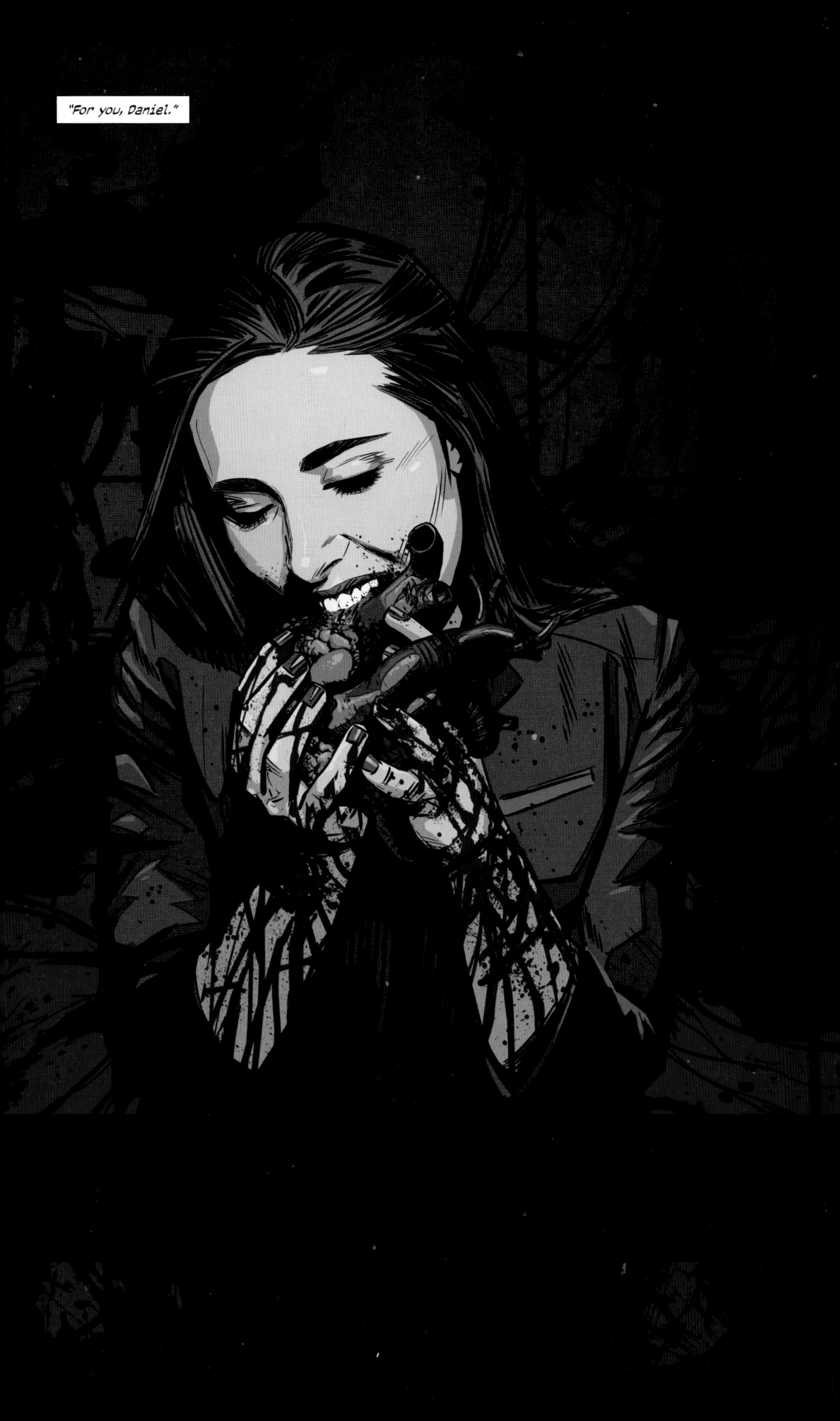
"For you, Daniel."

(a,b)

(c,d,e,f)

(g,h)

BALANCING THE SCALES (a,b)

(c,d,e,f)

THE PRINCIPLES AT PLAY
IN THE TRANSFER OF POWER

(g,h)

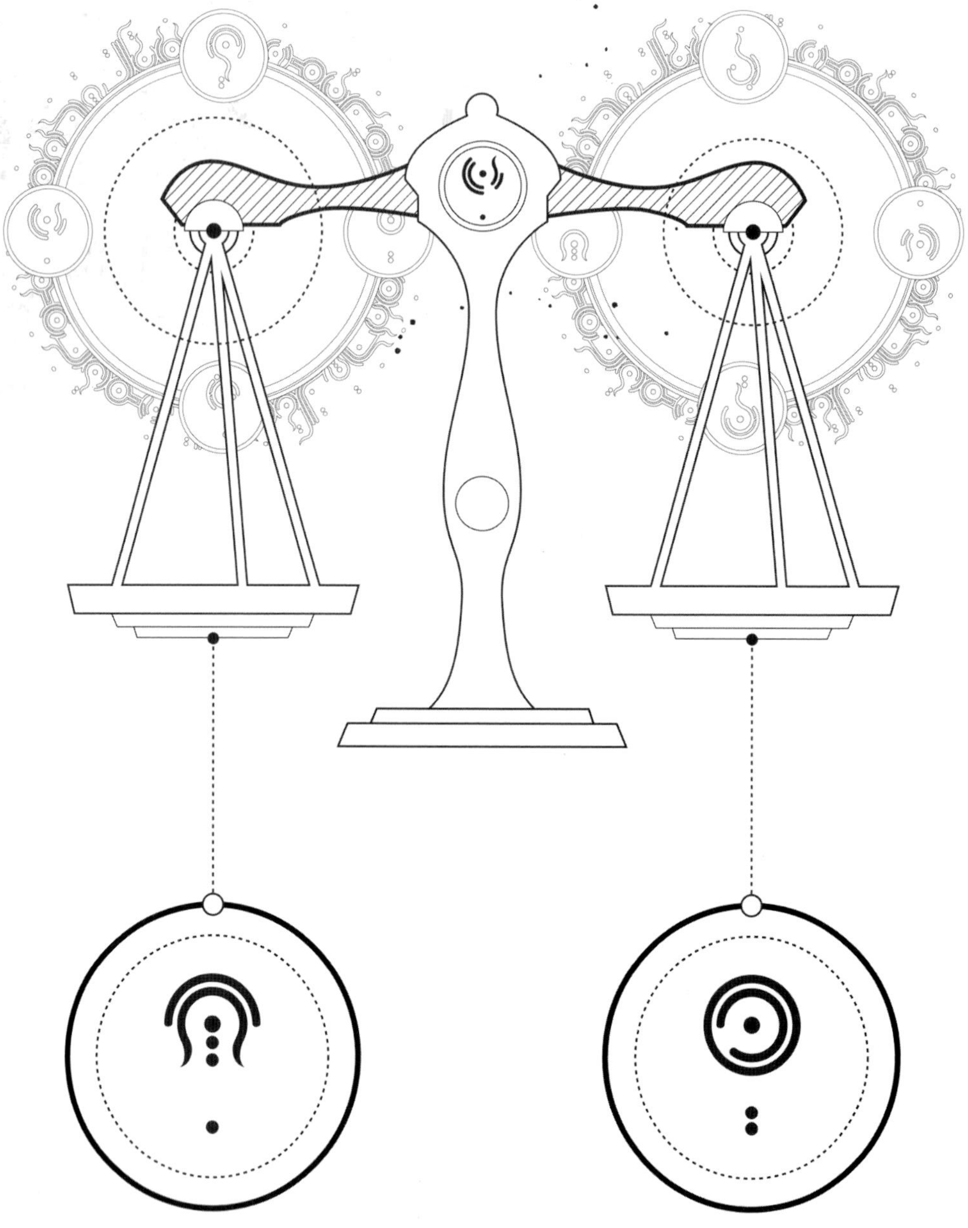

 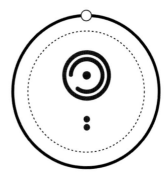

THE GREATER SCALES

This is commonly understood to be a term encompassing the entirety of all transactions between this earthly realm and the other. The Greater Scales are the physical manifestation of the eternal fluctuations of universal expansion.

Like any well-managed, expansionist market that eliminates old, poorly performing companies and replaces them with younger, more vibrant ones, we now understand that the erroneous belief in red shift (universal contraction) was a failure of both scale and vision.

What appeared to be an observed - and provable - theory was actually just a blip on a longer timeline. The following are constant:

1.) The universe always expands.
2.) The market always wins.

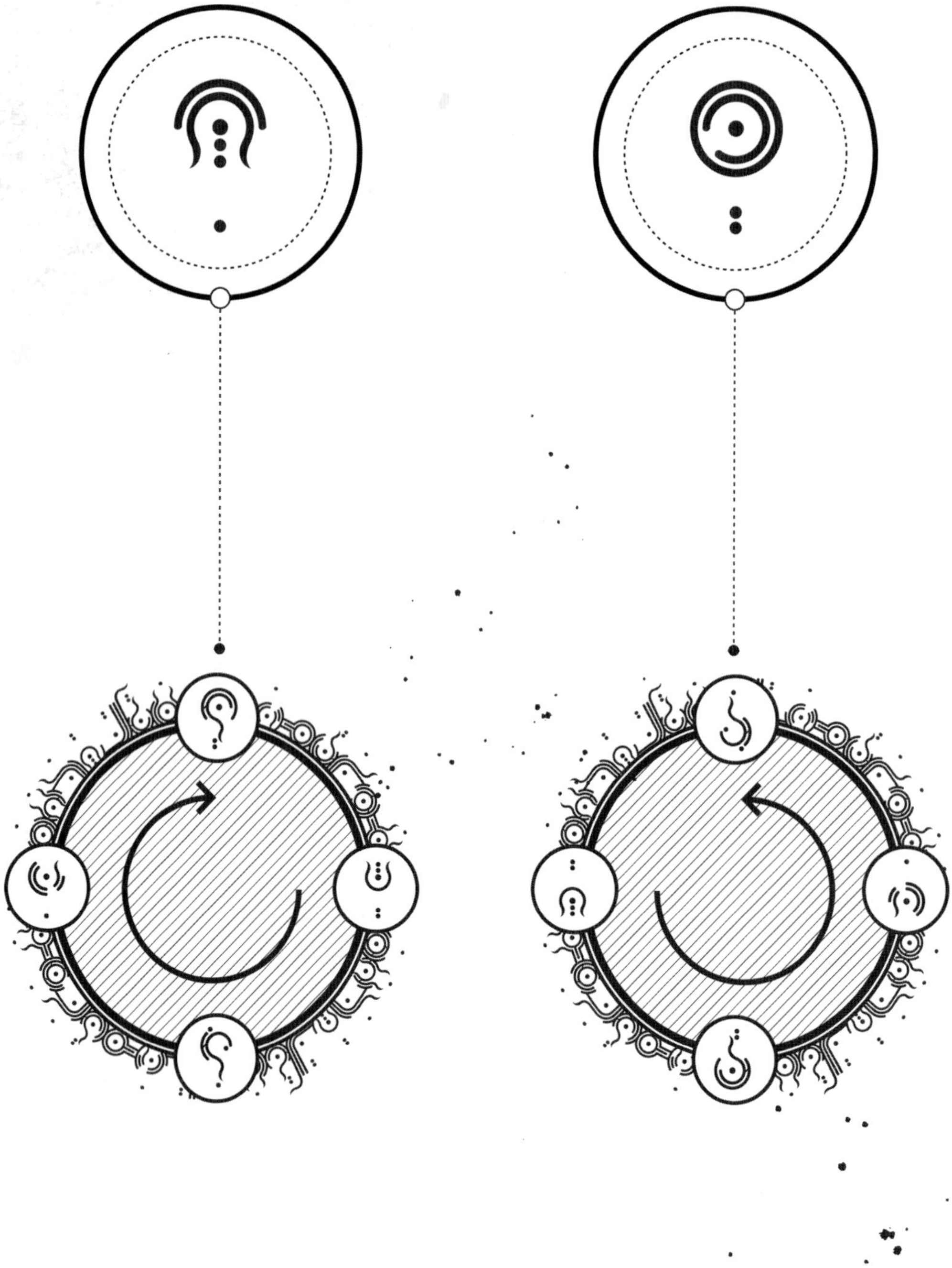

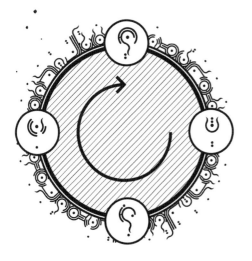 

THE LESSER SCALES

This is commonly understood to be a term encompassing all singular transactions between practicing members of various schools. It is the physical arena in which practitioners engage in both hostile and mortal takeovers.

(Neither of these are to be confused with "The Scales," which is a rotating position held in some Western schools. This position carries with it a physical totem capable of measuring the activity of both the Greater and Lesser Scales.)

(In the arena of the Lesser Scales.)

1.) A challenge can only be initiated by blood.
2.) A challenge can be refused without penalty.
3.) The challenger may not withdraw a challenge.
      a.) A challenger may be replaced by a
      familiar.
      b.) If replaced, the familiar will
      operate at half capacity (this is often
      referred to as a "familiar sacrifice,"
      and usually occurs in challenges between
      juvenile practitioners).
4.) Once agreed upon, a challenge does not begin until both practitioners have passed over the Scale walls.
5.) A challenge does not end until there is a victor.
6.) To the victor go the spoils.
      c.) In the case of surviving progeny, the
      victor may choose to impart seed capital
      if the children are allowed to stay
      within the school. If the children are
      exiled, the victor must provide a
      generational stipend to all survivors.

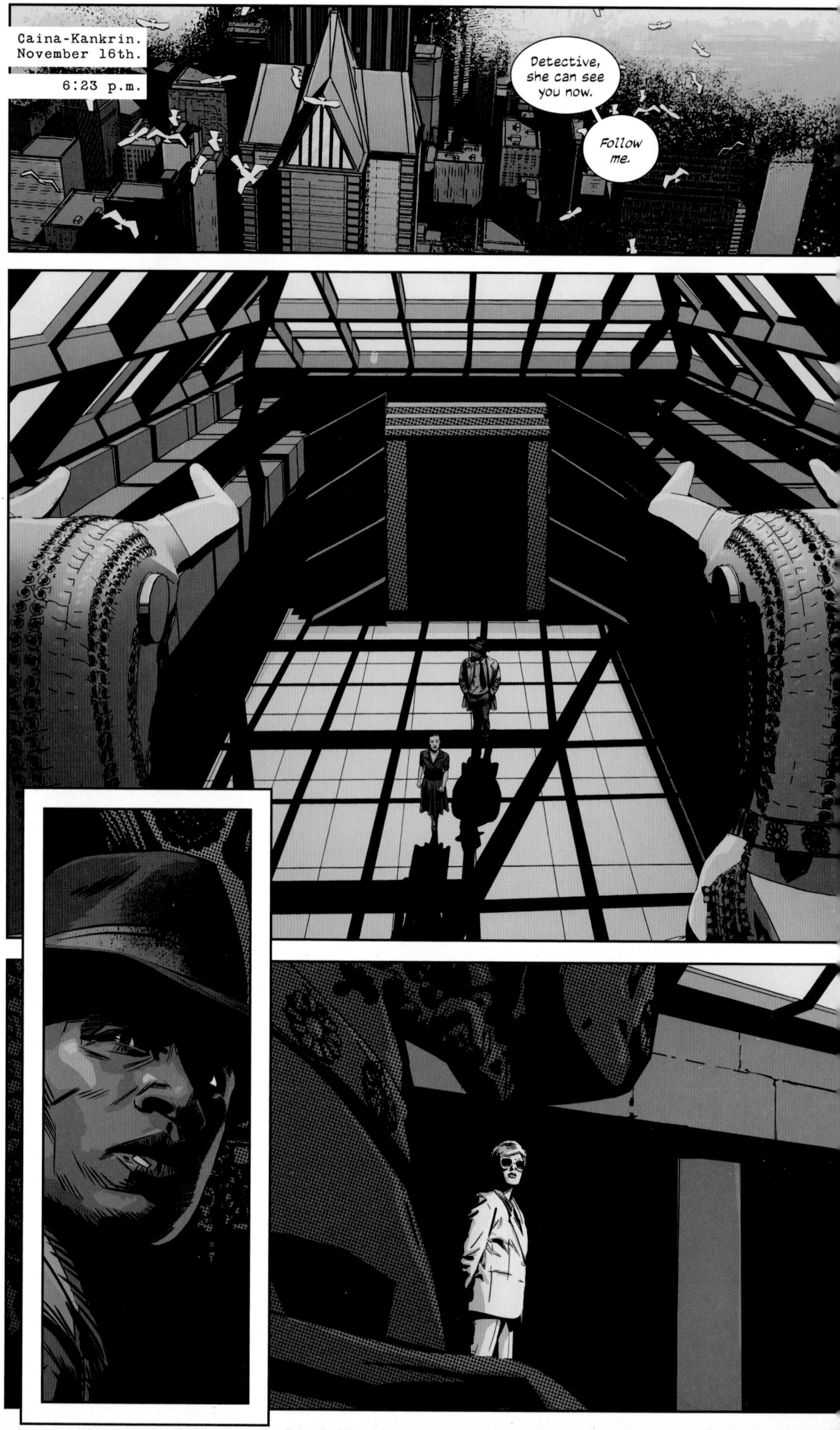

Caina-Kankrin.
November 16th.
6:23 p.m.
Detective, she can see you now.
Follow me.

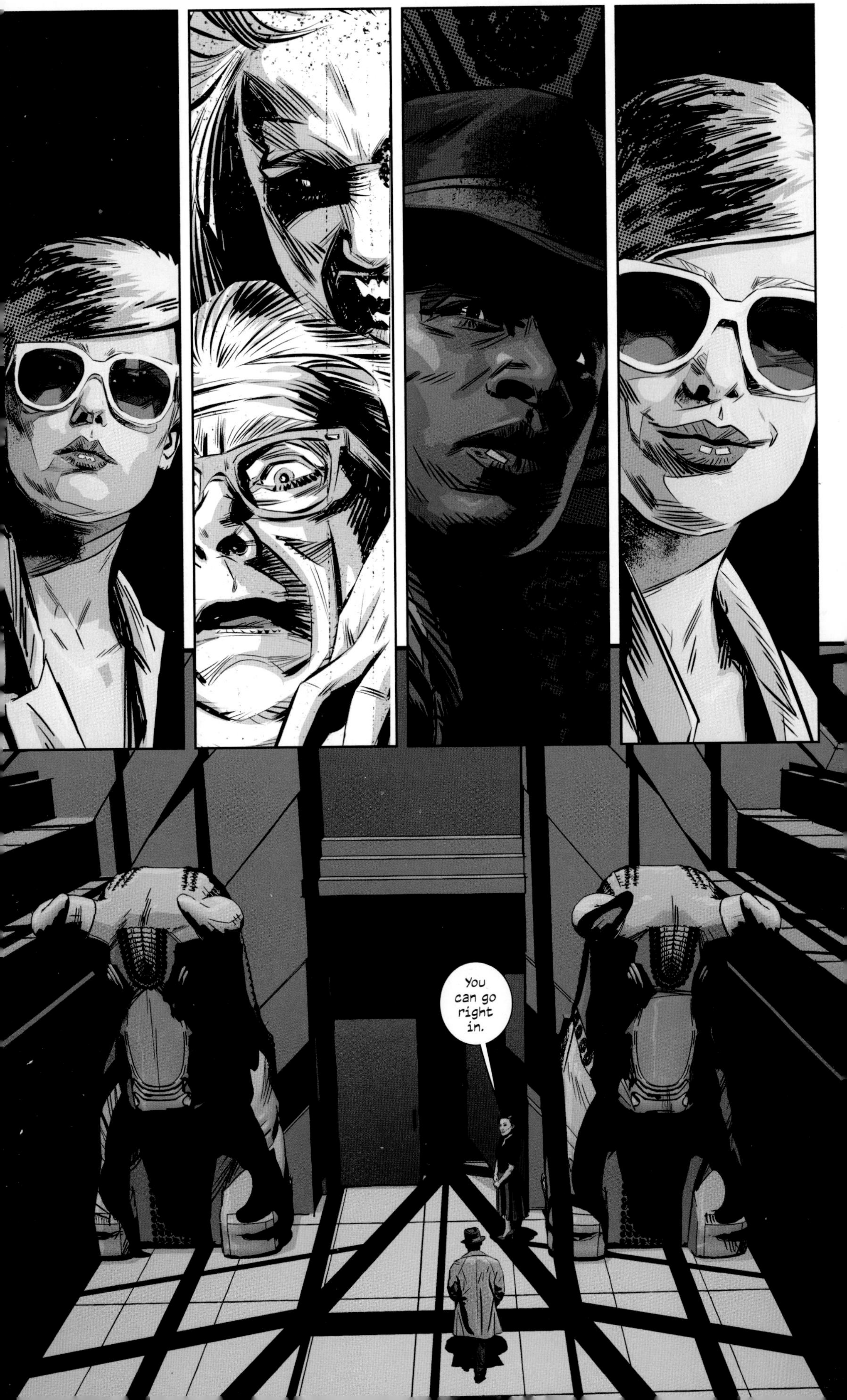
You can go right in.

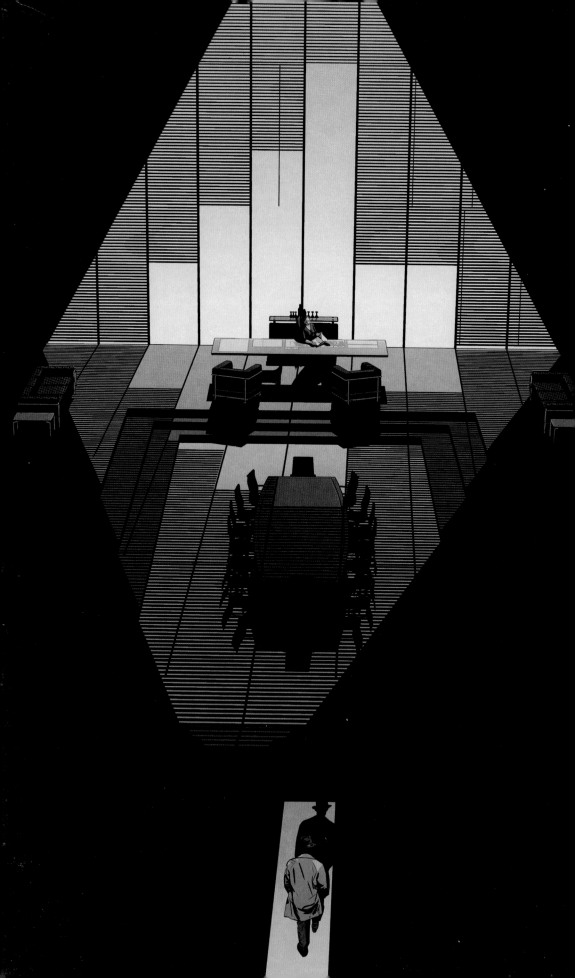

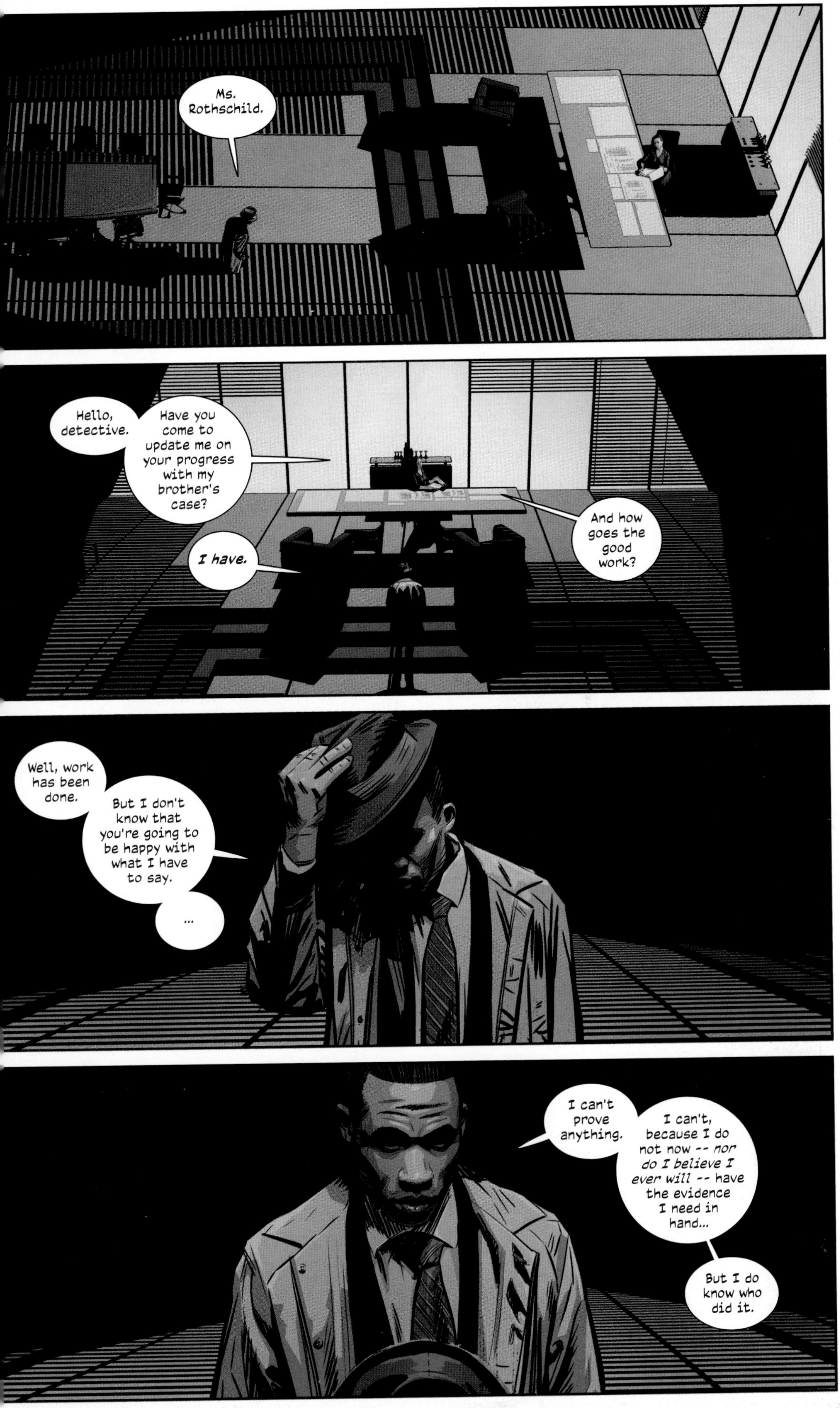
Ms. Rothschild.
Hello, detective.
Have you come to update me on your progress with my brother's case?
I have.
And how goes the good work?
Well, work has been done.
But I don't know that you're going to be happy with what I have to say.
...
I can't prove anything.
I can't, because I do not now -- *nor do I believe I ever will* -- have the evidence I need in hand...
But I do know who did it.

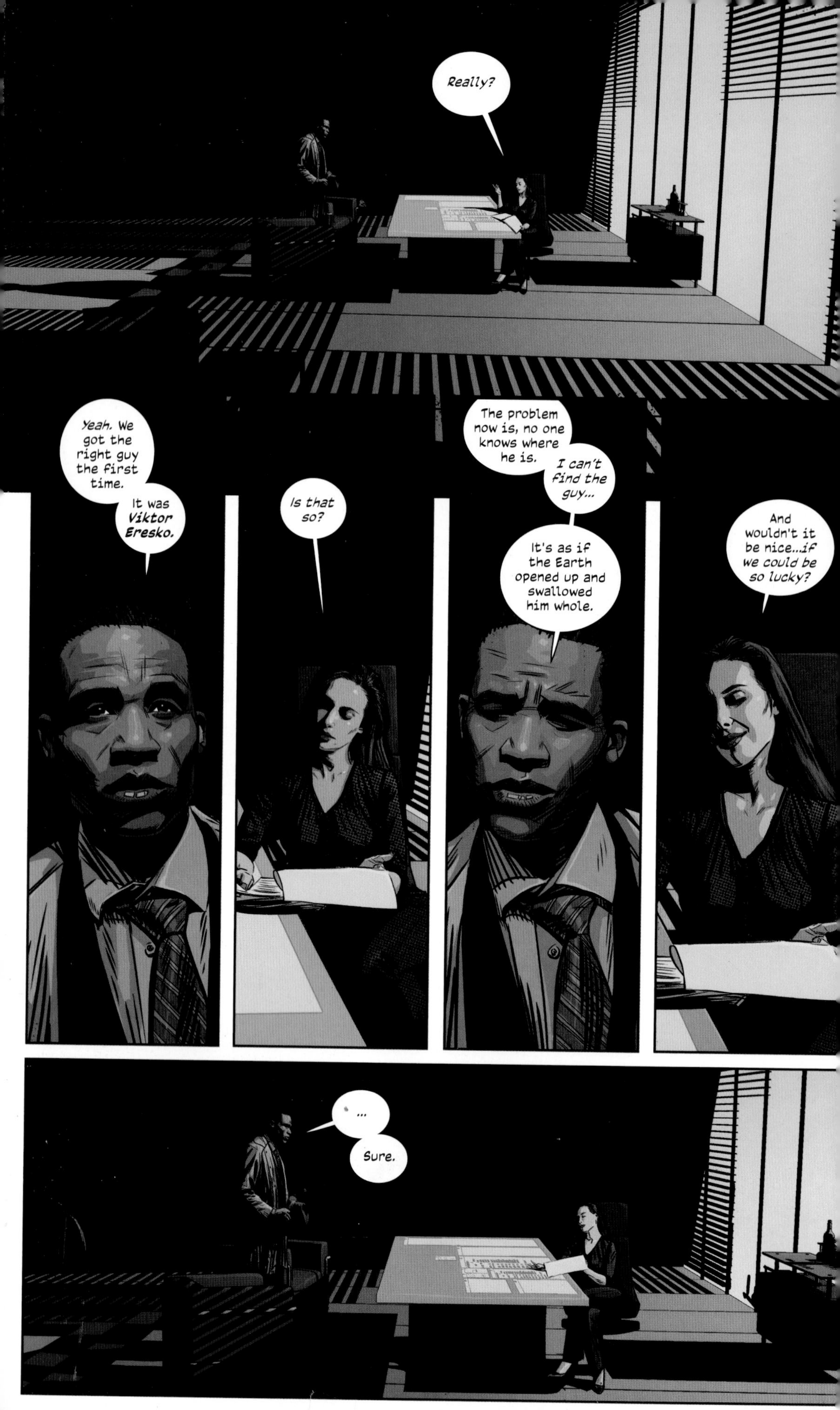
Really?
Yeah. We got the right guy the first time.
It was Viktor Eresko.
Is that so?
The problem now is, no one knows where he is.
I can't find the guy...
It's as if the Earth opened up and swallowed him whole.
And wouldn't it be nice...if we could be so lucky?
...
Sure.

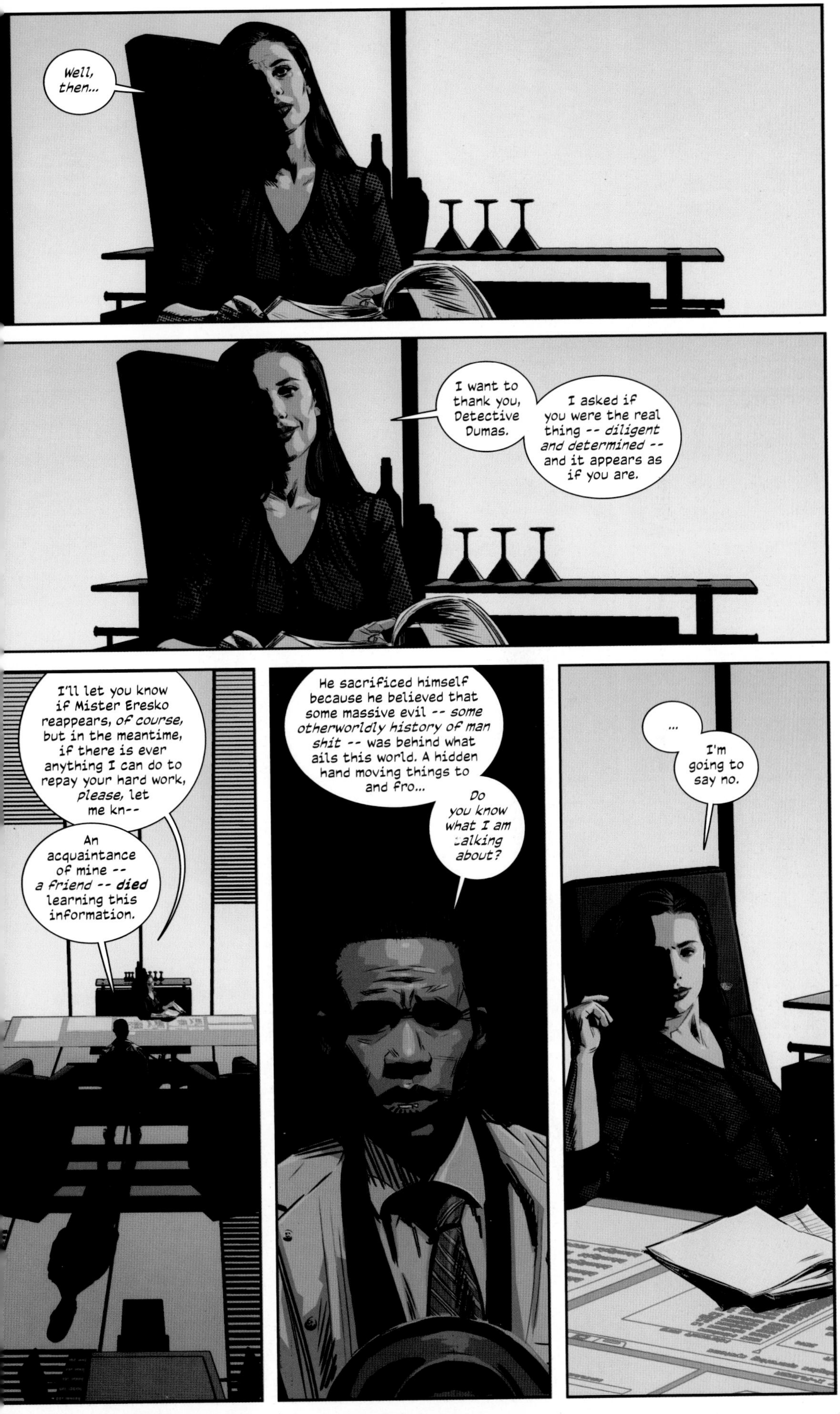
Well, then...
I want to thank you, Detective Dumas.
I asked if you were the real thing -- *diligent and determined* -- and it appears as if you are.
I'll let you know if Mister Eresko reappears, *of course,* but in the meantime, if there is ever anything I can do to repay your hard work, *please,* let me kn--
An acquaintance of mine -- *a friend* -- ***died*** learning this information.
He sacrificed himself because he believed that some massive evil -- *some otherworldly history of man shit* -- was behind what ails this world. A hidden hand moving things to and fro...
Do you know what I am talking about?
...
I'm going to say no.

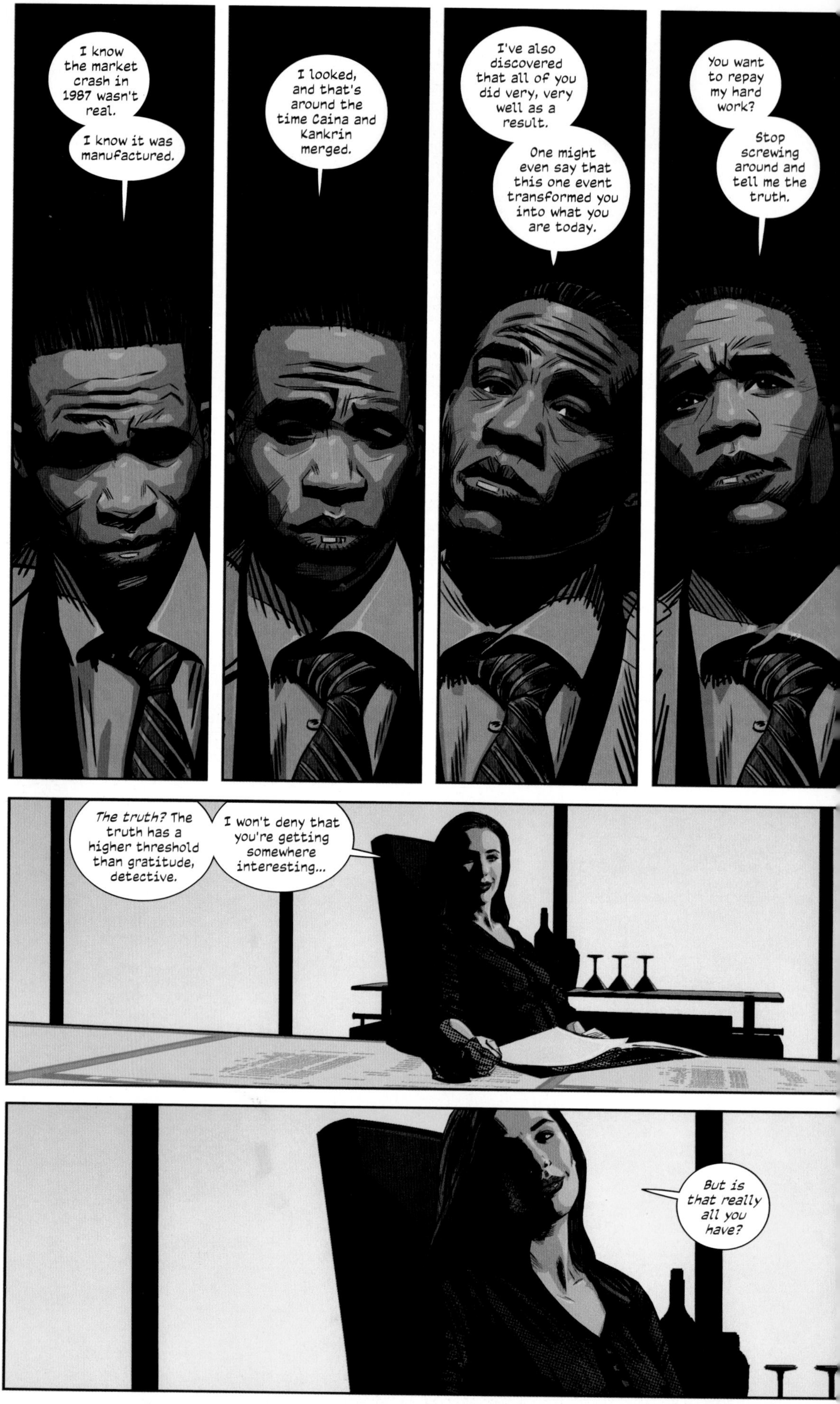
I know the market crash in 1987 wasn't real.
I know it was manufactured.
I looked, and that's around the time Caina and Kankrin merged.
I've also discovered that all of you did very, very well as a result.
One might even say that this one event transformed you into what you are today.
You want to repay my hard work?
Stop screwing around and tell me the truth.
The truth? The truth has a higher threshold than gratitude, detective.
I won't deny that you're getting somewhere interesting...
But is that really all you have?

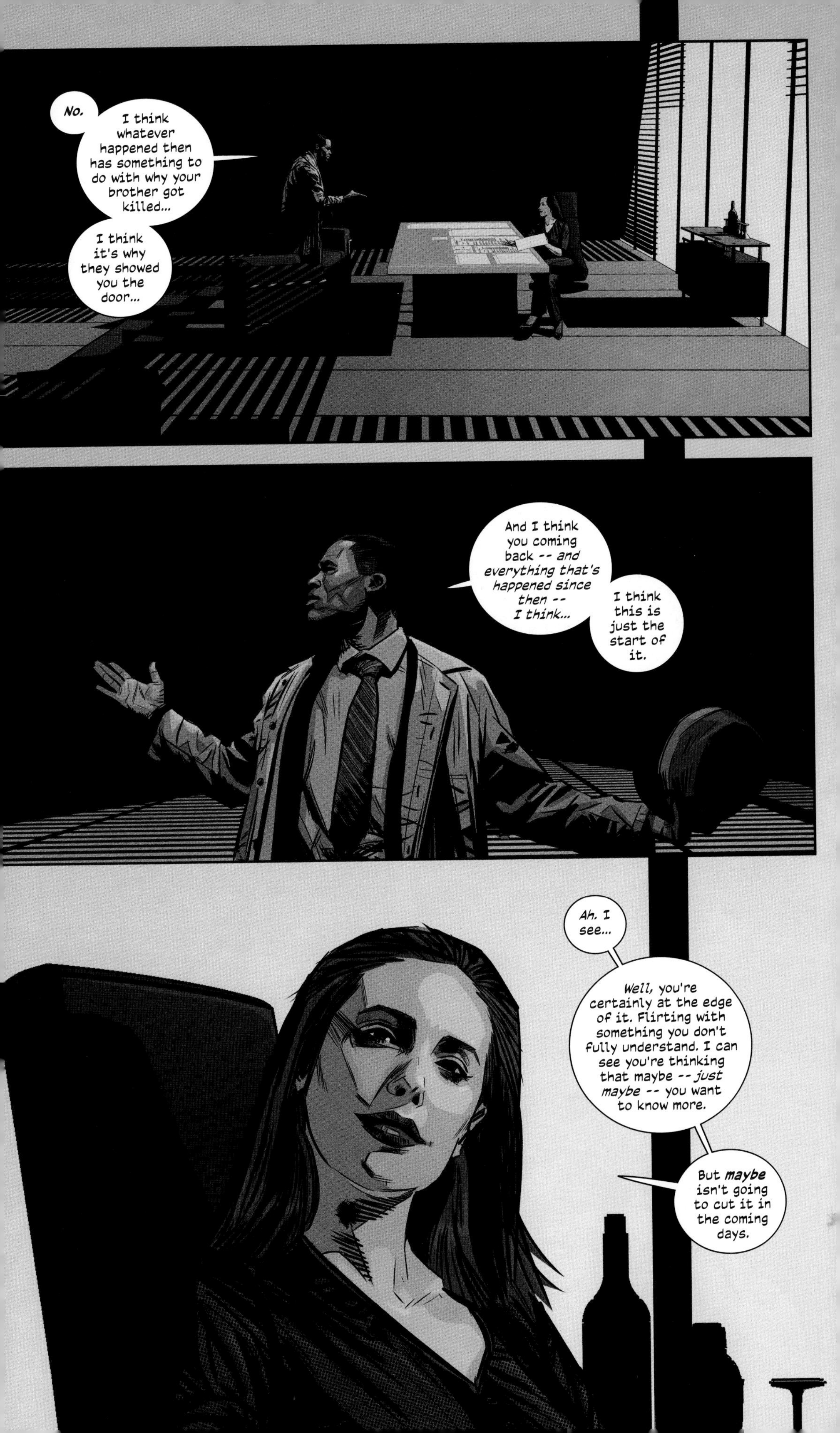
No.
I think whatever happened then has something to do with why your brother got killed...
I think it's why they showed you the door...
And I think you coming back -- *and everything that's happened since then* -- *I think...*
I think this is just the start of it.
Ah. I see...
Well, you're certainly at the edge of it. Flirting with something you don't fully understand. I can see you're thinking that maybe -- *just maybe* -- you want to know more.
But ***maybe*** isn't going to cut it in the coming days.

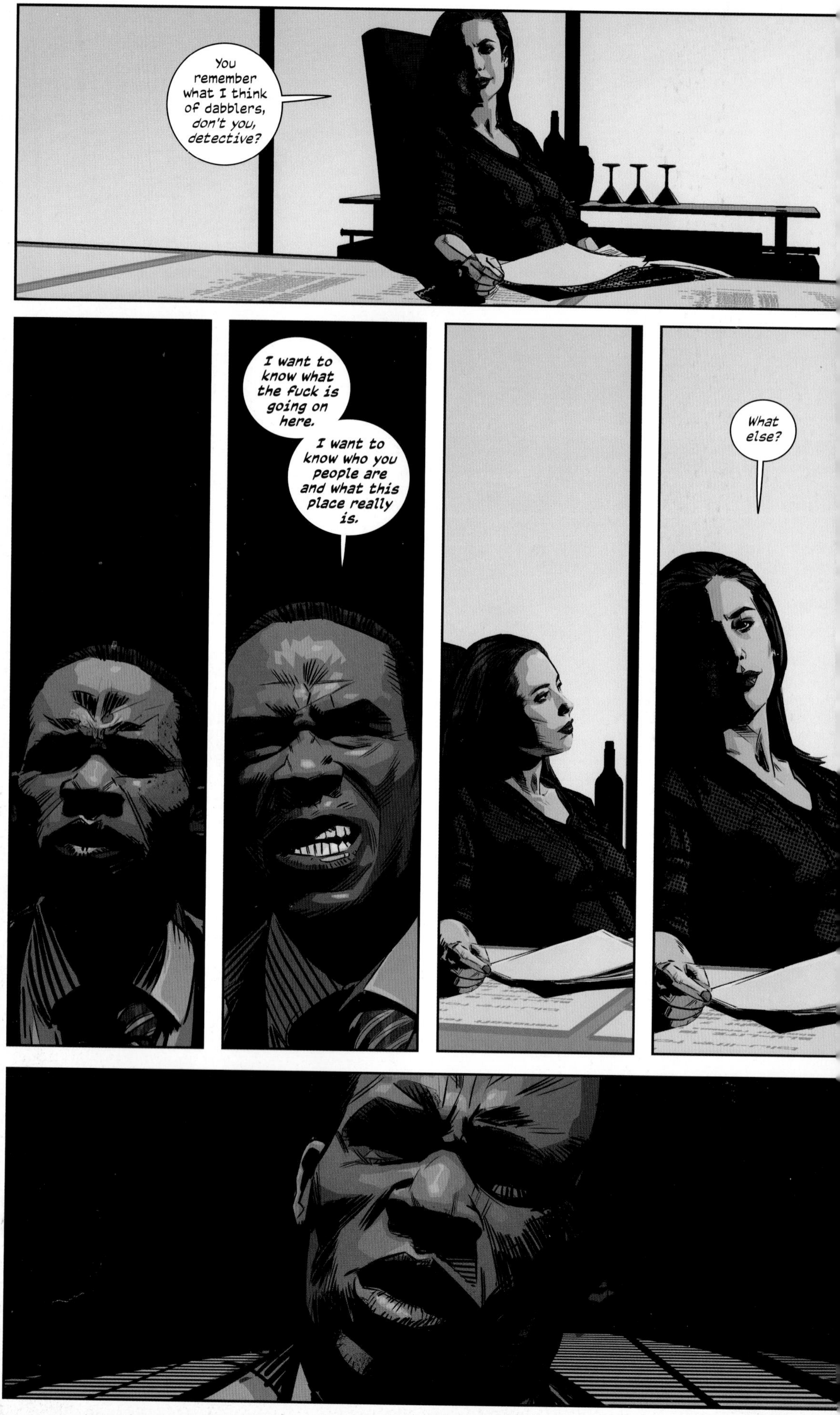
You remember what I think of dabblers, don't you, detective?
I want to know what the fuck is going on here.
I want to know who you people are and what this place really is.
What else?

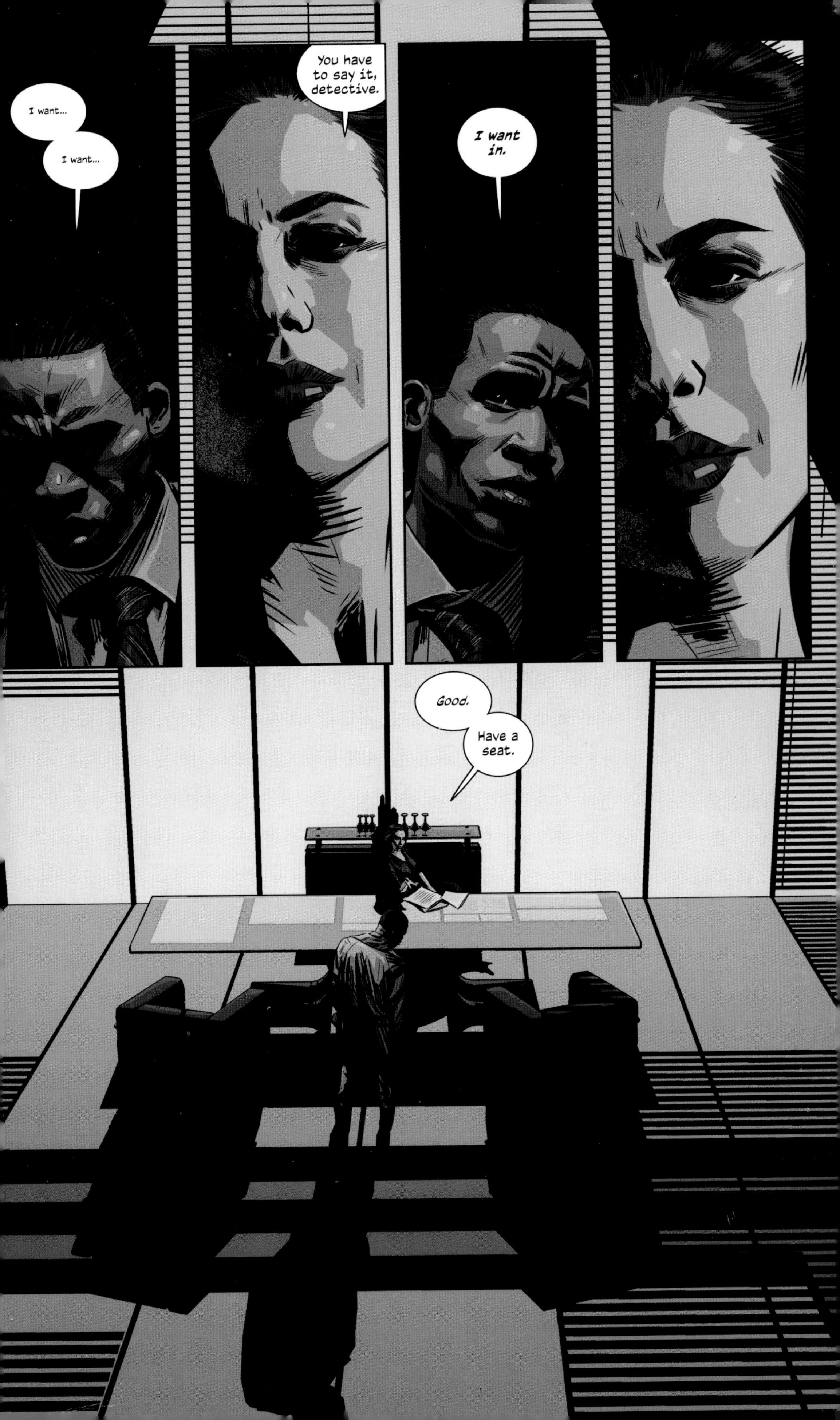

I want...
I want...
You have to say it, detective.
I want in.
Good.
Have a seat.

EPILOGUE

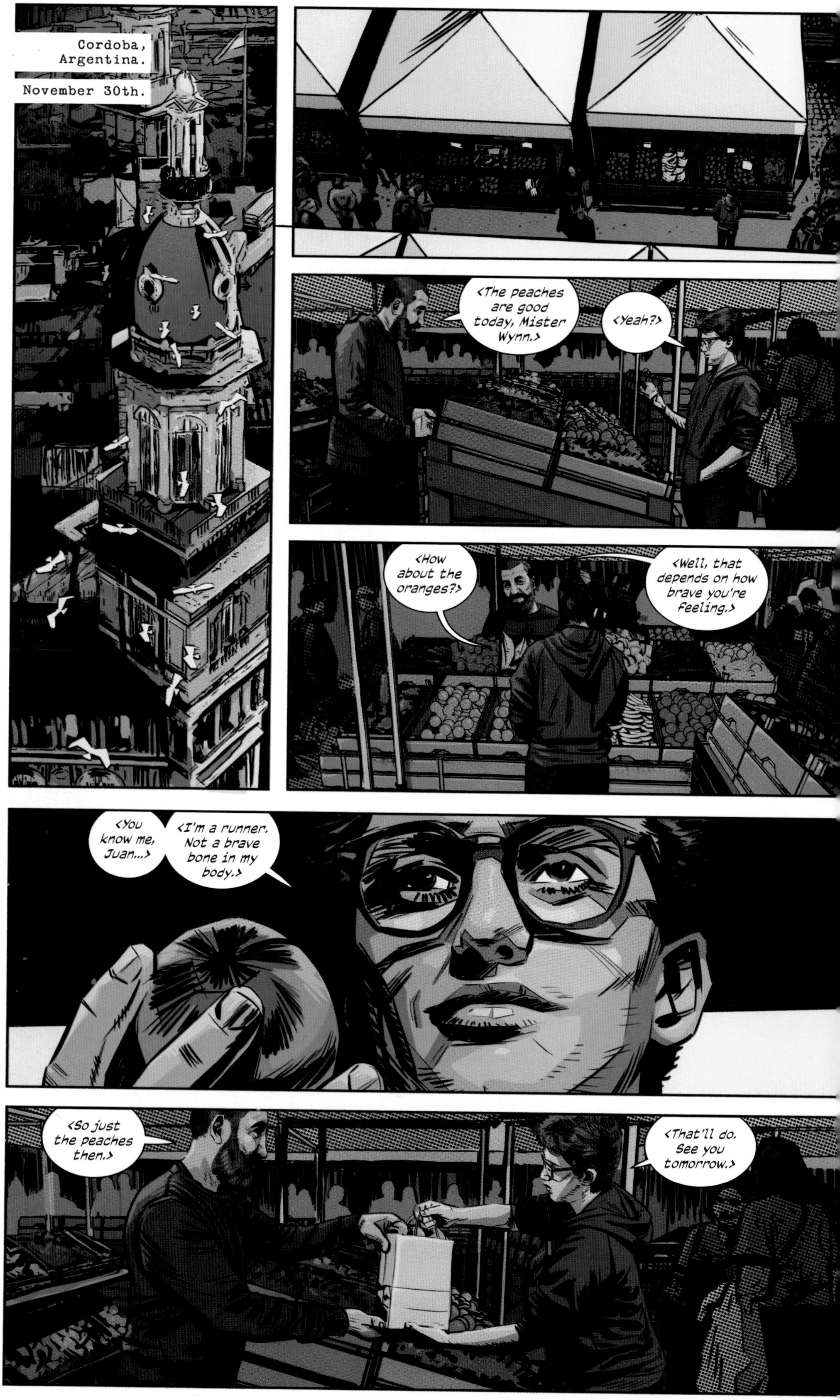
Cordoba, Argentina.
November 30th.
<The peaches are good today, Mister Wynn.>
<Yeah?>
<How about the oranges?>
<Well, that depends on how brave you're feeling.>
<You know me, Juan...>
<I'm a runner. Not a brave bone in my body.>
<So just the peaches then.>
<That'll do. See you tomorrow.>

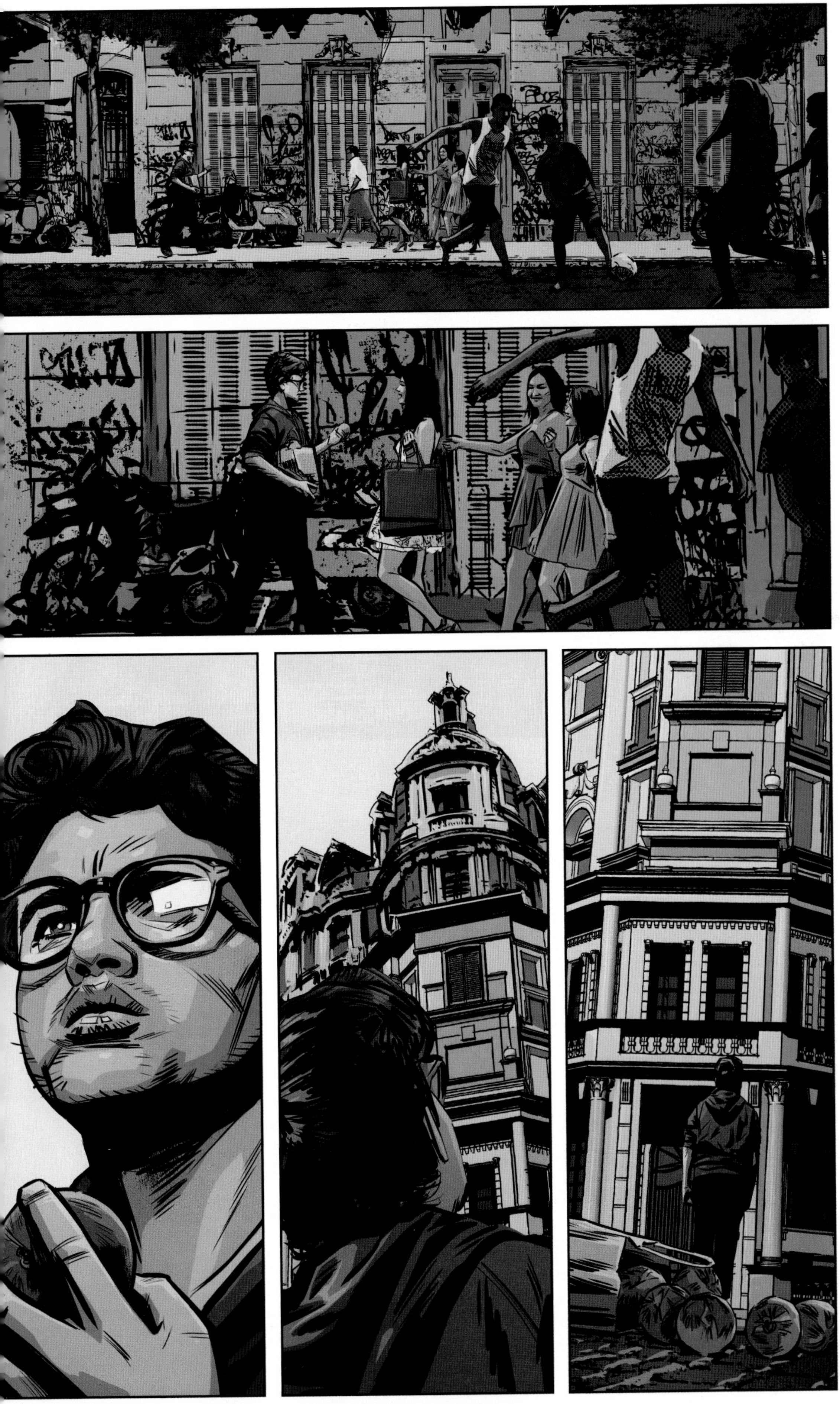

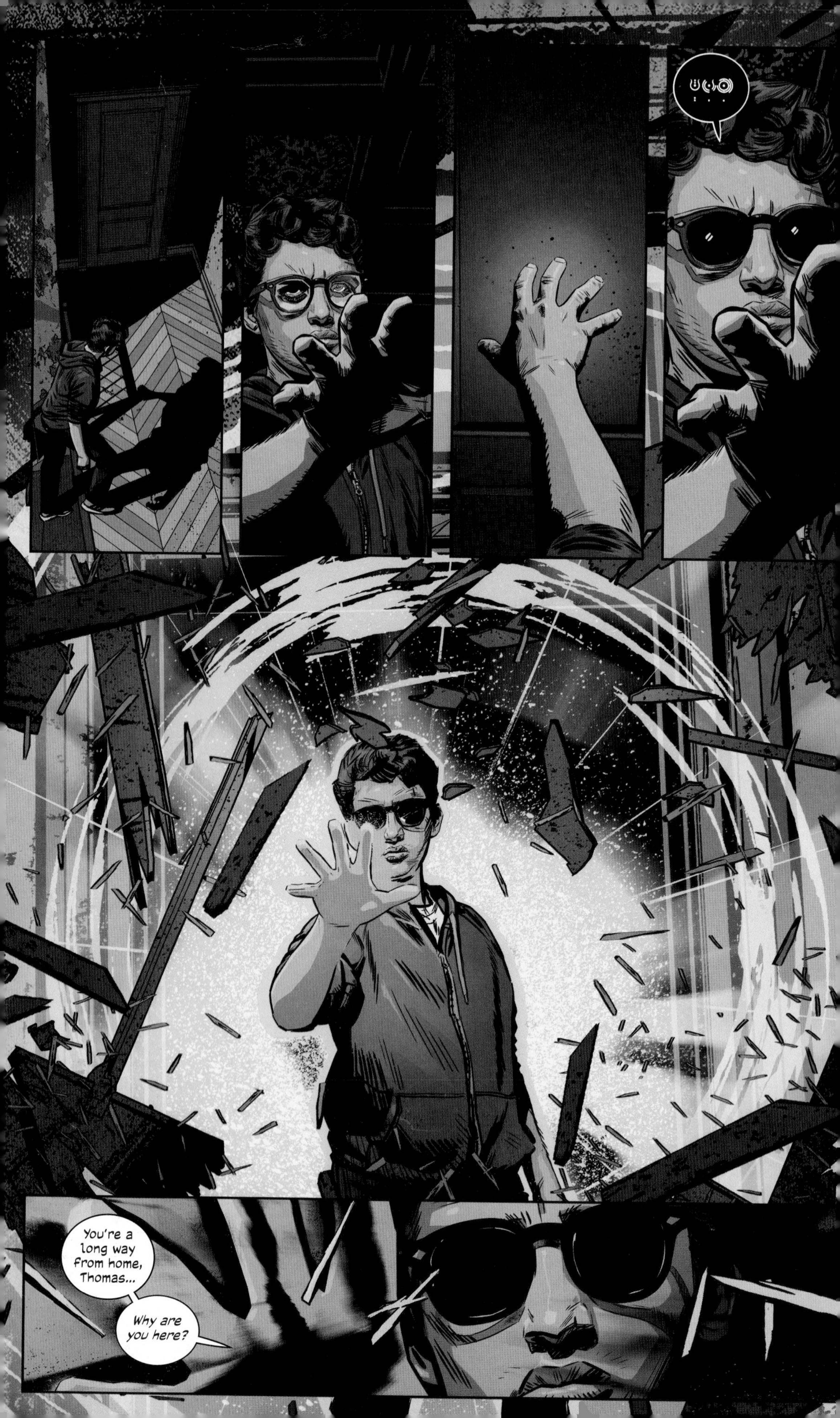
You're a long way from home, Thomas...
Why are you here?

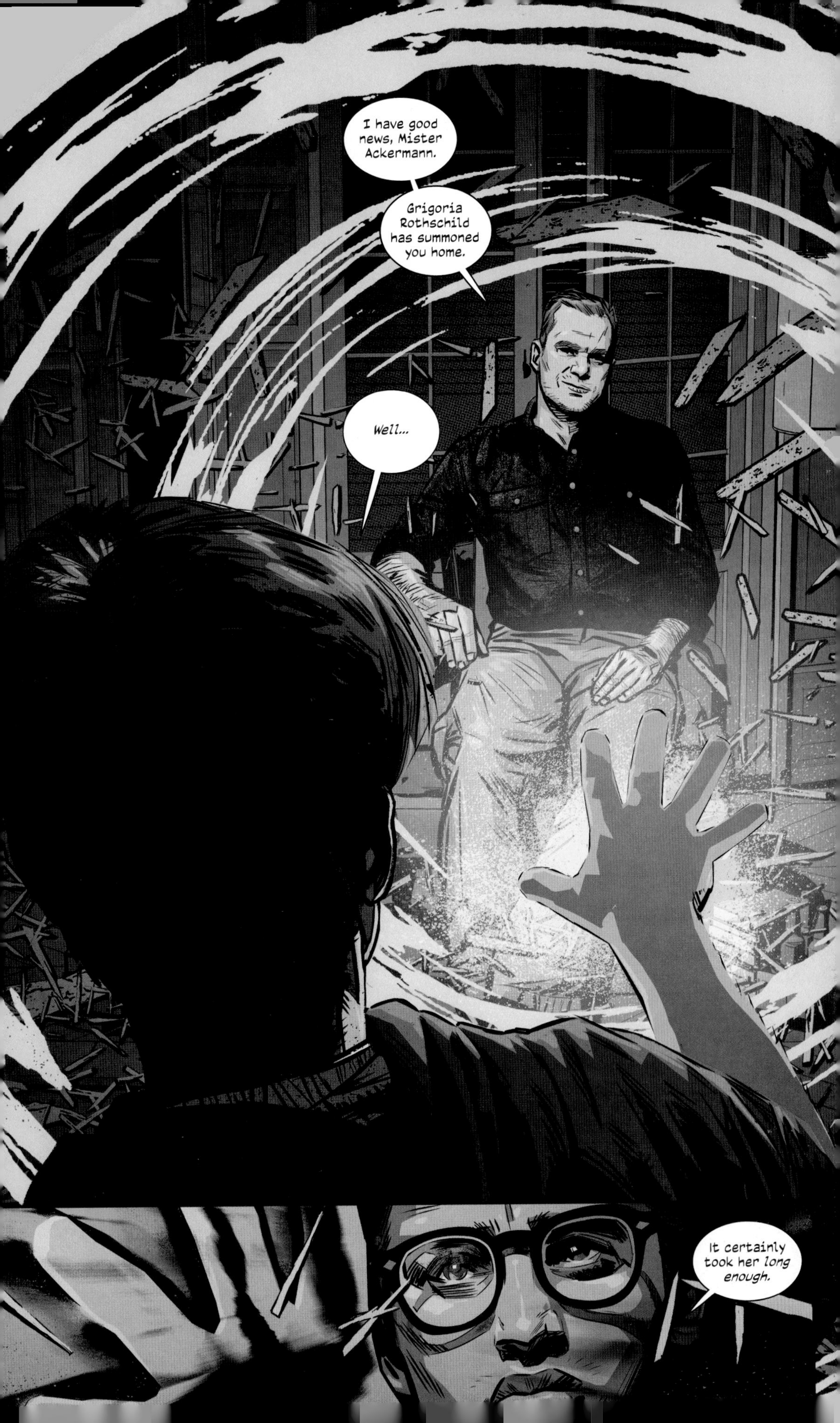
I have good news, Mister Ackermann.
Grigoria Rothschild has summoned you home.
Well...
It certainly took her long enough.

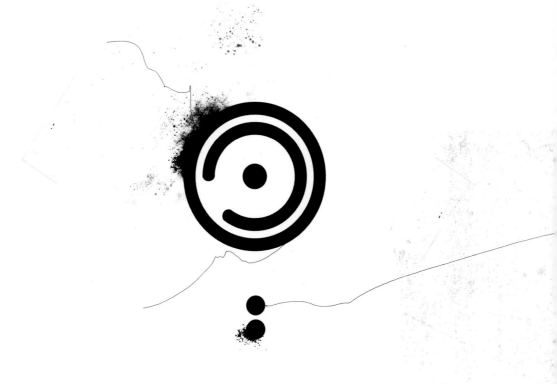

SKETCHES

Artist: Tomm Coker **Title:** TBMM **Issue:** 007 **Page:** 06

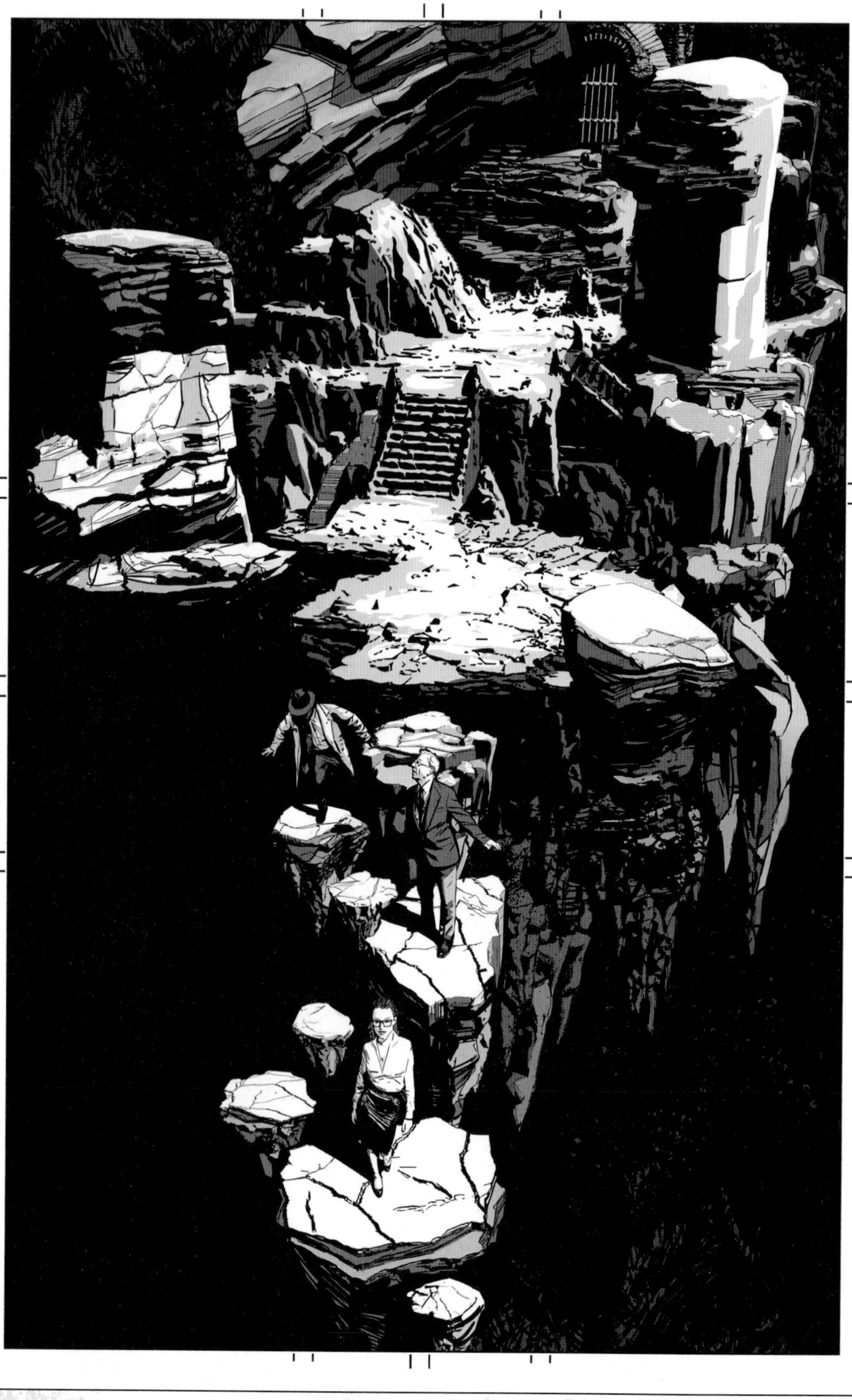

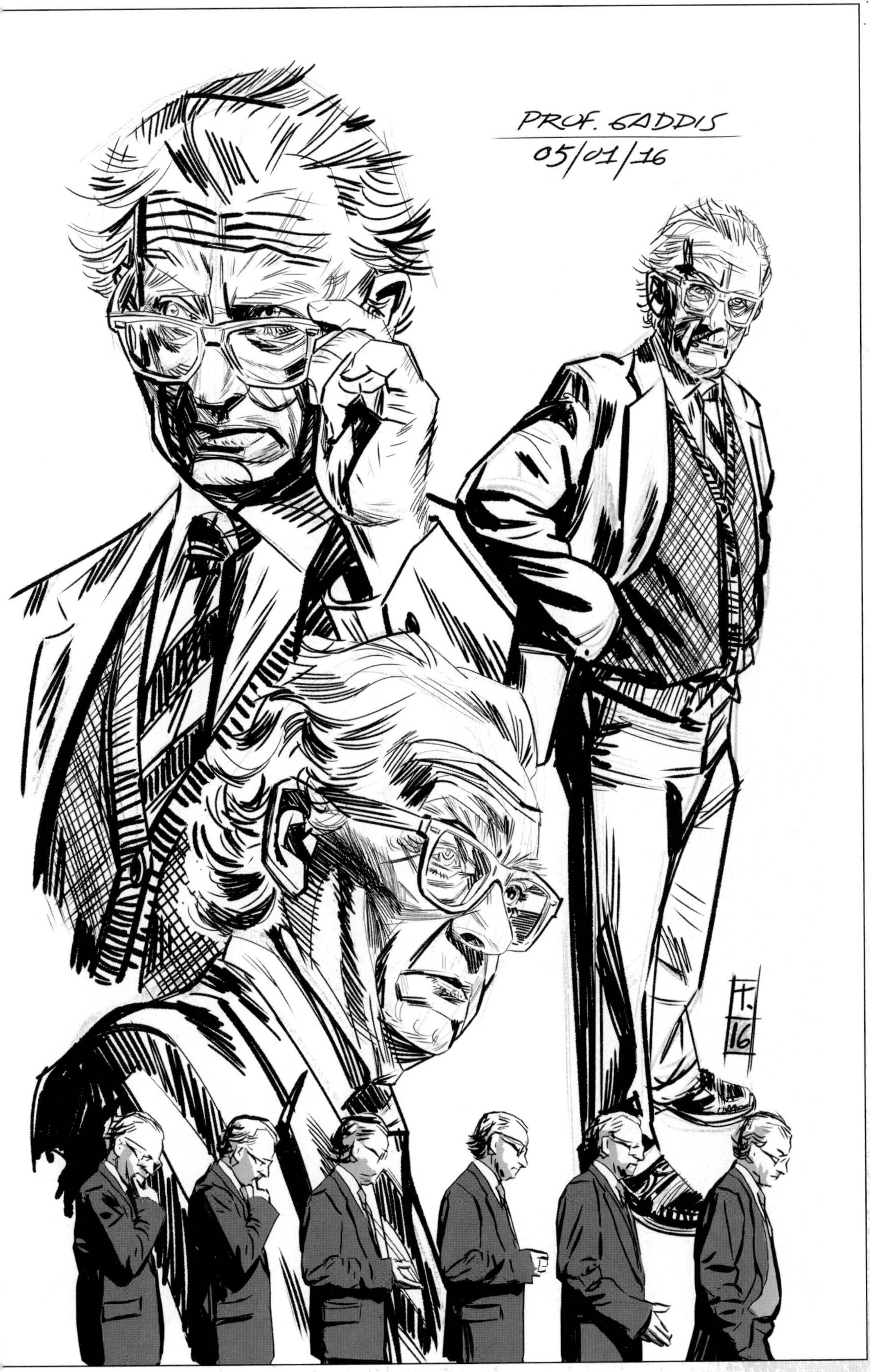
PROF. GADDIS
05/01/16
H.
16

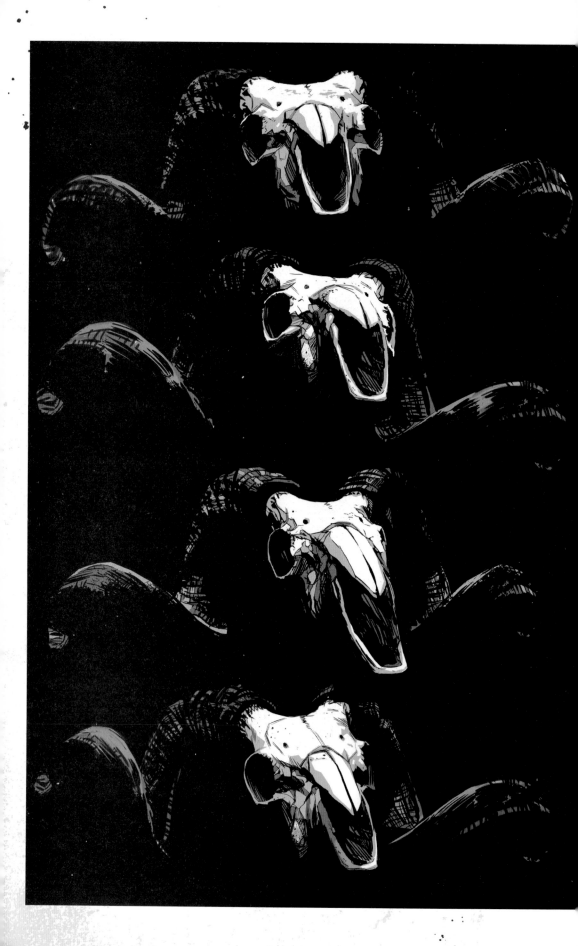

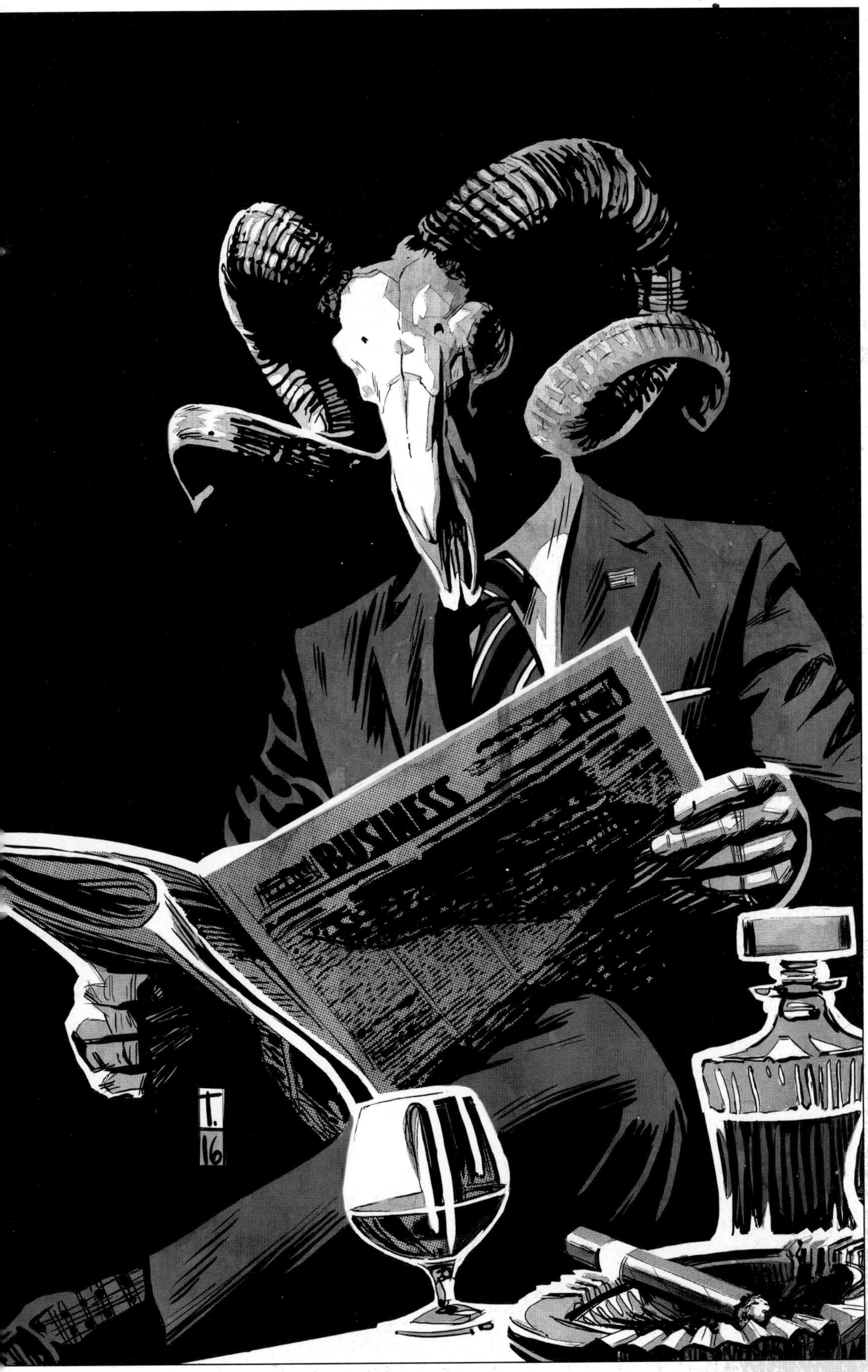
BUSINESS

Jonathan Hickman [redacted] lies [redacted]

Tomm Coker [redacted] is [redacted] a [redacted] thief [redacted]

Michael Garland [redacted] has [redacted] blood on [redacted] his [redacted] hands [redacted]

Rus Wooton [redacted] cannot [redacted] be [redacted] trusted [redacted]